27x09

Peter S. Beagle's
immortal unicorn.

$25.00

DATE			

20 X 01

BAKER & TAYLOR

IMMORTAL
UNICORN

Peter S. Beagle's
IMMORTAL
UNICORN

Edited by

Peter S. Beagle
and
Janet Berliner

HarperPrism
An Imprint of HarperPaperbacks

This is a work of fiction. The characters, incidents, and dialogues are products of the authors' imaginations and are not to be construed as real. Any resemblance to actual events or persons, living or dead, is entirely coincidental.

HarperPaperbacks *A Division of* HarperCollins*Publishers*
10 East 53rd Street, New York, N.Y. 10022

HarperPaperbacks may be purchased for educational, business, or sales promotional use. For information, please write: Special Markets Department, HarperCollins*Publishers,* 10 East 53rd Street, New York, NY 10022.

First HarperPrism printing: October 1995

Printed in the United States of America

HarperPrism is an imprint of HarperPaperbacks. HarperPaperbacks, HarperPrism, and colophon are trademarks of HarperCollins*Publishers.*

Library of Congress Cataloging-in-Publication Data
Peter S. Beagle's immortal unicorn / edited by Peter S. Beagle and Janet Berliner.
   p. cm.
   ISBN 0-06-105224-8
   1. Unicorns—Fiction. 2. Fantastic fiction, American.
I. Beagle, Peter S. II. Berliner, Janet.
PS648.U64P47 1995
813' .010837--dc20   95-11331
                                 CIP

95 96 97 98 99 ❖ 10 9 8 7 6 5 4 3 2 1

ACKNOWLEDGMENTS

The editors wish to thank both Harpers—Laurie Harper of Sebastian Agency and HarperPrism—for their support and enthusiasm, and Martin H. Greenberg, arguably the world's most renowned anthologist, for his advice and confidence. And, as always, there's the (mostly) unflappable "Cowboy Bob," Robert L. Fleck, without whose assistance this volume would probably still be in the pipelines. They wish to thank each other for keeping every promise made, the most important one being: "We're going to have fun, stay friends, and create something unique."

Peter sends his special love and gratitude to his wife, Padma Hejmadi.

Yet one more time, Janet Berliner extends unending love, affection, and gratitude to Laurie Harper for all of the long hours she put in, the countless conversations, and her invaluable input; to Bob Fleck, her personal assistant; her feisty mother, Thea Cowan; her daughter, Stefanie Gluckman; and her mentor and friend, Dr. Samuel Draper. You'll love *these* stories, Sam. To paraphrase, methinks that, "Age shall not wither them, nor custom stale their infinite variety."

TABLE OF CONTENTS

PREFACE

As Peter has written in his foreword to this volume, the range and
literacy of the stories we collected is nothing short of mind-boggling.
Clearly, the theme of immortality, together with the symbol of the unicorn, tapped a vein in the writers we approached. For that I am
extremely grateful.

More clearly, and this is something which Peter-the-modest would
never say himself, they would not dare to have given us anything but
their very best, their unique efforts. Some of them know him well and
are old friends; all of them stand in awe of his modesty and his talent.

I first met Peter more than fifteen years ago, at a writers conference
in Los Altos Hills, California. Of course I didn't know it was Peter, as I
stood near the campus swimming pool on that hot summer's day,
eaveswatching a man who looked like a bearded Jewish magician con-
verse with a shaggy mongrel.

"I talk to dogs, you know," the magician said, when he noticed my
presence. "And they answer me." Addressing, I suspect, the skepticism
on my face, he said, "Look, I'll prove it. I'll tell the dog to jump in the
pool, swim across, get out at the other side, and then walk around the
pool back here." He turned to the dog. "What's your name?"

"So you've trained your dog," I said. "Terrific."

"This isn't my dog. I've never seen it before in my life."

The dog obeyed, I became a believer, and Peter S. Beagle—con-
verser with dogs—and I have been friends ever since.

Before I left the campus that Sunday, I had purchased copies of two
of Peter's books, *A Fine and Private Place* and *The Last Unicorn*.
Those dog-eared, well-read copies have gone with me on every journey.
I have long wanted to find a project that would enchant us both. It is my
particular joy to have been the instrument that has reunited Peter with
the unicorn.

As for the theme of immortality, it too comes directly from Peter's
soul. One of the many things I have admired in him over the years is his
insistence upon keeping in touch with old, "forgotten" writers. Those
who perhaps wrote one opus, and then hid away, thinking themselves

unloved and unremembered. It is he who consistently reminds them that, though they may not be immortal in the physical sense, the words they have created are.

I can't tell which I love most, the heart of the man or his incredible talent; I can tell you that it's been a true joy putting this book together with him.

Thank you, Peter.

One more thing: The alphabetical-by-author order of the stories was pure synchronicity. We had no intention of creating an almost-encyclopedia of immortal unicorn stories, but so be it. Whatever works.

—Janet Berliner
Las Vegas, Nevada
April 1, 1995

FOREWORD

> ... and great numbers of unicorns, hardly smaller than an elephant in size. Their hair is like that of a buffalo, and their feet like those of an elephant. In the middle of their forehead is a very large black horn. Their head is like that of a wild boar, and is always carried bent to the ground. They delight in living in mire and mud. It is a hideous beast to look at, and in no way like what we think and say in our countries, namely a beast that lets itself be taken in the lap of a virgin. Indeed, I assure you that it is altogether different from what we fancied ...
>
> —Marco Polo

In the first place, I blame Janet Berliner for everything. This book was her idea from the beginning: she did the vast bulk of the editing, the telephoning, and all the other grunt work; and if you like *Immortal Unicorn,* it's mostly Janet's doing. If you don't like it, I'm covered.

In the second place, I could happily live out the rest of my time on the planet without ever having another thing to do with unicorns. Through what I persist in regarding as no fault of my own—my children were enjoying the chapters as I read them aloud, so I just kept going—I've been stuck with the beasts for some twenty-seven years now. First begun in 1962, published in 1968 (worlds and worlds ago, in a culture that measures time by elections and Super Bowls), *The Last Unicorn* is the book people know who don't know that I ever wrote anything else. Never a best-seller, never so much as a reliable annuity, it's been translated into fourteen languages, made into an animated film, and dramatized in half a dozen versions. People have written wonderfully kind and moving letters to me about it over the last twenty-seven years. I ran out of shyly spontaneous replies around 1980, I think it was.

But what amazed me as these stories began to come in is the eternal command the unicorn retains over the human imagination. Whether they turn up in the classic tapestry guises of Susan Shwartz's Arthurian tale, "The Tenth Worthy," or Nancy Willard's poignant variation, "The Trouble with Unicorns"; as dangerously attainable passions, in such works as P. D. Cacek's "Gilgamesh Recidivus" or Michael Armstrong's "Old One-Antler"; or as a source of karmic aggravation and cranky wonder to a rural community in Annie Scarborough's delightful "A Rare Breed," the damn things continue somehow to evoke astonishingly varied visions of soul-restoring beauty, indomitable freedom, and a strange, wild compassion, as well as the uncompromised mystery and elusiveness without which no legend can ever survive. Bigfoot, Nessie, Butch and Sundance, the unicorn . . . they leave footprints and dreams, but never their bones.

The title of this book has far less to do with physical immortality than with the unicorn's wondrously enduring presence in some twilight corner of our human DNA. From the European horned horse or dainty goat/deer hybrid to the ferocious, rhinoceros-like *karkadann* of Persia, India, and North Africa, to the Chinese *k'i-lin,* whose rare appearances either celebrated a just reign or portended the death of a great personage, there are surprisingly few mythologies in which the unicorn, or something very like it, does not turn up. India was the great medieval source of unicorn sightings; but over the centuries there have been accounts out of Japan, Tibet, Siberia, Ethiopia (Pliny the Elder and his contemporaries had a distinct tendency to stash any slightly questionable marvel in Ethiopia), Scandinavia, South Africa, and even Canada and Maine. Entirely regardless of whether they exist or not, something in us, as human beings, seems always to have needed them to be.

(It's worth mentioning that men have for centuries been manipulating the horn buds of cattle, sheep, and goats to produce a one-horned animal—with evident success, if that's your idea of success. Judith Tarr's story, "Dame à la Licorne," deals movingly and realistically with an eminently believable version of this ancient practice. But horns don't make the unicorn; it's the other way around.)

The possibility that unicorns might need humans just as much, in their own way, is well worth a moment's consideration. In *Through The Looking Glass,* after all, Lewis Carroll's unicorn says to Alice, ". . . Now we have seen each other, if you'll believe in me, I'll believe in you. Is that a bargain?" And there is a very old fable which holds that the unicorn was the first animal named by Adam and Eve, and that when they were barred from Paradise the unicorn chose to follow them into the bitter mortal world, to share their suffering there, and their joys as well. You might think about that legend when reading Robert Devereaux's story "What the Eye Sees, What the Heart Feels."

I've indicated earlier that I find the diversity of these stories as exceptional as their quality. What I expected (and after twenty-seven years of being sent cuddly stuffed unicorns, so would you) was an embarrassment of wistfulness, a plethora of dreamy elegies to metaphoric innocence betrayed, and a whole lot of rip-offs equally of *The Glass Menagerie* and the unicorn hunt scene in T. H. White's *The Once And Future King*. I couldn't have been more wrong.

The bulk of the tales in this book focus more on the power, and at times the genuine ferocity and aggressiveness of the unicorn—which is far more in keeping with the mythological record—than on its vulnerability. They range in setting from Lisa Mason's turn-of-the-century San Francisco to Eric Lustbader's all too contemporary Bedford-Stuyvesant district, to Cacek's Siberia, George Guthridge's linked Mongolia and Arctic Circle, Karen Joy Fowler's 1950s Indiana, Will Shetterly's nineteenth century American Southwest, Janet's own South Africa, and Dave Smeds' scarifying wartime Vietnam. Their tone cuts across a remarkable spectrum of action, style, and emotion, at one end of which we may with confidence place Robert Sheckley's quietly and profoundly flaky "A Plague of Unicorns." Somewhere in the middle we find Melanie Tem's tender and haunting "Half-Grandma," Fowler's "The Brew," Marina Fitch's lovely "Stampede of Light," Kevin Anderson and Rebecca Moesta's "Sea Dreams," Shetterly's "Taken He Cannot Be" (which swept away my grim resistance to reading one more flipping word about Wyatt, Doc, and the O.K. Corral), and Lucy Taylor's "Convergence"—stories less about unicorns *per se* than about generosity, courage, loneliness, love, and letting go: all immortal realities embodied by those aggravating creatures I appear to be stuck with. A little way along, a splendidly unique fantasy like Mason's "Daughter of the Tao" shades into "Dame à la Licorne," science fiction in the best sense of the term. (Incidentally, no man would have been likely to produce that one, by the way—I speak as the father of two daughters.)

Tad Williams' elegantly original "Three Duets for Virgin and Nosehorn" fits comfortably on the near side of "Daughter of the Tao," as does my own "Professor Gottesman and the Indian Rhinoceros." I'm honored to be in such company, and pleased that we've done our bit to restore the glamour (in the old Celtic sense of enchantment) of a noble beast, maligned and derided from Marco Polo through Hemingway and Ionesco. (Ionesco, by the way, had never seen a rhinoceros when he wrote the play that made the word a synonym for insane conformity. Introduced to two at the Zurich Zoo, I was once told he studied the creatures for a long while, and finally bowed formally, saying, "I have been deceived, and I apologize." Then he shook his walking stick at them and shouted, "But you are not real rhinoceroses!")

At the furthest end of the book's reach stalk Lustbader's "The Devil on Myrtle Ave.," Smeds' "Survivor," Michael Marano's "Winter Requiem," George Guthridge's "Mirror of Lop Nor," and S. P. Somtow's astonishing "A Thief in the Night." These are violent stories, as much or more in tone and vision as in action; and in these, too, unicorns as unicorns are less crucial than the central characters. The unicorn of "Winter Requiem" is a demon, plain and simple; the one literally depicted in "Survivor" is nothing more than a tattoo on a soldier's chest; while Somtow's unicorn is a shadow, a hoofprint, only seen fully for a moonlit moment at the end of this encounter between the Messiah and a strangely sympathetic Antichrist on the boardwalk at California's Venice Beach. For that matter, the unicorns of "Sea Dreams" are nar-whals, the steeds of undersea princes in a young girl's fairy tale; in Dave Wolverton's "We Blazed," there is no immortal beast at all, but a rock singer searching for his wife through the universe of her dreams. You won't find these unicorns up at the Cloisters museum, but you may very well recognize them all the same.

Strangers still ask me whether I believe in unicorns, really. I don't, not at all, not in the way they usually mean. But I do believe—still, knowing so much better—in everything the unicorn has always repre-sented to human beings: the vision of deep strength allied to deep wis-dom, of pride dwelling side by side with patience and humility, of unspeakable beauty inseparable from the "pity beyond all telling" that Yeats said was hidden at the heart of love. Even in my worst moments, when I am most sickened by the truly limitless bone-bred cruelty and stupidity of the species I belong to, I know these things exist. I have seen them, and once or twice they have laid their heads in my lap. In their very different manners, the stories in this book—altogether differ-ent indeed from what we fancied—express this old, foolish, lovely dream of the unicorn.

As I said at the beginning, any praise for *Immortal Unicorn* rightfully belongs to Janet Berliner. Me, I'm happy to be what used to be called, in the New York City garment trade, the "puller-in"—the guy who stood right outside the store and literally yanked people off the sidewalk, you absolutely got to see what we got here for you, fit you like custom-made. Not all of these tales may fit the unicorn of your imagining; but come inside anyway, come in out of the flat, painful sunlight of our time, blink around you for a bit, and see what might almost be moving and shining in the cool shadows.

—Peter S. Beagle
Davis, California
March 25, 1995

KEVIN J. ANDERSON & REBECCA MOESTA

SEA DREAMS

Peter: Kevin J. Anderson and his wife Rebecca Moesta are best known for their work on various *Star Wars* projects, both separately and as a team, but their story "Sea Dreams" has absolutely nothing to do with George Lucas or Darth Vader. It's about friendship, about storytelling, and about the ineffable place where magic and madness sometimes become one.

Janet: Kevin and Rebecca are dear friends of mine. I have long had the sense that their combined writing voice would contain some of the charm of their unique relationship with one another . . . which is why I solicited this coauthorship. It's so nice to be right!

Sea Dreams

JULIA CALLED ME TONIGHT AS SHE HAS SO MANY times before. Not on the telephone, but in that eerie, undeniable way she used since we met as little girls, strangers and best friends at once. It usually meant she needed me, had something urgent or personal to say.

But this time I needed her, in a desperate, throw-common-sense-to-the-wind way . . . and she knew it. Julia always knew.

And she had something to tell me.

Alone in the tiny bedroom of my comfortably conservative Florida apartment, I felt it as surely as I felt the cool sheets beneath me, and the humid, moon-warm September air that flowed through my half-opened window. At such times, common sense goes completely to sleep, leaving imagination wide awake and open to possibilities. And she called out to me.

Julia had been gone for five years, gone to the sea. Others might have said "drowned," might have used "gone" as a euphemism for "dead." I never did. The only thing I knew—that anyone *could* know for certain— was this: Julia was gone.

It had begun when we were eleven. That year, my parents and I left our Wisconsin home behind to spend our vacation at my grandmother's oceanside cottage in Cocoa Beach, Florida.

I had grown up in the Midwest, familiar with green hills and sprawling fields, but nothing had prepared me for my first sight of the Atlantic: an infinite force of blue-green mystery, its churning waves a magnet for my sensibilities, a sleeping power I had never suspected might exist.

Excited by the journey and the strange place, I was unable to sleep that first night in Grandmother's cottage. The rumble of the waves, the insistent shushing whisper of the surf muttering a white noise of secrets, vibrated even through the glass . . . and grew louder still when I got up and nudged the window open further to smell the salt air.

There, in the moonlight, a young girl stood on the beach—someone other than Grandmother, her friends, and my parents, talking about grown-up things while I patiently played the role of well-behaved daughter. Another girl unable to sleep.

I put on a bikini (my first) and a pair of jeans, tiptoed down the stairs, and let myself out the sliding glass door onto the sand. As I walked toward the ocean, reprimanding myself for the foolhardiness of going out alone at night, I saw her still standing there, staring out into the waves.

She seemed statuesque in the moonlight, fragile, ethereal. She had waist-length hair the color of sun-washed sand, wide green eyes—I couldn't see them in the dark, but still I *knew* they were green—and a smile that matched the warmth and gentleness of the evening breeze.

"Thank you for coming," she said. She paused for a few moments, perhaps waiting for a response. As I carefully weighed the advisability of speaking to a stranger, even one who looked as delicate as a princess from a fairy tale, she added, "My name is Julia."

"I'm Elizabeth," I replied after another ten seconds of agonized deliberation. I shook her outstretched hand as gravely as she had extended it, thinking what an odd gesture this was for someone who had probably just completed the sixth grade. Which, I discovered once we started to talk, was exactly the case—as it was for me.

We spoke to each other as if I had been there all along and often came out for a chat, not like strangers who had just met on the beach after midnight. Within half an hour, we were sitting and talking like old friends, laughing at spontaneous jokes, sharing confidences, even finishing each other's sentences as though we somehow knew what the other meant to say.

"Do you like secrets? And stories?" Julia asked during a brief lull in our conversation. When I hastened to assure her that I did—though I had never given it much thought—she fell silent for a long moment and then began to weave me a tale as she looked out upon the waves, like an astronomer gazing toward a distant galaxy.

"I have seen the Princes of the Seven Seas," she said in a soft, dreamy voice, "and each of their kingdoms is filled with more magic and wonder than the next. . . . The two mightiest princes are the handsome twins, Ammeron and Ariston, who rule the kingdoms of the North."

She had found a large seashell on the beach and held it up to her ear, as if listening. "They tell me secrets. They tell me stories. Listen."

Julia half closed her green eyes and talked in a whispery, hypnotic voice, as if reciting from memory—or repeating words she somehow heard in the convolutions of the seashell.

"They have exquisite underwater homes, soaring castles made of coral, whose spires reach so close to the surface that they can climb to the topmost turrets when the waves are calm and catch a glimpse of the sky. . . ."

I giggled. Julia's voice was so earnest, so breathless. She frowned at me for my moment of disrespect, and I fell silent, listening with growing wonder as her story caught us both in a web of fantasy and carried us to a land of blues and greens, lights and shadows, beneath the shushing waves.

"Each kingdom is enchanted, filled with light and warmth, and the princes rarely stay long in their castles. They prefer instead to ride across the brilliant landscapes of the underwater world, watching over their realms.

"Their loyal steeds are sleek narwhals that carry Ammeron and Ariston to all—"

"What's a narwhal?" I asked, betraying my Midwestern ignorance of the sea and its mysteries.

Julia blinked at me. "They're a sort of whale—like unicorns of the sea—strong swimmers with a single horn. Ancient sailors used to think they were monsters capable of sinking ships. . . ."

She cocked her head, listening to the shell. Her face fell into deep sadness for the next part of her story, and I wondered how she could make it all up so fast.

"The sea princes enjoy a charmed existence, full of adventure—they live forever, you know. One of their favorite quests is to hunt the kraken, hideous creatures that ruled the oceans in the time before the Seven Princes, but the defeated monsters hide now, brooding over their lost empires. They hate Ammeron and Ariston most of all, and lurk in dark sea caves, dreaming of their chance to murder the princes and take back what they believe is rightfully theirs.

"On one such hunt, when Ammeron and Ariston rode their beloved narwhal steeds into a deep cavern, armed with abalone-tipped spears, they flushed out the king of the kraken, an enormous tentacled beast twice the size of any monster the two brothers had fought before.

"Their battle churned the waves for days—we called it a hurricane here above the surface—until finally, in one terrible moment, the kraken managed to capture Ammeron with a tentacle and drew the prince toward its sharp beak, to slice him to pieces!"

I let out an unwilling gasp, but Julia didn't seem to notice.

"But at the last moment, Ammeron's brave narwhal—seeing his beloved prince about to die—charged in without regard for his own safety, and gouged out the kraken's eye with his single long horn! In agony, the monster released Ammeron and, thrashing about in the throes of death, caught the faithful narwhal in its powerful tentacles and crushed the noble steed an instant before the kraken, too, died."

A single tear crept down Julia's cheek.

"And though the prince now rides a new steed, his loyal narwhal companion is lost forever. He realizes how lonely he is, despite the friendship of his brother. Very lonely. Ammeron longs for another companion to ease the pain, a princess he can love forever.

"Ariston also yearns for a mate—but the princes are wise and powerful. They will accept none other than the perfect partners . . . and they can wait. They live forever. They can wait."

We watched the moon disappear behind us and gradually the darkness over the ocean blossomed into petals of peach and pink and gold. I was awed by the swollen red sphere of the sun as it first bulged over the flat horizon, then rose higher, raining dawn across the waves like a firestorm. I had never seen a sunrise before, and I would never see one as beautiful again.

But with the dawn came the realization that I had been up all night, talking with Julia. My parents never got up early, especially not on vacation. Still, I was anxious to get back to my grandmother's house, partly to snatch an hour or two of sleep, but mostly to avoid any chance of being caught.

I knew exactly what my parents would say if they knew I had gone out alone, spent the quiet, dark hours of the night talking to a total stranger—and I wouldn't be able to argue with them. It *did* sound crazy, completely unlike anything I had ever done before. *Irresponsible.* Even thinking the terrible word brought a hot flush of embarrassment to my cheeks.

But I wouldn't have traded that night for anything. Though I resisted such silliness for most of my life, that was the first time I ever experienced magic.

The vacation to Cocoa Beach became an annual event. Even when I went back to Wisconsin, Julia and I were rarely out of touch. My parents taught me to be practical and realistic, to think of the future and set long-term goals. Julia, however, remained carefree and unconcerned, as comfortable with her fantasies as with her real life.

We wrote long letters filled with plans for the future, and the hopes and hurts of growing up. We weren't allowed to call each other often, but whenever something important happened to me, the phone would ring and I would know it was Julia. She knew, somehow. Julia always knew.

During our summer weeks together, Julia spent endless hours telling me her daydreams about life in the enchanted realms beneath the sea. She had taught herself to sketch, and she drew marvelous, sweeping pictures of the undersea kingdoms. After listening to her for so long, I gradually learned to tell a passable story, though never with the ring of truth that she could give to her imaginings.

From Julia, I learned about the color of sunlight shining down from above, filtered through layers of rippling water. In my mind, I saw plankton blooms that made a stained-glass effect, especially at sunset. I learned how storms churned the surface of the sea, while the depths remained calm though with a "mistiness" caused by the foamy wavetops above.

I learned about hidden canyons filled with huge mollusks—shells as big and as old as the giant redwood trees—which patiently collected all the information brought to them by the fish.

Julia told me about secret meeting places in kelp forests, where Ammeron and Ariston went to spend carefree hours in their unending lives, playing hide-and-seek with porpoises. But the lush green kelp groves now seemed empty to them, empty as the places in their hearts that waited for true love. . . .

One day we found a short chain of round metal links at the water's edge. What its original purpose was or who had left it there, I could not fathom. Julia picked it up with a look that was even more unfathomable. She touched each of the loops again and again, moving them through her fingers as if saying some magical rosary. We kept walking, splashing up to our ankles in the low waves, until Julia gave a small cry. One of the links had come loose in her hand. She stared at it for a moment in consternation, then gave a delighted laugh. She slid the circlet from one finger to the next until it came to rest on the ring finger of her right hand, a perfect fit.

"There. I always knew he'd ask." Julia sent me a sidelong glance, a twinkle lurking in the green of her irises. She loosened another link and slipped it quickly onto my hand.

"All right," I sighed, feeling suddenly apprehensive, but knowing that it was no use trying to ignore her once she got started. "Who is 'he,' and what did he ask?"

"I am betrothed to Ammeron, heir to the Kingdom of the Seventh Sea," she said proudly.

"Sure, and I'm betrothed to his brother Ariston." I held up the cheap metal ring on my finger. "Aren't we a bit young to get engaged, Jule?"

Julia was unruffled. "Time means nothing in the kingdoms beneath the sea. When a year passes here, it's no more than a day to them. Time is infinite there. Our princes will wait for us."

"You really think we're worth it? Besides, how do they know whether or not we accept?" I challenged, always adding a completely out-of-place practicality to Julia's fairy tales. But my sarcasm sailed as far over Julia's head as a shooting star.

"Wait," she said, grasping my arm as she swept the ocean with her intense gaze. Suddenly, she drew in a sharp breath. "Look!" Her eyes lit up as a dolphin leapt twice, not far from where we stood on the shore. "There," she sighed, "do we need any more proof than that?"

Even in the face of her excitement, I couldn't keep the slight edge out of my voice. "I'll admit that I've never seen dolphins leap so close to shore, but what does that have to do with—"

"Dolphins are the messengers of the royal families beneath the sea," she replied in her patient way. Always patient. "One leap is a greeting. Two leaps ask a question. Three leaps give an answer." She flashed a smile at me. There was certainty in her voice that sent a shiver down my back. "And now they're waiting for us to respond!"

I struggled for a moment with impatience but couldn't bring myself to answer with more of my cynicism. I tried my most soothing voice. "Well, I'm sure Ammeron will understand that you—"

But she wasn't listening. Before I could finish my thought, she was running at top speed along the damp, packed sand. I looked after her, and, as I watched in amazement, she executed three of the most graceful leaps I had ever seen, strong and clean and confident. I knew I would look foolish if I even tried something like that. I'd probably fall flat on my face in the sand.

By the time I caught up to her, Julia was looking seaward, ankle-deep in waves, with tears sparkling on her lashes—or perhaps it was only the sea spray.

In her hand she held two more of the metal links from the chain she had found. Silently she handed me one of the links, then closed her eyes and threw the remaining one as far into the water as she could. I did the same, imitating her gesture but without the same conviction.

"Elizabeth," Julia said after a long moment, startling me with her quiet voice, "you are a very sensible person." It sounded like an accusation—and coming from Julia, it probably was.

We moved to drier sand and sat for a long time watching the waves, letting the bright sun dazzle our eyes. Perhaps too long. But Julia's hand on my arm let me know that she saw it, too.

Far out in the water a dolphin leapt. Three times.

*   *   *

Our lives were divided each year into reality and imagination, north and south, school and vacation, rationality and magic, until we finished high school.

I planned my life as carefully and sensibly as I could. My parents had taught me that a woman had to be practical—and I believed it. I chose my college courses with an eye toward the job market, avoiding "frivolous" art and history classes (no matter how much fun they sounded). After all, what good would they do me later in life?

My one concession to the lifelong pull the ocean had exerted on me was that I chose to go to school at Florida State. Luckily, it was a perfectly acceptable school for the business management and accounting classes I intended to take, so I wasn't forced to define my reasons more precisely.

And it allowed me to see Julia more often.

Julia, on the other hand, always lived on the edge of reality. My parents disapproved of her, and I grew tired of defending her choices, so we came to the unspoken agreement that we would avoid the subject entirely . . . though even I couldn't help being a bit disappointed in my friend. To me, it seemed Julia was wasting her life at the seaside.

I tried to help her make some sensible choices as well. She wasn't interested in college, preferring to spend her days hanging out near the ocean, making sketches that she sold for a pittance in local gift shops, doing odd jobs.

I convinced her to learn scuba diving. With her love of the sea, I knew she would be a natural, and in less than a year she was a certified instructor with a small, steady business. I even took lessons from her, as did one of my boyfriends, though that relationship ended in disaster.

As for romance, I occasionally went out on dates with men I met in classes, since I felt that our mutual interests should form a solid basis for long-term partnership, but my dating resulted only in passionless short-term relationships that usually ended with an agreement to be "just friends." I never let on how much these breakups really hurt me, except to Julia.

After each one, I would call Julia and she would meet me at The Original Fat Boy's Bar-B-Que, waiting patiently while I drowned my sorrows in beer and barbecued beef. Then we would drive to the beach, where I'd cry for a while, tell her the whole miserable tale, and vow never to make the same mistake again. Sometimes she drew tiny caricatures of my stories, forming them into comical melodramas as I spoke, until I was forced to acknowledge how silly or inconsequential each romance seemed as I dissolved into laughter and tears.

Julia dated often, drifting through each relationship with little thought for the future, until the inevitable stormy end—usually (I suspected) sparked by Julia's spur-of-the-moment nature and consequent unreliability that frequently frustrated men. Somehow on those nights, she would call to me and, no matter where I was, I would feel the need to go walking on our beach. And she would be there.

Once, particularly burned at the end of a tempestuous relationship, she asked what she was doing wrong—a rhetorical question, perhaps, but I answered her (as if *I* had had a better track record in love than she). "You're spending too much time in a fairy tale, Jule. I used to really love your stories about the princes and the sea kingdoms, but we're not kids anymore. Be a little more practical."

The ocean breeze lifted her pale hair in waves about her face as her sea-green eyes widened. "Practical? I could say you're living in just as much of a fairy tale, Elizabeth. The American Dream . . . following all the rules, taking the right classes, expecting to find treasure in your career and a prince in some accountant or lawyer or doctor. Doesn't sound any more realistic to me."

I felt stung, but she just sighed and looked out to sea, getting that lost expression on her face again. "I'm sorry. I didn't mean to dump on you like that. Don't worry. I guess I shouldn't be so upset either. It doesn't really matter, you know. After all, I'm betrothed to the Prince of the Seventh Sea."

And I managed to laugh, which made me feel better. But Julia had a disturbing . . . *certainty* in her voice.

The last time I ever saw Julia, her call was very strong. I was studying late on campus preparing for a final exam when for no apparent reason I felt an overpowering need to get away from my books, to talk to Julia. It had been months since I'd seen her.

No—she needed to talk to *me*.

Even though there was a storm warning in effect, I ran out the door without even stopping to pick up a jacket, got into my car, and sped all the way to Cocoa Beach. As I sprinted down to the beach behind Julia's house, I saw her standing on the sand. Dimly silhouetted against the cloudy sky, wearing nothing but a white bathing suit, her long hair blew wildly in the wind as she stared out to sea. It reminded me of the first time I had seen Julia as a little girl, standing in the moonlight.

When I came to stand beside her and saw her startled expression, I abruptly realized that something was very wrong: Julia hadn't expected me.

"You called me, Jule," I said. "What's going on?"

"I . . . didn't mean to." She seemed to hesitate. "I'm going diving."

Then I noticed the pile of scuba gear close by, near the water. I understood Julia's subtle stubbornness enough to realize that she placed more weight on her feelings than on simple common sense, so I stifled the impulse to launch into an anxious safety lecture and kept my voice neutral. "I know you have plenty of night diving experience, but you shouldn't dive alone. Not tonight. The weather's not good. Look at the surf."

For a while, I thought she wouldn't answer. At last she said softly, "David's gone."

"The artist?" I asked, momentarily at a loss before successfully placing the name of the current man in her life.

She nodded. "It doesn't really matter, you know. He fell head-over-heels for a pharmacist. It hit him so hard, I almost felt sorry for him. Don't worry; I don't feel hurt. After all . . ." Her voice trailed off. Her fingers toyed with the plain metal ring that hung from a silver chain around her neck. She had kept it all these years.

Her face was calm, but the storm in her sea-swept eyes rivaled the one brewing over the ocean. "After all," she finished with an enigmatic quirk of her lips, "I think tonight is my wedding night."

Uneasy, I tried for humor, hoping to stall her. "Don't you need a bridesmaid, then? I'll just go get my formal scuba tanks and my dress fins and meet you back here, okay?"

After a minute or so she looked straight at me, clear-eyed and smiling. "Thank you for coming. I really did need to see you again, but right now I think I need to be alone for a while."

"I'm not so sure I should leave," I said, stalling, reluctant to let her go, unable to force her to stay. "Friends don't let friends dive alone, you know?"

"Don't worry, Elizabeth," she said, barely above a whisper. "Remember, no matter what happens . . . I'll call you." She put on her diving gear, letting me help her adjust the tanks, kissed me on the cheek, and waded into the turbulent water. "I'll call you in a week—probably less. I promise."

As I left the beach I looked back every few seconds to watch her until I saw her head disappear beneath the waves.

Later, Julia's tanks and her buoyancy compensator vest were found in perfect condition on the shore a few miles away. And a plain silver neck chain. That was all.

* * *

That was five years ago. And tonight, when I needed her the most, I heard her call again.

Now, sitting on the damp sands, I listened to the hushed purr of the waves and stare at the Atlantic Ocean under the moonlight.

At times like this, here on the beach where Julia and I used to sit together, I wondered if I really was the sensible one. Yes, I made all the "right" choices, earned my degree, found a suitable job, got a comfortable apartment—though no dashing prince (accountant, lawyer, or otherwise) seemed to notice. I had been supremely confident that it would only be a matter of time.

But then, with a simple blood test, I ran out of time. Next came more tests, then a biopsy and a brief stay in the hospital. And behind it all loomed the specter of more and more time spent among the other hopeless cancer patients, walking cadavers, with the ticking of the deathwatch growing louder and louder inside their heads.

I would rather listen to the ocean.

It wasn't fair!

I raged at the universe. Hadn't I done everything right? Then why I had fallen under a medical curse, with no prince to kiss my cold lips and dislodge the bit of poisoned apple from my throat?

I needed to hear Julia's stories again. I longed to know more about the princes and their sea-unicorns, the defeated kraken, the tall spires of coral castles, in that enchanted undersea world where everyone lived forever.

I found a seashell on the shore, washed up by the tide, as if deposited there for me alone. I picked it up, brushing loose grains of sand from the edge, held it to my ear . . . and listened.

Far out in the water, I saw a dolphin make a double jump, two graceful silver arcs under the bright light of the moon.

My heart leapt with it, and I stood, blinking for a moment in disbelief. Then, feeling surprisingly restless and full of energy, I decided to go for a run along the beach.

And if I happened to leap once, twice, or three times . . . who was there to know?

ABOUT THE AUTHORS

Kevin J. Anderson's Jedi Academy trilogy—*Jedi Search, Dark Apprentice,* and *Champions of the Force*—has sold nearly three million copies and the books are the three top-selling science fiction novels of 1994 (according to *USA Today*). He is at work on other projects for Lucasfilm, including editing anthologies, cowriting a young-adult series of six books with his wife Rebecca Moesta, a new hardcover novel, a lavish coffee table art book, and a twelve-issue comic series for Dark Horse Comics, Dark Lords of the Sith.

Anderson's 1994 novel *Assemblers of Infinity*—written with Doug Beason—was nominated for the Nebula Award for best science fiction novel. Also that year his solo novel, *Climbing Olympus,* launched a new paperback line from Warner books and has been published in a fine leather-bound edition from the Easton Press. It will be produced unabridged by Books on Tape. Other major novels include *Ill Wind* (also with Beason) and *Blindfold,* both published in 1995.

Anderson has been to the top of Mount Whitney and the bottom of the Grand Canyon. He has been inside the Cheyenne Mountain NORAD complex; inside a Minuteman III missile silo and its underground control bunker; on the floor of the Pacific Stock Exchange; inside a plutonium plant at Los Alamos, New Mexico; and out on an Atlas-E rocket launchpad. He also, occasionally, stays home and writes.

Rebecca Moesta knew that she wanted to be an author since she was in her early teens, but it wasn't until five years ago that she began writing seriously. She has numerous *Star Wars* projects currently in the works. With her husband, Kevin J. Anderson, she has written a series of six young-adult novels (Young Jedi Knights), a series of four illustrated science books for grade-schoolers (Star Wars Cosmic Science), and two high-tech pop-up books. She has also written several science fiction stories, both on her own and with her husband, and cowritten three science fiction and fantasy novels under a pseudonym.

Moesta has worked for over five years as a technical editor and writer at the Lawrence Livermore National Laboratory, a large government research laboratory. Born in Heidelberg, Germany, to American parents, and raised in Southern California, she has traveled extensively in central Europe, and her research has taken her onto the set of a major motion picture (where she worked for a week as an extra), deep inside the Cheyenne Mountain NORAD complex, and into countless European castles and cathedrals.

She has one son, Jonathan, who keeps her busy nearly every minute that she doesn't spend writing. Her remaining time is spent serving as final reader and copy editor on all of her husband's manuscripts. In addition to her many fiction credits, she has had photographs, computer art, and nonfiction articles published in numerous science fiction magazines.

MICHAEL ARMSTRONG

—◦◦◦◦—

OLD ONE-ANTLER

Peter: As I implied in the foreword, the essence of the unicorn is independent of the form one culture or another may clothe it in. The one-antlered bull caribou of **Michael Armstrong**'s story shares in full the dignity, ferocity, and magical nature of its legendary counterpart, as well as the unicorn's capacity for pity and profound generosity. Michael Armstrong lives in Homer, Alaska, with his wife Jenny Stroyeck. He teaches English through the distance education program of the University of Alaska Anchorage, and has got to be the only writer included in this book who has also taught dog mushing.

Janet: Like so many of the writers in this book, Michael and I go way back. I remain constantly amazed by the breadth of his interests, which doubtless has more than a little to do with the depth of his insights.

Old One-Antler

~⟪ ⟫~

THROUGH THE OPEN FLY OF THEIR TENT, SAM watched his son peeing in the fresh snow. Malachi had grown about eight inches in the last year, Sam noticed, and some of the growth had been in places Malachi probably hadn't expected. Sam smiled as Malachi gingerly zipped his pants shut. The kid's learning about pubic hairs and the little brass teeth of jeans, he thought. Malachi handled his penis like it was some new toy that he hadn't quite worked all the bugs out of yet. And he probably hadn't, not at thirteen.

As Malachi walked over to the cook tent, Sam savored the warmth of the sleeping bag for a few moments, but then gave in to the same urge that had defeated Malachi minutes earlier: the son had inherited the weak bladder muscles of his dad, but Sam had learned a few things over the years, learned control, a little bit, and not to drink so much the night before.

Standing outside the tent, watching his pee shower down in a gentle arc and steaming in the chill air, Sam laughed at the obscenity Malachi had peed in the snow. That was good, he thought, a kid using urine like ink to express his frustration at waking to five inches of new snow on a late-August morning. A creative lad. Malachi would learn soon enough that snow was a pretty good thing when you were hunting caribou.

Sam finished up and poked his penis back into his pants, nestled it up against his single testicle. It had been fifteen years since he'd lost that nut to cancer. Just when he thought he didn't notice the loss anymore, fondling the lone ball in the floppy scrotum would bring the memory back. Hell with it, he thought. He zipped his fly and stretched, and gazed out at the tundra. They had made it, he realized.

Sam smiled at the sheer conspiracy of the trip. Each summer he got

Malachi for exactly five weeks, no more, no less, and he had to connive to make those five weeks last, had to figure out some way to impress upon Malachi that he, Sam, was his father, and that he, Sam, was a swell guy, and that he, Sam, knew a whole lot of things about life that Malachi's mother Roberta could never teach Malachi. Sam was a man and Roberta was a woman and Malachi was a boy becoming a man, and though Roberta insisted that she was teaching Malachi to be a good person, Sam knew that she could never teach Malachi what he had to be before he could be a good person; Roberta could never teach Malachi to be a good man. Although, Sam had to admit, he wasn't sure he could teach Malachi that, that any man could teach a boy how to be a good man. Sometimes only the boy could do that, learn himself.

The conspiracy was that Roberta thought Sam had taken Malachi up to the Arctic to look at birds, Sam having told his ex-wife some imaginative lie about migrating geese and the splendors of the fall tundra. Dumb bitch, he thought. If she knew anything about the Arctic, she would have known that the animal that sucked tanik outsiders up to the ass end of nowhere to Alaska in the fall was not birds, but big game, herds and herds of great animals with rippling muscles and wily minds and hearts and lungs just begging to be ripped to shreds by the sure shot of a 30-06 bullet. But if Sam had said to Malachi's mother, "Robbie, I'm taking our son up to the Arctic to blow away caribou," she would have dreamt up some court order—and he would have paid for it—that would have kept Sam from seeing his son for another year.

So Sam lied. He'd lied even to Malachi, which hurt him most of all. He didn't like the look on Malachi's face the night before when Waldo, their bush pilot, had set them down on a flat gravel bar along the braided Hula Hula River, and they'd set up camp and Sam had pulled out the two Ruger rifles, one new, one old, and gently handed the old one to Malachi.

"My first rifle," he had said. "It's yours now, son."

"Dad," Malachi had said, "it's a gun. I can't shoot it. What would Mom say?"

Sam had smiled, thinking what Mom would say. Robbie would say that guns were horrible things and that Malachi should never, ever, touch one, not even if an eight-hundred-and-fifty pound crazed grizzly was coming at you like a runaway locomotive and you knew the bear was going to rip your face off. But Robbie had never had to face a grizzly like that, and Sam had, and he knew what he would do, because he'd done it: he'd killed the bear, and apologized later, and then cut the bear's heart out and ate it, like Eskimos did.

"Hell, Mal," Sam had said. "You don't have to tell your mom."

Malachi had taken the rifle, held it gently in his soft hands, sighted down the barrel, clicked the trigger a few times, and smiled. Sam felt proud, and hopeful, too, because he knew that the bond was there, a faint spark he'd patiently fanned for all Malachi's life, a bond between father and son that no mother could quench. They were men and there were certain things men said and did to and with each other that women just couldn't understand.

Thinking of all that as he stared at the tundra, Sam breathed in the glory of the Arctic morning. He looked out at the hills dusted—no, covered in deep white snow—imagined the 'boos crawling across the tundra like ants on sugar. He almost went back in the tent to get his binoculars and glass the hills along the river, but shook his head. No hunting today, he thought. Today we throw thunder to the hills. Today we learn about rifles.

Malachi had learned a few things over the summers, and the lesson he'd learned well because Sam had screamed it into him one trip until Sam knew the words were scorched on Malachi's eardrums—the thing Malachi had learned was that the first guy up boiled water. Just like that, no thought, dump some snow in a pot, or walk to a creek, and boil water, even if you hated coffee or tea, because you had to boil water in the wilderness, boiled it unless you liked beaver fever, giardia, ripping your guts out for months after. Sam walked over to the cook tent—really, a tarp suspended over a gas stove on a box of food, the tarp sagging with snow—and smiled to see his son had primed the stove and started water boiling. Maybe he'd learn to drink coffee this summer, too, Sam thought. Maybe.

"Sleep well?" he asked Malachi.

"No," Malachi said. "Damn snow. It sounded like mosquitoes suiciding on the tent."

"Sure snowed a fuck of a lot, didn't it?" Malachi winced at the obscenity and Sam smiled.

"Yeah," Malachi said, punching the underside of the tarp and knocking damp snow off the shelter. "We going to get socked in?"

Sam laughed. "This isn't real snow, son. Not enough to stop Waldo from picking us up." He waved an arm at the expanse of white. "Besides, this will all melt by the afternoon. The serious snow won't come for another month or so."

"What if we get stranded?" Malachi asked. "What if like Waldo forgets us?"

Sam clapped him on the shoulder. "Then I guess we'd have to build an iglu or something, eh?" And Sam grinned at the horrified look on his son's face, at the thought that they might have to spend a winter there on that tundra. Horrors, horrors: a winter with his dad.

They made a quick breakfast—pancakes with blueberries picked the night before—and cleaned the kitchen and then got rifles and shells and went off to shoot. Clouds still covered the hills to the south, but the sun over the Beaufort Sea to the northeast promised to burn off the fog and soon the snow.

Father and son walked to the end of the little bush airstrip Waldo had dropped them off at the day before, away from the spike camp they would hunt from, to a pile of empty fuel drums at the edge of the gravel clearing. The airstrip had been an old military strip, abandoned barrels and stuff the way the military used to just chuck trash on the tundra, but the local Native corporation had picked it up in a land deal. You had to have permission to use it—the locals didn't mind outsiders hunting there, but liked them to pay for the privilege—and since Sam had done some programming work for the village, they let Waldo take him out there gratis.

It disgusted Sam to come here and use the strip, because it didn't seem like real wilderness, but he had to admit the airstrip had its advantages for a good caribou hunt. A few days later it'd be packed with caribou hunters guided by local villagers. For the moment, though, Sam hoped to get some peace with his son. The bulls might not come through for a few days, but that didn't matter, not yet. Today Malachi had to learn to shoot.

Sam dragged an old packing flat out a hundred yards from a drum, tacked a target to the gray wood, and went back to Malachi. The two rifles still lay flat on the top of the drum, still in the open cases, their chambers open. Good, Sam, thought, Malachi hadn't been tempted to touch them. He remembered the first rule Sam had drummed into Malachi four years ago before Robbie got weird about what Sam could do with his son and he could still take Malachi to the shooting range. Never touch a gun when a person is downrange, leave the gun in its case and with an empty chamber.

He patted his son on the shoulder, took the old Ruger out of the more battered of the two cases, and handed it to Malachi. The Mauser-style bolt had been pulled back, the chamber open and ready to take a cartridge.

"You know how to load it, Malachi?" Sam asked.

Malachi gave his dad a hard look, a little-boy tough-ass glare, said, "Sure," and reached for the box of brass rounds. Handloads, Sam's special mix of bullet and powder. He picked out a shell, held it away from him as if it were a spider, and gingerly slid it into the open chamber. Malachi turned the bolt up, started to slide the bolt forward.

"Son," Sam said, "seems to be a little glare out. You might shoot better with some glasses."

Malachi turned to Sam, and Sam had slipped on a pair of amber shooting glasses, big aviator-style shades that made him look like an evil genius. The boy nodded, reached into his parka pocket, and took out his own pair of glasses, slipped them onto his big nose—a nose like his momma's. He reached for the bolt again.

"And son," Sam said again, "I know you've gone deaf from all those years of being plugged into a Walkman, but if you want to save what hearing you do have left . . ." He held out his hand and opened up a palm in which four little foam earplugs nested.

"Right, Dad," the boy said, taking a pair of plugs and cramming them into his ears. Nice ears, Sam thought, earlobes separate, like his dad's.

"Okay, son," Sam said loudly, and the boy nodded.

Malachi slid the bolt forward and down, locking the shell in, then stepped around to the butt end of the gun, staring at it, looking at it, wondering what to do with it. Sam tapped him on the shoulder, waved him aside. He took the new Ruger down from the drum, laid it on a knapsack on the ground, snapped the old case shut, and put the stock of the old rifle on top of the case. Pulling an earplug out, Sam pointed at Malachi's ear, and the boy took one plug out, too.

"Okay, Malachi," the father said, "the scope's off this rifle, so you have to use the sight. Remember what I taught you years before? Think of the back sight as a valley, the forward sight as a mountain, and the target as the sun. Put the mountain at the head of the valley, and have the sun setting on the mountain. Not behind the mountain—it's setting on the tip of the mountain. "

"Line them up?"

"Line 'em up, one, two, three. You've got good eyes. Let the end of the stock rest on the case, hold the stock with your left hand. Right hand around the grip, index finger hooked slightly against the trigger. Got it?"

"Got it." The boy leaned against the drum, and Sam could see his legs shake slightly. Not good, he thought, the boy would have to get over that.

"Now, remember how you pulled the trigger on your old twenty-two?" Did he even remember his old .22? Sam thought. Did he remember his mother throwing the little pump rifle out the second story window of their house, fully loaded, the rifle discharging and putting a round into their chicken coop? Did he remember his mother unloading the rifle—smart woman, Sam thought—and smashing it with a splitting maul? Probably.

"Yeah, Dad. 'Don't jerk, pull.' One smooth movement."

"Good, son. Pull, then." Malachi put his earplug back in, and Sam smiled at the command. Pull, son. Try. Do it. Put me in front of the rifle and pull the trigger. Put your mother in front of the rifle and pull the trigger. Imagine it, boy. Imagine.

"Trigger won't pull, Dad." Malachi reached up, turned the safety off, and then Sam put his earplug in.

"Good, Malachi," he shouted. "Now try it. Relax. Breathe in, hold the breath, pull, exhale. Relax. Breathe, hold—fire!"

Sam watched the rifle end, always the clue. Watch how the rifle tip moved, watch how the movement of finger translates into eye movement, into focus, into breath, into shot. If the boy is relaxed, the tip will kick up slightly. If the boy is tense, it won't move, his muscles will hold it, fight the discharge, and he'll have a bad shot.

Malachi pulled the trigger. The rifle kicked, smoke rose up around them, and Sam heard the air fold around the bullet, heard the crack and the explosion that propelled the bullet. He always listened for that crack first, that satisfying flight of lead pushing air before it, sound collapsing behind lead. And the tip of the rifle: the tip swayed up, gentle for a 30.06, the boy's left hand riding up with the barrel and not fighting it. Good, boy, good, thought Sam. My son.

"All right, Malachi," Sam said. "How'd that feel? You feel loose?" He looked over at his son, his son sliding the bolt back already, opening the chamber, ejecting the shell.

"Yeah." Malachi looked up at his dad, a little grin on his face. You had to have that grin or you couldn't shoot, Sam thought. You had to feel the power and be in awe of it, not afraid, but in awe, or you wouldn't respect the rifle, respect the death in it. "Yeah. It felt fine, Dad. I felt relaxed, cool, Dad."

"Let's see how you did." Malachi got up, walked around in front of the rifle, glanced back at his dad, at Sam standing still and not moving. "Say the magic word, Mal."

Malachi smiled. "Clear, Dad. All clear." He pointed at the rifle, at the open breech, at the bolt pulled back.

Father and son walked downrange to the target, to the pallet a hundred yards away on the gravel strip. The smoke from the shell hung in the air like the clouds, and the sound of the firing still echoed from the hills. The violence of the firing lingered over the tundra, an unknown sound in a land of roaring winds. Malachi got to the target first, turned—grinning—and pointed at a little hole in the paper between the second and third rings under the bull's-eye.

"Good shot, son," Sam said. He took a pen from his parka and drew an X through the hole. "That'd be a lung shot on a 'boo if you had fired at it, if a 'boo would be obliging enough to stand still while we happened to be by that old drum there." Sam smiled. "A good shot, son. Let's keep trying, okay—you and me. We'll sight in the scopes, and then"—he looked out at the rolling tundra, at the hills he imagined treed with the velvet antlers of bulls preparing to rut—"and then maybe tomorrow we can look for some 'boo, maybe get one, okay? Maybe we'll find old One-Antler, huh?"

"Old One-Antler . . ."

Sam smiled at his son, as the memory lit up the boy's face. Years ago, Sam had told Malachi the story of Old One-Antler, a fable he'd made up, a tanik myth told as if it had been an Inupiaq legend. A great bull caribou roamed the Arctic, the story went, its antlers twisted together in one great rack, a single curved horn on its forehead. Legend had it that Old One-Antler could never die, that if you shot it and ate of its flesh or drank its blood before it miraculously healed itself, its immortality would be imparted to you. Even the antlers it shed yearly could serve as an antidote to pain and sickness—or give a tired old man new virility.

"Sure," Malachi said. "Maybe we can get Old One-Antler." And he walked—no, strode, Sam thought—strode back to the barrel and the rifle. He could see the pride in his walk, Sam thought, could see the confidence rippling through the boyish awkwardness, could see the strength firming up his downy legs, his clean cheeks. My son, Sam thought, my son.

They set out the next day to go hunting, the day clear and relatively warm, with a slight breeze blowing down from the north, enough to keep the bugs down. Mal and Sam packed light day packs—rain suit, gloves, lunch, water bottles, emergency blanket—strapped to bare backpack frames, the "torture rack" they'd haul out meat with, if they got a caribou. Sam carried a ground-to-air radio and they both had their rifles, of course, and ammunition.

Sam led the way up the creek valley that flowed into the Hula Hula River, over a small pass, and along another creek and around another mountain, to a set of terraces on the west flank of the mountain, each terrace like giant steps up the mountain—the site. The mountain had no name on the local topographical quad map, only an elevation: 1204 feet. As they hiked through ankle-deep wet bog, Sam counted drainages coming off the sides of the valley, so he'd know which drainage to take coming back if fog came in and hid the more identifiable ridge peaks.

Worst case scenario, Sam thought, if the fog came in so deep and they got totally lost, they could hike up to the ridge tops, and find their way back by the cairns set along the ridge. That's how he had found the site in the first place, found the ancient hunting camp: he'd been hiking over the ridge two summers before, had found the cairns, had followed them down and they led like exit signs to a creek and up to the old Inupiaq Eskimo camp on the lower of the terraces below elevation 1204.

Or, Sam thought, working his way up out of the bog to drier land below the valley ridge to his left, if they really got lost, they could just follow the caribou trails.

Along every hillside, along every creek, over passes and through valleys, generations of caribou, millions of caribou, had etched foot-wide trails in the tundra. Ground through the thin vegetation, through the moss and lichen and willow and grass, muddy trails wound over the country. Nothing guaranteed that the same caribou or the same herd would pass along the same trail year after year, but it was a safe bet, Sam knew, that some caribou at some time that summer would grace this ground with the chevrons of their hooves.

After walking several hours, Sam and Malachi stopped at the head of the creek valley, where it split beneath 1204 and wrapped around the bottom of the terrace. They had a view of the site up on the terrace, and of the tundra beyond. Sam unshucked his pack, brushed away snow from a rock, and sat down. Malachi remained standing.

"Hey, take five, son," Sam said.

Malachi nodded, took off his pack, but remained standing.

"Whatever," Sam grumbled. He pointed down at a clump of droppings, about the size and shape of raisins. With the tip of his hunting knife, he poked at the pellets. "Squishy," Sam said. "Recent, since last night's storm." Sam then noticed tracks, each pair of curved cuts in the snow like two scimitars mirroring each other. Two round dots about the size of a dime were at the base of each set of tracks. The wind had blown over part of the tracks, giving Sam an excuse for not noticing them earlier.

"Boo, Dad?" Malachi asked.

Sam nodded. "Big one. Maybe Old One-Antler," he joked. The father took out his binoculars and glassed the far terrace, then the hillside across the creek valley, where the tracks had come from. "Just stragglers now, Malachi. The lone bulls coming to meet the ladies as they head back south. The tracks seem to head up to the site." Sam smiled. "Let's follow them up there, set up a watch, and see what comes."

The site hadn't looked like an archaeological site when Sam had first found it: no mounds, no crumbling sod huts or whalebone jaws sticking out of the ground. But if you looked at the bones littering the tundra, their very number indicated something cultural. Someone had killed a lot of caribou in the past there, and not just a pack of wolves or a ruthless grizzly. The middles of longbones had been crushed into unidentifiable fragments, while the ends bore the marks of stone or metal knife cuts. Skulls had been bashed in at the face to get at the delicate brains, and the antlers had been cleanly sawn away. Humans had been there, had hunted many caribou over more than one season, and they had left behind the bones of their butchery.

A more trained eye could detect the depressions of tents, or the rings of stones that held down the tents. Higher up on another terrace, where the grass didn't grow as thick and where the wind swept away soil so that only lichens could take bloom, clear signs of human passing had been more obvious: sled parts, a knife handle made of bone, a steel point, or dozens of blue and turquoise trade beads. And more bones, human bones, the gracile bones of the lower arm and upper leg, or ribs, or the high dome of a skull. None of that remained now, Sam remembered; all the surface artifacts and much of the subsurface stuff had been plotted, excavated, numbered, bagged, and taken away to museums.

Sam had found the site, had led a team of archaeologists back there and helped them dig it, and had developed the computer program to map the locations of bones and beads. Two summers ago he had come out there with one of the archaeologists, and a friend, to do some follow-up testing, and it was then that he had discovered the incredible caribou hunting the ancients had known long ago. Better, he had discovered that the knoll a half-mile across from the site could be used to land a Cessna 185, if the pilot knew his stuff, like Waldo, and if the passengers dared enough. Sam hoped they could get a caribou in the general area, butcher it, and cache the meat on the knoll, then hike back to the airstrip and get Waldo to swing by to recover the meat on the return home.

A side fork of the creek rose up to a little valley to the north, and Sam and Malachi worked their way across the creek and up to the terrace. They spread out, following the tracks, noting the progress of the caribou. There, the bull had stopped to drink from the open creek. Then, it had run for a brief moment, spooked by who knew what. Finally, it traversed the side of the terrace, and over the edge—could still be there. The storm front had broken, and bright sunshine lit up the slope. The bull could be basking in the sun, glad for the respite from flies and mosquitoes, glad for the moderate warmth before the long winter and the longer migration south—or so Sam imagined.

The wind blew into their faces, carrying their scent behind, and the slope hid them as they worked their way up. An old bleached caribou rack lay on the tundra, its tips spotted with orange lichen. Sam picked it up and held it to his head, waggling it. Malachi giggled at Sam's joke, but Sam shook his head. He pointed at his son's rifle, slung across the top of the boy's pack, and then at Malachi. The boy nodded, and took down his rifle. He had the scope on now, sighted in the day before, and five rounds in the magazine, none in the chamber. Sam took his new rifle out, but kept it slung over his shoulder. With his left hand, he held the caribou rack to his head, and then they went up the hill.

At the crest of the terrace, where Sam guessed a caribou might see this rack coming over the top, he motioned to Malachi to stop. Sam had no idea if there even was a caribou above, but he had heard of the trick before. Distract the game with antlers, draw it in at the curiosity of another bull. It would be just before the rut, when any bull would be wary of another bull, and be drawn to the challenge. Or so he hoped. The tracks looked fresher going up the terrace, and even if there was nothing, the 'boo had to be close.

"Ready," Sam whispered, and they went up.

Sam held the old antlers high, brow tines dipped in challenge, and he quickly ran up the slope. Malachi came after him, rifle raised. Father and son came over the crest, to the broad flat slope of the main terrace on the site, and came upon—nothing.

Malachi lowered the rifle, and Sam let the antlers droop down, not holding them as high. The snow still clung to the terrace, white obliterating the bones the archaeologists had not collected. The memory of the site came back to Sam then: the cluster of tents at the far edge of the terrace, the big cook tent surrounded by smaller pup tents, and the mast of the radio antenna central on the site. Lines had been strung up and down the slope, marking the transects, and he could still remember tripping over them in the fog. Now the site was empty, empty but for a plain of snow and a few rocks burning their way to the surface as the snow melted.

Scanning the field, Sam made sure the bull didn't rest in some slight depression, or hadn't bolted away from them. Malachi saw the bull first. He tapped his father on the shoulder and then pointed up. There, on the next ridge, the barren ridge where the archaeologists had found the trade beads and the grave, a massive bull caribou stood. Its off-white coat barely stood out against the bright horizon, but the massive dark rack— still maroon in velvet—revealed its presence. It held its face away from them, the rack most prominent. Even in the glaring light, Sam could count a dozen points. A legal kill, certainly, and a trophy, no doubt. Definitely a trophy.

Sam waved his arm down, back below the ridge, out of sight. Malachi nodded. Sam pointed at the ridge rising up to the base of the higher terrace. His son smiled, understanding: they would work their way along the ridge, staying out of the big bull's vision, and then come up the base of the terrace until they were below where the bull had been. If it didn't move, they would be able to rise up to it, pulling the same antler trick again.

Malachi kept to Sam's right and behind as Sam took the point, skirting the very edge of the ridge, keeping just enough of the higher terrace in view to maintain their bearings. The face of the higher terrace rolled down to the top of the little creek valley, meeting the ridge of the lower terrace. One slab of the upper terrace's face had fallen away, and sheets of purple shale showed the geology of the structure: sandstone and shale topped with soil and tundra. Sam remembered that the terrace had been mostly free of permafrost, the ground too well drained to hold water and freeze.

They walked up to the ridge, up to where the face of the upper terrace had fallen away, to where they would most be hidden. There, Sam paused, adjusting the old antlers. Both of them panted with the exertion, with the excitement. Sam held up a hand, and Malachi nodded, understanding again. Wait. Catch their breath. Don't let the rush of adrenaline spoil what would be a good shot, perhaps an only shot. After a few minutes, Sam jerked his head up the hill, then pointed at Malachi's rifle and mimed jacking a round. Malachi grinned, slid the bolt up and forward, but kept the safety on.

Sam held up five fingers, then slowly let each finger fall down, counting to one. As he raised his index finger, he pointed at the hill above, and they charged. The father stayed to Malachi's left, great rack on his head and leading the way. The son followed Sam, a step behind, and they came up.

The bull held its back to them, head turned away from them and staring at the foothills beyond, the breeze in its face. Its rump faced them, a narrow profile and a hard shot. Sam wiggled the rack, trying to get the bull's attention—to get it to move, a side profile and a clear shot. He wiggled the rack again. Nothing. The bull ignored them. Malachi raised his rifle, clicked off the safety. Sam quickly shook his head, whispered, "Hold." Malachi waited. Sam waved the antlers again, and started to throw them down in disgust at the great bull's disregard of them. He'd throw a rock at it to get its attention. But then the bull turned.

Slowly it turned its head to them, bringing its body around, a clear shot, almost begging for the bullet: low rump, massive hind legs and forelegs and chest, its head nearly the size of a bear's, and its rack four, no five feet high off its head. Sam dropped the old antlers and pulled up his rifle, all the while shouting "Shoot! Shoot!" Malachi held his fire, though, even though Sam had stepped back, even though Malachi now stood in front, rifle held steady and in a perfect firing stance. And he did not shoot.

"Goddamn it," Sam shouted, pulling up his own rifle and jacking a round in, to hell with giving the boy the honor of the first shot. The bull turned to them, and Sam saw what made Malachi hold, why he stood transfixed by the caribou—as the caribou now held Sam in his gaze and he, too, could not move.

The bull caribou's antlers rose from his forehead, the two antlers set a hair's width apart, so that they twisted and grew together, one antler, really—Old One-Antler, Sam now saw. The legend made real. Part of him debunked the mystery of it, calculated how it would be possible for a caribou's antlers to be set close together, so that they grew as one. Enough radiation from atomic testing, from failed nuclear power plants, had dusted the Arctic so that such a mutation could arise. But another part of Sam's intelligence tossed away rationality, and glorified the mystery. Old One-Antler, the immortal single-horned beast, the imaginative tanik's legend that had turned out to be true.

Old One-Antler held them like that, kept them stunned in its gaze, and then it came toward them, a great leap and then a horrible rush. He lowered his horn, the dozen points red with velvet and red, Sam saw, with something else—with blood, its own blood or the blood of others. Even though Sam had faced down a dozen grizzlies, and had the steady nerve to calmly kill them, he found himself trembling at Old One-Antler.

Finally Malachi fired. The bullet cracked in the stillness of the vast tundra, lead flying, and Sam heard a slight thwick as the bullet nicked a point off Old One-Antler's brow tine. A good shot, and had Malachi been an inch lower, a killing shot to the brain.

Sam fired then, but his hands still shook, and the shot went wild, not even passing near the old bull. Old One-Antler turned to the father, his attention distracted. Malachi fired again, getting his range, and he shot off another tine. The bull turned away from Sam, saw the source of danger, and came upon the boy.

"No!" Sam yelled, trying to distract it, seeing what the caribou intended. He took a deep breath, calming himself, aimed, and pulled the trigger again. The feeling came back to him as he pulled, the knowing that he had aimed true and steady, and that the bullet would find home. A hollow click came from the chamber. Sam slid the bolt back, and saw an empty chamber. The next brass round in the magazine hadn't advanced. He worked the bolt, but couldn't get the cartridge to come up. Jammed. Sam cursed at his hand rounds, wondering if he had crimped the bullets properly. He reached into his pocket for another round, inserting it into the open chamber as he looked over at his son.

Malachi kept shooting, the last of his shots hitting, but not killing, breaking off tines but not coming any lower. For a moment Sam wondered if Malachi intended to break the antler and not kill, wondered if he could have pumped every one of his rounds into the bull's head and chest. As the bull bore down on his son, though, Sam saw that Malachi shot to kill, that his last desperate shot had been aimed to kill, but that for some reason the boy just couldn't adjust his aim right. The last shot grazed the bull's forehead, and then the bull came down on Malachi, on his son.

With its massive antler, the bull gored the boy in the stomach, catching the tip of a broken tine on Malachi's rib cage, and throwing the boy up in the air. Old One-Antler held his son—impaled, like a trophy—looked over at Sam, and then dropped the boy. In that moment Sam had a shot, and took it. His son free, the caribou presenting its flank to him, Sam held his breath, let instinct guide him more than thought, pulled the trigger, and heard the satisfying hard-metal click of hammer hitting primer.

A bullet hit finally, its energy hardly shed by the four- or five-yard flight through air; it hit hard on, tearing through lungs and heart and backbone, and the bull toppled to the ground. Malachi writhed on the snowy tundra, his hands bloody and the snow bloody as he clutched at his ruined stomach. Intestines rolled through his fingers, the smell of barely digested food stenching the warming air. And Old One-Antler writhed on the ground, too, legs kicking and a huge hole dappling its skin where the bullet had come out. Sam ignored the dying caribou and walked over to his son.

"Good shooting, Dad," Malachi said, grimacing.

"Shh, boy, shhh." Sam took off his pack and ripped off his parka and shirt, pressing the wadded-up shirt to the boy's stomach. A gut wound, and a hundred miles from a health clinic: the boy was dead. Sam hoped he'd die before he understood that there was no saving him.

The thrashing of the caribou behind him angered Sam. That damn bull should have died by now, he thought. He turned from his son for a moment, and looked at Old One-Antler. The big bull still kicked his legs. Kicked them, Sam saw, not jerking them—not the dying throes of severed nerves. Kicked them. Sam drew his knife to cut the bull's throat, to end its misery as he wished he could end his own son's misery.

Old One-Antler rose.

It rose on good legs and came to them and snorted hot blood into Malachi's face. The boy pulled back at the onslaught of foamy fluid, but the bull's blood streamed down his face. Malachi licked at it, and for a moment quit groaning. Old One-Antler stood, sneezing blood until its lungs ran clear. The wound in its chest closed up, until it was no more than a red stain on white fur. Even the broken tips of its antler seemed to come back.

Malachi groaned again, his stomach still bleeding. The foamy blood had been only a temporary salve. Sam looked at his son, at the healed caribou, at the knife in his hand. Old One-Antler stood panting. Sam looked at his rifle, still loaded, and at the knife. The caribou couldn't be killed, he saw—not long enough or fast enough. But . . .

Sam raised the knife, held the old bull in his gaze. The bull didn't move or couldn't move, he never did know, but Sam didn't care. Calmly he strode to Old One-Antler, until he was at the caribou's side. Sam stared at the caribou, its eyes almost pleading, and then he quickly hacked off a foot-long hunk of flesh from the caribou's right thigh. The wound closed even as Sam pulled away the steaming meat. Old One-Antler nodded its great rack to them, turned away, and disappeared over the edge of the terrace.

The meat dripped in Sam's hand as he came to his son. Malachi licked at the blood of the steak, and his groans quieted. Sam cut off small chunks of the steak, feeding them to his son. At first, Malachi chewed slowly at the raw flesh. With each bite he chewed harder: greedy, devouring. The boy took the last bit of steak from Sam, but Sam held it back.

It would give immortality, he thought. Some logic of the legend told him, though, that a body had to be nearly whole for the magic to work. It would work on him. For Malachi, it would only heal. Sam dared to look at his son then, wiped away blood from his boy's gaping wound. It had closed up, the intestines had wound back into his abdominal cavity, but the wound still bled. Just a taste, he thought, feeling his age, his stiff bones—the loss of that testicle so long ago.

The loss of his nut still pained, and he realized why: it meant the loss not only of part of his manhood, but of his marriage, of a loving woman. Things had started to go bad with Roberta right after Sam had licked the testicular cancer, as if the sacrifice of a testicle wasn't enough. The empty scrotum seemed to symbolize so many bonds broken. In that moment, Sam realized that what hurt most was that the greatest loss of all might have been of what mattered most: his son.

Just one taste, Sam thought, and perhaps he could be like Old One-Antler, could be whole—and live forever. Perhaps he could recover all that he had lost.

Malachi reached up for the last bit of steak, and Sam held it back, and then he smiled; he knew what he had to do, what fathers did, and he let his son take the last of the meat. He let his son lick Old One-Antler's blood from his hand, let the boy gently clean the blood from Sam's knife blade. Almost every drop went to Malachi. The wound closed up then, Malachi's blood drying up and only the shredded ends of his shirt testimony to the goring.

Sam reached into the bloody snow, the snow where Old One-Antler had lain, and he wadded up the snow and sucked on it. A surge of energy washed through him. The father stood, staring at the blood on the snow, at his son's blood and the caribou's blood. Even as he watched the snow steamed away, the late-summer sun heating the ground. Malachi slept, the sun warming his face.

On a far ridge, Old One-Antler looked down at him, as if warning him, as if playing with him. Sam understood. He took his rifle, worked the bolt, and the jammed round and the remaining rounds in the magazine fell to the tundra, more artifacts for the ancient's site. He left the rifles where they were, then hoisted his own pack, taking Malachi's day pack off the frame and lashing it to his own pack. Then with renewed strength, he lifted Malachi up in a firefighter's carry and took the boy across the terrace and over to the knoll where Waldo would land the plane.

On the knoll Sam held his son in his arms, stroking the boy's hair as he slept. The backpack lay on the ground, the radio on top of it. Sam waited for the distant hum of Waldo's plane as he shuttled another load of hunters onto the tundra. He knew they would find no trophies that year. Sam smiled, though, for Old One-Antler had given him something more wonderful than wild meat or some great set of antlers.

He had given him back his son.

ABOUT THE AUTHOR

Michael Armstrong was born in Virginia and raised in Florida. He now lives in Homer, Alaska. A graduate of New College, the University of Alaska, and the Clarion Writers Workshop, he wrote the novels *After the Zap, Agviq,* and *The Hidden War*. His short fiction has been published in *The Magazine of Fantasy and Science Fiction* and *Asimov's*. He has also had fiction in several original anthologies, including *Afterwar, Cold Shocks*, and *Rat Tales*. He teaches English through the distance education program of the University of Alaska Anchorage, and has also taught dog mushing and writing. Michael has also worked on archaeological digs in Arctic and south-central Alaska. He and his wife, Jenny Stroyeck, live in a small house they built themselves, and have a small sled dog team, a large house dog, and one cat.

PETER S. BEAGLE

PROFESSOR GOTTESMAN AND THE INDIAN RHINOCEROS

Janet: I said my piece about my personal relationship with **Peter S. Beagle** in the preface to this book; his official bio can be found at the end of his story. Since he (not unsurprisingly) refused to write this introduction to his own story, let me insert here what he wrote for what was originally intended as a coeditor's note for this volume: "Just because my stuff usually turns up on the fantasy and science fiction shelves doesn't mean that I keep up with the field worth a damn. A few years ago, when I was visiting in New York City, my closest old friend and I drifted into the bookstore Forbidden Planet, and found ourselves gaping at serried ranks of books written by nobody we'd ever heard of—and we both grew up on this stuff. I can still hear my friend asking in a hushed and anxious tone, 'Peter, who *are* these people?' I hadn't a clue then, and I haven't much of one now; but some of them can write up a storm . . . "

Peter is correct about the stories in this book. However, what *he* writes is more like the soft murmuring of breezes across the sensibilities of readers from seven to seventy. Regarding his story in this volume, Peter said, "I didn't intend it to, but it came out an homage to Robert Nathan, who was my friend and a wonderful writer." Outside of that, I'm safest if I paraphrase what Peter said about my story: "Anything I might say about 'Professor Gottesman and the Indian Rhinoceros' would at best be taken as seriously biased." All that's left, therefore— and this, at least, I must say—is that "Professor Gottesman" is uniquely, inimitably, Peter S. Beagle. That I love it goes without saying. Now go ahead. Read it. I dare you not to delight in it as much as I did.

Professor Gottesman and the Indian Rhinoceros

PROFESSOR GUSTAVE GOTTESMAN WENT TO A zoo for the first time when he was thirty-four years old. There is an excellent zoo in Zurich, which was Professor Gottesman's birthplace, and where his sister still lived, but Professor Gottesman had never been there. From an early age he had determined on the study of philosophy as his life's work; and for any true philosopher this world is zoo enough, complete with cages, feeding times, breeding programs, and earnest docents, of which he was wise enough to know that he was one. Thus, the first zoo he ever saw was the one in the middle-sized Midwestern American city where he worked at a middle-sized university, teaching Comparative Philosophy in comparative contentment. He was tall and rather thin, with a round, undistinguished face, a snub nose, a random assortment of sandyish hair, and a pair of very intense and very distinguished brown eyes that always seemed to be looking a little deeper than they meant to, embarrassing the face around them no end. His students and colleagues were quite fond of him, in an indulgent sort of way.

And how did the good Professor Gottesman happen at last to visit a zoo? It came about in this way: his older sister Edith came from Zurich to stay with him for several weeks, and she brought her daughter, his niece Nathalie, along with her. Nathalie was seven, both in years, and in the number of her that there sometimes seemed to be, for the Professor had never been used to children even when he was one. She was a generally pleasant little girl, though, as far as he could tell; so when his sister besought him to spend one of his free afternoons with Nathalie while she went to lunch and a gallery opening with an old friend, the Professor graciously consented. And Nathalie wanted very much to go to the zoo and see tigers.

"So you shall," her uncle announced gallantly. "Just as soon as I find out exactly where the zoo is." He consulted with his best friend, a fat, cheerful, harmonica-playing professor of medieval Italian poetry named Sally Lowry, who had known him long and well enough (she was the only person in the world who called him Gus) to draw an elaborate two-colored map of the route, write out very precise directions beneath it, and make several copies of this document, in case of accidents. Thus equipped, and accompanied by Charles, Nathalie's stuffed bedtime tiger, whom she desired to introduce to his grand cousins, they set off together for the zoo on a gray, cool spring afternoon. Professor Gottesman quoted Thomas Hardy to Nathalie, improvising a German translation for her benefit as he went along.

> This is the weather the cuckoo likes,
>   And so do I;
> When showers betumble the chestnut spikes,
>   And nestlings fly.

"Charles likes it too," Nathalie said. "It makes his fur feel all sweet."

They reached the zoo without incident, thanks to Professor Lowry's excellent map, and Professor Gottesman bought Nathalie a bag of something sticky, unhealthy, and forbidden, and took her straight off to see the tigers. Their hot, meaty smell and their lightning-colored eyes were a bit too much for him, and so he sat on a bench nearby and watched Nathalie perform the introductions for Charles. When she came back to Professor Gottesman, she told him that Charles had been very well-behaved, as had all the tigers but one, who was rudely indifferent. "He was probably just visiting," she said. "A tourist or something."

The Professor was still marvelling at the amount of contempt one small girl could infuse into the word *tourist*, when he heard a voice, sounding almost at his shoulder, say, "Why, Professor Gottesman—how nice to see you at last." It was a low voice, a bit hoarse, with excellent diction, speaking good Zurich German with a very slight, unplaceable accent.

Professor Gottesman turned quickly, half-expecting to see some old acquaintance from home, whose name he would inevitably have forgotten. Such embarrassments were altogether too common in his gently preoccupied life. His friend Sally Lowry once observed, "We see each other just about every day, Gus, and I'm still not sure you really recognize me. If I wanted to hide from you, I'd just change my hairstyle."

There was no one at all behind him. The only thing he saw was the rutted, muddy rhinoceros yard, for some reason placed directly across from the big cats' cages. The one rhinoceros in residence was standing by the fence, torpidly mumbling a mouthful of moldy-looking hay. It was an Indian rhinoceros, according to the placard on the gate: as big as the Professor's compact car, and the approximate color of old cement. The creaking slabs of its skin smelled of stale urine, and it had only one horn, caked with sticky mud. Flies buzzed around its small, heavy-lidded eyes, which regarded Professor Gottesman with immense, ancient unconcern. But there was no other person in the vicinity who might have addressed him.

Professor Gottesman shook his head, scratched it, shook it again, and turned back to the tigers. But the voice came again. "Professor, it was indeed I who spoke. Come and talk to me, if you please."

No need, surely, to go into Professor Gottesman's reaction: to describe in detail how he gasped, turned pale, and looked wildly around for any corroborative witness. It is worth mentioning, however, that at no time did he bother to splutter the requisite splutter in such cases: "My God, I'm either dreaming, drunk, or crazy." If he was indeed just as classically absent-minded and impractical as everyone who knew him agreed, he was also more of a realist than many of them. This is generally true of philosophers, who tend, as a group, to be on terms of mutual respect with the impossible. Therefore, Professor Gottesman did the only proper thing under the circumstances. He introduced his niece Nathalie to the rhinoceros.

Nathalie, for all her virtues, was not a philosopher, and could not hear the rhinoceros's gracious greeting. She was, however, seven years old, and a well-brought-up seven-year-old has no difficulty with the notion that a rhinoceros—or a goldfish, or a coffee table—might be able to talk; nor in accepting that some people can hear coffee-table speech and some people cannot. She said a polite hello to the rhinoceros, and then became involved in her own conversation with stuffed Charles, who apparently had a good deal to say himself about tigers.

"A mannerly child," the rhinoceros commented. "One sees so few here. Most of them throw things."

His mouth dry, and his voice shaky but contained, Professor Gottesman asked carefully, "Tell me, if you will—can all rhinoceri speak, or only the Indian species?" He wished furiously that he had thought to bring along his notebook.

"I have no idea," the rhinoceros answered him candidly. "I myself, as it happens, am a unicorn."

Professor Gottesman wiped his balding forehead. "Please," he said earnestly. "Please. A rhinoceros, even a rhinoceros that speaks, is as real a creature as I. A unicorn, on the other hand, is a being of pure fantasy, like mermaids, or dragons, or the chimera. I consider very little in this universe as absolutely, indisputably certain, but I would feel so much better if you could see your way to being merely a talking rhinoceros. For my sake, if not your own."

It seemed to the Professor that the rhinoceros chuckled slightly, but it might only have been a ruminant's rumbling stomach. "My Latin designation is *Rhinoceros unicornis*," the great animal remarked. "You may have noticed it on the sign."

Professor Gottesman dismissed the statement as brusquely as he would have if the rhinoceros had delivered it in class. "Yes, yes, yes, and the manatee, which suckles its young erect in the water and so gave rise to the myth of the mermaid, is assigned to the order *sirenia*. Classification is not proof."

"And proof," came the musing response, "is not necessarily truth. You look at me and see a rhinoceros, because I am not white, not graceful, far from beautiful, and my horn is no elegant spiral but a bludgeon of matted hair. But suppose that you had grown up expecting a unicorn to look and behave and smell exactly as I do—would not the rhinoceros then be the legend? Suppose that everything you believed about unicorns—everything except the way they look—were true of me? Consider the possibilities, Professor, while you push the remains of that bun under the gate."

Professor Gottesman found a stick and poked the grimy bit of pastry—about the same shade as the rhinoceros, it was—where the creature could wrap a prehensile upper lip around it. He said, somewhat tentatively, "Very well. The unicorn's horn was supposed to be an infallible guide to detecting poisons."

"The most popular poisons of the Middle Ages and Renaissance," replied the rhinoceros, "were alkaloids. Pour one of those into a goblet made of compressed hair, and see what happens." It belched resoundingly, and Nathalie giggled.

Professor Gottesman, who was always invigorated by a good argument with anyone, whether colleague, student, or rhinoceros, announced, "Isidore of Seville wrote in the seventh century that the unicorn was a cruel beast, that it would seek out elephants and lions to fight with them. Rhinoceri are equally known for their fierce, aggressive nature, which often leads them to attack anything that moves in their shortsighted vision. What have you to say to that?"

"Isidore of Seville," said the rhinoceros thoughtfully, "was a most learned man, much like your estimable self, who never saw a rhinoceros in his life, or an elephant either, being mainly preoccupied with church history and canon law. I believe he did see a lion at some point. If your charming niece is quite done with her snack?"

"She is not," Professor Gottesman answered, "and do not change the subject. If you are indeed a unicorn, what are you doing scavenging dirty buns and candy in this public establishment? It is an article of faith that a unicorn can only be taken by a virgin, in whose innocent embrace the ferocious creature becomes meek and docile. Are you prepared to tell me that you were captured under such circumstances?"

The rhinoceros was silent for some little while before it spoke again. "I cannot," it said judiciously, "vouch for the sexual history of the gentleman in the baseball cap who fired a tranquilizer dart into my left shoulder. I would, however, like to point out that the young of our species on occasion become trapped in vines and slender branches which entangle their horns—and that the Latin for such branches is *virge*. What Isidore of Seville made of all this . . ." It shrugged, which is difficult for a rhinoceros, and a remarkable thing to see.

"Sophistry," said the Professor, sounding unpleasantly beleaguered even in his own ears. "Casuistry. Semantics. Chop-logic. The fact remains, a rhinoceros is and a unicorn isn't." This last sounds much more impressive in German. "You will excuse me," he went on, "but we have other specimens to visit, do we not, Nathalie?"

"No," Nathalie said. "Charles and I just wanted to see the tigers."

"Well, we have seen the tigers," Professor Gottesman said through his teeth. "And I believe it is beginning to rain, so we will go home now." He took Nathalie's hand firmly and stood up, as that obliging child snuggled Charles firmly under her arm and bobbed a demure European curtsy to the rhinoceros. It bent its head to her, the mud-thick horn almost brushing the ground. Professor Gottesman, mildest of men, snatched her away.

"Good-bye, Professor," came the hoarse, placid voice behind him. "I look forward to our next meeting." The words were somewhat muffled, because Nathalie had tossed the remainder of her sticky snack into the yard as her uncle hustled her off. Professor Gottesman did not turn his head.

Driving home through the rain—which had indeed begun to fall, though very lightly—the Professor began to have an indefinably uneasy feeling that caused him to spend more time peering at the rear-view mirror than in looking properly ahead. Finally he asked Nathalie, "Please, would you and—ah—you and Charles climb into the backseat and see whether we are being followed?"

Nathalie was thrilled. "Like in the spy movies?" She jumped to obey, but reported after a few minutes of crouching on the seat that she could detect nothing out of the ordinary. "I saw a helicopiter," she told him, attempting the English word. "Charles thinks they might be following us that way, but I don't know. Who is spying on us, Uncle Gustave?"

"No one, no one," Professor Gottesman answered. "Never mind, child, I am getting silly in America. It happens, never mind." But a few moments later the curious apprehension was with him again, and Nathalie was happily occupied for the rest of the trip home in scanning the traffic behind them through an imaginary periscope, yipping "It's that one!" from time to time, and being invariably disappointed when another prime suspect turned off down a side street. When they reached Professor Gottesman's house, she sprang out of the car immediately, ignoring her mother's welcome until she had checked under all four fenders for possible homing devices. "Bugs," she explained importantly to the two adults. "That was Charles's idea. Charles would make a good spy, I think."

She ran inside, leaving Edith to raise her fine eyebrows at her brother. Professor Gottesman said heavily, "We had a nice time. Don't ask." And Edith, being a wise older sister, left it at that.

The rest of the visit was enjoyably uneventful. The Professor went to work according to his regular routine, while his sister and his niece explored the city, practiced their English together, and cooked Swiss-German specialties to surprise him when he came home. Nathalie never asked to go to the zoo again—stuffed Charles having lately shown an interest in international intrigue—nor did she ever mention that her uncle had formally introduced her to a rhinoceros and spent part of an afternoon sitting on a bench arguing with it. Professor Gottesman was genuinely sorry when she and Edith left for Zurich, which rather surprised him. He hardly ever missed people, or thought much about anyone who was not actually present.

It rained again on the evening that they went to the airport. Returning alone, the Professor was startled, and a bit disquieted, to see large muddy footprints on his walkway and his front steps. They were, as nearly as he could make out, the marks of a three-toed foot, having a distinct resemblance to the ace of clubs in a deck of cards. The door was locked and bolted, as he had left it, and there was no indication of any attempt to force an entry. Professor Gottesman hesitated, looked quickly around him, and went inside.

The rhinoceros was in the living room, lying peacefully on its side before the artificial fireplace—which was lit—like a very large dog. It opened one eye as he entered and greeted him politely. "Welcome home, Professor. You will excuse me, I hope, if I do not rise?"

Professor Gottesman's legs grew weak under him. He groped blindly for a chair, found it, fell into it, his face white and freezing cold. He managed to ask, "How—how did you get in here?" in a small, faraway voice.

"The same way I got out of the zoo," the rhinoceros answered him. "I would have come sooner, but with your sister and your niece already here, I thought my presence might make things perhaps a little too crowded for you. I do hope their departure went well." It yawned widely and contentedly, showing blunt, fist-sized teeth and a gray-pink tongue like a fish fillet.

"I must telephone the zoo," Professor Gottesman whispered. "Yes, of course, I will call the zoo." But he did not move from the chair.

The rhinoceros shook its head as well as it could in a prone position. "Oh, I wouldn't bother with that, truly. It will only distress them if anyone learns that they have mislaid a creature as large as I am. And they will never believe that I am in your house. Take my word for it, there will be no mention of my having left their custody. I have some experience in these matters." It yawned again and closed its eyes. "Excellent fireplace you have," it murmured drowsily. "I think I shall lie exactly here every night. Yes, I do think so."

And it was asleep, snoring with the rhythmic roar and fading whistle of a fast freight crossing a railroad bridge. Professor Gottesman sat staring in his chair for a long time before he managed to stagger to the telephone in the kitchen.

Sally Lowry came over early the next morning, as she had promised several times before the Professor would let her off the phone. She took one quick look at him as she entered and said briskly, "Well, whatever came to dinner, you look as though it got the bed and you slept on the living room floor."

"I did not sleep at all," Professor Gottesman informed her grimly. "Come with me, please, Sally, and you shall see why."

But the rhinoceros was not in front of the fireplace, where it had still been lying when the Professor came downstairs. He looked around for it increasingly frantic, saying over and over, "It was just here, it has been here all night. Wait, wait, Sally, I will show you. Wait only a moment."

For he had suddenly heard the unmistakable gurgle of water in the pipes overhead. He rushed up the narrow hairpin stairs (his house was, as the real-estate agent had put it, "an old charmer") and burst into his bathroom, blinking through clouds of steam to find the rhinoceros lolling blissfully in the tub, its nose barely above water and its hind legs awkwardly sticking straight up in the air. There were puddles all over the floor.

"Good morning," the rhinoceros greeted Professor Gottesman. "I could wish your facilities a bit larger, but the hot water is splendid, pure luxury. We never had hot baths at the zoo."

"Get out of my tub!" the Professor gabbled, coughing and wiping his face. "You will get out of my tub this instant!"

The rhinoceros remained unruffled. "I am not sure I can. Not just like that. It's rather a complicated affair."

"Get out exactly the way you got in!" shouted Professor Gottesman. "How did you get up here at all? I never heard you on the stairs."

"I tried not to disturb you," the rhinoceros said meekly. "Unicorns can move very quietly when we need to."

"*Out!*" the Professor thundered. He had never thundered before, and it made his throat hurt. "Out of my bathtub, out of my house! And clean up that floor before you go!"

He stormed back down the stairs to meet a slightly anxious Sally Lowry waiting at the bottom. "What was all that yelling about?" she wanted to know. "You're absolutely pink—it's sort of sweet, actually. Are you all right?"

"Come up with me," Professor Gottesman demanded. "Come right now." He seized his friend by the wrist and practically dragged her into his bathroom, where there was no sign of the rhinoceros. The tub was empty and dry, the floor was spotlessly clean; the air smelled faintly of tile cleaner. Professor Gottesman stood gaping in the doorway, muttering over and over, "But it was here. It was in the tub."

"What was in the tub?" Sally asked. The Professor took a long, deep breath and turned to face her.

"A rhinoceros," he said. "It says it's a unicorn, but it is nothing but an Indian rhinoceros." Sally's mouth opened, but no sound came out. Professor Gottesman said, "It followed me home."

Fortunately, Sally Lowry was no more concerned with the usual splutters of denial and disbelief than was the Professor himself. She closed her mouth, caught her own breath, and said, "Well, any rhinoceros that could handle those stairs, wedge itself into that skinny tub of yours, and tidy up afterwards would have to be a unicorn. Obvious. Gus, I don't care what time it is, I think you need a drink."

Professor Gottesman recounted his visit to the zoo with Nathalie, and all that had happened thereafter, while Sally rummaged through his minimally stocked liquor cabinet and mixed what she called a "Lowry Land Mine." It calmed the Professor only somewhat, but it did at least restore his coherency. He said earnestly, "Sally, I don't know how it talks. I do not know how it escaped from the zoo, or found its way here, or how it got into my house and my bathtub, and I am afraid to imagine where it is now. But the creature is an Indian rhinoceros, the sign said so. It is simply not possible—not possible—that it could be a unicorn."

"Sounds like *Harvey*," Sally mused. Professor Gottesman stared at her. "You know, the play about the guy who's buddies with an invisible white rabbit. A big white rabbit."

"But this one is not invisible!" the Professor cried. "People at the zoo, they saw it—Nathalie saw it. It bowed to her, quite courteously."

"Um," Sally said. "Well, I haven't seen it yet, but I live in hope. Meanwhile, you've got a class, and I've got office hours. Want me to make you another Land Mine?"

Professor Gottesman shuddered slightly. "I think not. We are discussing today how Fichte and von Schelling's work leads us to Hegel, and I need my wits about me. Thank you for coming to my house, Sally. You are a good friend. Perhaps I really am suffering from delusions, after all. I think I would almost prefer it so."

"Not me," Sally said. "I'm getting a unicorn out of this, if it's the last thing I do." She patted his arm. "You're more fun than a barrel of MFA candidates, Gus, and you're also the only gentleman I've ever met. I don't know what I'd do for company around here without you."

Professor Gottesman arrived early for his seminar on "The Heirs of Kant." There was no one in the classroom when he entered, except for the rhinoceros. It had plainly already attempted to sit on one of the chairs, which lay in splinters on the floor. Now it was warily eyeing a ragged hassock near the coffee machine.

"What are you doing here?" Professor Gottesman fairly screamed at it.

"Only auditing," the rhinoceros answered. "I thought it might be rewarding to see you at work. I promise not to say a word."

Professor Gottesman pointed to the door. He had opened his mouth to order the rhinoceros, once and for all, out of his life, when two of his students walked into the room. The Professor closed his mouth, gulped, greeted his students, and ostentatiously began to examine his lecture notes, mumbling professorial mumbles to himself, while the rhinoceros, unnoticed, negotiated a kind of armed truce with the hassock. True to its word, it listened in attentive silence all through the seminar, though Professor Gottesman had an uneasy moment when it seemed about to be drawn into a heated debate over the precise nature of von Schelling's intellectual debt to the von Schlegel brothers. He was so desperately careful not to let the rhinoceros catch his eye that he never noticed until the last student had left that the beast was gone, too. None of the class had even once commented on its presence; except for the shattered chair, there was no indication that it had ever been there.

Professor Gottesman drove slowly home in a disorderly state of mind. On the one hand, he wished devoutly never to see the rhinoceros again; on the other, he could not help wondering exactly when it had left the classroom. "Was it displeased with my summation of the *Ideas for a Philosophy of Nature*?" he said aloud in the car. "Or perhaps it was something I said during the argument about *Die Weltalter*. Granted, I have never been entirely comfortable with that book, but I do not recall saying anything exceptionable." Hearing himself justifying his interpretations to a rhinoceros, he slapped his own cheek very hard and drove the rest of the way with the car radio tuned to the loudest, ugliest music he could find.

The rhinoceros was dozing before the fireplace as before, but lumbered clumsily to a sitting position as soon as he entered the living room. "Bravo, Professor!" it cried in plainly genuine enthusiasm. "You were absolutely splendid. It was an honor to be present at your seminar."

The Professor was furious to realize that he was blushing; yet it was impossible to respond to such praise with an eviction notice. There was nothing for him to do but reply, a trifle stiffly, "Thank you, most gratifying." But the rhinoceros was clearly waiting for something more, and Professor Gottesman was, as his friend Sally had said, a gentleman. He went on, "You are welcome to audit the class again, if you like. We will be considering Rousseau next week, and then proceed through the romantic philosophers to Nietzsche and Schopenhauer."

"With a little time to spare for the American Transcendentalists, I should hope," suggested the rhinoceros. Professor Gottesman, being some distance past surprise, nodded. The rhinoceros said reflectively, "I think I should prefer to hear you on Comte and John Stuart Mill. The romantics always struck me as fundamentally unsound."

This position agreed so much with the Professor's own opinion that he found himself, despite himself, gradually warming toward the rhinoceros. Still formal, he asked, "May I perhaps offer you a drink? Some coffee or tea?"

"Tea would be very nice," the rhinoceros answered, "if you should happen to have a bucket." Professor Gottesman did not, and the rhinoceros told him not to worry about it. It settled back down before the fire, and the Professor drew up a rocking chair. The rhinoceros said, "I must admit, I do wish I could hear you speak on the scholastic philosophers. That's really my period, after all."

"I will be giving such a course next year," the Professor said, a little shyly. "It is to be a series of lectures on medieval Christian thought, beginning with St. Augustine and the Neoplatonists and ending with William of Occam. Possibly you could attend some of those talks."

The rhinoceros's obvious pleasure at the invitation touched Professor Gottesman surprisingly deeply. Even Sally Lowry, who often dropped in on his classes unannounced, did so, as he knew, out of affection for him, and not from any serious interest in epistemology or the Milesian School. He was beginning to wonder whether there might be a way to permit the rhinoceros to sample the cream sherry he kept aside for company, when the creature added, with a wheezy chuckle, "Of course, Augustine and the rest never did quite come to terms with such pagan survivals as unicorns. The best they could do was to associate us with the Virgin Mary, and to suggest that our horns somehow represented the unity of Christ and his church. Bernard of Trèves even went so far as to identify Christ directly with the unicorn, but it was never a comfortable union. Spiral peg in square hole, so to speak."

Professor Gottesman was no more at ease with the issue than St. Augustine had been. But he was an honest person—only among philosophers is this considered part of the job description—and so he felt it his duty to say, "While I respect your intelligence and your obvious intellectual curiosity, none of this yet persuades me that you are in fact a unicorn. I still must regard you as an exceedingly learned and well-mannered Indian rhinoceros."

The rhinoceros took this in good part, saying, "Well, well, we will agree to disagree on that point for the time being. Although I certainly hope that you will let me know if you should need your drinking water purified." As before, and as so often thereafter, Professor Gottesman could not be completely sure that the rhinoceros was joking. Dismissing the subject, it went on to ask, "But about the Scholastics—do you plan to discuss the later Thomist reformers at all? Saint Cajetan rather dominates the movement, to my mind; if he had any real equals, I'm afraid I can't recall them."

"Ah," said the Professor. They were up until five in the morning, and it was the rhinoceros who dozed off first.

The question of the rhinoceros's leaving Professor Gottesman's house never came up again. It continued to sleep in the living room, for the most part, though on warm summer nights it had a fondness for the young willow tree that had been a Christmas present from Sally. Professor Gottesman never learned whether it was male or female, nor how it nourished its massive, noisy body, nor how it managed for toilet facilities—a reticent man himself, he respected reticence in others. As a houseguest, the rhinoceros's only serious fault was a continuing predilection for hot baths (with Epsom salts, when it could get them.) But it always cleaned up after itself, and was extremely conscientious about not tracking mud into the house; and it can be safely said that none of the Professor's visitors—even the rare ones who spent a night or two under his roof—ever remotely suspected that they were sharing living quarters with a rhinoceros. All in all, it proved to be a most discreet and modest beast.

The Professor had few friends, apart from Sally, and none whom he would have called on in a moment of bewildering crisis, as he had called her. He avoided whatever social or academic gatherings he could reasonably avoid; as a consequence his evenings had generally been lonely ones, though he might not have called them so. Even if he had admitted the term, he would surely have insisted that there was nothing necessarily

wrong with loneliness, in and of itself. *"I think,"* he would have said—
did often say, in fact, to Sally Lowry. "There are people, you know, for
whom thinking is company, thinking is entertainment, parties, dancing
even. The others, other people, they absolutely will not believe this."

"You're right," Sally said. "One thing about you, Gus, when you're
right you're really right."

Now, however, the Professor could hardly wait for the time of day
when, after a cursory dinner (he was an indifferent, impatient eater, and
truly tasted little difference between a frozen dish and one that had taken
half a day to prepare), he would pour himself a glass of wine and sit
down in the living room to debate philosophy with a huge mortar-colored
beast that always smelled vaguely incontinent, no matter how many baths
it had taken that afternoon. Looking eagerly forward all day to anything
was a new experience for him. It appeared to be the same for the
rhinoceros.

As the animal had foretold, there was never the slightest suggestion in
the papers or on television that the local zoo was missing one of its larger
odd-toed ungulates. The Professor went there once or twice in great trepi-
dation, convinced that he would be recognized and accused immediately
of conspiracy in the rhinoceros's escape. But nothing of the sort happened.
The yard where the rhinoceros had been kept was now occupied by a pair
of despondent-looking African elephants; when Professor Gottesman
made a timid inquiry of a guard, he was curtly informed that the zoo had
never possessed a rhinoceros of any species. "Endangered species," the
guard told him. "Too much red tape you have to go through to get one
these days, Just not worth the trouble, mean as they are."

Professor Gottesman grew placidly old with the rhinoceros—that is
to say, the Professor grew old, while the rhinoceros never changed in any
way that he could observe. Granted, he was not the most observant of
men, nor the most sensitive to change, except when threatened by it. Nor
was he in the least ambitious: promotions and pay raises happened, when
they happened, somewhere in the same cloudily benign middle distance
as did those departmental meetings that he actually had to sit through.
The companionship of the rhinoceros, while increasingly his truest
delight, also became as much of a cozily reassuring habit as his classes,
his office hours, the occasional dinner and movie or museum excursion
with Sally Lowry, and the books on French and German philosophy that
he occasionally published through the university press over the years.
They were indifferently reviewed, and sold poorly.

"Which is undoubtedly as it should be," Professor Gottesman frequently told Sally when dropping her off at her house, well across town
from his own. "I think I am a good teacher—that, yes—but I am decid-

edly not an original thinker, and I was never much of a writer even in German. It does no harm to say that I am not an exceptional man, Sally. It does not hurt me."

"I don't know what exceptional means to you or anyone else," Sally would answer stubbornly. "To me it means being unique, one of a kind, and that's definitely you, old Gus. I never thought you belonged in this town, or this university, or probably this century. But I'm surely glad you've been here."

Once in a while she might ask him casually how his unicorn was getting on these days. The Professor, who had long since accepted the fact that no one ever saw the rhinoceros unless it chose to be seen, invariably rose to the bait, saying, "It is no more a unicorn than it ever was, Sally, you know that." He would sip his latté in mild indignation, and eventually add, "Well, we will clearly never see eye to eye on the Vienna Circle, or the logical positivists in general—it is a very conservative creature, in some ways. But we did come to a tentative agreement about Bergson, last Thursday it was, so I would have to say that we are going along quite amiably."

Sally rarely pressed him further. Sharp-tongued, solitary, and profoundly irreverent, only with Professor Gottesman did she bother to know when to leave things alone. Most often, she would take out her battered harmonica and play one or another of his favorite tunes—"Sweet Georgia Brown" or "Hurry On Down." He never sang along, but he always hummed and grunted and thumped his bony knees. Once he mentioned diffidently that the rhinoceros appeared to have a peculiar fondness for "Slow Boat to China." Sally pretended not to hear him.

In the appointed fullness of time, the university retired Professor Gottesman in a formal ceremony, attended by, among others, Sally Lowry, his sister Edith, all the way from Zurich, and the rhinoceros—the latter having spent all that day in the bathtub, in anxious preparation. Each of them assured him that he looked immensely distinguished as he was invested with the rank of *emeritus,* which allowed him to lecture as many as four times a year, and to be available to counsel promising graduate students when he chose. In addition, a special chair with his name on it was reserved exclusively for his use at the Faculty Club. He was quite proud of never once having sat in it.

"Strange, I am like a movie star now," he said to the rhinoceros. "You should see. Now I walk across the campus and the students line up, they line up to watch me totter past. I can hear their whispers—'Here he comes!' 'There he goes!' Exactly the same ones they are who used to cut my classes because I bored them so. Completely absurd."

"Enjoy it as your due," the rhinoceros proposed. "You were entitled to their respect then—take pleasure in it now, however misplaced it may seem to you." But the Professor shook his head, smiling wryly.

"Do you know what kind of star I am really like?" he asked. "I am like the old, old star that died so long ago, so far away, that its last light is only reaching our eyes today. They fall in on themselves, you know, those dead stars, they go cold and invisible, even though we think we are seeing them in the night sky. That is just how I would be, if not for you. And for Sally, of course."

In fact, Professor Gottesman found little difficulty in making his peace with age and retirement. His needs were simple, his pension and savings adequate to meet them, and his health as sturdy as generations of Swiss peasant ancestors could make it. For the most part he continued to live as he always had, the one difference being that he now had more time for study, and could stay up as late as he chose arguing about structuralism with the rhinoceros, or listening to Sally Lowry reading her new translation of Cavalcanti or Frescobaldi. At first he attended every conference of philosophers to which he was invited, feeling a certain vague obligation to keep abreast of new thought in his field. This compulsion passed quickly, however, leaving him perfectly satisfied to have as little as possible to do with academic life, except when he needed to use the library. Sally once met him there for lunch to find him feverishly rifling the ten Loeb Classic volumes of Philo Judaeus. "We were debating the concept of the logos last night," he explained to her, "and then the impossible beast rampaged off on a tangent involving Philo's locating the roots of Greek philosophy in the Torah. Forgive me, Sally, but I may be here for awhile." Sally lunched alone that day.

The Professor's sister Edith died younger than she should have. He grieved for her, and took much comfort in the fact that Nathalie never failed to visit him when she came to America. The last few times, she had brought a husband and two children with her—the youngest hugging a ragged but indomitable tiger named Charles under his arm. They most often swept him off for the evening; and it was on one such occasion, just after they had brought him home and said their good-byes, and their rented car had rounded the corner, that the mugging occurred.

Professor Gottesman was never quite sure himself about what actually took place. He remembered a light scuffle of footfalls, remembered a savage blow on the side of his head, then another impact as his cheek and forehead hit the ground. There were hands clawing through his pockets, low voices so distorted by obscene viciousness that he lost English completely, becoming for the first time in fifty years a terrified immigrant, once more unable to cry out for help in this new and dreadful country. A faceless figure billowed over him, grabbing his collar, pulling him close, mouthing words he could not understand. It was brandishing something menacingly in its free hand.

Then it vanished abruptly, as though blasted away by the sidewalk-shaking bellow of rage that was Professor Gottesman's last clear memory until he woke in a strange bed, with Sally Lowry, Nathalie, and several policemen bending over him. The next day's newspapers ran the marvelous story of a retired philosophy professor, properly frail and elderly, not only fighting off a pair of brutal muggers but beating them so badly that they had to be hospitalized themselves before they could be arraigned. Sally impishly kept the incident on the front pages for some days by confiding to reporters that Professor Gottesman was a practitioner of a long-forgotten martial-arts discipline, practiced only in ancient Sumer and Babylonia. "Plain childishness," she said apologetically, after the fuss had died down. "Pure self-indulgence. I'm sorry, Gus."

"Do not be," the Professor replied. "If we were to tell them the truth, I would immediately be placed in an institution." He looked sideways at his friend, who smiled and said, "What, about the rhinoceros rescuing you? I'll never tell, I swear. They could pull out my fingernails."

Professor Gottesman said, "Sally, those boys had been *trampled,* practically stamped flat. One of them had been *gored,* I saw him. Do you really think I could have done all that?"

"Remember, I've seen you in your wrath," Sally answered lightly and untruthfully. What she had in fact seen was one of the ace-of-clubs footprints she remembered in crusted mud on the Professor's front steps long ago. She said, "Gus. How old am I?"

The Professor's response was off by a number of years, as it always was. Sally said, "You've frozen me at a certain age, because you don't want me getting any older. Fine, I happen to be the same way about that rhinoceros of yours. There are one or two things I just don't want to know about that damn rhinoceros, Gus. If that's all right with you."

"Yes, Sally," Professor Gottesman answered. "That is all right."

The rhinoceros itself had very little to say about the whole incident. "I chanced to be awake, watching a lecture about Bulgarian icons on the Learning Channel. I heard the noise outside." Beyond that, it sidestepped all questions, pointedly concerning itself only with the Professor's recuperation from his injuries and shock. In fact, he recovered much faster than might reasonably have been expected from a gentleman of his years. The doctor commented on it.

The occurrence made Professor Gottesman even more of an icon himself on campus; as a direct consequence, he spent even less time there than before, except when the rhinoceros requested a particular book. Nathalie, writing from Zurich, never stopped urging him to take in a housemate, for company and safety, but she would have been utterly dumbfounded if he had accepted her suggestion. "Something looks out for him," she said to her husband. "I always knew that, I couldn't tell you why. Uncle Gustave is *somebody's* dear stuffed Charles."

Sally Lowry did grow old, despite Professor Gottesman's best efforts. The university gave her a retirement ceremony too, but she never showed up for it. "Too damn depressing," she told Professor Gottesman, as he helped her into her coat for their regular Wednesday walk. "It's all right for you, Gus, you'll be around forever. Me, I drink, I still smoke, I still eat all kinds of stuff they tell me not to eat—I don't even floss, for God's sake. My circulation works like the post office, and even my cholesterol has arthritis. Only reason I've lasted this long is I had this stupid job teaching beautiful, useless stuff to idiots. Now that's it. Now I'm a goner."

"Nonsense, nonsense, Sally," Professor Gottesman assured her vigorously. "You have always told me you are too mean and spiteful to die. I am holding you to this."

"Pickled in vinegar only lasts just so long," Sally said. "One cheery note, anyway—it'll be the heart that goes. Always is, in my family. That's good, I couldn't hack cancer. I'd be a shameless, screaming disgrace, absolutely no dignity at all. I'm really grateful it'll be the heart."

The Professor was very quiet while they walked all the way down to the little local park, and back again. They had reached the apartment complex where she lived, when he suddenly gripped her by the arms, looked straight into her face, and said loudly, "That is the best heart I ever knew, yours. I will not *let* anything happen to that heart."

"Go home, Gus," Sally told him harshly. "Get out of here, go home. Christ, the only sentimental Switzer in the whole world, and I get him. Wouldn't you just know?"

Professor Gottesman actually awoke just before the telephone call came, as sometimes happens. He had dozed off in his favorite chair during a minor intellectual skirmish with the rhinoceros over Spinoza's ethics. The rhinoceros itself was sprawled in its accustomed spot, snoring authoritatively, and the kitchen clock was still striking three when the phone rang. He picked it up slowly. Sally's barely audible voice whispered, "Gus. The heart. Told you." He heard the receiver fall from her hand.

Professor Gottesman had no memory of stumbling coatless out of the house, let alone finding his car parked on the street—he was just suddenly standing by it, his hands trembling so badly as he tried to unlock the door that he dropped his keys into the gutter. How long his frantic fumbling in the darkness went on, he could never say; but at some point he became aware of a deeper darkness over him, and looked up on hands and knees to see the rhinoceros.

"On my back," it said, and no more. The Professor had barely scrambled up its warty, unyielding flanks and heaved himself precariously over the spine his legs could not straddle when there came a surge like the sea under him as the great beast leaped forward. He cried out in terror.

He would have expected, had he had wit enough at the moment to expect anything, that the rhinoceros would move at a ponderous trot, farting and rumbling, gradually building up a certain clumsy momentum. Instead, he felt himself flying, truly flying, as children know flying, flowing with the night sky, melting into the jeweled wind. If the rhinoceros's huge, flat, three-toed feet touched the ground, he never felt it: nothing existed, or ever had existed, but the sky that he was and the bodiless power that he had become—he himself, the once and foolish old Professor Gustave Gottesman, his eyes full of the light of lost stars. He even forgot Sally Lowry, only for a moment, only for the least little time.

Then he was standing in the courtyard before her house, shouting and banging maniacally on the door, pressing every button under his hand. The rhinoceros was nowhere to be seen. The building door finally buzzed open, and the Professor leaped up the stairs like a young man, calling Sally's name. Her own door was unlocked; she often left it so absent-mindedly, no matter how much he scolded her about it. She was in her bedroom, half-wedged between the side of the bed and the night table, with the telephone receiver dangling by her head. Professor Gottesman touched her cheek and felt the fading warmth.

"Ah, Sally," he said. "Sally, my dear." She was very heavy, but somehow it was easy for him to lift her back onto the bed and make a place for her among the books and papers that littered the quilt, as always. He found her harmonica on the floor, and closed her fingers around it. When there was nothing more for him to do, he sat beside her, still holding her hand, until the room began to grow light. At last he said aloud, "No, the sentimental Switzer will not cry, my dear Sally," and picked up the telephone.

The rhinoceros did not return for many days after Sally Lowry's death. Professor Gottesman missed it greatly when he thought about it at all, but it was a strange, confused time. He stayed at home, hardly eating, sleeping on his feet, opening books and closing them. He never answered the telephone, and he never changed his clothes. Sometimes he wandered endlessly upstairs and down through every room in his house; sometimes he stood in one place for an hour or more at a time, staring at nothing. Occasionally the doorbell rang, and worried voices outside called his name. It was late autumn, and then winter, and the house grew cold at night, because he had forgotten to turn on the furnace. Professor Gottesman was perfectly aware of this, and other things, somewhere.

One evening, or perhaps it was early one morning, he heard the sound of water running in the bathtub upstairs. He remembered the sound, and presently he moved to his living room chair to listen to it better. For the first time in some while, he fell asleep, and woke only when he felt the rhinoceros standing over him. In the darkness he saw it only as a huge, still shadow, but it smelled unmistakably like a rhinoceros that has just had a bath. The Professor said quietly, "I wondered where you had gone."

"We unicorns mourn alone," the rhinoceros replied. "I thought it might be the same for you."

"Ah," Professor Gottesman said. "Yes, most considerate. Thank you."

He said nothing further, but sat staring into the shadow until it appeared to fold gently around him. The rhinoceros said, "We were speaking of Spinoza."

Professor Gottesman did not answer. The rhinoceros went on, "I was very interested in the comparison you drew between Spinoza and Thomas Hobbes. I would enjoy continuing our discussion."

"I do not think I can," the Professor said at last. "I do not think I want to talk anymore."

It seemed to him that the rhinoceros's eyes had become larger and brighter in its own shadow, and its horn a trifle less hulking. But its stomach rumbled as majestically as ever as it said, "In that case, perhaps we should be on our way."

"Where are we going?" Professor Gottesman asked. He was feeling oddly peaceful and disinclined to leave his chair. The rhinoceros moved closer, and for the first time that the Professor could remember its huge, hairy muzzle touched his shoulder, light as a butterfly.

"I have lived in your house for a long time," it said. "We have talked together, days and nights on end, about ways of being in this world, ways of considering it, ways of imagining it as a part of some greater imagining. Now has come the time for silence. Now I think you should come and live with me."

They were outside, on the sidewalk, in the night. Professor Gottesman had forgotten to take his coat, but he was not at all cold. He turned to look back at his house, watching it recede, its lights still burning, like a ship leaving him at his destination. He said to the rhinoceros, "What is your house like?"

"Comfortable," the rhinoceros answered. "In honesty, I would not call the hot water as superbly lavish as yours, but there is rather more room to maneuver. Especially on the stairs."

"You are walking a bit too rapidly for me," said the Professor. "May I climb on your back once more?"

The rhinoceros halted immediately, saying, "By all means, please do excuse me." Professor Gottesman found it notably easier to mount this time, the massive sides having plainly grown somewhat trimmer and smoother during the rhinoceros's absence, and easier to grip with his legs. It started on briskly when he was properly settled, though not at the rapturous pace that had once married the Professor to the night wind. For some while he could hear the clopping of cloven hooves far below him, but then they seemed to fade away. He leaned forward and said into the rhinoceros's pointed silken ear, "I should tell you that I have long since come to the conclusion that you are not after all an Indian rhinoceros, but a hitherto unknown species, somehow misclassified. I hope this will not make a difference in our relationship."

"No difference, good Professor," came the gently laughing answer all around him. "No difference in the world."

ABOUT THE AUTHOR

Peter S. Beagle was born in New York City in 1939. He has been a professional freelance writer since graduating from the University of Pittsburgh in 1959. His novels include *A Fine and Private Place, The Last Unicorn, The Folk of the Air,* and *The Innkeeper's Song.* When *The Folk of the Air* came out, Don Thompson wrote in the *Denver Post,* "Peter S. Beagle is by no means the most prolific fantasy writer in the business; he's merely the best." His short fiction has appeared in such varied places as *Seventeen, Ladies Home Journal,* and *New Worlds of Fantasy,* and his fiction to 1977 was collected in the book *The Fantasy Worlds of Peter S. Beagle.*

His film work includes screenplays for Ralph Bakshi's animated film *The Lord of the Rings, The Last Unicorn, Dove,* and an episode of *Star Trek: The Next Generation.* He has also written a stage adaptation of *The Last Unicorn,* and the libretto of an opera, *The Midnight Angel.*

Peter currently lives in Davis, California, with his wife, the Indian writer Padma Hejmadi.

JANET BERLINER

THE SAME BUT DIFFERENT

Peter: Anything I might say about **Janet Berliner**'s "The Same But Different" would be at best taken as seriously biased. We've been friends for a long time, and I'm very fond of her. Writer, teacher, superb editor, onetime agent, first-rate pool player, she hustles more determinedly, on more fronts, and in a tougher ballpark than anyone I know; and if she occasionally hustles me into gigs that I have no business taking on—such as this book—they tend to work out surprisingly well. Crazy as a jaybird, of course, but a real artist and one hell of a human being. I wouldn't have missed knowing her for anything. I wish she'd get some more sleep, is all.

The Same But Different

K NOW WHAT I WANT, LEGS-BABY? YOU
want to make me happy, get me ethnic. Ethnic's what's happening....
Alex "Legs" Cleveland tried not to feel irritation with his partner.
Ethnic, he thought. Made sense to *him.* He had spent a lifetime letting go
of the Reservation. Every time he believed he'd succeeded, the universe
decreed otherwise.

Still, it had taken him no time at all, and embarrassed him only
slightly, to nod, smile at his partner, and agree to find *ethnic* for the new
showroom at the MGM. Something like Mirage's Cirque de Soleil. *The
same but different.*

*Find me ethnic, with some tits and ass on the side, and I'll love you,
Legs-baby. Vegas'll love you.*

Maury was so damned L.A. Even worse, so Hollywood. He could
look into the eyeballs of a full-blooded Navajo, say, "Ethnic's what's
happening," and expect to be taken seriously.

Which, in this case, Legs thought, looking out of the window at the
Christmas lights strung across Hollywood Boulevard, he was. Though
what drove Alex to choose to go to South Africa on his search for *ethnic*
was not entirely clear to either one of them. Whatever the reason, once he
thought of South Africa, it felt like his only choice.

Next thing he knew, he was in Johannesburg, renting a car so that he
could drive to Bophuthatswana and scour Sun City—the Las Vegas of
South Africa, the brochure read—for *ethnic.*

Oh well, he thought, laughing at himself. This was no more or less
foolish than last year's trip to Madagascar, a fruitless search for a Roc's egg
inspired by the awesome success of *Jurassic Park;* or the year before,

spending his vacation in the Grenadines searching for buried treasure at the bottom of the Caribbean. He had found neither the egg nor the treasure; he *had* discovered little Marsha McDonald belting out "Going Under" in a Calypso tent in Grenada. At fifteen, she was the youngest Calypso Queen ever. Cute little thing. If only he'd gotten to her in time, before she signed on with that funny little German, Wolfie, and his Tobago Cabaret.

The good part was that, inevitably, he found something in each place to rationalize the journey. Mostly after the fact. So although what he thought he might find in Bophuthatswana was right now anybody's guess, he knew from experience that he would find something.

Which, he reminded himself, was how he had come to be driving on the left side of a road somewhere near Bechuanaland, in a rental car which put-putted like an old camel and whose air-conditioning was, to be kind, substandard.

So, apparently, were other things. He got as far as the outskirts of Krugersdorp before steam started pouring out of the hood and into the low desert.

After a suitable amount of time devoted to expletives, and the doffing of a layer of clothing, he decided that sitting around and humidifying the desert was not the way to go. He studied the map the car rental company had given him, and the touring guide next to the name of the town: Three hotels, a couple of gold mines, and daily tours of Sterkfontein Caves.

Not knowing what else to do, he stuffed his camcorder into his overnight bag—all the luggage he'd brought—and left the car.

He stood outside in the hot sun, sweat trickling down his neck, thumb in the air. After ten minutes, the driver of a small truck picked him up.

The driver, a tall, extremely black man, was a man of few words. He answered the questions put to him, but volunteered nothing.

"What's your name?"

"Sam Mtshali."

"Where are you headed?"

Thus prodded, Sam explained that he was a Zulu, a mine worker, and the sometime lead dancer of a troupe of dancers who called themselves The Zulu Warriors, and that yes—with what was almost a smile—he *had* finished school, *had* matriculated. He had even, he admitted, spent four years at the University, getting a degree in "something useful." And no, he knew nothing about cars.

"What do you suggest I do?" Legs asked.

"Might as well take it easy," Sam said. "It will take the rental car company a day, two maybe, to find another car and send it from Pretoria."

One phone call, made at the side of the road, proved the Zulu right. "Meanwhile, Mr. Cleveland, why not relax." Rolling her *rr*s. "See a little of our beautiful country. Go to the Caves, it's cool in there. Take a bus to the Voortrekker Monument."

Turned out that The Zulu Warriors were about to give a performance. With little much else to do, Legs was fairly easily persuaded to go and watch.

He was sitting half-asleep in rudely constructed bleachers, exposed to the midsummer African sun and daydreaming about a clean room, a soft mattress, and a very cold shower, when a simple drumroll echoed the distant thunder of an electrical storm.

At once the dusty arena was filled with bodies—jumping, arching, twisting, shaking the dusty earth with the pounding of feet and drums. Lunging, retreating, thrusting their marquise-shaped, cowhide shields forward and waving their clubs. Their beaded headbands catching the sun. Red and white goatskin bands on their legs and arms, copper bangles to the elbows, moving forward in unison, crouching, standing, bowing.

Enchanted, Legs imagined them in a showroom. Mine dumps in the background, dust rising from their feet, a backdrop of steel and glass high-rises on the horizon. What a set it would make. Wait till America gets a load of these guys, he thought, happy again at life's synchronicity. He'd pick up a couple of acts from the local shebeen, some women dancers to satisfy the tits and ass requirement, and a canary—not necessarily Miriam Makeba, but good enough. Afro was in. Caribbean was in: the Caribbean Allstars, with their reggae and calypso; Zulu Spear, with their steel drums; the West African Highlife Band, O. J. Ekemode and the Nigerian Allstars, with their Afrobeat. But no one, *no one,* had anything like this.

When they'd wanted legs, he and Maury had given them legs. When they'd wanted tits, he and Maury found them tits. Now they wanted African-authentic, *the same but different.* Well, they would get the same but different: The Zulu Warriors. The real thing. Just what "they" were looking for. Radio City would be calling him after The Zulu Warriors had made a couple of Vegas appearances. After that, a world tour, Hollywood. . . . One thing was certain, this wasn't the same old thing. They could stop telling him that. This wasn't leggy showgirls, cross-dressers, comics on the way up, the way down. This would bring in the Afro-American audience.

Legs wasted no time finding Sam when the dances were over.

"Who's your manager?" he asked.

"I am." A lithe African of indiscernible age stepped out of the shadows. "Nkolosi, also head of AFI, Africans for Independence." He put out his hand European fashion. "What do you think of my boys?"

He stared at Legs, his eyes expressionless. "Think you can do something for them?"

"Can I do something for them?" Legs grinned at Nkolosi, buying himself time while he tried to dredge up what he knew about the AFI and about this man.

"Can I do something for them?" Legs repeated. "Does a dog piss on fire hydrants?"

"Don't struggle so hard, Mr. Cleveland," Nkolosi said. "You have read of me. I am called revolutionary. Witchdoctor. Keeper of Ngwenya, the Mother of all Lightning Birds." His accent was cultured, Anglicized. It was that which reminded Legs of what he had read. This man was educated in the halls of Oxford—or was it Cambridge? No matter. He was dangerous, or so the *Time* article had said. Educated in the ways of the white man and in the lore of his father and his father's father. Unsatisfied with Mandela and the coalition . . . there was more, but Legs couldn't quite remember what. Politics wasn't his bag, nor was voodoo. No more than spirit magic. Bunch of crap. Far as he was concerned, Nick—or however you pronounced it—was the manager of The Zulu Warriors. Still, it was a good pitch, he thought. Nice and *ethnic*. Meeting Nkolosi was a quirk of fate, one he intended to use for his own aggrandizement.

"Very well, then, Mr. Cleveland," Nkolosi said. "In that case we'll meet later. Sam will tell you where and when."

"Right." Legs waved his hand. "Later, Nick."

Overhead, a cloud obscured the sun. Legs looked up. Shook his head. Took off his sunglasses and cleaned them. This African sun was a pisser. Did strange things to a man, worse than when he was a kid out in the middle of the Mojave. He could have sworn he'd seen a dragon up there, belly on fire, wings jagged.

He looked at his wristwatch. Four o'clock in the afternoon in Johannesburg. Subtract ten hours, that made it six in the morning in L.A.

He grinned. He should call Maury. Wake him up. Serve him right. *Give me ethnic, baby*. He'd give him ethnic all right. Maybe he'd even get lucky and catch Maury in the middle of plunking some honey-blonde chorus line wannabe.

He wiped the sweat off the back of his neck. "I need a telephone and a beer," he said.

"There's a small Greek café half a mile or so from here," Sam said. "When you're done there, find your way to the Sterkfontein Caves. Go on the tour. Amuse yourself by playing tourist. You'll like it. It's cool inside." He looked at Legs and smiled for the first time. "I mean temperature, not what you Americans call cool. There's an old mine dump behind the caves. You'll see a house. When the mine was working, the supervisor lived in it. Now I do. Meet me there in a couple of hours. If you get there first, just hang around."

Legs found the café with no trouble. The beer was warm, but at least it was wet. He took his bottle with him into the phone booth outside. The receiver was greasy and the booth smelled of old hamburger. Legs gagged, and held the door open with his foot. It didn't help much; the day had grown older, but no cooler.

"I'm bringing them in," he said, when Maury answered. "Ethnic, just like you wanted." He explained who and what they were, cutting to the chase so that he could get out of the telephone booth. "I'll have the contract signed over to me for eight of them. We'll leave sometime over the weekend. Private plane—part of the deal. We'll give them a day to get over jet lag, get them used to the stage. They'll be ready Tuesday night. Dingaan's Day."

"You did good, baby," Maury said, his voice raw. "Just one thing, what the fuck is a Dingaan?"

"You asked for ethnic. Go to a library, Maury. Look it up."

Chuckling at the thought of Maury in a library, Legs went back to the café. He used the bathroom, which was anything but clean, bought another beer, and asked for directions to the Caves. The last tour had already started, so he paid for a small, overpriced tourbook that lay atop a souvenir showcase near the entrance, and wandered inside.

Immediately, as if it called out to him, something drew him through an opening to his right and toward a cave painting at the far end of a small cavern.

The hair on his neck, on his arms, stood on end, and he shivered. He opened the guide book and identified the painting. "**Gemsbok**." *Cave painting of an oryx antelope, discovered by Sir John Barrow who. . . .*

His vision blurred. Without realizing what he was doing, he sat down on the floor of the cave and crossed his legs Indian fashion, the way he had sat as a young boy in the Mojave, waiting for his spirit guide to show itself.

Which it had. A black buck, with a single horn—black and white and crimson.

His hand, scrabbling nervously in the dirt floor of the cave, touched something hard and cold. He picked it up and looked at it. Striated. Black at the bottom, white in the middle, the tip of the piece of horn red as blood.

Unhurriedly, Sam packed away his stilts, showered, changed, and left the compound. In his hand he held a map and a set of car keys. He left the area, turned the car around, and drove down the hill. At the first fork in the road he made a right and drove around the outskirts of one of Pretoria's prosperous white suburbs. It would take him less than half-an-hour to get back to the meeting place. Plenty of time. He slowed down and thought about the dragon-child of Negwenya, the Mother Lightning Bird.

He was half-brother to the dragon-child, or so it was said. As it was said that when the time was right the dragon child would come for him, Sam Mtshali. Might be, he thought, she would have to fly a sizable distance to find him.

Strange, how things worked out. He was finally part of the *in* crowd, a Zulu, a voter of consequence, and here he was about to go off with a red man to dance in the United States.

Besides, it was all just a story, told around the night fires. He had seen Negwenya once, during his sojourn in the Karroo; he had never seen her child, his half-brother. His childhood memories were of music and dancing, of fighting and loving. He hadn't even met their master, Nkolosi, until he'd joined the AFI, and then only briefly until the witch-doctor appeared today to take over The Zulu Warriors and inform him of his duty.

He started to turn up the music on his car radio, thought better of it, and headed down the stretch toward his destination, the abandoned mining compound. He had known it would be deserted, yet today he found its air of desolation disquieting. Letting his gaze travel over the low-slung barracks, their corrugated roofs buckled by the sun, he peopled the compound. He imagined it filled with black men who spent their days in the belly of the earth and their nights on cement bunks, longing for families departed for the homelands. Wondering if their babies had become children, their children young men and women with families of their own.

Driving past the end of a barbed wire fence, he turned off the road, and took a narrow dirt track to a house that lay hidden behind bulges of sand that grew like breasts out of the Transvaal dust. Usually, he thought, there are children around places like this, using the dumps as their personal playground. Here not even a stray dog or cat broke the silence.

The quiet disturbed him enough that he found himself actually looking forward to his meeting with Nkolosi, and the red man who was taking them to America.

The front door key slid in easily and he walked inside. Because this was the last night he'd be spending here, he took stock—seeing it with the red man's eyes, and saying his farewells. There was a table. A couple of chairs. A bed with a *coir* mattress and, downstairs in the cellar, rifles wrapped in blankets and lying like corpses on the dank floor.

He wandered aimlessly back upstairs, found a small transistor radio, and turned it to Springbok Radio. Since it was hotter than hell inside, he opened the front and back doors and plugged in the only fan he owned.

Later, when an early evening thunderstorm darkened the sky, he sat at the window and watched the dust divert the rain into channels that ran down the grimy window panes. Then, wondering briefly what had become of Legs Cleveland, he lay down on the cot and dreamed of the smell of baking bread that sometimes masked the odor of poverty of his mother's kitchen. The sound of the rain on the tin roof had an hypnotic effect, and he was soon asleep. When he awoke, the sun was setting over the mine dumps and someone was knocking at the front door.

Sam opened it. "Come in, Mr. Cleveland."

"Call me Legs. Nick here yet?"

The red-skinned American put out his hand. Sam ignored it.

"Sorry I'm late," Legs said. He sounded nervous. "Fuckin' spooky around here."

Sam led him into the kitchen. There were only two chairs. Legs took one and indicated to Sam that he should take the other. When Sam did not do so, Legs said, "Okay, buddy. If you prefer to stand."

The Zulu lounged against the wall.

"Tell me about the Mining Company," the American said.

"They pay us well, by South African standards," Sam said. "In exchange, they demand a year's contract. Most of the time, the men don't have any idea what they're signing. They think they want to get out of the *kraal* and think they're going to get rich."

"I don't understand. They're equal now. They don't have to do it anymore."

"Do what?"

"Live in a compound, eat off tin plates, sleep on cement bunks . . . ?"

And laugh, and sing, Sam thought. And play the pennywhistle. Deprived and happy, until they begin to lust after the city and the cars— He said nothing.

"Hey, listen," Legs said. "We're gonna be working together. I need your cooperation, need you to keep the troops in line, if you know what I mean." Legs grinned. Put out his hand. "Can't we be friends?"

Still Sam said nothing.

Legs pressed on. "Don't hold it against me that I'm an American. My heart's the same color as yours." He gestured at Sam. "Besides, I'm Navajo. I understand what being different means, just like you men in barracks 536."

Sam moved gracefully away from the wall. "What is it you really want from us?" He looked at Legs and felt a fleeting compassion. He knew of Navajo, and of the Reservations where the red man, like the Zulu, allowed himself to be turned into a performing bear for the tourists.

Legs flashed a gold-toothed smile, then grew serious. "Your war dances are something, Sam. All the beads and feathers and paint. Assegais waving. Terrifying the audience. Your ancestors and mine were probably related."

"Is that what you believe?"

Nkolosi had entered the room silently. His eyes held the hint of a smile at the look on Legs' face as the American whirled around in surprise.

"Here's your contract," Nkolosi said. "Signed and stamped. I even went to a shebeen and found you some pretty ladies who love to dance, and a good singer."

Legs took the contract from him, folded it carefully, and put it in his pocket. "Guess that's it then," he said, moving toward the door. "Have the men at the airport—"

"Today is Sunday," Nkolosi said. "Tuesday is Dingaan's Day, Mr. Cleveland," Nkolosi interrupted.

Legs shrugged.

"You have surely heard of Chaka Zulu?"

"Yeah, Nick. I saw the made-for-TV movie. Helluva fighter."

Nkolosi's smile did not reach his eyes. "Over a hundred years ago, Dingaan—Chaka's brother—defeated the Boer leader, Piet Retief. . . . Never mind. The details aren't important. To you. Just listen to me carefully. You'll see in the contract that I have stipulated that The Zulu Warriors must dance on Dingaan's Day." He paused for a moment, then went on. "No matter what happens or where they are, they have to dance—to remind themselves of their heritage."

"They'll be dancing. Don't worry about that."

"Yes. They will, Mr. Cleveland."

Fascinated by the encounter between snakes, Sam watched Legs walk out of the front door, stop, and pull out the contract to check it over. The light from the house stopped at the American's feet and he had to kneel to see the writing. As he did so, a lizard darted across the path of the light. He jumped. "Sooner we get of this country, the better—"

"For all of us, Mr. Cleveland," Nkolosi said softly. "For all of us."

The next morning, Sam led his fellow dancers through the service entrance of the Mining Company's working compound, a carbon copy of the deserted one, except that it was peopled by flesh-and-blood men rather than by his imagination.

Things went almost too smoothly. They wandered out of the same service gates he'd driven through the day before, astounded at the new lack of security under the coalition. No one stopped them, questioned them, asked to see IDs. Sam had the strange sensation that he didn't exist at all, that he was a figment of Legs' and Nkolosi's imaginations—not even his own. It was not so much a nightmare quality, but a disembodiment, as if he had nothing whatever to do with what was happening. Even on the flight, his first, he did not lose that sensation.

They were less than an hour away from Las Vegas when Legs appeared. He perched on the arm of the seat across the aisle from Sam. "Don't panic," he said.

"Panic?"

"The pilot just let me know that we're making an unexpected landing. I'm not sure what it's all about. Something to do with heavy rains in Vegas. Flash floods at the airport—"

Legs looked pale, worried, but all Sam could feel was relief that he'd be able to walk around for a while, stretch his long limbs—anything that might force his mind and body to fuse.

Alex "Legs" Cleveland was the first to admit that he thrived on luxury. He was, therefore, not surprised that he was less than thrilled at the idea of sleeping on a rock in the middle of nowhere.

Well, not exactly nowhere. Don Laughlin's private airstrip was in the Mojave Desert, on the outskirts of Laughlin, the southernmost town in Nevada, right on the border of both California and Arizona. Hottest spot on earth where people actually live. Rarely got below one-twenty-five in midsummer. Still it was close enough to Las Vegas to be somewhere in Alex's lexicon.

Could be worse, Legs thought. It often had been.

He walked to the far end of the runway, leaned on a fence, and watched a helicopter marked "Riverside" take off in the direction of Vegas. Then he lit a cigarette, and glanced enviously at Sam Mtshali, sleeping comfortably on a large, flat rock just the other side of the fence.

Sam stirred and opened his eyes.

"That helicopter belongs to the man who built this town," Legs said.

Sam said nothing. He stared out into the desert.

He could see nothing around him except dust and sand and, in the distance, the blinking lights of a few high-rise hotels. He thought about the Karroo, where he had once spent a month listening for the voice of his ancestors. "Do you understand spirit-seeking, red man?" he asked.

"I have been part of it," Legs said. He pulled something out of his pocket, looked at it, and seemed about to show it to Sam.

"Then you know the desert. We are brothers after all."

Legs rubbed whatever it was he held in his hand, then replaced it in his pocket. In strangely companionable silence, he joined Mtshali on the rock. They lay together and contemplated the stars. Later, they talked quietly for a while of weeks spent alone in the desert, at the time of their initiations.

"I was taught that my ancestral guide would come to me in the form of an animal," Sam said.

"Did it?"

"Yes."

Sam was pleased when Legs did not ask for more explanation than that.

"My spirit guide came as a beast with one horn," Legs said. Again, he reached into his pocket. "I didn't know exactly what it was until the other day." He held up the small gemsbok horn—striated, black at the bottom, white in the middle, and tipped with red. "I found this in the cave in Sterkfontein, buried near that painted figure of a one-horned oryx antelope Sir John Barrow found on the cave wall, at least according to the guidebook."

He paused. "Can't imagine why someone hadn't found it before. An archaeologist. A paleontologist. A tourist. It was lying right there, saying pick me up."

"It was waiting for you," Sam said, matter-of-factly. "Africa is like that. Things do not call out *Mfune,* pick us up, until *they* are ready." He was silent for a while. "I, too, have only seen my ancestral guide once," he volunteered, surprising himself by his own loquacity. "She will come to me again when she is ready. Even here, the Lightning Bird will find me."

He stopped talking, and soon fell into an uneasy sleep, interrupted by voices and dreams—ancient voices and ancient dreams, of Africans and Indians, of white men and black, of blood and revenge.

Legs listened to the Zulu's sleep-mutterings. Sam mumbled a couple of times and rolled over. The Zulu was so different from him and yet, as it turned out, so much the same.

The same but different.

The night desert was cold, the sky brilliant with stars. He lay back down, closed his eyes, and allowed the stored daytime warmth of the rock to penetrate between his shoulder blades, but sleep eluded him.

Opening his eyes, he looked at the sleeping Zulu, examined the man's ear and earring, and imagined the close-up on *Geraldo.* A tall and stately man, dressed in a terra-cotta loincloth, earlobes embedded with circular discs which so stretched the lobes that they hung below the level of his jowls. He and Maury would license the sale of those earrings. Half of America would be wearing them. The new liberal button. He'd be rich. Very, very rich. And a hero for taking the troupe away from the Mining Company, where—he would say to *Entertainment Tonight*—they worked underground all week and made a mockery of their heritage for the tourists on Sunday afternoons. And all for pennies. He'd get them real money. Make them rich, what the hell. Maybe he'd run for political office, go back to his roots—

Mayor Alexander Cleveland. The key to Los Angeles. Better yet, Vegas. Maybe he'd marry, make a whole shitload of emancipated little Navajos. On the other hand, with all those broads, hanging around for a handshake, begging for a fuck . . .

. . . Yeah, Alex thought, as Sam stirred next to him. You'll love me, everybody will love me. I'll get stinking rich, send a big check to the Reservation—and stop making promises before I have the means to fulfill them. One of these days, I'll even stop looking for yesterday. Stop needing my Show Biz fix.

In a pig's eye.

He had tried every high—coke, morphine, booze. There was no high like this. Maury would love it. Vegas would love it.

Legs Cleveland was back in business.

He debated the walk into Laughlin, and quickly abandoned the thought. Hell, everyone else who'd been on the private jet, including the pilot, was sleeping. No point in doing anything until dawn, except try to rest. Just so there weren't any snakes around, he thought, lighting another cigarette. He reached into his pocket and once again removed the piece of gemsbok horn. What was it that Sam had said? *In Africa things do not say* Mfune, *pick us up, until* they *are ready.*

Mornings are no time for conversation, Sam thought. He shifted so that his back was squarely facing Legs, and opened his eyes. For a moment, as he'd awakened, Sam had thought he was at home. The thought was fleeting but comforting. He watched the mountains come alive into the dawn. This desert, the Mojave, Legs had called it, was like the Karroo. Yet it was different, too.

The same but different.

The real question was, why was he here?

Searching for an answer, he forced himself to relive what had happened in his life since he'd picked up Alex "Legs" Cleveland at the side of the road, mostly because he had never seen a red man in the flesh before. There was Nkolosi's appearance, the dances, the meeting—

—A streak of light brought the mountains into relief. The smell of Legs' cigarette penetrated Sam's retrospection. Keeping his back to the red man, he actively relived the rest of the time between the meeting with Nkolosi and the present. When he had caught up, he turned over, propped himself up on one elbow, and looked over at Legs. Then he stood up and stretched to his full height.

"It is Tuesday," he said. "Today we must dance."

Damn plane, damn storm. Damn everything, Legs thought, scrambling back over the fence. His relatively benign mood was disappearing fast with the renewed realization that he was stuck out here until noon. He headed for the plane to pick up his video-cam and to speak to the pilot.

Their conversation did not improve his mood any. No amount of effort had rustled up a bus that was available before noon. He was hot. Hungry. Thirsty. Vegas was only an hour or so away by car, yet he felt like he was stranded in the middle of Hell. Some place for an opening performance; bullshit, this Dingaan's Day stuff—like insisting on celebrating Custer's last stand.

How was he supposed to know how to deal with this bunch of fucking Zulus who insisted on dancing, right here, today.

A noise overhead broke the desert silence. He looked up, expecting to see Don Laughlin's helicopter returning.

"PRESS. CNN," he read out loud. "Come on down, guys. It's . . . da-da-da-da . . . Showtime!"

The helicopter banked to the right and circled.

Shifting his gaze a little, Legs blinked and refocused.

He got up and walked quickly toward the plane, where The Zulu Warriors were dressing. All he wanted was to get out of this place. His heart hadn't regained its natural rhythm since they got here.

He sat down and tried to concentrate on the voice booming over the plane's PA system. A familiar voice. Sinister. Sibilant. Nkolosi's, though it could not be.

"More than one hundred years ago," the voice said, "a band of Zulus attacked and destroyed Piet Retief and his white followers. The war dances which preceded that bloody battle are about to be recreated for you."

He hadn't authorized the announcements, Legs thought. Or had he? Suddenly he couldn't remember. He felt confused, lucky to remember his own name. If my friends could see me now, he thought wryly: Alexander "Legs" Cleveland, entertainment King of Laughlin, Nevada.

"Let's go," he yelled. He applauded too loudly. "It's showtime."

Sam listened to Legs' clapping and wondered if it reached into the barracks, to the friends he had left behind. He looked at the troupe, The

Zulu Warriors, waiting to make their entrance. Their stage a desert airstrip. Only they weren't warriors. They were urbanites, whose ancestors once were warriors. Though he knew it shamed them to make a mockery of their tribal rituals, there were those among them who had long not given a damn.

Suddenly, he knew why Nkolosi had sent him here. Now. To get American television coverage for Nkolosi's statement against the Botha-Mandela coalition. Proof that the tribal heritage was being sublimated. This would be Nkolosi's platform statement, as the American called it, his first official bid for leadership of the new South Africa.

Sam mounted his seven-foot stilts, took out the knife he'd hidden in his belt, and conjured up feathered warriors, readying poison darts, and secreting them in plumed headdresses. Somewhere in the deepest level of his gut, he sensed their assegais quivering with the scent of blood.

He looked upward. Overhead, the sky had darkened and the circling helicopter had given way to his ancestral guide. At her side flew his half-brother, son of the Lightning Bird. Together, they had come to remind him and the other dancers that happiness in the afterlife depended upon having lived this life with pride.

"Kill the Wizards!"

Sam's cry broke out, loud and clear. An ancient cry, Dingaan's, it rose from his throat as it had risen from Dingaan's over a century before. He stared straight at Legs. "Kill the Wizards, and the world will bow before you and your ancestors!"

Legs sank to the ground. Cross-legged, sun beating down on his bare head, he stared through his video-cam lens at the bodies of the dancers—skin glistening with oils and unguents, assegais held loosely, tapping the beat with balls of unshod feet . . . the beat itself, moving from legato to staccato in preordained rhythms and played by one lone drummer. Behind the men stood the women, breasts exposed, heads raised, voices harmonizing in a language of loss.

Slowly, their movements ordered by centuries of tradition, eight men drove their bodies to the beat, drove them until they became Dingaan's marshals reborn.

They were all tall men to begin with. In their feathered headdresses, bobbing and gyrating as they circled the musician, they appeared gigantic. As for Sam, elevated above the highest head by his wooden stilts, Legs knew that the Zulu could see beyond the airport, across the desert that so closely resembled the land that had belonged to his father's father . . . the land of Legs' own tribe. In his own mind's eye, Legs saw cattle grazing and sensed that he was seeing what Sam saw. Feeling what Sam felt.

The rhythm picked up. Legs glanced across at the far end of the airstrip where a group of security guards stood stiffly erect. "Kill the Wizards!" Sam cried out.

"I am an American. I am one of *you*," Legs shouted, as the guards advanced and he realized he was sitting directly in their path. Move, schmuck, move, he told himself. He could sense the danger he was in, yet he sat on, his head filled with visions of axes and arrows—

And then it was too late.

The dancers were dancers no longer. Warriors now, they charged. Swaying, Sam commanded his troops, and a guard's bullet found its mark.

Clutching his head, the Zulu began to totter. For a moment, impossibly, he maintained his balance. Raising his hands in the air, he released his assegai in what he thought to be the direction of the advancing guards. But the blood from his wound obscured his vision.

Legs, standing now, felt the assegai impale him. He watched the flow of blood from Sam's wound. Then together, like two telephone poles struck down by an electric storm, the black man and the red man fell to the ground.

Lying in the dust, Legs watched Sam trace his fingers in a pool of blood, theirs, and wet his lips. Our blood tastes the same, Legs thought, wondering why that had never occurred to him before.

He thought longingly of Las Vegas, the danger of the tables, the wonderfully blatant kitsch. Then he looked up at the Mother Lightning bird, its cousin the helicopter, and the child Lightning Bird, come with its Mother to guide the spirit of their son and half-brother, Sam Mtshali. Where the hell was *his* spirit guide when he needed it?

He reached into his pocket for the gemsbok horn. His hand came up empty. As the pain began, he narrowed his eyes and looked across the tarmac. A brightly colored object lay near the spot where he had climbed the fence. By sheer force of will, he dragged himself over to where it lay. He picked it up and lifted his head to the sky. For a moment his vision blurred and the three birds, the same but different, became one. Then his pain stopped. He looked down at his wound. To his amazement, the flow of blood had ceased.

Slowly, testing every movement, he stood.

"Black, white, Native American. All the same magic, isn't it, Mr. Cleveland?" Nkolosi's voice was soft inside Legs' head. Soothing. A grandfather, healing the cut on his grandson's knee by the gentle persuasion that a kiss could make it better.

Bloodsucking magician, Legs thought, knowing Nkolosi could hear him. He used me. *Used* me. Now what am I supposed to tell Maury?

He brushed himself off. For one thing, he thought, as he ambled toward the plane—stepping gingerly around several bodies, including Sam's—he would tell Maury to watch CNN News. He patted the video in his pocket, the one he had made of the one-and-only performance of The Zulu Warriors in the US of A. That would take care of *ethnic*, for the moment. They ought to be able to sell plenty copies of that, a few million at least, what with the killings and all. More than pay for the trip to Africa which, he decided, he personally would avoid in future.

So where next? He was fresh out of ideas . . . except, well, there was that kid he'd heard about, the one who claimed he could fly—no tricks, no gimmicks. A regular Mary Martin.

He took the piece of gemsbok horn out of his pocket, kissed it, and chuckled. "One thing you gotta say, Maury," he rehearsed out loud, patting his chest where the wound had been and holding the video-cam on high, "Alexander 'Legs' Cleveland puts on a helluva show."

ABOUT THE AUTHOR

Janet Berliner Gluckman is the coeditor, with David, of *David Copperfield's Tales of the Impossible* (HarperPrism, due Fall '95). She also had a hand in Peter S. Beagle's *Unicorn Sonata* (Turner Publishing, due Fall '96). She recently completed work on *The Michael Crichton Companion.* Among her current projects are *And So Say All Of Us,* an episodic psychological thriller, *Prism,* a dark novel about androgyny, and *Dance of the Python,* a novel in the tradition of H. Rider Haggard, about treachery and witchcraft in modern tribal South Africa.

In 1961, Janet left her native South Africa in protest against apartheid. After living and teaching in New York, she moved to San Francisco's Bay Area, where she started her own business as an editorial consultant, lecturer, and writer. She now lives and works in Las Vegas. Her last novel was *Child of the Light,* coauthored with George Guthridge (St. Martin's Press, April 1992). She is under contract to White Wolf Books for *The Madagascar Manifesto,* which completes the Child trilogy.

Janet's short fiction and nonfiction has appeared in many anthologies, magazines, and newspapers, including the *San Francisco Chronicle.* She is the author of the political thriller *Rite of the Dragon*, and coauthor of *The Execution Exchange,* and *Timestalker* (TV Movie-of-the-Week). She served as personal and developmental editor of *Don Sherwood: The Life and Times of "The World's Greatest Disc Jockey"*—a No. 1 bestseller on the West Coast—and as coordinating writer on *The Whole Child* series from Enrich.

In her copious free time, she travels (most often to the Caribbean), dances (preferably the lambada), and plays the occasional game of poker.

EDWARD BRYANT

BIG DOGS, STRANGE DAYS

Peter: **Edward Bryant** is one of those people—Judith Tarr and Octavia Butler are two others—whom I am always running into at fantasy and science fiction conventions, am delighted to see, have a pleasant drink and an intriguing conversation with, and don't see again for several years at a clip, until we run into each other in some other crowded hotel lobby in some other town. I think of Ed as the only cowboy I know, and if he isn't really one, I don't want to hear about it. He was raised in Wyoming and has worked as a stirrup-buckle maker, so there you are. Of his dozen or so books, his *Particle Theory* is one of my favorite short fiction collections, and his *Cinnabar* remains one of the very best novels of the last twenty years. He has adapted his own stories for *The Twilight Zone,* and had others adapted for Lifetime Cable's *The Hidden Room. Flirting With Death,* a major collection of his suspense and horror stories, should be out by the time you read this. See you next time, Ed . . .

Janet: My friendship with Bryant goes back to a small convention in Denver circa 1977, a little piece of forever ago. It was there that I read the first chapter of *Cinnabar* and determined to meet this man whose voice spoke so loudly to me, intellectually and viscerally; there that he taught me about the virtues of drinking Irish coffee out of paper cups; there that I saw first drafts of his stories emerge from his typewriter (yes, *typewriter*) reading better than most final copy I'd ever seen. Edward does this "thing" when he writes. He uses universal buzz buttons to force the reader to bring baggage to his stories, thus adding a dimension that both does and doesn't exist on the actual page. More than that, he once sent me a Valentine that depicted a man lying in the desert, his guts exposed to the world, vultures feasting. Who could resist such a man, who manages to turn even his bloodiest tales into love stories?

Big Dogs, Strange Days

H E SAT ALONE IN HIS APARTMENT AS HE had for so many days and nights, and painted. It occurred to him that practice was good for his art; he did not consider himself all that accomplished an artist. So he played with various effects and different media.

This year he was amusing himself with acrylics.

Those paints had not existed when he first took up the brush. As best he could recall, that would have been about the year 1810. The man reckoned he was close to 221 years old. One spitting devil of a long while . . .

Never be an old master, he thought, and smiled. An old amateur, probably.

He glanced up above the old wooden desk where he'd hung the first piece he'd ever painted. It was a crude rendering of two men struggling in a fight to the death, rolling over and over in dust and cactus spines. The man in the breechcloth had a knife and the naked man didn't, but the unarmed man had twisted the hand with the knife around so that the blade sank to its hilt in the armed man's belly.

The artist remembered sketching out the scene on a thin sheet of aspen bark in Manuel Lisa's fort, a rough place that lay in the center of what someday would be Montana.

His artistic media had been berry juice, charcoal, and a little blood. He had used bird feathers as brushes. After this long, the colors had faded, but the artist could fill in their hues in his mind.

He turned back to his current canvas. The artist had only this afternoon begun to sketch the rough figures. This was not a realistic scene. He was attempting to evoke ghostly figures, masked by wind and spitting snow. From different directions, the figures approached a roadhouse. The artist knew—had known—the location well. It lay a mile outside Casper, Wyoming. He believed it had burned to the ground sometime around the turn of the century—the twentieth century, that is. Good riddance. The owner had been a real shit.

The most spectral of the figures was the equine head that overshadowed all else. The human beings approaching the warm sanctuary of the roadhouse included a man in ranching gear, a woman wearing Shoshoni buckskin, an elderly Chinese gentleman in a dark broadcloth suit, and the artist himself.

The image of the artist would be the last executed. The man in the apartment hated self-portraits, but he knew this one was necessary. He had to be true to his materials. And to his memories . . .

Good work as ever, Coyote, said the voice in his head.

"I am not Coyote," he said aloud, irritated, but familiar with this routine.

You're sure you're not Coyote?

"Yes."

Well, the hand of Coyote, then. Paw of Coyote . . .

"Stop bothering me," he said. "I'm trying to concentrate."

Ferret, then. Saved from extinction by dint of extraordinary circumstance.

He ignored the voice and, after a while, it went away.

The artist shook his head, wondered why supernatural beings rarely communicated with him through dreams, as normal gods were supposed to do. He was never quite sure about this business of talking to the divine in broad daylight, right in the middle of his apartment on Patchin Place, just off 10th Street and Sixth Avenue. This was Manhattan, for the love of God, and he was a onetime hunter from the Shenandoah Valley of Virginia who'd had an adventure or two long ago.

Many adventures, he thought, and they continued imposing themselves on his life. He shook his head. Adventures were good. With 221 winters under his belt, it was probably a useful idea not to get bored.

Well, tedium had not yet set in.

The artist glanced up at the row of reference sketches thumbtacked to the edge of the bookshelf just beyond the canvas.

He cocked his head a moment, and stared at the image of the old Chinese man, trying to recapture the detail of the stooped body, the wrinkled face, the sunken eyes that still appeared as dark and shiny as *go* stones.

∞   ∞   ∞

Dr. Wu's body ached in every one of his atoms.

He sat on one of the hard wooden benches in Denver's cavernous Union Station. The bench was one of a number informally set aside for the use of Chinamen, Negroes, and Mexicans.

He listened for the wail of the locomotive whistle that would herald the arrival of the northbound Union Pacific train to Cheyenne, Wyoming, and then on to Casper. Right now, he heard only the ghost of a whistle's call; it reminded him of being a bit more than a quarter century younger, standing with his quiet fellows at Promontory Point, Utah. It had been May 10, 1869, and Wu had spent a hard year driving spikes and wrestling creosoted ties into place so that the westbound and eastbound tracks could finally meet.

Never mind the stories, there had been no golden spike.

Building a railroad . . . *That* had given him aches. But then so had working on the sluice boxes of the Gold Rush of twenty years earlier, and so had logging and laundering, and performing all manner of other menial tasks. Work had been a blessing. With only one Chinese woman for every hundred Chinese men, marriage had been out of the question.

And now Wu was Dr. Wu. Chinese medicine was what he practiced, and so he added the honorific in the American manner. It seemed to help business. He had learned his art at the feet of a master in his home village back in the Pearl River Delta in the province of Kwangtung. His medicine was that of South China.

Wu's thoughts wandered. They had that right. He was eighty-two years old, after all.

He knew his Western counterparts had a wise saying: physician, heal thyself.

Wu wished he could do that.

His muscles ached, his joints agonized, the pain vibrated in the marrow of his bones.

The worst of it though, the very worst terror of all, was that he feared he was too old to approach the Widow Cho. This beautiful celestial woman had lost her beloved husband a decade before, when their tailoring shop had been set afire by drunken Irish—or perhaps it had been drunken Italians. Wu could no longer remember that specific detail. He simply knew that the Widow had been without male companionship for ten years, certainly long enough to consider introduction to a new potential husband.

At eighty-two, Wu possessed certain apprehensions.

Because of this, he had allowed his colleagues in the six companies to prevail upon him to undertake an important mission. If good fortune smiled, then the Chinese Consolidated Benevolent Association would make a great deal of money, income which Dr. Wu would share.

There was something else the mission might accomplish for him, though, a reward of an acutely personal nature. That was his hope. He already had enough money for the rest of his days. It was his pride that needed a cushion.

The cry of the big steam locomotive shivered the old man's bones as it surely must be shaking the heart and liver of every other human being in this place. Dr. Wu got to his feet and painfully hefted his satchel. He touched the inner pocket of his jacket. He felt the crisp square of paper that instructed him how to find a certain roadhouse a mile or two from the Casper station.

With a little hope and a great deal of pain, Dr. Wu joined the throng straggling toward the waiting train.

∞ ∞ ∞

The artist brewed himself a cup of coffee. He made it the old way, heating a percolator on the stove burner. Mr. Coffee was not welcome in this home.

No cream for the artist. If there were a few grounds in the cup, so much the better. It gives body, he told himself.

When he returned to the canvas and settled himself in his chair, he critically scrutinized what he had done already. Touch-up could come later. For now, he wanted to rough things in.

He raised his head and glanced at the study of the big man in rancher's garb. The broad brim of his Western hat was creased and stained, certainly weathered for more than a few hard winters. The man's forehead was broad, his eyes wide as though constantly surprised by what he saw. Crow's feet fanned out from the corners of those eyes.

The rancher was dressed for cold weather. His long coat was lined with fleece. He wore gloves. A hint of blowing snow swirled around his exposed face.

The artist couldn't help but shiver.

∞ ∞ ∞

Barlow Whitaker had come west from Pennsylvania when he was twelve. He was on his own, having no desire to continue reaping his father's harvest of beatings, and more, having no wish to spend the rest of his life working with the hope of inheriting the old man's dirt-poor farm.

Not that Barlow was doing all that much better in southeastern Wyoming. He had worked like a dog for other men, to get enough cash to secure a homestead east of Cheyenne. He had married his nearest neighbor's daughter; that had doubled the size of the spread. Love had come later, but it surely *had* come. Barlow was glad for that. Children had not yet arrived, no heirs, and that bothered him. His wife and he possessed no issue, but it wasn't for lack of trying.

Besides his wife, Barlow's great love was horses. He would rather raise a herd of horseflesh than cattle, any day of the week. He loved watching the stallions breed the mares; he loved helping the mares foal their colts. There was nothing to compare with watching the spindly-legged offspring struggling upright, lurching uncertainly, then tottering off to nurse at their mother's side.

Most of all, Barlow loved breaking the horses to saddle. Every two-year-old was a challenge, each one a tough problem to solve. His neighbors said that Barlow was real good at what he did. He had the reputation for knowing what a bucking horse was going to do the second before it did it. He could ride like the wind.

Maybe he could even ride a tornado the way Pecos Bill could in the old story. He'd never tried that.

His wife said he rode so well, he could be a centaur.

Barlow had to think about that.

Right now, though, he was a little worried. He was a bit apprehensive about leaving the big bay stabled for a week in Cheyenne while he took the U.P. northbound up to Casper. As he stood on the exposed platform of the Cheyenne station, clapping his hands together for warmth, he also thought about the letter from the bank. Last winter hadn't been a good one. Too much snow and cold; too many head of stock had died. That had been the heartbreaker—all those dead horses he'd known and raised, ridden and loved.

All the money he could scrap up in the world was a thin sheaf of greenbacks folded and hidden in the money belt around his waist. He also had a set of directions to find a roadhouse outside Casper.

Barlow was going to buy horses. The Boer War was heating up and suddenly the British Army was combing the U.S. of A. for good horseflesh. The rancher knew the Shoshoni had a wealth of herds right now.

He would buy one. And if they wouldn't sell their horses satisfactorily, well—Barlow didn't want to think about that. He was basically an honest man. He did not wish to use the Colt .45 tucked into his belt beneath the bulky coat.

The man glanced up at the steel-gray sky, which had begun to spit snow. These weren't soft flakes drifting down slowly. The clouds were offering up what was turning into cold sleet.

Barlow heard the distant whistle. Good. The train would be here soon.

∞ ∞ ∞

The artist stretched; his muscles registered exquisite pain, his joints cracked luxuriously.

This wasn't going all that badly. What looked back at him from the canvas was not as clumsy as he'd anticipated. Still, there was considerable left to evoke with his paints.

He could stop and brew some fresher, hotter coffee. No, he looked up at the working sketch in the center. Coffee could wait. He was on a roll now. He didn't think the woman would be tough to paint at all.

After all, he knew her well.

∞ ∞ ∞

Her name was Storm Soother and she was a medicine woman of the Wind River band of the Shoshoni. For two days now of increasingly ominous weather signs she had ridden the black stallion called Lightning Tree east toward Casper. She had started out in bright sunshine from Fort Washakie on the Wind River Reservation. She left, not exactly in secret, but still while the Indian Agent was sleeping off his heavy lunch. There was no law that bound her to the reservation, but the whole sorry episode of the dubious prophet Wovoka and the desperate appeal of the Ghost Dance movement was only a handful of years in the past.

Government agents were still nervous; and Storm Soother did not want this spirit errand to be delayed. Thus she left her home under cover of the light. The Indian Agent didn't notice for an entire day.

The journey wore worse on the woman than it did the horse.

Lightning Tree appeared as fresh as he had two days before the woman and he descended from the Rattlesnake Range, crossed through Emigrant Gap, and saw the dim, distant lights of Casper.

"We will rest in Bar Nunn," she said to Lightning Tree, as much as to herself. "The train must be on its way, but it won't arrive before the afternoon. We'll get some food."

The stallion whickered. She leaned forward and patted the side of his muscled neck.

Storm Soother thought ahead to the coming light, and beyond that, to the afternoon in which she would meet the three men at the roadhouse. She offered up a prayer that an agreement would be reached. The medicine woman had offered up many prayers since dreaming this situation that must be addressed.

It was a knotty problem. It was her task.

∞ ∞ ∞

The artist frowned. His attempt to fill in the shadings on the medicine woman was dismal.

He would do better. He realized he would have to examine the innermost workings of this painting.

He'd have to go inside.

∞ ∞ ∞

The man who called himself John Colter was already waiting when the other three arrived. He had ordered a shot of rotgut from the surly proprietor of the nameless roadhouse, and had drunk it down with dispatch. There was no purpose in attempting to savor so foul a brew. Colter suspected the drink was perhaps only hours old.

The manager and he were the only people in the establishment. Colter wondered if the weather was putting travelers off. More likely this place was simply not one that drew passersby through its sterling reputation. Fine, then. Privacy would be useful.

The others arrived. The two men came through the door almost in company with each other. Colter knew the elderly Chinaman must have had to hurry to keep up with the big, bluff cowboy. It was a hike of a mile or more from the station. The two men looked around in the dim interior. Black eyes and blue eyes, both expressions questioning.

The roadhouse proprietor was stacking enough wood in the huge fireplace to burn a witch. He grunted. "No Chinamen."

"I have money," said Dr. Wu.

"Don't need your money," said the proprietor. "*Could* maybe use some laundry done."

Wu said nothing.

"He stays," said Colter. He opened his jacket slightly and let his fingers rest on the hilt of the large Bowie knife lying sheathed against his thigh.

The big rancher laughed. Everyone else turned to stare at him.

"Name's Barlow Whitaker," he said. Barlow gestured at the Bowie knife. "My daddy named me for the knife. Thought it'd be lucky for me. He should have picked that one."

"Barlow knife's got a good blade," said Colter. "Nothing to be ashamed of. Bowie's good too," he said reflectively.

The proprietor mumbled something and retreated to the bar.

They heard the sound of a horse, hoofbeats approaching, an imperative whinny. A minute later, the woman came through the door.

"No Indians," said the roadhouse proprietor. " 'Specially no squaws."

It was the rancher's turn to open his coat slightly. He set his ham-sized hand on the ivory grip of the .45. "She's still a lady," Barlow said. "She stays."

"Then you all better buy something," said the proprietor.

"You stock any sarsparilla?" said the medicine woman.

Dr. Wu had been watching all the goings-on with some curiosity. "I am supposed to meet a person here . . ." he began.

"Me too," said Barlow.

"I think we need names," said the medicine woman.

Colter made the round of introductions without faltering. Barlow and Dr. Wu both stared at him with some evident suspicion. Storm Soother stared at him with frank interest.

He stared back at her. Her hair and eyes were equally dark and lustrous. She was a handsome woman, body soft and capable. "I believe some of us know much more than the rest, Mr. Colter," Storm Soother said.

"Then let's get to it." Colter gestured toward a rough plank table. All four took seats. Barlow chivalrously pulled out the chair for Storm Soother.

Colter took a deep breath. "You all got directions to come here. You all think you're here for a specific reason. Well, you're wrong." He smiled across the table. "Except for maybe Storm Soother, there."

"Please explain," said Dr. Wu.

"Okay," said Colter. "Settle back. Barlow, I think you're a man who wants some sort of future for his family. You want children, right? Heirs?"

Barlow slowly nodded.

"You think you can make a small fortune out of selling off all the horses you can lay your hands on to the British, so's they can ship them to Africa where they're fighting with the Boers." He paused. "I've got to tell you something. What you want to get by hook or by crook from the Shoshoni is more valuable than you could ever pay for. It's too valuable to sell to Mr. John Bull."

"What are you saying?" said Barlow. "What's more valuable than horses?"

"Dr. Wu can tell you that," said Colter. He turned to the small, elderly man. "I think, sir, you and your celestrial brethren have heard some mighty interesting stories about a special breed of horse up here in Wyoming."

Dr. Wu slowly nodded.

"They are, of course, not really horses."

"Wait a minute," Barlow cried.

Colter said to the medicine woman, "You want to bring your steed in here?"

"God *damn* it!" cried the roadhouse proprietor, who had been eavesdropping. "No horses. You're not going to bring that thing in here."

Colter spun something sharp and glittery through the air straight at him. The proprietor reflexively caught it. He stared at the ten-dollar gold piece. He looked up and shrugged.

Colter held the door wide while Storm Soother led Lightning Tree inside. The stallion clopped across the wood floor.

"If he makes a mess . . ." said the proprietor.

"Take it out of the gold eagle," said Colter.

"Fine stallion," said Barlow, "but he looks like a horse to me."

Colter said, "Back to Dr. Wu. Horses that aren't horses; horses with a single horn comin' out of their head. They kindle a real desire in the children of heaven."

"What Mr. Colter is trying to say," said Dr. Wu, "is that we value the powder of that horn for its medicinal properties."

"It's an aphrodisiac," said Colter. He grinned. "I just learned that word. It means any kind of thing that lights up a man's passion." He glanced at Storm Soother. "And I guess a woman's, too."

"Actually," said Dr. Wu, "the value is immense."

"When you find them," said Colter. "And when you poach them."

"I don't get this at all," said Barlow.

"Be patient a moment. 'Long about the sixth century, an Irishman named St. Brendan seems to have landed in the New World. Along with a small crew, he brought over a cargo that just sort of galloped away when they hit the beach. How he ever made it across the Atlantic in a coracle— that's not even a full-size ship—with a breeding pair, I don't know. But I guess he did, and the beasts bred here."

"Beasts," Barlow said hopelessly. "Irishmen?"

"The critters moved west for about a thousand years. They were pretty lonely. Then in 1600 the Spaniards brought horses to Santa Fe. It was only a matter of time before the Indians got over the belief that the Conquistadores and their horses were one creature. The Indians caught on pretty fast that horses could be used for everything from hunting to war. When the Lakota got them, they called them shun-ka-ka. Shun-ka is dog. Shun-ka-ka is big dog. By about 1690, the Shoshoni had horses, and it wasn't long after that when the horses and the Irish critters met up. Guess you can figure what happened then." He paused. "They bred true, not like mules. They're still around, and slowly growing in numbers." He smiled at Storm Soother. "They seemed to take to the Shoshoni. It was a good match."

"There are some reasons," said Storm Soother. "The reasons go back."

"A long way back," said Colter. "Did you men know there were horses here before the Spaniards came? There were horses here in the New World until about seven thousand years ago. Scientists from the East have found their bones encased in stone. Those horses weren't very big; I guess they were smaller than ponies. But they were part of the family."

Storm Soother looked down at the floor. "This is the part that shames me."

"Not you," said Colter. "Ancestors. All the horses died out after about eight thousand years of Indians hunting them like deer and eating them."

"So there is a debt," said the medicine woman.

"And every tribe pays on that debt by caring for their horses," said Colter, "and especially caring for the crossbreeds."

"What about you, Mr. Colter," said Dr. Wu. "Where do you enter this tale?"

"Well, a while back I had a bad time with a band of Blackfoot. They were a mite upset that I'd been helping out their enemies, the Mandan. So they stripped me naked and gave me a head start to run across a godawful plain full of rocks and cactus. Then they chased me. One brave caught up, but I killed him. I hid from the rest under a beaver dam in the Madison River. It wasn't too long after that, I found a place I called Colter's Hell. You call it Yellowstone. And when I was there, I found the crossbreed critters. Didn't kill'em. Didn't eat'em. I befriended them, and then brought a couple back to the Shoshoni. I didn't know it then, but they decided to give me a gift."

"The Shoshoni?" said Barlow.

"The critters. They're not good just for aphrodisiacs. They can offer other things. Maybe it's a blessing, maybe a curse. I don't know yet."

Dr. Wu quietly, respectfully waited for a pause before speaking. "How will we resolve all this?"

"Poaching and killing are out of the question," said Colter. "So's selling 'em off to the British." He met Barlow's eye. "Here's the deal. You've got the finest horse ranch in the state. The Shoshoni'll give you some breeding mares and a stallion. You just take care of them. Give them space and food, and maybe a little love. Won't take long for you to build up a herd."

"They've got to eat," said Barlow. "So do my wife and me. Should we make it a tent-show and charge admission?"

"Hell no," said Colter. "This is where Dr. Wu comes in. Every other season or so, the critters shed their horns. Just like deer, only not as frequent. Anyhow, the properties are still there. I think Dr. Wu and his friends will buy whatever you supply for a fair price."

Their eyes turned toward the old Chinese man, who slowly nodded. "I could agree to such an arrangement."

"So how can we know if we're all shootin' straight?" said Barlow reasonably enough.

"There's an old belief," said Colter, "from back there in the Dark Ages. Those folks knew that you could use the horn to tell if something was poison. It doesn't have to be just a drink."

"What horn?" said Barlow.

Dr. Wu's eyes narrowed as he stared at Lightning Tree.

Colter said, "Storm Soother?"

The medicine woman nodded solemnly. She pushed back her chair, stood, and slowly walked around the table, passing her hand before each of their eyes.

"Well, I'll be god—" Barlow stopped himself in time.

Dr. Wu said nothing.

"Behold," said Colter.

The horn sprang true and straight from the center of Lightning Tree's forehead. It was at least a yard long. Black at the base, the shaft was a brilliant white, the tip bright crimson.

"Now," said Colter, "every one of us, grasp the horn with our right hands."

They moved from the table to form an arc around Lightning Tree's head.

"I am left-handed," said Dr. Wu tentatively.

"Then use your left hand." There was only mild exasperation in Colter's voice. "If there is poison in anything one of us has said, then the horn will find it out."

No one hesitated. The four of them reached, twenty fingers curling tightly around the proud horn.

Light exploded.

The four of them staggered back, reeling, electrical fire seeming to shoot from hands and hair. Colter was reminded of the men he'd seen reeling in the generator building down in Telluride. He'd taken a short job working for the crazy, brilliant, European scientist Tesla, helping to build the huge DC power source for the new mine. One of the workers had accidentally shorted one of the motors during a test phase. It was extraordinary fortune that no one had been killed. But the effects had lingered after the electrical dance had ended and the participants scattered across the plank floor. It had taken Colter hours to shake off the effects of the electrical power; much longer to remove all the splinters.

They stared at the aptly named Lightning Tree.

The creature snorted, met their stares, started snuffling in Storm Soother's proffered hand, velvet lips searching for grain. With her free fingers, she dipped into the slung pouch, extracted golden corn, drizzled them into her other palm. Lightning Tree inhaled them, his mane shaking with satisfaction.

"Did it work?" said Dr. Wu.

"Is anyone dead?" Colter smiled.

All stared at one another.

"So," said John Colter, looking straight at each of his companions in turn. "Is each of you satisfied?" He could see the high color in each of their faces, even that of Dr. Wu.

Barlow shook his head wildly for a moment like the motion of a spooked horse, then controlled himself. "Yes," he said.

Dr. Wu nodded slowly.

Storm Soother looked back from her steed, met Colter's gaze, and smiled.

Barlow Whitaker had his long sheepskin coat wrapped around him. He set his Stetson forward on his head, obviously readying it for the stiff winter wind that still howled outside the roadhouse.

"You going on to Wind River?" Colter asked curiously.

Barlow shook his head. "Got things to attend to at home. I believe there is a U.P. steamer heading south later tonight. No snow's heavy enough to stop that train." He hesitated, as though unsure if he wished to continue. "And there's the missus. I've got some business I need to carry out with her."

Colter noted with amusement that the six feet six inches of rancher appeared to be blushing.

"Listen," said Barlow. His voice lowered. "Man to man, I've got to ask you something."

Colter nodded seriously.

"When we all grabbed hold of that critter's horn?" The rancher almost stuttered. "Was that like holding on to the supernatural grand-father of all johnsons, or what?"

"That's about it," said Colter. "The power there's considerable. It's why the Chinamen so value the powder of the horn." He held out his hand. "Good luck to the missus."

Barlow's pause was only momentary. He took Colter's hand in his much larger one and shook it vigorously.

"Oh," the rancher said as he turned toward the door. "I guess maybe I'll share a compartment down to Cheyenne with Dr. Wu."

"He's Chinese," said Colter without inflection.

Barlow smiled. "He's just a man. So long as I don't have to eat his food, it'll be fine."

"Then wait a moment for me to bid my good-byes," said Dr. Wu. The stooped, wizened man took Storm Soother's hand, then Colter's. To the Shoshoni medicine woman, he said, "I thank you for this evening's entertainments. I believe we have reached agreement. Our bargain will be the bargain." As he spoke the last, he looked at Lightning Tree. "The Chinese Consolidated Benevolent Association—and I especially—will be grateful for the shed horn you share with us."

Storm Soother nodded.

Dr. Wu hesitated, then allowed a small smile to creep across his lips. Colter thought he could almost hear a slight sound like stiff papyrus crackling. "Now I will go. Like my compatriot, Mr. Whitaker, I have business to transact at home. I feel it is a good time to attend the Widow Cho." He bowed slightly to woman, horse, and man, and followed Barlow Whitaker out the door.

"And now," said Colter to Storm Soother, "what about you?"

"Yeah." Almost forgotten, the roadhouse manager grumbled from behind the bar. "No horses, no Indians."

"Be silent," Storm Soother told him. He was. She turned back to Colter.

Ferret was snared by the warm, night-black gaze.

"It is my understanding," she said, "that you knew the grandmother of my grandmother."

"Sacajawea?" said Colter. "She was a magnificent and strong woman. She convinced her people—your people—to aid us. Without that help, I fear we wouldn't have prevailed."

"It is my understanding that you knew her very well." Storm Soother's meaning was clear.

"She was one of the two squaws of Toussaint Charbonneau, one of the expedition's interpreters," said Colter. "She brought her papoose. Meriwether Lewis and Bill Clark ran a tight ship."

"You knew her *very* well." Storm Soother's smile did not vary.

The logs shifted in the fireplace. Flames shot up toward the flue. Colter suddenly wondered if he was blushing brighter than the fire. "We had our times, she and I," Colter finally said. "I've never loved anyone more."

Storm Soother's voice and eyes were both level with his. "I'm not minded to start riding back to Wind River at night, in the middle of a December storm."

"There are rooms here," said Colter.

"Now hold on just a damned minute," the roadhouse manager started to say.

"Innkeep, shut up," said Colter. The man shut up.

"We need only one room," said Storm Soother.

"You're young," said Colter. "I'm not."

"Her spirit is with my spirit. It'll do."

He took her hand. Storm Soother's skin seemed hotter than the heat radiating from the conflagration building in the fireplace. "This works out, you realize, there's a chance Lightning Tree won't be resting his head in your lap."

"I'll take my chances," she said.

∞   ∞   ∞

The artist set down his brushes. The painting was looking pretty darned good, and he was surprised. "You're no Albert Bierstadt," he said aloud to himself. "Not even a Charlie Russell." This would do. Time for a breather.

He went downstairs to get the mail. Rarely did anything more than advertising circulars arrive in the box, but the afternoon was sunny and it would be good to sit on the steps for a while.

But today there was an envelope in the black metal box.

The artist sat on the step below the landing and scrutinized what he'd received. It was a creamy number ten envelope with only his name and address on the outside. He held it up to the light. The postmark told him it had been sent from the Wind River Reservation in Wyoming.

Inside him, a spark flared fiercely.

He carefully ripped open the envelope and took out the piece of folded notepaper. Handwritten, big loops. The ink was blue. He sniffed. No scent. Dated the previous week.

Dear Mr. Colter, it read.

He skipped to the end of the page. It was signed Mallory Storm. He retraced to the beginning.

> *You don't know me, but I believe you have known some members of my family. I have read references to you in the journal of my great-grandmother, Storm Soother. I know you must be getting well along in years now—*

The artist laughed aloud with delight.

> *—but I wondered if I might ask you a favor. I will be coming to New York soon as I have been accepted into graduate school at Columbia University. I'll be seeking a*

*doctorate in American Studies, specializing in political
structures of the plains tribes and how they were affected
by indigenous religious beliefs. I would very much like to
meet and talk with you. I hasten to assure you that I will
not take up much of your time or energy. But I would still
very much enjoy the privilege of meeting you.*

He heard the voice in his head. *Hey, Ferret, recall that last conversation with her great-grandmother?*

Indeed he did. He had said, "You know I'm always on the move."

She had nodded. "Just keep in touch once in a while. Safeguarding spiritual concerns shouldn't take up all your time." The sarcasm was very light, almost playful. "An occasional card would be nice. A visit would be even better. Two of the Spoonhunter boys have been showing signs of tipi-tapping, but I'm not interested."

"I will try," he had said.

He had done that, though Storm Soother and he never saw each other again. But she had received his cards, and sometimes they had spoken and held each other in dreams.

The artist realized the letter was shaking in his fingers, so much so that he could barely read the rest. He frowned, concentrated.

*If you would be agreeable to seeing me, my home
address and telephone number are above. My great-
grandmother passed on some years ago, but I know she
would have wanted me to relay her best wishes. I look
forward to doing that.*

*Very Sincerely,
Mallory Storm*

The artist folded the letter, but did not slip it back into the envelope. He could feel the muscles of his face relax from the frown into first a smile, then a broad grin.

The afternoon sunlight burned his face now, hot as fire, and he welcomed it.

He stood, then, and turned to go back to his apartment. He had never really taken to Mr. Bell's invention, though he had learned to use all sorts of newfangled gadgets. His desk held a barely unpacked Macintosh PowerBook loaded with a full graphics package.

Today, he thought, perhaps the telephone would justify its entire miserable existence.

ABOUT THE AUTHOR

Edward Bryant, though born in White Plains, New York, grew up on a cattle ranch in southeastern Wyoming. He attended a one-room rural school for four years before starting classes in the small town of Wheatland. He attended the University of Wyoming, receiving a B.A. in English in 1967 and an M.A. in the same field a year later.

He began writing professionally in 1968 and has published more than a dozen books, starting with *Among the Dead* in 1973. Some of his titles have included *Cinnabar* (1975), *Phoenix Without Ashes* (with Harlan Ellison, 1975), *Wyoming Sun* (1980), *Particle Theory* (1981), and *Fetish* (1991). *Flirting with Death*, a major collection of his suspense and horror stories, will appear in 1995, simultaneously with a new edition of *Particle Theory*.

Bryant's short stories have appeared in all manner of magazines and anthologies, including the prestigious *Norton Book of Science Fiction*. He's won two Nebula Awards, and in 1984 made it onto the map—literally—when he was placed on the Wyoming Literary Map by the Wyoming Association of Teachers of English.

He has worked as a guest lecturer, speaker, writer-in-residence. He frequently conducts classes and workshops. He occasionally works in film and television as a writer and as an actor; in 1994, he played the Bard's parody of himself-as-opportunist-writer, Peter Quince, in *Ill Met by Moonlight,* a feature film version of *A Midsummer Night's Dream.* He has also been a radio talk show host, a substitute motel manager, and a stirrup-buckle maker, among other jobs. These days he lives with two Feline-Americans in a century-old house in North Denver along with many, many books. Presently he's working on a feature film script, a start-up comic book, and trying to finish a novel.

P. D. CACEK

GILGAMESH RECIDIVUS

Peter: **P. D. Cacek**'s work has appeared in a lot of magazines with spooky names, yet most people, I should think, would not call her "Gilgamesh Recidivus" a true horror story—depends on your attitude towards immortality, of course. . . .

Janet: P. D., aka Trish, was a valued member of that same Bay Area writer's workshop I have mentioned before, The Melville Nine. She is a fabulous writer, another one with a unique voice which stems from her bizarre and, in my opinion, all too accurate way of looking at the world. She is also my friend, which is why I took such particular joy in introducing her to Manhattan, to bagels and lox, and—through this book—to a whole new readership.

Gilgamesh Recidivus

THE COLD WAS A LIVING THING, STALKING HIM from the blue shadows, its icy breath encircling his feet as he trudged along the narrow swath of black ice that doubled for a footpath.

He had never liked the cold—once fearing its final embrace, then seeking it out. *For so very long.* But now the cold knew him and teased him like a coy lover, allowing him only the slightest touch before scurrying away.

"My, haven't we gotten poetic in our old age," he chided himself, his breath adding another layer of ice to his mahogany-colored beard. "Fool."

Cresting a small rise, he stopped and looked back over his shoulder. The railway village he had left that morning, huge in comparison to most of the Siberian settlements he'd seen dimly through the train's ice-coated windows, had been swallowed by the cold night. If anyone in the village remembered the tall stranger who had stopped only long enough to ask directions of the stationmaster, it would be a false memory . . . one that he had fashioned on the spur of the moment. A new identity. A new name. And a manufactured life to go with it.

He had done it so many times before that it was second nature. So *many* times before that if he put his mind to it, he could almost forget who he really was.

Almost. And never.

Hunching his shoulders beneath the bulky, post-Afghani War parka he had bought from an enterprising black-marketeer, he turned back to the path before him. There was no evidence that another human being had made the same journey since the first snow. The ancient stationmaster, once they found a dialect they both could mutilate just enough to understand, had warned him of the outpost's intentional isolation. There would be *no one* to help him if he became lost. *No one* to carry him out.

No one to watch him die.

Finally, to die.

He shook his head and laughed, the sound startling the cold away from his face. He had become foolish in his old age. If his journey was successful, he would have more than enough witnesses to his death.

While the lieutenant studied the documents that showed a different identity than the one he'd given to the stationmaster, he studied the men.

There were three others besides the officer—all identically dressed in the drab brown uniform and woolen greatcoat of the Home Guard, each wearing a rabbit-fur hat with the ear-flaps down and tied beneath cold-reddened chins. Each with a rifle slung over one shoulder.

A smile tugged at his lips beneath the frost clinging to his beard. He had witnessed this scene so many times before—the self-important officer, his soldiers, their weapons—that it gave him a comforting sense of déjà vu.

He let the smile fade as the officer looked up. Slumped his shoulders and eased deeper into character. Waited for his cue.

"Biogenetic engineering," the lieutenant said, nodding as if the term were as familiar to him as the small cast-iron stove his men were huddled around.

"Yes," he answered, but gave no further explanation. He could have, of course, gone into the most intricate details of gene-splicing—one of the *benefits* of such a long life was in having the *time* to learn these things—but, as with his total acquiescence during the soldier's rough-handed search, he didn't like to show off.

Unless he had to.

"A very remarkable field. Your papers seem to be in order, however . . ."

The soldier tapped the forged documents with a gnawed pencil stub and cleared his throat. His accent came from the south; perhaps as far as the Caspian or Black seas . . . thousands of kilometers from the Siberian Hell he had been consigned to.

"It must be difficult to be so far from your home, Lieutenant, especially in so inhospitable a place as this."

The soldier looked up through the glare of the kerosene lantern on the desk beside him.

"With such primitive amenities. Don't you miss the sun?"

The narrow face moved away from the light, the almond-shaped eyes going from sea-green to azure. The pencil stub *pinged* when it hit the desk top.

"Why are you here, Doctor . . . "

"Ambrose," he said, filling in the pause. He'd chosen the name as a final jest . . . a pun to defy the gods who had abandoned him so long ago.

He didn't realize he'd been smiling until he felt it stop—at the same instant the lieutenant gathered up the documents and placed them in the desk's center drawer. The sound the lock made when it slid home was still echoing in the chilled air when the soldier stood up, his gloved hand going to the thick gun belt cinched at his waist.

Ambrose took a deep breath and waited. He hadn't planned on killing the men, they were to be his storytellers. But if their deaths meant that he might finally die . . .

He let his hands slowly ball into fists.

"You will be so kind as to tell me how you knew to come to this place, *Doctor* Ambrose. We are not generally listed in any Intourist publications." The lieutenant's gloved hand moved to the flap on the front of the holster. Ambrose shifted his weight to the balls of his feet. "I suggest you answer now, Doctor. And please . . . the truth."

You wouldn't accept the truth *if I told you, boy.*

Sighing, his breath steaming in the frigid air, Ambrose unclenched the fingers of his right hand and reached toward the parka's inside breast pocket. Matching his movements precisely, three SKS semiautomatic rifles took aim at his heart.

. . . if their deaths mean that I can finally die . . .

No. Not yet.

He lowered the heels of his boots to the wooden floor.

"Peace, friends," he said, more to the lieutenant than to the armed men. "There is an item in my pocket that may explain things to your satisfaction, sir. May I get it?"

A curt nod. "But do so slowly, *Doctor* Ambrose, the boredom of this place has made my men seek diversion where they can find it."

"Boredom?" He forced his hand to stop at the pocket's lip. "*Here?* In the presence of the greatest biological discovery of all time? May God forgive your men, Lieutenant."

The man's eyes flashed and Ambrose pretended not to notice. The ideological wounds the lieutenant must have suffered when first communism and then the Marxist ideal fell were undoubtedly still too fresh for an invocation to *God* to hold much meaning.

But it will, Ambrose promised silently. *By the end of this night it will.*

"I must admit that I heard of . . . this through less than official channels, sir."

Tucking himself deeper into the character of obsessed scientist, Ambrose pulled a five-by-ten-centimeter news article and its corresponding photograph from his pocket and laid it on the desk facing the lieutenant. The picture was overexposed and grainy, showing only the vaguest outline of an elongated neck and flowing mane. But the *horn* was still visible—stark white and pointing straight at heaven like an accusing finger.

"Of course I don't usually *buy* this sort of journalistic trash," he said, urging his voice into breathless wonder, "but the headline . . . and picture. My G— Lieutenant, if this story is true then all I need are just a few cells . . . a simple scraping of the inside of the animal's mouth and . . . I . . . I can . . ."

Panting, his breath almost as thick as the frozen mist outside, Ambrose patted his chest and smiled. Weakly. He regretted that with the present government in financial ruin there would be no opportunity to video-tape him. It was the performance of a lifetime. A very *long* lifetime. And his last performance.

With any luck.

"I apologize, Lieutenant," he said sheepishly, still feigning vulnerability, "but I'm sure you can understand my excitement."

The officer grunted as Ambrose leaned forward, compensating for his six feet, three inches, and tapped the article with his finger, drawing the man's attention back to it.

The story had appeared in one of the more "reputable" American tabloids, the brazen headline

RUSSIAN UNICORN DISCOVERED

peaking Ambrose's interest just enough to buy the paper and suffer the smirks of an overweight supermarket cashier. In lifetimes past, he had discovered that truth, like Edgar Allan Poe's purloined letter, occasionally could only be found where you didn't look for it.

"I know, I know," he went on, "these papers usually tend to vie for the record of Elvis Presley sightings and UFO abduction stories . . . but you have to understand, Lieutenant. If there is *any* validity to the article—"

His guts twisted over on themselves when the lieutenant looked up.

There was surprise in the man's eyes, yes . . . naturally, considering the publication . . . but there was something else as well. Incomprehension. He didn't recognize the animal in the photograph.

Ambrose forced himself to remain calm as the soldier shook his head. *Are you gods not done with me yet?* It was a lie. Another lie and he should have known better after so many centuries. He almost laughed out loud.

But there was still *something* about the three other soldiers' nervousness . . . the way their eyes kept shifting from his face to the small
locked door to his left.

. The way sweat kept beading upon their brows despite the coldness of
the room.

Something.

He sighed, decided to continue the illusion a while longer.

"So." The pain in his voice sounded so real that even he was moved. "I
have come all this way in what is usually referred to as a wild-goose chase."

"I am familiar with the term, Doctor Ambrose," the lieutenant said,
moving his hand from the holster, the chair's frozen springs screaming as
he leaned back. "I have not been assigned to Siberia all of my life."

Ah.

Go on, Ambrose. *All they can do is shoot at you.*

All illusion faded.

"Then why *are* you here, Lieutenant—if the article is false, that is?"
He smiled. "I doubt that even a government in transition would assign
men to guard an empty Siberian hovel."

His smile was matched.

"I am but a *humble* officer in the Russian Army, Doctor Ambrose,"
the lieutenant shrugged, "and I do what I am ordered. Without question
. . . even in a transitional government. It is not a lucrative profession, but
it keeps food in the bellies of my wife and children."

A man three months in the grave would not have missed the *subtle*
hint. A communist he may have been born and bred, but the lieutenant
was willing to make the "sacrifice" to capitalism for the sake of his wife
and children.

If he even had a wife and children. Not that Ambrose cared. He had
never been a moralist.

Pushing up the left sleeve of his parka, Ambrose quickly removed the
gold watch he wore. Time, after so many centuries, meant little to him,
and gold was still a highly negotiable commodity.

"Of course, I would not ask for the privilege of seeing what may be
behind that locked door without . . . showing my appreciation."

"Even if there is nothing there, Doctor?"

"Even so."

The lieutenant shifted in his chair just enough to hide the transaction
from his men and slipped the watch into the front pocket of his greatcoat,
nodding.

"Then follow me, Doctor Ambrose."

The three soldiers never lowered their rifles as their officer stood up
and, taking the kerosene lantern from the desk, led the way across the

room. Ambrose imagined the weapons aimed at his back. The sensation reminded him of fleas crawling across his skin; a mild distraction, but of no consequence.

The sound of the hasp opening cracked in the still air . . . still except for the muffled sound of unshod hooves coming from the darkness beyond the door.

"I cannot give you permission to take anything from the animal, doctor," the lieutenant said, blocking the door with his body, the hand holding the ring of keys again resting upon the holster, "not even a picture, and I apologize for the lack of heat. It—it seems to prefer the cold."

The door opened and Ambrose inhaled the scent of fresh dung and musk and hay. *Alive. Whatever was in there was actually alive.*

"Stay away from the horn, Doctor," the lieutenant said, standing to one side. "It has already killed one scientist. A *biologist,* like yourself."

With the light at his back, Ambrose entered the room first.

And froze.

The animal lifted its shaggy head and stared at him through the clouds of steam rising from its nostrils. *Alive.* The light from the lantern turned its dun-colored hide to gold.

The single horn to polished hematite.

It was real.

"I . . ." For the first time in his life Ambrose did not need to pretend wonder. "I thought from your expression when you saw the photograph that . . . that it was just another fairy tale."

"It was the picture that confused me, Doctor Ambrose," the lieutenant said, giving the makeshift wooden corral in the center of the room a wide berth as he walked to a workstation directly opposite the door. "This animal does not look at all like the one in the photograph."

"No," Ambrose said, "it doesn't."

Tiny and compact, ten hands at the shoulder if that, the unicorn resembled a stunted Mongolian pony more than the sleek, alabaster creature of myth. Even the horn, pushing its way through the thick forelock, was different. Where the "mythical" alicorn was supposed to be spiraled like that on a narwhal, the "living" horn resembled the protuberance on a rhinoceros. Black as the heart of a Sumerian whore and curved back toward the tufted ears like a scimitar.

Ambrose took a deep breath and let it out as a laugh. *It was a hoax. And a pathetic one. Some psychotic veterinarian's idea of a joke.* Shifting his eyes, he caught the lieutenant's wide-eyed stare and laughed again.

"My compliments to the designer," he said, tipping his head in a mock bow, "or was this done by committee? That might explain the choice of animal. I'm sure that obtaining an Arab or Lipizzaner, even though it might have looked more like a unicorn, was too much of an expense for the new government to justify. Am I right?"

"You . . . don't *believe* what you see?"

Shaking his head, Ambrose walked to the corral and lifted his hand to the animal. Three things happened simultaneously, only two of which he could understand. One was the lieutenant's sudden shout—something about staying away from the corral—the second was the scream coming from the animal itself as it reared up on its hind legs and struck out at the air between them.

The third was the blinding blue light that knocked him to the floor and left behind the smell of ozone and singed horsehide.

—tor ambrose are you

"—all right?"

Ambrose blinked his eyes and for a moment saw only an afterimage of the animal—its color reversed, finally looking like the fantasy creature it was supposed to be.

"What?"

"We put an electrified grid along the inside of the corral. He, the animal kept . . . there was no way of holding him without it. The voltage . . . It isn't capable of hurting him, but he doesn't seem to like it."

I can understand why, Ambrose thought as he allowed the lieutenant to help him to his feet, his own flesh tingling uncomfortably. It was then that he noticed a second gas generator beneath the workstation and the thick cable that ran from it to the corral. A bright red alligator clamp attached the cable to the chicken wire mesh that had been nailed to the inside of the wooden railings. It seemed a makeshift design, but very effective.

Ambrose felt a drop of moisture touch his chin an instant before it refroze and wondered exactly how high the voltage was, even though the lieutenant was right about it not seeming to effect the animal.

The unicorn had settled down, shaking its brushlike mane and pawing at the trampled straw. *That,* at least, Ambrose noticed, concurred with the legend. The hoof, although almost completely covered with thick, black "feathers," was cloven like a goat's.

Like those he had once seen being woven into a tapestry.

So long ago.

"I can understand the need for such security measures, Lieutenant," he said. "You certainly don't want anyone to get near enough to see the suture marks around the horn or study the surgically altered hooves."

Brushing off his sleeve where the man's hand had been, Ambrose turned and began walking to the door. "Thank you for your time. And the sideshow."

"This is no sideshow, Doctor Ambrose."

It was the *way* the lieutenant said those words that made Ambrose stop and walk back to within an inch of the corral. At that distance, he could hear the electricity humming through the wire mesh—could feel it prickle the hair on his arms and legs even through his clothing. His beard and eyebrows felt like they were standing at attention.

"Watch," the lieutenant said.

And Ambrose watched.

Watched the lieutenant remove the sidearm from its holster and take aim at the animal. Watched, with a sensation of compressed time, the bullet leave the muzzle and tear a hole in the quivering chest.

Watched, too, as the shredded flesh curled back in around the wound and closed.

The unicorn snorted and pawed the ground, undisturbed by either the shot or the armed soldiers running into the room.

"It is all right," the lieutenant told his men. "I was just giving the doctor a demonstration. Dismissed."

Ambrose only heard the sounds of their boots striking the wooden flooring as they left. He couldn't take his eyes off the animal. Didn't dare.

"By the gods. How . . . *old* is it?"

He could hear the lieutenant replace the handgun and snap the holster flap back in place.

"The biologist . . . the one who was killed . . . wasn't sure, he never got a chance to collect much data. But he thought it was old. Very old."

"Is it immortal?" Ambrose whispered.

This time it was the lieutenant who laughed.

"Of *course* not, Doctor. No. Nothing is immortal."

"Are you so sure?"

The smile faltered slightly around the edges. "Yes, Doctor, I am. This animal was found in one of the most hostile environments known to man. It's only natural that it would . . . develop certain natural survival skills that our scientists haven't encountered before."

"Yes," Ambrose said, looking again at the animal's barreled chest. Where the bullet had impacted the hair had re-formed in the shape of a star. "I would think that spontaneous tissue repair is not something most scientists deal with on a regular basis. How then do they explain it? Or the animal?"

The lieutenant's grin acquired some of its former glory.

"I'm sorry, Doctor, but the tour is over." Nodding once, he spun on his heels and walked to the worktable. His gloved fingers were closing around the lantern's wire handle when the unicorn suddenly nickered.

Ambrose backed away from the corral and into the lengthening shadows as the lieutenant crossed the room. The cold fingered his throat as he unzipped the parka.

"Ah, do you hear that, Doctor Ambrose?" The lieutenant asked, increasing the lamp's brightness. The shadows slunk back and Ambrose joined them. "That moaning sound? It's only the wind, but sometimes out here a man can imagine . . . many things. A storm is coming and our friend here wants to be out in it. We found him in a storm, did the newspaper mention that? No? Oh, well. It's that sound, I think . . . it's like it calls to him." A shudder passed over the lieutenant's bowed shoulders. "Foolishness. Now, Doctor, if you would be so kind to accompany me back to my desk I can—"

The shock in the lieutenant's eyes bordered on fear when he turned and found himself staring at Ambrose's naked form. Darkness crept closer as the lantern made a shaky decent to the floor. Ambrose followed the dark, closing the gap between them.

Underlit, the lieutenant's face took on the visage of a death mask.

Ambrose nodded his head. It was a good omen.

"It is not so foolish to hear voices in the wind, Lieutenant," he said, feeling the cold wrap itself around him like a lover. "That is how the gods speak to men. And drive them mad."

"HERE!" The lieutenant shouted and, like the well-trained dogs they were, the soldiers came running.

Ambrose felt the sensation of fleas tickling his spine once more. And smiled.

Lifting his hands away from his sides, he glanced back over his shoulders, just to make sure his instincts hadn't failed him after so many centuries. They hadn't. The rifles were level and not even a blind man could miss at that distance. The smile grew.

"Get his clothes and handcuff him to one of the chairs out there!" The lieutenant seemed less afraid now, with the men in the room. Or maybe it was the rifles that made him brave. "Then call down to the village and have them send someone to take him off our hands. I don't want this pervert here any longer than he needs to be."

Ambrose lifted his chin, the smile fading as he closed his eyes as one set of boots began moving toward him.

"No," he commanded.

The boots stopped.

He opened his eyes and saw beads of sweat on the lieutenant's face.

The unicorn was prancing nervously within its electrified enclosure—tossing its head, the lantern light flashing across the midnight horn.

It knows.

"Wh-what do you want?" the lieutenant asked, his voice almost lost to the howl of the wind.

Ambrose nodded. "You're direct. I've always appreciated that and will answer in kind. I've come to kill the unicorn."

"NO!" Despite his obvious fear, the officer placed himself between Ambrose and the corral. Gun coming clumsily to his hand. Shaking. One more inch and the back of his greatcoat would brush against the electric mesh. "Are you *mad*? You saw for yourself that it can't be killed. This is the last of its kind . . . you can't kill it. Besides, I'm not afraid of a crazy man. I warn you, *Doctor,* that if you take one more step toward this creature I *will* kill you."

Smiling, Ambrose took that step.

And the room exploded with sound.

He heard and memorized each one: The trumpeting scream of the unicorn, the paper-tearing *rippp* of the assault rifles, the hollow *thump* as bullets punched holes through his body.

The wet sound of retching as the bloodless wounds repaired themselves as fast as the unicorn's had.

Finally, a whisper.

"Who are you?"

Looking down, he ran a hand over his unmarked flesh; brushing away the last remnants of the Ambrose impersonation.

When he looked back up, Gilgamesh smiled at the lieutenant.

"Just an old man who has grown tired of living," he said gently, using the tone he remembered from countless storytellings and lullabies. "If I am successful in killing the unicorn, then I may find the secret of killing myself. Or, perhaps the unicorn will kill me . . ." He took a deep breath and listened to the storm's growing rage. "Either way I shall be dead."

The lieutenant took another step toward the corral, sobbing now, shaking his head.

"No. Y-you can't."

"What do you mean? Kill or be killed? I have done so much of the former that it means nothing. And as for the latter . . . "

Gilgamesh closed his eyes, trying to blot out the memories, but they were still there—as fresh and solid as if he were living through them at that very moment. Again.

"Read the legends if you want about a man not much older than you who *so* feared death that he usurped the powers of the gods.

"See a plant that gave eternal life. You would look for such a thing, wouldn't you?" he asked through the darkness of his closed eyes, not expecting an answer. Getting none. "Of *course* you would. Any man terrified of death would."

When Gilgamesh finally opened his eyes, he didn't look at the man, only watched the animal. The unicorn was calm—neck arched, heavy tail swatting lazily at its golden sides, ears pitched forward as if it, too, were listening.

"Imagine then finding out how much you have given up to become immortal . . . the *last* of your kind . . . to see all that you ever loved wither and fade to dust while you stand forever unchanged."

Smiling as he once had smiled at a precocious carpenter's son in Jerusalem, Gilgamesh reached over and removed the empty gun from the limp hand.

"I will tell you another secret, Lieutenant," he whispered. "That part of the legend where the serpent is supposed to carry off the plant of eternal life is wrong. It never did."

The look on the man's face had shifted from fear to confusion. Gilgamesh chuckled softly.

"Forgive an old man his digressions, Lieutenant," he said, and tossed the gun into the shadows at the far end of the room. When it struck the floor, the unicorn shied and the ends of its tail brushed against the wire. Blue sparks danced across the mesh.

"I'm sorry," Gilgamesh said, not sure whether he meant to address man or unicorn. "Please, stand aside, Lieutenant, and let me give the story the ending it deserves."

Round eyes the color of broken ice met his.

"You're out of your mind," the lieutenant screamed over the building storm. "Legends can't die."

"Why not?" Gilgamesh asked as the man swung at him.

He hadn't meant to protect himself, there was no need—blows were as meaningless as bullets—but he did. Gilgamesh caught the man's closed fist and pushed. He reacted, and heard the gods laugh.

"NO!"

But it was already too late.

A halo of blue-white flame blossomed around the lieutenant's body as he fell backwards into the wire. Steam and sparks, the color of urine in the lantern light, erupted from the generator beneath the worktable as the overloaded circuits shut down.

Silence. For a moment. And then the muffled sound of cloven hooves on straw. Building up speed.

The unicorn's back hoof shattered the lantern as it leapt over its smoldering protector and charged.

Gilgamesh felt the same jolt of energy he had experienced when he had accidentally brushed against the electric barrier, but this was a hundred times worse. It drained him instantly. Collapsing, Gilgamesh rolled into a ball and groaned. It felt as if all the centuries he'd lived through had finally caught up with him.

He was panting, barely able to hear the hysterical shouting of the soldiers above the pounding of his own heart. *No . . . it wasn't his heart . . . his heart hadn't beat in two millennia.* Lifting himself to one elbow, Gilgamesh watched through growing flames as the tiny, dun-colored unicorn cocked its hind legs and kicked out another wall plank.

The building was old, probably constructed in haste against the coming of a long-past winter, its timbers rotted. In less time than it took Gilgamesh to push away from the hungry fire, the unicorn was free.

He thought he heard it once . . . whinnying its triumph to an uncaring sky . . . but it might have been only the storm. The gods laughing at his defeat.

Again.

The flames were already feeding on the dead lieutenant when Gilgamesh was finally able to stand. The clothes he had worn to the outpost had been the fire's first course, but that didn't matter; if there were no extra uniforms in the building he would simply "appropriate" one from its current owner. Being just another faceless soldier in a country still tottering from years of suppression would make it easier to track the unicorn.

To find it and—

He stumbled over a crack in the floor and pitched forward, grabbing the doorframe to keep from falling. *Oh yes, tracking down the unicorn would be child's play compared to simply walking out of the building.*

Then he noticed his hand in the wash of firelight.

It looked *different.*

He raised the second and turned them slowly from back to front. They *were* different.

His hands had always been a source of pride to him—smooth and strong enough to crack two hard-shelled nuts or a man's skull; but the hands before him now were wrinkled flesh, the fingers knobbed and curled in toward the palm.

Gilgamesh stretched out his fingers as far as they would go and watched them tremble.

They were the hands of an old man.

old

He didn't have to feel his face or look down at the sagging flesh that hung from his limbs. He knew. He had *aged.*

From one brief touch, the unicorn had leeched away centuries.

Throwing back his head, suddenly lighter from its lack of hair, Gilgamesh laughed until the sound caught in his throat and tried to strangle him. *So this was what it felt like to be old.* He didn't care much for it, but it was a start.

Pushing away from the heat-blistered doorframe, Gilgamesh shuffled through the empty outer office and into the howling night. A naked old man wandering through a storm would be a pitiable sight to anyone who saw it, but he knew there would be no one foolish enough to venture out on a night like this. And if one did, he would have clothing and a new identity—either by guile or the knife, which ever was easiest.

He was even less worried about the dead lieutenant's men. They were probably already halfway back to town.

With stories to tell about the unicorn and the stranger who appeared as if by magic and could not be killed.

The stuff of which legends were made.

Bracing himself against the howling cold, Gilgamesh faced into the worst of the storm. It would be hours . . . days more than likely . . . before any of the townspeople braved the elements . . . and story . . . to come up this far. By then the building would be nothing more than snow covered ash—whatever truth it held burned away. The tracks left by his bare feet and the unicorn's hooves long since buried beneath the drifts.

Just another story to keep the children from wandering too far into the woods.

Just another joke played on a tired, *old* man.

Gilgamesh raised his fists to the storm just as something moved through the wind-driven snow directly ahead of him, a living shadow—its body the color of old cream, its ebony mane and tail whipping shadows out of the lighter-colored storm . . . the scimitar horn rising into the night as the shadow creature reared.

"WAIT!" he shouted, pleading with it as he opened his arms. "COME BACK!"

The shadow dissolved.

"You aren't finished with me yet," he yelled, looking past the skuttering clouds to the blackness beyond. "Are you?"

Only the wind moaned an answer.

Ignoring the cold, Gilgamesh hunched his bony shoulders and headed north, away from the tiny knot of civilization and into the empty Siberian wastelands.

Following . . . the . . . unicorn.

Back into legend.

ABOUT THE AUTHOR

P. D. Cacek was born and raised in the sunny climes of California (many, many years ago), but she recently had her belly button surgically removed and replaced with an "I-♥-Colorado" bumper sticker. Writing "ghostly" tales since the age of five (a fact that had both family and teachers worried), P. D. has, if the Internal Revenue Service is correct, actually been making a living as a freelance writer for the past ten years.

Still a "ghost" writer by nature, her work has appeared in a number of small-press magazines as well as *Pulphouse, Deathrealm, The Urbanite, Bizarre Bazaar, Bizarre Sex and Other Crimes of Passion, 100 Wicked Little Witches, Newer York, Deathport, Grails: Visitations of the Night,* and *Return to the Twilight Zone.* She is currently editing an anthology of short fiction.

CHARLES DE LINT

SEVEN FOR A SECRET

Peter: As an occasional singer/songwriter/guitarist, it interests me to discover that several contributors to *Immortal Unicorn* have worked as far more professional musicians than I ever was. **Charles de Lint** is one: He currently plays in an acoustic band called Jump at the Sun, along with his wife, MaryAnn Harris. His consistently admirable fiction (*The Ivory and the Horn, Memory and Dream*) aside, I'm shamelessly envious of the fact that he plays Irish flute, fiddle, whistles, button accordion, bouzouki, guitar, and bodhran. He is also the proprietor/editor of Triskell Press, a small publishing house that prints fantasy chapbooks and magazines. Later for that— I want to find out how you get a sound out of that damn button accordion. . . .

Janet: I had read some of Charles de Lint's work before inviting him into this anthology, but obviously not enough. After reading this story, he's got me. I intend to read everything he has ever written. Since Charles is Canadian, I chose to leave the British spellings in his story. I think they add to the flavour.

Seven for a Secret

———⟨⟨⟨⟨ ∿ ⟩⟩⟩⟩———

"It's a mistake to have only one life."
—Dennis Miller Bunker, 1890

- 1 -

LATER, HE CAN'T REMEMBER WHICH CAME FIRST, the music or the birds in the trees. He seems to become aware of them at the same time. They call up a piece of something he thinks he's forgotten; they dredge through his past, the tangle of memories growing as thick and riddling as a hedgerow, to remind him of an old story he heard once that began, "What follows is imagined, but it happened just so. . . ."

- 2 -

The trees are new growth, old before their time. Scrub, leaves more brown than green, half the limbs dead, the other half dying. They struggle for existence in what was once a parking lot, a straggling clot of vegetation fed for years by some runoff, now baking in the sun. Something diverted the water—another building fell down, supports torched by Devil's Night fires, or perhaps the city bulldozed a field of rubble, two or three blocks over, inadvertently creating a levee. It doesn't matter. The trees are dying now, the weeds and grass surrounding them already baked dry.

And they're full of birds. Crows, ravens . . . Jack can't tell the difference. Heavy-billed, black birds with wedge-shaped tails and shaggy ruffs at their throats. Their calls are hoarse, croaking *kraaacks,* interspersed with hollow, knocking sounds and a sweeter *klu-kluck.*

The fiddle plays a counterpoint to the uneven rhythm of their calls, an odd, not quite reasonable music that seems to lie somewhere between a slow dance tune and an air that manages to be at once mournful and jaunty. The fiddle, he sees later, is blue, not painted that colour; rather the varnish lends the wood that hue so its grain appeared to be viewed as though through water.

Black birds, blue fiddle.

He might consider them portents if he were given to looking for omens, but he lives in a world that is always exactly what it should be, no more and no less, and he has come here to forget, not foretell. He is a man who stands apart, always one step aside from the crowd, an island distanced from the archipelago, spirit individual as much as the flesh. But though we are all islands, separated from one another by indifferent seas that range as wide as we allow them to be, we still congregate. We are still social animals. And Jack is no different. He comes to where the fires burn in the oil drums, where the scent of cedar smudge sticks mingles with cigarette smoke and dust, the same as the rest of us.

The difference is, he watches. He watches, but rarely speaks. He rarely speaks, but he listens well.

"They say," the woman tells him, "that where ravens gather, a door to the Otherworld stands ajar."

He never heard her approach. He doesn't turn.

"You don't much like me, do you?" she says.

"I don't know you well enough to dislike you, but I don't like what you do."

"And what is it that you think I do?"

"Make-believe," he says. "Pretend."

"Is that what you call it?"

But he won't be drawn into an argument.

"Everybody sees things differently," she says. "That's the gift and curse of free will."

"So what do you hear?" he asks. His voice is a sarcastic drawl. "Fairy music?"

The city died here, in the Tombs. Not all at once, through some natural disaster, but piece by piece, block by block, falling into disrepair, buildings abandoned by citizens and then claimed by the squatters who've got no reason to take care of them. Some of them fall down, some burn.

It's the last place in the world to look for wonder.

"I hear a calling-on music," she says, "though whether it's calling us to cross over, or calling something to us, I can't tell."

He turns to look at her finally, with his hair the glossy black of the ravens, his eyes the blue of that fiddle neither of them has seen yet. He notes the horn that rises from the center of her brow, the equine features that make her face seem so long, the chestnut dreadlocks, the dark, wide-set eyes and the something in those eyes he can't read.

"Does it matter?" he asks.

"Everything matters on some level or other."

He smiles. "I think that depends on what story we happen to be in."

"Yours or mine," she says, her voice soft.

"I don't have a story," he tells her.

Now she smiles. "And mine has no end."

"Listen," he says.

Silence hangs in the air, a thick gauze dropped from the sky like a blanket, deep enough to cut. The black birds are silent. They sit motionless in the dying trees. The fiddler has taken the bow from the strings. The blue fiddle holds its breath.

"I don't hear anything," she says.

He nods. "This is what my story sounds like."

"Are you sure?"

He watches as she lifts her arm and makes a motion with it, a graceful wave of her hand, as though conducting an orchestra. The black birds lift from the trees like a dark cloud, the sound of their wings cutting through the gauze of silence. The fiddle begins to play again, the blue wood vibrating with a thin distant music, a sound that is almost transparent. He looks away from the departing birds to find her watching him with the same lack of curiosity he had for the birds.

"Maybe you're not listening hard enough," she says.

"I think I'd know if—"

"Remember what I said about the ravens," she tells him.

He returns his attention to the trees, the birds all gone. When he looks for her again, she's already halfway down the block, horn glinting, too far away for him to read the expression in her features even if she was looking at him. If he even cared.

"I'd know," he says, repeating the words for himself.

He puts her out of his mind, forgets the birds and the city lying just beyond these blocks of wasteland, and goes to find the fiddler.

- 3 -

I probably know her better than anyone else around here, but even I forget about the horn sometimes. You want to ask her, why are you hiding out in the Tombs, there's nothing for you here. It's not like she's an alkie or a squatter, got the need for speed or any other kind of jones. But then maybe the sunlight catches that short length of ivory rising up out of her brow, or you see something equally impossible stirring in her dark eyes, and you see that horn like it's the first time all over again, and you understand that it's her difference that puts her here, her strangeness.

Malicorne, is what Frenchy calls her, says it means unicorn. I go to the Crowsea Public Library one day and try to look the word up in a dictionary, but I can only find it in pieces. Now Frenchy got the *corne* right because she's sure enough got a horn. But the word can also mean hoof, while *mal* or *mali* . . . you get your pick of what it can mean. Cunning or sly, which aren't exactly compliments, but mostly it's things worse than that: wickedness, evil, hurt, harm. Maybe Frenchy knows more than he's saying, and maybe she does, too, because she never answers to that name. But she doesn't give us anything better to use instead so the name kind of sticks—at least when we're talking about her among ourselves.

I remember the first time I see her, I'm looking through the trash after the Spring Festival, see if maybe I can sift a little gold from the chaff, which is a nice way of saying I'm a bum and I'm trying to make do. I see her sitting on a bench, looking at me, and at first I don't notice the horn, I'm just wondering, who's this horsy-faced woman and why's she looking at me like she wants to know something about me. Not what I'm doing here, going through the trash, but what put me here.

We've all got stories, a history that sews one piece of who we were to another until you get the reason we're who we are now. But it's not something we offer each other, never mind a stranger. We're not proud of who we are, of what we've become. We don't talk much about it, we never ask each other about it. There's too much pain in where we've been to go back, even if it's just with words. We don't even want to think about it—why do you think we're looking for oblivion in the bottom of a bottle?

I want to turn my back on her, but even then, right from the start, Malicorne's got this pull in her eyes, draws you in, draws you to her, starts you talking. I've seen rheumy-eyed old alkies who can't even put together "Have you got some spare change?" with their heads leaning close to hers, talking, the slur gone from their voices, some kind of sense working its way back into what they're saying. And I'm not immune. I turn my back, but it's on that trash can, and I find myself shuffling over to the bench where she's sitting, hands stuck deep into my pockets.

"You're so innocent," she says.

I have to laugh. I'm forty-five and I look sixty and the last thing I am is innocent.

"I'm no virgin," I tell her.

"I didn't say you were. Innocence and virginity aren't necessarily synonymous."

Her voice wakes something in me that I don't want to think about.

"I suppose," I say.

I want to go and get on with my business. I want to stay.

She's got a way of stringing together words so that they all seem to mean more than what you think they're saying, like there's a riddle lying in between the lines, and the funny thing is, I can feel something in me responding. Curiosity. Not standing around and looking at something strange, but an intellectual curiosity—the kind that makes you think.

I study her, sitting there beside me on the bench, raggedy clothes and thick chestnut hair so matted it hangs like fat snakes from her head, like a Rasta's dreadlocks. Horsy features. Deep, dark eyes, like they're all pupil, wide-set. And then I see the horn. She smiles when she sees my eyes go wide.

"Jesus," I say. "You've got a—"

"Long road to travel and the company is scarce. Good company, I mean."

I don't much care for weird shit, but I don't tell her that. I tell her things I don't tell anybody, not even myself, how it all went wrong for me, how I miss my family, how I miss having something in my life that means anything. And she listens. She's good at the listening, everybody says so, except for Jack. Jack won't talk to her, says she's feeding on us, feeding on our stories.

"It's give-and-take," I try to tell him. "You feel better after you've talked to her."

"You feel better because there's nothing left inside to make you feel bad," he says. "Nothing good, nothing bad. She's taking all the stories that make you who you are and putting nothing back."

"Maybe we don't want to remember those things anyway," I say.

He shakes his head. "What you've done is who you are. Without it, you're really nothing." He taps his chest. "What's left inside that belongs to you now?"

"It's not like that," I try to explain. "I still remember what put me here. It doesn't hurt as much anymore, that's all."

"Think about that for a moment."

"She tells you stuff, if you're willing to listen."

"Everything she says is mumbo-jumbo," Jack says. "Nothing that makes sense. Nothing that's worth what she's taken from you. Don't you see?"

I don't see it and he won't be part of it. Doesn't want to know about spirits, things that never were, things that can't be, made-up stories that are supposed to take the place of history. Wants to hold onto his pain, I guess.

But then he meets Staley.

- 4 -

The fiddler's a woman, but she has no sense of age about her; she could be thirty, she could be seventeen. Where Malicorne's tall and angular, horse-lanky, Staley's like a pony, everything in miniature. There's nothing dark about her, nothing gloomy except the music she sometimes wakes from that blue fiddle of hers. Hair the colour of straw and cut like a boy's, a slip of a figure, eyes the green of spring growth, face shaped like a heart. She's barefoot, wears an old pair of overalls a couple of sizes too big, some kind of white jersey, sleeves pushed up on her forearms. There's a knapsack on the ground beside her, an open fiddle case. She's sitting on a chunk of stone—piece of a wall, maybe, piece of a roof—playing that blue fiddle of hers, her whole body playing it, leaning into the music, swaying, head crooked to one side holding the instrument to her shoulder, a smile like the day's just begun stretching across her lips.

Jack stands there, watching her, listening. When the tune comes to an end, he sits down beside her.

"You're good," he tells her.

She gives him a shy smile in return.

"So did you come over from the other side?" he asks.

"The other side of what?"

Jack's thinking of Malicorne, about black birds and doors to other places. He shrugs.

"Guess that answers my question," he says.

She hears the disappointment in his voice, but doesn't understand it.

"People call me Jack," he tells her.

"Staley Cross," she says as they shake hands.

"And are you?"

The look of a Michelle who's been called *ma belle* too often moves across her features, but she doesn't lose her humour.

"Not often," she says.

"Where'd you learn to play like that?"

"I don't know. Here and there. I just picked it up. I'm a good listener, I guess. Once I hear a tune, I don't forget it." The fiddle's lying on her lap. She plays with her bow, loosening and tightening the frog. "Do you play?" she asks.

He shakes his head. "Never saw a blue fiddle before—not blue like that."

"I know. It's not painted on—the colour's in the varnish. My grandma gave it to me a couple of years ago. She says it's a spirit fiddle, been in the family forever."

"Play something else," he asks. "Unless you're too tired."

"I'm never too tired to play."

She sets the bow to the strings, wakes a note, wakes another, and then they're in the middle of a tune, a slow reel. Jack leans back, puts his hands behind his head, looks up into the bare branches of the trees. Just before he closes his eyes, he sees those birds return, one after the other, leafing the branches with their black wings. He doesn't hear a door open, all he hears is Staley's fiddle. He finishes closing his eyes and lets the music take him to a place where he doesn't have to think about the story of his life.

- 5 -

I'm lounging on a bench with Malicorne near a subway station in that no-man's-land between the city and the Tombs, where the buildings are falling down but there's people still living in them, paying rent. Frenchy's sitting on the curb with a piece of cardboard cut into the shape of a guitar, dark hair tied back with a piece of string, holes in his jeans, hole in his heart where his dreams all escaped. He strums the six drawn strings on that cardboard guitar, mouthing "Plonkety, plonkety" and people are actually tossing him quarters and dimes. On the other side of him Casey's telling fortunes. He looks like the burned-out surfer he is, too many miles from any ocean, still tanned, dirty-blond hair falling into his face. He gives everybody the same piece of advice: "Do stuff."

Nobody's paying much attention to us when Jack comes walking down the street, long and lanky, hands deep in the pockets of his black jeans. He sits down beside me, says, "Hey, William," nods to Malicorne. Doesn't even look at her horn.

"Hey, Jack," I tell him.

He leans forward on the bench, talks across me. "You ever hear of a spirit fiddle?" he asks Malicorne.

She smiles. "Are you finally starting a story?"

"I'm not starting anything. I'm just wondering. Met that girl who was making the music and she's got herself a blue fiddle—says it's a spirit fiddle. Been in her family a long time."

"I heard her playing," I say. "She's good."

"Her name's Staley Cross."

"Don't know the name," Malicorne says. There's a hint of surprise in her voice, as though she thinks she should. I'm not the only one who hears it.

"Any reason you should?" Jack asks.

Malicorne smiles and looks away, not just across the street, it seems, but further than that, like she can see through the buildings, see something we can't. Jack's looking at that horn now but I can't tell what he's thinking.

"Where'd she go?" I ask him.

He gets a puzzled look, like he thinks I'm talking about Malicorne for a second, then he shrugs.

"Downtown," he says. "She wanted to busk for a couple of hours, see if she can't get herself a stake."

"Must be nice, having a talent," I say.

"Everybody's got a talent," Malicorne says. "Just like everybody's got a story."

"Unless they give it to you," Jack breaks in.

Malicorne acts like he hasn't interrupted. "Trouble is," she goes on, "some people don't pay much attention to either and they end up living with us here."

"You're living here," Jack says.

Malicorne shakes her head. "I'm just passing through."

I know what Jack's thinking. Everybody starts out thinking, this is only temporary. It doesn't take them long to learn different. But then none of them have a horn pushing out of the middle of their forehead. None of them have mystery sticking to them like they've wrapped themselves up in double-sided tape and whatever they touch sticks to them.

"Yeah, well, we'll all really miss you when you're gone," Jack tells her.

It's quiet then. Except for Frenchy's cardboard guitar, "Plonkety-plonk." None of us are talking. Casey takes a dime from some kid who wants to know the future. His pale blue eyes stand out against his surfer's tan as he gives the kid a serious look.

"Do stuff," he says.

The kid laughs, shakes his head and walks away. But I think about what Malicorne was saying, how everybody's got a story, everybody's got a talent, and I wonder if maybe Casey's got it right.

- 6 -

"Blue's the rarest colour in nature," Staley says.

Jack smiles. "You ever look up at the sky?"

They're sharing sandwiches her music bought, coffee in cardboard cups, so hot you can't hold the container. If Jack's still worrying about magic and spirit fiddles, it doesn't show.

Staley returns his smile. "I don't mean it's hard to find. But it's funny you should mention the sky. Of all the hundreds of references to the sky and the heavens in a book like the Bible, the colour blue is never mentioned."

"You read the Bible a lot?"

"Up in the hills where I come from, that's pretty much the only thing there is to read. That, and the tabloids. But when I was saying blue's the rarest colour—"

"You meant it's the most beautiful."

She nods. "It fills the heart. Like the blue of twilight when anything's possible. Blue makes me feel safe, warm. People think of it as a cool colour, but you know, the hottest fire has a blue-white flame. Like stars. The comparatively cooler stars have the reddish glow." She takes a sip of her coffee, looks at him over the brim. "I make up for all the reading I missed by spending a lot of time in libraries."

"Good place to visit," Jack says. "Safe, when you're in a strange town."

"I thought you'd understand. You can put aside all the unhappiness you've accumulated by opening a book. Listening to music."

"You think forgetting is a good thing?"

She shrugs. "For me, it's a necessary thing. It's what keeps me sane."

She looks at him and Jack sees himself through her eyes: a tall, gangly hobo of a man, seen better times, but seen worse ones, too. The worse ones are why he's where he is.

"You know what I mean," she says.

"I suppose. Don't know if I agree, though." She lifts her eyebrows, but he doesn't want to take that any further. "So tell me about the spirit in that fiddle of yours," he says instead.

"It hasn't got a spirit—not like you mean, anyway. It comes from a spirit place. That's why it's blue. It's the colour of twilight and my grandma says it's always twilight there."

"In the Otherworld."

"If that's what you want to call it."

"And the black of a raven's wing," Jack says, "that's really a kind of blue, too, isn't it?"

She gives him a confused look.

"Don't mind me," he tells her. "I'm just thinking about what someone once told me."

"Where I come from," she says, "the raven's an unlucky bird."

"Depends on how many you see," Jack says. He starts to repeat the old rhyme for her then. "One for sorrow, two for mirth. . . ."

She nods, remembering. "Three for a wedding, four for a birth."

"That's it. Five for silver, six for gold. . . ."

". . . seven for a secret never to be told. . . ."

". . . eight for heaven, nine for hell. . . ."

". . . and ten for the divil's own sel'." She smiles. "But I thought that was for crows."

He shrugs. "I've heard it used for magpies, too. Guess it's for any kind of blackbird." He looks up at the trees, empty now. "That music of yours," he goes on. "It called up an unkindness of ravens this afternoon."

"An unkindness of ravens," she repeats, smiling. "A parliament of crows. Where do they come up with that kind of thing?"

He shrugs. "Who knows? Same place they found once in a blue moon, I guess."

"There was a blue moon the night my great-great-grandma got my fiddle," Staley tells him. "Least that's how the story goes."

"That's what I meant about forgetting," he says. "Maybe you forget some bad things, but work at it hard enough and you forget a story like that, too."

They're finished eating now, the last inch of coffee cooling in their cups.

"You up to playing a little more music?" Jack asks. "See what it calls up?"

"Sure."

She takes the instrument from its case, tightens the bow, runs her finger across the strings to check the tuning, adjusts a couple of them. Jack likes to watch her fingers move, even doing this, without the music having started yet, tells her that.

"You're a funny guy," she says as she brings the fiddle up under her chin.

Jack smiles. "Everybody says that," he tells her.

But he's thinking of something else, he's thinking of how the little pieces of her history that she's given him add to his own without taking anything away from her. He's thinking about Malicorne and the stories she takes, how she pulls the hurt out of them by listening. He's thinking—

But then Staley starts to play and the music takes him away again.

"I was working on a tune this afternoon," she says as the music moves into three-four time. "Maybe I'll call it 'Jack's Waltz.'"

Jack closes his eyes, listening, not just to her music, but for the sound of wings.

- 7 -

It's past sundown. The fires are burning in the oil drums and bottles are being passed around. Cider and apple juice in some, stronger drink in others. Malicorne's not drinking, never does, least not that I can ever remember seeing. She's sitting off by herself, leaning against a red brick wall, face a smudge of pale in the shadows, horn invisible. The wall was once the side of a factory, now it's standing by itself. There's an owl on top of the wall, three stories up, perched on the bricks, silhouetted by the moon. I saw it land and wonder what owls mean around her. Jack told me about the ravens.

After awhile, I walk over to where she's sitting, offer her some apple juice. She shakes her head. I can see the horn now.

"What's it with you and Jack?" I ask.

"Old arguments never die," she says.

"You go back a long time?"

She shakes her head. "But the kind of man he is and I do. Live long enough, William, and you'll meet every kind of a person, hear every kind of a story, not once, but a hundred times."

"I don't get what you mean," I say.

"No. But Jack does."

We hear the music then, Staley's fiddle, one-two-three, one-two-three, waltz time, and I see them sitting together on the other side of the fires, shadow shapes, long tall Jack with his raven hair and the firefly glow of Staley's head bent over her instrument. I hear the sound of wings and think of the owl on the wall above us, but when I check, it's gone. These are black birds, ravens, a flock of them, an unkindness, and I feel something in the air, a prickling across my skin and at the nape of my neck, like a storm's coming, but the skies are clear. The stars seem so close we could be up in the mountains instead of here, in the middle of the city.

"What are you thinking about?" Malicorne asks.

I turn to her, see the horn catch the firelight. "Endings," I find myself saying. "Where things go when they don't fit where they are."

She smiles. "Are you reading my mind?"

"Never was much inclined for that sort of thing."

"Me, either."

That catches me by surprise. "But you . . ." You're magic, I was going to say, but my voice trails off.

"I've been here too long," she says. "Stopped to rest a day or so, and look at me now. Been here all spring and most of the summer."

"It's been a good summer."

She nods. "But Jack's right, you know. Your stories do nourish me. Not like he thinks, it's not me feeding on them and you losing something, it's that they connect me to a place." She taps a finger against the dirt we're sitting on. "They connect me to something real. But I also get you to talk because I know talking heals. I like to think I'm doing some good."

"Everybody likes you," I tell her. I don't add, except for Jack.

"But it's like Scheherazade," she says. "One day the stories are all told and it's time to move on."

I'm shaking my head. "You don't have to go. When you're standing at the bottom of the ladder like we are, nobody can tell you what to do anymore. It's not much, but at least we've got that."

"There's that innocence of yours again," she says.

"What the hell's that supposed to mean?"

She smiles. "Don't be angry."

"Then don't treat me like a kid."

"But isn't this like Neverneverland?" she asks. "You said it yourself. Nobody can tell you what to do anymore. Nothing has to ever change. You can be like this forever."

"You think any of us want to be here? You think we chose to live like this?"

"She's not talking about you, William," Jack says. "She's talking about me."

I never heard the music stop, never heard them approach, Jack and the fiddler, standing near us now. I don't know how long they've been there, how much they've heard. Staley lifts her hand to me, says hi. Jack, he's just looking at Malicorne. I can't tell what he's thinking.

"So I guess what you need is my story," he says, "and then you can go."

Malicorne shakes her head. "My coming or going has nothing to do with you."

Jack doesn't believe her. He sits down on the dirt in front of us, got that look in his eye I've seen before, not angry, just he won't be backing down. Staley sits down, too, takes out her fiddle, but doesn't play it. She holds the instrument on her lap, runs the pad of her thumb along the strings, toys with wooden curlicues on the head, starts to finger a tune, pressing the strings against the fingerboard, soundlessly. I wish I had something to do with my hands.

"See," Jack's saying, "it's circumstance that put most of these people here, living on the street. They're not bad people, they're just weak, maybe, or had some bad luck, some hard times, that's all. Some of them'll die here, some of them'll make a second chance for themselves and your guess is as good as mine, which of them'll pull through."

"But you chose to live like this," Malicorne says.

"You know, don't you? You already know all about me."

She shakes her head. "All I know is you're hiding from something and nobody had to tell me that. I just had to look at you."

"I killed a man," Jack says.

"Did he deserve it?"

"I don't even know anymore. He was stealing from me, sent my business belly-up and just laughed at me when I confronted him with it. Asked me what was I going to do, the money was all spent and what the hell could I prove anyway? He'd fixed the books so it looked like it was all my fault."

"That's hard," I say.

I'm where I am because I drank too much, drank all the time and damned if I can tell you why. Got nobody to blame but myself. Don't drink anymore, but it's too late to go back. My old life went on without me. Wife remarried. Kids think I'm dead.

"It was the laughing I couldn't take," Jack says. "He was just standing there, looking so smug and laughing at me. So I hit him. Grabbed the little turd by the throat and started whacking the back of his head against the wall and when I stopped, he was dead. First time I ever saw a dead person. First time I ever hit anybody, except for goofing around with the guys in high school." He looks at me. "You know, the old push and shove, but it's nothing serious."

I give him a nod.

"But this was serious. The thing is, when I think about it now, what he did to me, the money he stole, none of it seems so important anymore."

"Are you sorry?" Malicorne asks.

"I'm not sorry he's dead, but I'm sorry I was the one that killed him."

"So you've been on the run ever since."

Jack nods. "Twelve years now and counting." He gives her a long, steady look. "So that's my story."

"Do you feel any better having told us about it?"

"No."

"I didn't think you would," she says.

"What's that supposed to mean?"

"You've got to want to heal before you can get out of this prison you've made for yourself."

I'm expecting this to set him off, but he looks at the ground instead, shoulders sagging. I've seen a lot of broken men on the skids—hell, all I've had to do for years is look in a mirror—but I've never imagined Jack as one of them. Never knew why he was down here with the rest of us, but always thought he was stronger than the rest of us.

"I don't know how," he says.

"Was he your brother?" Staley asks. "This man you killed."

I've been wondering how she was taking this, sitting there so still, listening, not even her fingers moving anymore. It's hard to see much of anything, here in the shadows. Our faces and hands are pale blurs. The light from the fires in the oil drums catches Malicorne's horn, Staley's hair, awakes a shine on her lap where the blue fiddle's lying.

Jack shakes his head. "He was my best friend. I would've given him anything, all he had to do was ask."

"I'm sorry for you," Malicorne says, standing up. "I'm sorry for you both, the one dead and the other a long time dying."

She's going then, nothing to pack, nothing to carry, leaving us the way she came, with her hands empty and her heart full. Over by the oil drums, nobody notices. Frenchy is rolling himself a cigarette from the butts he collected during the day. Casey's sleeping, an empty bottle of wine lying in the dirt beside his hand. I can't see the black birds, but I can hear them, feathers rustling in the dark all around us. I guess if you want to believe in that kind of thing, there's a door standing open nearby.

"Let me come with you," Jack says.

Malicorne looks at him. "The road I'm traveling goes on forever," she says.

"I kind of guessed that, what with the horn and all."

"It's about remembering, not forgetting."

He nods. "I know that, too. Maybe I can learn to be good company."

"Nobody ever said you weren't," she tells him. "What you have to ask yourself is, are you trying to escape again or are you really ready to move on?"

"Talking about it—that's a start, isn't it?"

Malicorne smiles. "It's a very good start."

- 8 -

Staley and I, we're the only ones to see them go. I don't know if they just walked off into the night, swallowed by the shadows, or if they stepped through a door, but I never see either of them again. We sit there for awhile, looking up at the stars. They still seem so big, so near, like they want to be close to whatever enchantment happened here tonight. After awhile Staley starts to play her fiddle, that same tune she played earlier, the one in three-four time. I hear wings, in behind the music, but it's the black birds leaving, not gathering. Far off, I hear hoofbeats and I don't know what to make of that.

Frenchy gets himself a job a few weeks later, sweeping out a bar over on Grasso Street, near the Men's Mission. Casey goes back to the coast, says he's thinking of going back to school. Lots of the others, things start to look up a little for them, too. Not everybody, not all of us, but more than tried to take a chance before Malicorne came into our lives.

Me, I find myself a job as a custodian in a Kelly Street tenement. The job gives me a little room in the basement, but there's no money in it. I get by with tips from the tenants when I do some work for them, paint a room, fix a leaky faucet, that kind of thing. I'm looking for something better, but times are still hard.

Staley, she hangs around for a few days, then moves on.

I remember thinking there's a magic about her, too, but now I know it's in the music she calls up from that blue fiddle of hers, the same kind of magic any good musician can wake from an instrument. It takes you away. Calls something to you maybe, but it's not necessarily ravens or enchantment.

Before she goes, I ask her about that night, about what brought her down to the Tombs.

"I wanted to see the unicorn," she says. "I was playing in a pick-up band in a roadhouse up on Highway 14 and overheard somebody talking about her in the parking lot at the end of the night—a couple of 'boes, on their way out of the city. I just kind of got distracted with Jack. He seemed like a nice guy, you know, but he was so lonely."

"The unicorn . . . ?"

For a minute there I don't know what she's talking about, but then Malicorne's horsy features come to mind, the chestnut dreadlocks, the wide-set eyes. And finally I remember the horn and when I do, I can't figure out how I forgot.

"You know," Staley's saying. "White horse, big spiraling horn coming out of her forehead."

"But she was a woman," I begin.

Staley smiles. "And Jack was a man. But when they left, I saw a white horse and a black one."

"I didn't. But I heard hoofbeats. . . ." I give her a puzzled look. "What happened that night?"

Staley shoulders her knapsack, picks up her fiddle case. She stands on tip toes and kisses me lightly on the cheek.

"Magic," she says. "And wasn't it something—just that little piece of it?"

I'm nodding when she gives me a little wave of her hand.

"See you, William," she says. "You take care now."

I wave back, stand there, watching her go. I hear a croaking cry from the top of the derelict building beside me, but it's a crow I see, beating its black wings, lifting high above the ragged roofline, not a raven.

Sometimes I find myself humming that waltz she wrote for Jack.

Sometimes I dream about two horses, one black and one white with a horn, the two of them running, running along the crest of these long hills that rise and fall like the waves of the sea, and I wake up smiling.

ABOUT THE AUTHOR

Charles de Lint was born in the Netherlands and is presently a citizen of Canada. His father's job with a surveying company allowed him to grow up in places as diverse as the Yukon, Turkey, Lebanon, and the province of Quebec. A full-time writer and musician, he currently makes his home in Ottawa, Ontario, with his wife MaryAnn Harris, an artist and musician.

He was a professional musician for fourteen years in a band called Wickentree. After a four-year break, during which he could still be found at local sessions, he and MaryAnn formed a new band, Jump at the Sun, with two other local musicians, still specializing in traditional and contemporary acoustic music. His instruments are Irish flute, fiddle, whistles, button accordion, bouzouki, guitar, and bodhran (an Irish goatskin drum). He is also the proprietor/editor of Triskell Press, a small publishing house that prints occasional fantasy chapbooks and magazines. His writing includes novels, short stories, comic book scripts, poetry and nonfiction, as well as reviews and columns for many magazines and newspapers. His short fiction has appeared in hardcover and paperback anthologies as well as in numerous magazines. He is the recipient of multiple awards, has served on many awards committees and juries, and is an ongoing reviewer: "Books to Look For" for *The Magazine of Fantasy and Science Fiction* and "The Eclectic Muse" for *Pulphouse, A Fiction Magazine*.

He served as vice president of the Horror Writers Association, 1992–1994, and will be the writer-in-residence for the Ottawa and Gloucester Public libraries for the calendar year 1995. His most recent books are *The Ivory and the Horn* and *Memory and Dream*, both published by Tor Books.

ROBERT DEVEREAUX

◄━◦ᴜᴍᴌ∫ᴌᴍᴍ◦━►

WHAT THE EYE SEES, WHAT THE HEART FEELS

Peter: **Robert Devereaux**'s story, "What the Eye Sees, What the Heart Feels," deals with the human-unicorn link in a gentle, affecting manner that I'd hardly have expected from a writer who publishes in anthologies like *MetaHorror, Love in Vein, Splatterpunks 2* ("Peter, who *are* these people?"), *Book of the Dead 3,* and *It Came from the Drive-In.* He is the author of the novel *Deadweight,* and has a second, *Walking Wounded,* due out in 1996. Robert lives in Fort Collins, Colorado, ". . . working as a software engineer by day and letting his imagination run wild by dawn . . ." It seems to be having a very nice time.

Janet: This is a very gentle man, Peter, and a damn hard worker at his craft. I herewith thank you, Robert, for your extraordinary patience with my "editorial interference." I hope you agree that the results were worth it; I know the readers will . . . you sentimental slob, you.

What the Eye Sees,
What the Heart Feels

———✦———

THE DEATH THAT TURNED OUT TO BE THE LAST one she witnessed belonged to an old woodcutter. And that one, because of her mounting accumulation of ills, she nearly missed out on.

Did the others think her odd? No doubt they did. She saw them infrequently these days, their flashing white bodies glancing through the world, partaking of life. *She* partook of *death*. Or, more precisely, she bore witness to the skimming of life, the final throes, blunting the pain that so often accompanied them. If that was odd, then odd she was and proud to be so.

Her aches made the world seem smaller than it was. Distances, once easy to judge, tended these days to deceive her. As she hastened onward, a hard-packed roadway drove spike after spike into her striking hooves. Her heart, a surging red fury, pounded out of control in her breast. Even so, she pressed at top speed toward the woodcutter's cottage, praying she'd arrive on time.

The wood she entered seemed familiar. That wasn't surprising. By now, all the world seemed—indeed was—so. Beside the cottage's shadowed east wall, an unassuming grave marker belonging to the woodcutter's wife brought to mind her death years before, a gray sigh in his huddled arms. Without a moment to spare, she burst silently through the thick oak door as a last ray of sunlight faded on his face. Their eyes met. The dying man was a worn husk of wrinkle and bone, his axe idle by the fireplace. Plump misshapen pillows angled him up. Tattered blankets, gray as dust, clung to him. Through one last exhalation, he shivered, his lips thin and dark.

His eyes melted upon hers.

Eons before, when she and the world were young, this witnessing, this absorption of pain, had made her feel superior. She, of all her kind, lived deeper, felt more profoundly, probed life to its roots—or so she had imagined. The others? They drank from far shallower waters, their fluff-white manes tossed carelessly in the wind. They scattered their attention hither and yon, squandering it. Ah, but she—and one other, the one who witnessed births—had chosen, more wisely, to fix on one thing only. For too many millennia, that had been her view. But since her disorders had begun to gather and spread, she'd grown to honor, to envy, the others. Depth, she understood finally, could be gained through sidewise means, glances at experience that seemed superficial but weren't. So they in their way had mined life's riches, and she in hers.

The dying man's eyes widened.

The air about him refused to be drawn into his nostrils, into his gaping mouth. "Accept it," she said, her ribs hurting from how swiftly she'd arrived. Her words took the edge off his panic, softened him, even as lances of pain shot through her, heightening the misery of founder and strangles, the botfly larvae and tapeworms that infested her tract, the colic, the arthritis, the disorders ravaging her lungs. Her coat glowed with the light of immortality. But inside, she harbored accretions of death.

A shiver rose from the woodcutter's body and he lay still. His eyes, dull cuts of emerald, saw no more.

Above him, without tears, she wept.

She understood now what had to be done.

Centuries past, he'd mastered the art of indirection, those quick evasive sidesteps that kept him always a touch beyond their peripheral vision. Eluding detection by one of them was a cakewalk; two were slightly harder, three a tough yet manageable challenge. But escaping notice when four of them were around—particularly if they began to sense your presence—*that* was a major test of one's skills.

Many of his compatriots were retiring sorts, shyly tucked deep in the wild, backing farther into solitude whenever bands of rovers rumbled through the woods. Not he. And not a select few he'd chanced upon, or dallied with, in his long lifetime—those who, like him, had discovered how to hide in plain sight, whose deepest joy lay in witnessing, close up, the strange and wonderful doings of mortal folk.

He stood now in shadow, beyond a roaring hearthfire. These three—the midwife, her scrawny henlike helper, the fat-legged, gap-thighed peasant woman before whose widening vulva the pair soothed and coaxed, waiting in practiced wonder—were much too intent to even *try* to notice the benevolent creature watching over them.

"Come now," the midwife said, her big hands working the woman's flesh like an impatient cook kneading dough. "Just relax into it." Anger sat sharp upon her tongue. He couldn't tell if it was meant for her assistant, for the peasant woman, or for the world at large.

"I can't do it," whined the mother-to-be, her forehead bathed in sweat, wet black curves of hair sweeping like knife blades above it.

"You'll be fine," came the response, muted, mothering. The assistant's head turned in wonder. It was clear she'd never heard the midwife's voice soften that way. Or *any* way. The midwife, too, looked surprised, raising a hint of eyebrow, then resuming more gently her massaging. "That's right," she said. "That's the way. You're doing fine."

"You think so?" A twist of hope fluted up.

"I do." And she was telling the truth.

This part gave him great satisfaction. His presence, like the fire's forgiving light, softened edges, broadcast warmth, infused with blessings everything he gazed upon. Although his immortality derived from wholly other causes, it felt forever linked to the births he witnessed, to the new blazes of life flaring up. It seemed to him too that those amassed witnessings flew out from him as he watched, giving the mortal players in that drama a confidence and strength far beyond their best capacities.

The midwife sculpted an opening—wide, taut, wet with emerging hair and scalp. "That's it," she coaxed, "that's the way."

"Unh," the peasant woman said. "Mmmn."

"It's coming," the midwife's assistant chimed in.

The woman's labia stretched, a wide thin o of taut flesh. Her baby crowned, its head purple and slick with vernix. From the sweep of his tail to the swirled tip of his horn, he knew it was a girl. Mortals didn't know—despite their comical feints at divination—but *he* always knew, the moment he saw a laboring woman's belly, which gender her infant would be.

"Come on, sweetheart," the midwife urged gently. "It's time to be born." One huge palm supported the infant's head; the other worked to help its swiftening passage out. Caught it, an expert catch and swaddle! He thrilled at the sight, the spills of liquid, the squirming of new flesh—a blend of three, then four, bodies. Firelight danced upon fabric and skin. Faintly, like loam, the aromas of blood and life arose. Sounds of delight and relief interwove. Then all was business and love. A bond fixed them to this time and space, a bond never in his memory, nor in theirs, to be broken.

Joy swept along his horn, a rush that filled him to the heart. Tearlessly he wept.

Then abruptly, cutting through his joy, a summons sounded in his head.

The women carried on, oblivious.

He raised his horn to the signal. His ears twitched at its strength.

Before thought could intercede, he sped away, hurtling silently through earthen walls into the darkness of night. Turning, he galloped at once unerringly east.

As she left the woodcutter's cottage, she heard the moans of the dying, clamoring as ever for her attention. Impossible. For her, the end had come. As much as she owed them her presence, she simply couldn't endure one more death. Time and again, she had relented, taking on her chosen task despite the ills it brought. But her agony had grown so great that words like guilt and selfishness had finally lost their hold.

The world stunned up into her hooves, shoots of pain struck from passing greens and browns, as she hurried back to the purest wood on earth. It was a place no one born of woman would ever reach, a place of trees and moss and generous sun, where night never fell, and where, so long ago, they had all burst forth upon the earth. That memory—how they'd come so swiftly into being, flurrying out of the circle, each of them different yet bound in mind and spirit to the others—emerged in all its beauty whenever she brought this clearing to mind. The wide ring of stones, cozy yet somehow beyond the mind's compass, gleamed with scatterings of mica caught in pure hard white rock, a vast jaw of molars set inevitably, artistically right. They'd been flung from these same stones, and the earth that tracked them before they lifted into the sky remained as soft as on that first day. Hoofprints that had bitten deep then into dirt—each of them unique, not one overlaid or obliterated—shone now with undiminished clarity.

Coming in over the circle of stones, she touched down on plush grass and found the center, the place of summoning. Her eyes, thick with rheum, cast a film over what she saw; but she felt the power there, the stones equidistant from her like the rim of a wheel brought into true. She stumbled. The parasitic pain had imbalanced her, had knocked her equilibrium askew. It couldn't be shaken off, her horntip making zigzags in the air, her erratic head slowing at last in resignation. Faltering, she lowered herself carefully to the ground (far more dignity was possible from that position) and brought her will entirely to the tip of her rising horn.

As he raced onward, the earth in all its splendor rehearsed itself in his sight. When he idled, when he slept or grazed—these ways of being bestowed their own peculiar grace. But to gallop lightly over the earth, to spin out road and glade and ribbons of sea beneath his hooves, passing through trees and towers, through huts of thatch and sod (their solidity more dream than real)—this movement, this thundering gallop, was a prayer indeed, a perfect blend of beauty and the awareness which affirmed it.

Summonings were seldom. The last one had occurred in the distant past, a celebration of a love the summoner had witnessed and in some way participated in. A svelte young filly had stood in the midst of the clearing, tossing her head and speaking of a rustic couple—how they'd met, how they'd fought, reconciled, found commonalities, nurtured them, all beneath the gaze of the teller. Unbounded happiness had swept through him, had swept through them all, even those who kept shy of humanity. As rare as summonings were, they always taught lessons worth learning, lessons that healed and affirmed.

New vistas rose before him, splitting right and left, joining behind him and vanishing over a rolling horizon. Within them—few at first, then increasing—streaks of white wove through blues and greens and browns. So brilliant and pure were they that they approached silver, liquid shards of mirror, reflecting himself. Random brushstrokes fell closer, quicker, multiplying, resolving into the joyous forms of those he knew so well.

Below, along flanks of thundering white, he watched early comers touch down. At the place of summoning, centered on the greensward, sat the summoner. He felt her in his horn as he had from the first—felt her call, her urgency. Why wasn't she standing, as summoners always stood? Circling with the others, he drifted down, watching those already earth-bound draw together in curiosity as latecomers flurried the air behind him. There sat the summoner, majestic, wise. But as she enlarged in his sight, as he saw her more clearly, other feelings arose in him, feelings of sorrow for what her outer majesty could not conceal.

Above her they sailed in, homing on her call. Doves flocking in obedience, they let through cuts of sun, the clearing mottled as those coming down touched hoof to turf. In the mundane world, they let gravity chain them to the earth. But whenever they were summoned here, the skyways afforded them purchase, gave lift and yaw and balance to their airborne bodies.

She'd considered standing. The thought alone shot a fistful of barbs through her breast. A realization stunned her. She would no longer stand, no longer use these four aching legs that had carried her through uncounted eons. They, and she, were finished. Used up. If the others couldn't release her—but surely they could, and would—she'd lie here until the world ended, alone at the place of her birth, beauty surrounding her, torment and suffering within.

As stragglers thinned in the sky, the ones that were earthbound shone with more light than shadow. Innumerable but nearly complete, the host swept from where she lay, across the grass, among wide flat birthstones and the pounded track, and farther out amidst oaks whose tall trunks pierced the heavens. Yet despite their numbers, rounded out by the last-dropped few from the sky, there was no sense whatever of crowding. At all sides, they had ample room to mix and wonder, casting an eye in her direction before settling down to hear what she had to say.

The amber oozings of her eyes had caked like candle wax down her cheeks, but her vision served. She relaxed, letting the signal fall away at last. White bodies swam before her, there, there, sharp, stable—yet impossible, in her dizziness, to fix upon. Every breath she took proved more difficult than the last.

She lowered her eyelids, unrushed, feeling in her heart for the right moment to speak.

He moved among the crowd, each face uniquely beautiful, and familiar as home. "What's it all about?" he asked.

"No idea," they said, or dumbly shook their heads, mane fluff floating like clusters of dandelion.

Wandering nearer to the summoner, he caught an intriguing face, asked again. The wide-flanked mare gazed up and said, "Look at her. You'll find a clue. Settle in beside me, okay? You're not half-bad-looking."

Why not? These gatherings often generated sufficient communal heat that foals joined their ranks eleven months afterward. The planet had plenty of room for more of their kind. None of them ever died, of course. That was strictly the province of men and women and the cyclic life that shared their earth. He and the others had dashed into the world fully grown, and their offspring, over idle centuries, grew to adulthood and stabilized there.

Lowering himself, he felt stiff grass blades brush his belly and soften under his weight. The mare, nuzzling him, smelled of sweet clover. He nuzzled back, a hint at what lay ahead. But his gaze, the mare's, too, fixed on the summoner. Her eyes were inflamed, her throat swollen. Pus lay thick about her nostrils. They called the disease the strangles. He imagined they'd all had brushes with one or another affliction, but they'd thrown them off quickly. Not she. He noted too the outward signs of founder: Around the hoof walls visible to him, and where horn met brow, diverging rings had developed, a crumbling of the laminae. Clearly, from the way she held herself, other ills plagued her as well.

"She's ailing," he said, astonished.

"It's her peculiar ways," said the mare, not judging, just noting, her breath as savory as new-mown hay. "She's weird. Like you. She's the one who tends to the dying."

"I could never do that." Yet he admired her. Always had. While the others—those not too shy to venture forth—had scattered their talents in many directions, preferring variety, only he and she had lent fierce passion to a single pursuit.

"It can't be healthy, her obsession with the dying, with *being there* for them." Nodding toward the summoner, the mare added, "There's the evidence."

Early in his witnessings, he'd seen mothers die in childbirth. He'd watched infants emerge stillborn or deformed or badly delivered, maimed in removal, deprived of limbs through a midwife's ineptitude. Those witnessings had hurt. Quickly he'd decided to be more selective, a plethora of births to choose from. Sensing the successes, he partook of them alone.

The murmuring started to die down. From this distance—though he suspected those farthest out could hear it too—labored breathing came to him, wheezes that betrayed lung problems, viruses past any hope of cure.

She craned about, surveying the crowd.

For the first time he understood. They were not here for their usual celebration, not at all.

"My friends," she said, but she had to clear her throat and repeat it. "My friends, seeing you here brings me great joy."

They listened without moving. Yet her eyes refused to hold them still. It was as though the earth and everything upon it had turned liquid in her sight. Whipped white meringue shimmied along withers and loins and horns. Myriad pairs of eyes jittered like cloves in pounded dough.

"You honor me with your presence," she went on. "Why are you here? I see the question in your faces. It's because I'm dying. For years I've been dying. Even so, my life continues. I go on—wrapped, as we all are, in immortality.

"Many deaths have passed before my eyes. Many deaths have pierced me. It's a thing of awe and wonder to witness how men and women abandon the burning houses of their bodies. I've borne witness to nature at her most natural and her most terrible, ugly and beautiful both. But the misery of the dying, and of those who grieve for them, have left an indelible mark on me."

She felt buoyed by the support that came to her from all sides. It assuaged her pain. She wished she could spend an eternity in the presence of these, her kind. But that, she knew, could never be. They had their chosen tasks to be about, their comings and goings upon the earth—and she had one final task to perform.

"I have summoned you to ask a favor." No one had ever told her of the power she wanted them to exercise, but she knew they had it and that they would know it, too. "I want you to grant me release. You alone, in concert, have the power to free me. You alone can let me die. This I now request."

Renewed murmurs caught the crowd. Sunlight plated them in gold, their mouths moving, their great heads swinging in conversation. Inside, she felt parasites crawl and bite, sapping her strength. Fresh wind swept the treetops.

One of those seated nearby, a male, rose to speak. Her gaze was untrustworthy, but she recognized the watcher at births, a well-meaning soul whose eyes sparkled with life. He too, as she, was regarded strangely by the others, the ones not so fiercely focused, not so single-minded, as they.

"Forgive my boldness," he said, trumpeting his words and lofting his head so that all could hear. "You surely don't expect us to kill one of our own kind. We can't possibly do such a thing. Our lives go on without end. I myself celebrate beginnings, as you know. This morning, I watched a woman open herself. She gave new life from her womb and cried at the pain and beauty of what she gave. I cried too. Each of us in this clearing is a beginning with no end. How can you ask us to close off one such beginning?"

His was a token resistance. She knew that. So did he. A special harmony bound their kind, a oneness of sensibility that had never left them, no matter how scattered the paths they'd taken from their first natal gallop around this ring and off into the world. "Your concern touches me, it honors me," she said. "But in giving what I ask, you won't be killing me. You'll be letting me die. That's the end I want and need. If you hesitate, you'll only prolong my suffering. Be generous. Please. Grant my request."

She knew, without looking at him, that he had resumed his place on the grass. Closing her eyes, she lifted her head toward the sun and offered her immortality to be drawn like dew from the spiraled surface of her horn. It resembled the summoning, but it differed: the focus of her energy—the focus of theirs—shifted, there where the air filled with lilac and the soft breezy lifting of manes.

"Poor thing," said the mare beside him. She had shut her eyes, and her horn pressed upward at a determined angle. The others, too, wherever he looked, had begun to show that same intense readiness-to-charge.

Letting his eyelids fall, he lifted his head.

It wasn't fair. Perhaps there was a way to save her. They might be able to halt her agony, reverse it, take—each of them—a portion of her pain into themselves and so renew her. But even as he maneuvered his horn just so, he knew there was no such way.

They owed her her end.

He imagined he heard a faint high whine, the sort of keening that might issue from a ghostly fiddle strung taut and drawn across with one thin horsehair, so near the threshold between sound and silence as to have been dreamt. Sunlight glowed through his lids. The others, attuned by a commonality of blood, drew closer.

Into his horn's tight twist, the thousandth part of her life's energy drained, an exchange multiplied manifold among the gathered masses.

He felt her eyelids drift open.

Her eyes rested on him.

Him alone.

He sensed her scrutiny but kept his own eyes closed, becoming more giving, more accepting, his ears twitching as he drew off his share of what she offered.

Had any of them held back, she couldn't have yielded what she needed so fiercely to yield. But the hard swirls that twisted from brows, the bold thrust of horns that unified them even in their disparity—these they offered, without exception, to her service.

And serve her they did.

In fancy, her cream-white spiral drew them toward her. The distance separating them shrank, until—haphazardly at first, then uniformly and upon every inch of surface—the blunt tip of each horn touched her horn, siphoning off a tiny part of her life. Her ills, encased until this moment in a shell of immortality, seeped through that crumbling shell. Released from confinement at last, they wracked her as they went.

In her mind's eye, she saw clearly the one who alone had made protest. A handsome steed. Robust. He'd spent his life witnessing births, avoiding the botched ones, the ones that ended badly. Many of those latter she'd seen, many attended. They had cost her much. But in the easing of sorrow, they had returned far more.

She felt herself weaken. No longer did she need to push her gift out. Instead, the others, homed in upon her, reached to embrace it, to accept it.

Slowly her eyelids rose.

There he sat, vibrant, beautiful, shut out from life's bitterness by a choice he'd made long ago. He and the others brought her to tears, shining so firm and heartwhole under daylight. In sorrow, they robbed her of what she'd asked them to steal. She saw it change them, change *him*, seeding riches deep inside him.

His head lifted.

She knew he felt her eyes on him.

The air smelled of sweet apples. Her body was shot through with pain. Through the razored claws of a breeze, sunlight scorched her back.

She watched his eyelids part. Dark pupils gleamed through curd-white slits. Their eyes met. It was *his* horntip that touched the tip of her horn, *his* the essence that drank most deeply of hers.

She gave.

He took.

Lightened of her burden, she let herself fly free, rising skyward without liftoff, even as the earth, unbroken, opened to embrace her.

Her weakening, as he witnessed it, happened gradually, a soft easing of the flesh. But her eyelids' last closing caught him unprepared. It began, as the others had, with the lazy downward drift of her lashes. Then, instead of their rise, her neck and head lowered through a slow roll that brought them, as gently as a feather falling through unstirred air, to rest upon the green.

For an eternity they sat there, fascinated by her unmoved corpse. A light breeze toyed with her mane. No other air moved upon her, nor any sign of it—no rib cage expanding, no flair of nostrils.

It seemed utterly wrong.

And nothing less than right.

Shadows passed over him. He glanced up. The ones at the outskirts of the clearing had begun to lift off. He saw their grim-set faces, the broken-stilted waggle of their legs as hooves caught air. His eyes found the summoner's corpse, refusing to believe the stillness that surrounded it.

The sea of white bodies gradually evaporated upward, leaving flat green. Shadows crisscrossed, thinned, and were no more. At one point, he felt the mare nuzzle him. He knew she was speaking words of farewell, but he heard only the kindness of her tone before she, too, was gone.

Another eternity passed.

Reluctantly he rose.

Walking was an effort. Before him lay a pure white ruin, her fallen body. "Please, not me," he tried to say, but no sound escaped his lips. He raised his head, taking in the warmth and comfort of the clearing and the sun's generosity overhead. Already suffering, his heart hurt worse for the beauty of the setting.

Perhaps if he . . .

His neck hung low, a steep white slope which his mane, were it not attached, might curl along like a carpet of snow hurtling downhill. Her horn tilted upward at an odd angle. The tip still pulsed feebly; he found it, by instinct, with his own horntip, a sure solid touch.

The final release of her voice, when it came, was neither sudden nor shocking.

Its warmth entered him and the entirety of his body enclosed it, an infant's mouth meeting its mother's nipple for the first time. "There's no one else," her voice spoke. Then it dimmed and fell silent.

Her flesh turned to granite before him, her horn a twist of white gold. The world had changed in the last hour. The hub at the center of their ring of birthstones, once empty, bore a monument—her transmuted body—to the summoner's devotion. Could he tread lightly in her hoofprints? She'd lived a full long life. *His* life, he felt, was just beginning, on the verge.

He had to try it.

He could always (*he could never!*) change his mind.

He backed away and sprang skyward, catching the air where the summoner's hooves had made their imprint coming in.

On all sides, voices called to him.

Here the births, there the deaths.

With a resolve not solid, but firm enough to see him on his way, he made his choice.

ABOUT THE AUTHOR

Robert Devereaux has had stories in such publications as *Pulp-house, Bizarre Sex, Iniquities,* and *Weird Tales*. He has appeared in *Meta-Horror, Love in Vein, Splatterpunks 2, Book of the Dead 3, It Came from the Drive-In,* and various Year's Best anthologies. *Deadweight*, his first novel (Dell, 1994), at once brutal and lyrical, provoked strong response across a wide spectrum of readers. *Walking Wounded,* out mid-1996, ventures into the more contemplative but no less lyrical realms of psychological horror.

Robert has lived for nearly three years in Fort Collins, Colorado, working as a software engineer by day and letting his imagination run wild by dawn. A lighthearted devotee of the sacred and the sensual in everyday life, Robert has an extensive collegiate theatrical background and a grounding also in choral singing. He loves most types of music but has a special fondness for opera, particularly late Wagner and early Strauss. He accumulates far too many books and CDs and lives in bliss without a TV.

Finally, long an admirer of the deceptive simplicity and visual lyricism of Peter S. Beagle's prose, Robert counts it a signal honor to be included in this anthology.

MARINA FITCH

STAMPEDE OF LIGHT

Peter: I think of **Marina Fitch** as practically a neighbor, since she resides and works with children in the farming town of Watsonville, California, where I lived for sixteen years. It is therefore a matter of chauvinistic local pride to present her "Stampede of Light" here. But it is also a matter of admiration, since her story is a completely original vision of the nature of unicorns, as well as a genuinely moving view of the terrible kind of loneliness that only children know, and the capacity for friendship and stubborn courage that belongs to the occasional real grown-up. . . .

Janet: Marina is another former member of The Melville Nine. She lived in Santa Cruz in those days, and used to drag herself by train and bus to our monthly meetings. She quit to move to Oregon, came back to California to get married, and, later, moved to Watsonville. Thank heavens she never stopped writing.

Stampede of Light

I DON'T KNOW WHEN I STOPPED BELIEVING I
would live forever.

"Open a child's mind and heart to the world, and you achieve immortality," my sixth-grade teacher Mrs. Rodriguez once told me. "Whether they remember you or not, you'll live forever."

I remember Mrs. Rodriguez. I guess that makes her a saint.

I shaded my eyes with my hand and scanned the kids racing across the blacktop, smashing tetherballs, clambering over metal play structures. At the edge of the grass two boys raised clenched hands. I brought the whistle to my lips—they tossed dried leaves at each other. I removed the whistle. Then the boys scooped up more leaves and dumped them on of one of my second graders.

He ignored them. I frowned, trying to remember his name: ginger hair, gray eyes, square face, freckled nose. Alone. . . .

Corey Ferris, one of this year's forgotten children. The one I couldn't place when I saw his name on my roll sheet the first month of school. The one who never caused trouble, never answered questions. The invisible child in a class of thirty-two.

I was a forgotten child, too. Until Mrs. Rodriguez.

Corey stood with his back to me, gazing across the field. I joined him. With a squint, I peered over his head. All I could see was the far corner of the cyclone fence.

"Corey," I said, "what are you looking at?"

He started. Shuffling away from me, he stopped, looked at the corner, then at me. "Don't you see her?" he said.

I looked again. This time I saw her.

The woman sat in the corner, her manzanita-red hair spilling over her shoulders, dark swirls against her turquoise blouse. Her skirt, vibrant with green, raspberry, yellow, and blue, fanned across her knees. She bent over slightly, her hands skimming across her lap.

A child stood beside her. A dark-haired girl, one of Peggy's third graders—Heather Granger. I headed toward them. The woman was probably Heather's mother, but it never hurt to check.

An image flashed through my mind: *smiling, the woman opened her arms wide. The girl rested her head in the woman's lap* —

The image vanished. A sense of loss touched me. . . .

The bell rang.

I glanced back at the worn, art deco school. My second graders were already lining up near the back stairs. Corey hovered at the end of the line, separated from the others by two paces. I turned a slow circle, searching the far corner, then the playground. Heather and the woman were gone.

I finally caught up to Peggy in the staff room after school. "Peggy, did Heather go home sick?"

Peggy shrugged into her jacket, then took the sheaf of papers out of her mouth. "Heather?"

"Heather Granger. Dark hair, quiet."

Peggy sucked in her cheeks. "I don't have any Heathers this year." She frowned. "I had three last year. No Grangers. . . ."

I blinked. "You sure?"

Peggy shook her head. "Nope. No Heathers."

I stared at the toes of my shoes, trying to recall Heather's face. I couldn't.

"Mary," Peggy said, "are you okay?"

"Did you—did you see that woman on the playground at lunch?" I said, looking up. "The one sitting in the corner of the field?"

Peggy's frown deepened. "What woman?"

I left around four. As I clattered down the wide front steps, I saw someone blur out of sight behind the potted rosemary on the landing. I stopped, then walked over and peeked.

Corey Ferris cowered behind the Grecian planter.

I squatted. "Corey, what are you doing here?"

He looked up at me, his mouth twisted in a lip-trembling pout.

I waited, head cocked to one side. Finally, he scuffled from behind the rosemary, dragging his backpack. He mumbled something.

"Say it again?" I said.

He glanced at the curb. "Waiting for Dad."

I stared at him. "Is he late?"

"Is it five yet?" he asked.

"No, not—is that when he picks you up?"

He nodded. I took a deep breath, held it, let it go. Students aren't supposed to be alone on the school grounds after two-forty-five.

"Does he—" I thought a minute. "Is this unusual?"

He shook his head.

I sat on the step. "What do you do?"

He hesitated, then sat beside me. He shrugged.

I glanced at my watch. I was supposed to meet a friend at five-thirty. . . .

So I'd meet her in my school clothes. No big deal. I dug through my school bag and pulled out a book. *The Stone Fox.* I nodded, impressed with myself. Good book. "Listen," I said. "I don't have to be anywhere. Would you like to help me read this?"

Corey stood beside me on the playground the next day, not really talking, just standing nearby. As recess wore on, he slowly inched closer. "Do you think?" he said. "Do you think the Stone Fox gave Willy one of the white dogs?"

I pondered this. "I don't know. What do you think?"

Corey grinned, a sudden, gap-toothed smile. "Yeah, he did. The best one."

"What do you think Willy named—?"

"Teacher!" someone wailed.

I turned. A group of kids ran toward me in geese formation. The girl in the lead scrabbled to a stop. "Teacher," she said, "Kevin threw my softball over the fence!"

Kevin slid to a halt. "Can I help it if Gabby can't catch?"

"First things first," I said. "Where did it go over the fence?"

Kevin and Gabby pointed, then glared at each other. I sighted down their fingers . . . to the far corner and the rainbow woman.

A child stood beside her, a boy with a buzz—Josue Hernandez. I'd had him two years ago. He stood beside her, intent on her hands as they skipped like pebbles across her lap.

An image seared through me: *Josue resting his head in the woman's lap. He dissolved like steam —*

By the time the image faded, I was halfway across the field, the gaggle of students squawking behind me. I froze five feet from Josue and the woman. Josue seemed . . . faded, as if he'd been stonewashed. His eyes were no longer chocolate dark, but faint as a shadow on sun-dried mud. He gazed at the woman's hands.

Long and slender, her hands were crosshatched with tiny nicks. She wore porcelain thimbles on her left thumb and forefinger. She wielded a golden needle with her right, embroidering something onto her skirt with a dark thread. I stepped closer. Her lap glittered as if appliquéd with mirrors. I took another step. No, not mirrors—tiny unicorns that sparkled like distant stars. The newest one, a dull, black unicorn on a field of green, lacked its horn. The woman's hands stopped. I looked up—

"Ms. Scibilin! Ms. Scibilin!" someone yelled. "Gabby threw Kevin's shoe over the fence!"

Little hands dragged me to the fence and pointed out the ball, embedded in a pumpkin, and the shoe, dangling from a bare guide wire. When I turned back to the woman, she and Josue were gone.

I walked onto the playground and scanned the field as I had every day for the past week. There was no sign of the woman. I frowned, disappointed. Juanita Vargas, the principal, had promised to call the police next time the woman set foot on the school grounds.

Even if she couldn't remember Josue or the girl.

Corey fell in step beside me. We'd shared three more books after school—two on dogs and one on magic tricks. He'd taken home the magic book.

"I figured out the Kleenex trick," he said. "How to make it disappear? But I can't get the penny one."

"That's a tough one," I said. "I'll help you with it after school."

He grinned at me. I smiled back, then did a quick survey of the field.

A chill wind whistled across the playground, rearranging the fallen leaves. A string of girls threaded their way between Corey and me, chasing orange and gold maple leaves. I scanned the play structures, lingering on a possible fight, then circled slowly. A football game skirmished along the edge of the field. Beyond the grass-stained players, Corey leaned against the fence, watching the woman.

I snatched at Gabby's wrist as she walked by. "Gabby," I said. "Go to the office and tell Ms. Vargas I need her to make that phone call. *Now.*"

Corey inched closer to the woman.

My chest constricted. I ran toward Corey. I glanced at the woman. She had another child with her, not what's-his-name, Josue, but a blonde second grader, one of Kristy's. Amanda Schuyler. The woman looked up, and even at that distance, I could swear she was looking at me—

"Ms. Scibilin! Watch out!"

Three hurtling bodies tackled me in the end zone. They tumbled over the top of me, then scrambled away. "Teacher, are you all right?" someone said.

I spat out a mouthful of grass. "I'm fine."

I swayed to my feet, then sat down abruptly. I knew if I glanced at the corner, Amanda and the woman would be gone.

I limped into the office an hour after the last bell. Panic muted the pain. The police had found nothing, no bits of thread, no embroidery needles, no matted grass. I'd sent them to Kristy's class to talk to Amanda Schuyler. Kristy told them she didn't have an Amanda Schuyler and never had. . . .

I winced, lowering myself into the secretary's chair. I went through the roll sheets, then the emergency cards. I even hobbled over to the filing cabinet and searched the cumulative folders. According to the Cayuga Elementary School records, Josue Hernandez and Amanda Schuyler did not exist. Not even in their siblings' cum files.

I struck the filing cabinet with my fist.

Juanita poked her head into the office. "You okay?"

"Fine," I muttered. I slipped Jason Schuyler's cum folder back in place, then slammed the filing cabinet.

Juanita studied me. "They hit you pretty hard. You're going to Doctors on Duty."

"I'm fine, Juanita. Really—"

She raised two elegantly penciled eyebrows. "District'll foot the bill if you go now. Something shows up later, you'll need a paper trail."

I hesitated. She was right, but—

"You're going," she said. She jangled her keys. "Come on. I'll drive."

Juanita insisted I drape my arm around her neck as we crept slowly down the front steps. I hunched deeper into my jacket, hoping no one was watching. "Juanita," I said in a low voice, "it's just a bruise. I'll be stiff for a few days, then it'll disappear."

Juanita grunted under my weight. "Could be fractured."

Fractured. I grimaced. "Great."

We passed the potted rosemary. Corey peeked between its branches, his face pale in the shadows. He bit down on his lower lip and withdrew.

I twisted my head to try to catch another glimpse of him. This is where I needed to be. With Corey, not in some clinic. "Juanita, I'm fine, really. It's just a bruise—"

Juanita stopped. She eyed me coolly. "I'm not worried about your leg. I'm worried about your head."

My cheeks flamed. My head—because no one else remembered Amanda Schuyler.

*   *   *

No fractures, leg or skull, just a bruise the size of a cantaloupe. Between the wait, the exam—complete with X-rays—and Juanita's unwillingness to release me unfed, it was almost seven when I made it back to the school. I waited until Juanita sped away, then got out of my car and limped up the steps. I searched behind the rosemary. No Corey, but tucked between the planter and the wall was the book of magic tricks.

Corey veered away from me when he walked into the classroom next morning. Head down, he put his backpack in his cubby and shuffled to his desk.

At one point Lily, the girl seated next to him, opened his desk and took his crayons. "Lily," I said. "Put those back and ask Corey if you may borrow them."

"He's not here—" Lily sat up, startled. Her eyes grew as round as slammers when she saw Corey. Backing away, she dropped his crayons.

Corey sat quietly, hands folded in his lap.

Within an hour, the class had forgotten him again.

It took me several minutes to find Corey when I went out for lunch recess.

He huddled ten feet from the woman. No one stood beside her this time. Her hands lay still in that colorful expanse of glittering unicorns. I imagined the one she'd been working on while the dark-haired boy hovered over her. I tried to recall the boy's name or face, but all I could remember was that dull, black embroidery amid the stellar unicorns.

I limped toward them. Girls. There had been two girls, too. But I could remember nothing but a sense of them, like perfume lingering in a closed room.

Corey took a step toward the woman. Her face tilted toward him. She seemed to be talking to him, coaxing him—

I gasped at the image: *Corey resting his head in the woman's lap, fading like mist in sunlight to become—*

I stared at Corey and the woman, not daring to shift my gaze. As if by watching them, I could keep that little head from lowering itself to that glittering field.

The woman's hands nested in her lap. Corey leaned into the fence; it bowed behind him like a hammock.

Gritting my teeth, I pushed myself to a lunging jog. The bruise throbbed along my hip. I cupped my hands to my mouth and called.

Corey flinched at the sound of his name, but refused to look at me. He stepped closer to the woman and knelt before her. She reached to pull his head into her lap. . . .

I lumbered toward them, tensing against the pain. Three, four yards and I'd be there. Sucking in a deep breath, I shouted, "Corey, get away from her!"

He snapped upright, swinging to look at me. The woman touched his leg. She murmured something. He glared at me, then bent toward her. The woman ran her fingers through his hair—

I grasped him by the arm. The woman pulled her hand back, plucking a lock of his ginger hair.

"Corey," I said. I dragged him away, reaching out to steady him with my other hand. With a growl, he wrenched away from me and ran toward the buildings. I sagged with relief, then turned on the woman. "Who are you?" I said. "What do you want—?"

She was gone.

I knelt beside the rosemary, parting its branches. "Corey?"

Reaching behind the planter, I patted the landing. I withdrew my dust-covered fingers.

I sat next to the planter. Late afternoon closed around me. "I have a special book for you," I said, hoping he was within hearing. The shadows deepened. I glanced at my watch. Four-fourteen. "It's about dogs," I said. If I stayed too late and he refused to come out of hiding, he'd miss his dad. "Corey, I'm sorry about yesterday," I said. "Ms. Vargas took me to the doctor. By the time I got back, you were gone." I glanced at my watch again. Four-thirty-five. A car pulled up to the curb. I sat up. A teenage couple got out and strolled across the front lawn, arm in arm. "Corey," I said. "I'm going. I don't want you to miss your dad." I pulled the book on Samoyeds from my book bag. "I'll leave this for you," I said. "Behind the planter. I'll see you tomorrow, okay?"

I arrived at school early the next morning, to see if Corey had taken the book. A shoe peeped from the planter's shadow. Puzzled, I squatted beside the rosemary. Corey curled around the planter, his backpack tucked under his head. His mouth hung slack, his eyes were closed. My heart lurched. I reached in and touched him. He murmured, then jerked awake, eyes wide.

I wound my arms around him and pulled him out. I hugged him. The chill of him seeped through my sweater. I smoothed the hair from his face. "Corey, have you been here all night?"

He nodded.

The breath went out of me. "Your father . . . ?"

He looked at me blankly. "Father?"

"My God," I whispered. I held him tight, rocking him. "What has that woman done?"

I had to look up his father in the phone book. Corey's emergency card was gone. So was his cumulative file. When Mr. Ferris answered, he had no idea who I was. "There must be some mistake," he said curtly. "I don't have a son—"

"But Corey—"

"Corey," he said. His voice grew wistful. "That was my grandfather's name." The curtness returned. "Sorry. Wrong Ferris." He hung up.

I weighed the receiver in my hand, then set it down. I went into the nurse's office. Corey huddled under a pile of blankets. I sat next to him. "Hungry?" I said.

He shook his head.

Peggy breezed in, glanced at Corey, yanked open the medicine cabinet. She took out a bottle of lotion. "New student?" she said.

Corey had worked his way to the end of the line by the time I led my students into the classroom. The boy just ahead of him shut the door in his face as if he weren't there. I opened the door and, taking his hand, led him inside.

When I took roll, his name wasn't listed. I flipped through the old roll sheets. According to these, he'd never been listed. I wrote him in and marked him "present."

During independent reading time, I walked over and crouched beside him. "She can't have you," I said. "I won't let her."

I kept him in during morning recess. I read to him; he stared out the window at the field. I moved my chair so that he had to look at me. "What did she promise you?" I said. "Where is she trying to take you?"

He turned away from me.

I touched his knee. "Corey?"

He slumped in his chair, staring at his desk.

The hair tickled along the back of my neck. On a hunch, I opened his desk. It was empty.

*   *   *

I followed him onto the playground at lunchtime. He ran across the field to the fence. I tried to keep up, but the bruise slowed me down. I gritted my teeth, trying to ignore the pain. He spurted ahead. The woman sat in the corner, waiting, her right hand raised slightly. A glint of gold winked between her fingers.

Corey stumbled to a stop in front of her.

"Leave him alone!" I shouted. "Leave them *all* alone!"

Neither Corey nor the woman turned.

I tripped, somehow caught myself. I winced, closing my eyes—

The image swept through me like a flash flood: *Corey, the boy, the two girls, countless other children, resting their heads in the woman's lap. One by one they blazed and disappeared like shooting stars, the only trace of them the bright unicorns on the woman's rainbow skirt—*

I forced my eyes open. Corey inched closer to the woman, his shins brushing her knee. The woman plunged the needle in and out of the cloth like a seabird diving through waves. I limped up to her, clenching and unclenching my hands.

Beneath the woman's needle, the outline of a unicorn was slowly taking shape on a field of blue, stitched in lusterless ginger thread. I searched the constellation of unicorns for the dull, black one, that other boy's, but couldn't find it. I finally located it on its field of green—now as bright as all the others.

Then a dull shape caught my eye. I took a step closer. Amid all the sparkling, prancing unicorns stood one small, brown horse on a field of blue.

Me.

I stood beside the rainbow woman. Her needle stitched the blue cloth with my hair, filling in the outline of the tiny unicorn. I knelt, my breath quick and shallow as I waited anxiously for her to finish. I would be someone. I would no longer be forgotten. I would become—

Corey dropped to his knees.

I tried to reel the image back, tried to remember. For Corey's sake. For mine.

I would become one of those gleaming unicorns that danced in her eyes.

I looked slowly from the woman's lap.

And trembled, that forgotten longing aching through me. Too frightened to take her in all at once, I started with her hair, that thick, manzanita-red mane that tumbled over her shoulders, then the perfect oval of her chin, the strawberry ripeness of her lips, the gentle slope of her nose. I steeled myself. Her eyes . . .

Her eyes had no color—not even white or black. I gazed into them, knowing what I would find there when my own longing had peeled away the layers of this world: unicorns, tossing their heads, light spiraling down their horns. . . .

I held my breath. They were more beautiful than I remembered. And so many—herds of them, streaking through the woodlands like a meteor shower. My ears rang with the drum of their cloven hooves.

If this is what Corey wanted, to join these magnificent creatures, who was I to stand in his way? I took a step back.

Rage kindled in me. Who had stood in *my* way?

I froze. Mrs. Rodriguez.

Kneeling beside me, she had forced my head up so that I could no longer see the gold needle pierce the blue cloth. "An illusion, Mary," she said. "There is so much in the world, so many things to discover and explore and create. Don't give up everything for an illusion."

I fought her, fought her words and the urging of her hands as she forced me to look. . . .

I swallowed, my throat dry and tight. But if this was what Corey wanted, who was I to deny him?

I am no Mrs. Rodriguez.

I am no saint.

The unicorns wheeled and galloped before me, a stampede of light. Then one of the unicorns stopped and faced me.

It yearned toward me, its eyes overflowing with a terrible loneliness. Another unicorn stopped, and another, until at least a dozen stared back at me. The first unicorn's longing echoed from eye to eye.

Their sadness sickened me. Without looking away, I groped for Corey. My hand clasped his shoulder. I drew him to me, caging him with my elbows and cupping his chin in my hands. I raised his head. "Look, Corey," I said. "Look into her eyes. If this is what you want, I'll let you go. But be sure."

He squirmed. More unicorns stopped to gaze at us.

"I want to be like them!" he said.

"Look *hard* at them, Corey," I said, reluctant to fulfill my promise. "See how lonely they are?"

"And is it any different here?" the woman said, her voice as husky as woodsmoke. "You are lonely here, Corey. There you will have others of your kind."

I wet my lips. "Corey—"

The woman hissed. "Leave us, meddler. You have nothing to offer him."

"Nothing," Corey said. But the word trailed with doubt.

My heart pounded. What had Mrs. Rodriguez said? What had finally reached me?

But I couldn't find the words. Frantic, I lashed out. "What does *she* have to offer you? An illusion, Corey. A lie. It's not real. It's like the Kleenex trick—"

Corey strained against my arms. The unicorns loped away.

"Let him go," the woman said. "He is mine. You have nothing for him. Absolutely nothing."

I loosened my grip slowly. My voice cracked. "Maybe *I* don't, but this world does. I saw you, Corey. I wanted to be your friend. Other people will, too. And they'll want to see that Kleenex trick. They'll want to know what Willy named his new dog."

The unicorns returned, gazing at me intently.

"They'll chase leaves," I said. "They'll throw balls and shoes over the fence. Your father will pick you up and take you out for ice cream. And I can—-I can teach you the penny trick."

Corey stood still as my arms fell away. The unicorns crept closer—

Their faces changed. Josue peered back at me, and Amanda and Heather. Jason from Peggy's class last year and Mindy from Kristy's class two years ago. More. Children I had never known. . . .

I doubled around the ache in my stomach. I had stopped trying and I had failed them, all of them. I had failed Corey.

The woman blinked. Her eyes became colorless once more.

Corey cried out. He grabbed me, burrowing under my arm, his breath hot and damp through my sweater. I clung to him, resting my cheek on his head. His hair smelled of rosemary. My gaze fell to the woman's hands.

She jerked the needle, snapping the thread. Dull and hornless, the ginger unicorn sank into a fold as she stood. "You've promised him much," she said. "Don't let him down."

She vanished.

Corey choked back a sob. His hands twisted the hem of my sweater. I held him with one arm. With my free hand, I fished a Kleenex from my skirt pocket. Footsteps stampeded toward us. I jerked to look. Unicorns . . . ?

Children.

"Ms. Scibilin! Ms. Scibilin!" a chorus of voices shouted. Small hands pulled at us, some patting me, some patting Corey. "What's wrong with Corey? Is Corey all right? Corey, you okay?"

"He's fine," I said.

Corey's chest shuddered with a deep breath. Tears beaded his lashes. I handed him the Kleenex. He stared at it a minute, then looked up at me. Eagerness and wonder dwelt in those gray eyes. So did Mrs. Rodriguez. So did I.

He held up the Kleenex so that the other children could see it. "Want to see me make it disappear?" he said.

About the Author

Marina Fitch's short fiction has appeared/will appear in *F&SF, Asimov's, Desire Burn, Tales from Jabba's Palace, Pulphouse,* and *Marion Zimmer Bradley's Fantasy Magazine.* She is currently trimming a novel and plotting new ones. . . .

She lives in Watsonville, California, with her husband Mark, about a mile from the oak tree where the Virgin Mary appeared a few years ago. She works as a PIP aide—playing with children one-on-one in a playroom filled with toys. Her previous "real" jobs included stints as editor, java jockey, bookstore clerk, secretary, journalist, luthier, busker, and publishing minion. She was once offered a job as a pitcher of Kool-Aid, a position which she now regrets turning down. Of her writing she says, "My experiences and my dreams shape my fiction. Who knows what I might have written had I danced in front of Kmart in that Kool-Aid suit."

KAREN JOY FOWLER

THE BREW

Peter: **Karen Joy Fowler**'s "The Brew," which deals with both the miraculous and the absurdly horrible side of immortality, is one of my favorite stories in this collection. But Karen is probably best known, not for science fiction or fantasy, but for the excellent and unusual historical novel, *Sarah Canary.* She has also published a book of stories called *Artificial Things.* Karen lives in Davis, as I do; along with my wife and myself, that makes at least three people I know of who don't teach at the local branch of the University of California.

Janet: After the first time I read a Karen Joy Fowler story, I wrote her an honest-to-God fan letter, enclosing the story and asking her to sign it. We have since become friends. I still read everything she writes, still send her fan letters, only now I'm hard-pressed to know what I like most, Karen or her work.

The Brew

─────⊸⊱❦⊰⊶─────

I SPENT LAST CHRISTMAS IN THE HAGUE. I HADN'T wanted to be in a foreign country and away from the family at Christmastime, but it had happened. Once I was there I found it lonely, but also pleasantly insulated. The streets were strung with lights and it rained often, so the lights reflected off the shiny cobblestones, came at you out of the clouds like pale, golden bubbles. If you could ignore the damp, you felt wrapped in cotton, wrapped against breaking. I heightened the feeling by stopping in an ice cream shop for a cup of tea with rum.

Of course it was an illusion. Ever since I was young, whenever I have traveled, my mother has contrived to have a letter sent, usually waiting for me, sometimes a day or two behind my arrival. I am her only daughter and she was not the sort to let an illness stop her, and so the letter was at the hotel when I returned from my tea. It was a very cheerful letter, very loving, and the message that it was probably the last letter I would get from her and that I needed to finish things up and hurry home was nowhere on the page, but only in my heart. She sent some funny family stories and some small-town gossip and the death she talked about was not her own, but belonged instead to an old man who was once a neighbor of ours.

After I read the letter I wanted to go out again, to see if I could recover the mood of the mists and the golden lights. I tried. I walked for hours, wandering in and out of the clouds, out to the canals and into the stores. Although my own children are too old for toys and too young for grandchildren, I did a lot of window-shopping at the toy stores. I was puzzling over the black elf they have in Holland, St. Nicholas' sidekick, wondering who he was and where he came into it all, when I saw a music box. It was a glass globe on a wooden base, and if you wound it, it played music and if you shook it, it snowed. Inside the globe there was a tiny forest of ceramic trees and, in the center, a unicorn with a silver horn, corkscrewed, like a narwhal's, and one gaily bent foreleg. A unicorn, tinted blue and frolicking in the snow.

What appealed to me most about the music box was not the snow or the unicorn, but the size. It was a little world, all enclosed, and I could imagine it as a real place, a place I could go. A little winter. There was an aquarium in the lobby of my hotel and I had a similar reaction to it. A little piece of ocean there, in the dry land of the lobby. Sometimes we can find a smaller world where we can live, inside the bigger world where we cannot.

Otherwise the store was filled with items tied-in to *The Lion King*. Less enchanting items to my mind—why is it that children always side with the aristocracy? Little royalists, each and every one of us, until we grow up and find ourselves in the cubicle or the scullery. And even then there's a sense of injustice about it all. Someone belongs there, but surely not us.

I'm going to tell you a secret, something I have never told anyone before. I took an oath when I was seventeen years old and have never broken it, although I cannot, in general, be trusted with secrets, and usually try to warn people of this before they confide in me. But the oath was about the man who died, my old neighbor, and so I am no longer bound to it. The secret takes the form of a story.

I should warn you that parts of the story will be hard to believe. Parts of it are not much to my credit, but I don't suppose you'll have trouble believing those. It's a big story, and this is just a small piece of it, my piece, which ends with my mother's letter and the Hague and the unicorn music box.

It begins in Bloomington, Indiana, the year I turned ten. It snowed early and often that year. My best friend Bobby and I built caves of snow, choirs of snowmen, and bridges that collapsed if you ever tried to actually walk them.

We had a neighbor who lived next door to me and across the street from Bobby. His name was John McBean. Until that year McBean had been a figure of almost no interest to us. He didn't care for children much, and why should he? Behind his back we called him Rudolph, because he had a large, purplish nose, and cold weather whitened the rest of his face into paste so his nose stood out in startling contrast. He had no wife, no family that we were aware of. People used to pity that back then. He seemed to us quite an old man, grandfather age, but we were children, what did we know? Even now I have no idea what he did for a living. He was retired when I knew him, but I have no idea of what he was retired from. Work, such as our fathers did, was nothing very interesting, nothing to speculate on. We thought the name McBean rather funny, and then he was quite the skinflint, which struck us all, even our parents, as delightful, since he actually was Scottish. It gave rise to many jokes, limp, in retrospect, but pretty rich back then.

One afternoon that year Mr. McBean slipped in his icy yard. He went down with a roar. My father ran out to him, but as my father was helping him up, McBean tried to hit him in the chin. My father came home much amused. "He said I was a British spy," my father told my mother.

"You devil," she said. She kissed him.

He kissed her back. "It had something to do with Bonnie Prince Charlie. He wants to see a Stuart on the throne of England. He seemed to think I was preventing it."

As luck would have it this was also the year that Disney ran a television episode on the Great Pretender. I have a vague picture in my mind of a British actor—the same one who appeared with Haley Mills in *The Moon Spinners*. Whatever happened to him, whoever he was?

So Bobby and I gave up the ever-popular game of World War II and began instead, for a brief period, to play at being Jacobites. The struggle for the throne of England involved less direct confrontation, fewer sound effects, and less running about. It was a game of stealth, of hiding and escaping, altogether a more adult activity.

It was me who got the idea of breaking into the McBean cellar as a covert operation on behalf of the prince. I was interested in the cellar, having begun to note how often and at what odd hours McBean went down there. The cellar window could be seen from my bedroom. Once I rose late at night and in the short time I watched, the light went on and off three times. It seemed a signal. I told Bobby that Mr. McBean might be holding the prince captive down there and that we should go and see. This plan added a real sense of danger to our imaginary game, without, we thought, actually putting us into peril.

The cellar door was set at an incline and such were the times that it shocked us to try it and find it locked. Bobby thought he could fit through the little window, whose latch could be lifted with a pencil. If he couldn't, I certainly could, though I was desperately hoping it wouldn't come to that—already at age ten I was more of an idea person. Bobby had the spirit. So I offered to go around the front and distract Mr. McBean long enough for Bobby to try the window. I believe that I said he shouldn't actually enter, that we would save that for a time when McBean was away. That's the way I remember it, my saying that.

And I remember that it had just snowed again, a fresh, white powder

and a north wind, so the snow blew off the trees as if it was still coming
down. It was bright, one of those paradoxical days of sun and ice, and so
much light everything was drowned in it so you stumbled about as if
there were no light at all. My scarf was iced with breath and my footprints were as large as a man's. I knocked at the front door, but my
mittens muffled the sound. It took several tries and much pounding
before Mr. McBean answered, too long to be accounted for simply by the
mittens. When he did answer, he did it without opening the door.

"Go on with you," he said. "This is not a good time."

"Would you like your walk shoveled?" I asked him.

"A slip of a girl like you? You couldn't even lift the shovel." I imagine there is a tone, an expression, that would make this response affec-
tionate, but Mr. McBean affected neither. He opened the door enough to
tower over me with his blue nose, his gluey face, and the clenched set of
his mouth.

"Bobby would help me. Thirty cents."

"Thirty cents! And that's the idlest boy God ever created. Thirty
cents!!?"

"Since it's to be split. Fifteen cents each."

The door was closing again.

"Twenty cents."

"I've been shoveling my own walk long enough. No reason to stop."

The door clicked shut. The whole exchange had taken less than a
minute. I stood undecidedly at the door for another minute, then stepped
off the porch, into the yard. I walked around the back. I got there just in
time to see the cellar light go on. The window was open. Bobby was
gone.

I stood outside, but there was a wind, as I've said, and I couldn't hear
and it was so bright outside and so dim within, I could hardly see. I knew
that Bobby was inside, because there were no footprints leading away but
my own. I had looked through the window on other occasions so I knew
the light was a single bulb, hanging by its neck like a turnip, and that
there were many objects between me and it, old and broken furniture,
rusted tools, lawn mowers and rakes, boxes piled into stairs. I waited. I
think I waited a very long time. The light went out. I waited some more. I
moved to a tree, using it as a windbreak until finally it was clear there
was no point in waiting any longer. Then I ran home, my face stinging
with cold and tears, into our living room, where my mother pulled off my
stiff scarf and rubbed my hands until the pins came into them. She made
me cocoa with marshmallows. I would like you to believe that the next
few hours were a very bad time for me, that I suffered a good deal more
than Bobby did.

That case being so hard to make persuasively, I will tell you instead what was happening to him.

Bobby did, indeed, manage to wiggle in through the window, although it was hard enough to give him some pause as to how he would get out again. He landed on a stack of wooden crates, conveniently offset so that he could descend them like steps. Everywhere was cobwebs and dust; it was too dark to see this, but he could feel it and smell it. He was groping his way forward, hand over hand, when he heard the door at the top of the stairs. At the very moment the light went on, he found himself looking down the empty eyeslit of a suit of armor. It made him gasp; he couldn't help it. So he heard the footsteps on the stairs stop suddenly and then begin again, wary now. He hid himself behind a barrel. He thought maybe he'd escape notice—there was so much stuff in the cellar and the light so dim—and that was the worst time, those moments when he thought he might make it, much worse than what came next, when he found himself staring into the cracked and reddened eyes of Mr. McBean.

"What the devil are you doing?" McBean asked. He had a smoky, startled voice. "You've no business down here."

"I was just playing a game," Bobby told him, but he didn't seem to hear.

"Who sent you? What did they tell you?"

He seemed to be frightened—of Bobby!—and angry, but that was to be expected, but there was something else that began to dawn on Bobby only slowly. His accent had thickened with every word. Mr. McBean was deadly drunk. He reached into Bobby's hiding place and hauled him out of it and his breath, as Bobby came closer, was as ripe as spoiled apples.

"We were playing at putting a Stuart on the throne," Bobby told him, imagining he could sympathize with this, but it seemed to be the wrong thing to say.

He pulled Bobby by the arm to the stairs. "Up we go."

"I have to be home by dinner." By now Bobby was very frightened.

"We'll see. I have to think what's to be done with you," said McBean.

They reached the door, then moved on into the living room where they sat for a long time in silence while McBean's eyes turned redder and redder and his fingers pinched into Bobby's arm. With his free hand, he drank. Perhaps this is what kept him warm, for the house was very cold and Bobby was glad he still had his coat on. Bobby was both trembling and shivering.

"Who told you about Prince Charlie?" McBean asked finally. "What did they say to you?" So Bobby told him what he knew, the Disney version, long as he could make it, waiting, of course, for me to do something, to send someone. McBean made the story longer by interrupting with suspicious and skeptical questions. Eventually the questions ceased and his grip loosened. Bobby hoped he might be falling asleep. His eyes were lowered. But when Bobby stopped talking, McBean shook himself awake and his hand was a clamp on Bobby's forearm again. "What a load of treacle," he said, his voice filled with contemptuous spit. "It was nothing like that."

He stared at Bobby for a moment and then past him. "I've never told this story before," he said and the pupils of his eyes were as empty and dark as the slit in the armor. "No doubt I shall regret telling it now."

In the days of the bonnie prince, the head of the McBane clan was the charismatic Ian McBane. Ian was a man with many talents, all of which he had honed and refined over the fifty-odd years he had lived so far. He was a botanist, an orientalist, a poet, and a master brewer. He was also a very godly man, a paragon, perhaps. At least in this story. To be godly is a hard thing and may create a hard man. A godly man is not necessarily a kindly man, although he can be, of course.

Now in those days, the woods and caves of Scotland were filled with witches; the church waged a constant battle to keep the witches dark and deep. Some of them were old and haggish, but others were mortally beautiful. The two words go together, mind you, mortal and beautiful. Nothing is so beautiful as that which is about to fade.

These witches were well aware of Ian McBane. They envied him his skills in the brewery, coveted his knowledge of chemistry. They, themselves, were always boiling and stirring, but they could only do what they knew how to do. Besides, his godliness irked them. Many times they sent the most beautiful among them, tricked out further with charms and incantations, to visit Ian McBane in his bedchamber and offer what they could offer in return for expert advice. They were so touching in their eagerness for knowledge, so unaware of their own desirability. They had the perfection of dreams. But Ian, who was, after all, fifty and not twenty, withstood them.

All of Scotland was hoping to see Charles Edward Stuart on the throne, and from hopes they progressed to rumors and from rumors to sightings. Then came the great victory at Falkirk. Naturally Ian wished to do his part and naturally, being a man of influence and standing, his part must be a large one. It was the sin of ambition which gave the witches an opening.

This time the woman they sent was not young and beautiful, but old and sweet. She was everyone's mother. She wore a scarf on her hair and her stockings rolled at her ankles. Blue rivers ran just beneath the skin of her legs. Out of her sleeve she drew a leather pouch.

"From the end of the world," she said. "Brought me by a black warrior riding a white elephant, carried over mountains and across oceans." She made it a lullaby. Ian was drowsy when she finished. So she took his hand and emptied the pouch into his palm, closing it for him. When he opened his hand, he held the curled shards and splinters of a unicorn's horn.

Ian had never seen a unicorn's horn before, although he knew that the king of Denmark had an entire throne made of them. A unicorn's horn is a thing of power. It purifies water, nullifies poison. The witch reached out to Ian, slit his thumb with her one long nail, so his thumb ran blood. Then she touched the wound with a piece of horn. His thumb healed before his eyes, healed as if it had never been cut, the blood running back inside, the cut sealing over like water.

In return Ian gave the witch what she asked. He had given her his godliness, too, but he didn't know this at the time. When the witch was gone, Ian took the horn and ground it into dust. He subjected it to one more test of authenticity. He mixed a few grains into a hemlock concoction and fed it to his cat, stroking it down her throat. The cat followed the hemlock with a saucer of milk, which she wiped, purring, from her whiskers.

Ian had already put down a very fine single malt whiskey, many bottles, enough for the entire McBane clan to toast the coronation of Charles Stuart. It was golden in color and ninety proof, enough to make a large man feel larger without incapacitating him. Ian added a few pinches of the horn to every bottle. The whiskey color shattered and then vanished, so the standing bottle was filled with liquid the color of rainwater, but if you shook it, it pearled like the sea. Ian bottled his brew with a unicorn label, the unicorn enraged, two hooves slicing the air.

Have you ever heard of the American ghost dancers? The Boxers of China? Same sort of thing here. Ian distributed his whiskey to the McBanes before they marched off to Culloden. Taken just before the battle, Ian assured them that the drink would make them invulnerable. Sword wounds would seal up overnight, bullets would pass through flesh as if it were air.

I don't suppose your Disney says very much about Culloden. A massacre is a hard thing to set to music. Certainly they tell no stories and sing no songs about the McBanes that day. Davie McBane was the first to go, reeling about drunkenly and falling beneath one of the McBanes' own horses. Little Angus went next, shouting and racing down the top of a small hill, but before he could strike a single blow for Scotland, a dozen arrows jutted from him at all points. His name was a joke and he made a big, fat target. His youngest brother Robbie, a boy of only fifteen years, followed Angus in like a running back, and so delirious with whiskey that he wore no helmet and carried no weapon. His stomach was split open like a purse. An hour later, only two of the McBanes still lived. The rest had died grotesquely, humorously, without accounting for a single enemy death.

When news reached home, the McBane wives and daughters armed themselves with kitchen knives and went in search of Ian. They thought he had lied about the unicorn horn; they thought he had knowingly substituted the inferior tooth of a fish instead. Ian was already gone, and with enough time and forethought to have removed every bottle of the unicorn brew and taken it with him. This confirmed the women's suspicions, but the real explanation was different. Ian had every expectation the whiskey would work. When the McBanes returned, he didn't wish to share any more of it.

The women set fire to his home and his brewery. Ian saw it from a distance, from a boat at sea, exploding into the sky like a star. The women dumped every bottle of whiskey they found until the rivers bubbled and the fish swam upside down. But none of the whiskey bore the unicorn label. Ian was never seen or heard from again.

"Whiskey is subtle stuff. It's good for heartache; it works a treat against shame. But, even laced with unicorn horn, it cannot mend a man who has been split in two by a sword stroke. It cannot mend a man who no longer has a head. It cannot mend a man with a dozen arrows growing from his body like extra arms. It cannot give a man back his soul."

The story seemed to be over, although Prince Charles had never appeared in it. Bobby had no feeling left in his hand. "I see," he said politely.

McBean shook him once, then released him. He fetched a pipe. When he lit a match, he held it to his mouth and his breath flamed like a dragon's. "What will I do to you if you tell anyone?" he asked Bobby. This was a rhetorical question. He continued without pausing. "Something bad. Something so bad you'd have to be an adult even to imagine it."

So Bobby told me none of this. I didn't see him again that day. He did not come by, and when I finally went over his mother told me he was home, but that he was not feeling well, had gone to bed. "Don't worry," she said, in response, I suppose, to the look on my face. "Just a chill. Nothing to worry about."

He missed school the next day and the next after that. When I finally saw him, he was casual. Offhand. As if it had all happened so long ago, he had forgotten. "He caught me," Bobby said. "He was very angry. That's all. We better not do it again."

It was the end of our efforts to put a Stuart on the throne. There are days, I admit, when I'm seeing the dentist and I pick up *People* in the waiting room and there they are, the current sad little lot of Windsors, and I have a twinge of guilt. I just didn't care enough to see it through. I enjoyed Charles and Diane's wedding as much as the next person. How was I to know?

Bobby and I were less and less friends after that. It didn't happen all at once, but bit by bit, over the summer mostly. Sex came between us. Bobby went off and joined Little League. He turned out to be really good at it, and he met a lot of boys who didn't live so near to us, but had houses he could bike to. He dumped me, which hurt in an impersonal, inevitable way. I believed I had brought it on myself, leaving him that day, going home to a warm house and never saying a word to anyone. At that age, at that time, I did not believe this was something a boy would have done.

So Bobby and I continued to attend the same school and see each other about in our yards, and play sometimes when the game was big and involved other people as well. I grew up enough to understand what our parents thought of McBean, that he was often drunk. This was what had made his nose purple and made him rave about the Stuarts and made him slip in his snowy yard, his arms flapping like wings as he fell. "It's a miracle," my mother said, "that he never breaks a bone." But nothing much more happened between Bobby and me until the year we turned sixteen, me in February, him in May.

He was tired a lot that year and developed such alarming bruises under his eyes that his parents took him to a doctor who sent them right away to a different doctor. At dinner a few weeks later, my mother said she had something to tell me. Her eyes were shiny and her voice was coarse. "Bobby has leukemia," she said.

"He'll get better," I said quickly. Partly I was asking, but mostly I was warning her not to tell me differently. I leaned into her and she must have thought it was for comfort, but it wasn't. I did it so I wouldn't be able to see her face. She put her arm around me and I felt her tears falling on the top of my hair.

Bobby had to go to Indianapolis for treatments. Spring came and summer and he missed the baseball season. Fall, and he had to drop out of school. I didn't see him much, but his mother was over for coffee sometimes, and she had grown sickly herself, sad and thin and gray. "We have to hope," I heard her telling my mother. "The doctor says he is doing as well as we could expect. We're very encouraged." Her voice wobbled defiantly.

Bobby's friends came often to visit; I saw them trooping up the porch, all vibrant and healthy, stamping the slush off their boots and trailing their scarves. They went in noisy, left quiet. Sometimes I went with them. Everyone loved Bobby, though he lost his hair and swelled like a beached seal and it was hard to remember that you were looking at a gifted athlete, or even a boy.

Spring came again, but after a few weeks of it, winter returned suddenly with a strange storm. In the morning when I left for school, I saw a new bud completely encased in ice, and three dead birds whose feet had frozen to the telephone wires. This was the day Arnold Becker gave me the message that Bobby wanted to see me. "Right away," Arnie said. "This afternoon. And just you. None of your girlfriends with you."

In the old days Bobby and I used to climb in and out each other's windows, but this was for good times and for intimacy; I didn't even consider it. I went to the front door and let his mother show me to his room as if I didn't even know the way. Bobby lay in his bed, with his puffy face and a new tube sticking into his nose and down his throat. There was a strong, strange odor in the room. I was afraid it was Bobby and wished not to get close enough to see.

He had sores in his mouth, his mother had explained to me. It was difficult for him to eat or even to talk. "You do the talking," she suggested. But I couldn't think of anything to say.

And anyway, Bobby came right to the point. "Do you remember," he asked me, "that day in the McBean cellar?" Talking was an obvious effort. It made him breathe hard, as if he'd been running.

Truthfully, I didn't remember. Apparently I had worked to forget it. I remember it now, but at the time, I didn't know what he was talking about.

"Bonnie Prince Charlie," he said, with an impatient rasp so I thought he was delirious. "I need you to go back. I need you to bring me a bottle of whiskey from McBean's cellar. There's a unicorn on the label."

"Why do you want whiskey?"

"Don't ask McBean. He'll never give it to you. Just take it. You would still fit through the window."

"Why do you want whiskey?"

"The unicorn label. Very important. Maybe," said Bobby, "I just want to taste one really good whiskey before I die. You do this and I'll owe you forever. You'll save my life."

He was exhausted. I went home. I did not plan to break into McBean's cellar. It was a mad request from a delusional boy. It saddened me, but I felt no obligation. I did think I could get him some whiskey. I had some money, I would spare no expense. But I was underage. I ate my dinner and tried to think who I could get to buy me liquor, who would do it, and who would even know a fine whiskey if they saw one. And while I was working out the problem I began, bit by bit, piece by piece, bite by bite, to remember. First I remembered the snow, remembered standing by the tree watching the cellar window with snow swirling around me. Then I remembered offering to shovel the walk. I remembered the footprints leading into the cellar window. It took all of dinner, most of the time when I was falling asleep, some concentrated sessions when I woke during the night. By morning, when the sky was light again, I remembered it complete.

It had been my idea and then I had let Bobby execute it and then I had abandoned him. I left him there that day and in another story, someone else's story, he was tortured or raped or even killed and eaten, although you'd have to be an adult to believe in these possibilities. The whole time he was in the McBean house I was lying on my bed and worrying about him, thinking, boy, he's really going to get it, but mostly worrying what I could tell my parents that would be plausible and would keep me out of it. The only way I could think of to make it right, was to do as he'd asked, and to break into the cellar again.

I also got caught, got caught right off. There was a trap. I tripped a wire rigged to a stack of boards; they fell with an enormous clatter and McBean was there, just as he'd been for Bobby, with those awful cavernous eyes, before I could make it back out the window.

"Who sent you?" he shouted at me. "What are you looking for?"

So I told him.

"That sneaking, thieving, lying boy," said McBean. "It's a lie, what he's said. How could it be true? And anyway, I couldn't spare it." I could see, behind him, the bottles with the unicorn label. There were half a dozen of them. All I asked was for one.

"He's a wonderful boy." I found myself crying.

"Get out," said McBean. "The way you came. The window."

"He's dying," I said. "And he's my best friend." I crawled back out while McBean stood and watched me, and walked back home with a face filled with tears. I was not giving up. There was another dinner I didn't eat and another night I didn't sleep. In the morning it was snowing, as if spring had never come. I planned to cut class, and break into the cellar again. This time I would be looking for traps. But as I passed McBean's house, carrying my books and pretending to be on my way to school, I heard his front door.

"Come here," McBean called angrily from his porch. He gave me a bottle, wrapped in red tissue. "There," he said. "Take it." He went back inside, but as I left he called again from behind the door. "Bring back what he doesn't drink. What's left is mine. It's mine, remember." And at that exact moment, the snow turned to rain.

For this trip I used the old window route. Bobby was almost past swallowing. I had to tip it from a spoon into his throat and the top of his mouth was covered with sores, so it burned him badly. One spoonful was all he could bear. But I came back the next day and repeated it and the next and by the fourth he could take it easily and after a week, he was eating again, and after two weeks I could see that he was going to live, just by looking in his mother's face. "He almost died of the cure," she told me. "The chemo. But we've done it. We've turned the corner." I left her thanking God and went into Bobby's room, where he was sitting up and looking like a boy again. I returned half the bottle to McBean.

"Did you spill any?" he asked angrily, taking it back. "Don't tell me it took so much."

And one night, that next summer, in Bryan's Park with the firecrackers going off above us, Bobby and I sat on a blanket and he told me McBean's story.

We finished school and graduated. I went to IU, but Bobby went to college in Boston and settled there. Sex came between us again. He came home once to tell his mother and father that he was gay and then took off like the whole town burned to the touch.

Bobby was the first person that I loved and lost, although there have, of course, been others since. Twenty-five years later I tracked him down and we had a dinner together. We were awkward with each other; the evening wasn't a great success. He tried to explain to me why he had left, as an apology for dumping me again. "It was just so hard to put the two lives together. At the time I felt that the first life was just a lie. I felt that everyone who loved me had been lied to. But now—being gay seems to be all I am sometimes. Now sometimes I want someplace where I can get away from it. Someplace where I'm just Bobby again. That turned out to be real, too." He was not meeting my eyes and then suddenly he was. "In the last five years I've lost twenty-eight of my friends."

"Are you all right?" I asked him.

"No. But if you mean, do I have AIDS, no, I don't. I should, I think, but I don't. I can't explain it."

There was a candle between us on the table. It flickered ghosts into his eyes. "You mean the whiskey," I said.

"Yeah. That's what I mean."

The whiskey had seemed easy to believe in when I was seventeen and Bobby had just had a miraculous recovery and the snow had turned to rain. I hadn't believed in it much since. I hadn't supposed Bobby had either, because if he did, then I really had saved his life back then and you don't leave a person who saves your life without a word. Those unicorn horns you read about in Europe and Scandinavia. They all turned out to be from narwhals. They were brought in by the Vikings through China. I've read a bit about it. Sometimes, someone just gets a miracle. Why not you? "You haven't seen Mr. McBean lately," I said. "He's getting old. Really old. Deadly old."

"I know," said Bobby, but the conclusion he drew was not the same as mine. "Believe me, I know. That whiskey is gone. I'd have been there to get it if it wasn't. I'd have been there twenty-eight times."

Bobby leaned forward and blew the candle out. "Remember when we wanted to live forever?" he asked me. "What made us think that was such a great idea?"

I never went inside the toy store in the Hague. I don't know what the music box played—"Edelweiss," perhaps, or "Lara's Theme," nothing to do with me. I didn't want to expose the strong sense I had that it had been put there for me, had traveled whatever travels, just to be there in that store window for me to see at that particular moment, with any evidence to the contrary. I didn't want to expose my own fragile magic to the light of day.

Certainly I didn't buy it. I didn't need to. It was already mine, only not here, not now. Not as something I bought for myself, on an afternoon by myself, in a foreign country with my mother dying a world away. But as something I found one Christmas morning, wrapped in red paper. I stood looking through the glass and wished that Bobby and I were still friends. That he knew me well enough to have bought me the music box as a gift.

And then I didn't wish that at all. Already I have too many friends, care too much about too many people, have exposed myself to loss on too many sides. I could never have imagined as a child how much it could hurt you to love people. It takes an adult to imagine such a thing. And that's the end of my story.

If I envy anything about McBean now, it is his solitude. But no, that's not really what I wish for either. When I was seventeen I thought McBean was a drunk because he had to have the whiskey so often. Now, when I believe in the whiskey at all, I think, like Bobby, that drinking was just the only way to live through living forever.

ABOUT THE AUTHOR

Karen Joy Fowler was born in Bloomington, Indiana. She now lives in Davis, California, with her husband and two children. Her novel, *Sarah Canary,* won the Commonwealth Book Award for best first novel by a Californian. It has been compared to E. L. Doctorow's *Ragtime.* The *New York Times Book Review* said of it, ". . . Ms. Fowler's prose is beautifully simple and evocative, and the narrative conception itself is a *tour de force.*" She has also published *Artificial Things,* a collection of short stories. She has written many short stories which have been published in all manner of magazines and anthologies.

Fowler's novel-in-progress is a feminist baseball novel.

GEORGE GUTHRIDGE

MIRROR OF LOP NOR

Peter: **George Guthridge**'s story is not necessarily an easy read; it *is* a worthwhile one. His own statement regarding his remarkable diptych, "Mirror of Lop Nor," is well worth including here:

> "Lop Nor: Reflection" and "Lop Nor: Refraction" are meant to stand on their own, but also, mirroring one another, to form a third story. A mirror is a triad: subject, image, object. A unicorn looks in the mirror; a narwhal stares back. They eye each other without blinking. Which is the image, which the reality?

Janet: George and I met in the early eighties because of his Nebula-contending African-based short story, "The Quiet." We have essentially been writing together ever since. For multitudinous reasons, we're often called the hot-and-cold team. That we come at things differently is not surprising. I am, by nature, more European gypsy than anything else; he is an Eskimo at heart, internal and cautious. My training is as a journalist, his as a researcher. What we do have in common is a serious love of words, a fascination for social and cultural anthropology, and an obsession with *The Great Gatsby*. George once counted the em-dashes in Fitzgerald's novel; I once fell in lust with a man—albeit briefly—simply because he, like Gatsby, looked wonderful in a pink suit.

Mirror of Lop Nor

For Noi

—reflection—

I
hear
your
hooves
above me,
cold as the
soul of the Khan.
Young, wild horses
brown as the land I
loved, manes the hair
of graves. Do not enter
here in search of Umber
or pasture, young horses.

THE AFTERLIFE IS A LIE. I KNOW: I AM DEAD, YET have no Khan to serve, no ghost horses to ride, not even the memory of women lamenting me. No one knows where I died except dust; and only wind wails for me, whistling in mockery at my stupidity and despair. *Umber, who captured the Lin and witnessed the whinnying of the Lung-Ta! In whose arms do you lie forever?*

Such voices fill the desert.

In my silence I scream for them to stop, but they do not stop, the wind never stops shrieking. My only hope lies in salty waters: that Lake Lop Nor will crawl across the desert, engulf my bones, evaporate my soul, rain it down on the grasslands of my beloved Mongolia, so far, far away.

Do you love me? Bragda asked. *Taste my blood.*

I lie in terror of dark desert.

Taste my blood, Umber, she said.

So hard do I yearn for the lake that sometimes I hear it spill slowly southwest toward my release, the wind scalloping the edge, its waters filling the created cavity. Then I realize it is only the wind, always only the wind, and I rail as I remember how I scoffed at water while I lived, reminding me as it did of my father's pathetic prayers for summer rains for his sickly winter wheat.

"He who prefers water over kumiss should seek an oasis and sell pottery," I would say to Bragda after I became a Mongol. Was I not one of the Khan's Lightning Messengers, able to ride for days without stopping, riding even while asleep, the rhythm of the horse like Bragda in her abandon, breathy but never moaning? On long rides, when the water in the goatskin gave out, had I not tasted the hot sweet suck of horse blood?

My pride brash as brass in morning sunlight.

Like flies on a dead man's face.

Do you love me, Umber? she asked. *Taste my blood. The Mongols say it holds the soul.*

Now my pride is sand searing a throat whose flesh has shriveled to parchment. Wind exposes a skull, pelts my jawbone with sand, a million stinging insults. Such is the final field of the farmer's son who fancied himself Mongol, the wretch who lassoed the Lin, the husband who loved his wife but never told her so.

Instead, I left her among Mongols while I rode in joy across empire, my love seemingly only for danger and distance. Alone, she waited for my return or word of my death, surely always fearful, her face framed by a traditional headdress whose braids and bangles were strange to her, cooking mutton instead of meals of summer cabbage and winter wheat, everything foreign to her stomach and soul.

Not room enough in this great grave for so many regrets.

Come Lake Lop Nor.

Breach my bones.

Send me home to Bragda.

Taste my blood, she said.

How many days and dreams have passed since that late-winter night when last I slept beside her, warm against her flesh, warm beneath the sheepskin? Even now I see her silhouetted against the wall of the ger as the oil-lamp flickers and the squatty burkan gods watch from near the door. She disrobes: taut breasts, belly that sadly never stored a child, buttocks like mounds of black bread. I have returned from a thirty-day ride, so exhausted I want to sob like a weak woman, giddy from the pitching and yawing of the pony and the endless hours without real rest. Naked, she bows and places the small fruit offering I have brought home into the spirit house we keep in honor of our original heritage.

Then she kneels beside me, opens the boogda bag, the marmot kettled in its own skin, and with forefinger and thumb brings meat to my mouth. I am too exhausted to chew. I down the meal with marmot-grease broth, reach for her.

"A bad time," she whispers. "I am sorry. . . ."

I ignore her protest and take her roughly, stuporous with desire, thankful to be between someone else's legs rather than the horse between mine. After, she squeezes a drop of semen from me, touches it to her tongue.

"You are my lord . . . Umber."

She has never grown accustomed to my new name, for I have been Umber only since my twentieth year, son of a farmer whose name I have not spoken since that day I welcomed the enemy. He lost a son and I an ancestry the instant I took an assassin's arrow meant for Otogai, the Khan's third son—and lived to become Mongol.

I put my arm around her waist.

"It did not bother you that I am bloodied?" she asks.

I say nothing. It bothers me, but I say nothing.

Her eyes are lowered. A sign of respect. In her, a sign, I sometimes imagine, almost of reverence. It frightens me, her faith in me, and I remember again that day she stood with me when the Mongols came.

How happy I was when the army of the Khan breached the Great Wall and overran the lands of my former ancestry with its barren, barefoot fields of sickly winter wheat! It seemed that only Bragda and I did not flee before the invaders. My neighbors shook their heads at my foolishness as they herded toward the cities. "You would stay and fight for this land that yielded so little?" Father begged as he bundled our family possessions in his cart. "The Mongols have no love for farming. They will not remain. Soon we will return, my son. Do not sacrifice yourself."

Sacrifice? I stay to see the land trampled.

"You will die quickly, uselessly," he said. "A sword slash, and I will have lost my only child. And do you know what they will do to your beautiful bride?"

Why did you remain beside me amid that desolation, Bragda? You would never say.

I draw my fingers along her silken back. She shivers—quietly smiles—then touches herself between her legs and holds two fingers close to my lips. "Taste my blood, Umber," she says. "The Mongols say it holds the soul. Know me as no other man ever has—or ever will."

No woman should dare ask a man such a thing. Yet her fingers remain extended, and her eyes plead.

Her words shake me not only for what she asks but for the memory they instill. Not virginal when we wed, which was why my father, a poor farmer, was able to buy me such a beauty, her face round as the moon, soft as moonlight among lilies in bloom, feet so small you would have thought them bound, toes flexible enough that she sometimes uses them to massage my manhood, and she giggling. She has never hinted about who took her before I did.

Time ticks, her heart beating against my chest, and I sense fear emanate from her like warmth from a candle.

She lifts her eyes—moist with love, as the rest of her has so often been for me. Demean myself this way for her, I sense, and I will never lose her love no matter how many rides I might require—of her, away from her. I know not why it is important to her, yet I sense a gateway of our lives hinges on this moment. Just as it did that sun-scorched afternoon when we stood together—she behind me, trembling; I could sense her trembling—and watched the Khan's cavalry march a hundred abreast across the fallow, hallowed ground on which my ancestors toiled and dreamed and died.

I lift my head toward her fingers.

Am interrupted by the tent's wood-framed flap slapping open.

Bragda jerks her hand away, desperate to squirm beneath the sheepskin as Jailspur enters without knocking. There is no need for the formality of knocking. Commander of the Messengers, the warrior to whom Otogai himself gave the task of teaching me how to ride, Jailspur has treated me as the son he never had, and in return I have accorded him the respect my real father deserved. As usual he is impatient, suspicious, his scant mustache and beard seeming to give his aged, weathered face a perpetual sneer, but beneath that demeanor dwells the man who not only showed me how to handle a horse and how to survive, but also lovingly drilled into me tales of honor and of the yasak, the Khan's code of laws.

He glances around the ger as if expecting treachery, then haughtily peers down on us, the wrinkled folds of his eyelids like hoods. "You ride," he says.

"But I just returned."

"You would disobey me?"

"Of course not." Already I am rising, pulling myself into sheepskin cloak and felt socks, my joints sore and stiff. "Where would you have me go?"

"Khwarezm. You will tell Temujin that we have captured an Uighur monk who ciphers symbols."

To bring such a message to the Khan himself? My heart should skip as joyfully as a flat stone. Not only is it the highest honor to serve him personally, he rewards Messengers regardless of their message—one reason for his warfare success—rather than adopting the Chinese custom of executing bearers of bad fortune. The news will delight him. For has he not said that those who read and write hold the power of gods? *Find a scribe who can pen our history,* he has declared, *and our glory will live forever.*

Instead of skipping, the stone sinks.

At least another three months without Bragda, who now pokes her head from under the covers, staring in horror from me to Jailspur. He looks away, abruptly ill at ease, and in that instant she briefly shakes her head at me in terror. Fear emanates from her in even greater waves.

When he eyes her again, his gaze registers contempt, as though he sees her nakedness despite the sheepskin cover.

And suddenly I *know*.

He has had her, against her will, while I was away.

He who taught me that warriors guilty of murder or adultery or urinating on water so respect the yasak that they will announce their transgression and expect to be put to death without ever having been accused.

My Mongol father.

Turning, he stalks into the night, me stumbling behind, pulling on boots. Wanting to kill him but knowing I cannot accuse, much less condemn. He is a commander. And I, after all, a foreigner.

Above us the Eternal Blue Heaven, ear to so many Mongol prayers, is but a black bowl crusted with icy stars that twinkle in mockery.

He reaches his tent, pauses, walks on. Perhaps he knows I am aware of what he has done but fears to involve his family. Perhaps he seeks a place where he can quietly murder me. If so, it would be a favor.

We wend through camp, he not acknowledging me behind him. The air, filled with the smell of smoke and butter and mutton, crackles with the cold. Snow snaps beneath our footfalls. I hear a woman humming, and I wonder what Bragda must be thinking. I wonder if she has snuffed the lamp and sits in darkness, humiliation emanating from her like heat.

When Jailspur reaches the edge of the huge camp, the clouds uncover the moon. It is as if he has ordered a curtain pulled back, nature acquiescing to his wishes. How many times in these five years since Bragda tugged the arrow shaft from my back and nursed me again to health have I witnessed Earth and Heaven side with the Mongols? I could kill him, but I cannot kill them all, and I have no power to fight the world.

On the grasslands, white-muzzled horses mill uneasily, many nervously pawing frozen ground, as if the renewed light has found out some conspiracy among them. There are five hundred of them—half the herd that was among the bounty from Kara Khitai, the enormous kingdom that once I called home. The rest are with the Khan. Rallying symbols as the Mongols march against Bukhara and Balkh.

Jailspur removes his caftan, tosses it onto the ground and, bare-chested despite the cold, spreads his arms, as if expecting the horses to come. They shy away, moving as with one mind.

"The finest steeds this side of eternity," he says, picking up his jacket and holding it in the crook of his arm as he gazes across the grasslands. "Were you or I born like the Khan, clutching a blood clot in our fist, then perhaps we, too, would own such an animal, eh Umber? Perhaps the Blue Heaven would smile on us as well."

I neither answer nor step up beside him as an equal. I remain behind, as a woman might. As an assassin might.

"I have delivered few messages these past years," he says. "I kept turning my responsibilities over to you. People have been laughing. I hear them say *old* behind their lips. What did you expect of me, Umber?"

"And yet you would have me go again."

This time it is his turn to be silent. He puts the caftan across his shoulder and, hunched as though burdened by the weight of the moon-light, saunters off toward a distant hill, the horses slowly scattering.

I watch him until he disappears into darkness, and when I turn to go back to my tent I am surprised to find Bragda behind me. She holds my leather armor and peaked metal helmet—my proudest possession other than the wife a poor, wise farmer chose for me—and I find myself trembling as I recall how she stood behind a husband branded a fool by his neighbors and insolent by his father, while the Khan's terrible cavalry came on. I tremble not from the fear I felt then but the love I feel now. Tremble so much that my teeth chatter. I clamp my lips shut.

She waits, eyes downcast, until I follow her cue and put on the armor and helmet. When she looks up at it there is a sad smile in her gaze. Perhaps she remembers how, when Jailspur gave me the helmet after a year's horseman-ship instruction, she said I was a Ki, the horned horse of Chinese legend.

From beside her feet—bare toes curled upon the snow—she lifts my saddlebags and leather drinking pouch. "I tucked a cabbage amid the dried meat and milk curds," she says. "I traded for it during"—the eyes again downcast—"during the time you were gone. It was to be your breakfast, after you were rested."

When she gives me the things our hands touch. The edges of her eyes tighten, a look of pain. "Go now, " she says.

"Bragda."

"Go. And do not look back, my love. The spirits will think you're not watching the trail, and will steal your eyes."

She backs away—hesitantly; now turning, hurrying off. I think I hear her crying, but it is only a mother humming a child asleep.

"I'll come back for you," I call out. "I will come back."

A dog barks. Smoke from a thousand tents rises into moonlight. I stand there until the day dawns violet against the hill toward which Jailspur walked, before I trudge to where the Lightning Mounts are hobbled and select the dapple-gray I often use for the first and last legs of journeys. I let the horse trot from camp, she seeming happy to be moving. Without nodding I pass women gathering dung for fires and boys tending horses and sheep. They eye me curiously. The ugly Chinese.

For three days I do not look back—not until I crest the summit of the eastern pass through the Heavenly Mountains and see Lung-Ta prayer-flags snapping in the wind, one color for each realm of the universe. All point back toward the northeast, the land of Khan. An odd, ill omen; winter winds usually blow south.

Rather than invoking the traditional prayer to the passes, I murmur to the Wind Horse, guardian of the elements of self-control: body, speech, mind. "Be a steed for the spirits, Lung-Ta," I beg him. "Carry them to watch over my wife."

I switch ponies at Barkol, the dapple-gray about to drop. I have long since worked past exhaustion; hatred drives me on. I suck my anger like a pebble in a parched mouth.

Days wing by like the birds that sometimes come squalling out of the infinite blue, angry with the intruder. Their cries shake me awake; for the first time since I learned to ride long distances, I have given myself over to the horse's rhythm out of frustration rather than love. A golden-brown mare, she trots along as though unaware she carries anyone, much less a Chinese.

At Hami we cross the Silk Road, the ruts of a thousand years and myriad caravans etched into the desert, and continue southwest toward Lop Nor and the southern route—faster but more hazardous than going west through Kashgar, where camel drivers and shopkeepers might see the pain behind my scowl. I break into a gallop when I see the great salt lake shining like a coin beneath the sun, and pretend I am in an even greater hurry than I am when I change horses at the outpost on the northern shore. The two men stationed there raise eyebrows in hope of news or kind words, but I offer neither, dismounting and sending the next steed, a piebald, galloping as I run and leap on, the animal wild-eyed at my insistence, splashing through the salt marsh.

Dusk has oranged the horizon when we come to the southern end of the lake, where I pull up so abruptly that I yank both reins and mane.

Drinking from the salt waters is a Lin.

Reddish and shaggy, the mare has muscular shoulders, a swayed back, and huge haunches, as if built for fertility. She does not look up as I slide from my horse and approach, but watches me coolly, only a slight shake of her head indicating she is aware of me. Her horn—except for its fleshy tip, translucent as an icicle—catches the waning light. I squat, knees cracking, as if a lowered level will power blood to my brain and enable me to see that she is merely mirage. Or hallucination.

Now she lifts her head, a bundle of rushes between her teeth, her jaw working, water falling from her muzzle and splashing, disturbing the stillness. Bragda, I realize, was right. The Ki and Lin, male and female of the species, are real. As real as my dreams were false.

She canters away across the desert, the land flat and nondescript here, not the wind-tortured landforms deep within the Takla Makan, the desert from which no living thing returns. As if Eternal Heaven, angry over the uncaring and ugliness of the people below, slammed a fist between the Heavenly Mountains to the north and the Himalayas to the south, then twisted knuckles in despair. Such is the wretched land of the Takla Makan.

I jump onto the piebald and ride after her.

For days I follow her into the desert, my heart racing faster the more my mount continues to tire. It has become apparent that the Lin is leading me rather than being followed, for she never lets me closer than the length of my father's field, speeding up each time I kick the piebald into a panting gallop but slowing should I fall behind.

Why, I wonder, has she led me into the desert? To keep her pursuer from returning to alert others that she exists?

The brown expanse tufted with brush gives way to land knobbed with sandstone forms so grotesque they look like evil idols. It is as if I have entered a supernatural world. Calcite is crusted like opium, and shale set on edge curves up like talons or scimitars waiting to slice open the unwary. The piebald limps along, head and tail drooping, legs nicked in a dozen places.

When the Lin pauses at a tall stickery bush jutting like a flame between two ragged hills, I also halt. I spear my helmet into the soil, line it with hide torn from my saddlebag, pour precious water within, again pull myself onto the horse, ride away and wait. The Lin stops cropping the bush and slowly serpentines toward the offering. Knowing I cannot catch her unawares, I hope to win her trust, so that—against all logic: sun, exhaustion, and desperation having warped my reasoning—she will come to me of her own will.

She examines the helmet but does not drink. Then she snorts as if in disgust and wanders away, her gait less certain now.

When at last, disheartened, I go back to the helmet she is again a farmer's field away. I drop to the ground and consider the water instead of replacing it in the bag. Sunlight reflects off the liquid as though off a coin. I remember the gleam of Lop Nor, the lake that moves, its marsh-rushes like lashes around a glassy eye staring up from the desert as if scrutinizing God.

Salt. That is what drew her to Lop Nor! Salt—together with water: symbols of life and immortality. Elixir for a horned horse.

Salt fringed a dry watercourse along what is now the horizon, I remember. Heart thudding, I leap onto the piebald and race him so urgently, backtracking, that twice he nearly falls. When we arrive he is lathered and gasping. I wrench off a boot, scoop in salt and dirt, the Lin again, insanely, a field away, and gallop back to the helmet, holding the boot like a chalice. The Lin, once more cropping the spike bush, eyes me as I filter salt from sand, my fingers a sad sieve. I have witnessed her look before.

"Bragda," I utter through parched lips.

The sound so startles me that I cease working, pour half the boot-sand into the helmet. If the lake has a sandy bottom, why not my capful? I mount the piebald and, watching one another, the Lin and I ascribe a cir-cle, she to the helmet, I to the bush. Up close I see that its main branches, white as poplar, are long and strong and straight. With my knife I whittle off the greatest length I can find as the Lin drinks, neighing her satisfac-tion, shaking her head, again drinking. From my saddlebag thongs I fash-ion a lasso, attach it to one end of the branch and at the other make a loop for my hand, reviewing with a kind of exultant anxiety the lessons Jail-spur taught. How to ride upside down, dangling from a stirrup; or on my head, a shoulder snugged in the saddle; above all how to lasso a takhi—a wild pony. My sorriest skill. As though I had captured myself one sun-scorched afternoon as the Khan's cavalry rode toward me, and I had not the heart to capture anything else.

"Bragda," I repeat, under my breath. The Lin whinnies as if in answer.

I pat the piebald. He is spent. What horseman am I, using him up like this? I resolve to make his anguish up to him should we capture the Lin. Give him the remaining water and curds, walk before him rather than ride as we return to the Lop Nor station, and there order him rubbed down and fed, then set free. Even now the men would obey me, but report me to be punished. With the Lin in tow they will obey *instantly,* report me with pride. I will own the finest horse beneath Blue Heaven.

"Soon," I whisper in the piebald's ear, and mount him, he stumbling to hold me.

I kick him and ride down on the Lin like a thunder, the piebald struggling to respond. The mare seems reluctant to move from the salt water, as if it has drugged her senses. This time she eyes me in fear, not condescension.

Then, as though breaking from a spell, she jerks up her head and starts to bolt, tension rolling the length of her, power gathered in her hind legs.

"Bragda!" I shriek in a cracked, croaky voice as the piebald's hooves pound and dust boils up around me. The Lin hesitates—an instant too long before she lurches left. I am now so near I can see the sheen of sweat upon her flanks. I thrust the lasso forward. The noose dangles in the sun.

Then it is around her neck. She swivels on all fours, facing me, straining against the leash, legs spread, like a dog worrying a rag. Her snorts are desperate, high-pitched; she jousts at the branch with her horn, twisting her head from side to side.

"I've come for you!" I yell at her. "You see I came back!"

She kicks the helmet, sending it catapulting end over end, water wheeling into the air. I am jerked off-balance. The piebald lurches, trying to adjust himself to the rider, and in his exhaustion, stumbles. The mare lunges back—too late. The piebald pierces its neck on the mare's horn—and instantly rears, screaming. I tumble from the saddle, unsuccessfully fighting to keep my feet in the stirrups, hit the ground so hard my breath exits in a whoosh. As I lie trying to suck in air, the Lin watches as if in horror as the piebald collapses. Then the mare flees, pulling me with her.

Dirt covers my face, choking me, rocks rumble against my back and buttocks. I hang on whether I want to or not, my hand trapped in the loop. Far behind me the piebald is on the ground, kicking spastically, crying its pain and terror. Shadows slant like ribs across my face and then I am pulled through the bush, branches and brambles raking my skin and eyes. She drags me onward, and I know I would not let go even if I could. The mare, like Bragda, is all I have. Other than delusion.

I will die this way, I decide, here in a realm rendered evil by the elements. Not that death much matters, except for my not seeing Bragda again. What was I thinking when I shirked my duty as Messenger and followed the mare? That she would make me so respected my position would be elevated above Jailspur's? That he would be forced to dissemble before me and fear for his life?

Suddenly the Lin stops.

And lies down.

I clamber to my feet, spitting dirt, wiping grime from my eyes. Her back is toward me, chest heaving. Surely the sojourn in the desert could not have weakened her so!

She turns her head toward me, nostrils flared, her gaze more that of victim than victor. In her eyes I see darkness spreading. The wind has picked up, whining past my ears. As I peer at the sky, fear twists my insides like rope. Black clouds drive across the desert, sand furling before them. Takla Makan storms, infamous for their severity, arise so quickly that the only warning experienced caravaners have is when the older camels abruptly halt and thrust their mouths into the sand.

I claw at the loop, squinting around anxiously for shelter. As if taunting me for my travail, the sandstone idols waver and disappear behind the onslaught of sand. It assaults my face like needles. I cry out in pain— unable to hear my voice above the wind—and clutch my jacket's felt liner against my cheeks. I collapse to my knees, nuzzle my head against the mare. She does not resist.

The sand beats a furious percussion against my leather armor while I huddle, as concerned now for the plummeting cold as for the sand. I wriggle my right hand, still attached to the loop, beneath her head, and snuggle ever closer against her flanks, not unlike how I used to lie with Bragda, my groin cupping her buttocks, my left arm around her torso, hand on a breast, my right hand pillowing her head.

Though my eyes are clenched shut, the insides of the lids seem coated with dirt. As I struggle for breath, the mare's heat is a heaven I can almost taste but not touch with my lips, separated as it is from me by felt. I wonder if the sky is also felt, behind which lives the warmth and heart of God.

Bragda, my mind moils, and I wonder if Jailspur is upon her, absorbing her heat—never her heart. Why did I not plunge my knife into his back!

As abruptly as it began, the storm subsides. Here in the Takla Makan it is not like in the Gobi, where storms rage for days, sand browning the sky yet leaving the land unchanged. Here, storms slash like a Mongol sword, delivering death, carving up the world.

When I look up, coughing against the grit in my mouth and shoving away at the sand cloaked to my shoulders, I seem to have arisen in some other world. The idol-shaped sandstone formations are aproned with dirt, as though their essence has been pulled out of them.

I stand, shaking off the sand and fear. The mare also gains her feet, weak-kneed and unsure on the impermanent earth, neighing her dismay, softly tossing her head. I start to unloop the thong from around my wrist but decide against it; she seems resigned to the fate of the pole and noose. We trudge through sand together, awkwardly, my right arm across my chest; I am on the wrong side of her.

We crest the rise.

No sign of the piebald. A dune has avalanched, its alluvial fans spread across the depression in which the animal died—if indeed I am facing the right direction.

Needing a focal point, I search for the bush from which I cut the pole. The bush is also gone, as though the wind uprooted it and sent it flying like the arrow of an assassin. I dig among the alluvial for my goatskin bag, but to no avail. We will have to reach the Lop Nor station without water.

I do not, dare not, let go of the loop. We head off in what I hope is the right direction. Above, as if in contradiction to the cold, the sun blazes. I have the ugly sense that the desert is how the sun wants the world: scoured clean of life, reduced to sandscape. Beneath the glare, everything looks white, the color of mourning. Not even the most hardened Mongol would enjoy such austerity. There is a greater feeling of death here than I have ever known. Temujin's bloodbaths pale beside it.

The mare and I stumble on, she perhaps as physically and spiritually lost as I, keeping close to me as we move across the barrenness. The cold continues to deepen. Plumes of breath hang momentarily from her nostrils like fine feathers, and in her horn, sunlight coalesces like warmth congealed. I am tempted to take hold of it, but I would no more touch it than I would a fellow Buddhist's head, highest point of the body and thus residence of the soul. For me, the highest point was not head but helmet, which I had thrust into dirt. Perhaps wisely, perhaps an insult to ancestors.

We crest another hill; beyond lies the sharpened shale, which seems to stretch forever. Was it such an expanse when we came? How obsessed was I with the Lin!

We start forward, though I know I will never survive the crossing. The shale will slice my boots, pierce my feet. The mare balks: from fear, I think at first, but when she tilts her head and then lowers it, throatily snorting, I grasp her intent.

Wants me to ride.

She shivers and turns in an uneasy circle as I mount, her eyes full of fear, her whinnying seemingly one of subtle lament, not insult. The storm seems to have scoured me of whatever pride or joy I should feel at mounting such sublimity, and yet a thought occurs: if I gifted the Lin to the Khan, could he not mate her with stallions of the Kara Khitai herd? Might he not elevate me to the top of the empire? Perhaps even make me his fifth son?

But the thought fades, another lone bird squalling above desert only to wing away, and for the first time in my life I feel at peace. The mare starts forward through the ragged rocks without my urging, hooves clinking against stone like the chime of a Buddhist bell. Who shod her, and why? The Eternal Blue Heaven, seeking to keep all creatures bound to the earth?

Around us, shale wavers like fingers of demons or the dead reaching up to protest our passing, and suddenly I know why the region seemed smaller before. Death is not to be denied. Was the area more compact during our first crossing, hoping to draw us into a trap—or wider now, attempting to hold us within?

The Lin provides a path.

Then I can see Lop Nor, shining in the sky and reflecting the ground —a trick not uncommon in the desert—though the lake is still many days away. There, salt water awaits the mare; and, too, a stall. For should we reach the station, I will never release her. I am not strong enough for that. I came for her; I will never let go.

We thread among shale for a day and into darkness. When dawn blooms along the horizon, sand and crusted earth greet us; we have completed the crossing.

The mare does not try to shake off her human weight, as I expected she might. Desire for the elixir of Lop Nor, I suspect, drives her despite the looming loss of freedom. Above us, the lake blinks in and out of existence, as though now and again closing its eye to the world.

"Bragda," I whisper, and pat the mare's neck.

Her head, already hanging, lowers even further as if in acquiescence.

That evening, as the first clouds I have seen since the storm lie like coiled cloth along the horizon, the winking of the lake escalates my thirst. I had thought myself no longer capable of saliva. Even now, though saliva spumes in my cheeks, I cannot swallow, so parched and swollen is my throat. As I lie beside the mare, seeking warmth, I fight the desire that pulses in that throat, that finally pulses up and down my body, like taut nerves struck with a tuning fork. I fight, but my body is too aflame with thirst. *Why not?* tolls like a bell in my brain. *Why not drink of her, Umber? What harm could come of it!*

I pray to the Eternal Blue Heaven, to Bragda, to my father son of a farmer son of a farmer for release from greed; but the day is dark, Bragda is not listening, the prayers to my father and my fathers before him are plaintive laments from beyond a far, far field.

I press tightly against her, trying to commune with her. What is she thinking? *How* does she think? The desire for water makes my heart race. Even my skin tingles with the craving. *Forgive me,* my inner voice whispers, but I do not mouth the words, for fear she will hear and, understanding, flee.

I slide my knife from its sheath, quickly cut a tiny slit along the right gaskin, and lower my lips to the wound. She neighs her dismay and starts to rise, but I am up with her, and then the effort seems to expel from her and she lies down again. The drug that is her lifeblood courses through me. My mind feels the emollient; though my limbs heat up, listlessness suffuses me—a reaction the opposite of what I would have believed.

As she gains her feet I easily stand, but the desert appears to slant to and fro, as if my mind is water a child is attempting to hold in a shallow pan. Careless yet careful, I again mount, aware with heightened senses of the world around me. Each grain of sand looms large. Each, a miracle.

How wonderful the elixir that is the blood of the mare!

We will make the station, I know; and I can give the Khan the essence of the Lin without my having to give her up. Sequester the mare, dole out her blood to Temujin a vial at a time. Who then would be the more powerful—he, or Umber?

I could buy my father and neighbors out of their bondage at Jinquan. Again they will have farms and freedom. I will send searchers into the opium dens, whose windows, below street level, look out on the world but see nothing. We will find Bragda's father, and surely with the goodness and grace of the blood of the Lin he will escape his addiction.

And Bragda will love me.

And forgive me for leaving her.

A distant whinny assails us, dissipating my daydreams.

The Lin halts. Together we look around, she seemingly as confused as I over the new sound.

Then we see a stallion, nimbused by the sun, upon a bluff whose stark sides have been riven by the wind. He lifts, kicking at the air. Fastened to his back, what at first looks like the spiked bush sparkles darkly. Not a bush, I realize, but a triad of wish-fulfilling jewels, elongated and egg-shaped, set as though in a lotus-flower saddle.

The Lin whinnies and keeps turning toward the stallion, regardless of how hard I kick her onward toward Lop Nor. Curiously, I feel no fear; perhaps the blood-drug lodged in my gut has calmed my heart. I blink at the realization of good fortune—who but the dead and dreamers have witnessed the Lung-Ta?—and close my eyes.

Drowsiness descends, and abruptly I am on the ground, gasping and looking up at Lop Nor shimmering in the sky directly above me. My reflection peers down from the lake. I could cry, had I moisture enough for tears.

The Lin lowers her head and nuzzles me as if to assure I am alive. I groan; the sound seems to spill from outside my body, echoing beneath the bowl of Heaven. "Go away," I manage to say.

She nudges my ribs more insistently, attentive even to an enemy.

"Bragda?" I ask, and let the loop fall from my grip.

I know now why Bragda stood behind me that day the Mongols came. Not in support but in hope that together we would run away.

Perhaps she will be better off with Jailspur: among Mongols, stealing another's wife is not so much infamy as tradition. He might not love her as I did but at least he if leaves her he will say good-bye.

When I stagger to my feet, I see the mare bound up the bluff toward the white stallion. How else but by freeing her could I keep her from the Khan?

I walk toward Lop Nor, and when darkness descends I lie down against the cold, my blood chilling, never to warm again. I have the spirit but not the physical skills to go on. In my dreams I see the Lin and Lung-Ta canter across clouds.

I awaken not into daybreak but into death. Sand whistles through my rib cage and fills the cavity of my pelvis. Desert-spiders and, once, a hare scuttle across the expanse and find sustenance in my shriveled flesh. The giving makes my jawbones sag open in a smile. I know the karma in that, know it literally in my bones, and when I look up through eyeless sockets at Lop Nor, I am not afraid. Not even of Mongols whose ghosts might ride the wind.

Another storm comes, so ferocious that it sends rocks running. I laugh at its weakness. Sand covers my bones, as though the world is incensed at my insult. I lie awaiting Lop Nor.

Instead of water, I hear hooves. They pass again and again across my grave, gradually revealing my face. The herd is golden brown, offspring of a silver-white stallion and a russet mare. So fine-limbed and sleek-bodied is the herd that their hooves barely touch the earth as they roam the Takla Makan—now home to mustangs not even a Mongol could ride. I am happy as I await the lake, for in dying I have learned to live; and by drinking the Lin's blood have learned that, except for escape, there is no evil.

—refraction—

I
am
amid
narwhals'
whistles and
terrified wheezes,
like elders coughing;
flukes slapping, kayak
creaking, ice converging
as froth and fear pull me
into waves in whose tangled
hair sea mammals breed and
bear: the world's watery roots.

I DO NOT FIGHT THE DROWNING. IT TROUBLES
me no more than the failure of the research project. Without sorrow or
solace I remember how, before the narwhals collapsed the kayak, this sea
and my soul were calm as a mirror, the narwhals mirrors of the world's
fragility, their flanks a map of time.

My eyes and lungs bulge, salt water and bile burst into my mouth,
bubbles escape as if seeking a higher life-form to inhabit. I am oddly at
peace despite the pain, as though, like water bending light, the fjord
refracts my past. As sea and ice give way to darkness, I imagine the
kayak's skirt hugging my waist, thinking *there is no life without winter.*
Moon the color of snow, glaciers lying like predators along the fjord.
Whalesong—and spray from the narwhals' spouting. Do only we Eskimos see the value of the white world? Jerac was right: women should
hold the animal's legs while their husbands skin. He was wrong about
everything else. As I was, about everything.

I imagine myself again paddling in the polynia, the narwhals in a
rosette around me, flukes toward the kayak, tusks outward. I barely dip
the paddles, awed by what might drive whales to such a geometric. Dis-
play of communal well-being, or does an enemy lurk? Will an orca surface or polar bear pad out from among icefall? I lift my paddle in an
absurd attempt at defending myself.

I sigh at my naïveté, put down the paddle; the whalesong is not one
of fear. I let the kayak drift as I admire the tusks. Slender and spiraled,
brittle and exquisite. Small wonder why Medieval Europeans used them
as scepters and believed them imbued with Grace: capable of curing
impotency or ague, able to detect and neutralize poison. Symbols of
imperial power, they brought a king's ransom.

Today, for as little as three thousand krøner, you can hang one in your
den; for only fools believe in unicorns. The educated pontificate about
rhinos being the basis of the myth, while the real unicorns go on dying—
harvested for horns, or their tusks caught in cod and salmon nets.

The wind comes up as if to chill my anger, reminding me that the
world of ice pack and ice cap, though filled with retribution, is without
remorse. The living cannot retrieve the dead.

I am chilled despite my polypropylene, sweater, down coat, anorak.
My perspiration has begun to freeze. As usual I am overdressed—as I
was at Copenhagen's Polytekniske except for my freshman year. After
Jerac left school, I discarded my jeans for skirts and pressed slacks. I
became the Eskimo who had discarded her culture. Jerac and the Arctic

taught me nothing, nothing; but I learned less at the university. Heat, not cold, kills earliest on the ice; I know that much. It is opposite in academe.

Maybe as a grad student I should have attempted to radio-tag Jerac instead of narwhals. Perhaps I could have kept track of him. And he, me.

We met at Polytekniste as freshmen, both never out of Greenland before. Right off the ice, as they say. He was gorgeous: skin like moist terra-cotta, physique that brought him the gold in the knuckle-hop at the Eskimo Olympics, eyes so dark our heritage could not account for their depth. "A magician in bed," my dormmates told me. "Makes your inhibitions disappear."

We became lovers back home the following summer, while working at the cannery in Godthåb. Rather, he worked—on the slime line sixteen hours a day—and I was paid for delivering coffee and bad jokes. "Happy slimers are safe slimers," I had convinced the corporation, proving to myself, and any worker I could browbeat into listening, that the fishing industry's executives had the brains of beat-up humpies seeking to spawn.

Perhaps if he were not always giving up precious sleep to sleep with me, our weekend on the tundra would have gone differently. Jerac packed the basics, I brought my usual: Walkman with mini-speakers, freeze-dried kung pao chicken, leather flask filled with chablis. And mushrooms, this time.

An experimenter back then, I was anxious to try some, but only if Jerac joined me. At first he shook his head. I delayed asking again until after we made love to exhaustion—my exhaustion, anyway—in that endless light while the summer wind sighed against our tent. At last he lay with his head on my belly as we talked and snacked on pickled mangtuk. "About the mushrooms," I asked again, and he became silent; lay looking at the ceiling.

"They say that's what caused her problem," he said bitterly.

"I thought you said she'd eaten too much stink flipper. Or was drunk."

"She *couldn't* have been drunk."

His face hardened, but it was I who was annoyed—he invoking *her* again. For someone who never existed, the woman from Qingmi-uneqarfik often came between us. For Jerac she existed.

He took the last piece of whale skin from his mouth, replaced it in the Tupperware. He had temporarily lost his taste for its flavor of hazelnut and cloves. "Only if we do it the old way," he said.

"God, Jerac."

I was not so town-Eskimo that I did not know the tradition. The woman ingested the mushrooms, her liver filtering out toxins but not the hallucinogens. The man drank her urine.

It was crazy. It was also *culture.*

I hesitated. I realized there were boundaries to what I'd try. That, more than the danger and attendant humiliation, gave me pause. I felt old. But not like Eskimos are supposed to feel old.

"Never mind," he said. After a moment he added, in an awkward attempt at levity, "If the sexism bothers you, we could switch roles."

I laughed, but it was forced, reluctant. I sighed, lay down alongside him, head to toe. I gathered my courage and foolishness. "Would you fill a cup, or would I have to drink from the faucet?"

"You're certain."

I wavered: finally shut my eyes.

"It's too gross."

I waited to be caressed and cajoled. But Jerac misunderstood; silence filled the tent. He slowly sat up, put the film canister containing the mushrooms back into the side pouch of my pack, and crawled from the tent. Head, shoulders, bare butt, bare feet, gone.

"God, Jerac," I said, to the ceiling.

There were tears in my eyes.

I wouldn't cry, I never cried. Not for a man, anyway. When my father died I was stone. Stone when my brothers and uncle died. As the boys in my high school at Godthåb dropped like dominoes—suicide and accident, accident and suicide; and how do you classify Russian roulette?— I had stonehood polished to perfection. The gleam in my eyes at graveside reflected my heart. It was not caused by tears.

I refused to follow Jerac outside. I crossed my arms as though to keep my will in place, and tightly shut my eyes.

Sleep slowly enveloped me. Not exactly sleep, but not daydreaming. I lay in the stupor of considerable sex and too little empathy. For the first time I could recall, I dreamed of deserts.

He lies on the ground while sand skirls in the wind, his tattered jacket and puffy pants billowing, the goatskin boots full of holes, his toes and hands and face shriveled to parchment. The lips are gnarled, eye sockets empty. Sand builds along the windward side of his legs, spreads over the knees and thighs, angles across the jacket. Only the feet and face remain uncovered. When the wind abates, a bird lands on his chest, and after walking around as though nervously testing the stability beneath its feet, tears off the upper lip as if pulling up a worm. The bird flies toward a lake lying on the horizon like a shiny coin. The ravage has unhinged the jaw; it sags open. The man appears to be desperately grinning. Dusk brings the wind. Shadows and sand fill the mouth.

When I awakened I felt a sense of loss, whether only from Jerac's absence I wasn't sure. I pulled on my things and crawled outside.

As if unmindful of the chill, he lay naked and seemingly asleep on the lichen-covered slope beyond the tundra marsh. I slogged over, padded up the hill, nudged his foot with my boot.

"Good way to get hypothermia."

He turned his face toward the ice cap along the horizon. The moon was silver-blue, the sun pale and distant. My watch buzzed. *Midnight.*

"You going to play *shrug*?" I demanded.

He would sometimes go silent and rigid, in the way Eskimo men often do, infuriating everyone with their silent fury, communication reduced to slight shoulder movements.

He shrugged.

I returned to the tent, lay remembering the discussions my girlfriends and I sometimes had. Many Eskimo men were dysfunctional. Was it wise to marry or have children by one? But there were voices that blew down from the ice cap, whispering *for the good of the culture.*

He returned an hour later. We shared the tent, but we might as well have slept on opposite sides of Greenland, the ice cap between us.

The wind lulled my anger away.

The man staggers against sand blowing across the desert, his cheeks so puffy with sunburn that his eyes are slits. A lake seems to shine in the sky, winking as he stumbles. He passes a swollen tongue across his lips. "Bragda," he utters, and collapses to his knees.

He crawls on, hands turned in, shoulders bowed like those of a lizard. Then his elbows give way; abruptly, his face is on the ground. When he lifts his face, sand covers his left eye, clinging to the mucous. He brushes desperately, again collapses. "Bragda." He clutches at sand.

I awoke to an ATV stuttering across the tundra. Outside, I found Jerac watching as the machine pitched and yawed across the niggerheads. His eyes were hard and narrow.

Jailspur was at the throttle, face burnished by the midnight sun. He shut off the machine and slapped his gloves down among the gas cans strapped to the rear luggage rack.

"Brought you something," he told Jerac.

He grinned, held up a baggie filled with fish strips. He was unshaven, his teeth green with grime, a front one missing.

"You came ten miles to bring smoked sheefish," I said suspiciously.

"Breakfast ready?" he asked Jerac.

Icily: "Tea and pilot bread."

"Sounds fine to me."

We ate sitting on rocks, not speaking. The slabs of snow and ice that dotted the summer camp seemed appropriate. Jerac stared at the bag of fish strips, holding it by the ends as if it were evidence. He ate nothing.

"You have the papers," he said finally, not looking at the older man.

Jailspur took a folded sheaf from his jacket and held it toward Jerac, arm's length, between forefinger and thumb. Jerac looked at the papers as if appraising their weight, the way he looked at the bar during gymnastic meets. He lowered his eyes and reached for the papers.

Jailspur pulled them back, Jerac's fingers closing on air.

The Dane laughed. Jerac seized the papers, held them before Jailspur's face as though to slap him with them, then walked to the edge of camp, where he clutched the papers against his stomach and stood looking across the tundra. A fulmar circled, screeching, angry at having humans near her nest. Jerac did not look up.

The papers, I was sure, were his long-awaited boat title and commercial permit. He could now sell fish on the open market. But Jailspur's unsubtle choreography with the fingers was not lost on me. Prohibitively expensive in our world of limited-entry cod and salmon openings, the papers had come at a price beyond the percentage of profits Jerac would owe his benefactor.

When Jerac was a boy, Jailspur briefly was his foster parent—until the courts decided Jailspur was not fit to be anyone's parent.

The Dane was back in Jerac's life.

Jailspur zippered his jacket, put on his gloves, slipped a leg over the machine with the exaggerated extension of someone mounting a Harley, yanked the starter cord. The ancient Honda roared into life.

I pulled the key from the ignition, the tundra again still except for the fulmar's cawing. "This could have waited," I told him. "He hasn't finished school. Tend to your fucking boat yourself. Leave him alone."

He held out his hand for the key, his body language insolent. I cocked my arm, ready to throw the key out into the tundra muck.

"Go back to Copenhagen—Bunnuq," he said, using my Eskimo name.

"Jerac goes with me," I answered.

"He knows where he's from. That's where he belongs."

Jerac had grown up in Qingmiuneqarfik—the village in which, it was said, a woman mated with dogs and produced the white race, nearly human outside but monstrous within. Only non-Eskimos would fail to understand such shame. Jerac's accomplishments paled by comparison.

"They should have locked you up," I said. "Jerac told me what you did."

Jailspur looked up at me from the tops of his sockets, brows pulled down.

"Never did nothing. The court said so. So did Jerac."

"Not anything anyone could prove. Or would testify to."

He smiled. It was haunting, and I sensed it would go with me when I returned to the university, even if Jerac did not.

I pitched the key as far as I could.

His face reddened even more. I thought he would hit me. I had been in a few fights, growing up in Godthåb, but they were mostly scratch-and-hair affairs, few fists. I never had been punched by a man. I wasn't ready, but in a way I wished it would happen.

Instead he sneered, reached into his rubber coveralls, withdrew a wallet, took out another key. He started the machine. "Jerac's a big boy."

He roared away, spewing mud and exhaust. The machine listed like a dog raising a leg as he traversed the nearest niggerhead. He raised a middle finger.

I looked for a rock or stick, but ended up throwing insults.

"He's not a boy! And he never was *your* boy!"

The finger remained up like a flag. I strode toward Jerac, thinking that perhaps I *had* eaten mushrooms, that the world was unreal. I wanted him to do *something*—tear up the papers, tear off Jailspur's finger.

His back to me, he was looking at the sun, red and diamond-shaped. "Only a share of the profits," he said. "That's all he'll want."

I looked around his shoulder—withdrew to keep from embarrassing him and having him walk away from me again. His eyes were so moist I half expected a tear to form upon his lashes. I put my cheek against his shoulder blade. "That's all he'll want," he said. He was quivering.

"You needn't accept what he's offering."

His body shook convulsively. "Even if I get a degree—how long before I raise enough cash for another chance like this?"

"You can always subsistence-fish."

"And my children?"

"You don't have children."

"But I will! And they will!"

He was talking crazy.

"You're sounding like a white man—always worried about the future."

"What am I, but a white man!—*masquerading*. What am I, anymore."

He walked away, and I couldn't have gone to him even had he wanted me to.

What were we—any of us—all of us.

When he returned to the tent, his reticence was more profound than before—he did not even shrug when I spoke to him. I ran my tongue along the length of his palm; he did not respond. Finally I eased his sweatpants down.

He was the only man I'd slept with who hated having orgasms. In bed he had an obsessive desire to please. I think Jailspur had taught him too well.

When he came, he gripped my hair.

"Leah," he said. "Leah."

It was my Christian name, and he hated it.

When I slept, the warmth and salt of him still in my mouth, I was again transported from the tundra to a hotter and far more foreign desert.

The man faces the wind, cheek crusted with sand, eyes and lips tight, arms out. His hands are fisted. Between him and the lake, amid the furling sand, rears a muscular reddish unicorn, forelegs kicking, its tusk translucent as an icicle. The man rocks as though inebriated and sits down in the sand, shoulders slumped, arms sagged, hands listless in his lap. "Everything I had," he mutters. "You ruined it all."

His eyes close as of their own accord. Sand peppers his face, but he seems not to notice. "If I get back to Mongolia . . . I'll kill you with my bare hands."

Back at the cannery, Jerac took to wearing mirror-like sunglasses, a baseball cap on backwards, jeans with holes in the knees: things he had seen on TV. He no longer laughed at my jokes or invented horrible similes to describe my coffee, and everyone on the line was faster with a fillet knife. We slept separately. When we were together we ate salmon instead of anything special, and did not talk much.

We flew back to Copenhagen, but he stayed less than a quarter. He skipped practices, and his grades slipped. None of my girlfriends asked about him anymore.

The night he left for Greenland, the Berlin Wall was officially coming down. Everyone who was anyone flocked to Germany, as though some Teutonic migration had begun. The flight to Reykjavik, where he would change planes, was nearly empty. "I'll stay if you beg me," he said. "I'll do anything you want if you beg me."

I reached to remove his sunglasses before he kissed me, but he backed away, hands up defensively, then compounded the slight by bowing and attempting to kiss my hand like some stupid European.

That night, Woman Without Face came to me for the first time.

The man staggers into the wind, snow, not sand, billowing around him. "Kill you," he mutters. At the edge of the lake in the distance stands a figure in a thick hooded coat, spear raised. The figure motions him forward. As he stumbles closer, he sees that the beckoning hand is the color of mourning. White as a fish's belly. He squints against the sun, trying to discern the figure's face, but except for a curve of slitted wood where the eyes should have been, the face is lost in the hood's darkness.

The figure points toward the lake—rimmed and chocked with huge ice chunks that float in a surface that mirrors the sun. Great fish-like creatures break the surface, noisily spouting, their geysers forming rainbows.

Jerac's promised letter-a-month became postcard-a-season, then ADDRESSEE UNKNOWN. The next summer I remained in Denmark, on a work-study stint that, appropriately, considering the omnipresence of Hans Christian Andersen, had me counting swans. That the other researchers called me Ugly Duckling did not stop several married ones from asking me out. I slept alone, and badly, and studied so much that I found myself with a galloping GPA I ultimately rode into grad school.

My proposed dissertation, *Echolocation: Acoustical Analogues in the Narwhal (Monodon monoceros),* was my undoing. The day my committee approved the topic I stood amid tanks that reeked of formaldehyde, and in concert before a hundred watchful specimens remembered with trembling clarity my last afternoon with Jerac, beneath the down comforter in my dorm room. The moment just prior to climax, I had told myself *he's only another partner only a partner* until I accidentally willed my orgasm away.

"You all right?" my committee head asked as she scrawled her signature.

Momentarily speechless, I pointed to the title, which I realized I had unintentionally typed in boldface. The subtext implied I would be returning to Greenland, for research. Straining against the weakness the memory instilled, I said, "I'll need money."

She stifled a smile at my non sequitur and glanced at her colleagues.

"Of course you do. All grad students do. Goes with the territory."

"What you're really here to learn," the second smiled at his own incisive humor, "is how to live with being poor. Then we watch you jump through research hoops."

The third, balding except for gray around his ego, had spent much of his research the past year trying to determine how to get into my pants. "You're *Eskimo,*" he said. "Apply for Northern Studies Institute funding. Americans love to throw money at anything *Native.* They think it assuages some collective guilt."

My non sequiturs. My youthful enthusiasm. My culture. Ultima Thule, the world they called Grønland. Such were the amusements in the mausoleum of higher education.

Under their tutelage and titles, I was to beg funding from some government, oil or Arctic shipping company, or environmental group. There was little difference, for money fueled them all; all knew the value of priming the pump with research. I would do most of the fieldwork, with one or more committee members occasionally visiting the research site. It would be a late-spring operation, when the ice pack had broken up enough to allow Zodiac launches but before the summer thaw made it difficult to locate the animals. I'd submerge hydrophones to record their songs, then put a year in the lab: decipher signals, check frequencies, search out correlations between songs, write the dissertation. Finally a journal article, my name bylined last.

Unless I proved exceptionally worthy, and a committee member fucked me not only intellectually but actually. Rather than my merely being the research assistant, the article then would be *coauthored*. Which meant my name would *still* be bylined last.

Woman Without Face had armed me for this moment.

"I have figured out how to radio-tag a narwhal," I said.

No one had succeeded at subjecting narwhals to telemetry.

The three monkeys looked up in unison from behind the lab table, so startled that Mr. Ego rocked on his stool.

Metaphorically I kicked the chairs out from under all of them.

"During winter," I said and, exiting, added, "A *lot* of money."

That night, Woman Without Face, as I had come to think of her, visited me again. As she had so many nights during the past four years, as mindful of my bedroom needs as Jerac had ultimately proved negligent.

Except for the slitted wooden sunglasses, her face, framed by the hood of wolverine and polar bear fur, is dark as death, her hands white as mourning. The man from the desert is gone. I am beside her. She shows me an agloo hole, where seals come to breathe, then faces me toward the narwhals, which arc in syncopated water ballet in an ice-free hole in the frozen sea rather than in a lake. Their tusks catch the sunlight.

She points to the dots arrayed along the flanks. "My children have a chance if I'm not their mother," she whispers. As the tails glide beneath the sea, she pushes me forward. "Approach their pain, not their pleasure."

When I awoke I lay looking at the Atlantic Whales poster above my bed. Over the years the picture had sagged on its pins, as if from the sea's weight. I, too, felt pulled down—by pride. I pushed my hair back and breathed deeply. *Stay centered.*

My center: into the ice-free polynia, like Alice through the looking glass, into the world where narwhals fed and moaned whalesongs as if in mourning for whatever narwhals mourn. Sometimes, staring at the poster, I imagined myself one of them, ugly duckling turned cetacean swan, jousting lance jutting, the dots along my marbled flanks like points on a map of eternity.

Those dots were what Woman Without Face wanted me to see. She was the woman from Qingmiuneqarfik; I had guessed the identity long ago. I was to look beyond lineage. Perhaps we are not products of our parents, she was telling me. Perhaps parents are merely *agloo* holes through which our centering spirit flowed—each child not a reincarnation but rather drawing into itself spirits of the dead depending on its capabilities and charisma, like a sculptor freeing a statue from the stone.

"My children have a chance if I'm not their mother."

As Jerac Johnnie would, if I raised enough research capital to buy out Jailspur's interest in the boat. I would give Jerac that chance as much for myself as for him.

I picked up the phone.

That Jerac proved easy to find did not surprise me. Most Eskimos do not drift far from their center unless alcohol absorbed them.

For Jerac, as with many, his center was his boat.

Even though it wasn't his.

Four months later he was showing me around *Qingmiuneqarfik;* Jailspur had insisted upon the name. An uneasy ebullience had displaced Jerac's depth. He prattled about draft and decking, ship tonnage and salmon poundage, weather along Inglefield Gulf. Jailspur watched us from the wheelhouse. Fishing regs dictated that the permit holder be aboard during the season, but the season was over. Jerac was a glorified deckhand.

"Why is *he* piloting?" I asked when we were behind the net winch. "That wasn't part of the deal."

"You told me you needed transport to . . . to Kangerlussuaq." He avoided saying "Qingmiuneqarfik," at the fjord's mouth. "You didn't insist on our going alone." He glowered, the ebullience gone like so much bilge, and lit a cigar, smoking Greenland-style: three puffs, put it out with spit, bite off the end of the ashed tobacco, chew. All the men in my family had smoked that way. First came the failure to wipe the tobacco juice at the corner of the mouth, then bathing declined, pants hardened with fish blood and snot went unwashed as each year the drinking extended further into the fishing season. "Why must you go *there*," he said morosely. "There're polynias . . . other places."

"Not in a fjord with so many narwhal, there's not."

"Fuck it." He glanced toward the wheelhouse as though needing an excuse to get away from me. Jailspur signaled with two fingers. Jerac gave me a hard look, climbed onto the main deck, and went inside.

Exhausted and discouraged, I slept that night in the bow's cramped cubby while the men loaded my equipment. Back in Copenhagen, everything seemed so straightforward. I would arrive in Thule, we would chug off into a bouyant sunrise, and after we reaped the research's rewards and I bought out Jailspur, I would only ask two things of Jerac.

That he rename the boat.

That, if possible, he love me.

My plan regarding the narwhals was simple, but required someone with knowledge of the fjord. Unlike other whales, narwhals do not migrate south during winter, except to journey from their summer range near Canada's Baffin Island to their winter quarters among Greenland's polynias—the never-freezing upwellings along the west coast.

Each year, narwhals entered Kangerlussuaq in search of halibut, their favorite food, but risked being trapped by advancing ice. That some trapped narwhals survived the winter was an enigma no one had studied. The expense, the isolation, and the possibility of not finding trapped narwhals were too great. Perhaps, some theorized, they escaped by ramming through the ice or by piercing it with their tusks. But a meter of ice imprisons a narwhal, and the tusk is too fragile to break anything except itself.

Woman Without Face, doomed by her sin never to enter the watery afterworld, had shown me the answer.

A polynia—usually an oceanic occurrence—existed in Kangerlussuaq Fjord. The animals would be trapped but not desperate, which meant they could be approached. Like other whales, narwhals love being scratched; crustaceans dig hooked legs into cavities not directly exposed to water flowing over the narwhal's body. Vigorous rubbing with a brush or even a hand seems to provide relief from an itching of literally leviathan proportions.

"... their pain, not their pleasure ... "

Attempts at telemetry had consisted of placing collar-like radios around the tusk. The narwhals slipped them off in minutes. I would glue a radio tag where the crustaceans thrived. The tag would be better protected, and perhaps the narwhal wouldn't notice it among the general discomfort.

The next day dawned cold and clammy, the stench of diesel so pervasive it seemed to cling to the skin, the engine's droning making my head drum. I peed in the coffee can Jerac had provided, pulled on my anorak, and climbed through the wheelhouse. I nodded to Jerac's grunted hello, stepped out into the stinging air, emptied the can overboard. Jailspur, at the wheel, stared at his reflection in the hole he had sleeved in the fogged-up front window, never looking at me.

We threaded among ice floes and icebergs, puttering through fog. The temperature continued to drop. Soon my teeth were chattering. Jerac exited the wheelhouse, crossed to my kayak, checked the straps binding it across the stern, stood contemplating the craft for several minutes. The kayak was traditional—walrus stomachs rather than fiberglass. I'd have thought he would examine it with a connoisseur's excited eye, but he just stared. Then he walked back to the wheelhouse. Before entering he gave me an ugly look.

Minutes later, Jailspur was laughing, his hand on Jerac's shoulder. Jerac stared into the windshield. When I went inside, wet and cold to the skin if not the soul, Jailspur stopped laughing and took his hand away. Jerac kept looking at the windshield. I went below. Condensation had formed along the bulkhead nearest my bunk; my bag was damp. I climbed in.

The only way to the rest of the boat was through the wheelhouse, so except for making sandwiches and emptying the can, I stayed in bed three days, ice occasionally sliding past the porthole. Woman Without Face brought dreams, and I thought about the man in the desert. Some relation to me, I was sure, but whether a literal or metaphysical one I couldn't tell. I thought about the dots on narwhal flanks.

Perhaps, like lineage, time is not a continuum but rather random acts the mind, seeking the satisfaction we call sanity, coalesces to sustain itself. Like beads threaded on a nonexistent string. Accept that the beads are scattered, and the past could lie ahead of us as easily as behind. We might impact not only the future, but the past.

Ibn Khaldun and Mahmoud Al-Hassan said as much a millennium before, in their appreciation of Allah—an idea only now catching on in the Western world, with its wormholes to parallel worlds whose time frame might not coordinate with our own. Though I felt little for Islam except scorn, given its excesses and view of women, I had found comfort in parts of its philosophy during the years of having Woman Without Face and not Jerac in my bed. Allah creates and destroys everything at each instant, but perhaps to demonstrate His omnipotence He leaves scattered beads.

The boat stopped. I went topside.

Qingmiuneqarfik's dozen tar-papered huts lay like crumbs before the fjord's maw, the village usually deserted during winter but now deserted permanently. The only sounds were from guy wires humming in the wind. No dogs came to investigate the boat out in the calm water.

"We'll anchor here," Jailspur told Jerac. "Then you take the skiff and find us a decent shack."

Check out your old place, is what he meant.

"The ice is firming up," I said hopefully, pointing toward the fjord's mouth. "Maybe we can get the radio tags in place sooner than I thought."

Savssats can occur quickly. Shore-fast ice is capable of growing across the mouths of fjords at a furious rate and expanding toward its head. It is not surprising that animals become trapped.

Moments later we were moored, and Jerac stood holding the line of the skiff we'd been pulling. His back was to the village; he was gazing across the fjord, his head hanging. Except for the tiny wake the skiff left, the sea was still, mirroring an orange sun bulbed atop the granite walls.

Jailspur slid open the wheelhouse door with a thud. "What's keeping you! She's paying you to do a job. Paying *us*."

Jerac let the skiff line go slack. The smaller craft drifted several meters before pulling around and creating another wake. Despite his bulk, Jailspur left the wheelhouse and bounded along the boat edge with a dancer's dexterity. He put a hand on Jerac's shoulder, and for a time the pair looked like father and son, the elder quietly giving advice. Jerac nodded as if in resignation and pulled the skiff alongside. Jailspur's hand trailed down Jerac's jacket to the back of his jeans. Jerac's head jerked up. He glared at the older man, and made a fist. Jailspur backed away. Jerac stepped down onto the bow of the skiff, crossed to the stern, lowered the motor, connected the gas hose, and pulled the starter cord.

He sat hunched, gray as the sea, as he puttered toward the village.

During the next hours I sometimes glanced at the launch sitting on that lonely snow-dusted beach before the empty houses, but mostly I watched the savssat. The ice spreading across the fjord's mouth looked like something created by time-lapse photography. One minute the sea was quiet and gray; seemingly the next it ran thin and shallow, as if a shelf had floated from the depths. Except for a couple of channels, the ice blocked the mouth and was broadening up into the fjord.

Now and again Jailspur emerged from the wheelhouse and watched the village, at first with coffee, then a cigarette, then with thumbs thrust into the sides of his coveralls. He rocked on his heels. "The little fuck. I have to beg him to get anything done right."

The sun had eased around the bowl of sky, never rising more than a few degrees off the horizon. It hung to the west, as clear as the day was cold. "I'll go see what's taking him so long," I said.

"The hell."

I didn't know if that implied agreement, but I unstrapped my kayak. I managed to lower it into the water without his help, climbed down, and climbed in with difficulty. As I pushed away with the paddle, he returned to the wheelhouse and yanked the door shut.

Wandering among the shacks was like being in a world of the dead. I half expected to see people peer from the windows or doors creak open, hands inviting me inside, but the windows just stared blankly and the only activity in the doorways was when a breeze rippled a plastic sack.

Jerac's footprints went from house to house, rarely in a straight line. Meandering. A quarter mile past the village, someone had built a traditional sod house, perhaps a desperate attempt to attract tourists. Such projects are common in remote villages, where even a few visitors a year can boost the economy.

The place was unfinished or, more likely, had fallen in. The whalebone stays looked bleached in the dying light. Seal and caribou hides lay haphazardly on the sides; others had slipped to the ground. The arctic entrance had no door.

Jerac's footprints led to the hut.

White people who hang themselves leave a question behind. Did they change their minds after stepping off the stool—panicking before their neck snapped? Among my people, there is no such issue. We tie twine or thin rope to a chair or door handle—any object—and, on hands and knees, lean forward, the noose around our necks. Change our minds, we stand up.

You have to *want* to die to die that way.

Jerac used his shoestrings, knotted together and neatly half-hitched around a whalebone. He still had on his tennis shoes, his legs tucked tightly beneath him, hands fisted as though in determination. Only after I untied him and laid the body on its side did I think to uncurl the fingers.

I opened the hands with difficulty. He had a treble fishhook in each fist, the barbs jammed into the flesh.

Until then my nerves had kept me moving, my emotions sealed in stone, but when the barbs tore from the skin I sank to the floor amid hides slick with rot and quietly cried, his head in my lap.

Had I not lowered my head, crying over him, Fric Jailspur would have killed me.

Somehow I never saw him crawl through the arctic entrance. He suddenly was standing over me, swinging a bone sled runner he had found somewhere. He missed my head, the bone slamming my shoulder. Pain screamed through me but I managed to lurch sideways as he swung again. Again he missed—hit Jerac across the top of the nose. There was a *thuuk* as bone shattered and blood splattered me.

"Now look what you've done," Jailspur said in a hollow voice, dropping the sled runner and falling to his knees. He lifted Jerac's hand and held it, fishhook and all, against his cheek. "You and your goddamn narwhals. Killed my precious boy."

He picked up the sled runner. I scrambled on hands and knees through the arctic entrance, then raced through the village, the empty houses watching unconcerned.

The *Qingmiuneqarfik* was moored close to the shore, the skiff beached beside my kayak. I chose the boat that best guaranteed survival, not speed, and pushed off, paddling furiously toward the savssat. Looking back to see Jailspur lumber from between the shacks, I cursed myself for not disabling the skiff. *Forget it. Stay centered.* I bent into the work.

The kayak hit the shore-fast ice with a bump I thought would crack the ribbing. The boat bellied, then slid into the slush and freestanding water atop the ice shelf. The ice was only a dozen meters wide; I jumped out, kept my weight across the kayak as best I could as I splashed along. I reached open water again just as Jailspur brought the skiff's motor screaming to life and sent the launch flying across the sea, spewing a rooster tail, the bow lifted.

I had thought the fjord would save me, but I was wrong.

Jailspur roared along the ice, found a lead, brought the skiff around in a spraying arc and headed up the channel. In an instant he would clear the savssat. My only hope was that he would run me down, killing me quickly.

Halfway across the ice shelf, the skiff bottomed out in a screech of metal, and Jailspur was abruptly without water. Cursing, he pulled up the motor, climbed from the boat, and shoved the craft forward. It moved easily across the ice, his strength apparent.

Suddenly he was not beside the boat. It sliced into freestanding water and slid forward. Only Jailspur's head and arms were visible. He was thrashing wildly. "Bunnuq! You bitch! Help me!"

I braced myself against my initial reaction and paddled forward. I climbed onto the ice, sloshed to his boat and somehow untied the launch line, then crawled toward him, the coiled rope slapping as I moved.

"That's a girl." He clawed at the ice shelf. "Keep coming."

When I was close enough to assure a good throw, I heaved the lifeline.

For a moment his thrashing stopped. He looked at the shoestring I had thrown, then at the rope still at my side. I smiled and backed away.

Few people can pull themselves from ice without help. There is nothing to grip. The hands bloody, the thrashing becomes more desperate. Cold inexorably seeps upward—Satan's frigid hand reaching through the torso for the soul thudding in the throat.

Jailspur almost succeeded in climbing out unassisted.

He had dug his nails into a tiny crack in stable ice, and his upper half was out of water when he discovered a new way to die.

There are three ways to kill a man who has fallen through the ice. You can leave him there, haul him out but let him freeze, or, if the weather is extremely cold, you can kick him in the spine and it will snap like a stick.

Fric Jailspur found another way.

I saw a man—or what had been a man—emerge behind him in the sea. The skin was parchment, the eye sockets empty, the upper lip torn off, revealing crooked teeth. Sand was crusted across the cheek, despite the water. He wore a tattered goatskin jacket from which water streamed as he rose—reaching around Jailspur's head, sinking gnarled fingers into

Jailspur's eyes, pulling him backward. Jailspur gurgled, clawing at the ice. Then both men were gone, only a small swirl to mark their passing.

Regardless of the thin ice, I retrieved Jerac's shoestring and slipped it into my pocket. Then I returned to my kayak and paddled into the fjord instead of recrossing the shelf.

It was almost dark. I could hear the honking of seals and the narwhals' pulsed whistling and clicks that bespoke social communication rather than the shrieked wheezes associated with fear or feeding. My paddle caressed the fjord's easy current. I was alone among the animals and the stars.

Somehow I knew the ice would continue advancing. The polynia would not hold. I could return to the gillnetter, but I kept heading east. The *Qingmiuneqarfik* was home beside the village whose name she bore. There was nothing for me there except legend, nothing anywhere beyond. I was home in Kangerlussuaq. I would drown when the ice closed in and frenzied fear seized the narwhals. But for the first time in my life, I would live.

ABOUT THE AUTHOR

In 1982, **George Guthridge** accepted a teaching position in a Siberian–Yupik Eskimo village on a stormswept island in the Bering Sea, in a school so troubled it was under threat of closure. Two years later his students made educational history by winning two national academic championships in one year—a feat that earned him the description as "Alaska's Jaime [*Stand and Deliver*] Escalante" and resulted in his being named one of seventy-eight top educators in the nation. Journalists have profiled his teaching techniques in such books as *Superlearning 2000*.

As a writer, he has authored or coauthored four novels, including the acclaimed Holocaust novel *Child of the Light* (with Janet Berliner, from St. Martin's Press, 1992) and the Western *Bloodletter* (Northwest Books, 1994). "The Quiet"—one of over fifty short stories he has sold to major markets—was a finalist for the prestigious Nebula and Hugo awards. He currently teaches English and Eskimo education at the University of Alaska Fairbanks, Bristol Bay.

ELLEN KUSHNER

THE HUNT OF THE UNICORN

Peter: **Ellen Kushner** is another person I'm always sure I know better than I do, because of having met her so often at science fiction and fantasy gatherings. She's the author of a fine fantasy novel, *Thomas the Rhymer,* which reflects her lifelong interest and experience with music, song, and singing. As I recall, that's mainly what we talk about in all those hospitality rooms. . . .

Janet: I echo what Peter said—I always feel that I know Ellen better than I do, and for the same reason. Also because we seem to have so many common friends and acquaintances. In the cover letter Ellen sent with her story, she wrote:

> This story is actually a sequel to the first story I ever published, "The Unicorn Masque." The month it appeared, another dream of mine came true: I got to meet one of my writing idols, Peter S. Beagle, at a convention in California. I nearly fainted when he told me that he'd actually read my story in the anthology (*Elsewhere,* Vol. 1, edited by Terri Windling, Ace Books 1980), and the generous praise he gave it still makes my heart beat fast. I think the Renaissance writers whose work inspired these stories would approve of the perfect circularity of my writing the next one in the sequence for him, and I thank him for the encouragement, and the opportunity to do so.

The Hunt of the Unicorn

B EROWNE ALSO IS HERE IN NANTES, EXAMINING *rugs newly off the vessels from Turkey. His family could well hire an agent to do this foreign collecting for them, to furnish the walls and tables of their houses at Hastings, Ardmere, Little River . . . not to mention his own apartments at court. Perhaps they assign him such tasks as consolation for the real work already being accomplished by his elder brother, whose movements I know you concern yourself with. What, after all, can the young Berowne do but occupy himself with ornament, being himself nothing but an ornament currying grace and favor at the court of the Baseborn Queen? My lord, you shall be kept well aware of his movements here, and those of all the rest of your countrymen as they touch these shores, to the greater future of our noble enterprise, which cannot fail to thrive.*

As for our Quarry, I have several reports to hand, but none of good repute. Your servant while I live—

∞   ∞   ∞

Lord Thomas Berowne was indeed in Nantes, though not at the moment examining anything particularly beautiful. He was in a dockside tavern where even the beer was stale to match the air. He wore a heavy cloak to hide the splendor of his clothes and was much too hot. With one gloved hand he cracked a vent in its folds for air, and received a warning glare from his manservant, Jenkin. Lord Thomas sighed, and looked around again for the stranger who earlier that day had offered him a chance at a rare carving. Berowne was on time for the rendezvous, and the stranger was not—unless he'd managed to disguise himself as a red-headed barmaid with a squint, or a one-legged sailor with a greasy beard. Over by the poor excuse for a fire, two men sat playing cards. One, with his back to the light, was nothing but a shape, and that not the shape of the antiquities dealer; the other was a heavy-built fellow who seemed to be mostly voice: he was on a losing streak, and as his cries of annoyance grew louder, other taverners emerged from the shadows to watch the fun.

"Yer an imp!" the loser roared. "Foreign devil, magicking away a sailor's good money, yer not a man at all!" This provoked predictable comments from the watchers that drowned out his opponent's answer. The loser was drinking heavily, and Jenkin muttered that there might be a fight toward, and perhaps they'd better go now?

Berowne cast another annoyed look toward the door. Still no sign of the stranger and his Hermaphrodite Venus.

"Yes, all right, Jenkin." But as the disguised nobleman rose, so did the drunken cardplayer, stumbling back from his bench and holding up a glittering knife. The spectators drew back, the winning cardplayer drew his sword—or tried to.

Thomas could see the other now. He was a study in black and white with his dark clothes and pale skin, pale hair. Only the low glow of the fire created a faint flush along his right side, running along his emerging blade, while above it his ivory fingers were sketched in charcoal, and his eyes a smear of shadow over high, wide-set cheekbones. Even the swordsman's movements were like the most graceful poses imaginable—and that was the problem: he moved as if he were in a court ballet, slow, deliberate, beautiful, and at about half the speed required for him to survive the encounter.

"Draw!" Lord Thomas ordered his servant; "I know this man!"

At the sight of two outsiders taking an interest in his quarrel, the drunken sailor turned tail and fled, stumbling and cursing his way out of the tavern.

The swordsman turned his head slowly to look at his rescuers. His eyes widened.

"Oh, no," he said.

But they managed to get him out of the smoky tavern and into the sharp night air. Jenkin lit their way down several streets, always away from the wharves. At length they stopped under a cooper's sign, leaning against the shuttered windows of his shop.

"I am not drunk," the beautiful swordsman explained meticulously. "Drink does not affect me. My hands are perfectly steady, and I know exactly where I am."

"Yes, yes." Berowne was delighted to free himself of the heavy cloak and wrap him in it. "I've heard this before, remember? When you were in my rooms at court, drinking my claret and beating us all at cards. You weren't well then, either, though I agree your hands were perfectly steady."

"I am perfectly all right."

"No you're not. You're white as a sheet, and you keep looking at your own hands as though you're not sure whether they're flesh or marble. Which they might well be; Carrara, I think, with the blue veining . . ."

"Ahem," said Jenkin.

"Yes." With an effort, the fair man moved his hand slowly down out of his sight. "Thank you, I must go now."

"I don't think you'll get very far," Berowne said patiently. "Besides, that sailor might have friends. You'd best come home with me."

And so Lazarus Merridon awoke the next morning in an enormous curtained bed, the kind he had slept in in his days at court, and in his master's house. The bed hangings were brocade, patterned with doves and ivy intertwined; he pulled them back and found a vase of white roses by the bed, and a pitcher of water flavored with rosemary, and a blue silk bedgown hung over a chair.

His own clothes were nowhere in sight, which was a pity; he couldn't leave the house clad only in silk, nor yet without his sword. Jenkin was no doubt washing and brushing the clothes; perhaps he was polishing the sword as well? Lazarus rose easily from the bed. He felt fresh and whole again. The tavern had been a regrettable mistake; most regrettable, now. He had thought no one from his past would find him there. A whim of fate had brought the young nobleman. For which he supposed he should be grateful, considering what a fool he had been, drinking more even than he could handle. He wished he were like other men, to whom strong drink brought the mercies of folly and forgetting.

He was thirsty, and drank nearly all the water that was in the pitcher. From the courtyard below his window, women's voices drifted up, laughing and bantering. He went to the casement, and looked out through the cloudy diamond panes. He saw the women as bright spots of color, fetching water at the well. He knew that their lives were not carefree, but in this moment they were happy in the day, in their task, in one another's company. He wished that he might join them then; but that choice had been lost to him.

"Ah, good! You're up."

Lord Thomas Berowne stood in the doorway, neat in brown satin modishly piped with velvet and trimmed with pearls.

Lazarus was wearing nothing. The nobleman was staring. In the moment when he realized it, Thomas turned to the roses and busied himself with rearranging them. The fair man crossed the room, and slipped the blue silk robe over his naked body. If he looked now like a Knight of Love resting between bouts, at least he resembled less a pagan god new-minted in flesh.

"Good morning," he said smoothly to his host. "I slept very well. I'm sorry I disturbed your household. If I might disturb them once more to the tune of my sorry possessions, I'll quit all disturbance hereafter."

"No, no." Thomas broke off a rose, occupied himself pinning it to his doublet. Lazarus couldn't help smiling, to see the young lord again with his hallmark. Last winter at court the nobleman had seldom been without his precious flowers out of season, just as Lazarus had seldom been without his lute. Thomas smiled back. "Your linen is drying, and you must be starving. Stay at least for a meal. This cook does a very nice omelette, and the rolls are fresh, I just tried one."

Lazarus nearly laughed at the man's disingenuousness. Instead, he set his teeth. "I will not strain your courtesy."

"Strain my—? No, it's no trouble, I'll be eating myself."

It was the fair man's turn to stare. "You are very bold, Lord Thomas. Stay me with omelettes, comfort me with apples if you will; I do trust that while you so stay me your hospitality does not extend to finding me better lodgings on a prison ship bound back for home, but only that you take some weird joy in dining with a traitor."

Lord Thomas looked evenly at his guest, all mirth gone from his round and pleasant face. "Are you a traitor, Master Merridon?"

"I loved the queen, it is well-known."

"As do we all."

"No." With one hard word Lazarus froze the practiced courtesy. "As no one else did."

"That is not treason. You served her majesty's pleasure," Thomas said quietly. "As do we all."

"And when she took sick, and like to die, I fled the court."

"That was unhappy."

"Poison was spoken of."

Berowne shrugged. "Strange if it had not been. But she will not hear it in the same breath as your name."

At that, the fair man's composure faltered; but only for an instant, while he drew a breath and closed his hands tightly on nothing.

The nobleman said carefully, "It was a wonderful winter for many, when you were there."

"If my love had been her death, you would not say so."

"I watched you all last year, and heard you play your music. The queen has many enemies. I never thought that you were one of them."

Lazarus turned away from his steady gaze. "Thank you."

"You're welcome."

"And yet," Lazarus Merridon turned his eyes full upon Thomas, "you do not know me at all." His eyes were wide, fringed with heavy lashes, the blue almost silver. Thomas met them, although it was not easy to look into them and speak at the same time.

"I would like to know you. I would like to be your friend."

"Would you?" Agitated, he paced the room, trying to keep his anger away from this generous man. "Because I play the lute, and sing, and can dance, and handle a sword, read Latin and some Greek; in short, play the gentleman in each and every part?"

Lord Thomas smiled fondly. "No, you fool. Because I like you."

"You—*like* me?" Even poised on the edge of confusion, head cocked, brow furled, hands taut, Merridon looked only as if he were performing some complicated dance turn. "What kind of reason is that?"

"The only reason. The very best."

Lazarus let the robe fall open. "Come, know me, then."

Berowne's face paled to match his own, then flushed. "Is this what you want?" he asked hoarsely. "I hadn't thought . . . "

"Come," said Lazarus Merridon, and sighed once as he felt the white rose being crushed between their two breasts.

∞ ∞ ∞

My lord, I dispatch this in haste only to tell you that the Quarry is Sighted.

∞ ∞ ∞

They awoke in the late afternoon sun, amid a tangle of sweaty sheets.

Thomas sighed. "I did not think that I could be so happy."

"You've had other lovers, surely."

"But none like you."

Lazarus smiled wryly. "Certainly none like me."

Thomas looked at his own well-tended hand; it seemed brown, even coarse against the man's pale, soft skin. "You are so beautiful. It's almost hard to believe that you are real."

"Let me help you to believe it." Lazarus kissed him, and they spoke no more until the sun was set.

A discreet tap at the door woke them only from their contemplation of one another.

"Yes?" answered Thomas, because it was his house.

Jenkin's rusty head appeared around the doorframe. "My lord, I wondered if you wanted supper. And if the gentleman wanted his clothes."

"Yes," said one voice, and "No," said the other.

Jenkin understood them perfectly.

There was bread, and cheese, and sausage, and white wine to wash them down with, stony and cold. Because they had slept enough, they lit the candles and they talked.

"I wish that I had known you all my life," said Thomas. "Come, tell me: what were you like as a little boy?"

"I don't remember," Lazarus answered.

"I was rather pious." Thomas rested on his lover's chest. "I like for people to like me, and most of the people I knew were adults. Even my brother, Stephen—he's always been very grown-up. He's virtuous and brave, like an old-fashioned knight: he's studied fighting, and tactics, and history and all. He is the heir, and a good thing, too. I am only a second son—a fifth, actually, but I'm the one that lived. Have you brothers and sisters?"

"No. I was hatched. From an egg—or maybe an alembic. I was an experiment."

Thomas laughed. "Of course. Your patron, Lord Andreas, always liked to dabble in the weird sciences." Lazarus shuddered. "Quite," said his friend. "Something about all those rings, crammed on his puffy fingers . . ."

"Oh, Thomas! You dislike him only because he is not beautiful."

"Well, I am sure that there are many other reasons to dislike him." Thomas rolled over, and wrapped his arms around his companion. "You let me talk and talk, and you don't say a word. You are so brilliant, so accomplished; is there not one good memory for you to share? Some piece of music heard for the first time; a kindly tutor; a lover; a warm spring night?"

Lazarus pressed his knuckles to his eyes, as though he would squeeze tears out of them. "Oh, do not ask me. Be my friend and do not ask me that."

∞   ∞   ∞

Of ships in the harbor here, full xiv are provisioning to the benefit of our enterprise under pretext of an Eastern Expedition, and idle men are easy come by to man them; expecting one profit, they will rejoice to find another! . . . Meanwhile, I will make it my business to create the occasion for some idle conversation with the Quarry, to know which way his mind tends concerning our affairs. That he is skillful and clever I well believe,

*since he contrived to elude me for so long. I will do all I can not to start
him into further flight, knowing his value to yr ldshp.*

∞ ∞ ∞

They woke to midmorning sunlight. The curtains were drawn, the
roses were fresh, and Lazarus' clothes lay neatly folded on a chest. Even
his sword had been polished.

Thomas Berowne said, "It's funny, how much more interested I was
in Turkey carpets two days ago. But I suppose I had better finish my deal-
ings, since I've begun. Dress and come with me; you can tell me which
ones to buy."

But Lazarus shook his head. "I think that would be unwise."

"Why? You have excellent taste."

The fair man smiled. "Thank you. But I will stay here."

"Ashamed to be seen with me, are you?" Berowne teased. "Afraid
we'll fall to it in the street, is that it?"

"That is exactly it."

"Oh, come, you're a model of self-control. I've seen you at court,
where the thing is truly tested."

Lazarus sighed, laughing. "Oh, Thomas . . . ! Just because you think
me blameless doesn't mean others do. Shall I spell it out? People are
looking for me. "

"But the queen has called off the search, I was there."

"Enemies of the queen, then."

"And you the great swordsman that you are, to fear them!"

"Much service I would do her, being taken up for quarreling and
murder in a foreign country."

"I can protect you, Lazarus. I promised."

"But who will protect you?"

Thomas raised his eyebrows. "You?"

"And there you have it"—Lazarus nodded—"a perfectly closed system. Pretty in two places only: philosophy and bed. Go on; be off with
you and buy your carpets. I will be here when you get back."

Lord Thomas looked at him gravely. "Will you?"

"Yes, I will. I like it here."

∞ ∞ ∞

*Welcome, my lord, to these shores, blessed by our most sovereign
lady. I rejoice in your deliverance from the realm of the Baseborn*

Queen, and hope you will return there soon in triumph at the side of our
gracious lady her sister, whose true right to the throne of her father is
incontestable.

∞   ∞   ∞

It was late that night under a full moon when Lord Thomas returned
to their room. What he saw made him catch his breath: a man seated on
the windowseat, fair head bent over a lute, all silvered by moonlight, the
strings shimmering like liquid as they were plucked.

He stood still, listening to the music, wishing it could go on and on;
but Lazarus looked up, and set the lute aside. "There you are. I went back
to my old lodgings to rescue a few things."

Around his neck a gold chain gleamed. Thomas approached, and
lifted from his chest a jewel, a heavy pendant of a unicorn crusted with
gemstones and pearls.

"The queen's jewel. You have it still."

"I was thinking of pawning it."

"But you did not."

"No." Lazarus laced his fingers with Thomas's, closed together
around the gaudy unicorn. For a long time, he looked at them. He opened
his mouth, closed it, then wet his lips and said, "Tell me—how is she?"

"Truly? She is sad. She reads philosophy, and speaks no more of
masques, nor yet of love."

"Poor lady."

"Her younger sister, the Gallish queen, has an eye to her kingdom as
well; rumors of invasion are common as starlings in June. Because the
Gallish woman has sons, and in her pride seeks kingdoms for them all,
while our sweet lady sits alone—"

"And will not wed. I know."

Thomas's fingers tightened around them both. "She still wants you.
My family serves her, and always has," he said earnestly. "Lazarus, I can—
I can arrange certain things. A passage. A pardon. You might return to her."

"No. It would kill her."

Thomas knelt at his feet, to look up into his moon-silver eyes. "Sweet,
why do you say so? I know you are a good man. You may not love her, but
you value her happiness, as I do. You would never seek to harm her."

Lazarus looked back at his friend. His pupils were huge and dark. "It
has to do with Andreas. With my guardian, my patron."

"He is no longer your patron. He cast you off when you fled."

"No. He did not," Lazarus said bitterly. "Never mind what he told the
court. He did not cast me off and never will."

"Sweet, what is it? Are you his son?"

The fair man barked a laugh. "God, no! I made a bargain."

"It can be broken. Whether you are bound by money, honor, duty—Lord Andreas is a rotten man, and a greedy one; it is not right for such as you to owe him anything! Tell me, only tell me, and I will see to it; I am not so very unworldly that I cannot do that for you."

"No. This bargain cannot be broken. And if it were to be, you would not like it." Lazarus smiled thinly. "I promise you that."

"Riddles, my love." Thomas unknit his fingers from the overwrought jewel, and smoothed his hand like a kitten, or a rumpled sheet. "I wish that you could tell me. I wish that I could help. . . ."

"You do." Lazarus' voice was muffled by Thomas's shirt. "Oh, you do. But there are things I cannot say—I cannot *tell* you, Thomas!"

Thomas kissed the back of his neck, where the fine hair grew like down. "What is it? What is so terrible? Are you a murderer? An adulterer? Father of a hundred bastards?" Lazarus laughed against his chest. "I know you do not kick small children in the street. What is this terrible thing you cannot tell?"

But the glib-tongued man was silent.

"Let me ask you questions, then. These painful secrets, kept too long, will fester; and, like old worms, begin to feed on that which is their home. I will ask, and you will answer as you may." He felt the fair man stiffen in his arms. "Right. Then cut straight to the heart. Lazarus, why did you flee the court?"

"For the harm I did the queen."

"What harm is that?"

"I did not mean to—I did not know—And when I knew, I fled."

"What did you do?

He turned his head away. "I poisoned her."

"You did. And by what means?" Thomas asked patiently.

Lazarus swallowed, and in a muffled voice said, "It is my love. My love that poisons."

Thomas nearly shook him, but wrapped his arms around him tighter instead. "Nonsense! People have only told you that . . . angry people, people you've hurt who want to hurt you. But you mustn't listen to them," he soothed; "they are wrong, it isn't true—"

Lazarus wrenched himself from his lover's grasp. His face was nothing but eyes and hollow angles, unnatural and lovely, like cut glass. "But it is true, Thomas. Not some quaint conceit—or maybe that is exactly what I am: the poetic *love that kills* made flesh, walking the earth. A lover's song incarnate."

"How is that possible?

"To be a dream made flesh? I do not know. Ask Andreas and his alchemical friends. But I am perfect, am I not? You have said so yourself. Created for a queen to be her death. And maybe I will be yours as well."

"How?" Lord Thomas only stared. "I do not understand."

"Because you do not want to understand! Look at me, Thomas, only look at me and think. I have no past, no childhood, no store of memories but dreams. I cannot get drunk, I cannot be killed, by poison or by the sword—instead of getting drunk, I go to sleep; my wounds close up as soon as they are made. I am not a man, Thomas, so do not waste your sympathy and your kind understanding on me. I'm not a man like you, or Jenkin, or the beggar in the street!"

Thomas sat, impassive. "And the queen?"

"I carry poison in my flesh. For others, not for me."

"I see." Thomas nodded. "Yes.

Moonlight flashed across his lover's body as he paced back and forth between the shadows and the window.

"But you were mortal once?"

"Of course. Only God can make a human soul from nothing," Lazarus said scornfully. "Do not ask me what I was before; it comes to me in dreams, but that is all."

Thomas said slowly, "I've taken no harm of you thus far."

"Nor did the queen, at first."

"Yes."

Lazarus stopped his pacing. He stood in the shadows, watching Thomas in the moonlight. Thomas rose, and turned from him, pressing his forehead to the moon-washed glass, hands raised above his head against the panes.

"There," Lazarus said. "You asked, and now you know." Lord Thomas's eyes were closed, his face washed blue, like someone in a tomb. "You will not want to see me, now. It is disgusting, I know."

"No," Thomas spoke, his cheek against the cold glass. "Oddly enough, that isn't true. I've heard all that you have said, and I think that I believe it. But I find I do not care. It makes no difference. And that surprises me."

"Ah," said Lazarus with a bravado he did not feel. "I have frightened you at last."

Lord Thomas smiled. "Oh, no, my dear; you do not frighten me." His face was warm enough to melt the coldness of the glass; but still he stood where he was, cheek pressed to the night.

Lazarus came to him, slowly and gently, and turned him in his arms, and sat him down, and laid his bright head in his lap.

∞ ∞ ∞

It is a wonderful thing, how Berowne scarcely ventures from his house, and yet he is not Ill, save with that disease common to bride-grooms and green girls! Neither do any come in to him, and so yr ldshp's thought that he might be passing and receiving information under cover of his collecting may be disproved. Let him do our work for us the whiles, for as a Keeper he does excel any that Art or Nature could provide!

∞ ∞ ∞

They had flowers and wine, music and conversation, darkness and light, and the warmth of one another's breath in the silences in between action and talk; they had all that they needed to make them happy.

In the dark, they talked of everything that came to them, or ever had. Thomas learned to know the rhythms of his lover's body, his breathing and his silences; when he needed comfort, when passion; when he might be taken, and when it was necessary to give.

Lazarus, too, learned to see without eyes, and to make music for one person only. *Pretty fool*, Thomas called him; and, knowing he could out-match Thomas at anything but love, Lazarus found he liked that.

Thomas tended his love like a garden. He pulled the weeds out from among the fragile shoots, careful not to tangle with their roots. Thomas asked, "Is it true you cannot die?"

Lazarus shrugged. "Only time will tell. It adds a certain spice to life. I think that I cannot be killed—except, perhaps"—he frowned—"by those who made me. My making was expensive; they told me so many times. They are unlikely to waste their labor by undoing me."

Thomas stroked the length of his body, infinitely precious now in light and dark. "I would like to think no one can touch you now."

Lazarus laughed gently. "No one but you."

∞ ∞ ∞

My lord has in the past had the kindness to credit me with some good sense, and so will not think me derelict or negligent, particularly when the good resolution of our enterprise is so very near, that I have not con-trived, by accident or by design, to meet with and hold some conversation with the Quarry. And yr ldshp's warnings about his prodigious skills at arms and clever speech have not made me timid, nor lax to do yr bidding, but only cautious not to betray my interest lest some word of this come to

Berowne. After all, the thing now is under way, and cannot be stopped, least of all by two such inward-turning fellows. Yr ldshp's concern that the Quarry not return to his Baseborn love, lest he in his great gifts should prove of service against us, I think unfounded. Your further uses for him you may achieve when you sit at the hand of the True Queen, whose enterprise will surely thrive. Meanwhile, so long as he remains the chief toy and jewel of the young lord, and they do content themselves with one another, then why not trust the words of the old adage, and "Let sleeping dogs lie"?

∞   ∞   ∞

But the end came, as it so often does, with news of the outside world. They were at breakfast, a meal of honey and golden sunlight, both making golden patches on their skin, and oranges, and country butter on rolls hot from the oven.

Thomas wiped a trickle of honey from the other's chin, and regarded him critically. "Hmm," he said; "you are, if possible, even paler than before. Fresh air is what you need, and if you must go out disguised, it won't be in that ridiculous black hooded cloak."

"I must not be recognized with you—"

". . . too dangerous, I know, I know. We must find some way of altering your looks that does no lasting harm—a wig? A wig . . ." The nobleman's smile stretched into a gloat of pure mischief. "Certainly a wig; a nice long one, and a veil, and paint to your eyes, and a lovely gown, green, I think!"

"Oh, excellent!" His friend's hilarity held a note of near-hysteria. "Disguise me as that I am!"

"Well you're hardly a courtesan, my dear, though some might call you my mistress—"

"My lord."

Jenkin stood holding a folded parchment bound about with tape and wax. "This is new come off the boat for you, my lord. A man waits below for your reply."

Thomas broke open the heavy seals. Lazarus knew the device stamped into them; the family crest was on Berowne's dagger, his goblets, his plate. He waited quietly across the room, until Thomas lifted a drawn face to him.

"My father—My brother—It seems I must come home."

"Are they ill?"

"No, no. But this is not a time for me to be abroad." Lord Thomas glanced down at the letter, and forced a smile. "They like the rugs I chose."

Lazarus felt it then, the hard-edged border between what he was to Berowne, and what a man's family was: the loyalties held, the confidences understood. "Well," he said. "You will close up this house?"

"I must." Thomas walked around the room, rapping at things with the parchment: the wall, a chair, a chest, the bed. "From what they say, I will not be back soon."

Lazarus felt his stomach lurch with understanding. "Good. I'll send you some music."

"Music?" Thomas looked at him with amazement. "What music?"

"For the procession. The banquet." With pride, Lazarus noted that his own voice held light and steady. "It will be a gift between us."

"My dear, what on earth are you talking about?"

"Now that your family has found you a bride."

"A—Oh!" Thomas laughed with his fingers spread over his face. "Oh, no. I wish it were that simple, that would be easy."

Lazarus saw that he was not laughing after all. He knelt at his side. "My dear, tell me—what is it?"

Thomas handed him the letter. Skimming over the salutations, the family news, Lazarus Merridon read:

". . . that Her Majesty's sister plans invasion is now certain, and the time will be soon. Although we could wish you safely away, your place is here."

∞ ∞ ∞

Berowne is closing his house up very suddenly. Doubtless he returns home to join ranks with the Baseborn Queen. Should the Quarry seek to accompany him thither, I will take those measures yr ldshp instructed me in.

∞ ∞ ∞

"Come with me," said Thomas. "Please come."

"I will be more use to you here. Hidden in the taverns, I can collect reports—"

"I do not care for use! I want you by me."

In the dark, Lazarus put his fingers to his lover's mouth, stilling the words on his lips. "I dare not come. I dare not. If the queen sees me— Or anyone thinks I've hurt her—If those who made me find me . . . "

"Come under my protection—Come disguised—Do you mean to live an exile all your life?

"An exile? You speak as though I had a home."

"In love, you do. In love and honor."

"Oh, Thomas . . . ! I am not a man of honor. I am not noble, as you are, in any sense of the word."

"You are loyal, to those you love. You would not suffer the queen to be harmed through you."

"Pride," Lazarus dismissed it. "I would not be used. If I go back, they will try to use me to harm—to harm those around me.

"You will not let them. You know now that you did not know before. You're strong, my love, and true."

The slender fingers clenched in upon themselves, biting half-moons in his perfect flesh. "*I do not know what I will do.* You must understand, Thomas, try—I do not know fully what I am. My limits or my strength. Andreas knows. I am afraid, Tom: afraid of him, afraid to let him find me."

"My dear, how long must you live thus?"

"I need time, I must have time to find out what I am in truth."

"I will kill Andreas when I see him! He is a traitor, and a pig besides. He never told you, he and his friends, what you were made of?"

"They gave me what they promised me."

"Lazarus—what did they promise you? What did you trade yourself away for?

"It was to be that which I am. The form, the grace, the gifts, the skills—all of it. I desired it above all things," the beautiful man said with bleak defiance. "I thought I would be happy."

"Poor Lazarus!" He heard the smile in Thomas's voice, but the man's warm hands were all comfort and affection. "You may not be mortal, but I fear that you are human after all."

Lazarus rolled in his lover's arms. And where one held the other and where one was held, was a thing indistinguishable as hair from hair in a braided coronet, or the interlaced twining of vines in the bower.

Lazarus spoke at last. "Go home and do what you must do. If it is done well, I will be free to return. If ill—then you will come to me, and we will go adventuring together the wide world over."

∞ ∞ ∞

The Quarry is fled. The trail is cold. I rejoice in your victory, and that of our most Sovereign Lady.

∞ ∞ ∞

In a tavern in another harbor town, Lazarus Merridon heard of the fall of the crown, and the death and attainder of many of its noble supporters. Among the dead, the Berowne heir; the parents fled to friends across the sea. And their surviving son, attainted traitor, awaiting now the new prince's judgment in a little room behind the thick walls of a tower, encircled with woven rushes in a field of flowers.

ABOUT THE AUTHOR

Novelist and public radio personality **Ellen Kushner** grew up in Cleveland, Ohio, and attended Bryn Mawr and Barnard Colleges. After graduating from Columbia University, she found a job in publishing at Ace Books as fantasy editor, and then went on to edit fiction at Pocket Books/Simon & Schuster. When she quit her publishing job to write, she supported herself in New York City freelancing as a book reviewer, copywriter, literary scout, and artist's representative. In her spare time she sang in choirs and folk coffeehouses.

In 1987, Ellen Kushner moved to Boston and began a career in public radio at WGBH-FM, as a music host. From 1989-91, radio audiences across America heard her as the offbeat and popular host of *The International Music Series* on American Public Radio. Other national work includes cowriting *Which Way's Witch: A June Foray Halloween Spell* (starring the famous voice from *Rocky & Bullwinkle*). She produced/hosted/directed/wrote three award-winning Jewish Holiday specials which have become annual favorites from APR (now renamed Public Radio International). She has also been heard on National Public Radio as a contributor to *A Note to You* and *Performance Today*.

In winter of 1995, Public Radio International will launch Ellen as the host and producer of a new national weekly series, *Sound and Spirit,* a musical exploration of the human spirit.

Ellen Kushner's most recent novel, *Thomas The Rhymer,* winner of the 1991 World Fantasy Award, as well as the Mythopoeic Award, is a fantasy based on British folklore and balladry. Her first novel was *Swordspoint: A Melodrama of Manners.* Her short fiction has often appeared in *The Year's Best Fantasy And Horror* (ed. Datlow & Windling) and in the "Punk Elf" *Bordertown* series (ed. Windling). Her latest book is *St. Nick And The Valley Beyond The World's Edge, A Christmas Legend,* illustrated by Richard Burhans (Viking Studio, 1994).

ERIC LUSTBADER

THE DEVIL ON MYRTLE AVE.

Peter: **Eric Lustbader**, best known to a general audience as the author of bestselling novels that include *Black Heart, The Ninja,* and *Second Skin,* is another one of those people who somehow pack several other people's careers into their résumés. He spent fifteen years in the music industry in various capacities, including working for both Elektra and CBS Records, as well as Cash Box Magazine, and running his own independent production company. Somewhere in there, amazingly, he also taught in the All-Day Neighborhood School Division of the New York City public school system, developing curriculum enrichment for third and fourth grade children. He has also taught preschoolers in special early childhood programs. He lives in Southampton, New York, with his wife Victoria, who works for the Nature Conservancy.

Janet: When Victoria Schochet—onetime editor-in-chief of science fiction and fantasy at Berkley Books—announced some years ago that she was marrying someone talented, handsome, and famous, I was impressed. Little did I imagine that it was *the* Eric Lustbader, or that down the road I would be asking him to write a story for this volume. The story is a standout. It will, I believe, surprise many and shock others with its theme. As for working with you, Mr. Lustbader, Suh, I can hardly wait for the next project.

The Devil on Myrtle Ave.

I T WAS RAINING CHILL NEEDLES THAT KNIFED
to the bone when Garland Montgomery found his mother. She was curled
up like a baby on the threadbare rug of their Bedford-Stuyvesant housing
project apartment. She was cool and still and there was a ball of bubbly
froth at the corner of her mouth. The used syringe lay, milky and evil as
whitey's face, at her side.

Garbage was heaped helter-skelter every which way and the room
had that too familiar smell of old grease, rotting food, and rank human
flesh. In the weeks since he had been here rats had begun to rustle in the
shadows.

Without a second thought, Garland turned and ran out of the filthy
apartment, down the bare concrete stairs, almost tripping over old Mrs.
Blank, who slept on the landing between the second and third floors,
wrapped in grease-smeared newspaper. Mrs. Blank was nuts, raving
about little pink men from Mars when she was awake, so no one paid her
any mind. They were sure she was dreaming of whitey. Her breath
smelled of lighter fluid.

Out in the rain, Garland ran as fast as he could. He slipped in a gutter
filled with all kinds of shit and slammed hip-first into a wildly braking
car. Lights flared and an angry horn blared. Then he had vaulted across
the car's hood, crossed Myrtle Ave. as a truck coming the other way
veered away from him, and was racing around the corner. He ducked
down a side street and into a back alley, filled with vermin and not much
else.

Garland, who was fifteen, had seen his brother shot dead in this alley,
because he was trying to sell a bag of cocaine. Garland had two other
family members he knew about. His oldest brother, Derryl, was in Attica,

in prison for three counts of manslaughter. His sister, who was seventeen, lived in Pittsburgh with two squally children and a common-law husband who most nights beat her. Garland, who was the man of the family, had wanted to go down to Pittsburgh and pistol-whip the man into shape but his sister had said no. "My life ain't so bad," she had said to him by phone. "At least he ain't run out on me."

A bitter comment about a father neither had known.

Garland found the building, reached up through the pouring rain for the iron fire escape ladder. He scrabbled upward, a familiar journey, until he reached the roof. He broke through the skylight without much trouble, cut through the wire mesh beneath the glass with cutters, and dropped to the floor. He was in Dr. Gupta's office, the Indian, who he and his pals from the Bloods made fun of every time they saw him. The doc and his fat wife lived in the two-bedroom on the ground floor. The place always stank from curry and weird spices.

The building was important because it was in a kind of no-man's land between Blood turf and Crip turf. The two gangs were mortal enemies, and there wasn't a man alive Garland hated worse than Levar, the rival gang's leader. He'd bludgeoned to death two Bloods single-handed. For Blood or Crip, coming here was an act of heroism.

Garland knew Dr. Gupta's office like the palm of his hand; it'd been here he'd made his initiation into the gang, breaking and entering, stealing some shit—opium and morphine—to prove his feat. In celebration they'd pierced the soft bony stuff between his nostrils and stuck through a thick silver chain. He'd been nine; three weeks before, he'd been given a gun by his mother, who'd wanted him to have protection in a neighborhood filled with danger and death.

He was strapped; he never went outside without his gun. He touched it now, then fingered the unicorn charm that hung from his nose chain like it was a sacred talisman that could keep away harm. Within minutes, he had gathered up the things he needed. Then he vaulted back up through the skylight, ran across the rooftop, and climbed back down the fire escape.

He made his way through the courtyards of the project. Looking at the graffiti-covered brick buildings, you'd never know they hid a whole other world inside. Old Mrs. Blank heard him coming full tilt and pulled her head into her shoulders like a tortoise. More than once there'd been gunplay in her stairwell.

Back at his mother's apartment, he knelt down beside her. She hadn't moved. Water dripped from him onto the carpet as he got to work. He ripped the paper off the disposable syringe, broke out the vial of epinephrine, drew it into the syringe. He turned his mother onto her back, pounded her rib cage with his fist, slapped her cheeks hard. Her head lolled loosely from side to side but she didn't open her eyes.

He felt for the soft places between her ribs, counted, was so nervous he had to start all over again. Counted, *three, four, there!,* got the spot where her heart was, and jabbed the needle through the skin. He moved the needle very slowly between her ribs. He'd once seen this done with a sharp jab and the needle had broken off as it struck bone.

When he was into the spongy layer beneath, he drove home the needle. He made the injection. Had he got the heart? His mother's eyelids fluttered and he heard a rattling in her chest. He put his ear against her breast, heard her heartbeat thundering like a runaway chopper. It was much too fast, out of control.

He jumped up. In the kitchen, he took down a canister of salt, mixed it with warm water until the crystals were dissolved. He poured half the liquid into another glass, filled the syringe with the salt water, making sure there were no crystals in the syringe. Then he opened the freezer, put a tray of old, smelly ice under his arm.

He found the vein into which she'd injected the heroin and pumped in the salt water. Then he jammed the ice against her crotch. Her eyes flew open.

"Mama?" he said, shaking her. "Mama?"

She stared wide-eyed at him. Did she know who he was? Her mouth gaped open, foam dripping onto her chin.

"Mama, yo' gotsta get on yo' feet."

A sudden seizure gripped her and she began to quiver.

"Mama!" Garland cried, holding her tighter.

Another spasm made her teeth clack together, and her breathing became labored, ragged. She pulled a shuddering breath and never released it.

Garland began to cry. He knew it was definitely not the kind of thing the man of the family did. But he was also a kid, and he was so scared. He wiped the chain through his nose with the back of a hand made clumsy by fear. The silver unicorn that hung from it jingled lightly. For a long time, he couldn't move. He stared into his mother's wasted face. Just thirty-three and she looked as old as Mrs. Blank. That seemed so sad, he began to cry all over again.

He knew she was dead, but he was reluctant to leave her. He clung to whatever was left of her warmth and thought of how she had sung him to sleep when he'd been young. He tried to remember the song she sang to him, but he couldn't. It was gone with her. All he could remember was the moment she had given him the gun.

He had thought that being strapped made him a man, but the members of his gang had wasted no time telling him uh, uh, he'd have to do much more than just carry a gun. He'd have to shoot someone before he'd be a man in their eyes. He'd have to prove his courage by being master of life and death. This he had done most willingly during a gang scuffle, firing off two shots and wounding two of the enemy. He'd been cut off from the rest of the Bloods, all alone without backup. From that incident, he'd gotten the street name of Unicorn.

But he'd never killed anyone.

On the morning after his mother's OD, Garland lay in wait on Myrtle Ave. It was a wide street used by maybe a hundred trucks a day servicing the independent supermarkets and corner groceries from Fort Greene to Bushwick. Because they weren't part of big chain stores, they had to pay cash for their deliveries. That meant more often than not the truck drivers were holding big bucks. But not always. One of Garland's gang homeboys had shot a driver in the neck for twenty-three dollars. It seemed stupid, except that his status in the gang had skyrocketed.

The trucks had certain set routes and schedules, so they were easy marks. All the gang members had memorized the routes and times of deliveries. Garland turned his head as a black Camaro jounced down the street spewing rap from its speakers. It paused for a light, then cruised through it, leaving a cloud of blue exhaust in its wake. Just down the block from where Garland crouched in hard morning shadow, colored plastic pennants cracked in the stiff breeze. They were strung from nylon lines in front of the Associated market and wound around a lamppost. A nasty-looking yellow mutt with a damaged leg limped in the gutter, rooting for breakfast. Old Moses, a grizzled black man in a tattered mackinaw, was doing his thing, selling hijacked gloves out of a Dumpster. But he was chilled; he wouldn't make a move. As Garland waited for the potato chip truck to come by, his mind was completely blank. It was like he didn't want to think.

A blue-and-white squad car from the 79th Precinct cruised by and Garland smiled. The cops were under mounting pressure from the papers and TV to do something about the hijackings and killings along Myrtle Ave. Too bad the cops didn't have a fucking clue.

The potato chip truck swung into view, slowing as it passed Garland. It stopped in front of the market, the big beefy white man swung down from the cab and rolled up the back door. Garland watched him as he began to unload the cartons of potato chips. The time to take him was after he'd made delivery, and, his pocket bulging with bills, he was just getting back into the truck.

Garland was patient, his mind filled with nothing, a red nothing that took his breath away. He was waiting to hear again that song his mother used to sing to him, but all he heard was an ambulance siren on Lafayette Ave. It screeched against his eardrums. The yellow mutt began to bark at Old Moses selling his stolen gloves.

Old Moses kicked at it. The mutt yelped in pain and loped clumsily away. Garland tried not to think of his three-month-old son, whom he'd never seen. His name was Marcus; Garland never even saw the mother, a thin, inky dark girl he'd fucked in the back of a friend's car. Once. It meant nothing to Garland, just another way to get off. The last thing he needed was to be burdened with a girl he barely knew and a squally kid. He'd be damned if he was going to end up like his sister.

Cool, Garland thought. Let's be cool.

In front of the Associated, the driver was wheeling his loaded-down hand truck across the sidewalk and into the market. He was inside maybe ten minutes, then he came out, more nervous now. He rushed back to his truck, stowed the hand truck, banged down the rolling back door. As he went around the far side of the truck to the cab, Garland made his move.

By the time the driver slid behind the wheel, Garland, clinging with one hand to the outside of the curbside door, had his gun pointed into the cab.

"Oh, shit," the driver said. He was one of those big, flush-faced Irishmen, who drank too much and then went out looking for trouble.

"Here be trouble," Garland said.

The driver's hands were on the wheel. Garland was thrilled to see them trembling.

"I don't want none of that," the driver said. He was trying, unsuccessfully, to ignore the gun pointed at him. "Go ahead. Take my money."

His words might have been Russian for all Garland made sense of them. His mind, so recently drained of everything, was now seething with a fury he could not name. He saw his mother, dying. He saw himself helpless to save her. Helpless because he was not yet a man, for all the mannish pretense of his young life. Deprived of youth, he yearned for something beyond it, an adulthood for which he was wholly unprepared. But his thought was this: If he had been a man, he could have saved his mother. The red rage gathered around this thought and, given form, demanded an immediate and explosive outlet.

Garland stared hard into whitey's eyes and pulled the trigger.

When Tony Valenti heard the gunshot, he was on Myrtle Ave. just east of Bedford. He stamped on the accelerator of the truck and ran a red light. His pulse was running hard and it felt as if his heart was sitting in his throat. He wanted to gag with the apprehension.

He saw Jack Halloran's truck in front of the Associated. Halloran
was known as the potato chip man, just as Tony was the pie man. The
drivers' real names weren't used on the street. A small group was gathering while a grizzled old man scrabbled through a Dumpster, his back to
the commotion. Tony hit the brakes, swerving to the curb. He grabbed the
baseball bat he kept in the cab in case of trouble and, without turning off
the ignition, banged the door open and swung down into the street.

Vehicles were stopping or slowing down, their occupants rubbernecking
as they crept past Halloran's truck. Tony ran through the thickening crowd.
He knew Halloran well. Besides working for the same wholesaler, they
were friends. They had dinner once a week, their wives exchanged gossip,
their kids played together. They'd even spent this Thanksgiving together.

He reached the cab and, for an instant, hesitated. Then he climbed up
and stared in.

"Oh, Christ," he whispered, and ducked his head back out. He closed
his eyes but he could not block out the inside of the cab, splattered with
blood and bits of bone and brain. Jack Halloran's face had been blown
away. Tony felt a pressure in his chest. Maybe he was having a heart
attack. His face was flushed and his hands shook as he held on to the outside of the truck.

"Someone call the police?" he asked.

He felt a firm hand on his shoulder, and a voice say, "The police're
here, bud."

He turned to see a pair of uniforms, their squad car behind them,
lights flashing. A black and white duo, very PC, he thought.

"Yeah?" he said, addressing the white one. "Where were you when
my buddy got his face shot off?"

"Easy does it," the white cop said. Then, "Would you mind standing
down from there?" When Tony had complied, the black one, eyeing the
baseball bat he gripped with white knuckles, said, "You better put that
weapon away before someone confiscates it."

"This?" Tony hefted the bat. "A Christmas present for my boy. He's
in Little League."

"You witness the shooting?" the white cop broke in.

"No," Tony said. "I heard the shot, though. I was just passing Bedford."

The white cop nodded. "Well, stick around, anyway."

The black cop, on his way past Tony, said, "And all you could afford
was a used one? Tsk, tsk."

Tony went back to his truck, stowed the bat in its spot behind the
seat. As he did so, he watched the black cop systematically going through
the crowd, looking for witnesses. Tony saw him saunter over to the grizzled man beside the Dumpster. Even then, the old guy kept his back to the

street and Jack Halloran's truck. The black cop kept asking questions and the old guy kept shaking his head from side to side, no, I ain't seen nothing. But Tony suspected that he was lying. Something in the way he refused to turn around, look at the scene of the murder, like he'd already seen more than he wanted of it.

Tony waited patiently until the black cop got around to him, was reassured that Tony did not, in fact, witness the shooting.

"What is it?" The black cop stared right into Tony's eyes. "Do I smell bad or something?"

"What?"

"You got this look on your face, like you smell a bad smell, you know, like rotten meat."

"Hey, just a minute," Tony said, trying to recover. He had, in fact, been wanting to speak to the white cop, who he assumed was in charge. "My buddy's been shot to death on a route we both use. I gotta right to be upset."

The black cop told him he could go.

Tony watched him walk away, then said, "That old guy at the Dumpster, he see anything?"

The black cop paused, folding away his notepad. "What's it to you?"

"Jack Halloran was a pal," Tony said. "We had Thanksgiving together not two weeks ago."

The black cop looked at him deadpan. "That a fact?" He glanced over at the grizzled old man, bent over his Dumpster. "Nah, he's so out of it I doubt he remembers what day it is. He's useless."

Tony nodded. "Listen. There's a photo in Jack's cab. Him and the family. I'd like to take it back to his wife."

The black cop sighed. "I understand, Mr. Valenti, but right now it's evidence. Soon as it's dusted for prints and we can release it, it'll go to the next of kin."

"But that's just it," Jack protested. "I don't want it to come to her from the police. It'll kill her."

"Sorry. It's regs."

Tony took a step toward the black cop. "Maybe I should speak to your partner."

The black cop gave him a dark and menacing look. "Take my advice, Mr. Valenti. Go home, get on with your work, whatever. But leave the scene now."

It was after six when Tony returned to the warehouse. Because of the incident, he'd been late delivering his packaged pies and cakes. Also, because he'd taken time out to call Katie to reassure her he was all right and to tell her to get over to Eileen Halloran's and give her what moral support she could. God knew Eileen was going to need it.

Tony's boss was waiting for him. "I want to see you in my office," he said as he turned his back. "Now."

Mr. Tolan's office was one of those old dusty spaces marked out by metal walls and frosted glass. Tony guessed it must date back to the turn of the century. Inside, it didn't look as if much had changed since it was built. Ancient file cabinets lined the walls, there were two metal and vinyl chairs and a chewed wooden desk on bare wooden floorboards so worn they had lost all color.

"So," Tolan said as soon as Tony walked in, "I heard about Halloran."

"Yeah." Tony shook his head sadly. "A helluva thing."

Tolan, balding, burly, in shirtsleeves and toting a massive cigar, advanced on him. "I also heard from the cops that you're toting a baseball bat."

That black bastard ratted me out, Tony thought. "Well, whadaya expect, Mr. Tolan, it's a fuckin' jungle out there. Look what happened today."

"Listen to me, Valenti. You chose this job, it didn't choose you. The situation on Myrtle Ave., it's part of the job, nothing more. What makes you different than the other drivers on my payroll? You know the rules. You're expressly forbidden to carry weapons of any kind. And if you want to keep your job, you'll get rid of yours immediately."

"But what about Jack Halloran? For Christ's sake, look what happened to him. If he'd been armed—"

Tolan shouted down Tony's protest. "What happened to Halloran is tragic, no doubt. But it's over. The police'll do their job—"

"The police, that's a laugh," Tony grunted. "The police can't catch these gangsta kids. They melt into the jungle of the projects and the police come up with zilch every time. One of these days they're just gonna forget about trying."

Tolan went back behind his desk. "None of this is your problem, Valenti. You gotta forget about Halloran, forget your anger. You gotta think about yourself—and all the other drivers who work here." Tolan shook his head. "Look, I explain this to every rookie who signs on. You been here, what, twelve years? By now you know it as well as I do. I got a whole company to think about. My guys start holding and what happens? They get carried away, bust up some citizen by mistake, and who gets sued? This company gets sued, that's who. With liability insurance what it is I can't afford that, Valenti. None of us can. That kinda suit would put this place out of business, then where would you an' all the other drivers be?"

Tony clocked out and went home. But he couldn't forget Jack Halloran and he couldn't let go of his anger. He came from a poor background. His father had worked hard—fourteen hours a day to feed his family and put them through school. College for all of them, had been his motto. Whether they had wanted it or not. Tony hadn't, had hated all four years of it. In fact, he'd spent most of his senior year working in a gas station, which was where he developed his love for big engines and trucks.

Tony had never told his father; the old man would never have understood. But that basic gulf between him and his children hadn't stopped Tony's father from loving them, providing for them. He'd been an honest man, a man who'd lived by his ideals. And he'd passed those ideals down to his sons and daughters. Tony did not believe in environment excusing behavior. His father had taught him to fight against adversity, not use it as an excuse to sin.

Katie and the kids were over at the Hallorans'. She had left him dinner in the oven but he had no appetite. He nearly choked on a beer, poured himself some whiskey instead. That didn't taste good, either, but at least he could get it down. He had another. Then, he climbed the stairs and went into his kids' bedroom. He remembered waking up at night to the sound of his father's heavy boots striking the floorboards downstairs and, secure, drifting back off to sleep. As a father now, he recalled so many nights tiptoeing upstairs to look in on the peacefully sleeping faces of his children and feeling a warm glow inside knowing that they, too, slept in the security of his tread.

On Amanda's side of the room, he picked up her stuffed animals one after another: a penguin, a panda, a manatee, a unicorn with a rainbow-colored horn, three different kinds of bears. Each one had a place in the pantheon of her beloved pals. When she was frightened at night she'd call out to him and he'd hear her no matter how deeply he was sleeping. He'd pad in and, without her seeing, pick one animal in the dark, animating it. Pitching his voice high, he'd speak to her through it. Often, he'd tell her stories of his own father's life or fantasies he'd make up on the spot. Amanda loved them all. She never giggled, always took the playacting seriously, and soon she'd calm down, snuggling back down under the covers. Then, he'd put the animal in her arms, her eyes would close, and she would sleep.

On Kevin's side of the room, he saw the book of Maxfield Parrish paintings he'd given to his son last Christmas. On his day off, he'd trekked all the way to the Metropolitan Museum of Art in Manhattan to get it. He'd only meant to run into the gift shop but, dazzled, he'd drifted through the galleries the whole day. Picking up the book, he leafed from one gorgeously tinted page to another. If only the world were full of light and peace like the scenes Parrish painted. But it wasn't.

He had become afraid, not for himself or for Katie so much as for the kids. What kind of world had he brought them into? And if one of them should be killed, what then? This is what Jack's murder had shown him: he'd be unable to go on. Guilt burned him like inhaled acid. At the moment of Jack Halloran's death everything changed for him. He'd had enough of the chaos of his neighborhood. He was bound and determined to bring some form of order to a world gone completely mad. It was the best—the only lasting—legacy he could give his children.

He put the picture book on Kevin's bed, stroking it one last time. Then, he got up and, without looking back, went into the master bedroom. From the top shelf of his closet behind his winter boots, he dragged out an olive WW II metal ammo case. He took out the .38 and loaded it. Then he carefully put the case back, put the gun inside his waistband and zipped his plaid jacket over it.

The Hallorans' smelled of macaroni and gravy; Katie's doing, no doubt. He remembered Thanksgiving dinner. The old table around which they had joyously sung songs was draped in black crepe. An Irish ballad was playing on the stereo. He made the rounds. Eileen cried on his shoulder, he gave a pep talk to Jack's thirteen-year-old son, he felt tongue-tied around Jack's daughter, whom Katie held in her arms, and he got thoroughly depressed.

He talked to Amanda first, doing his best to reassure her, but he could see she was frightened.

"Willie was a little upset when we left the house," she whispered with her head in the crook of his shoulder. Willie was her stuffed penguin. "I didn't know whether to leave him but I didn't want to bring him here." No, she wanted to seem more grown-up than that.

"Is Willie scared?" Tony asked her.

She nodded. "A little."

"I'll speak to Willie." He snuggled her in his arms. "He's got nothing to worry about." He turned her face so she could see him smiling at her. "He'll believe me, won't he?"

She nodded, and an answering smile spread over her face. She threw her arms around him and his heart came close to breaking. He held her tight, feeling more certain than ever that his children's future was all that mattered.

"How you doin', buddy?" he asked Kevin when he'd let his daughter run off to the kitchen for some more cookies and milk.

"Okay, I guess."

Tony looked deep into his son's eyes and saw what he didn't want to see. "It's getting a little freaky out there, that what you're thinking?"

Kevin shrugged, not meeting his gaze.

"I mean, last week we were having Thanksgiving with Jack and now he's gone." He put his elbows on his knees, leaning forward. "I think that's kind of scary."

Kevin's gaze slid toward him. "You do?"

"Listen, son, any time someone we know dies it reminds us that bad things can happen." He struggled to think rationally, to keep his children secure in mind, body and soul. The words came so easily he had no time to dwell on their hollow ring. "It's part of life, and even if we can't understand it, we have to accept it."

"Mom said she doesn't want us out after dark for two weeks."

"She's right. Because of what happened to Jack, we have to be extra careful for a while." He ruffled Kevin's hair. "But, I'll tell ya what, we do that and everything'll be cool."

Kevin seemed to mull this over for some time. At last, he said, "I heard it was you who found Uncle Jack."

"We had the same route, y'know, so . . ." His voice trailed off. He knew he had to be careful here, say something Kevin would understand. "I held his hand."

Kevin nodded. "I would have liked to say good-bye to Uncle Jack."

Tony put his arm around his son's shoulders. "Yeah. Me, too."

He watched as Kevin got up and went over to the TV to watch *Ren & Stimpy.*

Then he got up and dragged Katie away from Eileen Halloran's mother. Because of worry, his wife's dark eyes seemed more deep-set than usual. Tony thought she looked very sexy.

"Come on," he whispered in her ear. "Let's get outta here."

She shook her head. "No way. I can't leave Eileen yet."

He put his arm around her and rolled his eyes heavenward.

Katie almost burst out laughing and her face got red. "Are you nuts? *Here? Now?*"

"Sure," he whispered. "Why not?" He was already leading her through the crowded living room and up the stairs to the deserted second floor.

"Sweetheart, this isn't the time—"

From just behind her on the stairs he reached around to cup one breast. "This is *just* the time."

Katie hesitated. She did not yet understand what finding Jack had done to her husband; she suspected he didn't know himself, but she knew he needed to find out. She turned back to stare into his eyes, and she saw a pain there that struck her through the heart. He needed to heal, and right now he needed her. She put her hand over his, squeezing her breast harder. She could not refuse him. Besides, there was something needful in it for her as well. So close to death she could feel its cold breath on her cheek, there was a kind of pressure from deep inside, an urge to prove that she and Tony were still very much alive.

When Tony felt her lean back against him, he scooped her up in his arms like he used to do when they were just married. He'd carry her everywhere through their tiny apartment. They'd both be naked and laughing like loons until the heat of their bodies impelled them into another round of feverish lovemaking.

As he carried her into a back bathroom and kicked the door closed, Tony felt feverish. It had begun when he'd walked into the Hallorans' with the .38 digging into his hipbone and had seen his wife across the bustling room. She'd looked as radiant as a rose in full bloom, her dark eyes dancing beneath the solemnity of her expression. In their long relationship Katie had always been the optimist; it was that eternal sunshine that got him through his darkest days of unemployment, bad jobs, and worse hours.

He needed a full dose of her now.

Without releasing her, he set her down on the edge of the porcelain sink. They kissed as long and passionately as they had in their teens. Tony felt familiar hands at his belt, and had to quickly take over so the .38 wouldn't go crashing to the tiles.

"Do you think we'll go to hell for this?" Katie's lips took on this bruised and bee-stung look when they'd been kissing. The sight inflamed him all the more.

"We're husband and wife," he said as he pushed up her dress. "We can do what we like."

"But isn't it a sin? This is a time of mourning. It's disrespectful of the dead." Her eyes fluttered closed as his hands closed over her breasts.

"There's no disrespect." Tony licked her ear as he entered her with a powerful rush. "It's life, baby. It's life. And there's no sin in that."

Afterward, they hung onto one another, even though the position was vaguely uncomfortable. It was like that moment when you awake, remembering a good dream, Tony thought, and you don't want to move, don't want to open your eyes for fear that the real world will come crashing in.

At last, Katie gave a little shudder, as if against a chill wind. She looked into his face as she smoothed down her dress as best she could, and he could see tears standing in the corners of her eyes. "I know I have to be strong," she said, "but I'm scared." She gripped him suddenly. "I'm scared for you."

"There's no need," Tony said. "I'll never end up like Jack."

Katie searched his face. "How do the kids seem to you?"

"They'll be fine," he reassured her as he dressed. "Don't worry."

He stepped back so Katie could hop down off the sink. She said, "There's got to be a better way."

"When you find it, let me know."

She turned around, examined herself in the mirror. "Look at me. Everyone will know what we were up to."

"Not everyone," he chuckled, kissing her neck. "Not the kids."

She began to wash up. "Maybe we could move."

He laughed mirthlessly. "Yeah? Like where?"

She looked at him in the mirror. "Florida, maybe." Her voice sounded hopeful. "Marjorie—"

"No offense to your cousin, hon, but she's not the most realistic person in the world. Look who she married, some used car hustler, who's been indicted twice. Besides, what could I do down there, be his assistant?"

She patted her face dry with a *Mighty Morphin Power Rangers* towel. "Drive a truck, same as you do here."

"But, hon, here's where I have a job. It may not be much, but it's all we've got. I've got seniority, which means I don't have to be driving nights or weekends. We got pretty good benefits. The kids're comfortable in school. They got their friends. Besides, we haven't got anything to fall back on. What if I can't find a job for three months, six, a year?" He shook his head. "Not to mention, all our close family's here. You want to leave them?"

Katie had no answer for that. Here's where they had made their life, and for good or ill, here's where they stayed.

Together, they went quietly down the stairs into the riot of the house. On the TV, *Ren & Stimpy* had been replaced by nonstop music videos.

He squeezed her hand. "Hon, I've got to get outta here for a while."

Katie nodded. Obviously, he needed more than her body to get his head straightened out. That was okay; she'd expected as much. But as she walked him to the front door, she was filled with a deep sadness she could not explain. She was struck dumb, tears rolling down her cheeks. There was so much she wanted to say, but she could not find the right words.

"It's going to be all right," he said. They both had to believe that now, or they'd have nothing. But in his heart of hearts he knew that his version of all right wasn't anything like hers. He moved as gently as he could out of her arms, and out the door into the cold, clear night.

Tony followed the sound of rap music as if it were a glowing ribbon. It led him inevitably to Myrtle Ave. A bunch of black kids seemed to be having an impromptu party outside the Associated. It looked to Tony as if it were on the spot where Jack Halloran had been shot to death. Rage gripped him anew and he fingered the .38 hidden beneath his coat.

He forced himself to look away. To rap's hard-edged beat he saw the grizzled old man dozing at his post by the Dumpster. Tony knew he'd find him here. People like that marked out their territory and rarely left it.

Like all street people he smelled. Tony tried not to concentrate on it. The man had his back to Tony until the very last minute. Then, as Tony approached, he whirled around, an unfortunate move, since it sent out a wave of garlic, alcohol, and rank body odor that made Tony dizzy.

"Hey, old man," Tony said.

"Hey, whitey." The old man laughed. "This here's my turf. Get yo' white ass outta my face."

"Now listen—"

"No, *yo'* listen." The old man whipped the blade of a long knife at Tony's throat. "Yo' don't count fo' shit here, motherfucker. So why don't yo' split 'fore yo' gets hurt."

Tony felt the pulse pounding in his temples as if it were screaming to get out. "My pal got shot to death today." His voice was none too steady. "Just over there, where the party's going on."

"Doan' mean shit t' me." The old man pushed the blade an inch forward. "Doan' change nuthin' 'tween yo an' me."

"You saw who did it, didn't you, old man?"

It was a question the grizzled man wasn't expecting. For just an instant Tony saw the light of a mute answer in his eyes. Then a kind of curtain came down. The old man spat. He had good aim for an alky; he hit the toe of Tony's workboot. "I didn't see shit. I'se a businessman; tha's all I see. Business."

"No." Tony shook his head. "You saw the murder. You know who pulled the trigger." He took a lurching step back. "Well, I got a message for you to deliver to this rat punk. You tell 'im Tony's lookin' for 'im." Very carefully, he reached inside his coat, drew out the gun. He held it at his side, the muzzle pointing at the pavement.

The old alky's eyes opened wide at the sight of the weapon. "What yo' got in mind's plain crazy," he said. "Sho' as I'm standin' here it'll get yo' dead."

Tony ignored him. He was playing to the balcony: the group of partying kids in front of the Associated. More than one of them must know who had shot Jack in cold blood. "You tell the murdering bastard that he won't get away with it. Enough's enough. When he gunned Jack Halloran down he stepped over the line. He's a dead man. You tell 'im that, old man. You fuckin' tell 'im that."

Then he turned and melted into the shadows of the shuttered stores lining Myrtle Ave.

For a time, the grizzled old man did nothing. He put away the knife and mumbled something to himself. He rooted through his Dumpster, still talking to himself. He withdrew a pint bottle of cheap booze, finished it off. Then he grabbed out a bottle of electric blue after-shave and drank that as well. He closed his eyes as his whole body shuddered. If Tony didn't have the red rage running through him, he might have felt a twinge of pity for the alky. But he didn't have time for that now; not with Jack Halloran's bloody, unrecognizable face looming up on the stage of his mind.

After what seemed a long time, one of the kids detached himself from the dancing, drinking crowd, and sidled up to the grizzled old alky. He looked about fourteen. Everything he wore was grossly oversized; his sneakers looked like they were size twelves. His black face shone in the glare of the streetlight and Tony could see his features were still unformed. The kid shuffled anxiously from one foot to another while he screamed at the old alky. Tony thought he heard the word "unicorn." Then the kid's face got mean and he barked something, drawing a gun. The old alky's face went white and he began to babble, pointing and gesticulating wildly. Now Tony did feel for him; adults in this neighborhood were at the mercy of teenagers with guns, knives, and the kind of unreasoning savagery that put them beyond any hope of redemption. What they lacked was any sense of conscience; their amorality was harder to penetrate than tank armor.

At length, the kid nodded, then with a casual flick of his wrist, sent the old alky staggering back against the Dumpster. With a contemptuous look on his face, the kid waved the gun threateningly in the old alky's bloodied face before he began to lope away.

Keeping to the deepest shadows, Tony followed him. His moment of compassion for the old alky vanished. Now he gave him not a thought; his mind was filled with the image of Jack Halloran's mutilated head.

Not surprisingly, the kid led Tony into the projects. The Marcy complex stretched from Myrtle Ave. to Flushing Ave., a warren of shadowed brickwork that housed a whole other world. Tony felt a moment's hesitation. He'd heard so many horror stories about what went on here at night—had read about them in the safety of his own home over coffee and a Drake's cake—he knew he was entering uncharted waters. Terrible danger lurked here, but so did Jack Halloran's killer.

As he pressed on, sprinting from shadow to shadow, he felt Jack's presence at his side, urging him on, confirming that what he was doing was right. Justice had many faces, Tony thought. Who was to say which one would show itself tonight?

A chill wind dragged soot and grit up from the concrete sidewalk, swirling it like black sleet as Tony crossed a courtyard eerily deserted. He felt a twinge of nervousness now; he was totally vulnerable, a white face in a black continent where everyone was either strapped or stoned or both. That made each person he saw a potential paranoid. He hurried past stringy plane trees eking out a mean existence from small squares of packed earth piled with candy wrappers, broken bottles, used syringes, and dogshit. Gangsta rap music drifted from a window, then was abruptly cut short. A gap between buildings revealed a group of kids smoking, hanging out. There were distant sounds of scuffling, and one brief shout. A car peeled out, roaring down Myrtle Ave.

The outer door of the building the kid went into should have been locked, but the lock was broken. Tony pushed through the door, watched the elevator rise to the fifth floor. He waited. It sat on five until he pressed the button. It returned to the lobby empty. He took it up.

He thought of Jack Halloran, the potato chip man, and the family he'd left behind: a son whose life would be scarred forever, a daughter who might never remember who her father was. Again, he felt a wave of red rage sweep over him. He reached for his .38 as the door opened on five.

He just had time to register a young black face with eyes that seemed to hold no emotion.

"Excuse me, I'm getting off—"

He saw the charm hanging from the thick nose chain and he remembered the old alky's word he'd overheard. *Unicorn.* This was the kid who'd blown Jack's face off. Then he saw the gun the kid was pointing at him.

"You sonuvab—" Tony began.

The explosion rocked him back, slamming him against the rear wall of the elevator. He felt no pain, nothing. His numb legs gave out and he slid down. He smelled something sickly sweet: his own blood.

"I hear yo' lookin' fo' me. Well, heah I is." The kid pointed the gun at him. There was a roaring in Tony's ears. "So long, sucka."

A second explosion sent Tony rocketing down a black hole so deep it seemed to have no end.

Tony opened his eyes. Blood pumped out of two holes in his chest. *Whoosh, whoosh,* rhythmic as a metronome. Tony, disembodied, looked down at his own bloody form and saw it in two separate places at once. Terrified, he looked around. In one scene, he could see himself with Katie beside him. His vantage point was dizzying, as if he were a fly on the ceiling of a green and stainless steel room. She was crying. Two—no four—people hovered over his body, gloved hands manipulating instruments. With a start, he realized they were doctors, that he was looking at a scene in a hospital emergency room. He saw a nurse lead Katie out. The doctors got back to work, operating on him.

Sickened, his mind half-numb, he turned his gaze in the direction of the second scene. There, he saw something entirely different.

He saw himself in a pastoral setting—Prospect Park, he thought at first. But no, it couldn't be, there were no familiar landmarks and all the trees were green in the lushness of midsummer. But this was December! What was he looking at?

As he watched, he felt himself drawing closer. This was the discorporate self. The self that saw and thought and moved, as opposed to the body of flesh lying in a Brooklyn hospital emergency room. And, as he stretched out his arms and looked down the length of his body—yes, he had a body—he saw himself as he had been when he was twenty-one, in his senior year of college.

He could feel a soft breeze on his face, hear the rustling of the ancient oaks that girdled the sun-dappled glade. High above the canopies of the trees, puffy white clouds drifted lazily in a luminescent blue sky right out of Kevin's Maxfield Parrish picture book. This scene reminded him of that kind of perfect, idealized world. Except for one thing. Though there was plenty of daylight, Tony could not find its source. No sun or any celestial body for that matter was visible. And the light itself was curiously flat, shadowless, as if it emanated from all directions at once.

Returning his gaze to the glade, Tony became aware of a great shadow where no shadows should exist. It dominated the far end of the glade, jumping and flickering like a flame in the wind, waxing and waning, its outline blurred and indistinct. It seemed humanoid, but its head was wreathed by a pair of what appeared to be huge curling horns, like a broken crown of thorns. It was large, almost as tall as the oaks. Before it, was a white horse. It was the most beautiful creature Tony had ever seen. The sheen of its snow-white coat was so pure it almost made him weep. This astonishing creature knelt in front of the shadow as if in obeisance.

Now, as Tony drew closer still, he could see that the great shadow had placed the knuckles of one hand hard against the horse's forehead, as if it were pressing the horse downward. Then, as if alerted that they were not alone, the horned head turned in Tony's direction. Perhaps the shadow spoke, because all the oak leaves began to tremble at once. The knuckles were removed from the horse and Tony saw that the animal had a spiral horn growing out of the center of its forehead. This horn was as black as pitch and gleamed and refracted light as if it were a faceted jewel just polished.

The shadow came toward him. As it did so, it became smaller, more clearly seen with each stride it took. It stood before him, a man, old but robust, with flowing white hair, a full beard, and apple-pink cheeks. The mouth was a cupid's bow and the eyes that fixed him in their gaze were ice blue.

"Do I know you?" the silver-haired man said.

"Who are you?" Tony asked. "God?"

"Close," the man said. "But not close enough."

Tony blinked. The scene seemed to have changed a bit. Behind where the unicorn knelt was a split-log fence and, to one side, a clapboard house with a wood-shingle roof. A wide wraparound porch held rough-cut cypress furniture with the bark still on. A shingle by the porch steps read: FRANCHISER. Tony sniffed. The tangy, luscious scent of barbecue was in the air. He'd once driven down to Florida with some buddies, what was it, twenty years ago. Along the way, they'd stopped in Georgia, turning off I-95 to find some mouthwatering pulled pork smothered in hot sauce.

"Look familiar, huh?" the man said, only he was no longer a man with flowing white hair, but a fat black woman with a red-and-white bandanna tied around her forehead, a greasy apron over a cheap calico dress.

"I met you," Tony said. "A long time ago."

He was remembering how during spring break in their senior year of college he and his buddies had trussed her up, put the pig's snout they'd carved off the smoked beast into her mouth while they stuffed their faces with its rich, fragrant meat. Then, laughing like loons, they'd painted, "Howdy, Nigger," across the front of her apron and, hopping into their car, had sped all the way across the border to Florida. Except for gassing up, they didn't stop until they reached Ft. Lauderdale. Even when Pete got sick from eating too much pulled pig, they hadn't slackened speed. Laughing, they'd rolled down the window and stuck Pete's head outside while he barfed his lungs out. But they hadn't meant anything by what they'd done; it was just a stupid prank. No one got hurt, not really. But Tony, seeing the fat black woman reincarnated in front of him, remembered the sinking feeling in his gut as he'd watched his buddy writing that phrase. *Howdy, Nigger.* Which one had actually done it, Billy, Pete? He found he could not remember, as if in some time past he'd tried to wipe his memory clean. What idiots they'd been, wanting so badly to be big shots by throwing their weight around. Against an old black woman? Unfortunately, she had presented the best target. But what could he do? He'd had to go along with them, otherwise they would have ostracized him.

"Time's got no meanin' heah-bouts." The fat black woman cut in on his thoughts. She had a curious look about her as if she knew what he was thinking. "That bein' the case, I thinks we should gets reacquainted."

She waved her arms, the loose flesh of their undersides flapping like startled chickens, and Tony could see the barbecue pit where she'd been smoking the pig. She waddled over to the pit, lifted up the corrugated metal lid, just as he had so many years before. But instead of a pig smoking on the rack, there was a human being.

Tony gagged, his mind frozen in disbelief.

Then the fat black woman took up a long-handled brush and painted the carcass with thick, tomato-red sauce. She turned back to Tony, her face wreathed in a grin. "Almos' time fo' lunch."

He let out a little moan. He could see what was scrawled across her apron, those two words, "Howdy, Nigger." She glanced down at herself and a look of profound sadness crossed her face.

"Yo 'an' yo' friens' did this to me, put th' tattoo t' me." She pointed to the one word that meant far more to her than it ever would to him. "Yo' know this here's the filthiest, most hateful word I can think of." She shook her head. "No, I don't s'pose yo' do."

She brushed her calico dress with knobby-knuckled hands as if it were the only one she possessed. "Yo' go' any idea what hurts the mos'? Fact yo' didn't even ask my name. But why should yo', sugah? I was no more 'n' a piece of meat to yo'. Barely human." The grin flitted across her face again, fugitive as a butterfly. "Din' stop yo' from gorgin' yo'self on my food, did it, sugah?"

Tony shivered. "What is this? Where the hell am I?"

The fat woman shrugged her meaty shoulders. "Why ask when yo' already knows?"

"How would I know?" And then it hit him like a shotgun blast. He was in hell.

"But I can't be!" He looked around frantically. Down there, as if seen through the wrong end of a telescope, he could still make out the doctors working over his body. Was it his imagination, or had their efforts become more frenzied?

"Is he going to die?" Katie's voice echoed as if through a mountain pass. So filled with sorrow and terror it sent a shiver through him. "Why won't you tell me whether he's going to live or die?"

"Because they don't know," the fat woman answered softly. "It's not up to them."

"Who *is* it up to?" Tony shouted. "You?"

The fat woman looked at him with profound pity. "I'm goin' show yo' the position yo' in, sugah."

At that moment, the unicorn made a sound. It was like a choir singing, a gorgeous blend of melody and harmonies, but as the fat woman turned toward it, the sound turned dissonant and a hard, unpleasant edge drove like a spike through Tony's ears. Its head bucked and its hindquarters rippled. Its back legs scrabbled against dirt and grass as it strove to rise from its bondage.

Without a word to Tony, the black woman strode toward the still-kneeling beast. With each step, her outline became less defined, darkening like a storm cloud, growing in size until it approached impossible proportions. A black hand reached out, sharp knuckles staining the unicorn's trembling white forehead until its head bowed and, trembling terribly, it settled back into the grass.

Tony almost cried out, for the moment the unicorn lowered its head he felt a sharp pain in his chest.

"Now where was I?" The fat black woman was back. "Oh, yas. It occurred to me that yo' needs a graphic illustration o' the position yo' find yo'self in."

The fat woman vanished. In her place was a man's head and torso. Without arms or legs it fit neatly into a handsome gilt frame of mitered wood.

"Does this give you the picture?" The man was dark-haired, with severe features, penetrating eyes, and an old-fashioned goatee that Tony had never seen except in films.

Tony looked from the strange limbless figure to the unicorn.

"What are *you* looking at?" The man seemed annoyed.

"What are you doing to that unicorn?" Tony could not help staring at the unicorn. "It looks so unhappy."

"I'm sure it *is* unhappy," the man said. "It is my job to make it so."

"Why don't you let it go?"

The limbless man smirked. "You haven't earned the right to ask, my friend." The smirk became a leering grin. "You have murder in your heart. That makes you my meat." He nodded toward the sign that swung from its post on the side of the porch steps. "I'm the original Franchiser. But what I franchise is damned hard work. You can't take shortcuts."

Tony made himself look at the quadriplegic in his fancy gilt frame. "Just what is it you franchise?"

That smirk was becoming irritating. "Oh, come on. You can't fool me. You're not thick as a brick. Look at what's smoking in the barbecue pit."

"I can't," Tony said. "It turns my stomach."

"You are a weak and wimpy boy."

As if a powerful hand flung him forward, Tony was pitched to the lip of the pit. He tried to avert his head but he couldn't. It was as if it were held in a vise. His eyes opened and he stared into the pit, at the body slowly smoking on the grill. It was the fat black woman. He blinked and it was the old black alky from Myrtle Ave. He blinked again and saw the kid from the Marcy projects, the one who had shot Jack Halloran. The thick chain through his nose was dark with soot and the unicorn charm had burned its imprint into his upper lip.

Tony groaned.

"That's your own mind you're looking into, my friend," the boxed man said. "Still feeling queasy?"

Tony tried, unsuccessfully, to look away from the horrific pit. Being pushed around by the quadriplegic, this lack of control was like a killing pressure, squeezing all the life out of him. He didn't like it one bit. But perhaps, given this creature's disposition, that was the point.

"That's what I franchise, my friend. Evil."

Tony stared. "Then you must be—"

"An angel." The quadriplegic smiled benignly. "Only an angel."

Tony smelled the fragrant grease dripping from the grill and he gagged. "Take it away. Please. I can't stand the stench."

"How hard it must be to live with yourself." Contempt turned the quadriplegic's voice to acid. "You mealy-mouthed—I can't franchise anything to the likes of you."

Abruptly, the killing pressure vanished and he was released. In his newfound freedom, Tony risked another glance downward at his life on Myrtle Ave.

"That's right," the quadriplegic said. "There's the place for you. Everything you love or have ever loved is right there in the O.R."

Awareness of Katie and the kids was overpowering. It was pulling him downward, back toward the operating room far, far below. He took a last look around. Surely this couldn't be death. A place where time had no meaning. What was it?

"Go on back where you came from," the quadriplegic said, "while you have the chance."

Tony turned to him. "What do you mean?"

"Hey! You need a road map? You're dyin' down there. That little sonuvabitch got you good, brother. Blood's pumping out of you like well water. You wait too long up here you won't be able to go back. Ever."

Tony wanted to cry. He thought of Katie; he thought of Amanda and Kevin, conjuring their faces one by one. His heart was breaking. He saw Katie's face as if it were veiled by tears. Just outside the O.R. she gripped the kids' shoulders with fingers of iron. *I know I have to be strong,* she had said to him, and she was.

It was at that moment that he heard again the exquisite music of the unicorn. It held within its subtle harmonics the pain of imprisonment that pulled at Tony's heartstrings. It spoke to him on a deeper level than he had imagined possible, and it seemed to break the spell he was under.

Though he still felt the pull from below, it was no longer overpowering. More like an old toothache, he thought, dulled to a background throb.

Tony knew he should be concerned about what was happening to his body, but this new world—wherever it was and whatever it might be— was at the moment so astonishing, so compelling that he could not bear to leave yet.

As if reading his thoughts, the voice of the quadriplegic broke through the unicorn's melody in a kind of music hall parody of an Irish accent: "It's a siren's song you're hearing now, m' boy. Best skedaddle 'fore it eats you for lunch."

Tony turned to look at the unicorn, which still lay in the same spot, gazing at him with eyes the color of clear, deep gemstones—emeralds he and Katie had once goggled over in the corner window of Tiffany's. He wondered if the unicorn could move at all or whether it was spellbound to the spot. He stared at it for a very long time, and suddenly a thought popped into his head. How could he be running out of time here where in this place time had no meaning? He was being lied to.

When he turned back to confront the quadriplegic, there was no sign of him or of the fat black woman or the amorphous crowned shadow. He-she-it had vanished.

Tony needed some answers and the only other creature here was the unicorn. As he walked toward it, he passed the huge, dreadful smoker, the front steps of the clapboard house, with its mocking sign: FRANCHISER. The frayed and scarred cowboy boots he'd worn all through college crunched on the blue-gray gravel drive. The noise, sharp as needles pinging against glass, caused the unicorn to look up. Its great horn swung around so that it was leveled at Tony. He paused in mid-stride. Until that moment he hadn't realized how menacing it could be. Now that he was this close he could see that the edges of the spirals were razor-sharp. Even a glancing swipe could flay skin and flesh from sinew and bone.

He took a step forward and the unicorn rose on its forelegs. He had never thought of the creature as being menacing. When he thought of unicorns it was in the context of a fairy tale; they were creatures of goodness and light, weren't they? Amanda's surely was. Like teddy bears, they were synonymous with comfort and warmth.

And purity of spirit.

He took another step toward the unicorn and it rose on four legs, backing away. The black and shining horn was aimed at the center of his chest. *Think*, Tony told himself. *What are you missing?*

Then he thought of something the Devil had said to him, for he was now convinced the creature of shadow and changeable substance he had encountered was, indeed, the Devil: *You have murder in your heart*. He did not want to be the Devil's meat; the thought sent shivers down his spine, assuming he still had one. Clearly, the Devil didn't think so.

He moved closer to the unicorn, who now stood alert and clearly restless. The powerful muscles along its flank jumped and spasmed as it bucked a little, backing up against the split-log fence. Its black horn lowered and it shook its head, clearly uneasy.

"I'm not going to hurt you." Tony took another step. "Don't be afraid."

Suddenly, the unicorn's forelegs collapsed under it, and it genuflected as it had earlier. Its eyes rolled in terror and its mouth opened.

"I'm not afraid, stupid. You are unclean. Unfit to touch me."

The voice, familiar in its mocking contempt, brought Tony up short. It seemed shocking and obscene coming from the unicorn's mouth. "Who ... who are you?"

"You know me," said the voice emanating from the apparently stunned unicorn.

"What do you want from me?" Tony asked.

"Climb aboard and we'll get things in gear," the Devil said.

Tony stood, transfixed until the Devil said, "Come on, don't be more of a wuss than you already are."

Slowly, hesitantly, Tony approached the unicorn. Its head was lowered, the tip of the long, black horn gouging a furrow in the grass. Tony climbed upon its back and, immediately, the unicorn rose.

"Hang onto your hat," the Devil advised.

Lacking one, Tony just had time to clutch the thick, white mane before the unicorn took off, paralleling the fence, heading away from the house. It soon came to a section badly in need of repair and, gathering its strength, leapt over the cracked top split log.

With a stiff breeze in his face, Tony was obliged to bend over the arched neck as the unicorn galloped at full speed across the vast expanse of undulating grasslands beyond the fence. Galloping was the wrong word, however, since it appeared as if the unicorn's hooves never touched the ground. Instead, it was flying, and not just flying but bursting through the air like a jet. Tony looked around, gaping, until they came to rest on the flat, dusty top of a mesa. Shards of glittering stone sparked beneath the unicorn's dancing hooves as its head came up.

"You know what I want," the Devil said, still speaking through the poor enslaved beast. "But you've got to give it to me willingly. It's the one thing I'm enjoined from taking."

It's my immortal soul he covets. Tony jumped as if bitten. "Never."

"We'll see," the Devil said.

Though the light in the sky had not waned, there was a sharp crack of thunder, accompanied by the unmistakable smell of buttered popcorn. Lights danced in front of Tony's dazzled eyes. When they cleared, he saw a small, stunted creature, dark-skinned, with a barrel chest and immense muscles. He had wild, black hair, matted and strewn with shards of bark and leaf. Into his forehead was tattooed a curious set of symbols. By the tools he held in each massive fist Tony could tell he was a metalworker of some sort. As Tony watched, dumbfounded, a pillar of fire flashed down from the heavens, enveloping the tattooed man. Flames crackled and licked greedily, feeding like a voracious animal. The tattooed man burned until all that was left was a pile of bones lying atop the blackened implements. With a spine-chilling rustle, the bones stirred, rising until they arranged themselves into a human pattern. The naked jaws clacked open and shut.

"Let's talk about you for a minute so we know where we stand," the skeleton said. "Why are you here? I'm certain you'd like to know."

Tony, who was already learning not to question the curious transformations of this place, said, "You bet I would."

Wind moaned eerily between the bones of the skeleton. "Evil stalks you, that's why."

"Are you another medium? Is the Devil using you like he did the unicorn?"

The skeleton shook his head, setting off a round of rattling. "Not a bit of it, though I suppose you could say I'm one of his many defeated incarnations. But you could look at yourself in the mirror just as well."

"Who defeated you?"

The skeleton deflected this question. "Irrelevant. This interview is about you." One bony hand lifted, pointing in Tony's general direction. "Take the incident that may very possibly lead to your death. All you thought about was taking revenge on Jack's murder. You didn't think about your job, your wife, your family."

"You didn't see what the . . . the animal did to Jack." Tony slid off the unicorn's back to ease the ache in his inner thighs. "He had absolutely no regard for human life."

The skeleton continued, unperturbed. "In fact, all of the responsibilities that made you a man, that defined life and your place in it were eradicated by the one bestial urge to take vengeance."

Though Tony refused to utter this admission, he knew what the skeleton said was true. It was as if one tiny but powerful part of his brain left over from a distant and primitive age had taken control, overriding any sense of prudence or conscience.

At Tony's side, the unicorn's tail flicked nervously, then was still. "At this moment," the skeleton said, "you are closer to the boy who killed Jack than you are to Jack himself."

Tony felt a surge of panic and he curled his hand into a fist. "That can't be."

"Oh, but it is. You have only to take a hard look inside yourself."

Something was stinking, like meat long gone rotten, and Tony turned this way and that, trying to locate its source. He finally realized it was coming from the spot where he'd secreted the gun. Its taint was on him like the mark of Cain.

"Christ, no."

The skeleton laughed. With a dry rattle, it collapsed into ash, which was quickly borne aloft by the wind. Soon there was no trace of it on the mesa beyond an insignificant charcoal smudge.

Tony looked at the unicorn. Its eyes were clear; the terror that had caused them to roll was gone. It snorted as it bucked in its newfound freedom.

Tony felt a great surge of empathy toward it. Filled with fear and self-loathing, he reached out. "Help me!" he cried. "You can save me! You have the power!"

The unicorn stamped its powerful forelegs. It stared at Tony with a pain beyond human comprehension. Music poured forth from its mouth like golden radiance. These most beautiful harmonies resolved themselves into words Tony could understand. "Once, perhaps," it said, "but no more. I am held spellbound; you have met my master." The great head bobbed up and down. "He has stripped me of most of my power. And he has put you beyond the possibility of redemption."

"I refuse to accept that!" Tony shouted.

"Give it all you've got, boy!" the Devil crowed in a peal of almost-deafening thunder that threatened to split open the sky. *"Fight on even under the most crippling of odds. I applaud you!"*

Tony covered his head as if he could hide himself away from the mocking voice. "It's not fair," he whispered, after the last echo had died away.

"I disagree," the unicorn sang in the myriad voices of a choir. "You had no compunction about using the old man. What did you feel for him when he was being beaten? Compassion? Did you go to his aid? No, you simply watched. Did you even think of him? What regard did *you* have for human life?"

"But that was different," Tony protested.

"Tell me how."

Tony opened his mouth to reply, but too late he realized that he had no answer. Except . . .

"I was frightened," he said softly. "That's what life on Myrtle Ave. did to me—to everyone in the neighborhood. We all lived in fear."

"Even the children."

Tony nodded at the unicorn. "Especially my children. I was going to do it for them."

"Better and better," the Devil cackled. *"Blood legacy's an eight-course banquet in itself."*

"I was speaking of *all* the children," the unicorn sang.

"You mean those teenage gangsters who rule the streets with their guns and their attitude."

"It's do or die for them, isn't it?"

Tony did not want to think about that. "If I'm really beyond redemption, at least let me help you," he pleaded. "Maybe that's why I was put here. Maybe we can heal each other."

"Look at you; you're a pathetic sight." The unlovely notes made Tony cringe. The unicorn snorted, steam rising from its velvet nostrils. "You can't even help yourself, let alone anyone else." The head waggled from side to side as it stirred up more dissonance with its restless hooves. "Here's my gift to you. It's all that's left of my power."

Suddenly dizzied, Tony put a hand to his eyes. There was a bright flare of greenish-white light and he blacked out. When he awoke he was looking at a cockroach the size of his thumb. He tried to react but his body wouldn't move. In desperation, he swatted at it with the back of his hand. A black hand. In fact, all of him was black. He saw his reflection in a windowpane. What was he, all of fourteen years old? Then he strained forward as he caught sight of the thick nose chain and the unicorn that hung from it, stinging his upper lip with half-frozen metal.

He looked around, saw that he was huddled in the corner of a ramshackle apartment. It was winter and the apartment was freezing. He wondered why the heat wasn't on, then remembered his mother didn't have the money to pay for it or for the electricity.

He started as the gloom was shattered by headlights on the street outside blazing through the cracked windows. That's when he saw his mother lying on the floor in a pool of frothy vomit. That's when he remembered trying to revive her after her OD, working on her, the cold sweat of desperation drenching his clothes. Her dead eyes stared at him like the blank windows of the project. He began to whimper. His mother was dead. What kind of life had she ever had beyond shooting heroin and being slapped around by a succession of boyfriends who acted as her sometimes pimp. Often as not, though it wasn't her fault, she forgot to have food for him and he'd have to scavenge around the neighborhood. His father he could remember not at all. In fact, the faces of all the men ran into one another like paint in the gutter. Where his father might be now was anyone's guess, but the simple truth was he had no interest in his son. In fact, none of the adults in this world did. They had no power.

Kids with knives, guns, and a belief in their own immortality had all of it. At least, that was what his two brothers had thought. One had been shot to death during a drug deal gone bad, the other was serving twenty-to-life in Attica for carrying out a blood vendetta. He also had a sister who seemed good for nothing but having babies. In fact, he had his own baby boy, but the very thought of it sent icicles of terror flashing through him. He'd fucked a girl, nothing more. It was a harmless night in the back of a car. Just a quick fuck. It should have been without consequence, right?

Vanished because they had never existed.

Tony never felt such terror in his life. He tried to cry out, but he was again overcome by vertigo. Another flash of greenish-white light crashed through his senses, stunning him. When he opened his eyes again, he was back on the eerie dark mesa top, confronting the unicorn.

Tony still saw torn bits of Unicorn's life, echoing in his mind as if the vision he'd been shown had somehow become part of him. This was a world without limits, without law, without anyone in authority to say this is the line across which you will not walk. There were no such lines for these new children of the street, armed, orphaned, pockets filled with drug money, and dangerous because none of the defining rules parents create for their children existed. Defining rules that a child might, at times, rebel against, but which, after all, allowed him the comfort and security of a dreamless sleep at night.

"You felt the fear."

"Yes." Tony squeezed his eyes shut. "It's terrible."

"This is not your fear," the unicorn sang. "It is *his*."

"Am I supposed to feel sorry for him now?" Tony asked, incredulous. "He's a *murderer*. He leveled a gun at my friend's head and calmly shot three-quarters of it away." Saying it still took his breath away, nothing had changed. "I still feel it. I can't stand it but I still have murder in my heart." He clenched his hands and raised them over his head. "I want to be healed! But you ask too much. You want forgiveness but there is none inside me."

"I said nothing of forgiveness," the unicorn sang.

"Don't listen to its honeyed song," the Devil thundered overhead. *"Of course it wants you to forgive the little savage. What else was it created for? But you know as well as I do that forgiveness is its own lie. It lets evil live on, untouched."*

Something burned hard and bright in the deepest part of Tony's heart. He looked at the unicorn and said, "I can't forgive him."

The echoes silenced the unicorn. It hung its head as if defeated.

"That's the kind of spirit I can sink my teeth into!" the Devil's voice exulted in a storm of cracked lightning.

The unicorn stamped its hooves as it trotted to the edge of the mesa.

Beyond, Tony could see a rock-strewn plain without end. It was studded with gnarled cottonwood and mature weeping willows, their cascades of leaves looking like bursts of spring rain. Streams rippled like liquid silver, here and there bubbling over rock-strewn rapids. But beyond, dimly seen, a set of dark, low hills chilled his bones.

"How cold and deserted the sky above my home looks," the unicorn lamented. "Once it was filled with stars, and the starlight bathed all of us in its brilliance. Once this place was filled with my brethren. Now all are gone."

An icy ball was forming in Tony's stomach. "What happened to them?" he asked.

The unicorn lowered its head, and its harmonies turned dark and nearly ugly, so that they caused a kind of pain that was almost physical. "As belief in them died, so did the stars. They began to migrate toward what stars remained until they approached the edge of the land of shadow. There they came under the spell of—what did *you* call him?"

"The Devil," Tony said.

"The Devil," the unicorn sang in a series of notes that hurt Tony's ears. "My people could not long live beneath his yoke, and, gradually, they perished."

"But what killed them?" Tony asked.

"A growing evil."

"Like kids with guns killing each other and people like me."

"Forget about a plague of locusts. This here's a fucking cancer," came the Devil's fierce rumble across the sky. *"You know all about that, doncha?"*

"I sure do," Tony said.

"Don't be so sure. It's more than that," the unicorn sang. "That form of evil has been around for centuries. This evil's different: a pervading sense of helplessness, an inability to act, to make the one, single selfless gesture that could begin again the chain of salvation. This is what killed us off."

"What d'you say?" the Devil chuckled. *"This beast is too much, ain't it? Some stinking nigger kid whacks you and all it wants you to do is forgive the sonuvabitch. That kinda shit doesn't cut it with me—and I can see it doesn't cut it with you, either."*

"Shut up!" Tony shouted. "You're manipulators, both of you. I refuse to be a soldier in this war."

Tony looked up into a sky filled with billowing clouds but no acid comments or cheap shots were forthcoming. Tony's gaze lowered to the unicorn. For the moment its song was stilled. Could he trust any being in this eerie world? Why would it have shown him Unicorn's painfully squalid life if not so he could find forgiveness in his heart?

And yet it had told him that it was not his fate to be redeemed.

"But the darkness didn't kill you," Tony said.

The unicorn snorted. "It will, eventually," it sang. "For now, I am waiting."

"For what?"

"For someone to bring back the stars."

"Don't look at me," Tony said. "It isn't going to be me. I don't have it in me to forgive Unicorn. He had a choice and he made it. There were so many other paths he could have taken."

The unicorn's head bobbed up and down. "There's no denying it. But the one who brings back the stars will see that it doesn't matter. Forgiveness doesn't matter. Beginning the process of change, the chain of salvation that will save us all, is the only thing that matters."

"Git on outta heah. Yo' mama's callin' yo'."

Tony started, saw the fat black woman had reappeared. She stood with tree-stump legs spread, her balled-up fists on hips wide as Myrtle Ave. There was a fierce scowl on her face. "Git back t' where yo' belong," she said. "Ain't no use yo' bein' heah, thas fo' *damn* sho'."

Far away, he could hear Katie sobbing, calling his name over and over, but her voice sounded odd, like an old 78, flattened and dusty, and filed away in some forgotten back room.

"Go on now, sugah," the fat woman urged. "Yo' ain't but got seconds left. Seems as if yo' dyin'." She took a step toward him, and Tony had the distinct notion that she was about to spit flames. "What chew waitin' fo'? Lissen to yo' po' missus. Boo-hoo. How she misses yo' sorry ass." She lifted an arthritic forefinger. "Then thas yo' children t' think of. 'Manda an' Kevin, right? Yo' doan' wanna up an' leave 'em now, do yo', sugah?"

There seemed to be a riddle here that had been posed in different ways by both the unicorn and the Devil. It was up to him to figure it out. He could chuck all this talk of chains of salvation and bringing back the stars. That was what the Devil wanted; judging by the persistent wheedling, he wanted it very badly. That meant Tony was a real threat to him.

Why? Could Tony really be the one to bring back the stars, to begin again the chain of salvation that would redeem the unicorn from eternal night? Yet, even if it were so, it meant leaving Katie behind—Katie and Amanda and Kevin. Leaving them to the jungle that Myrtle Ave. had become.

As Tony stared down onto the scene in the operating room far below he was struck by an odd thought. He had been able to fool himself that he'd been on a mission to provide a legacy for his children. How deluded could he have been? When he had set out to stalk the kid who'd murdered Jack Halloran what he'd really been about to do was to give up Katie and his

family. Dismaying at it might seem, going back to them now meant returning to the man he had been. No wonder the Devil was so eager for him to
do just that. *You've got murder in your heart. That makes you my meat.*

He'd be damned if he would let himself be the Devil's meat. Far better
to become a soldier in this as yet unknown war, to brave the unicorn's
challenge, whatever it might ask of him. And with that knowledge came
the realization that he could not return to his old life—he'd been changed
in some fundamental way. Even Katie would not recognize this Tony as
her husband. He'd made his choice without knowing it.

There was a spark of blue lightning, and he staggered momentarily as
if in response to an earthquake. In that instant of hollow silence after the
last echo rolled away, he heard Katie's wail of grief. But when he turned,
he found that he could no longer peer through the doorway into the operating room. It was gone, and Katie, the kids with it.

Thunder rumbled from a sky turned yellow. It resolved itself into a
voice filled with spite: *"You'll be sorry. Immortality isn't all it's cracked
up to be."*

But Tony knew he'd dealt the Devil more than a glancing blow, and
he was glad of it. "Now what?" he said to the unicorn.

"That's entirely up to you," the creature sang.

"I am here, for good or ill," Tony said. He threw his arms wide. "My
heart is my heart, but my spirit is delivered up to you."

"Oh, certainly not to me." The unicorn sang like a massed choir. "I
am but one link in the chain."

It looked upward and, following its gaze, Tony saw a sky now devoid
of all cloud. Clear and pellucid, the starless, indigo firmament seemed to
contain the infinite.

Tony heard a chord struck deep in the core of him, and he was dazzled by the essential truth flooding through him like celestial light. "That
was why I was brought here." He turned to the unicorn. "That's what this
struggle has been about. I am to become one of you."

"Too long beneath the yoke of darkness, I am dying," the unicorn
sang. "But you shall take my place. You are the one I have been waiting
for, the one who will return the stars to my sky."

He supposed in a way he'd known it all along. "But how?"

The unicorn dipped its head. "Forgiveness was never the issue, can
you understand that now?"

"I do," Tony acknowledged.

"Neither is redemption," the unicorn warned. "This transformation is
not about you; it's about everything else."

"I am a book waiting for words to fill it."

"In a moment, they will come flooding." The unicorn raised its head and, with a clip-clop of its hooves, came toward him. The long, black spiral horn was aimed at the center of his chest.

Overhead, the sky roiled. *"It's a trick!"* the Devil shouted. *"Don't just stand there! Run! Run or you'll be changed forever!"*

Tony knew better than to listen. Yet his muscles jumped and spasmed and a certain terror filled his belly.

The tip of the unicorn's horn touched Tony's chest. "Are you frightened?" it asked in a welter of fluting harmonies.

Tony nodded. "Yes."

And the unicorn sang him a glorious song as it impaled him. The gleaming black spiral went clear through him until he began to vibrate in response to a pulse, ancient of ancients.

Garland Montgomery and an entourage of four strapped teen gangstas were picking their way through the littered streets of Bedford-Stuyvesant when the winter rain changed to snow. In an instant, the hard, almost icy pellets were transformed into a dazzle of spiraling white flakes. The change broke in on Garland's thoughts, dark as nighttime shadows. Garland looked up, past the grimy brickwork, the blinking Christmas lights taped around window frames, the spiderweb of iron fire escapes draped with messages of whitey's Christmas, over the rooftops to watch the snow swirl down, pure as a bride's dress. He thought of nothing as he looked, unaware that merely being out in the snow might feel good.

He was late for a gang meet, a rally from which they'd get to the meat of tonight's entertainment: a street fight between them and Crips along one flank of the Marcy Projects.

But the snow just kept on falling until it was like curtains so thick they seemed suspended in the night. It was an amazing sight, even for Garland, and he stopped to keep the moment alive.

Through the snow he saw a spark of light. At first, he assumed that it was a low-flying plane on its way into La Guardia. Except that it did not move, did not blink. A star, then. Except how could starlight be seen through the snow and the nighttime city glow? Garland contemplated this question without success.

When he looked back down at the street he saw that he was alone. Where had his entourage got to? He whipped around and saw a shape moving toward him. Instinctively, Garland went into a semicrouch behind a row of galvanized steel garbage cans as he reached for his gun. He had two guns now—the one his mother had given him and the one he'd taken off the white man he'd killed in the elevator. With two shooting deaths to his name, he'd vaulted in status, leapfrogging others older than him, to become one of the leaders of his gang and a big man in the 'hood. People feared him; he could see it in their eyes. If they were smart, they feared him. Otherwise, he knew how to teach them fear.

Now, as the shape came toward him through the fast-falling snow, he clicked off the gun's safety. "I'll fuckin' clean yo' out, yo' take anutha step," he shouted. His voice sounded weirdly loud. He refused to believe that he might be scared; the leader of the Bloods couldn't be scared. So he shouted all the harder to cover his fear.

He took aim at the large shape approaching through the thick snow. He would have pulled the trigger, too, had he not been frozen in place by the sight. A big horse, whiter even than the snow, came toward him. Mist blew from its nostrils, icicles clung to the tufts above each ankle, and the water of melted snow ran down its spiral horn, black as the closet where Garland had once been imprisoned by one of his mother's pimps as he had his way with her. Not a horse, then: a unicorn. Unconsciously, he touched the cold silver pendant hanging from his nose chain.

As the huge snow-white animal loomed out of the night, Garland could see pinpoints of light sparkling like diamonds along the edges of that horn. He thought, *I'll kill this motherfucker and take its horn. Nobody else has a horn like that. What a weapon it would make! A symbol of power no one else's got!* He rushed from behind the trash cans and, aiming his gun at the unicorn's neck, pulled the trigger.

At least, he wanted to pull the trigger. In fact, nothing moved. It was like he was frozen in time, except that he could feel his heart fluttering in his chest as the snow swirled wildly between the buildings. The snow blotted out everything, leaving him alone with the white animal in a white world. Then he saw someone step out from behind the unicorn.

Wide-eyed, Garland watched his brother Derryl walk toward him. But something was wrong with him. He was leaning to one side like he'd been shot or his leg was broken. Then Garland saw that Derryl was dragging a body along behind him.

"Derryl," he breathed, "what chew doin' here. Yo' break outta Attica?"

Derryl, still in his dull prison overalls, spread his arms. "Check it out, bro'. I ain't never gon' get outta that hellhole." Then he pointed to the gun. "Wass up? Yo' gon' t' shoot yo' own blood?"

Suddenly self-conscious, Garland put the gun away, pointed to the body at Derryl's side. "Who yo' got there?"

"Don't you recognize him?" Derryl hauled the body in front of him. "Thas our brother Jovan."

Garland started as if slashed with a blade. "That ain't Jovan. Jovan be long dead."

"Look at his face, Garland." Derryl reached down, pulled the body up by its shoulders. "Jus' look at him."

Garland took a step toward his brother despite himself. But one look at Jovan's bloody face made his stomach turn over. "How this be happenin'?" he asked of no one in particular. "Jovan be dead, man. Dead an' buried."

Derryl was looking from Jovan to Garland. "Yo, I never noticed this before but yo' and Jovan could be mistaken for one 'nother." He let go of the body, which sprawled awkwardly at his feet.

Garland could see the point his brother was trying to make. But he knew Derryl was dead wrong. He'd never end up like either of his brothers. He shook his head vigorously. "Uh-uh, that ain't me," he said vehemently. "I gots the power now, bro.' I gots all the power I need."

"You a willful boy," Derryl said. "Yo' always was."

"Ain't no boy," Garland screamed into the howling wind. "I'se a man now, Derryl. A *man!*"

But the surging snow had already wiped out all trace of his brothers. In their stead he found himself in a tiny cramped cubicle in a crowded ward in Community Hospital. It was a dark place, dreary with the groans of the hurt and dying. He stood beside a bed on which lay a man so bony thin it was hard to believe he was human. In fact, judging by the size of his thick brow and his bull nose, this man must once have been big and robust. No more. His skin, scarred by bleeding sores, was so unhealthy it was charcoal gray.

As Garland watched, a white nurse entered through a gap in the curtain that hung from a stainless steel track in the low ceiling. She was wearing all kinds of protective shit: a mask and those thin rubber gloves. She checked the man's vital signs, checked on the fluids slowly dripping into his veins, shook her head. As she left the cubicle, Garland saw she stripped off not one, but two pairs of gloves. Just before she disappeared, he caught a glimpse of a sign pinned to the outside of the curtain: CAUTION. AIDS PATIENT WITHIN. EXTREME BIO-HAZARD.

Garland was wondering what he was doing here when he noticed two tattered photos on a ledge beside a stack of boxes containing sterile cotton gauze. When he looked closer, he saw a shot of his mother and, beside it, a photo of himself as a small child.

Garland stood still for what seemed an eternity. In his mind were two questions. Could this be his father? Could this be the man who broke his mama's arm in three places?

Garland's heart skipped a beat and he drew his gun, aiming it at the bony man's chest. "Yo' did that to her, I'll blast your sorry ass to Kingdom Come."

The bony man, of course, said nothing.

Something dark and terrible seemed to fill Garland's chest, making it so hard to breathe he sobbed with the awful weight of it. "Motherfucker. You broke my mama's arm and you walked out on me." He put down the gun. "A quick death's too good for yo'. Yo' gettin' what yo' deserve."

Then the snow came swirling back and, momentarily lost within that chilling fog, Garland had a vision that terrified him. It was years from now. He was an old man, forty or so, dying of some unnamed disease. Visited in a mean hospital bed by a young man, handsome, strong, vital. It was his son, Marcus.

"Marcus," Garland said in this vision. "I'm dyin'."

Bending over him, Marcus looked him in the eye and spat on him.

The snow came roaring back, hitting Garland full in the face, momentarily blinding him.

"Marcus!" he cried into the howl of the storm. "Marcus!"

As if he had been summoned by Garland's heightened emotions, a squally three-month-old boy-child appeared. Garland looked at his face through the falling snow and saw with a start that it was his own face.

Marcus.

Something inside him broke like a bowstring too tightly strung. It echoed through him like a gunshot. He took a halting step toward his son, if only maybe to get a better look. But, no, he had to get closer, take him in his arms, hold the baby tight. His terrible vision of the future lay before him like a smoking ruin. The thought of it made him sick to his stomach.

In fact, now he thought of it, ever since he'd seen that weird star pulsing electric white in the sky just before the unicorn appeared, he'd had a liquid feeling in his gut like he'd eaten something that was going to make him real sick. But now he realized that it was something he'd eaten a long time ago, a kind of poison that had been seeping through his veins like rainwater someone had pissed into. It was something that was making him do to his own son what had been done to him.

He could not let that happen. He could not abandon Marcus.

Garland reached out for his son. He could almost touch him now. In a moment, he'd set things right. He'd make sure that vision of the future never came to pass.

That was when the bullet spun him around. He never really heard the report, just the echo of it, half-muffled by the snow, as it ricocheted off the project walls. He was falling. His left knee struck the snow-covered pavement, jarring his spine, making his teeth clack together. He felt the blood spurting from his chest but, oddly, he felt no pain.

Lying on his side on the icy pavement, he saw the evil moon face of that fucker Levar striding toward him. Levar, the leader of the Crips, who'd been out for vengeance on the Bloods ever since Garland extended his gang's crack-dealing territory. Levar had sworn to kill Garland and now he was going to make good his promise.

Snow pattered onto Garland's cheek, cooling the feverish rush of blood. Something convulsed inside him and his legs drew up. He was coughing blood and Levar was laughing.

Levar leveled the 9mm at Garland's head and laughed. "Yo, it's the end, motherfucker." He moved closer, keeping the muzzle of the gun trained on Garland's head. "There's bets you'll crap yo' pants when the time comes. Here's where we gets to find out."

Garland looked up then, his heart beating fast as he watched the big old unicorn come prancing at him through the snow.

"Jesus," Garland muttered as, through pain-filled eyes, he saw the unicorn lower its head, bearing down on Levar. Levar, high on crack cocaine, had eyes for no one but his intended prey.

Then Garland heard this sound that made the small hairs at the base of his neck stand straight up. Levar heard it, too, because his attention wavered. A kind of singing like a choir of angels in full voice was coming from the unicorn's open mouth. Levar's gaze flickered once, the muzzle of the 9mm moving a little off its mark. The unicorn was almost upon Levar and, out of time, he pulled the trigger.

Garland screamed at the second explosion. Something slammed into the side of his head and, for a time, he passed out.

When his eyes fluttered open, he saw the unicorn at his side. It stood there for a moment, pawing the ground like it was undecided or something. Then it knelt, its huge forelegs folding in on themselves.

Garland had trouble seeing; all the blood running down the side of his head, he supposed. Pain overcame him and he cried aloud. He was very frightened as he looked into the unicorn's left eye. He thought of his brothers, one dead, the other locked away, and remembered what Derryl had said to him. He thought of his father, dying of AIDS. But, in the end, neither of them mattered. Only Marcus mattered. More than Garland could have imagined; more than he could say. His sole thought was this: to live another day so that he could hold his son in his arms; to live another week, another month, if possible, years, so that his son could have what he himself had never had and wanted more than anything else.

With his last ounce of strength, Garland climbed with terrible agony onto the unicorn's back. He steadied himself, but his thoughts kept running away from him. For sure if the pain kept up he'd be dead in no time.

He was already insensate when the unicorn rose and, snorting smoke, trotted through the thick and unnatural snow. It cantered down the eerily deserted streets of Bedford-Stuyvesant; it crossed Myrtle Ave. where, as

Tony Valenti, it had witnessed the death of the potato chip man, Jack Halloran; it trotted past the quiet courtyard of the Marcy Projects where, with murder in his heart, Tony had stalked Garland to his lair; it passed the fire escape Garland so often climbed on his way up to the vulnerable skylight that led to the doctor's office. The unicorn clip-clopped sound-lessly up the rutted stoop of the brownstone. No clods of snow were thrown up in its wake; no hoofprints appeared at all in the snowfall.

With Garland stretched out on its back, it passed through the closed front door as if it did not exist. In the hallway, the complex aroma of Indian spices could not quite hide the stench of rotting meat and stale grease. It walked down the meanly lighted tiles, chipped and colorless with age and neglect. With the tip of its black, shining horn it rang Dr. Gupta's bell. Then it knelt, lowering its burden carefully in front of the door.

Dr. Gupta's wife, a round, jolly Indian woman gave a little shout as she opened the door. Garland's dark, handsome head fell against her slip-pered feet and a touch of blood smeared her sari. Her husband, a very large, very dark Indian, appeared with a cigarette in one hand and a fork-ful of curry in the other.

"My God," he said, kneeling down beside the boy. His wife took his cigarette and fork from him as deftly as a surgical nurse plucks used implements from her doctor's grasp. His hands explored the areas around the gunshot wounds in chest and skull, widening in concentric circles until his preliminary examination was complete.

"I'll call the hospital," his wife said.

"Save your time," Dr. Gupta said. "He'll be dead by the time an ambulance arrives."

Without another word, he hoisted Garland over his shoulder in an expert fireman's lift and took him upstairs to his office.

"It's fate this snowstorm," the doctor's wife called up after him as he ascended. "If the weather hadn't changed, we'd be at your sister's in White Plains."

Once in his office, Dr. Gupta placed Garland in the back room—the surgery where, from time to time, he performed abortions as well as other minor operations.

Garland, very near death, kept watch over his son. He held that image close to him, clinging to it even when the snowstorm became terribly fierce, the howling winds threatening to rip the vision from him. He fought the snow, the wind, and the bone-chilling cold, desperate to keep Marcus close to him. Everything else slipped away: guns, crack, Bloods, Crips, power—all were cauterized, reduced to ash before his determina-tion to hold on to the image of his son. It meant a great deal to him whether he lived or died; more than he could ever say. Life was suddenly precious, and he had seen so little of it.

Marcus even less.

He fought and fought until he was utterly exhausted. What was it Derryl had told him? Only a child is willful; a man lets go of his willfulness to live in the world. Now Garland understood. He wanted so much to live in the world beyond Bed-Stuy.

He had fought. He had done all he could. It was time to give up being willful. It was time to put himself in the hands of something larger, something in which he could believe and, if he lived, teach his son to believe in. He felt the comforting weight of the silver pendant on his upper lip. He willed the image of the unicorn into his mind.

I am yours, he whispered in his mind, delivering himself into the care of that extraordinary beast.

When he woke, hours later, he felt sunlight streaming onto his face. It was dark and he could not see, but, sniffing, he smelled the combined odors of antiseptics and Indian spices and knew without looking around where he was. It will be clear tonight, he thought. There will be starlight.

He must have stirred because, a moment later, he caught an intense whiff of curry, and felt a presence at his side.

"You had me very worried, young man," Dr. Gupta said. "You are exceptionally lucky to be alive. But you'll be all right now. Do you understand me?"

"I can't see," Garland said in a voice that seemed throttled by cotton wadding.

"There are bandages over your eyes," Dr. Gupta said. "It cannot be helped."

Memory flooded back and he saw Levar standing over him, aiming at his head, about to pull the trigger. He heard again the terrifying explosion and he must have spasmed off the table because the next thing he knew, he felt hands on him and Dr. Gupta's voice saying, "Easy does it."

Then a needle slipped into the meat of his upper arm and he felt a soothing warmth seep through him.

"I got shot in the chest," he managed to get out. "And in the head."

"One bullet could have torn your heart to shreds," Dr. Gupta affirmed. "As I said, very lucky." There was a small hesitation. "The other creased your skull, nothing more. The bandages are a precaution only. Tomorrow, when I take them off, you will see as well as you ever could."

"Yo' mean I'm not blind?"

"No." Dr. Gupta said. "But your body has taken a nasty beating and you've lost a lot of blood. That's why you're so weak. Not to worry." He chuckled. "You know, my wife is already cooking you soup and curry, even though I told her oh so many times that I'll be feeding you intravenously for a while."

"Yo, doc, why'd you save me? Yo' shoulda let me die."

"Life is precious," Dr. Gupta said. "My profession preaches that, but it is my children who have taught me the real meaning. No matter how difficult life seems, it is still worth living."

Garland felt dark despair threaten to overwhelm him. "What yo' know, 'bout it? Yo' may be brown but yo' ain't no nigger."

"One of my children is autistic. Do you know what that means? There's something wrong with her brain. Chemicals missing or all messed-up. Chemicals you have and take for granted. She can't think right, can't develop or learn past the age of six, but she struggles on. She's almost twenty now."

Garland thought of his son. He sure didn't want anything like that to happen to Marcus. Thinking of Marcus, he forgot about himself and his despair subsided.

Dr. Gupta said. "You know, I've had my eye on you. Yes. 'There's a willful boy,' I told my wife many times. 'Once he learns to let go of that willfulness, to give himself over to life, he'll be okay.'" He tapped Garland's shoulder. "And now, here you are. Karma, as we Hindus say. Fate. You understand?"

And somehow Garland did. He reached up and fingered the pendant that hung from his nose chain. His fingertips traced the full outline of the unicorn and, in doing so, he was able to keep its image in his mind. Somehow this calmed him. In a very real way, he needed to know that it was still with him, for he felt a deep conviction that in the days and weeks to come, when he might be at low ebb, the unicorn or his memory of it would give him strength.

Clutching the pendant made him want to tell Dr. Gupta that it had been he who had broken in and stolen the doctor's opiates, that he had done far worse, killed as Levar had meant to kill him, but he was so weak, so full of drugs that made him feel weird and floaty that when he opened his mouth all that came out was a tiny, dry croak.

He remembered his brother Derryl calling him willful. At the time, he only dug in his heels and shut his ears. Now he could see that only children were willful. It was cool to be willful, he could see that as well. The gangs were cool, breaking rules and laws as they saw fit. Being willful. But the gangs' willfulness only extended so far. Death took some of the gangstas—as it had taken Jovan, as it had almost taken him. The cops took others, sometimes, like Derryl.

In a moment of sharp and painful insight, Garland saw just how limited willfulness could be. Because it was that spiteful willfulness that was cutting him off from his son, from all the days of a future he could not as yet imagine. And yet, with the unicorn's help, he knew it existed.

That was a step. Such a big step that he was suddenly terrified of what lay ahead of him. It was a new world where everything was unknown and, therefore, would be a terrible struggle. His new life would be far harder than it had been working his way up the gangsta hierarchy. And, in many ways, more dangerous. Would Levar or a gangsta from the Crips wanting to make a name for himself come after him? But he knew he had no other choice; he was committed now.

Committed. That world had a good sound in his mind, like music that stirred his soul.

Dr. Gupta said, "I must confess I've taken your weapons. I've never stolen a single thing from anyone in my life, but in this case . . ." He paused and Garland supposed he was debating with himself. "I propose a deal. You let me keep the guns and I promise not to report this incident to the police." He tapped Garland's shoulder again, and, this time, Garland had a vision of the unicorn pawing the snowy pavement with a white hoof. "Like I said, I recognize you from the neighborhood. You threw in with a bad lot but, as I tell my wife often enough, every child needs a chance at life, eh? Eh?"

Garland felt Dr. Gupta close beside him. "What do you say to my proposal?" Dr. Gupta asked.

Garland, thinking of Marcus, nodded as best he could. *Every child needs a chance at life.*

"Ah, delicious," Dr. Gupta said. "There's no going back on your word once it's given. That's the mark of a man, you know."

Garland wanted to tell Dr. Gupta he was not going to go back on his word. It was odd. Just as it was a chain that held the unicorn pendant close to him, he felt part of a chain now, one link in a long line that stretched so far away in either direction he couldn't see the end. Where this vision came from he had no idea, but he was certain that the chain existed and that he was part of it. This was what gave him the determination to be the right kind of man for Marcus no matter how hard it would be to walk away from the gangs, from Myrtle Ave., from everything he had known. When he thought about it that way, it seemed overwhelming, impossible even. He wanted to cry, feeling no older than his fifteen years.

He nodded again, and Dr. Gupta made more noises of delight.

Garland blinked beneath the tightly wrapped bandages. He was gripped by a peculiar kind of warmth that had nothing to do with the shit floating around in his veins. It was so strong he felt terrified. It must have shown on his face because Dr. Gupta slipped his fingers through

Garland's. His hand squeezed gently but forcefully until Garland felt Dr. Gupta's warmth running through him like a river.

It was a feeling wholly unfamiliar to him, but he knew it felt good. He knew it made him feel calm and protected. It made him feel like however scary and uncontrollable the world might seem, he'd be able to handle it. And he knew it was the feeling he must give to Marcus, because Marcus, too, was part of the chain.

And then something happened inside of him, as strange and magical as the star in the snow-swept sky or the appearance of the unicorn.

"I remember," he whispered in a dry and cracked voice.

"But what is it you remember?"

"I remember the song my mother usedta sing me."

From this, Dr. Gupta deduced that Garland's mother was gone. "That's good. Memories like that are what keep us going. To my mind it means you're over the worst." He kept a firm hold on Garland's hand. "In any case, I'm here now. I won't let anything bad happen to you."

All of a sudden, Garland began to cry.

ABOUT THE AUTHOR

Eric Lustbader was born and raised in New York City. He graduated from Columbia University in 1969. Before becoming the author of such bestselling novels as *The Ninja, Angel Eyes, Black Blade,* and others, he had a successful career in the music industry. In his fifteen years of work in that field, he wrote about and worked with such artists as Elton John, who later asked Lustbader to write the liner notes for his 1991 boxed set "To Be Continued . . ." He was also the first person in the United States to predict the success of such stars as Jimi Hendrix, David Bowie, and Santana.

He has also taught in the All-Day Neighborhood School Division of the New York City public school system, developing curriculum enrichment for third and fourth grade children. He currently lives in Southampton, New York, with his wife Victoria, who works for the Nature Conservancy.

Lustbader is currently hard at work on his next novel.

MICHAEL MARANO

WINTER REQUIEM

Peter: **Michael Marano** writes that he " . . . was born in 1964, the youngest of nine children. His interest in horror is, therefore, self-evident." Hard to argue the point. As a home-made, half-assed medievalist myself, it intrigues me to learn that he began studying alchemy and Kabbalah while pursuing a degree in medieval history at Boston University.

Janet: Nothing about Michael is simple. He is one of the most intense and loving people I have ever met. What's more, he supplies me with coffee beans and fascinating manuscripts, in about equal quantity. This may be the first time you read one of his stories. My guess is, it won't be the last.

Winter Requiem

—⊸⊸⊸⊸⊸⊸

—To the memory of Lee Marshall

David WATCHED A STREAK OF RED NOVEMBER sunset become a bloody serpent hung in the darkening sky.

He knew, sitting in the wine-colored dusk beneath the eaves of a great oak, that the serpent was an illusion conjured by the toxins in his blood. He did not dispel the vision by blinking or glancing away. It did not threaten him as did most others; it was neither disturbingly vivid nor clear, but had, rather, the quality of art. He found comfort in the serpent's rich color and its smoke-like undulations.

To him, it seemed a guardian of this time of change, ushering the day into night, summoning stars from the darkening east, and winter from the dying fall. He wished, in the way that he had once prayed, that such a guardian would see him through the coming end of his life.

When dusk gave way to moonlight, and the scent of autumn's dead leaves meshed with smoke from distant fireplaces, and the sound of the brook that ran through the grove of oaks to the south became sharper with the cold night air, David stood and leaned on the branch he used as a walking staff. In his youth, not so very long ago, he'd called this hill "Weathertop," and carried a tall branch of birch as a prop when he imagined himself a peer of Gandalf. Now he needed a staff to negotiate the terrain; the illness that had turned his blood to slow poison had also given him gout.

He hobbled down the hill toward the house where he'd grown up. By the time he reached the yard he was sweating with exertion, despite the night air. Drowsy grayness filled the corners of his sight, as if another phantom would step from the shadows to accost his senses. At the door, he stood a moment, and breathed deeply until the grayness passed.

When he entered, he saw his work, the sheets of music he'd been composing, crumpled and torn and strewn about the living room. The piano bench had been toppled and flung to a far corner. The piano itself was dented and banged, its rich wood splintered and scuffed from the blows of the poker that lay upon it. A bottle of ink had been thrown against the far wall, leaving a smear like a blue handprint upon the white paint and shards of glass upon the wood floor.

David stood aghast. The clatter of his staff as it fell from his hand brought him out of his shock.

He limped to the center of the room, turned in circles, filled with panic, filled with fear, filled with rage. He was about to phone the police when an ugly thought struck him.

He could have done this himself, while made drunk by the disease that was killing him—enraged that the degradation of his mind would not allow him to compose a musical legacy before his body destroyed itself. He had been frustrated, angry for most of the day, unable to focus on his work or play musical phrases on the piano.

He had no memory of what he'd done before he'd left the house—no memory of actually leaving. He recalled only a need to be outside, to feel wind and see the sky before he resumed composing.

He searched the house for signs of a break-in. Who would break into a house in the middle of the woods? There were no forced or broken windows, no splintered wood on the doors.

Fear washed over him. A fear of losing himself, his music, his identity to mumbling, premature senility, and madness.

Not wanting to cry, feeling lancing pain in his gouty joints as he kneeled, David gathered the sheets off the living room floor, unrumpled them, and placed them on the mantel. He righted the piano bench and took the poker away from the scarred piano. He cleaned and tidied the room, but left the stain on the wall, for fear that trying to wash it off would make it worse.

Afterward, he put on his favorite recording of Mozart's *Requiem* and pressed a razor against the blue veins of his forearm.

The hunt was on.

Across wailing regions of Hell, his pursuers mocked him by signaling the chase with horns.

The deposed commander of twenty-nine scattered legions ran through living muck that screamed and writhed under his monstrous footfall. He crossed a swampy river as a horse would ford churning waters, his head and neck craning and bobbing with the strokes of his arms. The horn set upon the brow of his equine face rose and fell like a mast without a sail.

A new crash of horns came like a storm wind across the marsh. He stopped swimming and listened, looking back the way he'd come. Through the thick, perpetual fog of that starless, sunless place, he saw a signal fire flash atop a watchtower on the shore he had just left.

Ahead he saw answering fires upon the ramparts of the city of burning red iron on the shore before him.

He wanted to bellow his rage, scream his fury. But he dared not give away his location. Then he thought to make his position known in a manner that could save him.

He sounded the brackish water, warm as fresh blood yet laced with Death's cold touch, and pulled from the slime at the bottom something corrupted and tortured.

He broke the surface, and held aloft by one hand the screaming ghost he had pulled from below, hiding most of his bulk under the water, yet keeping his gaze above the surface.

The debased soul, able at last to shriek the agony it had felt since it had dropped to this spiritual vomitorium, summoned the river's guardian. Fast as an arrow from a bowstring, the guardian's skiff skimmed the water. The twisted gray creature on board smiled, eyes alight with the color of ice as he poised his oar like a weapon at the screaming soul's breast.

"You are *mine!*" said the guardian.

The prince lashed out. Hurling the ruined soul aside, he crashed his head and his spiraling horn against the skiff's prow, and gripped the prow in his claws. The guardian shouted, raised his oar overhead, and was about to bring it down on the prince's claws when the prince hissed, "I'll sink you!"

The boatman froze, teeth clenched.

"I'll sink you!" said the prince. "Think how all your little charges will be upon you, biting, gnashing, and clawing."

From the shore, the crash of horns came again, so close it made the air shudder. The twisted boatman smiled and leaned upon his oar.

"There's no room in *this* ark for you, either."

The prince growled, splintered the prow's lip, and rocked the skiff to and fro. He spoke in an intonation he had used in cold defiance of the Archangels. "Enough theater. Take me to the safe shore."

Without a word, the boatman piloted the skiff along the shores of the city of burning red iron. In the shallows, far from the city's ramparts and gate, the prince let go the skiff and waded ashore through water choked with rotted souls, putrescent as stalks of decayed kelp. Standing upon the bank, he pried several of them from his limbs, his chest, back, and genitals.

Soon he was running again, the hoofbeats of creatures both two- and four-legged thundering behind him.

The razor broke David's skin as the voices of the chorus gave earthly expression to the sound of Heaven. Blood ran down his wrist, baptizing his hand in red warmth.

He stopped the razor's path through his flesh.

If I survive this, I won't be able to play, he thought. His riot of emotions fell quiet as he watched red drops make sudden blossoms upon the deep kitchen basin. *The tendons will be cut. I'll have nothing left. Nothing. Not able to play or compose. Or I'll be put in a ward somewhere, not allowed anything sharp as a pen to compose with on scrap paper. . . .*

If he died now, there would be no meaning or point to his life. Nothing left behind. A few minor compositions, already performed, that his teachers and a few critics had said showed a hint of greatness. But nothing that would endure as a testament to the sacrifices his family had made for him and his music.

He set down the razor and inspected the wound.

It was minor. No vein had been opened. He flexed his fingers. No tendon had been cut. He washed the wound under warm water, and watched currents of red flow within the stream. A thought struck him as the bloody water swirled into the drain and the *Requiem* played itself out. He took a wineglass from the cabinet beside the sink. He let his blood flow into it, clenching his fist around a dish towel as he did so. He made a tight bandage around his forearm with gauze, and carried the glass to the living room. There, he took from the shelves the books of magic bound in dusty leather that had belonged to his mother, and the large clay bowl she had had made for her by an artisan who lived near Jerusalem. Dust covered the vermilion lines of concentric letterings inside the bowl—letterings in Hebrew, Aramaic, and other languages David did not know.

He wiped away the dust and set the bowl in the center of the room. With dull pain in his joints, he knelt over the books and began to read.

The prince ran through a forest of those who had, in life, made a gibbet of their existences, and had ripped their souls from out of their bodies so that they dropped here and germinated to twisted, black trees. Knotted branches inlaid with tendons and veins quivered with unreleased suffering. Blood spurted from the branches that he broke as he ran, and the blood wept, vibrating softly as if each drop were a tiny throat pressed upon his skin.

The prince stopped and listened for his enemies. He did not hear them above the steady cries that hung thick in the forest's air, or filled the bloody trail he had beaten behind him. Harpies, perched in the upper branches, pecked at the trees, taking communion in small bites from the ruined souls transubstantiated to twisted wood.

The sounds of the forest were restful, calming to the prince. They reminded him of the dark places where the newly-dead congregated, wandering like sleepwalkers, mourning the sudden loss of their bodies. In happier days, he would often run through this antechamber, scooping up souls like bundles of wood to give as playthings to his followers.

The prince crouched low and rested, thinking of how he would orchestrate sufferings that would make his enemies envy the damned they'd once had charge over.

His punishments would be hailed as atrocities, legendary in their cruelty, even in Hell. He would make of his enemies living standards, erect cathedrals to his own honor from their bones.

Those who hunted him served The Enfolded One, the great unthinking idiot that held sway in this world, of late. He could elude and defeat The Enfolded One's lackeys, and in time he would partake of the route of The Enfolded One with other princes and their armies.

But first he had to escape the hunters who craved his blood and coveted his horn, the emblem of his power that he wore upon his brow.

The cries from the trees closest to him quieted. The cries of his trail fell into the regular rhythms of the forest. Absently, the prince etched his mark upon the trunk of a tree. The soul inside cried softly in a tune he found soothing as he pressed his claws into the bark. Perhaps he should enlist aid from the Master of Fraud, he thought. Sound a clarion call while riding on his back as they flew in a gyre to the deepest pit of the abyss. If he doubled back, Hell's Gatekeeper would allow him to weave music from the suspirations of the newly-dead that would—

A sound rose from the way the prince had come, like a great wave breaking, the fabric of thunder meshed with the roar of the sea. And beneath that sound, the screams of his enemies as they crashed through the wood and the cries of the trees they wounded. The prince stood and, with the speed of a hunting cat, climbed the tree he had been scarring.

In the distance, he saw hundreds of points of light spread in a line. Some were, he knew, the flames of torches held by those who hunted him, darting, curving in a wide ribbon among the bleeding trunks. Others were the burning faces of yith hounds, black hunting bitches maddened with the need to rend and tear and wound.

The prince dropped to the ground, but did not run. He was a strategist, a tactician. Nothing he did now could be without thought. He stifled the sound of his pursuers in his ears, reached out with his senses for *anything* in the ether that could help him. And found it. Something informed so slightly by the aura of this place of suicide that, at any other time, he would not dare pursue it.

He had no choice.

At the trunk of the tree he had climbed, he kneeled like one about to take communion and forced his hands into his mark, pulling open within it a portal made possible by the dim invocation of his name.

"There are no such things as demons, Mother. Or angels. There is only us."

His mother had taught him to believe in magic, that the world was full of hidden wonders. As he grew older, he believed only in the wonders of the mind, that what she called "magic" was the product of focused will. Ritual and formula were crutches to focus that will.

He needed such a crutch to free his mind and thought from his sickness. Kneeling on the living room floor, David read aloud the Latin incantations of his mother's books, and also the Hebrew she had phonetically scribbled upon sheets of yellow legal pad and inserted within the pages. Toward the end of his ritual, he took the wineglass that held his blood and poured a few drops in the center of the bowl, so they were surrounded by the concentric lines of script.

He turned the bowl over and read a final Hebrew incantation.

There was a change within David's mind. A flowering of images and feelings that unfurled like a white rose. A vista of alabaster filled his vision, and a sound, distant at first as the tread of a ghost, became louder and more tangible.

He knew it to be the sound of snow.

A memory rose like mist from his childhood, of lying with closed eyes upon the white blanket of a winter field. Even the wind itself had been hushed. In that unreal, timeless quiet, he heard the breath of the sky itself, the whisper of the dome of gray clouds above, and the voice of each crystalline feather of snow as it fell, alighting upon the earth, his face and lashes. The snow had a delicate poetry, but he could not fathom its language. It was a language he both heard and felt, that touched him as the morning of the year's first frost touched him, telling him of its presence the instant before he woke.

David remembered the sound of snow, and remembered the person he had been when he had heard it: the boy who believed, as his mother had taught him to believe, that magic lay hidden everywhere around him.

This, as revealed by the snow, was the essence of what he was trying to compose, yet he had not been able to name it before.

He could grasp it and give it musical form. He would make it a requiem, a remembrance of his mother's teaching created in the twilight of his own life.

David wept, with relief and joy. And with pain, for the memory had been pulled from his deepest sense of self.

The white vista faded from his sight, but in his mind the sound of snow maintained. Grew louder.

David wiped away his tears and listened. A shiver ran up his back as strands of mist, like wisps of white hair, streamed from beneath the bowl, flowing into a smoky pool by the hearth.

The wineglass vibrated as the sound grew, as if a tuning fork had been touched to it. The vibration had a rhythm separate from the sound that David knew. He felt it inside himself.

It was the rhythm of his own breath, as if the blood in the glass were still within his veins, pulsing with his body.

Winter filled him, coursed in a February wind through his torso, his limbs, filling each capillary, collecting in an icy fist in his heart.

He screamed. The sound endured past David's scream. He tried to stand and run, blindly, into the cold November night. But he couldn't rise from his knees; the rotting joints of his legs gave way under him.

A hump formed in the pool of white smoke by the hearth, as if the pool were a sheet and a man stood up from a crouch beneath it.

The form became solid. The sound fell silent.

A hunched abomination stood before David.

"Yes?" it said.

With that one word, the sanity of David's world was torn away.

I'm hallucinating, he thought. *Be rational. This is nothing. This is a dream. This is a ghost. It comes from the sickness.*

The thing rose to its full height, towering above him. Fine mist came off its heavily muscled body, off its chiseled legs, its arms, off the torso that looked as if it had been sculpted in marble. Up to its neck, its skin was white as bone. Coarse hair with the sheen of sea-foam grew over the throat and the bestial head was at once like that of a horse, and that of a deer and of a goat. A mane of human-like hair fell in foppish bangs around the great spiraling horn that grew from its brow and that glowed like mother of pearl in candlelight.

It's not real. It can't be. It's a demon from one of Mother's books. A demon. You saw its picture and you . . .

The monstrosity fixed David with eyes violet as the cusp of a January dawn. Again, it spoke.

"Yes?"

The square animal mouth moved, making human speech that didn't vibrate as sound in the air but *occurred* in David's mind, like a premonition given grammar and cogent thought.

David tried to speak. His jaw trembled, as if from cold, and the beast cocked its long, equine head, never taking its gaze from David's.

David clenched his jaw, turned his gaze to the floor and forced words from his lips.

"You're not real. I don't believe in you."

He looked up, hoping, knowing, his words had banished the thing with the other phantoms his sickness had created.

David was again held by the violet gaze.

"But I believe in you."

David fought the urge to drown in those eyes and made himself speak.

"You don't exist."

"Oh, but I do."

"I didn't call you. I didn't summon you. You're nothing. I'm dreaming you."

The demon glanced away, freeing David from its opiate stare. It leaned forward; its horn lowered like a pike before David's face. Its great lion-clawed hand lifted the bowl from the floor as David would lift a teacup from a shelf. It turned the bowl over in its palm and pointed with a claw of its free hand to the red inscriptions inside.

"You did call me. And politely, I came. If you look closely here, you will see my name. You invoked it. Of course, if you do look closely, you will also find the name of a very splendid Nazarene carpenter. I'm afraid he's too busy knocking together cabinets and tables for his dear tyrant of a father to answer your call. I, however, am free this evening, and so accept your invitation."

"I . . . revoke my invitation."

"After I have come all this way? Why? Have I been rude? Of course I have! I have come empty-handed. Allow me to give you a gift."

It brought its horn down on David's shoulder, as if the horn were a sword and the creature were knighting him. David's every muscle clenched, his every tendon pulled tight. From his knees, he fell backward, unmoving on the floor.

The thing stood above him, its horn almost touching the ceiling. "There. Now I am a decent guest. But I am sure there are other exchanges to be made between us. Does this go here?"

The thing held out the bowl to David, and turned partly to place it on the mantel. "Ah! You compose!" it said as it set down the bowl. It picked up the rumpled sheets and read. And David, gripped by nightmare paralysis, could not scream when he saw upon the thing's back another atrocity.

The thing turned to face David. It stepped forward, looked down at him and said, "I am a patron of composers. I have stood invisible at the side of great maestros, guiding their batons. I have revealed my secrets to composers whom you venerate. I have woven melodies from the footfalls and the clatter of wheels upon the cobblestones of great cities—melodies that have touched the entire world. I would be happy to help you with this." It held David's rumpled compositions out to him and made a bow, like a courtier. "I am Amduscias."

The thing that had clung to the demon's back fell wetly to the floor. David tried to shut his eyes, to look away as the spectral body of a young woman, torn in half, reached out to him. She tried to speak, but no sound came from her mouth.

The thing that called itself Amduscias snatched the torn woman by her hair. "I've tracked mud into your home," it said coolly. "Forgive me." The woman continued her wordless pleading. She raised her arms over her head, trying to free herself from the demon's claws.

The buzzing grayness of disease filled the edges of David's vision. He embraced it, willing it to blot out what he saw. The light in the room changed, became dappled, like afternoon light in a deep forest.

The demon held the mauled ghost aloft, almost level with its head. In the dappled light of David's hallucination, Amduscias looked like a poacher holding his catch in a wooded glen. The demon's animal face looked with sickeningly human contempt upon the woman. It looked back to David.

"Since, as you say, I do not exist, I am a product of your mind," it said. "Therefore, if you were to *allow* me to possess you, no harm could come of it. I would be one part of your mind returning home. A part of your mind you've lost touch with, that otherwise would help you create sweet music such as this." The claw that did not hold the woman held forward David's compositions. "Allow me to demonstrate my musical ability."

It drew the sheets over its heart and the room filled with snatches of music. David's music. The bars, the sketches, the phrases he'd been working on performed faultlessly by invisible musicians. The air shimmered as if from the heat of a fire. The dappled forest light glinted as it shook with the music's resonance.

The music stopped with a gesture of the demon's hand.

"Think what I could do inside your mind," it said. "Think what I could liberate."

It shook the woman as a sadistic child would shake a cat held by the scruff of the neck. Bits of cloudy, dust-colored flesh dropped to the floor.

The demon came down to one knee. "There must be blood here somewhere for you to have called me. If it's fresh, I can make a gift of her. A little aid to help with your composing. Ah! Just so."

It set David's sheets down and lifted the wineglass. The dappled light

grew dimmer as the demon held the glass to its eye. "I'll do what I am
able with this. Watch what is possible when two agents meet to create
something new and wonderful. Imagine what could happen if you and I
were to join."

It set the woman like a broken doll on its knee, and with one claw
forced open her mouth and poured the blood down her throat.

Her flesh shrank, took on the texture of a wet scab. The demon began
sculpting her, molding her as if she were clay. "She will be of great use to
you. For how long I can't say. We'll make the best of what we have."

Welcome hallucination suffocated David's senses, eclipsing the vio-
lation of sanity before him. He floated in a world of twilight. Among bur-
gundy clouds, he saw the red serpent again, and longed for the comfort it
had given him as he had sat upon the hill. Dimly aware of himself, he followed the snake to a place he knew was safe.

Amduscias watched dreams move like föhn winds through the ether.

After stepping over the inert form of the conjurer who had summoned him, he settled upon a wooded hill that overlooked the conjurer's
home. The place was special to the conjurer; he could smell the conjurer's spirit invested among the oaks. He hunched down beneath the
tallest oak to watch for signs of his pursuers.

It was then he saw the dreams rippling through the nonphysical landscape the way sunlight moves through water. The dreams were sent by
his enemies. They would drift through the night to settle upon the minds
of sleepers, and so make the sleepers the vessels of his enemies.

His enemies would clothe themselves in the sleepers' bodies and
souls, and so continue the hunt through the living world.

Amduscias tasted the dreams as they passed. They were dreams of
redemption, of hunting and coursing a snow-white beast with a divine
horn, and being made clean and whole and pure by the beast's blood. The
dreams would make the sleepers hungry for such healing, and this hunger
would be used to make the sleepers long for the prince's blood and horn.

The prince was not alarmed. This was expected. His pursuers could not
follow him here without being summoned into materiality. He would be
ready for them when they resumed the chase as avatars moving through the
bodies of others. Several nights would pass before the dreams took root.

By then, he would have safe harbor in a willing soul. The conjurer
had a ripe and fragrant soul, full of vibrancy and poetic insight. The
prince would use his soul both as a shield and a weapon. He would create
within it a fortified tower from which he could attack. He would cleave to
and cleave through the man's soul, make it a source of *élan* to face those

who hunted him and crush them for their arrogance in taking arms against him. He would descend upon them as the Great Archangel who routed him and his followers had descended, just before The Expulsion.

It was a simple matter of time before the little conjurer capitulated, before he invited the prince to transmigrate into the chamber of his soul where his music was born, into the realm of his spirit where the prince would have complete dominion. Forced or insinuated possession would shatter his soul, make it useless.

Soon the sickness of the conjurer, or the desperation it inspired, would vaporize the rich metal of his will. All just a matter of time.

David's fountain pen glided over the staff paper.

The requiem's first movement would be carried by the piano, creating a foundation for the sound of snow translated as music. Wagner's *Das Rheingold* was his model; he would invoke sky and snow as acoustic collage the way Wagner had invoked the slow, deep power of a river. The piano would build a layer of sound echoing the heartbeat and breath of the person hearing the snow. Slow heartbeat, quiet breath . . .

After waking in the entryway dazed and stinking of fear, David had found the pen on the living room floor, beside a stack of freshly transcribed notations, copies of the sheets he had destroyed.

. . . breath that is soon joined with the breath of the sky, articulated with a French horn . . .

Several steps away, he'd found a moist, thick bloodstain.

. . . and the breath of the sky would fall into harmony with the steady notes of a flute . . .

The bloodstain had the vague outline of a small human body.

("She'll be of great use to you.")

. . . and the flute would change, creating a counterpoint to the piano and the French horn . . .

("A little aid to help with your composing.")

. . . a counterpoint that would parallel the opening of the senses of the person hearing the snow . . .

David undid his stiff, brown bandage, to see if his cut could have produced enough blood to make a stain that size.

("Watch what is possible when two agents meet to create something new and wonderful.")

. . . and the soft notes of a guitar would paint the movement of snowflakes falling through still air . . .

The wound was closed.

("Let me give you a gift.")

... soon joined by another guitar to suggest layers of snow ...
The joints of David's legs no longer ached.
("You will feel like a new man in the morning.")
David's hand jerked; the nib of the pen cut through the staff paper.
"It didn't happen," he said out loud. He paced as dusk filled the room, and made arguments to himself that what he had experienced was delirium. When he had convinced himself, he sat down to work again.
He could not focus.
The feeling of guilt and unfulfilled obligation was too great for him to bear. He went to the trash and fished out the soaked, bloody rags with which he'd cleaned away the stain. He buried them in the yard, straining with the shovel to break the hard soil.
The pleading eyes of the torn woman stayed with him though, well into the night.

Amduscias walked among the trees.
He heard, among the sounds of the night, the voices of his enemies in a whispering cacophony. They were nearer, tonight. He could smell them wandering without substance, uttering murmuring orisons that would bloom into the dreams that would give them a foothold within living souls.
The foothold would not be enough. He would destroy them, their purloined bodies, and the stifled souls within those bodies. It would be a great victory, and great blow against The Enfolded One.
Perhaps he should shove the little conjurer's soul into one of these oaks when he was done with it. Give it a home like the one it would have had if the conjurer had taken a few steps closer toward the bloody wood where the prince had heard his call. He'd use the spent soul as a conduit, a portal to this wood if ever he had need to escape the abyss.
He walked to the edge of the wood and looked down at the conjurer's home. He felt in the ether the process of sickness, the touch of madness. The prince's host from the night before was having another of his episodes.
Splendid.
He could never resist a dramatic entrance.
The prince crouched down and waited for an opportune moment to leave his body and invade David's weakened mind, and so invade his soul.

David fought the coming delirium with his music. He stood up from the piano bench as his senses reeled, focusing on the sheets of his composition, reading his notes and willing the tranquillity of the sound of snow to fill his mind. He would not face another horrific episode like he had last night.

The music surrounded him, held him with joy and a sense of being healed. The layers of the requiem built upon each other, and the room changed, became from the peripheries of his vision a great concert hall. The hall was empty, but his music filled the air. He faced the orchestra pit, and read until he reached the end of what he had composed.

"Bravo!"

David spun around.

The towering thing he knew as Amduscias walked the aisle toward him. It walked erect, with a grace that belied the monstrosity of its form. Its grace offended David. Revolted him.

"Bravo! You are touched with magnificence."

The demon stood a few steps from David. It turned its animal head, looking about with human intelligence. "What a lovely hall you've made. A special place, is it? A place of hidden dreams and lofty ambitions? A lovely hall. With lovely acoustics."

The monster threw back its head and sang with many voices part of an *"Ave"* with impossible pitch and clarity, as if an angelic choir found outlet in its throat.

When it was done, it pulled its animal mouth into a sickeningly human grin.

David looked away, spoke in a steady, even tone.

"I banish you. I cast you out."

"Do you?"

He looked back at the demon.

"Our Father, who art in Heaven, hallowed be Thy name. . . ."

The demon cocked its head.

"Thy kingdom come, Thy will be done . . . "

"On Earth as it is in Heaven!" said the demon. "But this is neither Earth nor Heaven. This is the place of your dreams."

David gripped the sheets of music tightly in his hand. They were a tether to the world that was real.

"What do you want of me?"

"I want what you want. I want to be returned to you. I want to help you with your great work."

"You can't have my soul."

"Why not? You share your soul through your music. Let me return to your mind. Let me free what's inside your soul so it can touch the souls of others. So your music can be shared with the world."

"What do you gain from this?"

"Joined with you, I would be a heavenly creature again. I would be pure and splendid. Able to sleep again upon the laps of maidens and heal the sick. Able to resurrect kings and foretell the birth of prophets." It raised its powerful arms skyward and turned joyfully. "You would not wish to deny me salvation, would you? I have healed you, have I not? At least partly? Imagine what I could do within you, what healing powers I could liberate. I might be able to save your life."

"You don't exist."

The demon looked at David as it had looked at the torn ghost-woman who had writhed at its feet.

It made a slow fist with its clawed hand before his face. "What have you to lose?" it hissed.

David stepped backward, toward the pit. He heard his sheets of music fall to the floor.

"What you have to gain."

With incredible speed for a beast its size, the demon lunged at David and reached for his throat. Its claws were almost on him when it looked up, startled as the sound of hunting horns reverberated through the room. It turned and was gone as the hall faded to dim shadows.

Amduscias pulled himself from the conjurer's mind, stood, and looked down from the hill he had claimed for himself.

Scrambling up the hill from the west were the human vessels of his pursuers. He could see pressed around their fleshy bodies the shadowy forms of those who had hunted him across vistas of damnation.

Mass possession like this was not possible. Not so soon. The dreams could not have taken root.

The prince looked up and saw a churning cloud like a swarm of insects blotting out the sky.

The Enfolded One had come.

Horns crashed through the ether.

Amduscias ran, the thunder of many footfalls behind him.

David picked up his sheets of music from the floor. He would play part of the piece. Get his mind working on the fine points. Focus, and gain control.

The entryway door burst open, and Amduscias forced his towering bulk through.

"ENOUGH!" David shouted. He picked up the piano bench and hurled it at the monster. "GODDAMN YOU! *ENOUGH!* I BANISH YOU! I EXILE YOU! YOU'RE NOTHING! YOU'RE—"

David was seized in the beast's claws. Lifted. Pressed against the cold plaster of the wall. The spiraling lance on the demon's brow hovered inches from his breast.

"Enough theater!" it said. "Do you hear them? Listen! They'll be at the door. The barrier I evoked will not hold them. They are my enemies. They will destroy us both unless you admit me to your soul. I cannot ward them off without you."

"No. This isn't real! You don't—"

The demon pulled him from the wall and smashed him back against it. "You don't know what's at stake!"

There was a crash in the entryway and David saw, over the demon's shoulder, his neighbors, people from town, old teachers and classmates standing at the door.

They pressed into the room, and for an instant, David thought he was saved.

The monster that held him in its claws looked toward the people piling into the room, then back at David.

Rage burned like diamond fire in those violet eyes.

It bellowed and pulled David onto its horn.

David screamed, back arched, arms out to his sides. He felt the horn pass through his flesh, his lung, his heart, his back. A fire coursed through him. He began to die as the horn that was killing him cleansed his blood.

His mind was freed from the sickness as his lungs filled with blood. He tried to cry out to the people below.

The demon's claws gripped David, its voice echoed in his mind.

"Give me your soul! You will live! We will live!"

The people in the room snarled like dogs and leapt upon the demon, rending and biting and tearing.

David fought the demon, joined to it by its horn, its mind groping, lunging, trying to cleave to his soul as its horn had cleaved through his flesh. The horn kept him in his body. His soul did not rise. He felt his being change as he and his enemy fell to the floor under the crush of bodies.

"Yes! Give me your soul! I can spare you from this!"

Hands were upon David, pulling, ripping.

The demon pressed into David's spirit through his sundered heart, through the strength of its will and David's longing for the agony to end.

David felt the atrocity of the thing's mind within his own mind. With his last act of will as his body tore, David reached out with his soul, pleading for salvation. Before his dimming eyes, he saw the red serpent—the guardian of change and benevolent passage. David embraced it with his spirit as his arms were pulled from him.

Between life and death, David joined with the demon. The serpent moved through him, and he knew it to be a thing of his own creation, part of his own mind given form, his own strength given tangible shape.

He put the demon down as his existence ended. The serpent's red glow transmogrified him, burning away what he had been, cleansing the demon's contamination of his spirit.

In an unnamable limbo, he knew the quiet of snowfall . . . and the dead ethereal form of his enemy.

He made them both his own as he heard the cries of tortured living souls around him.

A November sunrise, burning with secret fire and the rich amber of autumnal light, touched the faces those who had been a mob as they drifted across the countryside, covered with blood, covered with flesh, covered with scraps of skin and torn clothing.

As the songs of larks echo across a valley at dawn, so did their screams, cries, and sobs echo among the fields. Some of the wanderers fell to their knees, some tore their hair, some curled into fetal balls upon the cold, hard ground.

Their souls had been mauled by the things that had possessed them and filled them with blind lust for the blood they had thought could redeem them.

Gray clouds drifted from the west, towering in the sky like cliffs of granite, dimming the sun's light. The cold rains the clouds brought drove the people home like slow-moving animals. The rain did not wash away the filth that clung to their spirits.

What happened among them was kept secret, in the way witch hunts and midnight lynchings are. The house where the torn flesh of their prey lay piled thick upon the floor was burned several nights later, as was part of the fields around it.

The fire's glow brought a false dawn to the moonless sky; the clouds of smoke carried with them the scent of sulfur and rot, of burned hair and sickness.

A spiritual plague hung like choking fog over the countryside. A plague that would have warped and killed the souls of all whom it touched, had it not been for the visitation in dreams of a magnificent snow-white beast that came to each of them. That touched their hearts and souls with the healing light of its horn at the moment when the burning clouds of sunset seemed to have coiled among them a great serpent the rich color of cinnabar.

The beast came to them atop a hill crowned with a grove of oaks that was held by the eternal rebirth of spring. The coming of the creature was heralded by music. Sweet music, reminiscent of the sound of snow falling upon quiet winter fields, of the breath of the sky, and the voice of each crystalline feather as it alights upon the earth.

ABOUT THE AUTHOR

Michael Marano was born in 1964, the youngest of nine children. His interest in horror is, therefore, self-evident. He began studying alchemy and Kabbalah while pursuing a degree in medieval history at Boston University. After an abortive (and mercifully brief) stab at academia, he held a number of positions, including college writing instructor, apartment building manager, rare book dealer, and punk rock DJ. Currently, as "Mad Prof. Mike," he reviews horror movies for the program *Movie Magazine*, which is syndicated throughout the United States over the Public Radio Satellite Network. In this capacity, he sees scores of B movies each year and is now unsuited for almost any other form of employment.

"Winter Requiem" is part of a cycle he is writing that applies medieval heuristics and hermeneutics to the modern horror story.

He loves his wife, Nancy Nenno, more than anything else in the world.

LISA MASON

━━◦⊸⊷⊶⊷◦━━

DAUGHTER OF THE TAO

Peter: All I know about **Lisa Mason** is that she lives in Marin County, California, and that her story "Daughter of the Tao," besides being lovely and sad and fluidly inventive, is one of only two stories in this collection ("Mirror of Lop Nor" is the other) to deal with the *k'i-lin*, the unicorn of China and Japan, which is more like an element, a force of nature, than it is like the European horned horse. I wish there had been more such tales, but I'll gladly settle for these two.

Janet: I, on the other hand, know Lisa well. Aside from being gorgeous, talented, an attorney, and another sometime member of The Melville Nine workshop, she's a prolific novelist and short story writer. She is also, I am happy to say, my friend. We talk at length on the phone, of shoes and sealing wax, cabbages, kings, and publishing. I wish she lived around the corner.

Daughter of the Tao

1. DRAGON

SING CHOY DARTS THROUGH FISH ALLEY SEEKING fresh shrimp for her master. She swings her basket joyfully, savoring ripe odors of raw sea creatures, ginger root, peanut oil smoking in someone's wok.

A *mooie jai* does not skip along the streets of Tangrenbu, not on most days. Certainly not on a day as crisp and sunny as this, which her master's cook would have savored for himself. But Cook injured his leg. Ankle swollen from Cook's misstep into a pothole on Dupont Street. Cook seized Sing Choy's skinny arm as she knelt on the kitchen floor scrubbing with her soap and brush, flung her to her feet, and said, "Here, stupid girl, go get two pound shrimp and make quick."

"Yes, Cook," she said.

Sing Choy carefully washed her hands and face, retied her queue, smoothed wrinkles from her *sahm*. And set out with coins and basket, joy bobbing in her heart. Shrimp good luck. Perhaps her master will permit Cook to give her one fried shrimp for supper along with boiled rice and greens. "You shrimp girl," Cook joked. "Master buy you for two hundred dollars gold, plus five pound shrimp."

Sing Choy pauses among the fish peddlers in Fish Alley. Peasants in denim *sahms*, that's what the peddlers are, with felt slouch hats or embroidered caps, the crudest ones in the flat straw cone of the coolie. Her master employs men like this. She can feel their eyes. After all, a *mooie jai* does not skip along the streets of Tangrenbu.

Fish Alley is not even a street but a narrow, mean passage between forty-niner shacks long abandoned to slum landlords, crowded with bach-

elors who shift in and out with the fickle tides of opportunity and poverty.
Weathered clapboard walls are plastered with vermilion bulletins, black
calligraphy announcing news near and afar. A gilt *t'ai chi* adorns a lintel.
A potted star lily mournfully turns to what sunlight it can glean before
shadows close over its corner.

Huge baskets bulge with the bay's bounty: black-speckled oysters;
green and pink crabs with slow-pinching claws; shrimp, of course, of
palest celadon before they go to the wok; silvery salmon, some flopping
still, tepid water streaming into the gutter. Sing Choy's heart catches at
the sight of their dying. She pauses, struck with sudden nameless shame.

"Hey, you girl, why such a sad face?"

Sing Choy turns. Another girl! Who ever sees a girl in Tangrenbu?
Yet it's true, another girl stands beside her. Black cotton *sahm,* basket
slung upon her arm, queue wound around her head. She is taller than Sing
Choy by a handspan and very skinny. Face like the moon, a laughing
mouth. Around her neck a black silk cord and a tiny gilt *t'ai chi.* Little
shadows beneath the bones in her cheeks, little shadows beneath the gentle
swells of her breasts. The fish peddlers gape at her as if she were a two-
headed pig.

"I . . . I sorry pretty fish must die."

"Your heart too soft. Salmon delicious! Your master so cruel he never
let you taste salmon?"

Sing Choy stares at her big bony toes. Peasant feet made for walking,
standing in fields planting peas, carrying loads of millet. She is nothing.
She is no one to taste salmon. "Sometimes my master give me one fried
shrimp with rice and greens."

The girl throws back her head and laughs like the tinkling of a bell.
The fish peddlers murmur. Sing Choy is only too aware of their eyes now.
"Don't laugh like that," she mutters to the girl. "They all looking."

The girl takes her arm, draws her beneath a balcony with curved railings painted the color of an egg yolk. "Who you?"

"I Sing Choy."

"I Kwai Ying. You *mooie jai?*"

"Yes."

"Me, too. Cook sick?"

The beautiful language of Cantonese embraces so many dialects that
Sing Choy, a girl from the north, can barely understand this girl from the
south. They both must twist their tongues around the language of Gold
Mountain.

"Cook step into hole!" Sing Choy suppresses laughter. A little awed.
This bold girl, *mooie jai,* too? And her master let her taste salmon?

The balcony shades them from sun and the fish peddlers' eyes but affords no relief from the stench rising from a spattered bin groaning with all manner of offal. Fish heads and fins and guts, husked shrimp shells, the small flat mitt of a manta that wandered into someone's net. Sing Choy wrinkles her nose. Kwai Ying peers in curiously.

"Look," she says.

There, amid the garbage next to the manta, is another small dead creature, mottled gray in color, serpentine like an eel. But the creature is not an eel. Four fragile legs lie slack, each tipped with delicate fingers and long curved claws as fine as needles. The dead face resembles a tiny ox. A tuft of dark scarlet bristles sprouts from its pate. Its jaws hang open, miniature roar silenced forever.

"Poor thing," Sing Choy murmurs. "What is it?"

"Your heart too soft," Kwai Ying says, voice thick with contempt. "That just *lung;* a dragon."

"A dragon!" Sing Choy's eyes widen.

"Sure." Kwai Ying says, a frown tugging at her mouth. "It one of the four fabulous creatures, but look at it. Caught in fisherman's net like worthless manta, thrown away like fish guts. No better than garbage."

"But a dragon!"

"Stupid girl, you know the four fabulous creatures?"

Sing Choy shakes her head, humiliated.

"Dragon, phoenix, unicorn, tortoise," Kwai Ying dutifully recites. "My teacher say. I have teacher once, you know. Teacher say each very good creature. Supposed to bring good luck. Supposed to show harmony with the Tao. Supposed to"—raising her eyebrows significantly—"bring magic."

Sing Choy's mouth falls open. "Magic!"

"But I see no harmony in Tangrenbu," Kwai Ying says. "I see no Tao. I see no magic for *mooie jai.*"

Sing Choy could cry at the bitterness in Kwai Ying's voice.

Kwai Ying only shrugs. "When you come to Tangrenbu?"

"In Year of Golden Tiger. *Swallow* take me."

Sing Choy gulps. Still fills her heart with grief how her father sold her to a man in Shanghai, the ship's master of a clipper with three sails named for a pretty bird. The *Swallow,* a coolie clipper carrying illegal human cargo. They stowed her belowdeck for so many miserable days she lost count after tying two bits of string on each finger of her hands. Was grateful when they carried her up into the cold sunshine of San Francisco. Was grateful when they shimmied off the stinking rags she'd huddled in. Was grateful when she stood naked and shivering on a block beneath gaslights and an auctioneer opened her mouth, spread her skinny legs. Was grateful to go to her master for two hundred dollars, plus five pounds of shrimp. She was *mooie jai,* destined to scrub floors, polish pots, clean night soil from the water closet. Is grateful for one fried shrimp with her rice and greens. This Tangrenbu, City of the People of Tan.

"Golden Tiger," says Kwai Ying. Her pretty black eyes gleam. Her tone is as tart as new oranges. "And how many celestial creatures you see before Year of Golden Tiger?"

Sing Choy grins. Likes this game. Cook asks her this, too, so she will know how old she is. "I remember Year of Dog, but only a little because *I* little." The girls giggle together. "Then came Boar, then Rat, then Ox. And at last Tiger, all in gold."

"I know more animals than you," Kwai Ying says. "I know Cock and Monkey." Stern, quizzing. "And after Year of Golden Tiger?"

Sing Choy thinks carefully. Cook only asks her year by year, not all at once. "After Tiger came Hare."

"Yes."

"After Hare came Dragon." Doesn't want to look at the little dead dragon anymore. Stares into Kwai Ying's eyes. "After Dragon came Snake. I don't like Snake."

"Yes, yes."

"After Snake came Horse. Now is Year of Ram."

"And new year coming?"

"New year coming is Monkey!"

"Good." Kwai Ying rewards her with a squeeze of her hand. "I born in Year of Monkey."

"Then new year coming is your lucky year," Sing Choy says. "Another Year of Monkey!"

"Yes," Kwai Ying says. A small wry smile like she has swallowed something sour. "I see twelve celestial animals come and go. That is why my master make me eat salmon till my belly can hold no more."

Sing Choy should be glad Kwai Ying can eat so well but her heart catches as painfully as when she saw the flopping salmon, the little dead dragon. "Why make you eat?"

Kwai Ying takes her arm, pulls her away from the reeking bin. Flies land on the dragon in a buzzing tribe.

"Because I am woman now."

2. PHOENIX

Sing Choy sprints back to her master's house with two pounds of fresh shrimp and change. Taking his ease, ankle propped on a cushion, Cook counts out the silver coins carefully. Glances up at her, smiling his black-toothed smile. "Very good, girl. I tell Master you not so stupid, after all."

"Thank you, Cook. Any other thing you want?"

"No." Cook studies her, calculating. Doles out a silver coin. The sun angles over Russian Hill, casting shadows over Tangrenbu. But the day is not yet old. "Yes. You go get salted plums for Master. He like plums. And a coconut candy for you. But just one. And bring change."

"Yes, Cook."

"And put jacket over *sahm*." Cook produces one of his, throws it roughly over her shoulders. "Wrap hair, take hat." Jostles her around, coils the queue into a bun at the nape of her neck. Jams a slouch hat over her skull. Hat much too big, she looks like a little old man. Giggles. Cook whirls her to face him, shakes his finger in her face. "No laugh. You must look like boy. I cannot send girl into Tangrenbu. Since *lo fahn,* the white devils, say we cannot bring our families from China to Gold Mountain, there no women, no girls in Tangrenbu. Only *mooie jai* and . . . "

"And who, Cook?"

"And daughters of joy." Cook shakes his finger again. "Listen, girl. Never go to Bartlett Alley. Never go to Spofford Alley. Never go to Waverly Place. I hear someone see you there, I thrash you till you cry no more. You *sabe*?"

There was a time when Sing Choy would have cringed before Cook's finger. She has passed by Bartlett Alley, Spofford Alley, Waverly Place. Forbidden places, always. Recalls the strange birdlike cries she hears whenever she passes by those places. And another recollection: the time in Year of Snake when she walked with Cook through Waverly Place and saw men dragging something out of a shack. Something small and dark, which they tossed in the back of a wagon like trash. Cook had made her hurry.

But Sing Choy is bold after her foray into Fish Alley. She does not cringe. She says, without blinking, "I *sabe*."

And sets out for salted plums, one coconut candy for herself. Brings back change, shows Cook the candy, which he splits in half and eats. No matter. Half a coconut candy is well worth freedom she never had before.

And this is how Sing Choy sees Kwai Ying again: darting down Stockton Street, turning the corner at Broadway, disappearing into a pottery shop on Dupont. Every now and then they meet and pause, dart beneath a balcony, talk in breathless whispers.

"I never had teacher," Sing Choy says as they lean against two bales of rags bound with thick straw cords. Ashamed of her ignorance, but curious. "What is the Tao?"

"My teacher say Tao is the Way," Kwai Ying says. "Tao is eternal female, mysterious and mutable. Tao is chasm *and* mountain. Tao is light *and* dark. You see?" She takes her tiny gilt *t'ai chi* in her fingertips, shows

Sing Choy the disk, half light, half dark. And within each half, a dot of the opposite.

They both giggle, unsure if they understand what Kwai Ying's teacher meant.

"And what is harmony with the Tao?" Sing Choy asks, thrilled with her friend's wisdom.

"Harmony with the Tao means all is well." Kwai Ying muses. "Tao means peace and prosperity. Tao means good luck and magic. The four fabulous creatures appear in the world when the world is in harmony with the Tao. The four fabulous creatures cannot live when there is evil. The four fabulous creatures die or disappear when the world is not in harmony with the Tao."

A dark look passes over Kwai Ying's face that makes Sing Choy's breath snag in her throat.

They can never talk for very long. Bachelors' eyes are everywhere in Tangrenbu. Perhaps Sing Choy may look like a boy, but Kwai Ying cannot conceal her burgeoning femininity. Worse, she does not even try. Her master has given her black silk to wear. The luminous fabric clings to every hill and valley in the changing landscape of Kwai Ying's body.

"You so pretty, Kwai Ying," Sing Choy says. Envious; also admiring. The sight of Kwai Ying makes her heart bob with joy.

"Master say 'eat, eat, you skinny girl,'" Kwai Ying says, and produces a coconut candy for Sing Choy. "For you, little Sing. I cannot eat cheap sweets. I am stuffed with shrimp."

One day Sing Choy is carrying a basket of new lettuce from the farms in Cow Hollow when she finds Kwai Ying standing on the corner of Sullivan Alley.

A knot of bachelors crouches on the cobblestones surrounded by a crowd of onlookers. The men grin and spit, the mood is tense and ugly, but no one cheers too loudly. Some illicit gambling game. The bachelors love to gamble. No one wants to attract the bulls of the Chinatown Squad. Dreadful squawking noises arise from inside the circle like the tumult of an unhappy barnyard.

"Hi," Sing Choy says.

"Hi, you little girl," Kwai Ying says. She has grown haughty lately.

"What is it?" Sing Choy says, putting down her basket. Standing beside Kwai Ying's beauty, she feels sweaty, unkempt. Annoyed, too, at Kwai Ying's aloof mood. Perhaps Sing Choy is just a peasant girl and once Kwai Ying held some higher station, but they were both sold by their families. They both sailed belowdeck in coolie clippers, both stood naked and shivering on a block beneath gaslights. Both *mooie jai* in Tangrenbu.

Perhaps aware of her friend's annoyance, Kwai Ying turns with a sunny smile. A beguiling smile as though she wishes to make Sing Choy do something she would not want to do. "It's a cockfight. Want to see?"

Sing Choy backs away. "No . . . no . . . "

"Come on! Leave your basket. No one will bother your stupid lettuce. I said, come on!" She seizes Sing Choy's hand, won't let go.

They slip through the crowd to the knot of crouching men. It is a horrible sight! In a makeshift plywood pen two blood-spattered birds confront each other in a struggle to the death. A rooster with a scarlet comb, dark scarlet feathers, huge vicious spurs struts around the other bird, which staggers pitifully. The gamblers toss gold coins at a croupier, a man who holds the money and calculates odds in a low monotone.

The rooster pecks and kicks. "Oh," Sing Choy groans but Kwai Ying squeezes her hand so tightly she does not dare cry out. The other bird is a beautiful thing with variegated crest, tail, and wings. The long swooping feathers drag in mud and blood, but Sing Choy sees cerulean blue, golden yellow, cinnamon red, ivory white, ebony black. The rooster kicks again, spur connecting with the bird's breast, and the bird shudders in agony. The men yell, gold coins clatter. As Sing Choy blinks away tears, the bird cocks its head at her and Kwai Ying. For a moment its bright suffering eye looks right at them.

The bird bursts into a ball of fire! Flames of blue, gold, red, white, black shoot as high as a house. The crouching men fall back on their heels. The onlookers press forward. The croupier scrambles for his collection of coins. A rending cry rises up, inhuman, ghastly.

Kwai Ying drags Sing Choy through the crowd.

Now men jostle and push. A thin boy tumbles to the cobblestones, his face and *sahm* dappled with blood. Little blue flames spring from the blood like sparks catching and ebbing in cooking oil. Shriek of the bulls' whistle and the bachelors scatter, footsteps ringing down the alley.

Faces drained, eyes wide, the girls press up against the window of a sweetmeat shop. As still as feral creatures, as quiet as shadows, they wait till the Chinatown Squad has rousted everyone out of Sullivan Alley. Kwai Ying's hand in Sing Choy's is as cold as Cook's iron pot on mornings when fog curls through Tangrenbu.

3. UNICORN

Since the phoenix burned, Sing Choy has not seen Kwai Ying. She searches Stockton and Dupont, jogs down Broadway and up Fish Alley, even goes back to Sullivan Alley though she does not stay there long. Year of Monkey passes by, Year of Cock comes, and suddenly Sing Choy is taller than Cook. Her rough cotton *sahm* dangles above her ankles and wrists. The slouch hat she wears while running errands fits her skull perfectly now. Her thick queue hangs to the backs of her knees.

One evening Cook comes into the pantry behind the kitchen where Sing Choy sleeps on a cot and eats her meals. He brings in her bowl of supper, bangs it down on the little side table. "Master say you too skinny," Cook says. Baleful glance. "Eat."

Sing Choy takes the steaming bowl. Rice and greens, as usual. To her astonishment, she sees the bowl is also heaped with steamed salmon, chunks of fragrant pink meat more enticing than coconut candy. She takes the bowl, digs in chopsticks, greedily devouring. She is always hungry these days. Delicious salmon!

But she pauses in her gluttony, struck with sudden guilt.

Kwai Ying, where are you?

Kwai Ying could have left Tangrenbu, of course. Her master could have moved to San Rafael, Sacramento, Salinas, Russian River. A *mooie jai* could disappear anywhere in Gold Mountain.

But when Sing Choy turns the corner at Pacific Avenue, she sees a tall, pretty girl turn the corner onto Broadway. In Fish Alley, she hears the tinkling of a bell and is certain she hears Kwai Ying laughing. When she pauses before a gilt *t'ai chi* tacked to a lintel, she remembers the *t'ai chi* Kwai Ying wore around her neck on a black silk cord.

Kwai Ying is still in Tangrenbu.

Sing Choy finishes her supper. Making a show of gratitude, she steals a half glass of whiskey from Master's bottle in the pantry, brings it into Cook's room.

Cook smiles his black-toothed smile. "Smart girl. You pour a little water in bottle, Master never notice." Sucks whiskey from the glass. "You good girl." Cook's eyes blur. He wipes a tear.

"I lock up, okay?" she says, annoyed. Sad old man, a little whiskey makes him cry.

"You good girl," Cook says again. Sorrow tugs at his mouth.

Sing Choy locks up the house for the night the way Cook would have done. But she leaves the pantry door open, leaves the back door to the kitchen open. Reties her queue, jams her slouch hat over her forehead, fastens the frogs of her padded jacket. And creeps into the fog-shrouded night, seeking the places she has always been forbidden to go.

She walks down Bartlett Alley, Spofford Alley, Waverly Place. Recalls the small, dark thing thrown like trash by men into the back of a wagon. Recalls how Cook made her hurry, how Cook tried to turn her face away, but she saw anyway. Saw the corpse of a woman. Hears the same strange birdlike cries she has heard whenever she passes by, "Two bittee lookee, four bittee touchee, six bittee doee."

Forty-niner shacks in these alleys have long been abandoned to brothels. The procurers have subdivided the shacks into cubbyholes with locked doors, windows without glass set with sturdy iron bars. Cubbyholes called cribs. In every crib beneath gaslights, at every barred window, stands a girl in black silk calling, "Two bittee lookee, four bittee touchee, six bittee doee."

Sing Choy carefully tours each alley, peering in at the faces. Sees a northern girl, her broad flat cheeks dappled with bruises. A mountain peasant, her thick wide mouth crusted with lip paint and sores. A crone, withered and hacking, death etched in her eyes, yet she cannot be more than seventeen years old. And at last a moon face, a laughing mouth, little shadows beneath cheekbones. Charm always charms no matter how dark the shadows.

Sing Choy has bargained with merchants over the time Cook has let her run errands. She has carefully saved change from shrewder bargains than even Cook would have expected. She gives the procurer six bits. The procurer, a buffalo of a man with a butterfly knife stuck conspicuously in his belt, lets her into Kwai Ying's crib.

Sing Choy takes off her hat and sits while Kwai Ying bustles about, not noticing who the visitor is. Dirt floor and clapboard walls. A tiny cot, a chamber pot, a pitcher of water, some cotton cloths. A pipe, the bowl gray with opium ash. Candles, incense, a bottle of expensive whiskey, another bottle filled with some other astringent smelling fluid. If Sing Choy spread her arms straight out, her fingertips could just about reach each wall. The crib is freezing cold. Shrine on a side table, a spray of brown star lilies. Tacked on the wall by its black silk cord, the tiny gilt *t'ai chi.*

"Oh, Kwai Ying, don't you wear it anymore?" Sing Choy says.

Kwai Ying whirls, a snarl disfiguring her face, a knife in her fist. Then her mouth drops at the sight of Sing Choy. "Little Sing," she cries. Runs to her friend, embraces her. Then flings Sing Choy away. Pretty girl deeply shamed. Covers her pale cheeks with her hands. Dark circles rim her eyes. "Your heart too soft. I am no longer *mooie jai.*"

"You what the bachelors call a daughter of joy."

"Daughter of joy." Kwai Ying's voice is as bitter as lye soap. "Master sell me to Chee Song Tong."

Sing Choy nods. She knows now. Chee Song Tong runs most of the cribs in Tangrenbu. Smuggles girls from China, buys *mooie jai* when they are old enough to become daughters of joy. Sing Choy says at once, "I buy you back. How much?"

"What money have you?"

"Cook send me on errands for a long time now. I save fifty dollars in gold and silver." This is a great fortune for a *mooie jai*. Sing Choy has never had so much money in her life. Carefully hoards it in a hidey-hole beneath her cot in the pantry.

"*Stupid* girl. Chee Song Tong pay my master a thousand gold coins for me."

"A thousand . . ." Sing Choy's heart catches.

Kwai Ying scornful. "Fifty dollars." Unfastens the frogs on Sing Choy's jacket, poking, probing with her hands. "You still like boy, but your time coming."

"No!"

Haughty Kwai Ying again, beautiful and imperious, as tart as new oranges. "You will be daughter of joy, too."

Sing Choy is incredulous. "You like this, then?"

"Oh, little Sing!" Kwai Ying shakes her head. Tears squeeze from her eyes. Her mouth falls slack in a mask of grief. "How bachelors come and go. Dozens, dozens, and dozens more. All day long, all night long."

"No, no!"

Cruel Kwai Ying. "How they come at you, one after the other." Rubs her belly. "How they hurt. How they numb. How they steal your soul."

"I run away!"

"You are *mooie jai*. Where can you go? There is nowhere you can go. Except my teacher once say . . . "

But Kwai Ying clamps her lips shut. Bows her head.

"Please tell me," Sing Choy says. "I never had teacher. *You* my only teacher. I know nothing."

Sharp knock on the door. "Time up," the procurer says.

Sing Choy hands another six bits through the bars. "More time, please."

"Okay," he says, taking the money.

But another sharp knock batters the door.

Kwai Ying springs up beside Sing Choy, leaning out the window. Mutters, "The lousy . . ."

A creature thrusts its snout through the window. The horn on its forehead strikes the bars with a resounding *clang*. The creature opens its mouth and speaks, a tumultuous sound like many bells ringing. Two cinnamon red tendrils hang down below its nostrils like a man's mustache. Bushy hair wreathing long pointed ears is cerulean blue. Its scaly skin glows golden yellow. The long swishing tail and dancing hooves are as black as ebony. It stares at them with eyes like ivory marbles.

The girls shrink back before the blind-white gaze.

"Go away!" Kwai Ying says. Tremulous; then firmer, "Go away!"

The creature pulls back. Sing Choy expects the clatter of hooves on cobblestones, but there is only silence, the distant singsong, "Two bittee lookee, four bittee . . ." Sing Choy dares to peek out. There is nothing but the fog and night and Spofford Alley.

The girls sit on the cot, stunned and trembling with fear.

At last Kwai Ying stands, gets down her whiskey bottle, tips a sip. Stern, quizzing. "And what was that, little Sing?"

"That was unicorn," Sing Choy says dutifully, but her heart still cannot contain her bewilderment. "Third of the four fabulous creatures. But, Kwai Ying. We saw dragon dead. We saw phoenix die. The unicorn; he . . . "

"He very much *alive*?" Kwai Ying tosses her head, offers the bottle.

Sing Choy refuses. She has only seen eleven celestial animals. Next year, Year of Dog, is *her* lucky year. She does not drink foul liquor of *lo fahn*.

"What you really want to know," Kwai Ying says, "is why unicorn has come for *me*."

Little shivers of shock pop all over Sing Choy's spine like the first time she saw and heard firecrackers. "Why does unicorn come for you?"

"Because I can be daughter of joy; I can allow bachelors of Tangrenbu to numb me, steal my soul; I can allow procurer and landlord to steal my gold. Or I can be daughter of the Tao. I can embrace the Way." Kwai Ying sips more whiskey. Sulky girl. "I can choose. My teacher say."

Sing Choy is appalled. "Then why you choose *this*?"

Kwai Ying whirls on her like a striking snake. "My father did not sell me. My mother did not sell me. I am orphan. I am raised by the Daughters of the Tao. You know Daughters of the Tao?"

Sing Choy shrinks back on the cot. "No. I never hear of this."

"Daughters of the Tao," Kwai Ying says, "are immortal sisters. They embrace the Way. They practice *magic*. How we lived, oh my! On a beautiful island off shore of Hong Kong. Small island with a curved back, forests and clear streams. Lovely houses, balconies and pools, flowers and shrubbery. Not like ugly streets of Tangrenbu. And shrimp and salmon to eat, all you want, little Sing! Fried rice and pretty greens such as you have never seen."

Sing Choy does not know. Glances at the opium pipe, the whiskey bottle, the awful crib. Surreptitiously takes the knife from the cot where Kwai Ying left it. Perhaps Kwai Ying has gone mad in her slavery.

"You think I gone mad?" Kwai Ying says, laughing at Sing Choy's astonished look. "Gone mad, yes. Daughters of the Tao gone mad, too.

They do not accept dynasty, do not accept patriarchy. Do not accept bound feet or concubines or dictators or daughters of joy. Or *mooie jai*."

"Then why they sell you?" Sing Choy says. Blunt girl, learning how to be hard, too.

"Daughters of the Tao did not sell me," Kwai Ying says. The bitter voice fairly tears Sing Choy's heart from her breast. "Daughters of the Tao could not themselves withstand the evil of the world. The opium; the slave girls; the coolies; the oppression. One day our island swam away."

"Swam away?"

"Our island," Kwai Ying says impatiently, "has a head, four legs, a tail. One day our island swam away into the Tao, fleeing from the evil of the world. No one could have foreseen the whims of tortoise, I suppose. My teacher and I had gone on errands in Hong Kong. We were left behind. Just like that."

Sing Choy considers her friend's wild story. Very sad, how addled pretty Kwai Ying has become in so short a time. This will not happen to Sing Choy. No. Never. But she asks because she must, "And what happened to your teacher?"

"My teacher waited for omens," Kwai Ying answers at once, though her voice is low and slurred. "Omens came. The four fabulous creatures: *lung* the dragon, *feng huang* the phoenix, *ch'i lin* the unicorn, *wang pa* the tortoise. They crept through the gutter, swam in cesspools. And when the time was right, my teacher allowed the unicorn to pierce her and take her back to the Tao. It was horrible, little Sing!"

"Kwai, what do you mean?"

"They found her. In an alley. Blood pooled on her breast, blood everywhere. And I had no one. I was sold to slavers. I came to Gold Mountain as *mooie jai*. And now I am here, daughter of joy. The Tao is lost to me."

Sharp knock at the door. The procurer growls, "Time up. You go."

Sing Choy jams her slouch hat over her face. "Okay," she calls to the procurer. To Kwai Ying, "Then your teacher die? She took her own life? That what you mean?"

"No," Kwai Ying says. Takes a final slug of whiskey, caps the bottle, wipes her mouth. "No, I mean unicorn sought her, unicorn came for her, unicorn pierced her breast. Unicorn took her back to the Tao. To the island of immortal sisters. Yet . . . immortality look very much like death to me."

"You make no sense," Sing Choy says harshly. "Once I love you, Kwai Ying. Now I see you weak. Mad; deluded. I *never* be like you." Fastens the frogs of her jacket. Turns to go.

"Fine, I am weak," Kwai Ying says, touching Sing Choy's hand as the procurer lets in another bachelor. She yanks the black silk cord from the wall, takes down the little gilt *t'ai chi*. Slings the cord over Sing Choy's neck. "I fear the unicorn more than I fear my fate in Tangrenbu."

4. TORTOISE

And this is how Sing Choy comes to meet her womanhood.

First, Cook finds Sing Choy's hidey-hole beneath the cot, takes the fifty dollars in gold and silver coins. "Thief! Thief!" His black-toothed scowl, baleful glare. "You think you smart? Too smart for girl!"

Next, Cook and Master strip her of her black cotton *sahm*. She fights till Master whips his knuckles across the back of her head. She wriggles, shamed and naked as a frog. She is frightened Master will take her *t'ai chi*, fingers the black silk cord of the amulet Kwai Ying gave her. But Master does not seem to see the amulet at all, though it burns upon her breast like a hot coal. Master shimmies the tunic of a black silk *sahm* over her head, sliding the luminous fabric over the changing landscape of her body. She reaches for the trousers, but Master bunches them in his fist. No trousers.

A man is there to see Sing Choy. What they call a highbinder, a man who buys and sells girls like Kwai Ying. Like Sing Choy, too.

"Smart girl," Master says to the man, a weary graybeard with deep wrinkles and one eye. "Pretty girl." Master takes the hem of Sing Choy's black silk tunic, lifts the fabric up, showing her burgeoning breasts. The rest of her, too; curved waist, lanky hipbones, thighs sturdy from walking errands. She is not like boy anymore.

The graybeard pokes her ribs, her hipbones. "Too skinny."

"We fatten her up before you take," Master says. "Two thousand in gold."

"One thousand for this skinny one," says the graybeard. He laughs, a barking sound. Hard fingers, poking everywhere. Poking in places no one has been since Sing Choy stood on the auctioneer's block.

"*Very* pretty," Master says. "*Very* smart. One thousand seven."

"One thousand five," the graybeard says.

Sing Choy says nothing. What can she say? She has no voice in this transaction. She is *mooie jai*. Kwai Ying said *I see no magic for* mooie jai. Oh, Kwai Ying, Sing Choy cries in her heart. Cook has taken Sing Choy's scrimped money, taken all her things. She has nothing. She has no one.

"Done," Master says to the graybeard. To Cook, "Fry shrimp and salmon for this girl. Fry rice and greens, too." To Sing Choy, "You good girl. Make Master happy."

Master and Cook lock her in the pantry that night with bowls of greasy food. Master is so excited at the prospect of one thousand five hundred dollars in gold for his little servant girl who has grown up so beautifully that he forgets to take his whiskey. He probably has whiskey in his own bedroom, anyway. Master is old. Master has been old since Sing Choy came to his house in Year of Golden Tiger. Master came to Tangrenbu before the railroads, before the Silver Kings. Master does not care about a young girl. He has suffered much himself in Tangrenbu though now he has a house, a business, gold, coolies, and *mooie jai*. Master can let Sing Choy go. He can buy another *mooie jai* for two hundred dollars, plus five pounds shrimp.

Sing Choy tries the pantry door again, desperate to escape. She has been sold to the graybeard, she understands this now. Bound where, for what crib? She does not know but can guess. Bartlett Alley, Spofford Alley, Waverly Place? The pantry door is locked up tight. There is no window, no other way out. The clapboard wall abuts Hangah Alley, a mean cobble-stoned passage slick with trampled offal and the waste of Tangrenbu.

Desolate, Sing Choy sits back down on her cot, sips a bit of Master's whiskey in the bottle he left behind. Wonders if she should get drunk and forget. Wonders if she should get drunk and kill herself. Kill . . . *They numb you, steal your soul.* Kwai Ying, Sing Choy thinks, I so sorry. I understand at last.

But with what can Sing Choy do this deed?

The knife she took from Kwai Ying, of course. Not a big knife, not a jagged knife. A very small knife but sharp enough to make blood flow from the little blue branches in the stems of a young woman's wrists. Sing Choy finds the knife where she hid it behind a jar of pickled onions in the pantry. A small knife but powerful enough to defy the cruelty of Tangrenbu.

Suddenly Sing Choy hears the clatter of hooves in Hangah Alley, the cacophony of a galloping creature.

Boom!

The horn of the unicorn slices through clapboard and cheap plaster, tearing a gap clear through the wall above her cot. The unicorn's head thrusts through the dusty aperture. Plaster dust spills off the tip of its horn in a fine cloud like her breath on a chill morning. The creature stares at her, snorting. Blind eyes like ivory marbles. Variegated colors—cinnamon red, cerulean blue, gold—stream from its wild mane. The mustache, the horn, the golden scales, stomping hooves of glossy ebony.

A dream? A nightmare? A reality Sing Choy cannot accept?

"What you want?" Sing Choy whispers to the unicorn.

Immortal sisters do not accept dynasty, do not accept patriarchy. Do not accept bound feet or concubines or dictators. Daughters of joy or mooie jai.

Is this the secret voice of the unicorn or only the desperation of her own heart?

Sing Choy does not care anymore. "All right," she says, heedless with despair and a sip of whiskey. Bold girl, haughty and disdainful of death. She tears open her black silk *sahm*. Presents her breast to the unicorn.

The unicorn bows its head at once and pierces her. The horn slides in easily. A tiny prick, then nothing. Sing Choy looks down, expecting the bloodbath Kwai Ying saw of her teacher in the alley. But there is nothing. Nothing but a gentle throbbing like grief ebbing away. Nothing but the unicorn's forehead cradled against her like a suckling baby.

Suddenly the unicorn flings its head up.

Sing Choy gasps as the horn impaling her lifts her from the cot and hurls her through the ragged gap in the wall. *Now* she feels the stab of immortality! Like the flaying of skin, like burning. Is she screaming?

Dizzy, tumbling through the air like a circus acrobat, she slides off the horn and lands astride the unicorn's back. The scaly skin of the creature is as coarse as burlap and freezing cold. Yet in an instant, leaning over the creature's neck and heaving for breath, she regains her balance. Looks up; there, the ragged gap in the wall, the pantry, her cot. Only she is outside now! There is a small, dark thing on the cot, too, a wet red stain on the sheets. She turns her head, does not want to see.

The unicorn shifts beneath her, backs away from the torn wall of Master's house, and slowly turns. Straddling the unicorn, Sing Choy feels immense power, like the one time she rode on a horse's back and felt the power of the creature beneath her. But this is not the mundane power of Horse. This a power unlike anything Sing Choy has ever felt before.

Riding the unicorn now, not merely straddling, Sing Choy trots out of Hangah Alley. Proud girl; she regards the familiar sights of Tangrenbu like the passing of a dream and feels no regret, no clinging to this place.

The unicorn knows the way. They gallop up Dupont Street, up the long angle of Columbus Avenue to the northern docks where fishermen drink and gamble the night away. Salty sea air smells like life and like death and very much like the Tao. The unicorn gallops past the piers to a place where the land tilts down to the bay. The unicorn picks its way through rocks and debris till it stands upon the shore and paws at the sand with its gleaming ebony hoof.

The bay shifts and sighs beneath the full moon. Sing Choy sees breakers curl like snippets of lace merging into dark velvet. Far off, she can see islands, huddled and black in the roiling bay. Platters of rock, immutable, placed into the deep waters of the world long before humanity ever made its mark.

Dark shapes move beneath the breakers around one of these islands. An ancient face on a leathery neck lifts in a spray of foam. Huge fins flap around this island, a tail as long as a clipper ship whips the waves. A pearlescent mist hovers. Sing Choy sees women gathered on the distant shore. Pale hands wave at her like the wings of moths. Beautiful faces peer anxiously from afar. Voices call. Is Kwai Ying's teacher there? Sing Choy spies her at once, a woman in silk as red as blood with a braid to the backs of her knees.

Sing Choy waves back, heart bobbing with joy. Perhaps she will have teacher now.

The unicorn does not hesitate. It paws at the waves. The unicorn steps upon the water without sinking and takes Sing Choy home.

ABOUT THE AUTHOR

Lisa Mason graduated Phi Beta Kappa from the University of Michigan School of Literature, Sciences, and Arts. After graduating from the University of Michigan Law School, she practiced law in Washington, D.C., and San Francisco. Now she lives in the San Francisco Bay area with graphic designer and fine artist, Tom Robinson, and three cats, and writes fiction full-time.

Mason is the author of four novels: *Arachne, Cyberweb, Summer of Love,* and *The Golden Nineties. Summer of Love* (Bantam Spectra, 1994) is about a far-future time traveler who must return to San Francisco during the summer of 1967 to save the universe. In *The Golden Nineties* (Bantam Spectra, 1995), a time traveler returns to San Francisco during the wild and extravagant 1890s. *Arachne, Cyberweb,* and the forthcoming *Spyder,* (William Morrow-AvoNova) are cyberpunk tales set in a future San Francisco.

Her acclaimed short fiction has appeared in numerous publications, including *Omni, Full Spectrum,* and *Year's Best Fantasy and Horror.* Most have received Nebula nominations, many have been translated into other languages, and "Tomorrow's Child" (*Omni* 1989), was optioned for film to Helpern-Meltzer Productions.

ELIZABETH ANN SCARBOROUGH

A RARE BREED

Peter: **Elizabeth Ann Scarborough** really was a near-neighbor of mine when I lived on Bainbridge Island, six miles of Puget Sound from Seattle. What I particularly like about her story, "A Rare Breed," is the manner in which she sketches her special part of coastal Washington: a uniquely funny and touching mix of tourists, Old Inhabitants, aging hippie burnouts, and the walking wounded of one war or another, declared or otherwise. . . . In the bio she sent us, she calls herself, ". . . a child of the sixties . . . gray, fat, and nearly fifty." *Nearly* fifty? *Gray?* In the words of today's youth, "Been there. Done that."

Janet: "Been there, done that," myself. I don't know Elizabeth personally, though after reading her story I feel as if I do—and wish I did. She made me laugh when I was under extreme pressure, and for that, alone, I thank her.

A Rare Breed

───❦───

I MET MY FIRST UNICORN, APPROPRIATELY ENOUGH, when I stepped into an enchanting forest glade. It was enchanting for a couple of reasons.

The first reason was that it was out of shouting and phone distance from my place, where an unexpected visitor snoring in my bed reminded me never to wish for anything too much lest it come not only to pass but to remain for an indefinite stay.

The other reason was that I normally don't venture out in the morning too far from the house because I take blood pressure medicine. This medicine displaces the pressure on your heart by creating pressure on another bodily system. That morning, however, I had to go out or go nuts, so even though I did think of it before I left home, I had a certain personal function to perform. The strategically placed trees surrounding the glade provided cover from the road as well as from the hiking trail.

It requires a little extra agility for a female wearing sweatpants to assume the position in semibondage without falling over, of course, but I'd had considerable practice while living in the woods in Alaska. With sufficient privacy, such a moment can be ideal for achieving a calm, earthy oneness with nature. However, the occasion is not, as I discovered, the ideal moment for a close encounter with a unicorn.

Up until recently, unicorns were never a problem. No one I knew had seen one except in the movies or in books. Then all at once, people started seeing unicorns. This was my first one. I wasn't crazy about its timing.

It lowered its head, its little goatee quivering and its long spiral horn aimed right at me. Before I could—er—point out to the beast that it was supposed to be mythical, extinct, or at the very least an endangered species and therefore should have better things to do than menace me, it charged. Fortunately it was a good few yards away—the enchanting forest glade was a largish one.

I stood, hastily rearranging my attire for maximum mobility, and did a bullfighter twist to one side at the last minute as the damned thing galloped past me.

Undeterred, it turned, gave me an annoyed look, and lowered its head to charge again.

Clasping my garments to my loins, not from modesty but practicality, since they weren't properly fastened and would hinder movement otherwise, I recalled my meager store of woods lore and pondered my strategy.

With a mountain lion, you're supposed to make yourself big like an angry cat and back, not run, slowly away. This will make the lion think you're too big to swallow in one handy bite-sized chunk. With a bear, you make a lot of noise and hope it really is as scared of you as you are of it (though it couldn't possibly be). If it's a mother bear, you don't interfere with cubs. If you're camping, you hide your food in a sack in a tree well away from where you sleep, praying the bear eats your food and ignores you, mummied in your sleeping bag. But what in the hell you were supposed to do in the event of a unicorn attack had never been covered in any literature I'd ever read.

The unicorn galloped forward again, an ornery look in its green eye. "Hey, you," I said to it, sidestepping awkwardly. "You just cut that out. I didn't do a damned thing to you that you should go harassing me. Go find a virgin to impress!"

Shaking its head and emitting a snort that sent a cloud of steam rising from its nostrils, it turned to charge again. I ducked behind a tree long enough to fasten my pants, and prepared to duck again, but by this time the unicorn was pawing—or rather hoofing—at the place where I'd formerly positioned myself. It was covering my—er—scent, the way a cat would cover its scat.

"Prissy damn critter!" I muttered, and used its preoccupation to scoot away back to the road. I was not followed.

I definitely needed human company then and a latté. My guest would no doubt follow his lifelong custom and sleep till noon, so I headed down to Bagels and Begonias Bakery. It was Wednesday and on winter Wednesdays particularly, when the tourists were all back at work in their own towns, groups of friends met to gossip and pour over the Port Chetzemoka *Listener,* our town's weekly newspaper.

I grabbed my latté and a plain bagel and joined a table. Conversation was already in full swing but I broke in, which was okay etiquette for Wednesdays at the bakery. "You'll never guess what happened to me!" I said to the two people nearest me while Ramona Silver continued to regale everyone with the problems her friend Cindy had been having since her fifty-something boyfriend had gone back to drinking. The AA group in Port Chet has a much larger and more prestigious membership than any of the lodges with animal names.

Ramona stopped in mid-sentence and turned to me, "What?" she asked.

"I got attacked by a unicorn."

"Where at?"

"Walking up the Peace Mile at Fort Gordon. It just came out of the woods and tried to gore me." I didn't mention the circumstances. It didn't seem important then.

"Oh, well. The paper's full of that this morning," Inez Sunderson said, and directed me to the front page.

Local authorities, the *Listener* said, attributed the recent proliferation of unicorns in urban areas to the effects of deforestation and development.

"It's said that a unicorn won't even step on a living thing," Atlanta, the real estate saleslady turned psychic reader told us.

I snorted. "If that were true, they'd only walk on concrete. The one I saw walked on grass and was getting ready to walk all over me—after it shish kebobbed me, that is. I think the only thing that kept me from panicking was that I couldn't believe it was real. I've been writing about unicorns for a long time now and I always thought they were make-believe."

"Oh no," Randy Williams said. "The Raven people have several legends in which the unicorn is an important transformative figure. Of course, they refer to unicorns as the One-Horned Dog."

"Surely they're not *indigenous*?"

He shrugged. "The legends are pretty old. Of course, they might have been prophetic instead of historic, I guess. I don't speak the Raven tongue very well."

"You mean the Indian legends maybe foretold that the unicorns would be here?" asked Ramona, a jeweler and artist who, like every other artist in town, works four minimum wage jobs to sustain herself. She twiddled the silk flower she always wore in her hair, an orange one today. She always twiddled when she was thinking particularly hard. Her "Wow" was so reverent I understood it to actually mean "Far out."

Lance LaGuerre, our former Rainbow Warrior and present head of the Port Chetzemoka Environmental Council, said, "That doesn't necessarily mean the unicorns are indigenous or even a naturally occurring species. Some Indian legends also foretell such events as space travel and nuclear disasters, isn't that true, Randy?"

Randy just gave him a look. He doesn't like Lance very much. Lance is the kind of guy who would probably have grown up to be a religious–right-wing industrialist if his father, whom he detested, hadn't been one first. So he brought all of his genetic judgmental Calvinistic uptightness over to the other side. Thus he was a liberal, except that he wasn't awfully liberal when it came to being empathetic or compassionate or even reasonable with anyone who didn't agree with all of his opinions. And he had an awful lot of opinions.

"I mean, now the forest service is acting as if they knew about the unicorns all along but up until now, who ever heard of them? I'll bet they're the result of a secret genetic engineering program the government's been conducting . . . "

"Yeah," Ramona said, "Or maybe mutants from toxic waste like the Ninja Turtles."

Lance nodded encouragingly, if a bit patronizingly. I doubt the patronizing had anything to do with the Ninja Turtles. I don't think he knew who they were.

"Well, whatever they are," said Inez Sunderson, "they've been stripping the bark from our trees, digging up my spring bulbs, and terrorizing the dogs, and I mean to plug the next one I catch in our yard."

The men gently, supportively encouraged her to do so. Inez, you have to understand, gets that kind of response to everything she says. I think the reason is that she is one of those incredibly ethereally beautiful Scandinavian blondes who look really good in navy blue to match their eyes. She used to be a model, I know, and was almost as old as me, but she looked about twenty-five. She is also intelligent and well-read in the classics and has a good knowledge of music and only watches PBS when she deigns to watch TV and never sets foot in a mall. All that is fine but sometimes her practical, stoic Norski side makes her sound like Eeyore.

I didn't say much more. I was still bemused—and amused, because by now the incident seemed funny to me—by my first meeting with a unicorn. I wasn't quite ready to go home and face my other problem, though, so I hung out till everyone left, though Randy was over at another table talking with some of his other friends. He's lived in Port Chet for years and has all these close personal ties with the other folks who worked for the Sister Cities group, were with him in South America with Amnesty International, or used to live in school buses at the same time he did.

My alma mater is a little different from that of most of my friends. I wasn't living in school buses and going to peace marches. I was nursing in Vietnam. So was Doc Holiday, whose real name is Jim, but since he was a medic in Nam, and has sort of a Sam Elliot–gunfighter presence, everyone calls him Doc. It's appropriate. He's the local Vietnam vet counselor, Amvet coordinator, *and* how-to-avoid-the-draft-should-it-come-back-into-fashion resource person. He's a Virgo, which Atlanta has explained means he's very service oriented.

He walked right past me and sat down at a table by himself.

I figured he didn't see me and I wanted to tell him about the unicorn, so I got up and walked over to his table and said. "Hey, Doc. How ya doin'?"

"Hey, Sue," he said, shaking his head slowly. I could tell right then that he'd sat down where he was because he figured he was best off alone. He gets these depressions sometimes, but then, so does Randy. They belong to the half of the town that isn't already on Prozac. "Not so good, lady. I lost another one."

"I'm sorry, Doc." He was referring to clients. He told me once that more than twice as many Vietnam vets had died from suicide since the war as died in battle during. He still lost several more the same way every year.

"Can't win 'em all, I guess," he said with a deep sigh.

Randy wandered back our way just then. "Doc, hi. Sorry. I heard about Tremain."

Doc shrugged. "Yeah, I'm sorry about your buddy, too."

I hadn't heard about that one. "Flynn?" I asked. They both nodded. "God. AIDS is so awful," I said completely unnecessarily. But then, most things you say about how someone dies are unnecessary.

Randy's mouth quirked. "Well, hey, we never thought we'd live to thirty anyhow and look at us—old farts now. I guess it's just the time when your friends start dropping. But we never thought it would be us."

"Too cool to die," I said. "Old Boomers Never Die They Just—finish that sentence and win a free all expense paid trip to Disney World."

They nodded. We all understood. The three of us were graying lone wolves. Armchair analysts would say we had each failed to bond due to post-traumatic stress disorder—Doc's and mine from the war, Randy's from a number of things including the wars he observed with Amnesty. Actually, I think I'm in the club under false pretenses—I bond only too well and stay bonded, whether it's a good idea or not. Doc and Randy didn't care, as long as I didn't try bonding with them in any significant way, but it was good having a woman in the group since they both felt they had a lot of shit to work out about women. So, okay, it's tokenism, but nobody ever asked me to make the coffee, so I didn't care.

"Doc, you know what happened to me this morning? I got charged by a unicorn."

He gave me a slow grin. Twenty, thirty years ago it would have made my heart flip-flop. Fifteen years ago it would have sounded fire alarms that my feminist integrity was about to be breached. But now I just waited politely as he asked, "Oh, yeah? What was the offense? Did you get his badge number?"

"Very funny. I see my first unicorn after all these years of writing about them and all I get is cop jokes."

Doc's known me for, what? seven or eight years now, but he still takes my joking kvetching seriously.

"Sorry, Sue. I'd be more impressed except that our facility down by Port Padlock is about overrun with the critters. They're all over the place, and they fight constantly. It's sort of hard to teach people to be at peace with themselves when there's all these unicorns going at it cloven hoof and horn out in the back forty. Makes me want to get out my huntin' rifle again, but I swore off."

"I think I'll go for a walk. See if I can spot any," Randy said, and left. I followed reluctantly. I didn't want to go home.

Jess Shaw, my houseguest, was on his first cup of instant coffee when I returned. He had the remote control to my TV in his hand and was clicking restlessly between channels. The MUTE sign was on the screen. None of the cats were in sight. I think the smell drove them off. They're not used to people who reek of cigarette smoke and whiskey fumes, half masked by men's cologne. There was a time I couldn't get enough of that scent. Now I wanted to open a window, even though it had started to rain and the wind was whipping up the valley from the Strait. It wasn't that I didn't care about him anymore, it was just that ever since my first youthful infatuation more than twenty-five years ago, the emotion I felt toward this man was something like unconditional ambivalence. It was requited.

After not bothering to pick up the telephone for the last couple of years, the man had just driven two thousand miles to see me. In the years I'd known him, he'd gone through several live-ins and marriages. Since my own divorce, I'd done a lot of thinking about who and what I was and who and what the man I'd married and the men I chose tended to be, with the result that I'd pretty much retreated into my own private nunnery. So I just said, "Is your own remote at home broken? Is that why you came to see me?"

"Mornin', darlin'," he said, his voice as soft and growly as ever. The darlin' was nothing personal, however. To him everything that can be remotely construed as being of the female gender is darlin'. He sighed deeply and kept flipping channels.

"You'll never guess what I saw on my walk this morning," I said.

He obviously didn't give a rat's ass.

"A unicorn," I said.

"That's nice," he said.

"It almost killed me," I said.

"Huh," he said.

But two cups of coffee later he was up pacing a dented place in my splintery softwood floors and talking a mile a minute. He wanted to get his gun out of his van and go looking for the critter.

"Not a good idea," I said. "In this wind, a tree could fall on you."

"Well, bring the sonuvabitch on then," he said in that bitter tone he gets when he's both grieved and pissed about something. "It's not like I'm gonna live that long anyway."

"You've made it farther than I thought you would," I told him, a little tartly. He's like a quadruple Pisces and prone to throwing pity parties, so I wanted to head him off at the pass.

He stopped pacing and sipping coffee long enough to look over at me and grin. "Yeah, me too," he said. Then he shrugged. "But I pushed the edge of the envelope, babe, and now the doc says I've ruptured the sonuvabitch."

"What do you mean?"

"The big C, darlin'."

"You've got cancer?" I asked. "Where?"

"Liver," he said. "Just like you always told me."

I used to warn him about cirrhosis but after all the ups and downs he'd been through, I figured he was probably made from good old pioneer protoplasm and would end up grossing out the staff of a nursing home some day. I also figured I might hear about it from one of the mutual friends I was still in contact with. Funny that I hadn't. Now I didn't know what to say. Finally, I resorted to being clinical. "Did you get a second opinion?"

He lifted and dropped a shoulder. "Yeah. No good. They wanted me to go through chemo and all that crap but I figured, hey, I'd rather keep what hair I got and go finish up a few things while I feel like it."

I swallowed. "You know, doctors are wrong about a lot of stuff. And I have several friends who were supposed to have cancer and just got over it. How about alternative therapies? Have you tried that?"

He just shook, kind of like a dog, kind of like someone was walking over his grave. Now I noticed that his color under his tan was terrible. He'd always been thin but now he looked like he was made of matchsticks. He took a long shuddering breath and said, "It hurts, Sue."

"I'm real sorry," I said. Another friend I would have offered a hug but though he always talked like he could barely wait to jump any woman in his vicinity, he was weird about hugs when he was upset. So I put my hand in the middle of the kitchen table and waited to see if he'd take it. It seems to me that we had always taken turns being White Fang. He being wild and needing to trust and me being, at least in some ways, blindly loyal.

He took my hand and gripped it hard for a moment, then got up to pace again. By that time the wind had died down a little and the rain was just a drizzle. "Look," I said, "do you want to walk someplace instead of just around the room? That way you can smoke and I'll show you where I saw the unicorn."

"It's still raining," he said.

"We'll be in the trees. Are you up to it?"

"I ain't dead yet," he said.

His breath was even shorter than mine but he enjoyed the walk and picked up the unicorn's tracks right away. We followed them back into the woods, but then it started pouring rain again and I felt bad because I'd encouraged him to come out and he was shivering, despite his Marlboro man hat and sheepskin jacket, by the time we got back to the house.

I felt worse (and so did he) when the his chill didn't go away, in spite of a shower and being tucked back in bed. The cats showed up again and curled up next to him. He seemed to appreciate the warmth. I asked him for the name of his doctor but he wouldn't give it to me, said he was going to "ride it out." Well, I respected that, but by the second day, when he still hadn't improved, I called my own doctor as well as the mutual friends to find out if any of them had any ideas. He had no kin left, I knew, except for a couple of ex-wives. Finally Brodie Kilgallen told me that Jess had walked out of the hospital, telling the doctors what they could do with their tests and treatments, and that was the last anyone had seen of him down there. Brodie knew the name of the hospital, so if everything went well, I could have my doctor call and get his records from there if need be.

He slept all through the day while the wind drove the rain against the windows, made the trees do the hula and the wind chimes ring. I tried to write but finally, after the storm outside caused two brownouts and one brief power failure, I gave it up for fear my computer would be ruined. The TV's old, though, so after dinner I settled into my nest of pillows on the end of the couch and with cats, remote, hard-wired phone and a bag of pretzels, flipped on the evening news. The wind was booming now, window-rattling, and house-shaking, a thug growing bolder in the dark.

According to the news, the storm was raging throughout the Puget Sound area. Trees were across the roads, across power lines everywhere. One motorist had been killed already. Highway 101 was closed along the Hood Canal, and both the Hood Canal Bridge and the Narrows Bridge, which joined the Olympic and Kitsap Peninsulas with the mainland, were closed. They often were, especially the Hood Canal Bridge, during high winds. Right after the bridge was built, the first big storm blew it away and people had to drive around or take a ferry for a couple of years until it was repaired. With 101 closed, you couldn't even drive around now.

Pretty soon Jess padded into the room, wearing only his jeans. He walked into the kitchen and put the kettle on for his first transfusion of the day, then, for a wonder, came and sat down on the couch next to me.

"I didn't know y'all got hurricanes up this far north," he said, and we sat in one of the only companionable silences I can remember in our association, just touching, watching the tube. He didn't drink or pace or smoke or anything but watch the tube, making a brief remark occasionally or responding to one of mine without rancor at me for interrupting the sacred broadcast.

Then the kettle went off and he got up to fix his coffee, even inquiring if I wanted any.

Just as he returned with the cup, the TV winked off, along with the lights and the fan on the propane stove and we were left staring at a ghostly blue screen.

I found a flashlight, lit a couple of candles, and called the power company. The line was busy, of course.

Jess started telling me about hurricanes he had lived through along the Gulf of Mexico and continued into a rambling story about his boyhood. I'd heard it before, many times. He always revises it in the retelling. I opened the blinds to try to see how far the power loss extended. The whole neighborhood was dark, as was the hill above us and the streets all the way into town, as far as I could see.

"Jess?"

"Yeah, babe?"

"Play me something, will you? I haven't heard you play since you've been here. You up to it?"

"Hell, yes," he said, and got out his guitar and began playing a song about the death of the Nez Perce Appaloosas. He kept on singing one after the other, songs he had learned since I'd last seen him, songs he used to play constantly, new songs he admired but had only learned bits of. I heard a sort of tapping sound and looked toward the window.

Four whiskery mouths were pressed against the glass, above them the tips of four horns. I touched Jess on the shoulder and turned him, still singing, to look. He caught his breath and gave me the same "Oh, my god," look he'd worn when we saw the Marfa Lights together. But he kept singing, segueing from "Blowin' in the Wind" to the Shel Silverstein unicorn song. At this the critters gave a collective snort and turned tail for the woods between my house and my northernmost neighbor's.

"I never cared for that one myself, actually," he said, shaking his head. "Damn, Susie-Q, what the hell do you folks do around here when this happens?"

"I was thinking we might go see my friend Doc and seeing if he's up to a visit," I told him. "He's a vet counselor who lives out in Port Padlock at old Fort Chetzemoka, which is a pretty interesting historical site. I think you'd like him and find the area interesting."

"Okay with me. You think he's got a beer?"

"Could be," I lied. Doc's been dry for fifteen years, six months and he'd have to tell you the rest. "We should take some candles though."

Soft light glowed from Doc's windows when we drove into the park grounds. Several pale four-legged shapes lurked at the edge of the woods, down by the water, and behind the house and the caretaker's buildings at the park. Randy's truck was in the driveway beside Doc's.

I felt immensely relieved. Randy and Doc would know how best to help Jess. I could get him medical help, of course, but Jess has been in the habit most of his life of turning over the unattractive practical details of daily existence to some woman until she had control over all of his associations, jobs, and where he'd be and who he'd be with at any given time. Then he'd rebel and sabotage her, chewing his own foot off to escape from the trap he'd laid for himself. I was too old for that game and he was too sick. I wasn't going to turn my back on him, and I didn't want to do a whole codependent number either. What was left of his life was his to do with as he wished and if he was going to drink it away, I was going to need backup to deal with it.

"Hi, Doc," I said, sticking my head in the door. Doc likes to adapt Indian ways when he's off duty and it's rude to knock. Usually you try to make a lot of noise outside the door but there was no way we'd be heard over the storm and I wasn't going to expose Jess to another chill.

Doc and Randy sat in the recycled easy chairs Doc keeps by the fireplace. A candle burned in the window and on the table between them.

"Don't you have sense enough to come in out of the rain, young lady? Getcher buns in here," Doc said.

I walked in, half pulling Jess behind me and as we shook the water from our ponchos I introduced him.

Randy said, "I was just warning Doc to start filling up water containers, Sue. I heard on the scanner that the floodwater's reached the point where it's within an inch or two of compromising the reservoir."

"Holy shit," I said. "That'll shut down the town *and* the mill."

"You betcha," Doc said. "I got some extra jerry cans though. I could let you have a couple."

"I wouldn't want to run you short," I said, "but I'd appreciate it."

Jess was standing at the window, staring out at the rain and the pale shapes dancing in it. Randy looked over his shoulder. "Wonder where they all come from."

"I don't know, but they're getting bolder," I told him. "Jess was singing me some songs and they came right up out of the woods and crossed the yard to listen."

"No kiddin'? They're music lovers?"

"Good to know they like something besides destroying trees and flower bulbs," Doc said. "You folks want some coffee?"

"Sure," Jess said, his hand going to the jacket pocket with his flask.

"I'll hold a flashlight for you while you find stuff, Doc," I told him, catching his eye with a meaningful look that he met with a puzzled one. But he nodded me toward the kitchen and we left Randy and Jess to stare at each other.

"So, you're going to tell me who this guy is, right? Long-lost love?"

"Close enough," I said. "He's lost anyway." I filled Doc in while he made loud noises crashing around the shelves of the white tin cupboard he packs both dishes and nonperishables in. The coffee was instant, not that big a deal.

Randy was regaling Jess with some of his better stories about Central America. Like Jess, Randy can be so quiet you can't get a word out of him or so garrulous you can't get a word in edgewise.

Jess seemed content to just sit and listen. Doc handed him his coffee and after giving his a splash from his flask, he offered it to the others. He didn't have any takers.

By the time the coffee was gone, Jess, Doc, and Randy were swapping stories. Jess felt compelled to keep his hand proprietarily on my knee, though I knew from long experience he had no interest in that knee at all—it was a territorial thing, about as romantic as your cat pissing on your shoe. But aside from that, everyone was getting along famously. Both Doc and Randy liked music and at one point someone said something that reminded Jess of a song with a yodel in it and he started singing again, but this time he winked and half turned to the window. Sure enough, there was a whole herd of unicorns out there, their faces blurred impressionistically by the rain.

"That's the damnedest thing I've ever seen," Doc said. He peered more closely at the creatures in the window. "You know, I haven't looked at these guys this close up before. There's something a little funny about them."

"Funny how?" Randy asked.

"Funny familiar," he said. "I'm getting one of those psychic things I used to get in Nam—"

"Maybe we ought to call Atlanta," I said facetiously. "We could have a storm party."

Doc turned away, chewing his lip. Without another word, he pulled on a slicker and went out in the yard. I watched through the window while Randy and Jess pretended not to notice he'd done anything out of the ordinary.

The unicorns scattered at first, then Doc hunkered down beside a mud puddle and waited. I thought, oboy, he's going to look like a sieve by the time they finish with him. A couple of them did feint towards him and I saw his mouth moving, his hands making gentling gestures.

After a bit Randy asked, "What's he doing?"

"Talking to the unicorns."

"What about?"

"Your guess is as good as mine." So then he had to go out, too, and Jess put on his coat again to join them. I wanted to say, don't go out there and stand around in the rain like the other damn fools, you'll catch a chill and die this time and then I guessed he probably knew that. I used Doc's phone book, found Atlanta's number, and called.

"Sue! How nice of you to call. Do you have power at your place yet?" she asked.

"Not that I know of. Actually, I'm out at Doc Holiday's in Port Padlock."

"He caretakes the grounds at old Fort Chet doesn't he? Is he okay? No trees down on the house or anything?"

"No. Nothing like that. But he said something about thinking he was having a psychic experience with the unicorns."

"Really? I haven't gotten close enough myself to pick up anything specific but there's definitely *something* about them. I'm not the only one who's noticed it, either."

"No," I said, looking out the window at the three men sitting on their haunches in the rain, a loose circle of unicorns surrounding them. "Do you think you could come out here?"

"In this?"

"Yeah, I know. And it might be for nothing. But it could be interesting, too."

"Okay."

I put on my own coat and went out in the yard to join the boys. Two unicorns danced skittishly sideways to let me inside the circle. They were learning manners since my first encounter, maybe? I was as skittish as they were. I didn't hunker down either. My knees aren't that good. The rain was letting up at least and the wind quieting a little.

None of the men said a word. They stared at the critters. The critters stared at them. Then the lights came back on and the unicorns, startled, scattered to the edges of the woods surrounding the house. About that time, Atlanta arrived.

Doc seemed to have a hard time snapping out of his trance but he did give her a little wave and say, "I was just thinking about you."

"So Sue said," she said, not smiling but looking sympathetic and receptive. "Where are the unicorns?"

He nodded toward the woods. Some of them were creeping back out, watching. A couple were brawling up in the north corner of the property.

"Will they let me touch them?"

"I think so, maybe. I'll come with you."

The two of them headed for the nearest of the beasts while the rest of us stayed behind for fear of spooking the one Doc and Atlanta were stalking.

"Well, so much for the virgin thing," I said, surprised to hear myself sound so disgusted. "They're not real unicorns."

"Of course they are," Randy said. "Just because they don't do what you were led to expect they would doesn't mean they're not real."

I felt let down and excited at the same time. On the one hand, they weren't turning out to be what I thought they should. On the other hand, it promised to be a kick seeing what they did turn out to be, other than a nuisance.

Doc approached the unicorn first, and it let him lay his hand on its neck in a friendly way. With his other hand, he took Atlanta's forearm and guided her hand toward the beast's nose.

The unicorn tolerated that closeness for a second or two before it bolted. Doc and Atlanta rejoined us.

When we went back inside the house, the phone was ringing and Doc's TV, set on our local news bulletin board, was saying that the recent rains had caused the flooding to overflow the reservoir and we should all used bottled water for drinking until further notice.

Doc apologized for not getting out his jerry cans sooner. I introduced Atlanta to Jess and he gave her the best of what charm he still had to call on, to which she responded with girlish confusion. I fought off a pang of jealousy and asked, "What did you think of the unicorn?"

"I think Doc's right," she said.

"Right about what?" Randy asked.

Jess just sank back onto the dilapidated couch and closed his eyes. His mouth and nose had that strained look about them I've seen so often on people who were suffering but afraid to ask for pain meds. After a moment, he drew out his flask but, from the way he shook it, I could tell it was empty.

Doc cleared his throat. "I know this sounds a little crazy, but the unicorns remind me of some of my clients. I'm pretty sure the one I was trying to talk to at first out there in the yard was Tremain."

"It would explain why you have so many of them around here, anyway," Doc said.

And these were the guys I turned to for practical help for Jess! "You think that's what they are too, Atlanta?" I asked her.

She did a Yoga inhale-exhale number then said, "They're frightened. Disoriented. And—I don't know how to say this. They aren't quite real."

"What do you mean, not real?" Doc asked.

"They're all adult males for one thing, and none of them seem to have been unicorns very long. They're not sure what to do, where to go, how to act. They're like souls in limbo."

"So you think they're reincarnations of the vets?" I asked. "Then why did one try to attack me while I was taking a leak in the park the other day?"

"Maybe that one was the reincarnation of LaGuerre's old buddy Jenkins? Remember? The guy who took potshots at the sewage plant when they started building over by the lagoon?"

"Yeah," Randy said. "He didn't want you polluting the pristine parkland, I bet."

"I still don't get it," I said. "Why should they come back as something that was just mythical before? I mean, even taking reincarnation as a given, why not come back as another person, or a worm if you've behaved in a pretty unevolved fashion, or one of my cats if you deserve to be spoiled?"

Atlanta shrugged. "I don't know. But it seems to me like maybe, well, because there's too many of them dying at once? Maybe there isn't really an established place for them?"

"Yeah," Doc said. "And a lot of these guys weren't bad or good, just confused. Maybe Great Spirit didn't know what to do with them either. Take Tremain. He was well educated, for awhile after Nam he was a mercenary, then he switched and became an agent for the Feed the Children foundation, meanwhile going through three families before he tried settling down and working as an electrician. Then he kills himself. Who'd know what to do with a guy like that?"

Atlanta nodded soberly. "There's a lot of people that way now. Too many maybe. Well educated, semi-enlightened, lots of potential but just never could quite find a place among so many others—even after, I guess . . ." her voice trailed off as she looked out the window toward the woods again.

"So all our contemporaries who are dying are coming back as horny old goats?" Randy asked, chuckling. "I like that. That's real interesting, folks. I think I'll wander over by Flynn's place and see if he's around. Maybe he'd like a game of ringtoss."

These were the people I was counting on for practical help with Jess? They were nuttier than I was. I just wrote about this stuff. They believed it.

"So what do you think of all that?" Jess asked in the car on the way back to my place.

"I hate to say it but I think the sixties were way too good to some of my friends," I said.

"Maybe that's why they're comin' back as unicorns," Jess laughed. "They're all hallucinations."

"Or something," I said.

"If I come back as one, I promise not to gore you when you try to pee, darlin'."

"Gee, thanks."

Just as we were pulling into the drive he said, "Susie?"

"Yeah?"

"Say your buddies are right about the unicorns. Why are they only around here?"

He was serious now. And it occurred to me that questions about the afterlife, however ludicrous they might sound to me, were probably of urgent interest to him right now. So I said, "I dunno. Maybe because there's such a high concentration of guys kicking off around here, but it's a small place. Maybe it's like some sort of cosmic test area or something."

He nodded, very soberly for him.

While he slept in the next morning I spoke with my doctor, with a friend in hospice work, trying to figure out what to do if Jess chose, as he seemed to be doing, to die at my house. I half wished they'd tell me it was against the law. It had taken me a lot of years and miles to find a place to work and be peaceful while I got over him. I didn't much want it polluted with his death. On the other hand, I wouldn't be able to live with myself if I sent him away. Ordinarily, I'd figure whatever ulterior motive brought him to me would take him on his way soon enough, but now he was dying and I knew about that. The bullshit stopped here.

Ramona called me about two that afternoon. "Sue, it's awful. They're going to start shooting the unicorns."

"Who?" I asked.

"The public works guys from the city. They're trying to get in to fix the reservoir and the unicorns won't let them."

"I don't think they can do that legally, Ramona," I said as soothingly as possible.

"They don't f-ing care! They're going to just do it and take the consequences afterward. I'm calling everybody to get their butts up there and stop it."

"Okay, okay. When?"

"Now!"

"What's to stop them from doing something after we leave?"

"I'm not leaving," she said, but she was a little overwrought. In her hippie days she could have chained herself to a tree. Now she's got a son to think of and an elderly mother to care for.

I was just debating whether to wake Jess or to go by myself and leave him a note when Doc and Randy drove up.

"Jess still here?" Doc asked, without even greeting me.

"Yeah," I said. "But he ought to be up soon. You can stay and wait for him if you want. Ramona just called and said the city workers are planning to kill the unicorns blocking work on the reservoir and they're organizing a protest."

"I know," Randy said. "I called Ramona."

About that time there was the sound of bare feet hitting the floor in the bedroom and Jess padded out and peered benignly but blearily around the corner before disappearing into the bathroom. A few noisy minutes later he was back out. In the light of day he looked worse than he had before, his skin stretched tight and dry over his cheekbones, his eyes feverishly bright. The smile he greeted us with was more like a grimace and he walked stooped a little, his hand pressed to his side.

I didn't want him to go, but for once he didn't insist on six cups of coffee. He took one with him. He threw it up on the ground outside when we got to the reservoir.

Armed men in uniforms squared off with Ramona, yellow silk flower quivering with indignation, and a small crowd of people, only some of whom I recognized from the bakery. Lance LaGuerre for one, Eamon the Irish illegal, Mamie who used to run the gallery downtown, lots of others. A rerun of the sixties, except for the unicorns stomping, splashing, bleating, fighting, kicking, biting, and diving in and around the reservoir and the flooded river overrunning it.

Doc strode over to talk to the city workers. Some of them were clients of his, others Amvet buddies. Gunhands relaxed a little. Randy hauled Jess's guitar out of the back of the truck.

He nodded at Jess, Jess nodded at him and spent a minute or two tuning.

"Shit, oh dear, they're gonna sing 'Kumbaya' at us," one of the city guys said.

Instead, Jess swung himself and his guitar into the back end of the truck while Randy started the engine. I joined the protesters, as Jess began to sing in a voice that never did really need a sound system.

The unicorns that were in the reservoir climbed out and dried off and followed the others, who were already trotting down the road after the truck while the pied piper of Port Chet sang the national anthem. Doc saluted and the city workers put their hands over their hearts while the unicorns, brown, black, white, spotted, dappled, gray, and reddish, their horns uniformly shining white, passed by. Jess kept singing the national anthem until they were well down the hill and into the trees (and out of rifle range). Then I heard him launch into Hamish Henderson's "Freedom Come All Ye" in lowland Scots with a fake Irish accent.

"Wow," Ramona said. "Some guy. How'd he do that?"

I shrugged. "He's been doing it all his life."

"For unicorns? He got some special thing with them?"

"I don't know. I expect a ghetto blaster with loud rock 'n' roll will work as well for some of them, or maybe the Super Bowl on a portable TV, but we already knew they were attracted to Jess's music so this'll get them out of harm's way while everybody cools off. Maybe someone would like to call a lawyer for the unicorns and get a restraining order against the city? Before Jess runs out of breath and the critters return?"

But that wasn't necessary. Five o'clock came first and the city workers climbed back into their vehicles and went home, and pretty soon the protesters did, too. Doc hitched back into town to help Ramona see about hiring the unicorns a lawyer. He asked me to stay and see if any of the beasts came back or new ones came. He said Randy and Jess were supposed to come back for us when they'd taken the unicorns safely off into the national forest on some of the back roads Randy knew.

It wasn't a bad wait. The water was so pretty and clear that even the turbulence of the river mingling with the still water couldn't mar its beauty. You could still see clear to the bottom, like in a mountain stream. And the reservoir was plenty deep.

It was getting dark by the time the truck returned for me, and it had started to rain. I picked up the lights all the way down the road and Randy parked and honked for my attention. When I stood up, Randy yelled, "We got to get back to your place. Jess wore himself out—he's running a fever and he's looking pretty bad."

But about that time there was a thump and a crunch of gravel and a splash.

"Where is he?" I asked, peering into the cab.

"Still in the back."

But he wasn't. His guitar was there. I ran to the reservoir. He was lying facedown in it, the ripples still circling away from him in the pallid moonlight beyond the truck's headlights.

When I pulled on his arm, it was hot as a poker. Randy leaped out and helped me and did mouth to mouth and got him in the truck. I couldn't help thinking on the way to the hospital that it was a blessing this had happened. He'd apparently gotten delirious from fever, half drowned himself trying to cool off, and now we *had* to turn him over to someone else.

My relief turned to anger and dismay when they took him away from us into ICU and not even Randy's friends on the nursing staff could help. Nobody but next of kin allowed. Randy took me home and I sat there crying and hugging my cats, waiting for a phone call to tell me my friend— my oldest, dearest love who was now my friend—had gone out with his boots on and was now, if Atlanta and Doc were right, on his way to unicorndom to be chased through a country where he had no real niche, even in the afterlife.

The call came at about six in the morning.

I scared all three cats grabbing for the receiver. "Hello?"

"Sue Ferman?"

"Yes?"

"Mr. Shaw in bed six wishes to check himself out now. He said to call you."

The damned fool, I thought, briskly brushing the tears away and cleaning my glasses so I could see to drive, he was determined to die here. I drove into the hospital lot and walked through the door, afraid of what I might see. What I saw was Jess arguing with an orderly that he didn't need a goddamn wheelchair, he could walk out on his own two feet.

"Susie-Q, get me outta here, will you?" he said. "I thought I told you no hospitals."

"Yeah, well, you didn't tell me you were gonna drown yourself," I said, hugging him whether he wanted me to or not. He did. And to my surprise his hug was strong, and cool, if not as fragrant as usual. I took a good look at him. His eyes were tired and lined and he was still thin, but the pain was gone from his face and when he stood up to get into the car, he stood erect as he ever had, moving with an ease I'd almost forgotten he possessed.

He hung around another day or two to see if the unicorns returned but you know, they never did. We're still not sure why. Then he said, "Well, darlin', I love the audiences you got around here but I guess if I ain't gonna die, I'd better haul ass home."

I surprised myself by laughing, not even bitterly. "Yeah, we already know we can't live with each other."

He grabbed me and hugged me and kissed my ear rather sloppily. "I know it. But I sure do love you. I don't know what the hell you see in me though, I truly don't."

I returned his hug and kissed him on the bridge of the nose where I kiss my cat and where his horn would one day sprout if the present trend continued. "I don't either except that you're almost always interesting as hell."

"I'll stay if you want me to," he said, like he was going to make the ultimate sacrifice. "You damn near saved my life."

"Nah," I said. "I love you more than I've ever loved anyone but you get on my nerves. Go back and find some younger woman who's not got to cope with you and menopause at the same time."

And he did.

He's called every so often since then, however, even though he hates the phone, just to stay in touch.

"How's our horny little friends?" he asked the first time he called back from the road in Boulder. "Do they miss me?"

"They must," I told him. "Since you led that bunch off that day, nobody's seen much of them. Do you suppose Atlanta was right and they were just on their way to some other place?"

"Either that or it was just the cosmic testing ground like somebody said and somebody else saw the test was failin'."

"Well, it's the city that feels it's flunked now," I told him. "Do you know, when they tested that water, even after the flood supposedly polluted it, they found it was free of all impurities? We had the taps turned on again right after you left. Three cases of hepatitis C, two cases of AIDS and several more cancers supposedly made miraculous recoveries in that time, but then, of course, the good water got all flushed out of the system. The city would *pay* the unicorns to come back now. But I guess you can't just have magic when you want it."

"Nope, which brings up somethin' I been meanin' to discuss with you. Do you know that ever since I got out of the hospital, I haven't been able to enjoy a good drink? It's like it turns to water the minute it touches me."

I expressed my sympathy with cheerful insincerity and hung up to take a couple of bags of daffodil bulbs out to the woods, just in case.

ABOUT THE AUTHOR

Elizabeth Ann Scarborough has written at least a dozen novels, one of which was the Nebula Award winner *The Healer's War*, drawn in part from her time as a nurse in Vietnam. Others include her quietly riveting take on Shangri-La, *Nothing Sacred*, and its sequel, *The Last Refuge*.

Scarborough writes full-time, but retains an enduring passion for folk music, its history, meanings, performance, and performers. She has written three books specifically about the music and musicians, but all of her work has been somewhat influenced by it. She is, she says, very much a child of the sixties, who grew up hearing her grandfather's stories about being a cowboy and the stories of her parents growing up in the Depression and seeing hobos, knowing that her daddy was a union man, a workingman proud of being a craftsman and refusing to go into management.

"All of the reasons I like folk music," she says, "also have to do with why I write fantasy. I love reading mysteries, but in fantasy writing I can use the full scope of my imagination to explain a very peculiar world to myself. But because my interest is in folk music rather than, say, classical, I like to write about ordinary people in my stories, not the kings and princesses and iron-thewed heroes but the regular folks, like the ones in the songs. These days we don't have many hobos, though we certainly have a lot of bums, not all of them unemployed. The cowboys mostly drive pickups and I doubt they sing to the cattle anymore, the way grandpa did. But people still try to hold their jobs against machines, the way John Henry did, and I see a lot of dignity in that. A lot of humanity and valor.

"Back in the sixties, when I was a much younger woman, before I went to Vietnam (I was way younger before that) and before the women's movement started making sense of my own life for me, all of the men looked so valiant to me. The doctors I worked with were godlike enough to make me rebel against their power, the soldiers I took care of later, baby-faced, heartsick, bored, lonely, immortal, and invincible even after they were wounded, the war protestors using art, and language, and colorful clothing and music to make their point; I was as in love with them as they were with themselves, probably. Music is the code for those feelings, rock for 'Nam, folk for the boys brave enough to stick to their principles and stay the hell home or go to Canada.

"We're all older now and most of us have let the years beat the hell out of us, but the music still stirs us and even now, gray, fat, and nearly fifty, I can look into the eyes of a man my own age, one who was in Nam or marching here at home, and if the right song is playing, the understanding that passes between us is as close as I've ever come to true love. Here's to you, guys, who's like you, damn few and they're all dead.

"Except, maybe, for a few unicorns."

ROBERT SHECKLEY

A PLAGUE OF UNICORNS

Peter: I first read **Robert Sheckley** in the early 1950s, when I was twelve or thirteen—*Untouched by Human Hands*, it was—and I've been a devoted admirer of his ever since. In that so-called Golden Age of science fiction (all Golden Ages are so-called, by definition), he and William Tenn and Avram Davidson stood out as, to my knowledge, the only writers who consistently dared to introduce humor, off-the-wall satire, and plain absurdity into their work. I used to read his short stories to my children, who were warped enough then to appreciate them, and are totally bent now, thanks in part to Mr. Sheckley, who remains, straight through his three recent collaborations with Roger Zelazny (*Bring Me The Head of Prince Charming, If at Faust You Don't Succeed,* and *A Farce to be Reckoned With*) the treasured weirdo he always was.

Janet: I know that Bob doesn't remember this, but I first met him when Ed Bryant took me to a party Bob threw in a Greenwich Village loft. It was a mighty strange party, which I'm sure was his intent. This story is almost as strange, but then anything else from Sheckley would be a profound disappointment.

A Plague of Unicorns

—❦—

CHILDREN, IT IS ONLY FITTING THAT YOU should know the stories of your ancestors. Here is the legend of Ctesiphon, who sought the unicorn's horn of immortality for his beloved, Calixitea.

Ctesiphon lived in the ancient days of our civilization, in the great city of Aldebra. One day while listening to speeches in the forum he met the fair Calixitea, daughter of Agathocles and Hexica. The attraction between them was immediate and imperative. Love struck them as unexpectedly and powerfully as lightning. From that first day they were inseparable. Within a month Ctesiphon had approached Calixitea's parents to ask her hand in marriage, asking for himself since his own parents had died in the great plague of '08. Since the young man was wellborn and had a reasonable income, the parents consented. A date was set. And then Calixitea fell ill.

The finest doctors were consulted, as well as specialists from Asmara and Ptolomnaeus, where men are skilled in such things. Their diagnosis was immediate and conclusive: Calixitea had contracted the rare disease known as galloping anisthemia. There was no cure. The victim would be dead within a week.

Ctesiphon was beside himself with grief and rage. When no reputable doctor would offer any hope, he went to the wizards, whose controversial practices were a frequent topic of discussion in the forum. And here he did not begin at the bottom, or even mid-list, but went straight to Heldonicles, reputed to be the greatest mage of his generation.

Heldonicles answered the door himself, since his latest apprentice had just recently left him after winning a million talents in the Aldebran

Lottery. Not even wizardry is entirely proof against good fortune, though if Heldonicles had anticipated it, he might have done something about it: Agatus had been a good lad, and might have made a decent wizard himself. But it was always difficult to keep a good apprentice.

"What can I do for you?" Heldonicles asked, ushering Ctesiphon into his sitting room and gesturing at one of the low blocks of marble that served for seating.

"It is my sweetheart, Calixitea," Ctesiphon said. "She is suffering from galloping anisthemia and the doctors say there is no cure."

"They are correct," Heldonicles said.

"Then how am I to save her?"

"It will be difficult," Heldonicles said, "but by no means impossible."

"Then there is a cure!"

"There is not," Heldonicles said. "Not in the generally accepted meaning of the word, anyhow. To cure her, you must go to the root of the matter. Mortality is the real problem here."

"And how am I to do anything about that?"

Heldonicles settled back and stroked his long white beard. "To preserve one from mortality, a state of immortality must exist."

"That's impossible," Ctesiphon said.

"Not at all," Heldonicles replied. "You've heard of the unicorn, no doubt?"

"Of course. But I always thought it was a myth."

"In the realm of magic," Heldonicles said, "myth is the merest statement of fact. Ctesiphon, there exists a country where the unicorn dwells. The unicorn's horn is an infallible conferrer of immortality. If you go to that country and bring back a horn, or even so much as a sliver of horn the size of your fingernail, that will suffice to save her."

"If this is possible, why is it not done more generally?"

"There are several answers to that," Heldonicles said. "Some men are simply too lazy, and would not stretch out their hands if heaven itself were within their grasp. Others might make the effort, but would not know that the opportunity exists. Because opportunity, young man, is a darting and an uncertain thing in the domain of magic. What was never possible may be done today, and not be possible again tomorrow."

"Is that the only explanation?"

"There are others," Heldonicles said. "Perhaps you'd care to study them someday. I have quite an interesting book on the subject. For now, there is a clear and immediate choice. Either you bring your beloved some unicorn horn or she is doomed."

"And how do I go about that?" Ctesiphon asked.

"Ah, now we're getting to it," Heldonicles said. "Follow me to my laboratory."

In the familiar surroundings of his laboratory, with its creaky wooden tables loaded with alembics, retorts, furnaces, and the bodies of small animals, Heldonicles explained that unicorns had once existed in this world, but had become extinct due to uncontrolled hunting of them. This had been a long time ago, and people had known a brief golden age when unicorn horn was plentiful, so the stories ran. Mankind had been extremely long-lived back then. What had happened to the Immortals? Heldonicles did not know. He had heard that ordinary people had resented them, for there was never enough unicorn horn for everybody. They had tortured many of them, and if they could not kill them, had contrived to make their lives so unpleasant that death itself seemed a tolerable alternative. Until at last the remaining Immortals had contrived a way to leave their home planet, to get themselves elsewhere, together with their herds of unicorns, to another world in another realm of reality, where unicorns could thrive in abundance and everyone shared in the benefits they brought.

"What is this place?" Ctesiphon asked.

"It is sometimes referred to as the country behind the East Wind."

"And how does one get there?"

"Not easily," Heldonicles said.

"I understand that. I suppose there's no regular service between this place and that one."

"Oh, there's regular service, but only spirits can avail themselves of it. This place exists in another region of space and time entirely, and has no regular connections with our own. Not even traveling on the back of a dragon could get you there. However, there is a way for a person of much determination who is willing to risk everything for his beloved."

"I am that person!" Ctesiphon cried. "Tell me what I must do."

"The first requirement for this, as for most other enterprises, is money. I will need all you have, all you can beg, borrow, or steal."

"Why is so much wealth needed?" Ctesiphon wanted to know.

"To buy the materials that will be used when I cast the spell that will send you where you want to go. I ask nothing for myself. Not at this point."

"Are you sure this magic will work?" Ctesiphon asked. "I have heard bad reports on magic."

"Most of it is plain humbug and tomfoolery," Heldonicles admitted. "But there is some, the very oldest, that works. To go that route is expensive, however, since the dearest ingredients are needed in conditions of utmost purity, and such does not come cheaply in this day and age."

Heldonicles had to find money to buy oil of hyperautochthon, and two tail feathers from the Bird of Ill Omen, and seven crystalline drops of anciento, wrought at great expense from the inner bark of the hinglio tree, itself rare, and stored in little flagons of amber, themselves worth a king's ransom. And there were more ingredients, the least of them too dear by half.

Ctesiphon procured these articles over a frantic two days, taking out a crippling loan at usurious rates to secure the final money he needed. At last, by the morning of the third day, he brought them all to the wizard, who declared himself satisfied and led Ctesiphon into his laboratory.

There he asked Ctesiphon if he was ready for this journey. Ctesiphon said he was but asked what price Heldonicles wanted for himself.

"I'll let you know when I'm ready to name it," the wizard said.

"But you won't tell me what it'll be?"

Heldonicles shook his head. "Magic is spur-of-the-moment, and so are the practitioners of it." And with that Ctesiphon had to be content. He had often heard that when you dealt in magical matters, you had to beware the double whammy. But he saw no way of avoiding that, whatever it might be.

"If you help me save Calixitea's life, you can have what you want of me. Even my life. Even my soul."

"Perhaps it won't go quite that far," Heldonicles said. "But you're thinking along the right lines."

The actual ceremony was elaborate and tedious and more than a little painful at times. But the wizard assured Ctesiphon that it was a one-shot; to return, Ctesiphon would need only click his heels together four times (reports of three heel clicks being all that was required are false; such reports have corrupted the ancient formula for the sake of a false simplicity) and say aloud, "Home again!"

Ctesiphon thought he could remember that. And then he was no longer able to think of anything, because the multicolored smoke of the wizard's fires, burning in tall braziers, curled around him and he had to squeeze his eyes tight shut and sneeze violently. When he opened them again, he was in a different place.

Ctesiphon found himself standing on a high mountain pass in a place unknown to him. Behind him were deep mists. Ahead, there were sloping meadows dotted with clumps of ancient oaks and cut through here and there with bright streams of water. Scattered across that plain in their thousands he saw herds of unicorn.

Like a man in a daze, Ctesiphon picked his way through the mild-eyed creatures, and the wonder of them was still on him when, further down the plain, he came across and entered the low stone city of the immortals.

The people had noted his progress and were waiting for him. "A visitor!" they cried, for even in the Land of the Immortals a tourist was a welcome sight. And this place was somewhat off the beaten track that leads to the twelve most famous sights of the Universe of Invention, and whose names cannot be spoken here.

In this land everyone looked about thirty years old and in the prime of life. There were no old people, and no children, either, for this race had lived so long that they had given up procreation as boring and old-fashioned, and even perversion had at last turned banal. But they were always ready for novelty, and the idea of giving some unicorn's horn to Ctesiphon was clearly the most novel idea that had come along in a long time.

Everyone knows that unicorns shed their horns from time to time, or lose them in battle with the griffins; and everyone remembered that the immortals picked up these horns whenever they came across them, and put then in a special place. But what place was that? Hadn't they buried them in a bronze casket under the northernmost point of the city wall? Or was that what they had done a century ago? No one could remember.

"But haven't you written it down somewhere?" Ctesiphon asked.

"I'm afraid not," said Ammon, a citizen who had appointed himself as spokesman.

Ammon hastened to reassure Ctesiphon, lest he think the less of them, that they all had excellent natural memories, nor had age robbed them of a scintilla of their intelligence. But the sheer accumulation of fact and detail, year after year, for uncounted centuries, left a mass of material in their brains too dense to navigate with the simple tool of natural recall. So they had all learned the art of forgetting old nonessential things so they could recall newer things, perhaps equally nonessential but at least current. One of the losses had been the location of all the shed unicorn horn.

Then someone remembered that they had devised a system to help them remember facts that weren't of immediate importance but might be wanted someday. But what was the system? No one could remember, and their voices rose in the air, arguing, disagreeing.

Then a man stuck his head out an upper story window and said, "Excuse me, I was asleep. Did someone ask something about remembering something?"

"We need to know where the unicorn horns are kept!" they called back to him. "We devised a system to help us find facts like that."

The man in the window nodded. "Yes, you devised a system, and you asked me to remember the system for you. That was my job and I am happy to say I did it well."

"Then tell us where the unicorn horns are!"

"I do not know anything about that," the man said. "I was only supposed to remember the system that would tell you who remembered that information."

"Out with his name, then."

"Do you want me to tell you the system?"

"No, you obtuse idiot, we only want the name of the man who remembers it for us and to hell with the system!"

"Don't get so excited," the man said. "What you need is safely stored in the head of Miltiades."

"Which Miltiades? Miltiades what?"

"The Miltiades you want is where you put him, in the Temple of Memory."

"Never heard of it. Temple of what?"

"Memory. You see, I remembered that for you as well, and it wasn't even required. It's straight down the street, first left, second right, can't miss it."

To many in the crowd it didn't seem the right way to go, but they followed the man's directions, and, bringing Ctesiphon with them, went to the indicated place.

It was an abandoned building. They entered it and went through to an inner courtyard. Here there was nothing except a largish box.

Ammon opened the box. Within was the head of a man, in his thirties like the rest of them, and apparently in the prime of life despite the loss of most of his customary parts.

"You've come for me at last!" the head cried. "But what took you so long?"

"Sorry, Miltiades," Ammon said, "I'm afraid we forgot you were here until that other fellow, I didn't catch his name, the one who remembered you, told us to come here."

"You mean Leonidas," Miltiades said. "Bless his incredible memory! But why did you come now?"

"This fellow here," Ammon said, indicating Ctesiphon, "needs a unicorn's horn, and we've got plenty of them somewhere, and by a natural chain of association we came to you to find out where they are kept."

"Unicorn horns?" Miltiades said.

"Yes, we always used to save the unicorn horns, don't you remember?"

"Of course I remember," Miltiades said.

"Didn't forget about the unicorn horns, did you, lying there in the dark?"

"Not a chance. What else was there to do but think about unicorns' horns?"

"Specialization has its merits," Ammon said, in an aside to Ctesiphon. "He would never have remembered otherwise."

He turned to Miltiades. "Now be a good fellow, Miltiades, and tell us where they are."

"Ah," Miltiades said.

"What do you mean, 'Ah'?"

"I mean, let me out and I'll tell you."

"Out of the box?" Ammon said.

"That's right, out of the box."

Ammon thought for a moment. "I don't know. I haven't thought about it."

"Well, think about it now."

"I can't. I'm thinking about this fellow and the unicorn horn he wants. And anyhow, what would you do outside your box? You haven't got a body, you know."

"I know. You fellows cut it off, back when you were fooling around. But it'll grow back once I'm free of the box."

"I still don't see how you lost your body in the first place."

"I'm telling you, you fellows cut it off when you wanted to get me to remember where the unicorn horns were kept. I didn't want to, you see. It was also an experiment to see how far you could push immortality."

"This far, anyhow, without trouble," Ammon said.

"That's right. But now I've done my turn. Now experiment on somebody else. Let somebody else remember for a while."

They decided that was only fair and so they set Miltiades free, and Miltiades told them what they needed to know and then closed his eyes, waiting for his body to grow back. So the rest of them left and followed his directions to a cellar door at the end of a tiny cul-de-sac deep within the city.

The place was empty. Half-concealed in the trash on the cellar floor there was a large bronze box.

They pushed back the heavy lid, and revealed by flickering torch light a veritable treasure trove of unicorn horns.

Ammon selected one horn and handed it to Ctesiphon. "Do you know how to use this?"

Ctesiphon said, "I think so, but please tell me anyhow."

"You shave off an amount equivalent to your thumbnail, powder it, and dissolve it in a glass of wine."

"Thank you," Ctesiphon said. "I'll be on my way now."

"It's been nice meeting you," Ammon said. "After you and your bride take the stuff, why don't you come back? It's always nice to live among your own kind."

Ctesiphon said he'd think about it. But the city of the immortals seemed to him like an old people's home. Although they looked young, yet there was a mixture of vagueness and querulousness about them that was more than a little off-putting.

Ctesiphon tucked the unicorn horn securely into his belt, clicked his heels four times, said the magic words, and so appeared again in his native city of Aldebra.

There was genial rejoicing when Ctesiphon returned with the unicorn's horn. The local savants declared that a new age had begun, one which would bestow the blessings of infinitely extended life on all citizens. Enthusiasm abated suddenly when it was realized that one unicorn's horn would only serve a limited number of people. Ctesiphon was criticized for not bringing back a sufficient quantity for everyone—though no one explained how he might have accomplished this.

Ctesiphon ignored this groundswell of popular opinion and went to his beloved's bedside. There he shaved scraps of unicorn horn into a glass of the famous black wine of the Eastern Provinces, itself said to have salubrious qualities. His beloved drank, and Ctesiphon waited anxiously for signs of its efficacy.

He did not have to stay long in doubt. Within minutes, Calixitea was ready to get out of bed and take up her normal life again.

Her parents, noticing the change, asked for unicorn horn for themselves. Ctesiphon couldn't refuse them, nor did he want to. He supplied them with the necessary shavings, and made more available for Calixitea's aunts and uncles and cousins and nephews and nieces, finally drawing the line at a third cousin twice removed.

Ctesiphon had planned to reserve some of the horn for the immortalizing of great geniuses and public benefactors of the sort that turn up only once or twice in a generation. But before he could carry out that scheme, a city official arrived at his door, demanding and receiving the municipality's due share, which was promptly ingested by the mayor, his wife and family and nearest relatives, and the foremost members of the town council, all of whom felt they deserved immortality due to their important positions and good intentions toward the public at large. Ctesiphon gave without stint, and was more than a little surprised to see how quickly the horn was dwindling.

And then the king of the region wanted his share, and some for his wife, her sister, his wisest councilor and his wiliest general.

Finally there was just enough unicorn horn left for Ctesiphon to take his own dose. But before he could do so there was a knock at the door. It was Heldonicles the wizard.

Ctesiphon was a little embarrassed because he hadn't called on the wizard since his return. He had been too busy handing out shaved unicorn horn to the many claimants.

"Went well, then, did it?" Heldonicles enquired.

"Well indeed," Ctesiphon said. "And I have you to thank for it. How can I ever repay you?"

"Easily enough. Just give me that bit of horn you have left over."

"But that's the last of it!" Ctesiphon exclaimed.

"I know. It makes it all the more valuable, and therefore desirable."

This was a difficult moment for Ctesiphon, and yet not so difficult after all, because he had already considered who would be his partners in immortality if he took the horn. They would be in-laws and politicians for the most part, and he had no great desire to spend immortality with them.

He gave the bit of horn to Heldonicles and asked him, "Will you take it now or later?"

"Neither," Heldonicles said and left.

Ctesiphon was confused by this but he had fulfilled his primary purpose—to save Calixitea's life.

However, when he visited her, he found that things had changed. Calixitea had decided, in consultation with her parents and relatives, that although Ctesiphon was a fine young man, and would no doubt make an acceptable husband for a single lifetime, he left something to be desired as a husband for all eternity.

Calixitea wasn't at all sure she would even want to marry another immortal—that could be sticky in a country with no divorce, and no death to substitute for it.

She needed, at the least, someone who could provide for her, not only in the years to come, but in the centuries that lay after those years, and the centuries after that. What the family had decided upon was a rich man who would already possess the basis of a fortune sufficient to keep Calixitea and her family secure throughout eternity.

There was nothing personal in this decision, and no criticism of Ctesiphon was intended. But circumstances had changed, and Ctesiphon had no one to blame but himself.

Feeling decidedly strange, Ctesiphon returned to his house to try to figure out what to do next. He wasn't home very long when there was a rap on the door and the wizard Heldonicles was there.

Ctesiphon asked him in, poured him a glass of wine, and asked him how it felt to be immortal.

"I wouldn't know," Heldonicles said. "I didn't take the powdered unicorn horn for myself, but to sell. The richest man in the country paid me a very good price for it."

"I'm surprised you didn't want to use it," Ctesiphon said.

"You shouldn't be. It should be apparent to you by now that immorality is delusive. In fact, it's a game for weak-minded people who haven't thought the situation through."

"What are you going to do?" Ctesiphon asked.

"With the money I got for the horn, I've bought the materials that will let me travel to the Land of Infinite Possibilities."

"I never heard of it," Ctesiphon said.

"Of course not. You're not a shaman. But it lies at the heart of all men's dreams and hopes."

Ctesiphon mused for a moment, then asked, "In this Land of Infinite Possibilities, is anything at all possible?"

"Just about."

"Eternal life?"

"No, that's the one thing the Land of Infinite Possibilities can't deliver. Without death, you see, nothing is really possible."

"But aside from that—"

"Yes, aside from that, anything is possible."

Ctesiphon said, "Wizard, will you take me along?"

"Of course," the wizard said. "That's what I've come here for. It's what I was planning all along."

"Why didn't you mention it before?"

"You had to suggest it yourself."

"But why me?" Ctesiphon asked. "Am I so special?"

"It's got nothing to do with that. It's difficult to find a decent apprentice these days. One with the necessary mixture of naïveté and cunning, but not too much of either quality. One who could be interested in the work of wizardry for its own sake."

And so the wizard and his new apprentice rode off into the blue in search of the ineffable, and for all we know are there still, exploring the kingdoms of the possible for new and ever newer knowledge and delight. They left behind Calixitea and her insufferable parents and a few rich people with their immortality, and from that choice all of us are descended, and all of us live out our endless years in boredom and apathy, because nothing new can ever happen.

Still, the outlook is not entirely grim, children. We believe that Death will return some day and relieve us of the vast tedium of our lives. This is a matter of faith with us. We can't prove the existence of Death, but we believe in it nonetheless. Someday, children, with a little luck and God's mercy, all of us will die.

ABOUT THE AUTHOR

Robert Sheckley was born in New York and raised in New Jersey. After serving with the U.S. Army in Korea, he attended New York University. He began selling stories soon after his graduation, and produced many short stories, which are represented in such collections as *Untouched by Human Hands* and *Pilgrimage to Earth*.

Sheckley's first novel, *Immortality, Inc.,* was recently made into the movie *Freejack*. His short story, "The Seventh Victim," was the basis for the movie and novel, *The Tenth Victim*. His complete short stories in five volumes were published by Pulphouse Publishing. He has written many novels in the science fiction and fantasy genres. Recently he completed three novels with Roger Zelazny—*Bring Me the Head of Prince Charming, If at Faust You Don't Succeed,* and *A Farce to be Reckoned With,* all published by Bantam Books.

Recently, Sheckley turned in *Alien Harvest,* a novelization in the Aliens series, and *The Laertian Gamble,* a novel in Star Trek's *Deep Space Nine* series, both of which will be available late in 1995. He lives in Portland, Oregon, with his wife, the journalist Gail Dana.

WILL SHETTERLY

TAKEN HE CANNOT BE

Peter: I know **Will Shetterly**'s work up to now entirely from the several Liavek collections, which he cocreated and coedited with his wife Emma Bull. Some years ago I had to write a magazine article on shared-world anthologies, and Liavek easily became my favorite of the ones I covered. I'm delighted by the unhurried, understated quality of his prose, the obvious originality of his mind, and the fact that he's the only writer in this anthology who has ever run for governor of a state. Minnesota, it was, and he came in a respectable third in a field of six. I always suspected I'd like Minnesota.

Janet: I confess that I did not know Will's work at all until Peter's request that I solicit a story from him for this anthology. I can now say, happily, that I know Will's voice—on the phone, and insofar as this dandy little story is concerned. Getting to know both voices better promises to be a fun exploration.

Taken He Cannot Be

THINGS DIE. THIS IS THE LESSON THAT EVERY-
one learns. Some do not learn it until the instant before death, but we all
learn it. We pass our final exam by dying. Dr. John Henry Holliday
earned his diploma from the school of life at a younger age than most. At
twenty, he had been told that consumption would kill him in six months,
yet at thirty, he still lingered around the campus. He supposed he was a
tenured professor of death, which made him laugh, which made him
cough, which made him think about the man they had come to meet, and
kill.

He rode through the midsummer heat beside his best friend, Wyatt
Berry Stapp Earp. They had both grown beards to disguise themselves, and
they had dressed like cowboys instead of townsmen. No one who saw them
pass at a distance would recognize the dentist-turned-gambler or Tombstone's former deputy sheriff, both wanted in Arizona on charges of murder.

They rode to kill John Ringgold, better known as Johnny Ringo.
Wyatt had said that Wells Fargo would pay for Ringo's demise, and Doc
had always believed in being paid to do what you would do cheerfully for
free. He did not know or care how much Wells Fargo might pay. He was
not sure whether Wells Fargo had made an offer, or Wyatt had merely
assumed the coach line would show its gratitude for the death of the last
leader of the Clanton gang. Doc knew Wyatt had asked him to come kill
Johnny Ringo, and that sufficed. Had anyone asked him why he agreed,
he would have said he had no prior engagements. The only person who
might have asked would have been Big Nose Kate Elder, and she had left
him long ago.

The brown hills stirred frequently as they rode. The two riders
always looked at motion—in a land where bandits waited for their piece

of wealth from the booming silver mines, you always looked. They never expected more than sunlight on quartz, or dust in a hot puff of wind, or a lizard darting for food or shelter. Vision was simultaneously more powerful and less trustworthy in this dry land. The eye saw far in the parched atmosphere, but it did not always see truthfully.

The unicorn showed itself on a rise. Doc never thought that it might be a wild horse. Though it was the size of a horse, it did not move like a horse, and he had never seen a horse with such white, shaggy fur, and that long, dark spear of its horn left no doubt, at least not in a person who lived by assessing situations instantly, then acting.

Doc acted by not acting: he did not flinch or blink or gasp or look away in order to look back. If this apparition was his private fantasy, he would not trouble Wyatt with its existence. If it was not, Wyatt would say something.

And Wyatt did. "Doc?"

"Eh?"

"What's that critter?"

"Unicorn."

"Eh."

They rode for another minute or two. The unicorn remained on the ridge. Its head moved slightly to follow them as they passed.

Wyatt said, "What's a unicorn?"

"In Araby they call it *cartajan*. Means 'lord of the desert.'"

"I can see that."

"'The cruelest is the unicorn, a monster that belloweth horribly, bodied like a horse, footed like an elephant, tailed like a swine, and headed like a stag. His horn sticketh out of the midst of his forehead, of a wonderful brightness about four foot long, so sharp, that whatsoever he pusheth at, he striketh it through easily. He is never caught alive; killed he may be, but taken he cannot be.'"

"Huh. Shakespeare or the Bible?"

"Some old-time Roman named Solinus, translated by some old-time Englishman who might've supped with Master Will and King Jim."

"I ain't never seen no unicorn before."

"Nor yet. That's a mirage. A will-o'-the-wisp. The product of a fevered brain."

"I reckon you're contagious, then."

Doc laughed, then coughed, then said, "Well, ain't no one known to've seen one before. Not for sure. All that's written down is travelers' tales, 'bout things they heard but never saw."

"We're the first to spot one?"

"In centuries. Far as I know."

"What do you think a circus'd pay for a critter like that?"

Doc laughed and coughed again. "Have to catch it first. It being a bastard of the mind, I reckon it'd race as fleet as a thought."

"Faster 'n horses?"

"S'posed to be."

"We could corner it in a box canyon, maybe."

"That horn ain't s'posed to be for decoration."

"Animal worth anything dead?"

"Depends on the buyer."

"Could stuff and stand it in a penny arcade. I seen a mermaid once. Looked like a monkey and a fish sewed together, but you got to admit, a sight like that's worth a penny."

"At least." Doc was rarely reluctant to tell anything to Wyatt, but he hesitated before he finally said, "Horn's s'posed to cure most sicknesses." He coughed. "Turn the horn into a drinking cup, and it takes the power out of poison. You can smear its blood on a wound, and the wound'll heal right up. Some say its whole body's magical. You're s'posed to eat its liver for something, but I forget what. There's folks who say it can make you young again, or live forever, or raise the dead."

"Any o' that true?"

Doc shrugged. "Three minutes ago, I would'a said it was all proof a lie lives longer than a liar. Now I'm not so sure."

"Let's find out." Wyatt drew on the reins. As his horse halted, he dropped to the ground and pulled his rifle from its boot on his saddle.

Doc said, "Ain't neither of us sharpshooters. One miss 'd scare it off for good."

Wyatt paused with the rifle butt at his shoulder. "You all right, Doc? Ain't like you to pass on an opportunity set before you."

"I do make some note of the odds, Wyatt. Leastways, when I'm anything like sober."

"Mmm. Your old Roman said they could be killed. There a trick to it?"

Doc considered the answers, and thought of Kate, and said, "We ain't got the means."

"Hell." Wyatt spoke with no particular emphasis. "Then there's no reason not to try what we got, is there?"

"No." Doc whipped his short-barrel Colt from its holster and fired in the general direction of the unicorn. It seemed to study him with disappointment while the sound of the shot hung in the hot, clean air. Then it danced aside as Wyatt's shot followed Doc's, and it tossed its mane and its horn in something uncannily like a laugh before it skipped back behind the rise.

"Damn it, Doc, if you'd'a waited till we could'a both took aim with rifles—"

"Why, sure, Wyatt. I reckon I could'a' taken me a nap, and once you had ever'thing to your liking, I'd'a risen well-rested to shoot ever so nicely, and we'd now be arguing whether unicorn liver'd taste best by itself or with a big plate o' beans."

Wyatt stared at him, then said grimly, "With beans," and slid his rifle back into its boot.

Doc laughed and coughed and holstered his Colt. Then he let his surprise show on his face. The unicorn watched them from the next rise. Wyatt swung back onto his horse, looked toward the unicorn, then looked toward Doc, who said, "It sure is pretty."

He did not expect Wyatt to answer that. Wyatt did not surprise him. The unicorn studied them as they rode by. When they had left sight of it, it appeared again on a further ridge that paralleled their ride.

Wyatt said, "If we could lure it in close, we'd plug it for sure."

"Mmm," Doc said, and then, "Maybe we should let Ringo live."

"Eh?"

"Ain't like he was one o' the ones who killed Morg."

"He stood by 'em. He planned it with Curly Bill. He was in on the attack on Virge."

"That ain't proven."

"Is to my satisfaction."

Doc laughed, said, "Hell, Wyatt, we'd have to kill half of Tombstone to get everyone who stood by the Clantons," then coughed.

When he lifted his head again, Wyatt was watching him like the unicorn had, with cool speculation. Doc wiped his mouth with the back of his hand and smiled. Wyatt said, "All right."

"All right, what?"

"All right, Ringo don't need to die. 'Less he insists on it."

"How so?"

Wyatt smiled. "Like I said. Depends on him."

Doc nodded, and they rode on. The sands stayed a steady white-hot glare, and the sky continued to leach moisture from their skin and their lungs. The unicorn accompanied them, always at a distance. Each time it disappeared, they thought it had abandoned them, but it always appeared again at a new, improbable vantage where only the most accurate marksman might take it.

Fred Dodge had said Ringo was on a drunk, and camping in a canyon in the Chiricahuas. Both of these things turned out to be true. Near a creek in the shade of a boulder, they found him reading aloud from *The Iliad* with an empty bottle and a pair of boots beside him. His outstretched feet were wrapped in strips of light cotton. He looked up as they rode near and switched from Latin to English to say, "Achilles and Patroclus, welcome."

"Hell, you are drunk if you don't recognize us," said Wyatt.

"Who you think you're playing?" said Doc. "Hardly Odysseus. Poor Hector? Brash Paris? The accommodating Panderus, perhaps?"

Ringo lifted his right arm from beside his body to show them his .45. "Anybody I damn well please. That's a good one, you two whoremasters calling names."

Wyatt said, "Doc, I forget. Why'd you want to warn him?"

"Seemed a fair notion at the time." Doc turned to Ringo. "You began the exchange of pleasantries, my Johnnie-O."

"Oh, all right, all right." Ringo waved the matter away in a broad circle with his Colt, then rose unsteadily to his feet. "So. To what do I owe the honor of this visit?"

Wyatt said, "Wells Fargo wants you dead."

"Wells Fargo?" Ringo drew himself erect and stated, precisely and indignantly, "I am a rustler, not a highwayman."

"It's the price of fame," Doc said. "A few hold-ups, they ask who's like to've masterminded 'em, and your name's sitting at the top of the heap."

Ringo blinked. "So why'd you two come in talkin' instead o' shootin'?"

Wyatt said, "Ask Doc."

Doc worked his lips and wondered at the impulse that had brought them under the gunsight of the man they had hunted. He said simply, "There's been a lot o' killin'. Mind if I water my horse?"

Ringo waved again. The weapon in his hand did not seem to be any more significant to him than a teacher's baton. Doc swung down from his horse, and so did Wyatt. Doc said, "I'll take yours," and led both horses toward the creek.

Ringo said, "So, I'm to infer you take no interest in the blood money?"

Wyatt said, "Why would you do that? We're hardly gonna let that money go to waste, not after we crossed back into Arizona."

"Hmm," said Ringo. He brought the barrel of his pistol to scratch his mustache, and Doc, moving toward the creek with his horse, wondered if the cowboy would shoot off his nose. "So, you're not after me, but you are after the reward on me. Am I to lie very still for several days? If you kept a bottle of good whiskey near my coffin, I might manage."

Doc squatted upstream from the horses to splash a handful of water against his face. As he lifted a second handful to drink, he saw the unicorn walking toward him.

Wyatt and Ringo were only a few yards away, talking about money and death. Boulders and brush gave Doc and the unicorn some privacy.

The horses noted the creature, but they continued to drink without a sound of fear or greeting.

The unicorn paused on the far side of the creek. It raised its head to taste the air. Its horn could impale or eviscerate buffalo, but if there was any meaning in the lift of the horn, it was a salute.

Wyatt was telling Ringo, "We'd meet in Colorado after they paid us. We'd give you your third, and you could go to Mexico or hell, for all we cared. Everyone'd be happy. You're gettin' a little too well-known to keep on in these parts as Ringo, you know."

"How would I trust you?"

Wyatt made a sound like a laugh. "How would we trust you? Our reputation with Wells Fargo will hang on you stayin' dead once we said you was."

"Huh," said Ringo, and then he laughed. "Hell, I ain't been dead before. Why not?"

The unicorn, if it heard the speakers, ignored them. It stepped into the creek. At the splash of its hoof, Ringo said, "What's—"

Doc heard them, but he kept his eyes on the unicorn, suspecting that now, if he looked away, he would never see it again. He thought of Big Nose Kate, and how she had cared for him, and he wondered if she had known any man who could not be said to have failed her.

Wyatt said, "Hell, Johnny, ain't you seen a unicorn before? That there's Carty John, the lord of the desert."

"Well, I never," said Ringo.

Doc heard the two men move closer, and saw the unicorn glance toward them. As it stepped sideways, ready to turn and run, Doc said calmly, "Back off. This is my play."

He heard Wyatt and Ringo withdraw a few feet. The unicorn's gaze returned to Doc's face. He extended his left arm, palm upward to show there was nothing in his hand. The unicorn took the last step, and its breath was warm on Doc's skin. He was afraid he would cough and scare it away, then realized he felt no need to cough.

Wyatt called softly, "Want me to fetch a rope?"

Ringo laughed, "Hell, ain't no need of that."

Wyatt said, "What do you mean?"

Ringo said, "Look at that! It'll follow Doc like a lovesick pup now." He laughed again, even more loudly, and Doc heard the sound of a man slapping his knee in delight as Ringo added, "And you know why?"

Wyatt said, "No. Why?"

Ringo said, " 'Cause there's one thing a unicorn'll fall for, and that's—"

Doc heard the pistol shot, then felt the pistol in his right hand. Ringo slumped to his knees and fell forward, hiding the hole in his face and exposing the larger one in the back of his head.

Wyatt went to calm their horses. The unicorn stayed by Doc. It had not spooked at the sound, sight, or smell of death. Doc let the pistol slide back into his holster.

Wyatt said, "Well, it'll be easier to convince Wells Fargo he's dead now."

"Mmm."

Wyatt squatted by Ringo, drew a knife, and cut a piece of scalp from Ringo's hairline. "What you want to do with Carty John there? Start up a unicorn show, or sell him?"

"He won't abide crowds."

Wyatt dropped his hand to the gun at his thigh. "You figure to shoot him then, or should I?"

Both pistols cleared their holsters at the same time. Neither fired. Doc and Wyatt stood still, Wyatt's pistol aimed at Doc's sternum, Doc's pistol aimed more toward Wyatt than anything else.

Time passed, perhaps slowly, perhaps quickly. Wyatt lowered his head, but not his gun, a fraction of an inch in a question. Doc answered by swinging his pistol behind him as he yelled, "Git!" The barrel struck something soft, and he thought it had been easier to send Kate away.

The unicorn did not try to impale him. It spun and ran. As it splashed across the creek and onto the sand, Doc holstered his pistol. He listened to the unicorn's hooves, but he did not turn to watch it go. He stepped forward, then fell coughing to his knees in the creek.

Wyatt took him by the shoulders to lift him and direct him toward the bank. While Doc sat on a boulder in the sun, Wyatt found Ringo's horse, saddled it, rolled Ringo's body in a blanket, then lashed it across the back of the horse. Wyatt said, "You want his boots?"

Doc looked where Ringo had been reading, then shook his head.

Wyatt said, "If they were all that comfortable, he'd'a been wearing 'em."

Doc said, "I'll take the book."

Wyatt picked up *The Iliad,* handed it to Doc, then said, "Ready to ride?"

"At a moment's notice," Doc said, and he stood, wondering if that was true. He tucked the book in his saddlebag, then swung himself onto his horse's back. "Where you taking him?"

Wyatt turned his horse back the way they had come. "I got a plan."

"As good as your last one?"

"I 'xpect."

"That's comforting."

"Killing Stilwell and Curly Bill so publicly just created messes for us. I figure to prop Johnny down by the road into town, which ought to get a story goin' that he up and killed his sorry ass hisself."

Doc considered several flaws in the plan, but said nothing. It would be a last joke on the town that had driven them away. He could hear people arguing why Ringo's boots were missing and whether a self-inflicted wound should be ringed with powder burns. It would be less than a joke, or more. It would be a mystery, and therefore it would be like life.

"Sure," Doc said, and coughed.

They left Ringo near a farmhouse and let his horse go free. Wyatt had hung Ringo's cartridge belts upside down on him, but Doc did not ask whether that was to make it look like Ringo had been extremely drunk, or was another little taunting detail for Sheriff Behan and Tombstone's legal establishment, or was simply a sign that Wyatt's mind was on other things.

When the scene of Ringo's suicide was complete, Wyatt said, "Doc, maybe we ought to split up for a while."

That would be prudent. If anyone decided Ringo had been killed, it would be best if no one could say that two men looking like Wyatt and Doc had been near these parts. Doc nodded.

Wyatt said, "I'll get your share to you."

Doc nodded again.

Wyatt smiled. "Half's better 'n thirds, ain't it?"

Doc coughed, then nodded a third time.

"You'll be all right?"

Doc said, "Sure."

"Well. Be seein' you."

He watched Wyatt ride away. A bullet in Wyatt's back would surprise no one, but Doc did not draw his gun. He loved anything that was simple and forceful and beautiful. Some things should live forever, and some things should die.

Coughing, he rode on alone.

About the Author

William Howard Shetterly was born in Columbia, South Carolina, on August 22, 1955. He has five novels and a few short stories and comic books to his credit. He presently lives in Minneapolis, Minnesota, with his beloved wife, Emma Bull. They run SteelDragon Inc., a part-time press which produces books, comic books, and music albums, including work by Cats Laughing and the Flash Girls. They have two cats, Chaos and Brain Damage, who have been allowed to live for reasons not immediately apparent to the outside world. It really isn't worth watching *Toxic Zombies* to see his very brief appearance in a very bad movie. In 1994, he ran for governor of Minnesota on the Grassroots Party ticket, and came in third in a field of six.

SUSAN SHWARTZ

THE TENTH
WORTHY

Peter: **Susan Shwartz** is the only writer in this anthology who chose to draw her story from the Unicorn Tapestries at the Cloisters. Her story is, therefore, more traditional than many of the others in this book. Her take is, however, unique.

Janet: I am sincerely and consistently filled with admiration and not a little envy at Susan's knowledge of medieval history and, in particular, of the Arthurian legend. I tend to store many pieces of knowledge in far-ranging arenas, while Susan is one of those people who takes pleasure in constantly widening her knowledge and understanding in particular ones. I often wish I had that kind of mind, that kind of memory.

The Tenth Worthy

M ICHAEL KAYE STOOD ON THE WEST TER-
race. His hands closed on the gray stone, the safe stone, of what was now
a parapet, not an ornamental wall. He tried not to think of grapnels and
ladders, siege engines wheeled up from the West Side Drive, or missiles
flung from the Palisades across the river.

Someone flung a rock up at him. It fell short of the walls, let alone
him and the shuttered windows, but he stepped back. He was glad he did
not have to look into the whites of the besiegers' eyes. Their soulless
eyes. So far, all this lot of Soulless had been able to manage was shouts
and stones.

The wasters across the river had more brains. There! Something
splashed into the Hudson, disturbing the patterns breathed into it by the
wind. Thank God, the Cloisters was still out of range. Thank God, too,
that no one had rediscovered artillery.

The wind drove a glowering phalanx of clouds across the horizon,
reddened from ground fires. The Wasting that had already destroyed
Manhattan burned now on the Palisades. A brazen sort of sunlight forced
its way beneath thickening clouds, and thunder growled.

Dimly from outside the Cloisters' walls came the shouts of the latest
mob to venture into Fort Tryon Park. Michael heard a shot. One of the
guards assigned to the gardeners must have fired. *Waste of a bullet.* Still,
what was one bullet wasted if they could scratch the last of the harvest
from their tiny fields?

At least, the defenders of Fort Tryon Park had stout walls to be thankful for. If the weather held just a little longer, they would also have rather
more food than they had feared. Still, it was problematic whether they
could hold out until Thanksgiving, let alone Christmas. Feasts would be

fasts. Surviving till next spring seemed past praying for, though they prayed in the Cloisters' chapels anyway.

Michael Kaye's prayers, instead, were for his daughter; but a rising tide of panic swamped them. *Gently, but quite, quite inexorably, the ragged old madman who had forsaken the subway tunnels for the gardens and now worked as orderly to the physicians lifted Michael's little girl from her mother's desperate grasp and carried her into the fresh-air ward that had been St.-Michel-de-Cuxa Cloister before this second, deadlier burning struck. His wife Ari had risen, running after the big, gentle, sorrowing man who bore her child away, perhaps to its death.*

"Tell Jennifer," she called over her shoulder. *"Laurie loves her. She'll come, I know she will! Please!"*

Brassy sunlight struck glints from the gray stone. Michael squeezed his eyes shut, and his tears were not for the brightness of the light. Laurie's eyes had been fevered, but there had been sanity in them. And soul. So many babies these days seemed to lack souls. So did the hollow folk who had devastated the world, caused the Wasting, and ended the world he knew.

Michael had valued his job as a very junior medieval researcher at the Cloisters—when so many elder scholars shuttled hopelessly from junior college to junior college—as a lifesaving chance at even a modest scholarly career. One day, he had brought his family here to visit, but that had been the day the Wasting had begun. As the city burst into flame and Soulless mobs roved the park, they had never dared to leave.

The mighty cables of the George Washington Bridge seemed to jangle in agony; the Brooklyn Bridge collapsed into the caissons that had claimed so many lives. Manhattan was cut off.

The last messenger from the main branch at the Metropolitan Museum of Fine Arts reported a city in flames. Too bad they could not carry some of the arms from Main uptown: spears and halberds, or My Lord Cid's sword. Jennifer was drilling all of them—the guards, scholars, and technicians who had worked here before the Wasting and the refugees who had fought their way to such safety as the Cloisters offered—with what arms any of them could invent.

The heavy, reinforced door banged open. Jennifer walked quickly to his side. "I heard about your little Laurie. I'll visit her this evening."

Like any good chatelaine, she knew what went on in her household without having to be told.

"At least, she's not Soulless." By their eyes, you knew well which children were the Soulless: infants whose eyes did not track; toddlers who, when their memories began to waken, remembered nothing. God help the world when they grew up. If they grew up. They might do such things as made the Wasting look like child's play. Having no memory and little mind, they saw no reason why they should not—or any reason at all.

He . . . but he remembered. Not just the memories of this current life, but fragments of what had to be another life. Today's Michael would have been happy as a minor academic or librarian. But serving the leader of this keep had waked his oldest memories: it was a dark guilt that, here at the end of his world, to know he had been fulfilled.

He turned toward his chatelaine, and she held up a hand.

"I wish," her voice was cool at his side, "I remembered more about siege engines. I remember staring out over the walls, watching the armies and hoping I had thought to lay in the supplies I needed most. Of course, I hadn't." The voice turned wry.

Jennifer had turned up here in the earliest days of the Wasting, stick in one hand, knife in the other, serviceable pistol tucked into her belt, and, in her pack, a box of jewelry, some of it ancient, as what she called her "dowry." When they had opened it, they had found in it torques, rings, and the Red Dragon of Britain.

It was mad, impossible—but it had to be true. He *remembered.* So Michael had shut the box, bowed to her in homage, and brought her before the Museum's Head. She had approved the Main Hall for its defensive capabilities and charmed the Head with the courtliness Michael remembered from the days he had been a sharp-tongued steward and fos-ter brother to a king. At least, he thought he remembered.

He soon got proof, as the Head insisted on taking his newest refugee on a tour of his domain.

"Here," the Head's dry voice ripened into warmth, "are our tapestries. The Nine Worthies, or Heroes, though not all nine tapestries survived the Revolution. Three pagan—Alexander, Caesar, and Hector. Three Hebrew—David, Joshua, and Judah Maccabee. And three Christian—Godfrey of Bouillon, Charlemagne . . ."

Jennifer looked long at the tapestries of the pagans and Hebrews. They were in remarkable condition, considering that they had been used to store vegetables. But then she came face to face with the remaining tapestry.

"Arthur of Britain," said the Head.

She turned on her heel and followed her guides into the room that housed the Unicorn Tapestries, her back almost too straight. It was the most dignified retreat Michael had ever imagined: or Kaye, as he had been in the life when they had bowed to each other across Arthur's hall.

Got you, Your Majesty, Michael thought her. Not Jennifer, but Guen-evere. The Queen. Drawn here, no doubt, by the King—and the tapestry—she would not face.

Michael, still in attendance, suppressed another chuckle. Taking the director's arm, Jennifer had strolled the wide, pegged planks past the huge fireplace as if she were at home in Camelodunum, agreeing in the way she had agreed with so many equally long-winded lords that Mr. Rockefeller had been absolutely right to love the tapestries so and nodding as he pointed out violets, periwinkles, and cherry trees in the rich backgrounds of the huge weavings.

Out in the Cloister beyond the paneled room, the madman saw Jennifer and started, shocked from his usual round of digging and fetching and carrying and murmuring to himself. The old street person tugged at his forelock and dipped his head. Jennifer blanched at the sight of him. Michael looked at him more closely, so used to seeing the familiar madman that he had never recognized his older guise. *Oh, I know you too, half-mad, wise in the ways of forests, devoted to your King.*

The Head pointed to the unicorn that dipped his horn into a fountain.

"Unicorn's horn was said to draw a serpent's poison from the water. It could even bring the dying back to life. I daresay we could use one about now."

But the age of wonders was past. Or was it? Why else had these old figures from Michael's past assembled here? Why was he here, hiding his old knighthood at the end of his world? *To serve my Queen,* he told himself, more Kaye than Michael in that thought.

Lacking unicorn's horn, some among the Cloisters' staff and refugees sickened. The Head collapsed, dying between one breath and the next. No one was surprised when Jennifer took over his responsibilities. She was, after all, trained for them.

A rattle of stones barraged the Terrace, given strength by a fresh gust of wind. They both ducked. Michael saw his hands flexing. Michael knew to duck. His former self had been a champion once and would gladly have snatched up one of the rocks and hurled it back. His skin prickled as lightning stitched itself across the sky. It was leaden now, though sunlight still pierced the edges of the clouds.

Jennifer put out a capable hand. "No point in goading them."

Abruptly, twilight replaced the day. Beneath them, the Soulless howled. A gust of wind howled louder.

"The madman said the cold's coming," Michael told the Queen.

"He'd know," she said.

The wind pressed against the thick door, reinforced with black iron. As the first squall hit, Michael motioned for the chatelaine to precede him into the safe long vault of the corridor up toward the paneled galleries.

She stalked past the tapestries of the Nine Worthies—Caesar presenting arms eternally in the faded weave—as if she were furious at them all.

The madman had carried the children from the Chapter House into the room housing the Unicorn Tapestries. How much he had changed from the homeless man who had staggered in here, sat, watching the gardeners, and then, like Jennifer, in the grips of his memories, taken charge. Even the trained horticulturists and doctors deferred to him. Did they know why? Maybe some of them, too, remembered stories of Merlin, wise in the ways of herbs.

The children sensed his love and needed no more. If the magician moved them, it was to a place where, at least, he could watch them as he went about his business in the various gardens. And the rain washed away the reek of smoke that wafted even this far uptown.

Michael watched him from the windows separating galleries from Cloister. The old man's hands were very sure, the three middle fingers almost of one length: such hands might well have belonged to a healer or scientist, not a gardener or grubber in trash cans.

Merlin had been right. The cold was coming in, even piercing what delicate equilibrium of heat, dryness, and air circulation that the engineers could force from the ever-crankier climate-control system. The tapestries had survived revolutions and decades in barns; the children were not so durable.

Jennifer threw herself down in the thronelike chair between two of the great tapestries, glancing from time to time into the next room or toward the Worthies of the pagan world.

Her eyes went to the doorway beyond which the children, the sick and dying children, huddled in winter coats harvested from the Lost and Found.

"They're so cold," she murmured. "And they'll get colder." She straightened. "That much I can cure right now."

Stalking over to the Arthur Tapestry, she looked the woven king in the eye for the first time. Seizing hold of the tapestry, she tugged one corner free of the frame that held it. The heavy cloth resisted.

"Damn you," she muttered. Then she yanked with all the strength of her body, her love, her anger, and her fear. The frame buckled, and, with a ripping sound, the ancient cloth tore free.

"Lady," Michael protested. Torn, after all those centuries, and by a hand that should have cherished it.

"For pity's sake," she told him, as if protesting the sorrow in his eyes, "you know their history. These things were used to cover vegetables for years. I wish we had the vegetables, too, to help get us through the winter. We'll be lucky if we don't lose half the children to starvation. At least, they'll be warm."

She tugged the heavy weaving up into her arms. Arthur's face looked up. The way the cloth was bundled up, his face seemed to grimace.

"He's of no use reigning from the wall. Let him protect *these* children." She began to drag the cloth into the next room.

"Are you going to help me or are you going to complain like you always do?" He followed her.

Waked by the noise, the children huddled together for reassurance, even more than warmth.

"We've brought you something nice," Jennifer reassured them.

Together, they spread the tapestry over five little bodies. Jennifer tucked it in at their feet. A ring from her trove gleamed on her hand in the candlelight. Michael looked down at the children. How quickly their shivering had stopped.

"Let's take the rest of them down and shake the dust out of them. Then we can start on the tapestries in this room," Jennifer said. "Michael?"

But Michael had hastened to the corner where his wife Ari restrained their daughter's hands—so hot that she, surely, had no need of tapestries. "Her fever's so high I'm afraid she'll have a seizure," Ari said. "I'd take her outside, but that's worse. The old man says we can cool her off in the fountain."

"I'll help you carry her," he offered. Thank God for ribs. Otherwise, his heart would burst out of his chest with fear. He heard Jennifer's footsteps, leaving the room, followed by the tugging and victorious crash as she pulled down another tapestry, the faint ripping sound (he winced) as she separated it from its frame, and the swish and drag as she dragged it along the floor, shook it, and piled it in a corner against need for it.

"Michael? Ohhhh . . ." she was at their side in an instant, her hands going out to the little girl.

"Laurie . . . Laurie . . ." A minor miracle: the child's eyes opened and recognized her. Her lips parted on Jennifer's name. Ari leaned forward, urging the child to drink, and Michael raised his daughter on his shoulder. In his past life, he had never been so gentle with children: well, live and learn—and Kaye had a lot to learn.

The child drank, sighed, then reached out with a free hand, attracted by the gleam of Jennifer's ring. She stripped it off and put it in the child's hand.

"Get better, sweetheart," Jennifer murmured. "We need you."

Laurie's smile almost stopped her father's heart. Acquiescent, she let herself be settled back into the nest of pillows and blankets.

"You don't think she'll swallow it, do you?" the chatelaine asked Ari, practical again.

"When she falls back to sleep, I'll take it and give it back to you." Ari reached up and clasped the older woman's hand. "Thanks."

"She's going to make it. She's got to. You want to get her under covers? I brought something warm."

Ari's eyes followed Jennifer's gesture toward the folds of tapestry.

"Not now; she's too hot. If we can bring her fever down, thank you."

"Good luck." Jennifer touched the child's forehead, then sped away.

Michael knelt beside his daughter. She murmured in a troubled sleep. Even in the dim candlelight, her face and hands were so pale, almost translucent, that it terrified him. But her fingers clutched the ring tightly, resisting his attempts to pull it free. He patted the little hand, then dared to meet his wife's eyes.

My gracious silence, he thought. Before the world changed, he had classmates and colleagues who had married, almost, as a form of professional advancement: doctors, lawyers, bankers. He had married not for income, but for peace: he for the library, she for the garden; both of them content to let the outer world flow around them as long as they could share their private sanctuary.

"What does Jennifer think she can do?" Ari's voice trembled.

I don't know, Michael wanted to say, but dared not. "Hold out, as long as we can," he said instead.

She looked at him. *Make it right again.*

I am not a leader, he protested silently. *I am an attendant lord!*

Dear Lord, was he going to fail Ari and Laurie in what he was as well as what he did?

Seeing his confusion, Ari took his hand. "It's all right," she said.

But he had only to look down at their daughter to know that it was not all right at all.

They sponged Laurie for hours in the courtyard's fountain, until her fever had broken. Shivering in his shirtsleeves—Ari had accepted his sweater as much because it was *his* as because it was warm and now slept beside their child wearing it for reassurance—Michael slowly entered the Nine Heroes' Room. The tapestry frames lay tumbled on the floor.

Footsteps and his shadow brought Jennifer's head up, and the candlelight cast her silhouette onto the emptiness where the Arthur Tapestry had hung.

She turned to face him. He hoped it was only the lamplight that made them too bright.

"It's not going to be enough, you know."

"We'll make it right." He offered her what reassurance he could.

"Ah God, my back." Her voice was the merest breath, and she twisted her shoulders as if she could shrug off some of her burden. It was presumption to touch her and cowardice to flee. Michael drew up one of the few chairs that had not been sacrificed yet to reinforce the shutters. He was glad of those shutters: it was witch weather out there tonight.

"You should sleep."

He shrugged.

Wax sputtered and fell to the base of the tarnished polycandelon standing on the table by the wall. They heard footsteps: a guard, no doubt, making the circuit of the halls and corridors, checking shutters and doors. The emergency generator hummed, powering the floodlights, keeping the Wasting at bay for one more night.

The guard stepped into the room, nodded, and went on. *All's well.* Only it wasn't. The guard's footsteps subsided as he padded down the hall.

"You should sleep too," he told her. "Let me tend to things."

She shook her head. Michael settled his hand on his cheek and fell into an uneasy doze.

A door banged open. He leapt up, but not as quickly as Jennifer.

"That's the West Terrace door," she said. "We've got a three-inch bar on it. And an armed guard."

That guard not only had one of their rare guns, but one of the last mobile phones that worked. He should have called out. They should have heard him. In the last extremity, he should have shot anyone who scaled the wall. *He should have died before letting anyone pass.* The words, older than he and darker by far, thrust themselves into Michael's consciousness. Those had been his instructions at Camelodunum.

The footsteps echoed, sure and measured. Up the dark corridor from the Terrace. Through the Pontaut Chapter House and into the Cloister, they *clicked* upon the stone.

"Do you hear? He's wearing spurs." Jennifer's words were almost a sob. Her hand came up to cover her mouth.

Michael reached within his pocket for his Swiss Army knife. *What an absurd toy,* the ancient memories protested. *You need a sword.*

I cannot use a sword! the mind of the graduate student, the urbanite, the survivor of the Wasting cried.

In the end, only the scholar's ravenous curiosity from his current life held him in his place. *You may indeed die in the next moment,* it told him, *but you will die* knowing.

Jennifer rose. She forced her hands to her side and stood before the thronelike chair, waiting as the stranger's armored feet drew nearer.

The intruder paused on the threshold. The candlelight flared. It illuminated his bright hair, brighter for the gold circlet with its Gothic trefoils that crowned it. It picked out the rich bullion of the three golden crowns—England, Scotland, and Brittany—woven upon his surcoat and drew a winelike glow from the great amethyst upon the pommel of his sword Excalibur.

Michael's chair toppled and he fell to his knees on the uneven floor.

"Sir," he whispered. "Beyond all our hopes, you've come back to us."

Maybe his King knew no English, the thought occurred to him. How would you translate that into Latin? He forced his voice to stay level. His King would not want him to weep.

Arthur spared him a glance, humor flickering in it for the briefest instant. "What happened to my Kaye's sharp tongue?" he murmured.

Then the King's attention was caught and held by Jennifer.

How not? If the tapestry had drawn his Queen to this place, she had drawn him and, in tearing down the tapestry, somehow released him. But then, she had always been his lure, trap, and beloved destruction of his hopes.

In this life, she might be Jennifer, refugee, then chatelaine of this pathetic fortress. But in her memories and the King's, she was his Queen.

She met Arthur's eyes without flinching. They were very much of a height.

"Well, and so you have called me to your side again. How may I serve you?"

Jennifer's shoulders relaxed as if a burden had been lifted from them.

She gestured at Michael, past him at the tapestried room beyond, the whole embattled fortress that had once been a museum. "These people are mine, and thus your charge. I beg you, save them."

The King smiled at her. Then, with a bow, he withdrew.

They found the door to the West Terrace untouched, its guard asleep. With nothing more to do until dawn, they went to the children's infirmary and helped the nurses with tucking in, washing down, soothing, and reassuring the sick children. Their numbers had grown during the night.

Jennifer tucked one last fold of tapestry in at the side of an eight-year-old boy, then sat and watched the children twitch and whimper in fevered dreams. If some slept, muttering, others lay awake, if you could call it that, their eyes vacant. It might be that, when their fever broke, they would be restored—but to what? Soullessness? Better that they die. Above them, the unicorn dipped his horn into the fountain, draining it of poison, before the hunt began. Later, they would have to take these tapestries down, too.

At least, Laurie still slept. *If the King returns, I shall wake her. I want her to see him. They used to say that the King's touch . . .*

Jennifer had taken over the task of trying to feed Laurie when Michael heard the clang and click of the King's footsteps outside. Through the leaded windowpanes, he could see the tall figure pace across the cloister. It stopped for a moment and gazed up at the sky. As if feeling Michael's eyes upon him, Arthur nodded greetings and moved on.

"Majesty . . ." New ceremony filled Michael's voice, and he bowed his head to her.

"Don't call me that," Jennifer said. "Don't *dare*."

The King stood poised on the threshold. His vitality filled the sickroom. Laurie opened her eyes, then opened them even wider at the sight of the splendid figure. She even managed a broad smile.

The King smiled. He had no children who had lived save the one, as soulless as those who yammered now outside. It had been a grief to him. Michael remembered talks of "Kaye, *my* son will grow up to be . . ." from when they'd been scarcely more than boys themselves, over much, much of the best wine in the cellars.

A beaker stood upon the table by the window. Wrought of a narwhal's horn, it was part of the furnishings of this room when it still had been an exhibition hall. With its special properties of healing—at least, if you believed it to be a unicorn's horn, not a narwhal's, it would do for Arthur. He filled it with wine and ventured forward. Arthur drank, returned the beaker, then beckoned his Queen and her seneschal out of the room.

"Your walls are sturdy," said the King. "You have done well to shield your windows . . . a foolishness, those wide panes of glass. I gather you are short on food?"

"We will be very thin by spring," the Queen replied. "Next year, I plan to clear more fields. Meanwhile, we can send out foragers under guard . . . "

Arthur frowned. "You have no horses. No weapons to speak of beyond what you have made and your guards' arms, though—my lady, you can hardly call those soldiers! While outside, in their tens of thousands . . ." He paused, looking at the place where his tapestry had hung. "It is like Camlann. Very like."

"So you counsel us to despair?" Jennifer's voice arched upward, haughty as her eyebrows.

"Lady, lady, lady, with *your* valiant heart? You invested Londinium against my son, and now you rule this keep. Surely, both times, you did not expect quick victory, or victory at all. I counsel you to hold off the long defeat. That is what kings are for. Why else did you summon me?"

"The world has better weapons now," Michael ventured, his voice faint.

"So it has. So tell me, my lord Seneschal, did you procure them, or do you take the darkest view of things as you always did since Merlin taught us both?"

In the next room, children, waking, began to cry and fret. The madman emerged from whatever shed he occupied at night. He had to bend to enter the room. Seeing the King, he blinked. Michael watched off as he sloughed off his familiar guises of madman, gardener, children's nurse to bow to the King. It was the bow of one used to courts rather than city dumps; and that, too, no longer surprised Michael.

"So my old friend Merlin found his way to you, too," murmured the King.

"Can you take down the tapestries in the Unicorn Room?" Jennifer asked the old man. "We can probably use them for blankets, if nothing else."

The madman bowed again and slipped away, moving as the leaves move. Michael thought he heard him mutter, "All shall be well and all manner of things shall be well."

It was good that someone felt optimistic.

"And you always thought he mistrusted you," Arthur the King told Jennifer.

"Well, wasn't he right to think I'd be the ruin of you?" For a moment, they glared at each other. Then, she made herself shrug. "What would you have me do now?"

"You shall send your guards to me," he said. "I shall review them. And then we shall see what we can see."

It was no answer at all, really.

"You should rest while you can," she told the King. "Michael will see that you have food. I shall call the guards."

She gestured to the chair. As he seated himself, she bowed. The courtesy had nothing of humility about it, as if a wave or a ridge of stone had bowed, a line of such sudden grace that Michael gasped. Arthur smiled as at a beloved memory.

That day, Michael helped take down the Unicorn Tapestries. Then he worked in their woodshop until every muscle ached as if the Soulless beat him with clubs. When he grew too tired to work, he wrapped himself in fabric that he rather thought had been a Spanish bishop's cope and curled up in a paneled corner. Perhaps Ari would call to him from the other room with something he could do for their child. When the sunlight faded, he stared at the candlelight for warmth. If only he could shut his eyes for a few moments before the evening meal.

When he awoke, they were talking, the chatelaine and his King. As Michael Kaye, he knew how long it had been since he had last walked the earth as Kaye, the knight. Here was his brother, and here his Queen. Perhaps the age of miracles was *not* past.

"It is no use. Of course, I honor you; of course, I am grateful," said the Queen. "But the stain is set, the vessel defiled, the gem cracked at its core."

The King bent forward. He caught her hand and kissed it, then her brow. "I, too, am a great sinner. But even if this time looks like the end of all things, I see it indeed as a new dispensation. Of grace, not law. Of forgiveness, even in the teeth of bitterest remembrance."

Arthur stood very close to the Queen, but she turned her head away from any comfort he might offer.

She shook her head. "So, here at the end of all things, you come to forgive me?"

"I tell you, this may not be the end. I say we march out and grasp what all we can, and thus hold off the long defeat . . ."

"And turn thief? If we do that, what becomes of *us*?"

"We fight. We heal. We rebuild, please God. Not just in body, but in soul. For I tell you, my heart, I have lived this long while with the heart cut out of me."

"Where have you lived?" the Queen asked. "And how?" Involuntarily, she held out her hands, then pulled them back before he could clasp them.

"Healing my wounds."

"Ah!" She turned away. It was not just the wounds to Arthur's body that he meant, but to his heart and soul. She had helped cause those wounds, and memory of that would haunt her till Doomsday.

"*I* have healed, my lady. Have you?"

Hearing armored footsteps and a rustle of cloth, Michael dared look up. Too often, Kaye's tongue had been harsher than his heart would have liked.

His brother and the Queen stood, stubbornly apart, facing each other. She whirled, her ringless hands flashing up to cover her face. Michael held his breath. For a moment, even the sheltered candle flames ceased their dance. Arthur leaned forward, bending over his wife's bright hair.

Were they embracing now, his brother and his errant wife? Did he kiss her hair? It was not a moment that brother or foster brother should witness.

That night, the frost clamped down upon Fort Tryon Park. Outside, fires danced. The fevered children woke, coughing out what strength they had left, then lapsed into listlessness and sleep, from which feebler coughing woke them. They were always cold, even through the protective warmth of the Unicorn Tapestries.

In the days that followed, the King sent out foragers. They ventured into Washington Heights and below it into Harlem, fought their way back within the stone bridge that guarded the park from the highway and back behind the Cloisters' walls with treasures of cough drops, OTC remedies that were now as rare as the roc's egg, and even (from an office from which the doctor had long since fled) a few precious antibiotics, and news of fires on every block, of Central Park stripped of its withered trees.

It was fine for the madman to speak of retreat in terms of a sick beast returning to its lair to eat herbs, lick its wounds, and wait for a healing spring; but what healing could there be when the whole world was poisoned?

They might as well expect what Arthur had suffered at Camlann: to line up knights against knights, soldiers against soldiers, in hope of treaty—and have a serpent strike from behind, shattering the truce.

Michael Kaye, helping nurse the furnace as well as sick children, watched Arthur fight. This time, he managed not to press for decisive battle; and the battle against his nature was perhaps the hardest he had fought. Day after day, he fought it and won. But Michael knew his foster brother: as they ran out of food, out of healing, out of time, he would order one last sortie. Already, he had begun to drill the guards for assault, not for defense.

It was too cold now to meet in the Pontaut Chapter House, too dark to meet in the Gothic Chapel now that the shutters guarded the windows. They were holding council of war in the Nine Heroes' Room. One of the Nine sat in the great carved chair, Jennifer standing beside the throne from where she had once ruled.

Came a crash, a shuddering of walls, and a scream from outside—the highway between the Terrace and the Hudson, Michael thought. He must run and check for damages.

"What's that?" asked the head of Arthur's guard, also poised to run, but obedient to Arthur's hand-slashed order: *stay.*

"You know," the madman said, "I tended those foragers who returned.

"They brought back news, which we need as much as we need medicines," the old man continued. "Even if the news is grave. Prepare yourself: the Soulless have learned to hurl fire."

"My shutters," Michael worried. "Please God they hold."

Again, the wall shuddered. Dust trickled from the ceiling of the apse. Outside, a shout went up.

The King cocked his head. "Too close," he judged. "Even if your shutters hold, brother, they mean to pen us within or keep us fighting fires until they're strong enough to overrun our walls."

He paused, looking toward the next room. This time of day, the children were at their best. None of them raved with fever, and one or two even could laugh.

The words came from him as if under torture. "Call out the guards."

"Oh no," said Jennifer. "No. At least, let us try to treat with them first."

Arthur raised his head. "I tried that last time, at Camlann," he told her. "And you know how it ended. One adder-strike in the foot, and another deep into the heart of all Britain."

"We have to try. You told me, we have to try!" She was gone before the King could forestall her, her footsteps ringing on the stone. They heard her struggle with the new bars on the door to the West Terrace. It crashed open . . .

"God, no," whispered the King.

Again the catapult wound and struck. Something whistled through the air, smashing against the parapet. Air rushed in, and stinking of smoke.

"No!" screamed Arthur. "NO!" He had screamed thus at Camlann.

Armored though he was, no man ever moved faster. He dashed into the next room. The sick children scarcely had time to whimper as he snatched up the first tapestry he saw, then raced toward the West Terrace.

He flung open the door, sending Jennifer reeling away from it across the scorched stone, her hands beating at her burning clothes. Arthur pounced. He wrapped her in the heavy wool of the tapestry, snuffing out the fire. The stinks of singed hair and flesh rose as the fire died. Drawing his dagger, he cut free Jennifer's burnt locks and tossed them aside. Her knees sagged, and he caught her. For a long moment, they held each other. Then he snatched her back through the door and kicked it closed.

"Merlin!" he shouted for the madman. "Merlin! Get in here!"

He swept her up into his arms, bearing her back into the room where he had sat such a short time ago and lowering her onto the table. She clung to him with her burnt hands, tears of pain running down the ash on her face, leaving clean streaks.

The tapestry, much charred, fell away from her body. The Unicorn at the Fountain, the creature imprisoned in a garden, had survived all those centuries. Now, in an instant, the fire had consumed the dry wool that had housed it.

They were all the losers for its death; but at least they had not lost Jennifer. The madman appeared loaded with supplies of bandage and aloe and water.

"Tell the children . . . oh tell them something!" Michael snapped when his wife came to the door, demanding information. He could hear the wails of sickly children. They would all die, God help them. But with Jennifer alive, they had a chance to live a little longer.

The captain of the guard watched the King for orders. Still, Arthur stared at Jennifer's streaked face.

"This time," she whispered, "you *saved* me from the pyre."

Arthur shut his eyes. "I would rather have cut my heart out than send you to it last time."

Jennifer put out a hand to touch the ruined tapestry.

"The poor unicorn," she mourned. "Like the sly girl in the weaving, I was its death." Then she wept as she had not done in all the days of terror, all the years of betrayal, war, and the long, long hallowed silences of her old convent at Amesbury.

"It's gone," she wept. "Destroyed. I was not fit to look upon the unicorn, and so it's gone."

"No, lady," said the magus. "Fire purifies. The pattern is complete. You wrought its first links, and you are its heart." He wound fragrant linen bandages about her hands and wrists, washed the soot from her face, then lovingly completed the hair trim that her husband had begun and botched.

And still she wept. Merlin gestured to the King to hold her. He moved with his powders toward the wine . . .

. . . A tapping sounded up the stairs, across the Cuxa Cloister, and toward them. A tapping of delicate, immortal hooves.

Released by the destruction of the tapestry that had imprisoned it, the unicorn appeared in the door of the Room of the Nine Worthies. This was not the tamed pet of fantasy, but a majestic white creature, at least sixteen hands high. No wonder they said the touch of a unicorn's horn could restore life to the dying. There was eternal joy, Michael thought, and grace in every flourish of its tail, strength in its bearing, and splendor as the candlelight played upon its horn.

"Lord," whispered Merlin, "shall these bones live? Shall these bones live?"

Jennifer gasped, tore free of Arthur, and fled into the hall where the listless children lay. The unicorn followed. It stood poised upon the threshold, as if announcing itself, until the children saw it. They exclaimed in joy as it paced within the room. Ceremoniously, it touched each sick child with its horn, leaving health in its path where fever had stalked. When it had touched them all, it turned to stand before the Queen, who stood with her back against the wall, her bandaged hands held to her mouth.

Queen and unicorn faced each other. Light filtered in and glinted off the unicorn's horn, held at the level of her heart. Jennifer pressed back against the mellow wood. Michael could see how she forced her gray eyes to remain open, in the high arches of their sockets. Behind her, he heard the unfamiliar buoyant gurgle of his daughter's laughter. He ran to sweep her up in his arms. Who would have thought the age of miracles was *now*?

"Go ahead," said the Queen. "Pierce my heart. After all these years, I'll be relieved."

Bending its stately maned head with its rakish goat's beard until the horn clicked upon the floor, the unicorn stretched its forelegs out and bowed. It raised itself, then stepped closer. When the Queen reached out and took its face between her hands, its horn blazed aloft in benediction.

The bandages dropped off her hands. The burst blisters shrank, then disappeared. Even the pink of tight-drawn new-healed skin subsided. Her hair, the color of an autumn leaf, flourished, waving down her back. The Queen sank down and wept as if she were a child that had been forgiven.

Arthur the King ran his hand along the unicorn's flank as if it were a favorite war-horse. The beast rested its head against his shoulder.

"Now," said the King, "we go forth. To the sea."

Jennifer rose. Arthur held out his hand to his Queen. Shabby though she was, she placed fingertips upon its back. The two of them walked from the room. The children, tended by the madman, followed then into the Great Hall, down the stairs, and into the park. Laurie broke out of Michael's arms, ran to the unicorn, and—before she could be stopped—clambered onto its back.

Outside, the Soulless yammered. Seeing the fortress door open, they abandoned their catapults and pressed forward hungrily. Arthur's drawn steel restrained them. Then the sight of the unicorn forced them into a silence that was oddly reverent.

It started forward—and there was Michael's daughter riding on its back! He lunged forward to protect her. The unicorn lowered its crowned head at him in warning, and Arthur held up a hand.

"Do you think I would let harm come to her?" asked the King. "Or that *he* would?"

Two of the Soulless stole up to the unicorn and held out shaking dirty hands. The mighty head bent, sniffing those hands, then nudging against them. The unicorn's horn gleamed. No longer soulless, the pair fell to their knees. They were a woman and a boy. Jennifer came forth to comfort them and guide them into line.

"Now," said the King, "to reclaim our world."

Arthur raised Excalibur. The amethyst on its pommel gleamed in the winter sunlight as he brought the blade to his lips, saluting the unicorn that led down the twisting road and out toward the city.

Shadows followed at their backs. Kings and princes guarded them. A man bearing the Cross of God upon his back sang a Crusader's hymn as a Hebrew king harped. An aged paladin with a mighty beard marched alongside, holding the fragments of his kinsman's horn. One or two people had seized food and blankets. Ari, Michael noticed, had caught up a piece of tapestry, now empty of figures.

South through Washington Heights, where even the timid oldest emerged from the older buildings and fell into step, they marched, and into Harlem. Vacant lots in the 120s, where untidy camps had been set up teemed as people raced toward the unicorn. The blocked-up houses disgorged squatters as if the last trump had been sounded and the dead were raised. The unicorn reared in greeting, and the little girl upon its back laughed with joy.

"What a rider we'll make of her, brother!" Arthur called to Michael where he marched with his wife.

The newcomers clustered around, petting the unicorn. Two adults carried a pallet out into the street and laid it at the unicorn's hooves. With a gentle touch of its horn, the unicorn released the old man on it from mortal sickness. He rose and walked alongside, steadying himself against the unicorn's flanks until he was strong enough to walk on his own. In another time, Michael would have recoiled at the stinks of sickness and fever that rose from the old man, but he pressed forward toward his daughter.

Her head was not so high above his now, and Michael, sharp-eyed as a seneschal must be, understood. With every touch of a child's hand, with every life-giving touch of the unicorn's horn, the creature's light and substance seemed to diminish. The unicorn was *dwindling*. No longer was it the size of a war-horse, but only the size of, well, the unicorn of legend, more delicate and vulnerable now than it had been.

Jennifer came over to him. "Do you see how small it's getting?" he asked her.

"We both saw, my lord and I," she whispered.

"Can't we stop it?"

"Only if we retreat," she said.

"We'll drain it," Michael warned.

Arthur had gone over to the unicorn, had laid his arm over its shoulders, and walked beside it. The unicorn arched its neck and caracoled for a moment, taking heart and strength from the King.

"It is the unicorn's privilege to spend its strength for the good of its world," said Jennifer. "It is very like a king in that respect."

Michael found himself laughing and weeping, both. "I thought King's Touch, surely, was for other things."

Jennifer shook her head. "All he can do is comfort the poor beast." She blinked once, then proudly raised her head. The King spent his life for the country; the unicorn for the world; and the chatelaine must look as if all were well.

Past 125th Street, they marched. Now the wasteland of Central Park gaped before them. Men and women, even a few sad beasts that survived from the zoo in the West 60s, thronged out to greet it. At the sight of the unicorn and its company, some fell to their knees. Others shuddered, stretched, and yawned, as if soullessness were a sleep from which they finally had waked. They watched as people in New York had watched parades long, long before the Wasting, but they watched in silence.

The silence drew out, becoming oppressive. Michael's little girl leaned forward, smoothing her cheek in the silk of the unicorn's mane, somewhat dingy now. Had she whispered something?

Again, the unicorn began to caracole. Arthur stepped away from it, again drawing Excalibur. He saluted the crowd, which responded with a cheer. Downtown they marched, toward the ruins that jutted like ruined teeth from what had once been called the Canyon of Heroes. Leading the parade was another Hero, the tenth—a unicorn now fragile, with a translucent brittle horn. Each time it touched someone, it lost more light and strength. Oh, it was so tired!

Its head swung toward the King, dark eyes imploring. Arthur signaled a halt. Michael lifted his little girl from the unicorn's back, winning thankful looks from King and beast. The creature's back was lathered. Michael laid his own coat upon it. Someone brought it water, warmed against his body. Arthur talked gently to it, walking with it up and down.

When the procession again moved, the sky had turned darker with clouds and the waning sun. There was no smoke—another miracle in a day full of them.

Murmuring rose from the throng, as if they were children who only now realized what they had done in a burst of temper and were now sorry. And down further, past the welters of twisting streets that each released its own survivors, eyes feasting on the unicorn walking beside the King and dwindling more and more swiftly. Arthur beckoned to the Queen. When she approached, the unicorn pushed against her outstretched hand, then leaned its head against her. Arms linked across its back, King and chatelaine urged it forward. It was no larger now than a pony. A sickly pony.

The walls guarding the tip of the island from the rest of the world opened its gates to let the unicorn and the former Soulless pass. One man threw down his gun, and then they all did. A woman in a tattered suit sobbed, then joined the line of march through the fortress that no longer saw the need to protect itself, eastward toward the Seaport with its ancient reek of salt and fish, where stubs of the masts of sunken ships protruded from the dark water, and so to the tip of Manhattan Island.

The sun was only the merest coal of warmth in a gray sky above where the East and the Hudson rivers flowed together when they reached Battery Park. The last flicker of sunlight and the first campfires sparked off the unicorn's horn one last time. With a groan, the unicorn sank to its knees. It shivered in the evening winds, chill from the water. Michael's coat was drenched; Arthur covered it with his own cloak. Some of the former Soulless, expert from far too much practice, kindled fires from the dried-out stumps of trees near where cannons had guarded New Amsterdam and then New York in its early days, trying to make their camp as comfortable as they might.

As if in response, the tiny islands across from the park set out lights of their own. Bonfires sprang from about the feet of the statue, its torch fallen, on the island across the bay.

Toward midnight, rain doused the remnants of the fires. Michael crept away from his wife and child to make certain that the unicorn was covered. Arthur's cloak was soaked through.

"Do you want water, friend?" Michael asked. "Grain?" There must be something he could do for it. When he had charge of Arthur's hall, he had always had a way with horses. Still, he wished he could call for Merlin. He remembered: the madman had a way of turning up when he was needed. If he were not here, it must be because he could do nothing. So, Michael must rely on hands and voice to comfort at least the unicorn's heart.

The unicorn snuffled once at Michael's hand.

"You don't want me to leave you, boy? Well then, I won't."

Arthur appeared, handlinked with Jennifer, blankets pulled like hoods over their heads. They, too, sank down beside the unicorn.

Near dawn, the rain subsided. A wind blew across the tip of the island, bracingly chill and salty. It seemed to cleanse whatever it touched. The unicorn's head turned; the dulled eyes brightened, and it looked up. Its body barely made a mound beneath the King's sodden cloak.

The wind scoured away the clouds, revealing the morning star. Light began to tremble where the sky touched the East River. The unicorn stirred beneath the heavy woolen folds.

Arthur pulled the cloak away. Michael's eyes filled. Was this ancient creature that struggled up onto unsteady legs the triumphant unicorn that had broken a siege and transformed its besiegers?

It was drained, dying, surely. But it shied away from Arthur's sustaining hands. The King nodded, then knelt before the beast. Together, they waited. The first rays of the rising sun struck the unicorn's horn, kindling fire along its whorls and ridges. The unicorn whickered welcome. It sounded stronger—didn't it?

And then, with a speed astonishing for a creature so withered and drained, it raced straight toward the shore, toward the barriers, vaulting them in a leap that did not end in the river, but soared instead into the gleaming sky. A mist shaped like a giant horse with a gleaming horn formed before the sun, then dissipated in the morning wind.

Sunlight struck the ground, kindling light like an ember in a dying fire. Michael's daughter raced over to it, pounced, and, a look of awe on her face, held up her hand.

On it gleamed a stone large enough to cover her palm. A gem of adamant, Michael thought. They would have to revise the folklore, wouldn't they, when they could spare the time from rebuilding their world.

"Give it to the King," he heard his wife urge the little girl.

She held it aloft like a torch, but brought it to Jennifer instead. The woman bent to take the stone. It shone pink through their joined hands.

"For your new crown," the lady told the King.

"No," he said, "for yours."

He leaned forward. Their kiss was almost a passage of arms.

Hand on his Queen's shoulder, Arthur started forward. "Well, brother Kaye," he called to Michael, "I have a mind to turn gardener."

He always could count on Arthur to come up with good ideas. Unlike the gardens on the Unicorn Tapestries, Arthur's gardens would reclaim a world.

ABOUT THE AUTHOR

By day, **Susan Shwartz** is a financial writer and editor on Wall Street. By night and in any spare minute she can scrounge, she writes, edits, and reviews fantasy and science fiction. She holds a Ph.D. in English literature from Harvard with a medieval specialization. Her writing ranges from high fantasy to nuts-and-bolts military SF and alternative history.

She has been nominated for the Nebula four times and once each for the Hugo and World Fantasy awards and is now working on her twentieth book. Her most recent anthology, *Sisters in Fantasy (vol. 1)* will be published by New American Library. Her past two novels were *The Grail of Hearts* (Tor) and *Empire of the Eagle* (cowritten with Andre Norton and also published by Tor). Her forthcoming novel is *Shards of Empire,* a historical fantasy of Byzantium. It will be published by Tor. She has written about sixty pieces of short fiction and published in the *New York Times* and *Vogue.*

DAVE SMEDS

SURVIVOR

Peter: I'm going to take the liberty of including in full **Dave Smeds'** statement explaining why he wrote "Survivor."

War is something that stays with soldiers even after they come home. That's especially true of the Americans who fought in Vietnam. Soldiers of the nation's other wars typically served for the duration. In Vietnam individuals were yanked from the field of fire whenever their DEROS date (Date of Expected Return from OverSeas) rolled around, often being thrust within twenty-four hours into a peacetime milieu they no longer felt a part of. That we ultimately lost the war is only part of the point. Those men never had the satisfaction of knowing they had stayed until the job was done.

May each of the half million guys who went find their closure.

Janet: Dave Smeds is a big guy with a black belt, a love of fantasy and science fiction, and the ability to be fully devoted to whatever he is writing, be it a novel or a short story. He is yet another member of The Melville Nine, one who became—and stayed—my friend after I said good-bye to the group and took off for the West Indies. As you will see from this story, he is an excellent and painstaking writer, with a hearty respect for the old traditions of storytelling. His stories inevitably have clarity, directness, a sense of knowing where they are headed. I like that. I also like the fact that, as a writer, he is never satisfied by giving anything but his best.

Survivor

————◦◦◦————

1967

G.I. BOB'S QUALITY TATTOOS, THE NEON SIGN declared, luring customers through the Bay Area summer fog with a tropistic intensity. Tucked between a laundromat and an appliance repair shop in lower Oakland, the studio was the only place of business on the block open at that hour. Troy Chesley scanned right and left as if he were on patrol, dropping into a firefight stance behind a parked car as a thin, dark-skinned man strode up to the nearest intersection.

"Easy, man." Roger, Troy's companion, grabbed him by the collar and yanked him toward the door. "We ain't back in 'Nam *yet.*"

Troy's cheeks flushed. He had been doing things like that all night. No more booze. It wasn't every grunt that got a furlough back to the mainland in mid-tour, even if it happened for the worst of reasons. The least he could do was stay sober enough to acknowledge he was out of the war zone.

Troy was no longer sure why he had let Roger talk him into this. Nabbing some skin art was one thing; doing it in such a seedy locale was another. He jumped as the little bell above the lintel rang, announcing their entrance.

A man appeared through the curtains at the back. "May I help you?" he asked.

The hair on the nape of Troy's neck stood on end. Or would have, except that his father had insisted on a haircut so that he would look like a proper military man for his mother's funeral. *("Your lieutenant lets you look like* that *on the battlefield?")* "Shit," he blurted, "It's a gook."

No sooner had the words left his mouth than he knew it was the wrong thing to say. Yet the tattooist merely blinked his almond eyes, shrugged, and said calmly, "No, sir. Nobody but us chinks here." He spoke with no more than a slight accent, and with an air that said he was used to the ill grace of soldiers.

"Sorry. Been drinking," Troy mumbled. But drunk or not, it wasn't like him to be *that* much of an asshole. For some reason he felt menaced. The man was such a weird-looking fucker. He appeared to be middle-aged, but in an odd, preserved sort of way. His shirt was highly starched and black, his skin dry as parchment, his fingertips so loaded with nicotine they had stained the exterior of his cigarette. He sure as hell wasn't G.I. Bob.

He had no tattoos on his own arms. What kind of stitcher never applied the ink to himself?

"Come on," Troy said, tugging Roger's sleeve. "Let's get out of here."

Roger slid free. "We came all this way, Chesley my boy. What's the matter? Are the guys in your unit pussies?"

Those were the magic words. Troy barely knew Roger—their connection was that they had shared a flight from Da Nang to Travis and, in seven hours, would share the return leg—but he was his buddy of the moment, and he couldn't let the man say he lacked balls. He was a goddamned U.S. of A. soldier heading back to finish up eight months more In Country.

"All right, all right," Troy muttered.

"Do you know what design you want?" the stitcher asked. When both young men shook their heads, he opened up his books of patterns. "How about a nice eagle? Stars and Stripes? A lightning bolt?" He opened the pages to other suggestions he thought appropriate. To Troy, he seemed to give off a predatory glee at the prospect of jabbing them with a sharp instrument.

In less than two minutes Roger pointed to his choice: a traditional "Don't Tread on Me" snake. The artist nodded, propped the book open on the counter for reference, and swabbed the infantryman's upper arm with alcohol. To Troy's amazement, he did not use a transfer or tracing of any sort. He simply drew the design, freehand, crafting a startlingly faithful copy. The needle gun began to whir.

The noise, along with Roger's occasional cussword, faded into the background. Troy turned page after page, but the designs did not call to him. It had finally struck him that he would be living with whatever choice he made. A sign above the photos of satisfied customers warned, A TATTOO IS FOREVER.

Whatever image he chose had to be right. It had to be him. He finished all the books: no good. They contained nothing but other people's ideas. He needed something he hadn't seen on anyone else's body.

It came to him clearly and insistently. "Can you do a unicorn?" Troy asked.

The artist paused, dabbing at Roger's wounded skin with a cloth. "A unicorn?" he asked, with the seriousness of a man who used powdered rhinoceros horn to enhance sexual potency.

"A mean son-of-a-bitch unicorn, with fire in its eyes and blood dripping from its spike." Troy chuckled. "That'd be hot, wouldn't it, Rodge?"

"That's affirmed," Roger said.

The stitcher lit a new cigarette, sucking on two at once, and blew a long, blue cloud. He closed his eyes and appeared to tune out the parlor and his customers. When he roused, he reached into a drawer and pulled out a fresh needle gun, its metal gleaming as if never before used. "Yes. I can do that. But only over your heart."

Troy blinked, rubbing his chest. He hadn't considered anywhere but his arm, but the suggestion had a strange appropriateness to it. "Yeah," he said. "Okay."

The artist pulled out a sketch pad and blocked in a muscular, rearing horse shape, added the horn, and then gave it the intimidating, man-of-war embellishments Troy had asked for.

"That's fabulous," Troy said. He bared his upper body and dropped into the chair that Roger had vacated.

The man penciled the design onto Troy's left breast, with the unicorn's lashing tail at the sternum and the point of his horn jabbing above and past the nipple. He performed his work with a frenzied fluidity, stopping only when he reached for the needle gun.

"Point of no return," he said, which Troy thought odd, since he hadn't given Roger that sort of warning. It was at that moment he realized why the symbol of a unicorn had sprung to his mind. During the funeral, while the minister droned on, Troy had been thinking of an old book in which the hero was saved from death by a puff of a unicorn's breath.

His mind was made up. He nodded.

The needle bit. Troy clenched his teeth until his mouth tasted of metal. As the initial shock passed, he forced himself to relax, reasoning that tension would only worsen the discomfort. The technique worked. The procedure took on a flavor of timelessness not unlike watching illumination rounds flower in the night sky over rice paddies fifty klicks away. Detached, Troy watched himself bleed. He could handle anything, as long as he knew he was going to survive the experience. Wasn't that why he was there—proving like so many G.I.'s before him how durable he was? To feel anything, even pain, was a comfort, with his poor mother now cold in her grave, with himself going back into the jungle hardly more than a target dummy for the Viet Cong.

To be able to spit at Death was worth any price.

"What the hell is *that*?" asked Siddens, pointing at Troy's chest.

The squad was hanging out in a jungle clearing a dozen klicks west of their firebase, enduring the wait until the choppers arrived to take them beyond Hill 625—to a landing zone that promised to be just as dull as this one. They had spotted no sign of the enemy for a week, a blessing that created its own sort of edginess.

Troy, bare from the waist up, held up the shirt he had just used to wipe the sweat from his forehead. The tattoo blazed in plain sight of Siddens—the medic—and PFC Holcomb, as they crouched in the shade of a clump of elephant grass.

"It's a unicorn," Troy said, wishing he had not removed the shirt. "You know, like, 'Only virgins touch me'?" He winced, too aware of being only nineteen. The joke had seemed so good when he thought of it, but in the past three weeks, the only laughing had been *at* him, not with him.

But Siddens did not laugh. "You got that back in the World?" he asked.

"Yeah."

The medic turned back to Holcomb, obviously continuing a conversation begun before Troy had wandered over to them. "See? Told you it had to be something."

Siddens and Holcomb were a study in contrast. Siddens was wiry, white, freckled, and gifted with a logic all his own. Holcomb was beefy, black, handsome, and spoke with down-home, commonsense directness. But Troy thought of them in the same way. Siddens was the kind of bandage-jockey a grunt relied on. Dedicated. He was determined to get to medical school, even if his family's poverty meant taking a side trip through a war. Holcomb was steady as a rock. He wrote home to his widowed mother and eight younger siblings back in Mississippi five times a week—he had a letter-in-progress in a clipboard in his lap at that moment.

Troy, who had dropped out of his first semester of college, and who had managed to write to his mother only three times between boot camp and her death, wanted to be like both these men.

"What the hell are you talking about?" Troy asked.

Holcomb smiled and pointed at the tattoo. "Doug here thinks that's your rabbit's foot. Your four-leaf clover. Ain't nothing gonna touch you now."

Troy laughed. "What makes you think that?"

"We been watching you since you got back. Remember that punji pit you stepped into? How do suppose you landed on your feet without getting jabbed by even one of them slivers of bamboo?"

"Just lucky, I guess."

"And where you figure all that luck comes from?" Holcomb asked. "You were never that lucky before. Remember your first patrol? You be such a Fucking New Guy you poked yourself with your own bayonet. You slashed your ankle on that concertina wire."

Troy nodded slowly. The story of his life. Broken leg in junior high. Burst appendix at fifteen. Nobody had ever called him lucky. Little mishaps plagued him all the time.

But not for the past three weeks. Not since he had acquired the tattoo.

"Causality," Siddens intoned. "Everything happens for a reason. Remember Winston?"

Troy remembered Winston very well. When Troy was first assigned to the platoon, the corporal had been a short-timer just counting the days until his DEROS. He used to meditate on which boot to put on first. Some mornings he started with the left, some days with the right. When he doubted his choice, he was jittery as a rabbit. On one patrol, his shoelace broke. His cheeks turned the color of ashes. A sniper wasted him that afternoon.

"He knew he was fucked," Siddens said. "Nothing could have saved him. You're just the opposite. You've got the magic right there on your chest. It's locked in. You're invulnerable, Bozo. You're immortal." His voice dropped. "And there isn't a damn thing you can do about it."

Troy rubbed his chest, frowning, wondering if the two men were just trying to mind-fuck him. But Holcomb just nodded sagely, adding, "Some folks get to know whether their time acomin'. The rest of us, we just keep guessing."

Siddens was right. It was as if there were a force field around Troy. Even the mosquitoes and leeches stayed off him. When he and some other grunts from the platoon spent an R&R polishing their peckers in a Saigon whorehouse, Troy was the only one who didn't need a shot of penicillin afterward.

Troy began leaving his shirt off, or at least unbuttoned, as often as possible, until he realized his tan was obscuring the tattoo, then he covered up again. He began to smile and make jokes. He even volunteered to be point man on patrols. At first the lieutenant let him, but later shit-canned the idea: Troy wasn't cautious enough.

Then, as the summer of '67 dribbled into late autumn, the North

Vietnamese began to get serious about the war. Suddenly the enemy's presence meant more than an occasional sniper, a punji pit, or a land mine in the road. It meant assaulting fortified bunkers in the face of bullets and heavy artillery.

As the whole Second Battalion was swept into the midst of the firefight in the hills surrounding Dak To, Troy huddled in a foxhole, trying to banish the noise of the bombs from his consciousness. A five-hundred-pounder from a U.S. plane had accidentally wasted thirty paratroopers over on Hill 875—"friendly fire"—trying to dislodge the NVA from their hilltop fortifications. A brown, sticky mass stained the crotch of his fatigue pants—it had been there for hours. Hunger gnawed at his stomach—no resupply had been able to reach them for two days. Over and over he repeated the words Siddens had told him: *"Don't worry. You got the magic."*

He so needed to believe.

Dusk was falling. Staff Sgt. Morris passed a hand signal back. The platoon was going to advance.

A cacophony of machine guns and grenades filtered through the vegetation ahead. Somewhere, other elements of the battalion needed help. Troy gripped his rifle tightly as he rose from his foxhole. Crouching, he joined Holcomb and Siddens. They sprinted forward a bit at a time, heading for the base of the next large tree.

Troy was consumed by the urge to shut his eyes and clap his hands to his ears. No sooner had he done so than the ground erupted in front of him. Blinking, ears ringing, he realized only after the fact what he had sensed.

"Incoming!" he shouted.

His yell came too late. The smoking crater was already there. He was covered with specks of heavy, red laterite clay. He whirled to his right. There, still upright, stood the pelvis and legs of Doug Siddens. The medic's upper body lay somewhere in the brush.

Troy spun to his left. Leroy Holcomb was trying to scoop his intestines back into his abdomen with his remaining arm. Troy caught him just as he fell. His buddy let out a sigh and went limp, his blood and life soaking into the ruptured soil. He didn't even have time to utter a last sentence.

Troy cradled Holcomb's head in his lap. Sgt. Morris was yelling—probably something about retreating to the holes—but the words sailed right past. Troy examined his arms, his legs, his torso. Not a single cut. He had been the closest man to the explosion, and all it had done to him was get him dirty.

"Who'd have thought those gooks could whup our asses like this?" muttered Warren Nance, the radio telephone operator.

Troy raised his finger to his lips. The RTO should not have been talking. The jungle was fearsomely still, but that did not guarantee that the enemy had all fled.

The Battle of Dak To had ended suddenly. One moment the NVA were there, blasting with everything they had; the next moment they had melted into the earth, leaving the cleanup to the Americans. At present, Troy and the other survivors were scouring the jungle for the wounded and dead, a gory process that a Special Forces sharpshooter at the base camp had called "Shaking the trees for dog tags" due to the unidentifiability of some of the remains.

After the adrenaline overdose of the past week, the quiet did not seem real to Troy. Coherent thought was impossible. He still touched himself here and there, confirming that no pieces were missing. He felt no victory, no elation, no horror, no fear. All he knew was that he was here. The only emotion he was sure of was relief: What was left of Siddens and Holcomb had been zipped into body bags and shipped off. The KIA Travel Bureau was the wrong way to leave Vietnam, but at least he knew they were no longer rotting on the ground a million miles from home.

Why them? were the words rolling over and over through his mind. *Why them and not me?*

Whenever he considered the question, his hand rose up and scratched the left side of his chest. Sometimes it almost felt as if the unicorn were rearing and stamping its feet. Today the impression was stronger than ever.

They came to a gully containing the body of a dead U.S. soldier lying on his side. Flies crawled from his mouth and danced above the gaping wound in his back. As Nance bent to roll the corpse flat to check the tags, Sgt. Morris grabbed him by the radio and hauled him back two steps. "Hold it!" he hissed.

Morris knelt down, shifted a few leaves next to the front of the dead man, and uncovered a trip wire. "It's booby-trapped."

"Damn," Nance said. "Sure saved my ass, Sarge."

A burst from an AK-47 blistered the foliage around them. Nance jerked and fell.

"Down!" Morris yelled.

The squad hit the ground. Instantly half a dozen men trained their weapons in the direction from which the attack had come and began emptying their clips as fast as they could without melting their gun barrels.

Troy knew the bullets would continue to fly for minutes yet, even longer if the sniper were stupid enough to shoot back rather than play phantom. Meanwhile Nance was lying next to him, choking. A slug had torn through the back of the RTO's mouth.

What do I do? Troy thought. Nance was dying, and they had no medic; Siddens had not yet been replaced.

Troy's tattoo quivered violently. Abruptly the knowledge he needed came to him. He checked in Nance's mouth and confirmed that his upper breathing passage was too damaged to be cleared. Surgeons would have to do that after the medevacs airlifted the wounded man to a field hospital.

Nance's skin was turning blue. Troy pulled out his knife, located the correct notch near his buddy's Adam's apple, and sliced. Holding the gash open with his finger, Troy nodded in satisfaction as air poured directly into Nance's trachea. The RTO's lungs filled.

The panic in Nance's pupils faded to mere terror. Sgt. Morris managed to get to the radio on Nance's back and used it to request a chopper. Troy sighed. His buddy would live.

And then, with brutal suddenness, he understood why he had felt so certain of a medical procedure he had never before attempted. A presence was hovering inside him. He had been aware of the sensation for days, whenever the tattoo stirred, but he had not realized what it was. All he had known was that, from time to time, he felt as though he were looking at the world with different eyes.

The presence was not always the same. There were two entities. The visits had begun the night Siddens and Holcomb had died.

His buddies had not left him, after all.

1972

Specks of red Georgia clay marred the knees of Troy's baseball uniform. He bent down and brushed with his hands, but the dirt clung. With an abruptness just short of frantic, he tried again.

"Chesley!" The booming voice came from the rotund, middle-aged man near the dugout. "Where do you think you are? Vietnam? Pitch the damn ball already!"

"Sorry, Angus," Troy called, straightening up.

Troy had made the mistake a few days back of telling Angus that a lapse of attention had been caused by thinking of the war. Now the old fart accused him of more of the same any chance he could.

Troy shrugged off both the insult and the distraction that had provoked it. The ball was cool and dry in his hand, a tool he knew how to use. He wound up and let fly. The batter, suckered by Troy's body language, swung high and missed. Strike two.

Angus nodded. That was the kind of quality he expected of a prospective pitcher. Troy tipped his cap at the talent scout. Everything under control.

Troy had been thinking of Vietnam, though. Specifically of a buddy named Arturo Rivas with whom he had served during his second tour.

"When I get out of this puto *country, I'm going to do nothing but play baseball," Rivas said, huddling under a tarp. Thanks to the monsoons, the platoon hadn't breathed dry air in four days.*

Troy noted his companion's ropy muscles and gracile hands and, with a friendliness borrowed from Leroy Holcomb, said, "You mean as a pro, don't you?"

Rivas shrugged and smiled. "Why not? My uncle, he played in the minors for five years, and I'm better than him." He winked, full of young man's bluster. Troy could tell he believed what he said.

"I want to see you get there," Troy responded with sincerity.

That was five weeks before Rivas lost three vertebrae and too many internal organs in a nameless village in the Central Highlands. He had been the last one. First Siddens and Holcomb, then Artie Farina, Stewart Hutchison, Dennis Short, and Jimmy Wyckoff. Seven men dead from bullets, mortar rounds, and claymores that could have, should have killed Troy.

Dirt on his pants. He could wash a million times, and never lose the traces of those men.

Troy wound up, reading the batter's desire for another sinker like the last one. Troy laid it in straight and fast. Strike three.

"I want to see you get there." When Troy had made that comment, it had been intended merely as polite encouragement, but it had since gone beyond that. Arturo was with him. He guided Troy's arm through its moves, told him what the batters might be thinking, gave him speed when he ran around the bases. He was the one Angus was impressed with, the one the scout might reward with a contract.

The tattoo itched. *No,* Troy thought. *Not now.* But his wishes were ignored. The mind-set of a pitcher vanished. Arturo had phased out. He was Troy Chesley again—an indifferent athlete with no real knack for baseball.

The new batter was waiting. Troy hesitated, drawing another of Angus's infamous glares. No choice but to pitch and hope for the best. He flung the ball toward the plate.

The gleam in the batter's eye said it all even before he swung. The crack of wood against leather echoed from one side of the stadium to the other. The ball easily cleared the left field fence.

The next few pitches were not much better. The batter let two go by wide and outside, then with a whack claimed a standing double. Luckily the player after that popped out to center field, sparing Troy any more humiliation.

That ended the three-inning minigame. Angus and his assistants reconfigured the players into a brand new Team A and Team B. Troy waited by the dugout for his assignment, but it didn't come. As the other aspiring pros hit the turf or loosened their batting arms, Angus pulled Troy aside.

The scout spat a brown river of tobacco juice onto the ground. "I know you don't want to hear this," he said gruffly. "You've got talent, Chesley, but no consistency. One moment you're hot, the next you're a meathead. Until you can keep yourself in the groove, you might as well forget about this camp. Put in some time on your own, get the kinks out, and maybe I'll see you here next year."

Angus turned back to the diamond. His posture said that as far as he was concerned, Troy no longer existed.

Troy slapped the dust from his mitt and trudged into the locker room. Next year? Next year would be no different. No matter how hard he tried to keep Arturo Rivas at the forefront, sooner or later he, Troy, would reemerge—he or one of the other six.

He was living a total of eight lives. Out there on the diamond, he had been Arturo, as intended. This morning while shaving Artie Farina had surfaced, and he had whistled a tune learned during a boyhood in Brooklyn, three thousand miles from where Troy Chesley had grown up. At least he thought it was Artie. Sometimes there was no way to really know. He simply *was* one guy or another, without any sort of command over the phenomenon, his only clue to the transition consisting of an itch or warmth or tingle in the area of his tattoo.

He opened his locker, took out his kit bag, and began shoving items inside, changing out of his togs as he went. No shower. He wanted out of this place. Already he knew what he would feel the next time Arturo emerged— the shame, the disappointment, the anger. The ambient stink of sweat and antifungal powder attacked Troy's nostrils, making him crave clean air.

"I'm sorry," Troy whispered. "I tried."

How he had tried. This time with baseball, for Arturo. Last year in pre-med courses, aiming for the M.D. that Doug Siddens had wanted. In his biochemistry class he had sailed through the midterm, propelled by the mental faculties of a man determined to learn whatever was required to become a doctor. On the final, the unicorn remained as flat and dull as plain ink, and as mere Troy Chesley he scored a dismal thirty-two percent, killing his chance of a passing grade.

As he peeled away his shirt, the tattoo was framed in the small mirror he had mounted on the inside of his locker door. He touched it, as ever feeling as though, no matter how much it was under his skin, it wasn't truly part of him.

A good luck charm? Oh, he'd survived all right. Through the war without a scratch. He had all the life and youth he could ever have imagined. Seven extra doses. But as usual, the rearing shape gave him no clue what he was supposed to do with so much abundance.

1975

Troy's dented Pontiac Bonneville carried him out of New Orleans, across the Pontchartrain Causeway, through the counties of St. Tammany and Washington, and over the boundary into southern Mississippi. As he drove along country roads beside trees draped with Spanish moss and parasitic masses of kudzu, the sense of familiarity grew ever more intense, though he had never been to this part of the South.

He unerringly selected the correct turns, having no need to consult his map. His destination appeared through the windshield. Hardly a town at all, it was one of those impoverished, former whistlestop communities destined to vanish into the woods as more and more of its young men and women migrated to the cities with each generation. By all rights he should never have recalled the place name; it had been mentioned in his presence no more than twice, all those years ago.

There were two cemeteries, the first dotted with old family mausoleums and elaborate tombstones—a forest of marble. He went straight to the second, a modest but carefully maintained site overlooking a river. The caretaker stared at him as if he had never seen a white man on the grounds before, but he was polite as he directed Troy to the graves belonging to the Holcomb family.

Leroy's resting place was easy to find. Eight years of weather had not been enough to mute the engraving of the granite marker. A few wilted flowers lay in the cup. He lifted them to his nose, catching vestiges of aroma. Not yet a week old. After eight years, someone still remembered this particular dead man. That brought a tightness to his throat.

He had a fresh bouquet with him, but he placed it at the head of a nearby grave marked Lionel Holcomb, 1919-1962.

"Rest in peace, Daddy," he whispered.

A woodpecker hammered in the oak tree on the river side of the graveyard. The air thrummed with an invisible chorus of insects that could never survive in the San Francisco Bay Area, where Troy had been raised. Seldom had he felt anything so real as the smell of the grass at his feet or the humidity sucking at his pores.

He turned and walked determinedly back to his car and drove into town. A block past the Baptist church, he pulled up at a house. The clapboard was peeling, but the lawn was mowed and the roof had been recently patched, showing that while no rich folk lived here, the occupants cared about the property.

Troy stepped up onto the porch. The urge to rush inside was next to overwhelming, but he stifled it. The body he inhabited was the wrong color, the wrong size. No matter what, part of him was always Troy Chesley, even when he didn't want it to be so. He knocked politely.

A stout black woman in a flower-print dress opened the inner door and stared at him through the screen mesh, her eyes widening at his stranger's face.

Mama! I love you, Mama! Troy forced down the words in his mind and uttered the pale substitutions circumstances allowed. "Mrs. Holcomb?"

"That's me," she said.

I missed you, Mama. "My name is Troy Chesley. I served with your son Leroy in the war."

The woman lifted her bifocals out of the way and wiped her eyes. "Leroy," she said huskily. "He was my firstborn, you know. Hard on an old widow to lose a son like that. What can I do for you, child?"

"I have a few questions, Ma'am. I was wondering . . . what kind of plans Leroy had? What he wanted to do with his life? What do you think he'd be doing right now, if he'd come back from over there?"

She shook her graying head firmly. "Now what you want to go asking me those kinds of things for? All that will just remind me he ain't here. The war is over, Mr. Chesley. Go on about your business and don't bother me no mo'." She shut the door.

"But—" Troy raised his hand to protest, but blank wood confronted him. *You don't understand, Mama. Troy's got all my chances.*

"I've got everybody's chances," he murmured as he turned, shoulders drooping, and stumbled back to his Pontiac.

1978

The bathroom mirror showed Troy a twenty-one-year-old self. No traces of the beer belly or the receding hairline his younger brother was developing. No need for the corrective lenses his sister had required when she reached twenty-five. His greet-the-day erection stood stiff as a recruit being screamed at by a drill sergeant: a kid's boner, there even when all he wanted to do was take a piss.

He was aging eight times slower than normal. He was thirty now, a point when other two-tour vets often looked forty-five. At least he *was* aging. That proved he wasn't literally immortal. Just as he wasn't totally invulnerable, or the razor wouldn't have nicked him the day before. He didn't think he could bear it if the tattoo didn't have *some* limits.

He showered, dried, and drifted into the living room/kitchenette wearing only a pair of briefs—the summer sun was already high, and the apartment had no air-conditioning. Slicing an apple and eating it a sliver at a time filled the next three minutes. The clock above the stove ticked: the heartbeat of the room.

So many years to live.

Troy pulled open the file cabinet in the corner of the room that served as his home office and ran his fingers across a series of manila folders marked with names. He pulled out one at random.

It turned out to be that of Warren Nance, the RTO whose life he had saved with the emergency tracheotomy. That is to say, the one Doug Siddens had saved using Troy's hands. Clippings dropped out onto the floor, covering the threadbare spots his landlord described as "a little wear and tear." He sat down cross-legged and glanced at them as he put them back in the folder.

Warren was a realtor these days. The first clipping was a Yellow Pages ad for his business, describing it as the largest in the Texas panhandle. A pamphlet of houses for sale listed Warren's name as agent more than two dozen times. The third item, a newspaper clipping, praised him for a large donation to help people with speech impediments.

A dozen files in Troy's cabinet told similar tales. Sgt. Morris was now an assistant county superintendent of schools. Crazy Vic Naughton, now clean-cut and much heftier than he had been in Vietnam, was a sports commentator for a television station.

The one thing the files did not contain was direct correspondence, save for a Christmas card or two. Troy had seldom attempted to contact old buddies; he had abandoned the effort altogether after the incident with Leroy Holcomb's mother. As happened throughout the veteran community, the connections he had established in Vietnam disintegrated within the milieu of the World, no matter how intense those ties had been in the jungle.

It worked both ways. Troy had received scores of letters during late '69 and early '70. All from guys still In Country. He barely heard from those men once they arrived stateside. As the saying in 'Nam went: "There it is." And there it was. Soldiers sitting in the elephant grass watching the gunships rumble by overhead needed to hold in their hands replies from someone who made it back, just to have written proof that it was *possible* to make it back. Once they came home themselves, they didn't want to be reminded of the war. Now, with North Vietnam the victor, the silence was even more entrenched. Troy saw no reason to disrupt the quiet, and many reasons not to.

But still he kept the files. The other drawer contained only seven, but they were inches thick, filled with all the information he could collect on Leroy, on Doug, on Arturo and the others who had died beside him. This morning that drawer remained locked. He was thinking about the men who had lived. The other survivors.

They were making something of themselves.

Here he sat. He didn't even have a savings account. He was employed as a short order cook at Denny's, a job he had had for two months and one he would probably quit before another two months had gone by. Where his buddies had found focus, he had found dissipation, his efforts spread too thin in too many directions.

Too many chances. Those other men knew the Grim Reaper would catch them sooner rather than later, so they got down to business before their youth and energy raced away. Troy was missing that urgency.

On the other side of the wall he heard the reverberation of feet landing on the floor beside the bed and padding into the bathroom. The toilet flushed. The shower nozzle spat fitfully into life, and a soprano voice rose in song above the din of the spray and the groan of the plumbing: "Carry On Wayward Son" by Kansas.

A hint of a smile played at the edges of Troy's lips. Troy let the folder in his hands close. He cleared the floor, stowed the materials in the file cabinet, and locked the drawer. Before sitting back down, he lowered his briefs and tossed them on the couch.

Maybe he could make some sort of progress after all.

Hardly had the thought coalesced in his mind than his chest began to itch. He scratched reflexively, fingernails tracing the outline of the unicorn. No. He would not let anyone surface. This was his moment. With a firm act of will, he drew his hand away, brought his attention back to the sound of faucets being shut off in the bathroom. The doorway to the bedroom seemed to grow larger and larger until his girlfriend emerged wrapping a towel around her glossy brunette mane, her bare skin rosy from the effect of the hot water.

Scanning his naked body with an appreciative eye, she migrated forward with the boldness that had originally lured him into their relationship. He clasped her wrists, easing her down beside him and patiently thwarting her attempts to fondle him.

"Lydia, do you love me?"

She tilted her head, humming. "I will if you let go of my hands."

"I'm serious."

She blanched as the gravity of his tone sank in. "I . . . oh . . ." She hiccupped.

"I take it that's a yes?" he said as he released her wrists.

Head turning aside, arms hugging herself, and cheeks ablaze with uncharacteristic shyness, she nodded. "You weren't supposed to know, you fucker." He realized the drops on her face were not drips from her wet hair. "Not until you said it first."

"Will you marry me?" he asked.

Her nose crinkled, as if she were going to laugh or sneeze. She lay back on the ratty carpet and spread her legs. "You sure I can't distract you enough to make you forget you said that?"

"Not a chance," he said firmly. "Does that mean you're turning me down?"

"I'm . . . stalling." Her features hardened. "I don't want you to say one thing today, and another tomorrow, Troy. If you mean to follow through, then of course I'll marry you."

The puff of his pent-up breath almost made the walls shake. Shifting forward, he accepted her body's invitation.

1983

"You can't be doing this," Lydia said, yanking at the tag on his garment bag.

"Don't. You'll rip it." As he snapped his briefcase closed, she let go of the tag, spun, and marched to the window of their apartment. The Minneapolis/St. Paul skyline stretched flat beyond her—the nearest mountain a billion miles over the horizon. They had moved here when she landed the hospital job, but after almost two years he still couldn't get used to the landscape. He wanted geographical features that could daunt the wind, and most especially slow the approach of the summer thunderstorms whose booms reminded him too much of artillery.

"Darling, we discussed this," he said. "I'll be back by suppertime tomorrow. It's a little late to change plans."

"You didn't even ask what I thought of the idea. You didn't even think about the budget when you bought the plane ticket." Lydia tugged the curtain to the side and frowned. "The taxi's here." She turned back, meeting him eye to eye, freezing him in place instead of tendering silent permission to pick up his luggage. "What is so important that you have to spend money we don't have?"

"We have the money."

"Barely. There are other things we could have done with that cash."

He sighed and, denying her spell, carried his things to the front door. "This is something I need to do. You act like I'm way out of line."

"You're going all this way for a guy you knew for a few months? Doesn't that strike you as a little obsessive?" She patted her abdomen, highlighting the prominent evidence of pregnancy. "Don't you think you have bigger priorities at home right now? Christ, Troy, I feel like I'm living with a stranger sometimes. I don't know you right now. You're someone else."

Troy turned away before she could see his reaction. Her glare drilled a hole through the back of his head as he walked out the doorway, and the wound remained open throughout the ride to the airport, the takeoff, and the climb to cruising altitude. How he wanted to tell her: about the unicorn, about the seven lives he lived besides his own. Everything.

Even Stu wanted to tell her. That's who had emerged earlier in the week. Stewart Hutchison, his squad leader after Sgt. Morris had rotated to the safety of rear echelon duty. Stu understood Troy's needs the way Troy understood his.

He lowered the lunch tray and tried to write his explanation out in a note. He began by admitting that he had lied: This trip was not for a funeral. But when it came to speaking of all he had been holding in throughout their relationship, he kept crossing out the sentences, finally giving up when he noticed the woman seated next to him glancing at the paper.

He wasn't the person he needed to be in order to write it. Much as Stu tried to cooperate, the words had to be Troy's and Troy's alone.

After a troubled night in a motel room, he reached his exact destination: the stadium bleachers at Colorado State University, Fort Collins. He was among the throng gathered for the graduation of the class of '83. Patiently he waited as the university president announced the names, until he called that of Marti Hutchison, highest honors, Dean's List.

Stu had *had* to emerge this week. This was an event the man would certainly have attended had he not been killed in the Tet Offensive. Marti Hutchison had been a toddler when Stu enlisted, an action he had taken partly in order to support his young family. That day at the recruitment office the war had been only a spark no one believed would flare into an inferno. He had never expected to be removed so far from his child; that was not his concept of the right way to do things. A man needed to Be There, as he had said when he learned he had knocked up his high school girlfriend and heard her suggest giving the baby up for adoption.

He was Being Here today. Troy kept his binoculars pointed at the freckled face until she reached the base of the podium and vanished into the sea of caps and gowns. The eyepieces were wet with tears as he lowered the glasses, and it felt like somebody was pushing at his rib cage from the inside. The sensation recalled an occasion when he had sat in a bunker all night, so scared of the incoming ordnance that his heart tried to leap out and hide under the floor slats with the snakes. Or was that something Stu had experienced?

It wasn't fear he was feeling now, though. It was pride. He let the emotion cascade through him, yielding fully, allowing his buddy to savor every particle of the joy.

A memory came to Troy hard and potent, one of those that he and Stu shared directly: *Stu was sitting next to him in the shade of a troop carrier, speaking fondly of his wife, who was due to rendezvous with him in the Philippines during a long R&R the sergeant had coming up.*

"Gonna try for a boy." He grinned. "On purpose, this time."

Troy shut his eyes tight, reliving the moment when the claymore wasted his buddy, ten days before that R&R came due. No boy. Perhaps Troy and Lydia's child could make up for that, though that was not something he could control. At least he had this much. He caught a glimpse of Marti over the heads of several female classmates—she was almost as tall as her father had been. Again came the heat to his eyes and the tightness to his throat.

"Do you feel it, Stu?" His murmurs were drowned by the din of the names continuing to boom from the loudspeakers, though to his right a grandmother in a hat and veil glanced at his moving lips with puzzlement. "It's for you, buddy. You gotta be in here, feeling this."

Stu felt it, indulged in it, and as a sharp throb hit Troy on the left half of his chest, the dead man slipped back into limbo.

A peace came over Troy, a faith that he had done what he was supposed to. Because of him, seven men had their own taste of immortality.

Lydia would tan his hide if he went on more trips soon. But there was so much more to do. He still had never been to the California/Oregon border, where Doug Siddens was from, nor to Artie Farina's old digs in Brooklyn, nor to . . .

Surely there was some way to balance it all.

1989

"Do you ever really feel anything for us?" Lydia asked.

The abrupt comment made Troy jump. He had been gazing at the clouds out of the windows of their rental suburban tract home, lost to the moment. He always seemed to be lost to the moment.

Outside, his daughter Kirsten, resplendent in ruffled skirts and pig-tails for her final day of kindergarten, swung vigorously to and fro, fingers laced tightly around the chains, calling to him to watch her Go-So-High as he had promised to do when she headed for the backyard. Had that been thirty seconds ago, or several minutes?

"What do you mean?" He cleared his throat. "Of course I do."

"Do you?" Lydia hid her expression by stepping to the stove to remove the boiling teakettle from the burner. "That's good." She said it deadpan, which was worse than overt sarcasm, because it implied a measure of faith still at risk upon the chopping block.

"What makes you ask such a question?" He wanted to let the subject drop, but somewhere he found the courage to listen to the answer.

"You let yourself trickle out in a million directions," Lydia said, reaching into a cabinet for the box of Mountain Thunder. She put two bags in her mug and poured the water. "But it's not because you don't know what discipline is. You make trips, you subscribe to all sorts of small newspapers, you make scrapbooks. You even hired a private detective that time—all to find out more about some guys in your past. If that isn't ambition, I don't know what is. But you don't apply yourself to what you've got right here."

Lydia's jaw trembled. "It's like you're not even you, half the time. You're a bunch of different people, and none of them are grown-up. When you're in one of those moods, it's like Kirsten and I don't count. Are we just background to you?"

"I love you both," he said. "I'm just . . . not good at remembering to say so."

Lydia turned away, sipped her tea, and spat the liquid into the sink because it was far too hot. Testily, she waved toward the backyard. "Go push your child. You only have half an hour before you're supposed to go to that job interview."

"Oh. The appointment," he said. "Almost forgot."

"I know."

1991

As Operation Desert Storm progressed and U.S. ground troops poised on the border of Kuwait, Troy grew painfully aware of the frowns of the senior citizens at the park where he walked on afternoons when the temp agency failed to find work for him. Those conservative old men were undoubtedly wondering why someone as young as he wasn't over there kicking Saddam Hussein's ass, showing the world that America hadn't forgotten how to win a war. There was no way to explain the truth to them.

Just as there was no way to tell Lydia, not after all this time.

The day the Scud missile went cruising into a Jerusalem apartment building, Lydia emerged from the bathroom holding an empty tube of hair darkener, the brand Reagan had used during his administration. "Do you want me to get the larger size when I go to the store?"

"What do you mean? You're the only one who uses that stuff," he replied.

She blinked. "Me? I'm not the one going gray."

Troy swallowed his answer. No use confronting her. Four years younger than he, she was having a hard enough time dealing with her entry into middle age. She smeared on wrinkle cream every morning. She examined her body in the mirror each night after she undressed, bought new bras with greater support features, wore a one-piece bathing suit instead of a bikini so that the stretch marks below her navel would not show.

"Hey," he said consolingly, "it's all right, you know. It doesn't matter to me how you look."

Slowly she held up the tube to his face, her expression a fluctuating mix of anger and pity. "Troy, Troy, Troy—*this isn't even my hair color.* When are you going to stop playing these games?"

She had said it once too often. "It's not a game, Lydia." He choked back, not daring to say more. He regretted saying that much, but he couldn't let something so important be denigrated that way.

She tossed the empty tube across the room toward the general vicinity of the wastebasket. "Troy, you're forty-four years old. No matter how well you maintain your looks, let's face it—you're getting old. I don't like it any better than you do, but there it is. I've put up with a lot of weird shit from you in thirteen years, but this little fantasy of yours has gone far enough. I think it's time you saw a therapist."

Troy just looked at her in stony silence. The unicorn reared and snorted, though if it heralded the arrival of one of the guys, the latter held back, letting Troy keep command.

"No?" Lydia asked. "All right then, try this: You move out. I've done what I can. You get help, you make some changes, then maybe you can come back." She whirled and stalked out of the room the way she had come.

Troy hung his head. He did not go to the bathroom door, did not try to get her to change her mind, though he knew that was what she was hoping for. She would give him a dozen more chances, if only he would promise to change. But how could he do that? The facts were the facts.

He dragged himself into the bedroom and began to pack a suitcase—just a few things, so that he could get out of the house. He would arrange to come back for other possessions when Lydia would not be home.

He did not want to leave. This was yet another casualty in his life, and he was tired of making up for a choice he had made when he was nineteen. When would he be through paying the price?

1995

July the fifteenth arrived in a blaze of heat and humidity that recalled the jungle. It was Saturday, one of the special days. He pulled up to the curb outside what had once been his home and honked the horn. Kirsten, a lean and spry eleven-year-old, bounded out to his car with a grin on her face.

She still idolized him. He gazed at her wistfully as she buckled her seat belt: flat-chested, a bit under five feet tall, not yet one of those adolescents who had no time for parents. She would remain his girl-child for another year or so.

Troy thought of all those times he had failed to be a good father. He used to fall asleep trying to read her books at bedtime. He would forget to pick her up after school. She always forgave him.

"Mom says I need to be back by ten," she reported.

"Good," Troy replied, drawing heavy, damp air into his lungs, letting the dose of oxygen lift his spirits. The deadline was later than ever; it was, in fact, Kirsten's weekend bedtime. "Is your mother feeling generous, or what?"

"I made a bet with her." Kirsten giggled. "She said you'd be late. I said you'd show up on time. She promised that if you did, I could stay out until ten."

He chuckled. Kirsten had, as usual, asked him to be on time when they had spoken over the phone on Friday, but he had to admit, most times he managed to be late no matter what.

They went to the lake for swimming and boating, then returned to town to pig out on pizza and Diet Coke.

"Mom always gets vegetables on pizza," Kirsten said with a scowl. She beamed as he ordered pepperoni, sausage, and Canadian bacon. One of the few good things about being a divorced father was that he didn't have to bother with the hard stuff like enforcing rules, helping with homework, taking her to the dentist. He got to be the pal.

They finished their evening at the bowling lanes, where Kirsten managed not to gutter a single ball, beating him two times out of three. She danced a little jig as she landed a strike in the final frame.

He hugged her, noting with regret that it was 9:30 P.M. "Come on, Shortstuff. Let's get you home."

"I had a great time with you, Daddy."

Yes, Troy thought. It had been a good day. He felt like a real father. A competent, mature person, seeing to his offspring's needs. He had hope there would be more days like it. Leroy and Doug and the others emerged less and less as the years went on. What was the point of living in his body when they couldn't truly follow their paths? Troy actually found himself looking forward to the next decade or two, to seeing what sort of adult Kirsten would evolve into.

Chatting with his girl, he drove along the familiar streets toward Lydia's house, through intersections and around curves that were second nature to him. Three blocks from their destination, he stopped at a signal, waited for the green light, and when it came, pressed on the gas pedal to make a left-hand turn.

Headlights blazed in through the right-hand windows of the car, appearing as if out of nowhere. An engine whined, the noise changing pitch as the driver of the vehicle attempted to make it through a light that had already changed to red. Kirsten screamed. As fast as humanly possible, Troy shifted his foot from accelerator to brake. He had barely pressed down when metal slammed into metal.

Troy's car, hit broadside on the passenger side, careened across the asphalt, tires squealing, the other car clinging to it as if welded. Finally the motion stopped. Troy, hands frozen on the steering wheel, body still pressed against his door, looked sharply to his right and wished he hadn't.

Onlookers had to pull him away from his seat to keep him from uselessly trying to stanch Kirsten's bleeding. Numb, he finally let them drag him to the sidewalk. Nearby lay the dazed, yet intact, driver of the other car. The reek of alcohol rose from him like fumes from a refinery.

Troy had a bruise on his left shoulder and had sprained a wrist. That was all.

The way Troy saw it a day later, Kirsten had been a natural target. What better life essence to steal than that of the very young? The unicorn had probably had it in for her from the moment she was born.

He should never have called the tattooist a gook. The man had cursed him. For so many years, he had seen the unicorn at least partly as a blessing, when in fact the tattoo must have instigated all those deaths around him.

Causality. Everything happens for a reason.

The warnings had been there yesterday, but he had been blind to them. First there had been his uncharacteristic promptness. Then, Kirsten's smile in the bowling alley had reminded him all too much of Artie Farina grinning over a joke right at the moment the bullet struck him. Troy should never have kept his baby out late, should have taken her home in the daylight, before the drunk was on the road.

It was his fault. If not for the curse, reality would have taken a different path. The drunk would have come from the opposite direction, would have smashed into the driver's side of the car. Troy would have died, and his daughter would have lived.

It had been his fault in Vietnam as well. If he had taken the death assigned to him then, maybe all of his buddies would have lived.

He would not accept the devil's reward this time. He would not continue on, wandering through the decades, living glimpses of Kirsten's life, the one she would never live directly.

Blood seeped from the edges of the bandage on his chest. He pressed the gauze down, added another strip of tape from his shoulder to his rib cage. Pain radiated in pulses all the way down to his toes, but he paid it no more heed than he had when the stitcher's needle gun had impregnated him with ink back at G.I. Bob's.

He had been afraid, when he picked up the knife, that his skin could not be cut, that the invulnerability would apply. But it was done now, and the tears of relief dribbled down the sides of his face. Soon he would pick up the phone—to call Lydia, or contact the hospital directly. The docs could patch him up whatever way they wanted, recommend plastic surgery or let the scars form. All that mattered was that the tattoo was gone.

He had done the right thing, he told himself, wincing. He knew he could have scheduled laser surgery, could have gone to one of those parlors advertising tattoo removal. But it needed to happen before anything came along to change his mind. Now that he had found the courage, even one minute's delay would have been too much.

And it was working. He leaned toward his bathroom mirror, his reflection sharpening as he came within range of his nearsighted vision. There—little crow's feet radiated from the corners of his eyes. Gray roots showed like tiny maggots at the base of his hair. His joints ached, and his midriff complained of all the years held unnaturally taut and firm. He was back in the time line, looking as if he had never left it. Tomorrow's dawn would mark the first time in twenty-eight years that he would wake up as Troy Chesley and no one else.

His breath caught. Over the bandage, he faintly detected a glow. It coalesced into a horselike shape with a spike protruding from its head. It hung there, letting him get a good look, then it sank into his body. As it did so, his spine straightened, his hair thickened, and an unholy vibrancy coursed through his bloodstream.

His newfound sense of victory drained away. The ordeal had not ended. Some part of him was still willing to do anything to have a suit of impenetrable armor. The marks upon him had long since gone beyond skin deep.

A tattoo was forever.

"No," he whispered. His hand flailed across the countertop until his fingers closed on the knife. "I won't let this go on." If cutting off the unicorn was not enough to destroy its power, there was another way, and he would take it. He raised the knife to his throat. . . .

The weapon clattered to the floor. Troy stared at his image in the mirror. It had changed again. Though it was his same—youthful—face, his aspect now radiated an impression of intimidating, heroic size, as if he were looking at himself from the perspective of someone smaller and dependent.

"My God," he moaned.

The glow over his wound had done more than restore his immortality; it had brought an entity to the forefront. Troy reached toward the floor, willing his knees to bend, but they would not. The person possessing him would not allow a knife to point at the flesh of the man she had adored her whole brief life.

Leroy and Doug and Arturo and the others might have permitted him to consign them to oblivion. But this new one did not understand. She was frightened of death. Whatever shred of existence remained to her, she wanted to keep.

How could he deny her?

Troy stumbled into the second bedroom, lay down, and tucked up his knees. Overhead hung posters of cartoon characters. The coverlet was pink and trimmed with ruffles. He pulled Brown Bear off the pillow and hugged him close, beginning to cry as only an eleven-year-old, afraid of darkness and abandonment, could do.

ABOUT THE AUTHOR

Dave Smeds lives in Santa Rosa, California, with his wife Connie and children, Lerina and Elliott. He is the author of two books, the fantasy novel *The Sorcery Within* and its sequel *The Schemes of Dragons*. His science fiction and fantasy works have appeared in such anthologies as *In The Field of Fire*, *Full Spectrum 4*, *David Copperfield's Tales of the Impossible*, *Return to Avalon*, *Magicks: Sorceries Old and New*, *Dragons of Light*, *Sword and Sorceress IV, V, VIII, IX, and XI*, *Warriors of Blood and Dream*, *Deals with the Devil*, and *Future Earths: Under African Skies*; and in such magazines as *Asimov's Science Fiction*, *The Magazine of Fantasy & Science Fiction*, *Realms of Fantasy*, *Ghosttide*, *Inside Karate*, and *Pulphouse*.

He has also contributed two titles to Faeron Education's series of booklets for remedial reading classes. His erotic works for such magazines as *Penthouse Forum, Hot Talk,* and *Club International* led to a Henry Miller Award in 1992.

His work, called "stylistically innovative, symbolically daring examples of craftsmanship at the highest level" by the *New York Times Book Review*, has seen print in Great Britain, Germany, France, the Netherlands, Italy, Finland, and Poland.

Before turning to writing, Dave made his living as a graphic artist and typesetter. He holds a third degree black belt in Goju-ryu karate and teaches classes in that art.

S. P. SOMTOW

A THIEF IN THE NIGHT

Peter: **S(omtow). P(apinian). Sucharitkul** is plainly a one-man show and a three-ring circus at the same time. His career as a composer and musician includes symphonic and operatic works, and conducting positions with the Holland and Cambridge Symphony Orchestras, the Bangkok Chamber Orchestra, and the Temple of Dawn Consort. He has published twenty-five novels. In his third life, he is a screenwriter and film director. I freely confess that I envy him his energy, his diversity, and the talent—not to speak of the moxie—that went into the extraordinary story he sent us.

Janet: I first stumbled across Somtow—a relative of the Royal House of Thailand—in the lobby of a hotel in Phoenix. It was around 120 degrees outside, and he was taking shelter at the keys of a grand piano, playing oldies but goodies, interspersed, if I recall it correctly, by jazzed-up bits of Liszt, Chopin, and Bach. I sat down next to him on the piano stool and started making requests. He spoke to me in a variety of languages as he played. Apologizing for what he called his lack of skill as a pianist, he addressed me in German, French, Dutch, Afrikaans, and was delighted when I answered him in kind. That was a lot of years ago. We still challenge each other by the language switches, we still talk of my joining him during one of his commuter trips to Thailand and showing him South Africa on the way back to the U.S. Beyond all of that, I consider Somtow to be one of the best contemporary writers around. Perhaps because of his classical education (Eton College and Cambridge), even the most thematically bizarre of his literary departures has a traditional beginning, middle, and end, and is highly readable. You'll see. You'll see. . . .

A Thief in the Night

⁓ⱮꙨⰟⰓ⁓

I

T'S TOUGH TO BE THE ANTICHRIST. NOBODY
ever feels for the villain.

Without the eternal dark, they can never shine, those messiahs with
their gentle smiles and their compassionate eyes and their profound and
stirring messages.

Without me, they have no purpose.

And I'm older than they are; I'm the thing that was before the billion-
stranded web of falsehoods that they call the cosmos was even a flicker in
some god's imagining . . . some *dark* god's.

In a house by the sea in Venice Beach, California, I wait for the second coming. Not really the second, of course; there have been many more
than one. But the millennium is drawing near, and one tends to make use
of the tropes of the culture one has immersed oneself in; ergo: in a house,
a white house, by the sea, a placid but polluted sea, I wait, by a sliding
glass door that opens to a redwood deck with shiny steps that lead down
to the beach, for the second coming.

A unicorn led me here.

I can tell that the unicorn is very near. I can't see him directly, of
course; I don't have the kind of stultifying purity that allows that. But
we've achieved a kind of symbiosis over the eons. He works for me.
What he does for me is very obvious, and very concrete. He leads me to
purity so that I can destroy it.

What *he* gets out of this I do not know.

Today, a summer day, a cloudless sky, an endless parade of
Rollerbladers down the concrete strip that runs beneath my window, I
feel him more than ever. When they breathe, there's a kind of tingling in
the air. Sometimes you see the air waver, as in a heat-haze. Today the

shimmering hangs beside the refrigerator as I pour myself a shot of cheap chardonnay.

"Where is he?" I ask the air.

I hear him pawing the carpet. I turn in his direction. But already, he's just beyond my peripheral vision. I don't know how he manages it. One day I'll be too quick for him. But it hasn't happened in three billion years.

I hear him again. To my right. I slide the doors open. I squat against the redwood railings. I look to my right.

Against the slender trunk of a palm tree, the sharp shadow of a horn. Only a moment, but it is disquieting. A shadow is all I can normally see, or sometimes a hoofprint in the sand, or sometimes a piercing aroma that is neither horse nor man. The one who is purity personified is very close. Like an arrow on the freeway, the horn's shadow points me home.

He is a youth with long blond hair. He is Rollerblading up and down the pathway. He wears only cutoffs and shades. I've seen many messiahs. This one does not seem that promising.

Sex is usually their downfall. I think that's how it's going to be this time. I go to my closet and pick out what I'm going to wear. I'm going to be as much like him as I can. His type. I select a skimpy halter top, and as I slip into it my breasts start morphing to strain against the cotton; I squeeze myself into Spandex leggings, strategically ripped; in the back of the closet, which after all does stretch all the way to the beginning of time, I find a pair of Rollerblades.

In the mirror, I am beautiful. Too beautiful to be true. I am California herself. The sandy beaches are in my hair. The redwoods are my supple arms and torso. My breasts are the mountain lakes and in my eyes is a hint of the snow on the summits of the Sierras. My scent is the sea, the forest, and the sage. I am ready to go to the new messiah and fuck him into oblivion.

Outside: I follow the hoofprints which linger but a moment before dissolving in the fabric of reality. I glide along concrete. The wind gathers my hair into a golden sail. I pass him. I don't think he recognizes me. His eyes are childlike, curious, wide. I whip around a palm tree, cross paths with him again; he looks longer, wondering if he's ever met before, perhaps; then, a three-sixty around the public toilets, a quick whiff of old piss and semen, passing him for the third time, calling out to him with my mind, stop, stop, stop, at the palm tree, tottering, slipping, slamming down hard against the pavement, have to make it look good now, me, the mother of all illusion.

I look up. Shade my eyes. The shadow of the unicorn crosses his face. You can tell; the sun is blazing, there's no shade, but his countenance darkens and then, moving up and down his face, the telltale stripe that shows the unicorn is standing between us somewhere, bobbing his head up and down, pawing at the sand perhaps, for there's a flurry of yellow dust about his heels.

Oh, he is beautiful.

Now, sensing something wrong, he shimmies across the concrete, smooth as the wind.

Bends over me. I groan.

"Are you hurt?"

"Only a scratch."

I look up with what I know to be a dazzling smile, one that has toppled empires. It is not a glad smile; it's a smile that knows all the sadness of the world. But he counters my smile with a smile of his own, a smile like sunlight, a smile like the sea. Takes off his shades, lets them dangle around his neck on a gold chain.

"Let me heal you," he says softly.

"Nothing can heal me," I say.

"It's a gift," he says.

He touches me where it hurts. I have made sure to be hurt only in the most strategic places; where he touches, I murmur arousal. He only smiles again. His hand wavers over my breast, just scabbing over, and the wound closes in on itself.

"How did you do that?" I ask him.

"It can only be temporary," he says. I know now that he must be the one I'm seeking. He has the long view. He really knows that the cosmos will crumble to nothing one day, and it grieves him. He has compassion.

I moan again. "What's your name?" I say.

"I don't know," he says, "I just live here."

"On the beach?"

"Mostly. Don't remember how I got here."

"You just popped into existence?"

"No, I do remember some things. Parents kind of a blur I guess. Social worker talked to me once, took me to McDonald's. I ordered a bag of fries. Everyone had some. It was cool how long those fries lasted, you coulda sworn there was five thousand people in that restaurant. Okay so the social worker, she's totally trying to dig some kind of trauma out of me, you know, drugs, molested by daddy, whatever, but she made me remember a couple of things."

"Like?"

"Dunno like, pieces of a jigsaw. Can't see the whole picture. There's a dove over my head. Keep thinking it's going to shit. That's good luck, isn't it? My mother . . . I only remember her a little. Kissing me good-bye at the bus station. I don't know who my dad is."

"Do you sometimes think he came down from above?"

"Oh, like an alien? Sure. But that don't make sense either, bad genetics. I ain't so dumb."

"I feel a lot better." The air is chill; it's the unicorn breathing down our necks. He's impatient, maybe. He doesn't like to work for me that much. He is a slave, in a way. His shadow crosses the boy's face.

How old? I still can't tell. So blond, you don't know if there's hair in his pits. "Old enough," he says, "if that's what you're thinking."

I'm thinking: what are you telling me, you stupid beast? After all these eons, you're coming down with Alzheimer's? This is the purest heart in the world, and he's staring at me with knowing eyes, and his smile turns into an earthy grin and I don't think he's any stranger to sexuality? I remember the one that got away, two thousand years ago. Now there was purity. Is this the best you can do? I cry to the unicorn in my mind; but though he hears me, he seldom answers.

But I might as well see this through. The Antichrist can leave no stone unturned.

"You've made me feel, I don't know, so *healed*," I tell him. "All warm and tingly." I'm not even lying. "Is there something I can do for you?"

"Is that your condo over there?"

"Yeah."

"Maybe Coke?"

"I'm all out. I might have enough for a couple lines."

"You're so funny. I mean Coke as in pop."

A smidgen of purity at least. I laugh. "Come on over," I say. There are possibilities in this after all.

So we're standing in the room by the glass door that leads to the deck with the stairway down to the sand and he has his soda in his hand and then, always smiling, he sort of drifts over to where I'm standing, almost as if he still has his Rollerblades on, that's how he moves. He kisses me; his lips are very sweet as if they've been brushed with cherry lip gloss; his kiss draws pain from me, each nugget of pain almost more painful to pluck out than it was when it lay festering inside me. I feel myself respond. It's a strange thing. I don't feel passion over what I do, but now, oddly, I'm vibrating like a tuning fork, and he hasn't even taken off his clothes, although I have, of course, temptress that I am, and yeah, there's a dick down there somewhere straining against those frayed cut-offs. But what's happening to me? Aren't I supposed to be sucking his purity out of him? Aren't I the vampire darkness that ensorcels, poisons, and consumes? I bite into sweat and sand. He laughs. It's like hugging a tree. I yank down on the denim, no underwear, pull him into the jungle chaos that seethes inside, and his eyes are closed and I think yes, yes,

yes, you see now, I am killing the god-child in you, killing the future, closing the circle of the world, shoving the serpent's tail into his jaws. Oh, I cry out in an ecstasy of conquest. I exult. One more that didn't get away. It's child's play, I tell myself, as I let him empty himself into me. I feel a fire down there. I've never felt that before. It's never been so good to destroy.

But then he opens his eyes and I know something has gone wrong. Because he doesn't seem to have lost his purity at all. What I see is not the dullness of a flame extinguished. I see compassion. We're still standing there, flesh to flesh. Perhaps the flame that raged through me was not victory. Perhaps I was not detached enough. Perhaps he has actually caused me to have an orgasm. I am not sure. My thighs are throbbing.

Gently he leads me to the futon. It's black, naturally, L.A.'s most fashionable color. The pine frame is glazed black, too. He sits me down. And he says, very softly, "Sex is a beautiful thing, you know. Sometimes, when I'm with a stranger, I feel I'm giving away all of myself, and yet there always seems to be more to give."

I stare at him dumbly. Have men evolved that much, then? Have I given them too much freedom of thought? It has only been the blink of an eye since St. Augustine equated original sin with filthy sexuality. In his purity, this boy is completely innocent of such an idea. To me, what has transpired has been a wanton reveling in flesh and fluids; to him, I realize in astonishment, it has been an act of love, even though it was consummated with a stranger.

"You needed me," he says. "I heal people."

And turns away from me, and whistles, and I see the pointed shadow on the wall, and he walks away in his cutoffs with his blades slung over his shoulder, and the shadow follows him, and I wonder who the unicorn works for, and what he is getting out of all this, after all.

At the sliding door he says, "Oh, later. And I'm Jess. I don't know *his* name." He can see that creature as clearly as I see him, and he assumes everyone else can. A sure sign of a prophet, the ability to see such things. In the nineties they also call it schizophrenia.

I don't look up. I hear him slipping the blades black on and thudding down the wooden stairs.

I work myself into a frenzy. He has to be destroyed. I sit by the sliding door and gaze down onto the sand, and I see him whooshing past, a can of soda in his hand, and his hair streaming.

Sex is still the answer, I tell myself. That's still what the Garden of Eden thing means, isn't it? Though he seems to have found a way out of the Augustinian dilemma. He's found a way of imbuing sex with the attributes of divinity. There's deep theology here somewhere, but what do

I know of theology? I am not God. The rules of the game keep changing. How was I to know you could have sex and still retain your purity?

Sex. But somehow it's got to be made more potent. And keep love out of it. And make it so I can't be healed.

I think I have an idea.

Evening.

It's easier to follow the unicorn in the night, in a crowded wharf, on a narrow walkway crammed with vendors of beachwear and hot dogs and incense and sunglasses and car shades. In a sea of faces, an equine shadow stands out. Practice it sometime. Watch the dark patches that ripple across walls, past people's gray complexions.

I follow. But I'm not a beautiful woman anymore. I'm a man old before my time. Too thin for the wrinkled Armani that sags on my skin and bones.

He's squatting between two trash cans; above his head, two dope dealers are squabbling. He looks up at me; I'm not sure if he recognizes me or not. He's mumbling something to the unicorn. The crack dealers hunch together over him and I realize that, shoulder to shoulder, they make the outline of a unicorn.

But the moment the image gels in my mind, the two men break apart. The one with the mohawk that seemed to be the horn of the beast, that one goes north while the other goes south, toward a hot dog stand. All that remains of the unicorn is the shadow of a torso in a pile of trash, flickering between the moonlight and the strident neon of a coffeehouse.

Does he recognize me? I think not.

"Hi," I say.

"You forgot 'sailor'," he says.

"Am I that obvious?"

"Do you need to be healed?"

"No."

"I think maybe you do."

"A drink somewhere?"

"A drink? But you're dying."

"Is it that obvious?"

"Yes," he says.

We go to a bar. It's a leather bar, sleazy as shit. I have a glass of Scotch, and he asks for a glass of Evian. "Nothing stronger?" I say.

"It's as strong as it feels," he says, and waves a hand over the long-stemmed goblet. I wonder if he's turned it into wine. "Do I know you? You remind me of someone I met once."

"I remind a lot of people of people."

The waiter leers at us. And why not? A dirty old man and a beautiful youth. Actually I thought he was going to get carded. But no. We sit on leatherette stools, swimming in smoke. It's grim. I'll be waiting forever if I don't charge ahead. "Do you know what I want?" I ask him.

I make my eyes still and cold. The way people imagine a serial killer's eyes to be, though in reality they are sad people, lost on the fringes of fantasy. "You want to fuck me?" he says. Ingenuous. He smiles again as if to say, sure, anything, because I'm here to make you whole, I'm the caulk that will bind your soul.

"I want to kill you," I say. "I've got it. You know."

"I know." Still the smile. He always knew and yet he followed me. Was that a swizzle stick in the bartender's tray, or was it the horn of the unicorn? The smoke swirls like the tail of the beast.

"I'm riddled with Kaposi's. I have lesions on my lesions. If I fuck you, you will die. But I don't want to play safe. I'm bitter. I'm angry. I want to kill the world. I want to kill God."

If sex is not enough, I think, then sex and death together should do it. They are the twin pillars of the human condition. The error in making the Word flesh is that flesh is necessarily flesh.

"Will it be enough," he says, "to kill me?"

"I don't know. I'm raging. I don't know if you'll be enough. I could pretend you're the world. I could pretend you're God. Maybe that's what it will take."

"I don't like to say that I'm God."

"Are you?"

"People have said it."

"What people?"

"The little girl that the one-eyed man was pimping said it. I healed her up inside, totally. She closed her eyes and said, *God, God.* The social worker found her on the beach. She was staring up at the sun. I think she's blind now. But when I visit her in the group home, she says she can see. I don't know what kind of seeing it is because she's always walking into walls and tripping over coffee tables. I know she sees me okay, she never bumps into me. Except when she needs to be held."

"Is that a parable?"

"You mean, did it really happen? When I say a thing, somehow it gets to be true. But I've never said who my father is."

He is a profound enigma, this youth with the flowing hair and the deep, unfathomable eyes. "But you mean it," I say. "You *will* consent to die." I know that he cannot lie to me. "You will yourself to die."

"If that's what it takes to heal your rage."

I take his cup from him. I drink it in one gulp. It *is* wine, one of the faceless California whites.

I take Jess back to the where I found him earlier, the trash cans, the sea; now there is no one there at all. Behind us, the unicorn canters; I can hear the hoofclacks on the concrete, not a clippety-clop of an iron-shod horse, but a softer sound. It is almost the sound of raindrops on the leaves of a banana tree. And then, with alarming suddenness, it *is* the sound of rain.

He bends over, spreads his arms across the garbage can lids, and I pull down his cutoffs. There is no love here. There is no compassion.

There is no desire save the need to kill. There is no passion except fury. The rain is our only lubricant. I am the battering ram with the horned head. I am all anger. I squeeze the disease into him, a billion viruses in every spurt of semen. If I can't suck the purity out of you, I think, I'll fill you to bursting with my own impurity. I'll soil you with sin. Sex may no longer be the ultimate crime, but surely I have tricked him in seeking out death, and that is a mortal sin. Surely, surely. The rules of the universe do not change that much.

The rain pours down. I feel the exultation of victory. I pull away, kick the trash cans, send them rolling down the pavement and Jess slumping to the concrete, facing the sea. I didn't just give him AIDS, it's a kind of mega-AIDS and it works right away. The lesions sprout up in a hundred places on that bronzed flesh, and they spread with every raindrop; he blackens; he shits blood; he vomits; he writhes; he is in utmost torment.

He crumbles. The rain washes him down to the sand and sea.

I go back to the condo and make myself a double espresso.

In three days he is back.

It's not by the sea I see him, but down in Beverly Center, uppermost level, food court, me coming out of one of those artsy Zhang Yimao movies, ice cappuccino in hand. He's standing in the window of Waldenbooks, at the foot of the escalator I'm about to go down. Rollerblades slung across the shoulder, black tee shirt blazoned with the logo of some Gothic band.

Why hasn't he gone away?

He's coming up and I'm going down, we're crossing paths, I look at him, he looks at me, perhaps he knows me; I reach over, a glancing, electric touch of hand on hand for a split second, and I say, "Aren't you supposed to be dead?"

And he says, "I heard a rumor about that."

And passes out of earshot.

I go back up the escalator. I catch him coming down again, this time in more of a hurry. "I know you," he says, grabbing on to me; I am not sure who he sees, because I have not had time to change my shape. I run down the escalator the wrong way. We reach Waldenbooks, and the unicorn's shadow crosses the entrance. "But I don't seem to know anything else anymore."

I stop. I'm getting an idea. "You lost your memory?"

"It's more than that. Sure, like, I wandered into a homeless shelter this morning and I didn't know my own name. They thought it was maybe I was off my medication? But they didn't have anyone with authority to dole out Xanax or whatever it is, flavor of the week. So like, I'm here."

"I can tell you who you are."

"Do I want to know?"

"You know the answer to that."

He looks at me. He is disoriented. I have no shape, and he has just awoken from the sleep from which there is no awaking. But behind his confusion I can see that that demon compassion is about to come to life. I don't have much time. I have to do it soon, or it will be like that fiasco in Jerusalem. But I need to prepare myself.

I tell him I'll pick him up where Venice meets the sea, tonight, Friday the thirteenth.

Moonrise. I go to him as myself. I can hear the unicorn's breath above the whisper of the Pacific. His Rollerblades are stashed against the wall of the public men's room, and he is squatting on an old recycle bin, speaking to a withered hooker. For a while, I stand beyond the periphery of his vision, listening to what he has to say.

"Tell you a story," he's saying to her. "Because you think you've thrown away your youth, lost your beauty, and now you're this mangy old bitch yapping at tourists for a ten-dollar handjob. I knew this rich dude back East, and one day his daughter runs away from home, and she ends up somewhere around Sunset and Cahuenga, turning tricks, not cheap tricks at first, but later when she's totally lost her looks and been around the block too many times to count, they do get cheap and like, she's doing crack and everything. And she starts to miss her dad, so one day when she's completely bottomed out, she checks out of the women's shelter and hitches all the way back. And thirty-nine blowjobs later she walks in the front gate of the estate, and her dad's all sitting at the dining room table with her brothers and sisters, and her mom's dishing out this pudding which is all flaming in brandy, because it's Christmas. And everyone's crying and saying, you walked out on us, see how much you made us suffer, what did we ever do to make you do this to us." I can't help smiling. The homespun stories never change. He goes on, "But the dad says, it's okay, honey. I'm not going to ask what you've been through. I'm just going to say I love you, and welcome you home." He plants a chaste kiss on the prostitute's brow, and says, "That's what you have to do, babe. Go home to your dad."

"My dad's dead."

"There's a dad in your heart. That's the dad you have to go home to."

She weeps, and I interrupt them. "Another true story?" I ask him. She takes one look at me, stifles a scream, scurries away across the sand. He looks at me too. I don't know if he is afraid; if he is, he hides it well.

"True story?" he says.

"Oh, I remember now. When you say a thing, somehow it gets to be true."

"That sounds familiar."

"This morning, before the sun came up, Jess, you were still dead."

"I knew it had to be something like that! I woke up and it was like I'd been in a dark place, fighting monsters. The whole place was on fire but the fire gave no light. Was that hell?"

"Yes, Jess. You harrowed hell."

"No kidding."

"I tell stories too, you know. You'll have to tell me if you think they're true. I've been called the father of lies, but that's kind of a sexist thing to say; I'd rather be the mother of invention."

The tide is coming in.

"You keep changing the rules on me," I tell him. "First I thought sex would do the trick; it's worked every time for a couple of thousand years. And then there was death. I was sure death would work, because to seek death is the ultimate sin. Death and sex together. But you screwed me over by letting your death purge me of the cancerous anger that I'd worked up inside myself."

"I don't remember," Jess says. "I can't even see you too clearly. I look at you and all I see is a void. I know you're there because I can hear you inside my head. Does that mean I'm a schizophrenic?"

"Most people like you are."

"Don't I know it."

"All right. Are you hungry? I'll take you out somewhere."

We go to a Mongolian barbecue on Wilshire because he seems a bit hungry. It's a no shirt no shoes no service kind of a place but I happen to have an old lumberjack shirt in the backseat of the Porsche that seems to have my name written on it in the Venice Beach parking lot, don't ask me how, probably just another of this world's whimsical illusions.

Jess eats a lot: a lot of meat, a lot of vegetables, about five ladles of each sauce, and a triple side order of rice. I watch him. Sipping my water, I detect a hint of the vintner; it's still him all right, and he's still full of the power that comes from his ultimate innocence.

"I'm starting to remember a bit more," he says. "I guess seeing you was, what do they call it, a catalyst."

"What do you remember?"

"I'm a healer."

"How do you heal?"

"Sometimes with love. Sometimes by letting the world fuck me.

Sometimes by telling stories. The stories just come to me, but I know they are true. I've got a direct line to the source of the world's dreams. Don't I? That's who I am."

He's starting to know. He's coming out of living dead mode. I toy with a piece of celery, flicking it up and down the side of the bowl with my chopsticks. "Did the unicorn tell you this?" I say, not looking into his eyes.

"No," he said, "we don't talk much. He doesn't, you know. He's not people. I do all the talking."

The shadow of the chopstick; the horn of the beast. In the distance, waitresses gibber in Chinese. But maybe it's Spanish. I say, "There is something you really need to know. You're dying to know. But you can't know it because you're not fully human. The thing that you want to know is a wall that separates you from the human race."

After sex and after death, there is only knowledge.

Knowledge is the greatest of all tempters.

"You know," he says, "you're right. Maybe."

He smiles. Is he humoring me, or does he already see it? The breath of the unicorn hangs in the air; it's not cigarette smoke, because it's illegal to smoke in restaurants in L.A. For a moment, his eyes lose that I-will-heal-you look. "But if I tell you what it is," I say, "then everything's going to change."

"How?" he says. "You might be lying. Tomorrow you'll still find me Rollerblading up and down the beach, pulling lost souls out of the fire. One day I'll rescue every soul in the whole world, and everyone'll shine like the sun, and the sea will part for us and we'll go into it and we'll see a crystal stairway and it'll lead all the people into the arms of our father."

"Whose father?"

Your father is not my father, I think. I pop a wafer-thin slice of lamb into my mouth.

"So tell me your story," he says.

But first he gets up, fills up a third bowl with goodies, and hands it to them to cook. The restaurant has emptied out. When he comes back, I can see the doorman switching the sign to CLOSED, but they don't seem to be kicking us out. Jess waits.

"Once upon a time," I say, "there was a perfect place."

"Like Paradise?"

"Kind of. You can imagine it as a garden if you want, but I'd like to think of it as a big mansion with hundreds of rooms. Super Nintendo. Videos. Edutainment. Roller coasters. Discovery and laughter everywhere you turned. And there were two children who lived in the house, a boy and a girl. They were like brother and sister. Their father was a weird old man with a long white beard, and he lived on the top floor, and he had a lab where he experimented with creating life. Every time he made a new creature, the kids got to name it. Every day was an adventure, but the estate was surrounded by a stone wall, and there was no gate. The father loved them so much that he wanted them to stay with him forever. He knew that there was only one thing that would cause them to leave. He shut that thing up in a room in the basement of the house. They weren't allowed to go into that room. Not that it was locked or anything. That would have been too easy.

"The kids played in the house for a million years. It wasn't boring. It wasn't that they lacked things to do. But somehow they started to get fidgety. It was time for me to come to them. And I did. 'Adam,' I said, 'why haven't you gone into that room yet?' And he said, 'It's against the rules.' And I said, 'If your father had really wanted you not to go into that room, he would have locked it and thrown away the key.' So the boy talked it over with his sister for a long time, and eventually I took them all the way down there, slithering down the clammy stone steps, and I watched them go in, and I watched the door close behind them, and I waited.

"Sex and death were in that room, Jess."

"I remember now!" He's exhilarated. "They were kicked out of the house, and I've come to fetch them home."

"Oh, Jess," I said, "that's the illusion I've come to strip away; that's the one piece of knowledge in *your* dark basement room—we all have them, those basement rooms—and I've come to give it to you."

"Oh," says the boy, and the light begins to drain from his eyes.

"You see, the boy and the girl went upstairs to tell their father they'd broken the rule. The old man was very sad. He said, 'You can stay if you want. We can work this out. I don't want to lose you.' Adam and Eve looked at each other. Strange and grand new feelings were surging through their bodies. At last, Eve said, 'We have to go, Dad. You know we do. That's why you didn't lock the door.' And the old man said, 'Yes. You're human beings. You can't be children forever. You have to break the rules. It's human to defy your parents. It's human to strive, to seek new worlds, to leave the nest, earn a living, make love and babies, filter back into the earth so that it can nourish more human beings. You're dust and you must turn into dust again one day. It's a sad thing. But it's not without joy. But look how dust dances in the light. You are beautiful because you are not immortal. I'm the one who can't change. I'm the one who has to go on forever. Pity me, children. Pity your poor old father.'

"The knowledge the children gained was the gateway through the stone walls and into the world outside. They lived in the real world after that. Not always happily, and not ever after.

"And Paradise became an empty nest, and the old man realized that the perfect place he had built was a private hell from which he would never escape."

Jess doesn't speak for a long time. They are turning out the lights, but a different light suffuses us, the light from the unicorn's eyes. At last he screams out, "Oh, God! Why did you send me here? Fuck you—you told me I was here to love them and redeem them and really you want me to chain them up and throw the key into the ocean and—"

"You're talking to the unicorn?"

"Sometimes I think the unicorn is my father."

That's never occurred to me in all those years.

"Good-bye," Jess says softly, and he's not speaking to me. I've robbed him of his innocence at last. And now, for a few brief seconds, it is I who am pure: I am all the goodness that was once in the boy, I am his hopes and dreams, I am his sacrifice, I am his redeeming love. Only in that moment, as his vision leaves him, do I see the unicorn.

The restaurant has dissolved into thin air and the great beast is running toward the waves. The sea splashes against his moon-sheened withers. His horn glistens. The wind from the Pacific whips Jess's hair across his bare shoulders. He looks down at the sand. "I'm naked," he says at last. "Can't you hold me?"

The unicorn has dissipated into mist.

I cradle Jess in my arms, and he weeps. In that embrace, without sex and without death, I drain the last dregs of divinity from him. We love each other.

Maybe God *is* their father. But they are my children, too, and I'm a lot older than God. Because darkness is the mother of light.

I love them just as much as he does. More. My nest is empty, too. But *he* just won't learn to let go. He just won't let them be. He always wants to meddle in their affairs. But he always lets me have my three temptations.

They think they want to live forever. They think they want eternal bliss. But what they really want is to love and to die. That is their real nature. That is the truth that God can never face, and that's why this little war has to go on, why there'll always be an Antichrist.

Yesterday he was the savior of the world, but today Jess is just another lost boy. Tomorrow I'll give him the keys to the Porsche and the title deed to the house by the sea, so at least he can go Rollerblading to his heart's content, and have somewhere to come home to when he falls in love and raises a family and forgets that he ever had the power to mend broken souls.

I'm not the villain in this war.

Tomorrow I'll go someplace far away and I'll sit and wait for a hundred years until one day I'll hear the leaves rustling and see the darting shadow and the hoofprints in the sand, or the snow, or the forest floor. It's always been this way and it always will be. World without end. Amen.

ABOUT THE AUTHOR

Somtow Papinian Sucharitkul (S. P. Somtow) was born in Bangkok and grew up in Europe. He was educated at Eton College and at Cambridge, where he obtained his B.A. and M.A., receiving honors in English and music. He has published more than twenty-five adult and children's novels, and much short fiction. He made his conducting debut with the Holland Symphony Orchestra at age nineteen, has since conducted, among others, the Cambridge Symphony Orchestra, and has been a director of the Bangkok Opera Society. He writes and directs movies, among them a gothic-punk adaptation of *A Midsummer Night's Dream* starring Timothy Bottoms.

Recently, Somtow handed in the long-awaited sequel to *Vampire Junction, Vanitas,* to his publishers. His semi-autobiographic *Jasmine Nights,* published in 1994 by the British literary publishing house Hamish Hamilton, will be made into a fourteen-million-dollar motion picture, filmed entirely in Thailand, by AFFS. It has just appeared in the U.S. from Wyatt Books/St. Martin's Press, and has received astonishing praise on both sides of the Atlantic.

Somtow's forthcoming writing projects include a new literary novel, a short story collection from Gollancz, *The Pavilion of Frozen Women;* and a fourth young adult novel, *The Vampire's Beautiful Daughter.*

JUDITH TARR

DAME À LA LICORNE

Peter: When I first put **Judith Tarr** on my wish-list of possible contributors to *Immortal Unicorn,* I knew her as the author of seventeen historical and fantasy novels, and as the holder of a doctorate in medieval studies from Yale. Reading "Dame à la Licorne" made it obvious that she lived with, loved, and understood horses. But I didn't know about the Lipizzan who owns her, out there in Tucson. . . .

Janet: Before the birth of this anthology, my only (semi) personal contact with Judith was through the occasional dialogue on GEnie. Though I have still never met her in person, this story makes me feel as if I know her just a wee bit better. The story is one of the few SF tales we received; it says something about the writer and her love of horses, and shows us a future where, though much changes, much that is human nature stays the same.

Dame à la Licorne

I.

THEY TURNED OFF THE RAIN AT DAWN THAT DAY. By early feeding the sun was on, the filters at their most transparent, and the sky so blue it hurt. The grass was all washed clean, new spring green.

Some of the broodmares had taken advantage of the wet to have a good, solid roll in their pasture. Old Novinha, pure white when she was clean, had a map of Africa on her side, and a green haunch. She was oblivious to it, watching with interest as the stallions came out for their morning exercise.

Novinha was thinking about coming into season. Some of the other mares were more than thinking about it. They paced the fence as the stallions danced past, flagging their tails and squealing at any who so much as flicked an ear.

The stallions knew better than to be presumptuous. Young Rahman snorted and skittered, but his rider brought him lightly back in hand. The others arched their necks, that was all, and put on a bit of prance for the ladies. Because they were dancers and this was Dancer's Rest, they pranced with art and grace, a shimmer of white manes and white necks and here and there a black or a bay or a chestnut.

There were horses already in the training rings, the great ones, the masters of the art that the others were still learning. They had gone through the steps of the dance, and for duty and reward were dancing in the air: levade, courbette, capriole; croupade and passade and ballotade. The names were as archaic and beautiful as the dance.

* * *

Marina should have been riding one of the young stallions, dappled silver Pluto Amena or coal-black Doloroso or fierce blood-bay Rahman who was fretting and tossing his head under Cousin Tomas' hand. Tomas had less patience than Rahman liked, and stronger hands.

But Marina was up on the hill beyond the broodmares' pasture, where she could see the whole of Dancer's Rest like an image in a screen. She had gone up there to watch the sun come out, and stayed longer than she should, because of the flyer that was coming from the west. West was City and Dome. West was the Hippodrome, where things raced and exhibited themselves and even tried to dance, that were called horses but were not horses at all. Not in the least. Not like the ones that danced and grazed and called to one another in spring yearning below and all around her.

She had seen the horse-things. Everyone at Dancer's Rest had, because Papa Morgan let no one in the family ride or train or handle the horses unless he or she had seen what had been done in the name of fashion and function and plain unmotivated modernity. Horses in the Hippodrome looked very little like horses at Dancer's Rest—and very little like one another. Those that ran were lean whippy greyhound-bodied things, all legs and speed. Those that exhibited could not walk, could not trot, could not canter or gallop, could only flail the air in the movement called "show gait." It was a little like a prance and a little like a piaffe and a great deal like the snap and ratchet of a mechanical toy. And those that were there simply to be beautiful, could stand, that was all, and pose, and arch their extraordinarily long necks. They could carry no rider; their backs were grown too long and frail. They could walk, but with difficulty, since their hindlegs were so very long and so very delicate. But they were lovely, like living art, pure form divorced from function.

After a long day in the Hippodrome, Marina had come home to shock and a kind of grief. The family's horses were old stock—raw unmodified equine. They looked small and thick-legged, short-bodied, heavy and primitive. Their movements were strange, too varied and almost too heavy, all power and none of the oiled glide of the racers or the flashing knee-action of the exhibition stock. They were atavisms. The world had passed them by. All that was new and bold and reckoned beautiful was engineered, designed, calculated to the last curve of ear and flick of tail.

"That's why," Papa Morgan had said when she came back too cold of heart to cry and too angry to be wise. "That's what you needed to see. What they've made, and what we keep."

"But why keep it?" Marina had demanded. "Why bother with old stock at all? Nobody wants it. Nobody likes the way it looks or moves or handles. It can't run, it can't show, it can't stand up and look correctly beautiful."

"And worse than that," said Papa Morgan, "it has a mind of its own." He sighed. "That's why. Because it's not what people want. It's what it is."

She had understood, as she should, because she was family and she had learned the lesson from infancy. But her understanding was a shallow thing. She thought too often of going away as so many of the cousins and the siblings did, leaving Dancer's Rest to live in the world of cities and domes and gengineered equines. Only the strongest-minded stayed, and the ones who loved the horses above anything in the greater world, and those like Marina who were too weak-willed to leave.

Weak-willed, and bound to the horses, however primitive or unfashionable they might be. She was family. She was bred to this as surely as racers to the track and show stock to the ring.

The flyer was close enough now to see. She scrambled up from the damp grass, brushing at blades that clung, and knowing but not caring that her breeches were stained as green as Novinha's haunch. She ran down the hill toward the road, to the delight of the yearlings whose pasture it was. They swirled about her, a storm of hoofs and tails and tossing heads, parting and streaming along the forcefence as she ran through. She felt the tingle of the field, though the gate-chip was supposed to make it invisible and imperceptible. But she always knew where the fence was, and in much the same way the horses did.

Horse-instincts, Papa Morgan said, had been in the family since long before gengineering.

And why, she wondered, did she want to rear and shy and run away from the flyer that was coming to rest on the family's pad? It was only the inspector from the Hippodrome, come as she did every year at the start of breeding season, to inspect the stock and approve the roster of breedings-to-be and enjoy a long and convivial visit with Papa Morgan and the rest of the family. Marina had honed and polished Pluto Amena's levade for the exhibition that would crown the afternoon—she should be in the stable now, seeing that he was clean and ready to be shown.

But instead of turning toward the stable she kept going toward the house. She was not the only one. Papa Morgan and the elders were waiting, of course, as was polite, but there were others about as well, who should have been in the stables or in the house. Tante Concetta was standing near the pad, and Cousin Wilhelm, and Tante Estrella in breeches and boots with a long whip in her hand. Tante Estrella was a wild one, as wild as the young mares she preferred to train and handle, and as beautiful as they were, too. She looked a little frightening now, as if her ears were laid back and her tail lashing, threatening to kick or strike at the person who had emerged from the flyer.

It was not round smiling grey-haired Shanna Chen-Howard, nor any of the people who had always come with her to Dancer's Rest. This was a stranger. No human person came with him; only a mechanical, a mute and blank-faced metal bodyguard and recording device. It looked slightly more human than the stranger did, to Marina's eye.

Pity, too. He was young and not bad-looking. Gengineered, of course, but not so as to be obvious. That was the fashion these days. His parents would have designed him to emerge au naturel, with any serious flaws or inconveniences carefully and unobtrusively smoothed away.

They did not seem to have included a module for good humor. He looked as if he never smiled. His eyes as they scanned the people and the place were cold, and grew colder as they passed Cousin Wilhelm. Cousin Wilhelm stayed at home mostly, not for shame or shyness but because he was more comfortable there, where he did not need eyes to know where everything was. Implants had never taken, and mechanicals, he said, were worse than nothing at all. Marina thought he preferred the dark he had been born to, as rich as it was in sounds and smells. He was a better rider than most men who could see, and a wonderful trainer of horses.

This stranger in the inspector's tabard saw none of that. He saw a blind man in antique riding breeches, leaning on the arm of a greying and unnecessarily plump woman. Marina could read him as clearly as if he had spoken. *Primitive,* he was thinking. *Atavistic. Outdated.* Like the house in front of him, and the stables and the pastures beyond, and the horses in them, crude unmodified creatures without even the grace to be clean.

He was at least polite to Papa Morgan. It was a frigid politeness, with a bare minimum of words. Papa Morgan, who was never flustered, moved smoothly through the formulae of introduction, and took no notice of the brevity of the responses. It was briefest of all in front of Cousin Wilhelm: a sharp dip of the head that Cousin Wilhelm could not see, thoughtless maybe, but to Marina's mind as rude as an outright insult.

Papa Morgan noticed. He showed no sign of offense, but Marina saw how he led the inspector into the house without offering the greeting-cup, the wine and the bread and salt that sealed a friendship. Shanna Chen-Howard would have known what that signified. This person, this Hendrick Manygoats Watanabe, did not even seem to realize that he had been slighted.

Marina trailed after them. She was not invited, but neither was she shut out. There was a smell in the air, a little like hot iron, a great deal like fear.

"Yes," Papa Morgan said. "We do unregulated breeding here. We have a license to do so—a dispensation under the Mandate, for the preservation of rootstock."

He should not have had to explain to an inspector who administered the Mandate. The inspector knew exactly how much and how far Dancer's Rest was permitted to depart from the laws that governed gengineering. But he was insisting on being obtuse.

There was nothing convivial about the meeting. He had refused refreshment, which meant that no one with him could have it, either: distressing as the day wore on and they all went hungry. He had also refused the tour of the stables, and declined the pleasure of the exhibition. He had come, he said, to investigate the breeding practices at Dancer's Rest. They would present the records, please, and explain the entries, and be quick about it.

Papa Morgan was the most patient person Marina knew. He had to be, to be the head of the family. She had never seen him lose patience. Nor did he now with this stranger who would not look at his horses, but there was a glitter in his eyes that she had not seen before. It made her shiver.

She could have left long ago. But she stayed, and the others stayed, too, unnoticed and unreprimanded. They were like a bodyguard, she thought, though what they were guarding against, except bureaucratic niggling, she did not know.

Hendrick Manygoats Watanabe was not a patient man. He would never make a trainer of horses, she thought as she watched him scan the records. She wondered if he knew anything about horses at all, or if he cared. Shanna Chen-Howard had been one of those unfortunates who lack both the balance and the talent to do more than haul themselves into a saddle and sit more or less in the middle, but she had loved to watch the horses, ridden and free, and she had known many of them by name.

This man who had come in her place, who had not troubled to explain why, would never know Novinha and Selene and Bellamira and Sayyida, nor care that Maestoso Miranda liked sugar but Rigoletto preferred apples. His whole world was a scroll of data, columns of numbers, files labeled by genetic type. The living flesh, the animal that was the sum of its genes, was an irrelevance.

He frowned as the files scrolled behind his eyes. "Random," he said to himself, but not as if he cared who heard. "Untidy. This string—" He called it to the wallscreen in the family's meeting room, which was an insult of sorts: they all had implants, they were not primitives or atavists who refused the seductions of the net. The pure flow of data resolved into an image, a helix of stars, each with its distinctive color and form.

Marina recognized the shape of it. One of the elders, Mama Tania, said what they all knew. "That's the Skowronek gene-line. Very old, very illustrious. Prepotent."

"And severely flawed," said Hendrick Manygoats Watanabe. "You see here, here, here." Light-pointers flashed. "This is worse than untidy. This is a possible lethal recessive."

"So it is," Papa Morgan said mildly.

"And you make no effort to remove it?"

Papa Morgan seemed to grow calmer, the more agitated the inspector became. "Of course you do understand, Ser Watanabe. It was explained to you. We preserve the old stock, the rootstock. Unaltered. Unrefined. Flaws and all."

"But that is against the Mandate," said Watanabe.

"We are exempt from the Mandate," Papa Morgan said.

"That," said Watanabe, "is a matter of debate."

There was a silence. Someone drew a long, slow breath. It was as loud as a rushing of wind.

Marina was too young to remember how the exemption had been granted, but everyone knew the story. Someone, the family had argued, should preserve the old stock—for antiquarian reasons, or sentimental ones, or for scholars and scientists who might find new modifications based on the old genetic materials. There had been a movement then in favor of such curiosities; the exemption had passed, and no one had challenged it.

Papa Morgan was not surprised to meet a challenge now. Nor were the other elders. They had expected this, then. They might even have expected the stranger who came in Shanna Chen-Howard's place.

She felt a flicker of anger. No one had told her. And how many of the others knew, who had kept it quiet because it could only upset the young and disturb the horses?

Elders' prerogative. She did not have to like it. She was here, when she could perfectly well have been told to leave—she had no place or position, and no authority beyond that of an assistant trainer.

So. She knew what this stranger was here for. Why he had been sent, and how he had gained authority for it—and also, within the rest, why Shanna Chen-Howard had not come. Her faction must have lost power in the Hippodrome. This was the new faction, and the new law.

"Your exemption is revoked," said Hendrick Manygoats Watanabe. "Your breeding patterns are invalid. You will be receiving instructions, which you will follow. This complex, for example," he said, tilting his head toward the wallscreen, "will be removed. There will be no further random breeding of live male to live female. You will conduct your program in accordance with the rules and regulations of the Mandate."

Papa Morgan did not bother to contend that there was nothing random about the family's choices. He only said, "The Mandate has no provision for the preservation of rootstock."

"The whole of the Mandate encompasses such a provision. Your stock has been allowed to proliferate without rule or regulation. It has no specific function—"

"On the contrary," said Papa Morgan. "It is the most purely functional of all the equids. It lives to dance."

Watanabe's mouth opened, then closed again. Marina wondered if he had ever been interrupted in his life.

"We will appeal the decision," said Papa Morgan.

Watanabe recovered himself with an air almost of pleasure. "Your appeal is denied."

"We have to fight them."

The family was gathered where the elders had been since morning, all of them down to the toddlers from the crêches. There had been food earlier, and there was drink going around, intoxicant and stimulant and even plain water. The inspector was gone. He had taken his mechanical and his flyer and flown back to the Hippodrome without ever once looking at the horses.

"We should have dragged him out there," some of the younger trainers were insisting. "If he could see—"

"He saw all he needed to see." Marina surprised herself by speaking out—usually she kept quiet and let the others do the talking. "He looked at the helices, he saw how untidy and unregulated they were, and he knew they couldn't be allowed to continue."

Up among the elders, the same argument was going on, at nearly the same volume. Papa Morgan said in his deep voice that carried without effort, "We've been fighting the Mandate since it was made. We've been appealing this decision at every level. The answer is always no. We can keep our rootstock—by which they mean the type we breed and raise here. But we have to clean up its helices."

"But if we do that," Cousin Bernardin pointed out, "it's not rootstock anymore. It's modified. You know—we all know—that the helices are untidy because they need to be. That's where the strength is. That's what makes our horses what they are."

"The Mandate believes otherwise," said Papa Morgan. He sounded tired.

Papa Morgan was never tired or impatient or, all divinities forbid, defeated. But now he was close to all of them. He looked as if he wanted to turn and walk away, but the press of people hemmed him in. He had to stay and listen to all this fruitless babble.

Marina was freer than he was, but she could not leave, either. Whatever had brought her here in the morning was not letting her go. Family intuition, Tante Estrella would call it. Tante Estrella had more than her fair share of it herself.

As if the thought had invoked her, she came quietly to stand by Marina, not doing anything, watching people argue. She was still wearing her breeches, but her long whip was gone, laid aside somewhere. She did not seem agitated at all. If anything she was amused.

"Wait," she said to Marina out of nowhere in particular. "See what happens."

II.

Nothing happened, that Marina could see. The gathering ended in disarray. The Mandate left no choice and no debate. Its rules were strict and its regulations precise. Genetic codes would be corrected according to its guidelines, animals bred without the untidiness of stallion courting mare in the breeding pen or the pasture, pregnancies monitored and embryos transferred with clean mechanical precision.

There was none of the usual springtime excitement, the pleasure of matching this stallion to that mare, the waiting for her to come into season and accept him, the beautiful randomness of conception in a living womb. It was all done in the laboratory, as coldly meticulous as a chemical equation.

One thing at least the Mandate did not forbid, though it did not encourage it, either. It could not keep mares from carrying their own foals. Their clean, derandomized, genetically perfected foals, each set of helices prescribed by the authorities in the Hippodrome. Hendrick Many-goats Watanabe himself, according to the signature, reviewed and approved each one. The family's breeding managers were not permitted to select the matches. Not this season. They would be shown, he had informed them, what they were to do; then in other seasons they would know what was correct and what was permitted.

In much older days an insult of that proportion would have led to a duel at least, and maybe to a war. This season, with their greatest power stripped from them and handed to strangers, the elders in the breeding pens said nothing whatsoever.

They did as they were told. They collected specimens, handed them to the inspectors who flew in from the west, stood by unspeaking while those same inspectors returned from the laboratory with technicians and racks of labeled vials. When the horses objected, they made no move and spoke no word. More than one inspector or technician discovered that these undersized, primitive creatures were remarkably strong and self-willed—and utterly unforgiving of insults from strangers.

When the tech who had tried to collect a specimen from Favory Ancona went home with a broken femur, Papa Vladimir, who looked only to Papa Morgan for authority in the breeding pens, was seen to smile slightly and observe, "He should have asked first."

There was only one mercy in all of it. Once breeding season was over, the inspectors and technicians went away. They had done all they needed to do. The rest they left to the mares, and to the family. In the spring there would be foals, genetically purified and officially sanctioned, each with the Mandate's signature in its cells.

Marina did not know why, but after the first shock she stopped being upset. Angry, yes. The family had been trampled on. Its horses had been relegated to the status of a disease in need of a cure, its beautiful old bloodlines condemned as unsanitary. She could sit in the library with the books scrolling behind her eyes, telling over the names. The breeds that they kept pure here, the old breeds, the horses of princes: Arabian, Andalusian, Lipizzan. The lines preserved in each. Skowronek whose helices Watanabe had sneered at, Celoso whose sons were all kings and whose daughters were all queens, Favory and Conversano and Siglavy who had danced before kings. Ghazala, Princesa, Presciana; Moniet and Mariposa and Deflorata. They were woven in the helices, flaws as well as perfection, a memory as deep as the bone and more lasting.

It was immortality, not of the single creature but of the species itself. And the Mandate wanted to kill it in the guise of perfecting it.

Novinha was the first to come into heat and the first to get in foal. On a day of early spring when snow had been allowed to fall, she showed signs that she would foal in the night. Marina had foal watch in the broodmares' barn, blankets spread on straw next to the foaling stall. In the Hippodrome she did not doubt that they left such things to monitors and mechanicals. Here it was reckoned that foals of the old stock grew and thrived best if they were born the old way, with human hands ready if the mare faltered.

As the old mare began to pace her stall, Tante Estrella slipped in past Marina. She always knew when it was time, and she always came, no matter how late the hour. In fact it was early for a foaling, not quite midnight.

The long waiting, close on a year from breeding to birth, ended as it always did, with astonishing speed. As Novinha went down, Estrella was there, Marina close behind her, moving in concert as they had so often before.

There was little actually to do till the foal had slipped free of its mother. Novinha knew her business. This was her seventh foal, her luck-foal as family superstition had it, and she gave birth easily and quickly, from the first sight of the hoof wrapped in glimmering caul to the wet tangle of limbs sorting itself out in the straw.

Marina and Estrella stared at the foal, the perfect foal, designed and conceived under the Mandate. It was struggling to its feet already, lifting its head with its delicate curled ears.

Novinha was a Lipizzan, and so was the sire of record, Favory Ancona who had left so lasting a mark on the technician from the Hippodrome. They were all born dark, and turned glimmering white as they grew.

This foal of theirs under the Mandate had bypassed the dark phase. It was silvery white already, though it was no albino: its skin was dark under the pallor of the coat.

It was a colt. He was a big one, substantial for one so young, with a big square shoulder and a solid rump. In that he was just as he should be. There was even a hint of an arch to his profile, the noble nose that distinguished his breed and his line.

And yet there was something odd . . .

Estrella was quicker than Marina, and maybe less unwilling to acknowledge what she saw. She inspected the small hoofs as the colt wobbled up on them, marking that each was the same and each preposterous, cloven like a goat's or a deer's. And the tail, not the brush of a normal foal but a tasseled monstrosity, and on the forehead where the silver-white hair whorled to its center—

Marina laughed with unalloyed delight. "Didn't we warn them? Didn't we, then? And they meddled with our beauties regardless."

All the mares were foaling unicorns. Every one. Colt or filly, Lipizzan or Andalusian or Arabian, each was the same: silver-white, cloven-hooved, with the bud of a horn on its brow. The Mandate had outsmarted itself.

"There was a reason," said Papa Morgan, "for the untidiness in the helices."

"We did try to tell them," Tante Concetta said. She kept to the house and seldom went among the horses, but she had gone down to the barn that first morning to look at Novinha's colt. She laughed as Estrella had, with the same high amusement.

None of the elders was at all surprised, no more than they had been by the lowering of the Mandate. They had expected this. It must be something one learned when one became an elder, a secret that had stopped being a secret when Novinha's foal was born.

He had a name from before birth in the ancient tradition of his breed. Favory Novinha: Favory for the ancestor of his line, Novinha for his dam who inspected him with as little surprise as the elders had shown, and a quietly luminous pride. If it disconcerted her to be mother to such strange offspring, she did not show it.

Marina was beyond surprise when they got him out into the light and she had her first clear sight of his eyes. They were not brown at all, not even the near-black of his heritage, but a deep and luminous blue. Nor did they change as he grew. They were part of him, like the goat-feet on which he walked and the horn that sprouted on his forehead.

She was more or less in charge of him. It was usual for whoever had foal watch on a particular night to inherit, in a manner of speaking, the foal who was born on that watch. There was not much to do when the foal's dam was as experienced as Novinha. Mostly Marina watched him. She never quite admitted that she was waiting for him to do something unusual, something magical.

But he never did, unless it was magic that he grew so fast and moved so light. Lipizzans grew into their grace. When they were young they were awkward, gangling, often heavy on their feet. This colt was graceful from birth. He was born knowing how to move, how best to dance.

That was his magic, she supposed. He knew what other foals had to learn.

The Mandate had no provision for such an eventuality as this. It had not intended to create a new—or recreate a very old—species. It had been meddling, that was all. Asserting its sense of order on a disordered breed.

Hendrick Manygoats Watanabe came back as the last of the mares waited to deliver their foals. This time he was accompanied by Shanna Chen-Howard. She, for once, was not smiling. He was looking remarkably humble.

"They retired me," she said to Papa Morgan as they walked away from the flyer that had brought her. She was direct as always, though Watanabe looked sourly disapproving. "They tossed me out on my ear, told me to take myself a vacation, gengineer some roses, take up locustkeeping in the Sahel—anything but get in their way when they decided to lay the Mandate on everybody who was exempt. I gather they did much the same to you."

Papa Morgan spread his hands, eloquent of resignation. "What could we do? We're subject to the law. If the law says we have to give in to the Mandate . . ."

Shanna Chen-Howard slanted a glance at him. Marina, following at a discreet distance, thought she saw laughter in it. "You were always law-abiding citizens," she said blandly.

They had turned the mares out in the wide green pasture that rolled down to the river. Two sides of it were fenced in water, with a forcefence to remind the bolder foals that they were not to go exploring. All the mares with foals at side, as it happened, were greys; none of the dark mares had been bred this year, again under the Mandate.

It was a pretty picture from a distance, white horse-shapes on green, the larger grazing peacefully, the smaller playing or nursing or lying flat on the grass in the sun. Closer in, one realized that the mares were ordinary enough, but the foals were odd.

Marina found herself walking just behind Watanabe. He stepped gingerly, as if he had never walked on a dirt road before. The glances he shot at the pasture almost made her laugh aloud. He must be having dreadful visions of hip-deep mud, reeking manure, creatures crawling up the grassblades to devour him whole.

The fence along the road was an atavism, a real post-and-rail fence, though there was a forcefence just behind it to keep it secure. One of Papa Morgan's predecessors had thought it worthwhile to have at least one old-fashioned fence for leaning on and watching the horses. Papa Morgan did just that now, and Shanna Chen-Howard kept him company. Watanabe hung back, with Marina still behind him.

The mares had been aware of them all along, but most were busy cropping the new grass. It was Novinha's colt who came forward first, curious to see who these visitors were. He took a circuitous way about it, showing off his floating gait, spiraling in toward the fence till he stood just inside of it, nostrils flared, head up, bright eye fixed on them all.

Shanna Chen-Howard took a while to find her voice. When she did, it wobbled a little, but then it was its forthright self again. "Well. You weren't exaggerating."

"Neither were the holorecords we sent you," Papa Morgan said.

"No," said Shanna Chen-Howard, "but somehow, in the flesh, it's more effective."

She stretched a hand over the fence. The colt sniffed it, thought about nipping, caught Marina's eye and behaved himself. He let Shanna Chen-Howard stroke his nose, and stood still for her to run her hand up it till it touched the base of the horn. She almost recoiled then: Marina saw how she tensed. But he leaned into her, encouraging her to scratch where it was always itching.

"It is real," she said as he obliged him. "It really is." She began to laugh.

The only one who seemed to need an explanation was Watanabe. He was not about to get one. She kept laughing when Papa Morgan let her into the pasture, the same way Tante Estrella had when the colt was born, and Tante Concetta. It was a grand joke on the Mandate.

"The trouble," she said as they lingered over dinner that evening, "is that the Mandate has no sense of humor whatsoever. You're exonerated—there's no sign of tampering, and every breeding was administered entirely by technicians from the Hippodrome—but you know how the law works. It has to cast blame on somebody."

No one looked at Hendrick Manygoats Watanabe. He had a plate in front of him as they all did, the elders and the trainers who had been admitted to the meeting, the senior trainers and the younger ones like Marina who were in charge of this year's foals. He had eaten nothing and said nothing. It was probably excruciating for him to have to dally like this, being endlessly inefficient, eating and drinking and hanging about instead of working on the problem at hand.

"I'd ask, Why not blame the Mandate?" said Tante Estrella, "except I'm not that foolish. We did warn you—them—of what might happen if they tried to meddle with old stock."

"So you did," said Shanna Chen-Howard, "but after all, the horses bred under the Mandate were meddled with, too, in the beginning. Why would these be any different?"

"Because they're old stock," Tante Estrella said. "The others had already been meddled with till they forgot where they came from. These never did. The Arabian is the oldest and purest of all. The others were bred from it by masters who knew better than any Mandate how to make perfection in the form of a horse. It's dangerous to meddle with perfection."

Shanna Chen-Howard shook her head. She was not arguing, at least not with Tante Estrella. "So. We tampered with something that was already finished. We turned it into something else altogether."

"Exactly," said Papa Morgan.

Shanna Chen-Howard sighed heavily. "This is not going to go over well with the committee in the Hippodrome. There's that clause in the Mandate, you see, that your predecessors helped write. The one that draws the line between modification and complete transformation. We can tidy up your horses' helices. We can't turn their offspring into something other than horses."

Papa Morgan smiled. There was nothing smug about it, but Hendrick Manygoats Watanabe got up abruptly, kicked back his chair, and stalked out.

III.

None of it was really about the Mandate, or about the Hippodrome's mistake. Marina's, too, for thinking that it was so simple. She had not been paying attention. That was a bad fault in a horse trainer.

It was a long summer. The weather was on a random cycle, which meant heat and sun and a daily explosion of thunder. The nights were steamily warm, with a crackle of lightning near the horizon.

Marina liked to walk the pastures at night. The horses were quiet then, grazing or drowsing. There were monitors set to catch anything out of the ordinary, but they were part of the forcefence, invisible and almost imperceptible.

She went out on a night when the moon was full and the lightning had sunk almost out of sight over the world's rim, and wandered from pasture to pasture. There were mares in foal again, bred the old way, without the Mandate to interfere. They were standing together at the far corner of their pasture, looking out into the next, where their sisters were, and the foals.

Novinha's colt had a horn now as long as Marina's hand. It was ivory, densely spiral-grained and keenly pointed. The elders had been talking about blunting the foals' horns or capping them like an elephant's tusks or removing them altogether, for their own and their mothers' safety.

While the elders failed to agree on what to do, the foals did each other no damage, though they loved to spar like swordsmen. They seemed to have an instinct, a sense of just how far it was wise to go. It held even with humans. And that, thought Marina, was the most unfoal-like thing about them. Young horses were reckless of their strength, but these were remarkably careful, for babies. It was as if they were born knowing how to conduct themselves in the world.

Novinha's foal called to Marina as she came down to the pasture, running along the fence with head and tail high, tossing his head with its moon-bright gleam of horn. The others followed more slowly. They had their own chosen humans; they acknowledged Marina but did not welcome her as the colt did. In that they were Lipizzans, but again they were young for it.

She slipped through the gate in the wooden fence. The colt was waiting for her. He followed her as she walked to the river, with the others trailing behind, and even a few of the mares.

She stopped as she always did at her favorite place, a stone like a chair, where she could sit and watch the water flow by. The colt lay down as he liked to do and laid his head in her lap. The moon glowed in his coat. She stroked it. It was the softest thing in the world, and warm, and it smelled of flowers. He closed his eyes and sighed.

He was not asleep, not quite. His ears flicked as the other foals and their mothers found things to do nearby. A pair of shadows moved softly through them, stroking a neck here, a nose there.

Tante Estrella and Tante Concetta sat on the grass near Marina's stone. Some of the foals circled, curious, even came to be petted, but none came as close as the colt had, or laid his head in a welcoming lap. Maybe it was Novinha who prevented it: she had come to stand over Tante Concetta, huge and white and quiet.

Marina's head was full of questions. There were too many of them; they crowded each other. They silenced her.

Tante Estrella only sat for a moment before she was on her feet again, stroking and talking softly to one of the younger mares. That one had a filly, who came to investigate Estrella, nibbling boldly on the hem of her coat.

"Look," Estrella said abruptly. Marina started. The colt opened an eye but closed it again, refusing to wake for anything as trivial as human chatter.

"Look around you," Estrella said. "Do you know what you see?"

She was expecting an answer. Marina groped for one. "A mistake," she said. "The Mandate carried too far."

"No," said Estrella. "You don't see."

Marina frowned. She had come here to be alone in the quiet, not to be put in the training ring and set on a circle.

"Estrella is saying," said Concetta from Novinha's shadow, "that you need to look harder. What do you see?"

"Twelve baby unicorns," Marina said sharply, though she tried to be light. "Next you're going to tell me you planned this."

"We did expect that it would happen, yes," Concetta said. "We thought the Hippodrome needed a lesson."

"It could have blown up in your faces," Marina said. "We could have been shut down. If they get angry enough, we could still—"

"No," said Estrella. She was smiling. It was the same smile Papa Morgan had had, that had driven away Hendrick Manygoats Watanabe.

Marina was not as easily routed, and she had a unicorn in her lap. She looked around as she had been told to, in the moon's bright light. The mares were all around them, and the foals, watching as if what she said could matter to them. And how could it? She had nothing wise or intelligent to say.

She had to say something. She said, "We're old stock, too. Aren't we? What happens if they put us under the Mandate?"

Estrella laughed. It was a silvery sound, but very human. "Not what you're afraid of! We turn into what we were to start with. Gypsies. Tinkers. Tamers of horses from Old Troy onward. No more and no less than we always were."

"But," said Marina. "I don't—" She stopped herself, started again. "I'm not seeing what I obviously should see."

"We're all blind when we're young," Concetta said. "We have to learn to see. Like foals."

"Not these," Marina said, ruffling the colt's mane. "We're custodians, aren't we? We were given them, and they us. We protect them."

"That's part of what we do," Concetta said. "We watch over the old arts, too, and the old lines."

"Which happen to go back to the old stories," said Estrella. She seemed to find the fact delightful. So would Marina, if she had time to think about it—if she were not so afraid. She had grown up under the Mandate. She could not imagine it giving way so easily. The family could not be that strong. No one was.

She said that last aloud. Estrella shook her head at Marina's foolishness. "We don't need to be. We have our horses. And," she said, "their children. Haven't you wondered what will become of them?"

"Often," Marina said.

"In an older world," said Concetta, "there would be no place for them. This world, that makes new species out of the rags of the old . . . there's room in it for a myth."

Marina looked at the colt asleep in her lap. He did not feel like a myth. He was warm and solid and inescapably real.

"Is he going to live forever?" she asked.

She had no idea where the question came from. It simply was, hanging out there in front of them.

One of the mares snorted and stamped. The sound swelled to fill the silence.

Estrella spoke softly, almost too soft to hear. "We don't know."

Marina widened her eyes. "You don't know? But you know everything!"

Estrella said nothing. Concetta sighed. "We only know what all the elders know. What we teach the young ones when they're ready. What we preserve here, as far as the world ever knew, is the old way of training horses, and the old lines. Now it knows what the old lines are, and what they come from. But what else we've let the Mandate make here . . . we don't know. They may just be very long-lived."

"How? Like their mothers, still strong at thirty? Or like us with our hundred years? Or more than that?"

They did not answer.

The colt stirred suddenly and scrambled to his feet. He shook himself all over. He scratched an ear with a hind hoof; scratched his rump with his horn. He nudged against Novinha and, with a careful twist of the head that kept the horn from her belly, began vigorously to nurse.

Miranda could see how he would grow, from the way the moonlight struck him: not tall but broad and sturdy, built to carry a rider, to pull a carriage, to stand in marble on a monument. He was not the delicate goat-creature of the myth. None of them was, even the ones who had been bred from Arabians. They were all as real as the stone she sat on.

"And they said," she said, "that the rootstock was a rhinoceros."

"That was a diversion," said Estrella, "to keep the secret safe till people were ready to know it. It's not how long one of them lives, do you see? It's that the line lives. Just as with us. One person dies, gives way to another, but the species goes on and on. Eventually it changes. Or if people meddle with its helices, it discovers what it would have been."

Marina nodded slowly. "I wonder," she said. "Will they breed true?"

"We don't know that, either," said Concetta, but not as if she were deeply troubled by it.

Marina thought of finding answers. Of breeding under the Mandate; of being exempt from it. Of discovering what they had, and what it would turn into.

Shanna Chen-Howard would come back. Others would come with her. They would try to meddle. They could not help it. Somehow under the moon it did not matter. The world was so much wider than it had been, the day the Mandate lowered itself on Dancer's Rest.

"It did better than it knew," she said.

"Oh, it knew," said Concetta. "It just didn't know how much it knew." She pushed herself up, shaking out her skirts. "It was meant, after all, to make the imperfect perfect."

"And when it found something that was exactly as it ought to be," Estrella said over the back of her favorite mare, "it made something completely new, that was as old as memory."

And they said the magic had gone out of the world. Marina shook her head and found herself smiling. It was hard not to smile, with mares and foals all around her, and one coming to rest his horn gently over her heart.

"I wonder," she said, "how you'll take to the training ring." He snorted and raised his head and stamped. And went up, smooth and sure, all silver in the moonlight: a levade as polished as any in the arena.

She laughed. His eye seemed to laugh with her. She had an answer to that question at least. It was quite enough to go on with.

ABOUT THE AUTHOR

Judith Tarr is the author of, to date, seventeen novels including the World Fantasy Award nominee *Lord of the Two Lands,* the historical novels *Throne of Isis, The Eagle's Daughter,* and *Pillar of Fire,* and the acclaimed fantasy trilogy, *The Hound and the Falcon.* She has published short stories in *Asimov's, Amazing,* and numerous anthologies, including *After the King*, *Horsefantastic,* and *Alternate Kennedys.*

She holds a doctorate in medieval studies from Yale, and degrees from Mount Holyoke College and Cambridge University. She handed in the page proofs of her sixth fantasy novel and the final draft of her doctoral dissertation on the same day.

She lives just outside of Tucson, where she raises and trains the Lipizzan mares, Capria and Marita, and Capria's half-Arabian colt. The colt was born with a star on his forehead—but not, as yet, any sign of a horn.

Asked why she wrote this story, Judith replied:

> Very simple. I wrote what I know. I own, or am owned by, a Lipizzan. My friend owns another. We agreed quite some time ago that these are not normal horses. They're a rare breed, one of the rarest in the world. They live long, for horses; they're luminously white; they move with power and grace, and live to dance. And they understand English. They hardly need the horn and the cloven hooves—but since the editors of this anthology asked for both, I took matters to their inevitable conclusion.

LUCY TAYLOR

CONVERGENCE

Peter: **Lucy Taylor**, like P. D. Cacek, is another one whose stories appear in anthologies with names like *Hot Blood 4: Hotter Blood,* and *The Mammoth Book of Erotic Horror.* She lives in the hills outside Boulder, Colorado, with her five cats—which, speaking as a person who has lived with a lot of cats over the years—could quite easily account for a propensity to write horror fiction. But her "Convergence" is no horror story at all: It's a love story with a wonderfully happy/sad ending. . . .

Janet: Lucy is attractive, bright, and ballsy. She's also a terrific writer and a consummate professional. Sometimes I fantasize that up-and-coming writers like Lucy—and Lisa Mason, P. D. Cacek, Marina Fitch, Robert Devereaux, Dave Smeds—all of them close to a generation younger than I, are the new breed of authors. In these fantasies, they dedicate themselves to the development of an intravenous which is plugged into young writers and pumps into their veins a solution containing equal measures of work ethic, respect for deadlines, willingness to pay their dues, modesty, vision, determination, and talent.

Convergence

A LITTLE AFTER ONE A.M., THE WORLD TEETERED and tipped onto its side like a badly spun top. Sable Finley jerked awake with a cry of pain and surprise. She found herself lying on the floor, disoriented and confused, still half-asleep. Where was she? For a moment, she thought she was in Dan's bed back in Charlotte, North Carolina, and somehow, maybe thrashing about in a dream, he had shoved her out of bed. Or that she and Dan were visiting her daughter Miriam and granddaughter Elise in Oakland and an earthquake—the Big One that everyone always talked about—had hit.

Then she opened her eyes and saw, by the light she'd left on in the tiny bathroom, that the room was canted crazily to one side. Her suitcases had tumbled down from the overhead rack—she'd barely missed being bashed by falling Samsonite. The things she'd left out on the desk the night before—her journal, a copy of *Redbook* turned to a page on exercise for women over fifty, the necklace Elise had given her and the photo of her and Dan taken at their wedding the month before—had all slid off onto the floor.

From outside came a great commotion, doors being slammed, voices clamoring. The thunk and scuffle of panicked feet, objects crashing, a man shouting "What's going on?" and a woman's voice, razor-edged with fear, "Oh my God, where are the life vests?"

Then Sable was more awake than she'd ever been in her life, because she remembered now where she was—somewhere between Harwich, England, and Hamburg, Germany, on the Dutch ferry the *Nieuw Amsterdam*.

Going to meet Dan at the software convention in Hamburg before they took off for a few weeks to explore Europe together.

With their first stop in Paris to pick out their new apartment.

To start their new life together as husband and wife.

Dear God.

She shucked off her pajamas, got into a pair of slacks and a shirt. She wanted to take the photo of her family with her, but that was impractical, under the circumstances, so instead she snatched up the necklace Elise had given her, just a child's trinket really, a small silver unicorn with a red rhinestone eye and glittery horn on a cheap metal chain ("To protect you, Grandma" Elise had said). Sable put it around her neck and then stumbled out of the cabin into the chaos of the corridor, up the stairs past the car deck. From where the vehicles had been loaded on board the ferry, she heard what sounded like a demolition derby, metal crashing and crunching against metal and—*no, it couldn't be, wasn't possible*—the roar of water rushing in.

She was pushed from behind and fell forward, banging her knee on the stair. A foot crushed her hand. She yelped, pulled herself to her feet, and made it the rest of the way to the upper deck and then outside into the black, steel-cold night.

The boat felt like it was taking roller coaster plunges off huge cliffs of water, crashing down into jagged crevasses of obsidian sea. More and more listing to starboard. Sable skidded on the slippery deck. Her feet were bare—in her panic, she'd been unable to find the pair of Reeboks she'd left by the bed.

No matter, she told herself, she wasn't going to need shoes. The sea would calm down, the ferry would right itself, and she'd go back to bed. And soon she'd be in Hamburg and Dan would pull her into his big arms and she'd tell him about this terrible night, how afraid she had been, and he'd comfort her, hold her, make it all right.

It was all a bad dream. They weren't sinking. They *couldn't* be sinking.

Someone—a crew member with a bright shock of blood in his hair—thrust a life vest at her.

"Put this on!"

She stared at him, not comprehending.

"What's happening?"

He didn't answer. He was too busy forcing her arms through the holes in the vest, buckling it in the front. He was a small man, dark complected, his eyes cartoonishly big, like an electroshocked owl. She tried to ask him again what was happening, but the ferry lurched violently and water crashed over their heads in a long icy spill. A man and woman, pale lumps of doughy white flesh in little more than their underwear, pushed past her, jabbering in German. Sable followed them, clutching at whatever she could to stay on her feet.

The crew and able-bodied passengers were lowering life rafts into coal-colored waves that bucked and writhed like the back of a sea monster.

Someone shoved Sable from behind. "Go, lady, go!"

She slipped in her bare feet and skidded, arms flailing wildly. She saw the rail coming up—the same rail where just yesterday morning she'd leaned over and tossed bits of brioche into the sun-dazzled sky for the seagulls to catch, daydreaming of Dan and their future—and she screamed as she almost plummeted headfirst into the water, but then hands gripped her and she was lowered, swung really, into a wildly rocking, pitifully small rubber raft with eight other drenched, terrified-looking people.

"Get away, get away before the ferry goes down!" a long-haired man yelled.

Those closest shoved the raft away from the *Nieuw Amsterdam*, which was almost completely capsized now, the starboard deck partially underwater. Many of those left behind dived into the sea. Sable thought she heard seagulls shrieking out words in a Babel of tongues and then realized it was the screams of women who'd jumped or fallen into the sea.

She reached up, fingered the unicorn charm at her throat, where she could feel her pulse beating.

I'll be all right. I'll make it. I have to make it. Dan's waiting for me in Hamburg.

The sinking *Nieuw Amsterdam* went suddenly dark as the electricity failed. Whoever was left aboard now, Sable thought, would be fighting their way through the maze of the luxury ferry's corridors, through its bars and restaurants and casinos, in tomblike blackness. Anyone who hadn't gotten off the ferry by now . . .

But I'm all right, she thought. *I got off the boat and I'm not in the water.*

She clutched at the unicorn charm with numb fingers.

Then a wave the size of a three-story building struck the raft broadside, flipping it over and dumping Sable and all the others on board into the churning North Sea.

"You sure you don't want to fly over with me?" Dan had said. "We can take an extra couple of days before the convention starts to see Hamburg."

Sable had laughed, shook her head. "Sure you don't want to sail over with me instead of flying?"

She and Dan were sitting out in the backyard of her town house in Charlotte, enjoying the benign bake of an Indian summer. They were taking a break from the gardening, snipping back the errant branches of Sable's roses and clipping the weeds, the better to impress potential buyers when the realtor started showing Sable's property the next week. A pitcher of iced tea and a small plate of lemon bars sat on the table between them. Sable's hands smelled of planting and soil, the loamy tang of turned earth.

"I'd love to come on the boat with you," Dan said, biting into a lemon bar, "but then I'd miss most of the software convention. Macro-Bite isn't hiring me to head up the Paris office so I can miss out on their international trade shows."

Sable was grateful he didn't offer his oft-repeated lecture on the safety of flying versus the take-your-life-in-your-hands risk of the freeway drive to the airport. She already knew the statistics proving air travel was safer than almost anything you could do besides sitting at home in an armchair, but that didn't change how she felt about it. She was terrified of flying, of rising into the seamless bowl of sky held aloft only by principles of aerodynamics she had little faith in and no understanding of.

"I'll leave the cruise ship at Southampton and take the train to Harwich," she'd said, thumbing the well-worn travel brochure. "There's a ferry between Harwich and Hamburg every three days."

"I'll meet you," said Dan. "The convention will be winding up then. There's so much I want to show you in Hamburg—the Fish Market and the Old Town Hall and the Rapierbahn, bless its scurrilous heart." He squeezed her hand. "Then we'll drive to Paris and start looking for an apartment."

He'd leaned over and kissed her, and she'd marveled at it all over again, the miracle of meeting the right person this late in life. His lips tasted of lemon and honey and she could feel the desire rising in her as she hadn't felt it since she was a young girl. Sixty-one and in love. In lust as well—to hell with all that platonic, companionate stuff the magazines touted for couples their age—in the bedroom, she felt like a teenager. She felt absurdly lucky.

Sable snapped back to full consciousness in the water. She could hear moans and cries for help and there were things floating—people, objects—all around her. The air tingled with the terror of people in the water. Even for those who wore life vests, thought Sable, how long could they stay alive in water this cold?

How long could *she*? All her life she had been a strong swimmer. She still swam two or three times a week at the health club near her home, but this wasn't about swimming. This was about keeping her head above water and not dying of cold.

The dark, lozenge shape of a lifeboat loomed near her. Sable reached out as it passed, but there was no way she could haul herself into it—the raft was upside down. A wave lifted her up and heaved her away like a bathtub toy in the hand of a child, sending her skidding down its steep slope into a trough. Her head went under. Her mouth filled with brine. The vest shot her to the surface, gagging and gulping for air.

And she was cold, so bone-jarringly cold, every pore quaking with the sensation of being stabbed with tiny hypodermics of ice.

There was no sign of the *Nieuw Amsterdam*. Just the screams and the thrashing of those alive and still in the water.

Oh, Dan, Dan, what should I do?

Cries came to her. She turned and saw another lifeboat approaching her, this one right side up. Someone leaned far out, reaching for her.

"Help me, please help!"

A wave came between them, slapped her away.

"Help!"

The hands reached again and got her this time, hauling her up into the raft, where she collapsed in a shuddering heap against the wet rubber.

In the boat was a man with a well-trimmed goatee wearing a sodden jacket and slacks. Beside him huddled a young woman wearing only a pullover sweater and a pair of underpants, clutching her sides and shivering so hard she looked as if a huge vibrator throbbed at her core.

"The ferry?" asked Sable.

"Gone," said the man.

"What happened?"

"I don't know. Somebody said there was a leak through the doors on the car deck . . . who knows, it all happened so fast."

The girl moaned and clutched her knees, rocking back and forth like an autistic child. Her wet hair, stringy and kelp-like, was plastered around her colorless face.

"Only the two of you made it into the lifeboat?"

"The others fell out," the goateed man said. "A wave hit and turned us over. The other people . . . I don't know what became of them."

"But the *Nieuw Amsterdam*," said Sable, "they must have had time to radio for help. They'll send ships, helicopters. They'll find us."

"They've got to . . . or the cold . . . even if we don't drown, the cold will . . ."

A wave bunted them high, smashed them down. Sable was almost dislodged. She clutched at the ropes crisscrossing the raft.

The girl cried out in French, invoking the names of the saints.

Sable laid a hand on the girl's quaking shoulder. "We'll make it," she said, not knowing if the girl understood her or not, but wanting to offer comfort. "They'll send searchers for us. They'll divert all the boats in the area to look for survivors. We'll be all right."

But what she thought was: *I can't die. Not now, not here. Let someone else die, please God, not me. Dan's waiting for me in Hamburg.*

She reached up and fingered the unicorn charm, wishing it were a crucifix. To distract herself from her terror, she tried to recall what she knew about unicorns. Only that they were partial to virgins, that they were immortal and ancient, and that her eight-year-old granddaughter was fiercely enamored of their mythical species.

And that, like all things miraculous, splendid, and deeply yearned for, Sable knew they didn't exist.

Please God, don't let me die.

"To protect you, Grandma."

Sable had sat with Elise in San Francisco's Golden Gate Park. Dan and Miriam had stayed at home, ostensibly to watch a baseball game but really to allow Sable some private time with her grandchild, a consideration she deeply appreciated. It was Saturday and the green was confettied with bright rectangles of picnic cloths, the blue sky a shifting geometry of Frisbees and kites. Children scampered and dogs raced after balls. A pair of teenage lovers, androgynous with their nose rings and tie-dyed tee shirts that looked like they'd been gleaned from a sixties' rummage sale, cuddled and smooched.

Elise had scowled at the lovers and snorted with disapproval.

At her age, she was still blithely contemptuous of boys and blessedly indifferent to sex, something for which Sable was grateful. She played shortstop on an all girls' softball team, wore her blond hair waifishly short, and populated her room, not with the culture of Barbie and posters of sexless young pop stars, but with unicorns—stuffed unicorns, books about unicorns, coy, bendable unicorns with curly latex manes meant to be combed out and styled. Around her neck she wore a silver unicorn with a ruby-colored eye.

"I wish you wouldn't move to Paris," Elise said. "It's too far away."

"Dan's new job is there," Sable said. "And don't forget, your mom promised to let you come over and spend next summer with us. So you'll be seeing me again in no time at all. And you'll like Paris. Dan says it's a wonderful city."

From the way Elise's lip pouted out, Sable knew she found the idea of Paris about as exciting as the stewed prunes that she'd rejected at breakfast.

"I tell you what," Sable said. "When you come to Paris, I'll take you to see a unicorn. How would you like that?"

Elise perked up. "A unicorn in Paris? Where?"

"A very famous unicorn, in fact. It's in a tapestry in the Musée de Cluny in the Latin Quarter. Dan says that—"

"Oh. I thought you meant a *real* unicorn."

"Honey, there are no real unicorns."

"You mean they're extinct? Like the dinosaurs?"

"I don't know. Maybe there were unicorns at one time or another, but not anymore."

Tears gleamed in Elise's eyes.

Sable said, "Oh, honey, I suppose anything's possible. Just don't cry because I said that there aren't any unicorns."

"I'm not crying about that," said Elise, close to sobbing. "I'm crying because you have to move so far away. I wish you hadn't gotten married. Do you think you'll ever get divorced and come back home?"

"No," said Sable firmly, "Dan and I won't get divorced."

"But Mom says you aren't even going to Europe on the plane together. You're going on a boat by yourself."

"That's because I've got a silly phobia about flying. It's why Dan and I had to take the train out here."

"Why are you afraid?"

"I'm not sure," Sable had answered. "Something to do with the fear that I'll fall. That it's not really possible for the plane to be up there in the first place and that it has to fall down."

And I'll die and that will be all there is, she had thought. *The end of my being, end of love, end of life, everything.*

"You won't fall," Elise had said. She reached up, removed the unicorn locket from around her neck and handed it to Sable.

"Here you go, Grandma. To protect you."

"I can't take this. It's your favorite."

"It's okay," Elise said. "You can keep it for me and give it back next summer, when I come to visit." She looked suddenly uneasy. "You won't change your mind, will you?"

"Of course not, sweetie," Sable had said. "And until you come visit, I'll hang on to the unicorn."

The young woman in the pullover sweater was dead. Sable knew even before the man checked her pulse. The girl's face had the gelid, boneless quality of aspic, like you could scoop out her flesh with a dessert spoon and it would quiver and sparkle with ice crystals.

The goateed man looked at her, shook his head. "Dead."

"But . . . what?" Sable said. "Was she hurt?"

"She was wet," the man said. He could barely get the words out for his teeth's savage clacking. "The cold killed her."

A wave one-two punched the raft, spewing brine into Sable's face, over her sodden clothes. She clutched the ropes as the raft skidded down the side of a wave and partway up another. It was all she could do to hold on. She could not feel her fingers, her toes.

In the distance, like a beam from some hovering spacecraft, a cone of greenish-white light angled down, illuminating the water.

Sable pointed and shrieked, "There! There they are! I told you they'd come! There they are!"

And she thought of the dead girl's family and how they'd have to be told that she died right before help arrived, that if she'd only hung on a few more minutes, just a little while longer, she'd have made it like the other two people in the raft. Sable found herself overcome with gratitude. *I'm going to be rescued.*

The light was joined by another. The two lights crisscrossed and zigzagged. They wove patterns of pearl on the crests and the swells. They cleaved rents in the great, towering black of the sky. Brighter than moonglow, more dazzling than a skyful of northern lights, quicksilver carving the night into ebony hexagons.

Then they moved away in the other direction.

Away from the raft.

"No!"

Sable opened her mouth and banshee-wailed into the night like a madwoman, moonstruck and feral.

"They've gone," said the man, as though the enormity of the horror must be articulated.

"But . . . they can't . . . "

Sable found herself barely able to speak. She sat mutely, staring into the black sky and the fierce, blacker sea, watching the lights of salvation grow thinner and smaller and finally disappear.

They floated.

At one point Sable closed her eyes and either slept or lost consciousness. When she woke up, the French girl wasn't there anymore. Sable didn't know if a wave had washed her out or if the bearded man, not wishing to share their lifeboat with a corpse, had tossed her overboard.

She hoped it wasn't the latter. If she died, she would want someone to find her, send her body home, bury her. Not leave her to rot in the sea.

Don't think like that. Don't.

She shut her eyes and prayed, although she was not a praying person—had grown away from the Faith of her childhood decades ago—but it was as much a bitter rebuke as a plea for mercy. She was angry at this God she did not believe in. How dare he or she! How dare he let her meet Dan, the love of her life, the first man who'd ever held her hand when they went out in public, the first man who'd ever kissed her down *there,* who'd ever moved inside her, slowly, slowly, and made her believe in the power of sexual love for the first time in her life, and let her meet him this late, and then—when they hadn't even had a chance to enjoy a few years together, a few months—take her away.

Unfair.

And Elise.

She must live to see Elise finish high school, finish college, get married or maybe stay single, but become a young woman with all the promise and passion of youth.

Unfair.

She touched her neck. For a second, she thought the unicorn wasn't there anymore, but it was only because her fingers were so cold that she could barely feel the dimpled curves of the metal flank, the tiny sharp point of the horn. She scraped her nails over its surface to assure herself it was still there.

Then white noise and cold night filled her head again. The raft and its other occupant disappeared, and she was clinging to the mane of a powerful unicorn whose jutting horn opened a path through the waves. Wonder and gratitude filled her, but the creature began to melt out from under her, its snowy withers and flanks liquefying into meringue-colored foam. "No!" she cried out as the unicorn's neck dissolved into a high, glistening wave and she was swept under the water.

When she awoke this time, the goateed man was sleeping, and a pale light shone in her eyes. Not the light of the rescue helicopters but the thin, salmon-gold streak of dawn.

The sunlight. The sunlight will warm me.

She felt strait-jacketed by the cold. It was hard to move and harder to think clearly, hard even to remember her exact situation. She'd read that was one of the signs of the last stages of hypothermia.

The sun nudged up into the clouds a bit, like an infected eye squinting up into grey brows, and Sable saw something else.

"My God, look!" she shouted to the goateed man. "Wake up, look!"

Land, a whole verdant shore of it. She tried to remember her geography, the map in the atlas back home. The *Nieuw Amsterdam* had been halfway through the journey when it went down. If the current was sweeping her eastward, then she might be near the Frisian Islands, a narrow necklace of land off the coast of West Germany and the Netherlands. She could see the waves breaking on what looked like a smooth, barrierless shore. The beach appeared deserted, but on the hillsides, she made out dark, rectangular shapes that might have been houses.

"Look!"

She tried to shake the goateed man awake. He slumped forward. Vomit and water ran out of his mouth, and he flopped facedown into the pool of water collected in the bottom of the raft.

"No!" Sable tried to turn the man over, but he was too heavy. She tried holding his head up in her lap and rubbing his head—*there, Dan, does that feel any better? It's late and I'm so tired. Let's go up to bed. Dan, please, help me upstairs*—but after awhile Sable realized the man wasn't Dan, but some stranger who wasn't breathing, who hadn't, in fact, been breathing for a very long time, and she let his head slide off her lap and plop back into the water.

Alone now, she gazed toward the land. It didn't look far away. If she were rested and fresh, she could make it. As cold and exhausted as she was, though . . .

She waited to see if the land grew closer, but the current seemed to be sweeping the raft further out into the sea, bypassing the shore that appeared so tantalizingly near.

I can do it, she thought. *I can make it.*

The life vest would keep her afloat, but prevent her from swimming efficiently. She squirmed out of it and did a few stretches to loosen her stiff limbs. Then she dove into the sea.

Dan is waiting. Waiting for me.

She plowed into the waves, forcing herself to deny the exhaustion and numbness in her muscles, fighting the urge to give up and let herself sink, to rest her weary limbs on the sea bottom. She wasn't going to be like the girl who had died in the raft last night or the man who had died this morning. She could stay alive a little longer. Long enough to get to the shore. To get help.

I can do it for Dan.

For Miriam and Elise.

For once, the sea seemed to side with her, the waves behind her now as she got nearer the beach, pushing her on. The water grew warmer. It felt almost springy and soft now, like a plush carpet, and it was filled with small speckled fish, bright, bug-eyed fish like calico clowns, and Sable knew they were just dots fizzing behind her eyes, rainbow-hued illusions, but that didn't matter—they were beautiful—and she swam with the beaded and calico fish and with hordes of nimble, pinwheeling starfish, she swam with the shimmering schools of them toward the land.

Her knee scraped something hard, a layer of pebbles along a gently inclined beach. She crawled through the surf, then collapsed in the shallows, coughing and spitting up water.

Thank God.

With her eyes still shut, she reached up to touch the unicorn charm. Somehow it had stayed around her neck throughout the ordeal. Maybe Elise had been right, she thought, dizzy with gratitude. Maybe she had been protected.

Surely that she had survived this nightmare, thought Sable, was as miraculous as the powers of any unicorn.

She opened her eyes.

And stared around her, blinking, because something wasn't right, was not as it should be.

The beach she had dragged herself onto appeared to be covered with a vast shallow lake. The smooth vista which, at a distance, she'd thought to be sand was actually the sleek, glassine surface of a huge tidal pool. What she'd taken for houses, she saw now, was really light playing off the facets of rocks on the distant hillsides.

But the water . . . the water was comforting as a bath. Rumpled skeins of velvet flowed around her hips, her wrists. Schools of the wonderful fish swarmed around her fingers, minuscule pinpoints of light in colors she'd never seen, thousands of iridescent fish in what amounted to a cup of seawater. Liquid fish rippling and pulsing beneath the water's sleek skin, around her skin.

Through her skin.

She gasped and stared at this marvel.

The sea of fish eddied and whirled, creating tracerlike patterns. She sat mesmerized by this resplendent geometry and felt a subtle unfurling of memory taking place, a re-weaving of time into one seamless coil.

And all the while the miraculous flood swirled around her, as though the entire lake, ocean, and galaxy were a single drop of semen swarming with sperm.

A pointillist painting created from billions of droplets of life.

Life commingling, reforming, resurrecting itself.

Resurrecting.

She was part of this now, she thought, had always been part of it, and realized with a kind of horrified awe that the solidity of her body was already in question. The world and her physical self were blurring at the edges, bleeding into each other like coloring book pictures crayoned in by a child with no regard for boundaries or lines.

The bright fish, these marvelous dollops and squiggles of life, now pulsed through her bloodstream, her bone marrow, her brain, pulling her into the ebb and flow of the tide, the life that continued, survived, even though it had no right in the world of logic and reason to do so, even though she had never believed such a thing could be possible, any more than she had believed a unicorn charm might keep her safe.

Yet she was safe, she knew, here on the edge of this vast sea of souls.

And she would wait.

As Dan must be waiting for her, even now, through the long, awful morning at the dock in Hamburg. As Miriam and Elise, when they learned what had happened, would wait for news.

She would wait on this strange, benevolent shore for her loved ones to join her.

Knowing, in time, they would come to her.

ABOUT THE AUTHOR

Lucy Taylor is a full-time writer whose horror fiction has appeared in *Little Deaths, Hot Blood 4: Hotter Blood, Northern Frights, Bizarre Dreams, The Mammoth Book of Erotic Horror,* and other anthologies. Her work has also appeared in such publications as *Pulphouse, Palace Corbie, Cemetery Dance,* and *Bizarre Bazaar 92.* Her collections include *Close to the Bone, The Flesh Artist,* and *Unnatural Acts and Other Stories.* Her novel, *The Safety of Unknown Cities,* has recently been published by Darkside Press.

A former resident of Florida, she lives in the hills outside Boulder, Colorado, with her five cats.

MELANIE TEM

HALF-GRANDMA

Peter: **Melanie Tem** is the author of five novels as well as much short fiction. She is also a grandmother and was a social worker for over twenty years. That figures. I find more and more that the fiction that reaches me most immediately tends to be written by people living real lives—not the alligator-wrestling, freight-hopping dust jacket sort, but lives connected to a daily world with other people in it, other lives to be concerned with. The wisdom, tenderness, and quiet authority that inform "Half-Grandma" didn't come from books or TV or the Internet. . . .

Janet: Once upon a time, in one of my many incarnations, I had a small literary agency. That was how I met Melanie. I was, I am proud to say, her first agent. She's a tough lady with amazing courage, an indomitable spirit, and an overdose of talent. I'll never forget how she reamed me out—firmly, but ever-so-gently—when I called her "Mel." She ain't scared of no one, this woman. I cried (happy tears) a couple of years ago when I happened to be present when she won a Bram Stoker Award. I cried again when I read the story you're about to read—because it touched my heart. I knew it would when I asked her to write one. I was right in the first place: She's a heck of a broad and a helluva writer.

Half-Grandma

T HERE WAS A STRANGE HORSE IN THE PASTURE.
White. White and swift. White as concentrated light and swift as sound.

Amelia had been gazing distractedly out her kitchen window at the backyard scene at which she'd gazed distractedly for so many years. It wouldn't have been accurate to say simply that she no longer really saw it; she saw it now in her mind's eye quite as clearly and in as much generous detail as with her physical eyes, and lived it in her bones.

Almost always there had been horses in the pasture—her sons', until they lost interest in horses, too; her younger grandson's, but that had been more her idea than his, and he probably hadn't ridden more than half a dozen times; her own until perhaps ten years ago when she'd decided, with surprisingly little disappointment, that she was too old to risk riding anymore; then a series of boarders. So it took a while this time for the fact to register that there was a horse in the pasture that didn't belong there.

She went on fixing supper for herself and Brandon—mostly, if truth be told, for Brandon; she was hardly ever hungry these days—and contented herself, for the moment, with a discouraged sigh. She'd rented the pasture for two horses, and now, without saying a word to her, they'd put in a third one. Pretty little thing, from what she could see through the trees, but nobody was paying for it to be there. Now she'd have to decide whether to charge extra for it or not, whether to have an unpleasant confrontation.

She resented being put in the position of having to make a moral choice which by rights was not hers. She just wished people would be honest. Maybe she was wrong, but it seemed to her that people as a whole had been more honest in her day. Odd, sobering way to think of it, as though *this* day were not hers.

The back door slammed and Brandon came clattering up the stairs, talking before he even got into the room. His energy delighted and tired Amelia. They were no kin to each other, had known each other only since his family had moved into the neighborhood—which was, though, more than half his life. He'd taken to referring to her as his "half-grandma." It gratified Amelia no end that people could consciously form relationships like that; sometimes, it also saddened her that they had to. "Look what I found!"

He had a bird, pin-feathered and apparently uninjured. His small grimy hands imprisoned it—carefully, tenderly, but imprisoned nonetheless. "Oh, he's beautiful, Brandon," Amelia told him, paying full attention. The waffles would wait. Trying to sound interested and not accusatory, she asked carefully, "Where'd you find him?"

The bird was emitting tiny frantic chirps that urged Amelia to set it free. But Brandon, clearly, was enchanted. He lifted the hollow ball of his fists to his ear and listened intently, face alight. "Hear him? He likes me!"

"He's scared," Amelia countered gently. She sat down at the table and pulled him onto her lap. He didn't resist, but he was far more interested in the bird than in her. "He might be hurt. Did he fall out of the nest?"

Brandon shook his head. Plush gray light through the south window played across the downy back of his neck and on his tousled sandy hair. "I climbed up and got him out."

Amelia caught her breath in alarm. Brandon squirmed when he felt her stiffen, but knew not to look up at her. "Where?" she asked, afraid to know.

Brandon said happily, "He's my *pet*," and slid down. Amelia started to object, but he was already out of the kitchen, down the noisy wooden stairs, out of the house. Temporarily bested, she went to plug in the waffle iron, mulling ways she might explain to a ten-year-old the concept of respecting another creature's place in the universe.

Brandon loved waffles. Whenever he came to her house, he wanted waffles—for breakfast, lunch, and dinner if he was staying a while, for snacks if he was just visiting. Amelia always added one or more healthful things to the basic batter, so he got bananas, bran, yogurt, walnuts, raisins, without her calling attention to them. Among his mother's numerous complaints about him was her assertion that he was a fussy eater, and Amelia guessed that was so, but she noted rather smugly that he'd never turned up his nose at her waffles, no matter what she'd sneaked into them. He'd been known to consume as many as eight at a sitting. Amelia hadn't mentioned waffles to his mother.

Now when she called out the window for him to come in for supper, he answered, "'Kay!" but he didn't come. She made another waffle, which pleased her by coming out in perfect quarters, and then called him again; he answered again, but he still didn't come. Less annoyed than amused by the vagaries of boyhood, predictable through at least four generations of boys she had more or less known—brothers and cousins; sons less well, as it had turned out; grandsons almost not at all—she stacked the waffles on a plate, covered them with a napkin, put them in the oven on "Lo," and went out to get him.

He was down the hill at the edge of the pasture, staring up at the roof of the shed with his arms crossed and a glower on his face. He was such a perfect picture of outrage that Amelia wanted to laugh, but of course she didn't. As she made her way to him she glanced into the pasture. The renter's two horses were there, the black filly and the bay, but she didn't see the white horse. Uneasily she wondered if it had gotten out, then told herself sternly it wasn't her problem, it wasn't even supposed to be there, and went to stand beside Brandon. "Waffles are ready."

"He ran away," the little boy announced unhappily.

Relieved, Amelia nodded. "He went back where he belongs."

Brandon shook his head vehemently. "He belongs to *me*. He was my pet."

"What if he didn't want to be your pet?"

This idea was quite beyond him. "Why not?"

"He's a wild thing. It's not in his nature to be anybody's pet."

"But I didn't want him to go away." Brandon was close to tears. He cried easily, a trait which Amelia found endearing although she guessed that many other adults—and, for different though related reasons, children—did not.

She took his hand, and together they walked back up the hill toward the house and the peach-yogurt waffles. Amelia felt and acknowledged the brief shooting pain in her chest that had lately become familiar. Acknowledged: did not welcome, but did not deny, either. It might be nothing. It might mean her heart, or something less discrete and definable than an organ at the heart of her old body, was preparing to stop.

Brandon wasn't done. "But I wanted to *keep* him!" he wailed.

"I know you did, honey." Amelia smoothed his hair, reflecting tenderly that there would be—probably already had been—countless other things in his life he would yearn to hold on to.

He stayed quiet and teary through his first waffle. After a few unsuccessful attempts to distract or cheer him up, Amelia did her best to respect his feelings and restricted herself to a pat on the hand and an extra dollop of sugarless strawberry preserves. By the time he'd started on the second waffle, hot from the griddle, he was chattering again, telling about his numerous friends at school, all of whom were, as far as Amelia could tell, his *best* friends. She tried to explain that "friend" was too important a word to be used carelessly, that people didn't become your best friends just by being in the same room at the same time, but he would have none of it.

When he pushed his chair back and pronounced himself full, he'd eaten only four and a half waffles, which worried her a little. Wasted food made her feel sad and guilty; maybe the horses or the little wild cats who lived in the shed would eat them.

Brandon wanted to watch TV. More than she ought to, Amelia found herself lying on the couch with the television on; the pseudo-presence of voices and activity assuaged loneliness if she didn't think too much about how phony they were, and often she just didn't feel alert enough to do anything else, even read. Sometimes she was mildly resentful when visitors dropped by, generally one of her three sons who currently lived in town or her older grandson; she did not always want to extricate herself from the murky state of semiconsciousness into which she more and more easily sank, and television provided a host of handy excuses: "I must have dozed off." "It really does turn your brain to mush."

There was practically nothing on that she thought a boy Brandon's age ought to be watching, and she was somewhat appalled by the number and types of shows with which he seemed to be on intimate terms. Finally they agreed on a nature show, and she settled down in the rocker to watch it with him.

For a minute she was dizzy and sick at her stomach. Gripping the arms of the chair and staring fixedly at the regular repeated pattern of granny squares in the last afghan her mother had crocheted, nearly twenty years ago, she dreaded another days-long siege of feeling not at all well. But it passed. There would come a time, she supposed, when such things would not pass. When that happened, she would manage, but she was just as glad it was not now.

As the television program and Brandon and her living room came back into focus, out of the corner of her eye she glimpsed a white horse's head. It wasn't there when she looked directly out the window.

The simple cast of light could give rise to odd shadows and reflections. Years ago she'd had a dog named Jake, one in a long line of dogs and cats all of whose names and idiosyncrasies Amelia remembered fondly, who'd chased mirror reflections and the double circle of a flashlight shined on the ceiling; at certain times of the day at certain times of the year, plain light through the picture window had kept him leaping and mock-snarling for half an hour at a stretch.

Sitting on the floor at her feet, Brandon allowed her to stroke his hair a few times before he pulled away. Obediently she put her hands in her lap, not wanting him to break contact altogether. Really, though, she didn't think that was likely. Brandon wasn't the least bit skittish or reserved; it wasn't as if she had to win him. Still, her satisfaction was deep and sweet when he tipped companionably back against her knee.

It wasn't necessary or even wise to pay close attention to the program, although Amelia was rather interested in astronomy. Brandon would tell her all about it anyway. His memory and enthusiasm impressed her, so that she could put up with, even enjoy, his determination to recount every detail, not necessarily in sequence, not caring if she'd heard it the first time from the primary source. He did that with movies he'd seen, too, and cop shows, which she found considerably less fun to listen to.

Last summer Brandon had gone with his parents on vacation to the Southwest, where he'd learned about Kokopelli, the hump-backed flute player of Navajo legend, whose likeness he'd seen everywhere, from ancient pictographs on the walls of Canyon de Chelly to postcards for the Santa Fe tourists. Brandon had brought her a pair of Kokopelli earrings. "He makes girls have babies!" he'd chortled, and Amelia had laughed, hoping he knew what really made girls have babies. "I told the man they were for my half-grandma, and he said Kokopelli makes people live a long time, too. Live forever." She'd heard a lot about Kokopelli for a while there, and she wore the earrings every time Brandon came over, though he didn't often notice anymore.

It still made her smile to imagine the clerk, doubtless bemused by Brandon's term of relationship to her. Frequently she was saddened— mildly most of the time, but once in a while profoundly, heartbreak- ingly—that she wasn't his *whole* grandma, his *real* grandma. But his exu- berant claiming of her, quite as though there were no need for blood or legal bonds between them, also raised her spirits and renewed her often flagging hope, for him, for herself, and for the world in general. All this from one small boy. Amelia smiled and reached around to pat his cheek. She felt him grin.

She dozed. The older she got the more irregular her sleep patterns became, so that she was asleep when most people were awake and awake when they were asleep a good deal of the time. This accentuated her feel- ing of being not entirely of this world, and for a while she'd struggled against it, forcing herself to stay awake when she craved sleep, lying sleepless in her bed because it was the appointed nighttime hour. But lately it had come to seem not a problem.

"I want a constellation on my bedroom ceiling," Brandon declared.

"Maybe we can find a poster or stickers," Amelia agreed.

"No, I mean a *real* constellation. Orion the Hunter." He made a sort of all-purpose gesture of aggression.

"A constellation is huge," she pointed out. Surely he knew that. "It wouldn't fit on all the ceilings of all the rooms of all the boys in the whole city."

"Okay, then a star." She could tell he was playing, but there was a real dreaminess in his expression that made her want, foolishly, to give him a star. A real star. "I want a star for my very own."

"Stars belong to everybody. They have their own places to be. When they fall to the earth they aren't stars anymore," Amelia told him, and immediately softened her tone. "You can't own a star."

He was openly unpersuaded, and he was also abruptly bored with TV, for which Amelia was glad. "Can I feed the horses?"

Amelia readily gave permission, and got herself up on her feet to accompany him to the pasture. His parents insisted he have supervision, a parental caution that Amelia recognized as more symbolic than functional, since she wouldn't be able to do much to protect him anyway. But she liked watching him, and she loved the horses, and it was good for her to have an excuse to walk that far. When she stood up her ears suddenly rang, her vision blackened, and her head swam, but she steadied herself on the unsteady arm of the rocker until the danger of fainting had receded, for now.

Brandon ran ahead down the hill and then circled back, solicitous of her without seeming to be. He stopped now and then to stuff his pockets with stuff—bugs, flowers, caterpillars, shards of shiny rock and metal—that wouldn't be the same when he put them on his shelf. A bit unsteady still, Amelia kept her gaze mostly on the ground and on her own feet, so Brandon was first to see the white horse in the pasture. "Oh, cool!" he cried. "You got a new one! And look! He likes me!" Indeed, the white horse had come right up to Brandon and was nuzzling his proffered hand. "Hi," he crooned. "Hi, there."

Setting aside her feeling of unwellness and her refreshed annoyance at being taken advantage of by the underhanded renter, Amelia stood back and gladly watched the boy and the horse. Such a lovely tableau they made that there was a sensation of etherealness about them, an out-of-this-world quality at the same time that they seemed utterly, thoroughly, *here* and *now* and of her life as well as their own.

The soft gray coverlet of clouds had come untucked in the west, and the setting sun made an edge there like yellow satin. Brandon's hair and skin shone, and he stood very still to receive the horse's greeting; Amelia almost couldn't bear his stillness, for she understood what it cost him and what he was longing for in return.

The horse's coat shimmered like mother-of-pearl. The animal's movements were so graceful that Amelia found herself thinking of them as poetic, musical. It was light-footed, sure-footed, and its neck arched finely, its mane and tail flowed. Amelia took a step and put her hand out to touch it, not wanting to displace Brandon but suddenly yearning to lay her palm on that smooth iridescent neck right where the flesh curved inward under the jaw.

"It's a unicorn," Brandon whispered, just as Amelia, too, saw the protrusion from the delicate forehead, above and between the huge limpid brown eyes.

Her heart sank, as much for Brandon as for the horse. Something was wrong with this creature. It had been injured. It had a parasite under its skin. It had cancer or some other terrible condition that would cause growths like that.

Now there was an ethical principle at stake far more important than honesty. Keeping animals was a responsibility not to be taken lightly. This poor thing needed medical attention, and, indignation at the renter flaming into outrage, Amelia thought she would just call her own vet to come tend to it and send the renter the bill.

"It's a unicorn, right?" His tone was obviously intended to have shed all awe, was almost taunting now. But he wasn't looking at her. He was fascinated by the horse, which was now making as if to eat out of his hand, never mind that he had nothing to feed it. Amelia all but felt the vellum-soft nose in the creases of her own palm, the warm breath so deceptively like her own and Brandon's from a creature utterly unlike them.

"No, something's wrong. Come here. baby. Let me see." She had enough time to note that the lump was hard and pointed before the horse tossed its head out of her reach, making its mane undulate with light fractured into rainbows more brilliant than she would have expected this close to dusk. It whinnied, peculiarly melodious and high-pitched, then pawed the ground in preparation for flight.

"No, no," Brandon admonished, as if he were training a dog, and put a restraining hand on the glimmering withers. "You stay right here."

The beast shivered his hand off and backed away, nostrils flaring, ears straight up and deeply cupped. It tossed its head again, and the knob below its forelock caught the fading light, sharpening and elongating.

"That's a good horse," Brandon breathed, gently, desperately. "You're not going anywhere."

The animal ducked its head in a gesture whose message was indecipherable—if, indeed, it had a communicative meaning and wasn't simply a muscle stretch or a quick survey of the ground for edibles. Amelia couldn't help but notice that the thing protruding from its forehead was long enough to score the earth, and that when it did so it bent.

"Look!" Brandon was thrilled. "It's bowing to me!"

But then the animal faded into the dusk. Amelia was a little shocked that it vanished so completely; she'd have thought its white coat would collect and reflect what little light remained.

"It was mine!" Brandon cried after it, outraged.

Amelia felt dizzy, found herself sitting and then lying on the ground. It didn't seem an unnatural position to her, and Brandon scarcely took notice. She shook her head against the moist twilit grass and dirt, but couldn't bring herself to enunciate anything.

Dimly she realized that she didn't know what to expect from him now, whether because she really didn't know him very well or because of the essential unpredictability of significant events. He might have sprung at her. He might have stalked away. Instead he sank beside her, the warmth of him seeping under her skin but not all the way into the reservoir where she was neither warm nor cold.

There was a silence that seemed long. Brandon ran his hand, then both hands very lightly over the tufted grass, barely disturbing it, not picking a blade. Amelia drifted with the motion of his hands, the motion of the grass. Brandon said finally, "I just want to keep things I love forever."

Amelia reached for his hand, not knowing whether she took it or not. They stayed there together until it was all the way dark.

Eventually she was able to get to her feet, with considerable help from Brandon. Vaguely it surprised her that she didn't mind relying on him for support and orientation, wasn't embarrassed by her own need or frightened by her own dependence. It seemed to her equally acceptable if they did or did not make it back to the house, equally likely that being with her in this way would prove of value to Brandon as that it would traumatize him.

"What's wrong? What's wrong?" he kept asking. Her arm around his sharp shoulders and her side pressed against his much thinner side, she could feel his whole body shaking.

It took several tries before Amelia could tell him clearly enough to be understood. "I think I've had a stroke," she meant to say, but only a single syllable actually emerged; she hoped it was a useful syllable.

Apparently it was, for he said, "What's that?"

"Something with my brain," was the best she could do, because, in fact, something untoward had happened in her brain, and this was her brain commenting on itself.

In the flat glare of the halogen light over the back door, she saw his wide eyes flicker up to the top of her head, as though he might see what was wrong with her brain. When his gaze slid back down, it didn't quite fix on her face. "Don't die," he said. She understood that she was supposed to assure him, but she had no desire to do so even if it had been possible.

They could not get up the steps. Interminably they tried it on foot, but Amelia, though it was clear to her that these were steps to be climbed, could not comprehend what was wanted of her or by whom. More than once Brandon exhorted, "Pick your foot up. Just pick your foot up." He even bent and grasped her ankle and lifted her leg and deposited her foot on the first step, but then they were stuck in that position, even more precarious.

Amelia, however, did not feel especially precarious; in fact, she felt quite safe. Knowing that the boy was increasingly anxious, she wished she could do something about that but knew she couldn't and was aware of the wish flowing out of her head.

They tried crawling. Brandon tried pushing and pulling her. By now he was panting, crying. Amelia was aware of being chilly, and of bumps and bruises and scratches where probably there had been none before, but the discomfort was minimal. "I can't," Brandon admitted. He sat down beside her, slightly above her on the step.

A warm breeze came over her like breath. Her pulse was like very distant hoofbeats, hesitant then quick. Something soft lay across the back of her neck, not moving away but becoming so immediately and thoroughly familiar that she wasn't aware of it anymore. "Call." This time she said as much as she thought, just the verb with no conception of an object for it or even, once she'd murmured it, of a subject.

Brandon was gone then. Maybe he'd gone into the house to call. Amelia lay in her yard. Her house rose above her, solid and out of her reach and therefore not her house anymore. There came the sensation of warmth above her, then beside her, as the white horse settled down. Amelia wasn't surprised, though she hadn't been expecting it, either.

Sleek hollows. Pliable horn tracing the outline of her face and body as the creature bent its head to her, and the rainbow fringe of its mane. The aroma of horseflesh and flowers without a name. A nickering at the border of words.

The creature snorted and leaped to its feet. A noose lowered around its neck and Brandon crowed wildly from the top step where he stood with braced feet and held the other end of the rope in both hands, "Gotcha!"

The animal reared, hooves like stars and high clear voice. The rope snapped. Brandon gave a heartbroken little shout and flung himself off the steps. He managed a handful of mane, pulling the horse's head sharply around and the lithe body offstride, so that he was knocked down and a flashing hoof just missed his back. He wrapped his arms around a stamping, glancing leg and held on like a much younger child, whimpering.

Amelia knew horses. This one, though she conceded it was not precisely a horse, was spooked. Either she maneuvered around to the side of the frantic beast opposite the frantic boy, or the two of them together whirled; she was now pressed against—into—the glistening, quivering flank.

The animal shrieked and spun on her, wrenching itself free of Brandon, who shrieked, too. Amelia thought to flatten herself among the flying hooves and fists, but couldn't be sure that she had. In some way, though, she was between beast and boy, protecting one from the other, and then the unicorn broke into a seamless canter that carried it between the dark earth and the dark sky where it disappeared.

"You let it go!"

Amelia intended to tell him, "Yes." She had the impression that he held her accountable not only for this abdication but also for the escape of the bird and the inaccessibility of stars. And there was something to that. She wasn't to blame for the impermanence of things, of course, but she had assumed the role of messenger, and she concurred with Brandon's instinct that a certain moral responsibility accrued.

So she made an enormous effort and gathered him to her. He came easily. She couldn't stay with him much longer. "Don't go," Brandon whispered.

She was floating and flashing like stars. She meant to tell him, "Good-bye" and "I love you," but there was no way for either of them to know if that was what she said.

ABOUT THE AUTHOR

Melanie Tem's first publications were short stories in various small and literary magazines. Her articles have been published in professional journals and popular magazines.

She has published short fiction in various anthologies and magazines. Novels are *Prodigal* (Dell), which won the Bram Stoker Award for Significant Achievement, First Novel; *Wilding* (Dell), *Making Love* (with Nancy Holder; Dell; Raven Books, London); *Revenant* (Dell; Headline, London); and the forthcoming *Desmodus* (Dell; Headline).

Born and raised in rural Pennsylvania, Melanie Tem lives in Denver with her husband, writer Steve Rasnic Tem. They have four children and a granddaughter. She was a social worker for over twenty years before retiring in 1992 to write full-time.

NANCY WILLARD

THE TROUBLE WITH UNICORNS

Peter and Janet: Nancy didn't want anything said about her, beyond giving her biographical data. We don't think, however, that she'll object to us saying that we are extremely pleased that she wrote a story for this anthology.

The Trouble with Unicorns

⸺◅◦ʊʊʊ\ ∫ ʊʊʊ◦▻⸺

THE LAST WEEKEND SARAH CAME TO VISIT HER
father before she left for Europe, Mack the white cat crawled under the
upstairs bathroom sink to die. The sink in Toby's apartment leaked and
was stained with purple streaks; the previous tenant had been a painter.
Mack neither ate nor drank. He had spread himself flat on the blue towel,
like an island about to be submerged. Sarah sat on the edge of the bathtub
and wept. The week she was born, seventeen years ago when they were
still a family, a white kitten had mewed at the door and stayed. Now on
an ordinary Friday in April he was dying.

Tk tk tk.

The faucet dripped slowly and steadily.

Toby lifted Mack into the cardboard carrier. He gave a thin cry deep
in his throat, and Sarah tucked the towel around him. On his honeymoon
Toby had stolen that towel from a hotel in Venice because he loved the
winged lion in the center, and Sarah's mother had said, "If you're going
to steal from a hotel, steal an ashtray. It'll last longer." They'd ended up
fighting about it.

Sarah sat rigidly beside her father in the car, embracing the carrier,
her long blond hair falling across her cheeks.

"Comfort him," said Toby. "Talk to him."

Though he did not care much for cats, Toby had learned to love this
one. After the divorce Sarah's mother suddenly discovered she was aller-
gic to all fur-bearing animals. Toby got complete custody of Mack and
custody of Sarah every other weekend.

He drove into the parking lot of the Hudson Valley Animal Hospital
with a feeling of dread.

"I'll take the carrier," he said.

"No, let me," said Sarah and jumped out of the car and walked ahead of him to the door of the animal hospital.

Toby was astonished to find the waiting room empty. The plump receptionist was sitting with her back to him, and he had to lean across the counter and call out, "We're here with Mack."

"Take room five," the receptionist said, and continued typing.

When Sarah tipped the carrier to coax Mack out, he looked as though he'd been poured onto the examination table. Dr. Wu bustled in, felt the cat's back, and peered into his yellow eyes, which gazed past all of them as if at a distant horizon.

"You've had this old fellow a mighty long time," he remarked.

"That's right," said Toby and wanted to weep.

"I know this is tough on both of you. Take your time saying good-bye."

Dr. Wu left them alone in the treatment room. Mack kept his eyes open as Sarah stroked him, but he did not purr or rub his face against her palm, and Sarah said, "Is he going to die?"

"I think so," said Toby. "Yes. He is going to die."

No point in telling her about the lethal injection, he thought.

"Can we bury him?" asked Sarah. She had stopped crying.

"Of course we can," said Toby, "Did you think we'd just leave him here? When they call me to come, I'll pick up his ashes—"

"Oh," said Sarah, "ashes."

"I think that's how they usually do it. When you go back to your mother's house, you can scatter them in the garden. Or wherever you want."

Sarah said nothing for a long time.

"Dad, when Mack dies, can we get a baby ferret?"

Toby was shocked.

"Sure we could get a ferret, but not right away. I mean, don't you think we should have a period of mourning?"

"Oh, sure," she said. "I didn't mean right away."

He knew she was only saying that to placate him. Still, he'd made his point, that someone who has watched over you since you were born deserves a few tears, a warm bed by the fire in your broken heart.

Saturday morning when he went to his job at the piano store, he saw the old cat's face in every gleaming surface, heard his faint mew behind every note he played to show customers why they should buy a Yamaha spinnet and not a Steinway grand. He left work early and drove to pick up the ashes.

"Name?" asked the receptionist.

"Toby Martinson."

A different day. The office was filled with elderly people and cats in cages. There were two poodles on leashes and a black spaniel inert on his mistress' lap. Today's receptionist was thin, blond, and efficient. She tipped her face up to him.

"And when did you bring Toby in?"

The vision of his own ashes being carried out in a cardboard box sent chills through him.

"I didn't bring Toby in," he heard himself shouting. "*I'm* Toby. I've come for Mack's ashes."

The receptionist stared at him. "You should have said so right off."

She disappeared through a room directly behind the desk. She was gone so long he wondered if she'd lost Mack or given him to the wrong person. God knows, he told himself, it would be easy to get ashes mixed up. What was that poem he'd had to memorize in freshman English? He'd forgotten the author, the title, the poem. All he could remember was a single line.

A bracelet of bright hair about the bone.

Turning his back on the waiting room full of beasts and their masters, he read and reread the notices on the bulletin board beside the receptionist's desk.

BROWN HUSKY, 12 weeks old, all shots, loves children, needs good home. Owner moving and can't keep her.

TWO CATS FREE to good homes. Neutered, declawed, 1 male, 1 female.

Must give away my baby male enrocinul. Call evenings.

Toby reread the third notice more carefully, a pale green index card. *Enrocinul.* A computer glitch, probably, for something as ordinary as a parakeet. But were parakeets ordinary or merely familiar? Nothing in the universe was ordinary if you really thought about it.

An interesting computer glitch. Then he realized the notice was handprinted.

He heard his name called and went forward to receive the plain brown box that held Mack's mortal remains. On his way out, he pulled the green card from the board, tucked it inside his coat pocket, and walked out into the May morning.

To his relief, Sarah was not home when he arrived. He left the box on

the backseat of the car—Mack had always loved riding in the backseat—
and hurried into the kitchen and put water on for spaghetti. Well, why not
get another pet? he asked himself. Another reason for Sarah to spend time
with you, said a voice in his head, but he dismissed it. But not a ferret.
Another cat, maybe. Unless she has her heart set on a ferret.

He locked the box of ashes in the trunk of the car.

Sarah was in the kitchen, talking on the phone.

"Gotta go," she said. " 'Bye, Mom."

"Honey, I've got Mack's ashes."

She stood very still.

"Can I see them?"

"There's not much to see," said Toby. "If you want the key to the
trunk, you're welcome to look. But the real Mack isn't in that box."

He could not tell how she was taking it.

"Can we go to Wendy's for supper?" she asked.

On the way, he talked about school and about the trip to Europe. Suddenly she said, "Were there pieces of bone?"

"What?" exclaimed Toby, startled.

"Were there pieces of bone in Mack's ashes?"

"No," he said. "I don't think so."

"I read that sometimes there are," said Sarah.

After supper while Sarah was watching TV, he pulled out the green
index card, kicked off his shoes, and standing in the kitchen full of dirty
dishes, he dialed the number. He counted the rings, four, five.

I'll give it ten, Toby told himself.

On the seventh ring, a woman's voice broke in.

"Hello?"

"I'm calling about the enrocinul."

"Oh, yeah," said the voice. "You want it?"

"I don't know. Could you give me a little more information?"

"What kind of information?" The woman's voice was veiled with
suspicion.

"I've never heard of an enrocinul. Could you tell me—"

"It's a horse," she replied. "A small horse."

"A horse is out of the question," he said. "I live in an apartment."

"So do I," said the woman. "Two Triangle Court. When will you be
coming?"

"How about two o'clock on Sunday?"

She answered him with a long silence.

"How will I know it's you?" she whispered.

"I beg your pardon?"

"When you come on Sunday, how will I know it's you? What do you look like?"

"I have blue eyes and short brown hair, and I'll be wearing a faded denim jacket. My daughter will be coming with me."

"And your wife?"

"No, that's over," he laughed. "Just my daughter."

He hung up the phone and padded barefoot into the living room. Instantly his daughter lifted the remote control and switched off the TV. He pretended not to notice.

"Honey, I've got a lead on a new pet," he said. "Not a replacement for Mack, of course. Nothing can ever replace Mack."

"A ferret? "she asked.

"An enrocinul," he said. "It's a small horse."

She stared at him, wide-eyed.

"The owner is keeping it in her apartment," he added. "I thought we could just drive over to Clintonville and take a look at it."

Though he'd grown up in Clintonville, Toby had never heard of Triangle Court. Probably one of those new suburban developments, he thought. But when he stopped at his favorite Mobile station and asked for directions, there it was, on the map on the wall in the office, a tiny road in the old downtown, behind the public library.

His heart sank. Half the murders in Clintonville happened within a three-block radius of the library. The evening hours had been canceled. Two weeks ago, a man was found shot dead on the library steps clutching a book on how to raise bonsai.

As he climbed back into the car, Sarah said, "Dad, when are you going to teach me to drive?"

"I thought your mom was going to teach you."

"No, she says it makes her nervous."

"Well, I guess we could go out on one of these country roads and get you started some evening," said Toby, hoping she wouldn't pin him down to a time. He had a recurring image of her climbing back into the car after the first lesson and driving away from him for good. "Lock your door."

They passed the Daily Treat Deli and the library and turned into the empty parking lot behind the library. On the far side of the lot stood a row of old apartment buildings, three of them boarded up. Someone had pinned a handwritten note to the PARKING FOR PATRONS ONLY sign:

This is Triangle Court.

"We're here," said Toby.

Sarah squinted out of the window.

"Dad, this can't be the place."

"Two Triangle Court. It's got to be that one."

The neighborhood looked almost benign with the sunlight gleaming on the budding branches of ascanthus, sumac, and honeysuckle, tangled in the small backyards behind the buildings. Toby searched for a buzzer.

"I don't see how we can ever locate—"

"Dad," said Sarah, "the door is open."

There were six mailboxes in the dark hall. The names had fallen off all but one of them.

"Number Two, Betty Belinsky," read Toby, "It must be that one at the end of the hall."

The corridor smelled of mildew; Toby had a brief but intense image of *National Geographic*s piled to the ceiling in the basement of the house where he'd grown up. Beyond the door of number two droned a voice, just below the level of comprehension. Toby knocked. Nobody answered.

"She can't hear me over the TV."

"She'll hear *me*," said Sarah and pounded the door with her fist.

The voice stopped droning.

The door opened.

Oh, my Lord, thought Toby, what a homely woman.

He was used to attractive women, like his daughter, who had the bloom of youth on her, and his ex-wife, who had short red hair and had dieted herself down to a size 8. Betty Belinsky was fortyish, tall, and chunky about the hips, and she wore her straight brown hair pulled back in a blue plastic barette. Both her Led Zeppelin sweatshirt and her jeans looked a size too small for her.

"I've come about the enrocinul," said Toby.

She squinted at him.

"Who are you?"

"My name is Toby Martinson." He slid a card out of his wallet and handed it to. "I sell pianos for Yamaha."

"Um." She did not take the card, and she did not close the door.

"Sometimes I tune them," he added.

"Come in," said Betty Belinsky. "Make yourselves at home."

She pointed to an overstuffed sofa that had long ago given up on the good life and was dragging its belly on the floor; the red plush cushions had bald spots. It rose forlornly above the open boxes of books that covered the floor. Toby could not resist glancing at the titles in the box nearest him: *The Joy of Cooking, The Collected Works of Plato, Selected*

Songs of Thomas Campion. Perhaps they weren't her books at all. Perhaps she was organizing a sale of the public library discards. But who would discard *The Joy of Cooking?*

Stepping over the cartons, Toby and Sarah sat down gingerly on the sofa, which smelled of cat urine.

As Betty Belinsky disappeared behind the red velvet curtain that separated her living room from all that lay beyond, Toby had the odd feeling they were about to see the first act of a play.

"Sorry about the mess," she called out. "I'm moving."

In a few minutes she stepped back into the room, holding the enrocinul in her arms.

A faint pang of disappointment filled Toby; he looked more like a goat than a horse.

Until she set him down, and then he saw the animal as he really was: a small white horse with a knob in the center of his forehead. No goat had hair this fine, with the sheen of loosened milkweed on it. Toby reached out and stroked the animal's back. It was soft as the fur under a cat's chin. The enrocinul's tail was long but stringy, a dull ivory; the exact shade of my great grandmother's hair, thought Toby, when she let me braid it before she went to bed.

Sarah sank to her knees beside him and stroked his bristly mane.

"Oh, he's adorable," she cooed. "Where did you get him?"

"He was standing on the center strip along Route 55, trying to cross," replied Betty Belinsky. "So many animals get hit crossing that road, I figured he wouldn't have a chance. I pulled over and went back and got him."

"He let you pick him up?" exclaimed Toby.

"Maybe he was somebody's pet," said Sarah.

"Well, of course he was somebody's pet. He was wearing a collar with his name on it. Enrocinul."

"Is that his name or the name for what he is?" asked Toby.

"Oh, who knows what he is?" said Betty Belinksy. "I figured if I ran an ad for a small horse, nobody would answer it. This building's due to be knocked down next month. Did you bring a pet carrier?"

"A carrier?" inquired Toby.

"I thought maybe you'd have one."

"He doesn't need a carrier," said Sarah. "He has me."

She led the way into the parking lot. The enrocinul shivered a little, though the air was not cold, and buried his head in the crook of Sarah's arm. Very carefully she climbed into the backseat.

"Well, good-bye, Miss Belinsky," said Toby.

In the rearview mirror, Toby saw the animal lay its head on his daughter's lap. He watched her hands stroke the creature's milky ears and fiddle with the golden collar. The sun caught the letters on the animal's golden collar; they were deeply engraved and easy to read: *L'Unicorne.*

Toby nearly hit a parked car.

"Dad!" cried Sarah.

"Honey, we have a unicorn!" he shouted. "Look at the writing in the mirror! We have a unicorn—a French unicorn!"

They decided not to tell anyone.

"Especially not Mom," said Sarah. "She'd let the whole world know. I wish I weren't going away for the summer."

Before they got out of the car, Sarah unbuckled the unicorn's collar. The unicorn whickered and scratched his incipient horn against Sarah's hand, as if it itched. Toby remarked that a golden collar was far too valuable to leave lying around the house. At his suggestion, they hid it in the icebox, behind a saucer on which sat one rancid chunk of butter.

"Not much of a hiding place," said Sarah. "I mean, your icebox is so empty."

Since the divorce Toby had gotten into the habit of ordering takeout, mostly pizza and Chinese.

The unicorn licked its lips.

"What does the unicorn eat?" asked Sarah.

Toby felt a little stab of guilt.

"I don't know. We could try him on granola." He took a soup bowl from the cupboard, filled it with water, and set it in a corner of the kitchen. "I need to stop by the A & P and pick up a few things," he added.

"I'll stay here," said Sarah, "with the unicorn."

He left them in the living room watching *Sesame Street.*

The A & P was thronged. Toby grabbed a cart and dodged his way first down one aisle, then another, hoping inspiration would strike him. The array of cereals daunted him: bright boxes emblazoned with children grinning over bowls that foamed with cornflakes or Wheaties, and waving their spoons for joy. What if the unicorn didn't like granola? What if it preferred Cheerios or Quaker Oats?

He passed the fruit juice aisle. The pet food. Kiblets for the Older Cat. Chow for Seniors: twenty-five percent less fat.

What if the unicorn ate hay? "Christ," he muttered, "I don't know a damn thing about unicorns."

He remembered the pay phone just outside by the rack of shopping carts, and when his hand found the green card in his jacket pocket, he left his empty cart in the pet food aisle, hurried out of the store and dialed Betty Belinsky's number. She picked it up on the first ring.

"Hello," said a soft voice.

"Is this Betty?"

"Who is this?" demanded the voice.

"Toby. I'm the man who came by your place today and picked up the unicorn."

"I gave you an enrocinul," said the voice. It sounded like Betty trying to disguise her voice by holding her nose.

A truck stopped at the curb, its gears screeching.

"What does he eat?" shouted Toby. "I forgot to ask you."

"Where are you? I can't hear a thing."

"I'm at the A & P."

"Hot milk with honey is good," said Betty dreamily. "That's what I'm having."

"Thanks," said Toby. "Sorry to bother you."

When he opened the front door, clutching his bottle of milk and jar of honey, the TV was on but there was no sign of Sarah or the unicorn.

"Sarah?"

"I'm in the bathroom."

The door was open. Sarah was sitting in the middle of the floor, with the unicorn beside her. He had tucked his legs neatly under himself and was watching a faint reflection of himself in the full-length mirror on the back of the door. How murky the glass had become! The three of them might have been gazing into a pool of dark water for all the clarity it gave them.

"He's lonely," she said. "Dad, your mirror is so dirty I can hardly see myself."

Toby left the unicorn looking for its reflection while he drove Sarah back to her mother's house. It was a custom they all accepted, that he said good-bye to Sarah at the curb and never entered the house. He felt sure her mother was at the upstairs window, watching them hug each other.

"Take real good care of the unicorn for me," said Sarah. "God, I wish I weren't going. He'll be all grown up next time I see him," she added in mournful tones.

"Maybe he's a toy unicorn," said Toby. "Betty said he could live in an apartment."

Maybe she was lying a voice very much like Betty's whispered from deep inside his head.

As he turned into his own street, he remembered Mack's ashes, locked in the trunk.

*   *   *

He unlocked the door of his apartment and headed straight for the bath-room. The unicorn was still gazing into the mirror on the back of the door. The glass looked less murky, now, or perhaps he was getting used to it.

"What do you see, little fella?"

Toby sat down on the tile floor next to the unicorn and scratched it between the ears, glanced up at the mirror, and gave a whistle of surprise. The sink, toilet, and bathtub had vanished, and in their place he found himself staring at a porphyry pedestal, an alabaster urn, and a marble pool ringed at the top with gold, sunk in a lush bed of violets and columbine and bleeding hearts. Seated cross-legged in the violets was a young man with snappy blue eyes and short brown hair and a jacket that might have been cut from the sky on a spring morning.

What right does that guy have to be so goddamn happy? thought Toby.

Then with a shock he realized the man in the mirror was himself.

He spun around, panicked. To his relief, the toilet, the tub, the sink with its purple streaks in his bathroom had not budged.

Holding his breath, Toby leaned closer to the glass. By sitting per-fectly still, he found he could bring the garden into sharp focus. Now he recognized some of the trees by the cut of their leaves: cherry and oak and linden, walnut and plum. Not since he'd gotten his first pair of glasses in seventh grade had he seen trees that clearly.

The man in the mirror had a lute slung over his shoulder and was picking fruit from a low tree that resembled a date palm. Under the tree spread a deep shadow; the tiny flowers dotting it had been pressed flat, as if someone had recently been sleeping there.

Unicorn. The only thing missing in the mirror was the unicorn, who had not moved from his place beside Toby.

The window in the bathroom was dark.

The mirror, too, was dark.

What a bizarre dream, he thought. How long have I been sitting here? He hated to have time slip away from him without telling him where it was going. The poor beast must be starving. Toby stood up carefully, so as not to disturb him, and tiptoed into the kitchen, poured milk into a saucepan without measuring it, and turned on the stove. Suddenly there rose before him a clear image of Sarah's mother, heating the baby bottle, testing the temperature of the milk on the inside of her wrist. The image filled him with melancholy.

He poured the milk into a cereal bowl, stirred in a spoonful of honey, and carried it into the bathroom.

Under the bathroom sink lay the unicorn, flat and still, his eyes closed, his head on his hooves. *An island about to be submerged. A lost continent.*

Tk tk tk.

The faucet dripped as steadily as a water clock, unheard until all the other sounds in the room have left it.

He set the bowl on the sink and ran back into the kitchen. The clock over the stove said half past ten.

I can't call her later than eleven, he told himself.

Without looking at the clock, he dialed Betty Belinsky. The phone rang one, two, three, four, five, six. He imagined her asleep on the saggy sofa, exhausted from packing books or hauling them to a place of storage. What if her house was gone? "I will stay calm," said Toby to himself. I will stay on this phone until she answers it.

"Argh," said a sleepy voice.

"Betty?"

"Who is this?" demanded the voice, no longer sleepy.

"It's Toby. Listen, I hate to bother you but the unicorn is sick."

There was a long silence.

"I'll be right over," she said.

Toby started to give her his address but she cut him off.

"I already know where you live," said Betty Belinsky. "I looked you up in the phone book."

When the doorbell rang, he was sitting by the unicorn, stroking its ears. As he raced to open the door, it opened by itself and Betty Belinksy stepped inside. She was wearing a plaid raincoat and a purple rain bonnet and clutching a freshly boxed pizza.

"I asked the cab to stop at Dominick's," she said. "I thought you might be hungry."

"I'm starved," said Toby.

"Where's the unicorn?"

"In the bathroom," answered Toby.

They decided to eat the pizza on the bathroom floor, so they could keep an eye on the unicorn. Toby pulled the last two napkins from a package in the cupboard. As he rummaged through the icebox for a beer, he caught sight of the unicorn's golden collar on a saucer behind the butter.

"Maybe he's missing this," he said and held it up to show Betty, who looked surprised.

"Why did you take it from him?" she asked.

"I thought he'd be more comfortable without it."

"Better give it back," said Betty.

The unicorn had not moved from its spot in front of the mirror. There was something touching about the way his hair thinned into a pale band where the collar had been, and he did not struggle when Toby buckled it into place.

"We're down to the Happy Birthday napkins," said Toby. He opened the pizza box and offered Betty Belinksy the first piece.

"He's lonely," said Betty. "Just like my parakeet. My parakeet used to spend hours looking at herself in the toaster."

"The toaster?" exclaimed Toby.

She nodded, licking her fingers.

"It was a Toastmaster, and I always kept it polished. When I let Henrietta out after breakfast, she liked to sit on the toaster and watch her reflection. She thought it was another parakeet. Just like the unicorn in the mirror—" Betty sucked in her breath. "My God, there *isn't* a unicorn in the mirror!"

The two of them sat huddled on the cold floor. Betty shivered a little. There were two people in the mirror now, the man and a woman. Not a woman you'd call pretty. But attractive, quirky, and full of surprises, like a path twinkling with rain caught in the hoofprints of running deer. Toby admired the woman's hair, tied back with a scarf the color of purple heather. It tumbled dark and shining over her plaid cloak.

Why couldn't I meet someone like her? thought Toby.

Betty leaned forward.

"What are *they* having?"

"Roast chicken and wine," said Toby.

Close to his ear, a man's voice crooned,

> *I care not for these ladies*
> *That must be woo'd and prayed.*
> *Give me kind Amaryllis,*
> *the wanton country maid.*

The unicorn lifted his head.

When did I turn on the radio? thought Toby. I don't even have a radio.

The man in the mirror laid aside his lute. Of course it was he who had sung.

"Please finish the song," begged the woman in the mirror.

"Alas, dear lady, I've forgotten the words," said her companion.

"Nature art disdaineth," sang Betty, and she ran her fingers through the unicorn's mane. "Her beauty is her own."

"You know that song?" asked Toby, astonished.

She nodded without missing a beat.

> *Her when we court and kiss,*
> *She cries, forsooth, let go;*
> *But when we come where comfort is,*
> *She never will say no.*

The man and woman in the mirror were feeding each other chunks of chicken breast.

"Our unicorn is perking up," said Toby. "If he were a cat, he'd be purring."

Betty stopped petting the unicorn.

"The trouble with unicorns is, they can't do anything for you," she muttered. "A horse can carry you. You can put your money on a horse. A dog can protect you. A cat can mouse for you. A parakeet can talk to you. But a unicorn is useless."

"Shhh," said Toby. "You'll hurt his feelings."

"What about *my* feelings? I brought that beast home, I fed him, I talked to him, I gave him my love"—she was almost shouting now—"and all that time he just sat around looking pleased with himself. What has a unicorn ever done for me?"

As if he'd been waiting for this moment, the unicorn seized her sleeve in his mouth and held it for an instant, savoring it.

Then he leapt straight into the mirror.

With a tremendous splash, Betty and the woman in the mirror shattered the dark surface of the pool and sank out of sight.

Toby jumped to his feet and dove in after them.

"What are you doing?" cried the man in the mirror. "I can't swim."

"Neither can I," gasped Toby.

He could not see the unicorn, but a pearly light shot with gold shivered and rippled around the four of them.

I'm dying, he thought. All the nights he'd fretted about losing Sarah, it never dawned on him that she could lose him.

He was floating on the water, which bore him up easily, as if he had left himself behind and become his own reflection.

Betty was paddling toward him. Toby held out his hand to her, and together they clambered over the edge of the pool.

They found themselves standing between the sink and the bathtub. In the mirror, a middle-aged man and a chunky woman were walking away into whatever country was home to the unicorn. Stout in her sweatshirt and jeans the woman in the mirror might have been Eve following Adam out of the garden. You could tell by the way the man walked that his fears and failures weighed heavily on him.

"There but for the grace of God go I," said Toby. He turned to kiss Betty Belinksy, who was laughing and shaking the spring rain out of her shining hair.

ABOUT THE AUTHOR

Nancy Willard has published two novels, *Things Invisible To See* and *Sister Water;* a book of essays on writing, *Telling Time: Angels, Ancestors and Stories;* numerous collections of poetry, including *Household Tales of Moon and Water* and *A Visit to William Blake's Inn: Poems for Innocent and Experienced Travelers.* Her most recent book for children is *An Alphabet of Angels,* which she also illustrated. Her work has appeared in *The New Yorker, Esquire,* and the O. Henry and Pushcart Prize anthologies.

TAD WILLIAMS

—⚬⚬⚬⚬—

THREE DUETS FOR VIRGIN AND NOSEHORN

Peter: **Tad Williams,** one of the best and best-known fantasists currently at work, writes that he "grew up in Palo Alto, a small but fiercely self-congratulatory (with some reason) town in Northern California . . ." (*Privileged editorial digression:* No, it *hasn't* any bloody reason—I've lived there myself.) He now lives in London, ". . . where they seem to have grown bored by the insane panoply of weather types with which we Americans indulge ourselves and have sensibly limited themselves to two: 'gray and wet,' or 'gray and very, very wet.'" After giving up on an early dream of being an archaeologist, having discovered that it involved work, he sensibly decided to settle for being hugely famous, "skip(ping) over all the irritating intermediary bits . . ." He is also half-owner of a multimedia company called Telemorphix, Inc. "We produce an interactive television show called *Twenty-first Century Vaudeville.* It's too weird to explain. . . ."

Janet: Here is another writer I have known forever, one of whom I can truly say, "I knew him when. . . ." Mostly we'd meet at BayCon, a medium-sized SF convention which I used to attend for pretty much the express purpose of playing catch-up with old friends. Tad was always there, hanging around, talking about writing, and being hopelessly intelligent and—dare I say it—*nice*. Then one year he announced that he was writing a novel. He did. And the rest, as they say, is (*New York Times* bestselling) history.

As for this story, it's an absolute delight—a little scary, a little history, and a lot Tad.

Three Duets for Virgin
and Nosehorn

F ATHER JOAO CONTEMPLATES THE BOX, A WOODEN
crate taller than the priest himself and as long as two men lying down,
lashed with ropes as if to keep its occupant prisoner. Something is hidden
inside, something dead yet extraordinary. It is a Wonder, or so he has
been told, but it is meant for another and much greater man. Joao must
care for it, but he is not allowed to see it. Like Something Else he could
name.

Father Joao is weary and sick and full of heretical thoughts.

He listens to the rain drumming on the deck above his head. The ship
pitches forward, descending into a trough between waves, and the ropes
that hold the great box in place creak. After a week he is quite accustomed to the ship's drunken wallowing, and his stomach no longer crawls
into his throat at every shudder, but for all of his traveling, he will never
feel happy on the sea.

The ship lurches again and he steadies himself against the crate.
Something pricks him. He sucks air between his teeth and lifts his hand
so he can examine it in the faint candlelight. A thin wooden splinter has
lodged in his wrist, a faint dark line running shallowly beneath the skin.
A bead of blood trembles like mercury where it has entered. Joao tugs out
the splinter and wipes the blood with his sleeve. Pressing to staunch the
flow, he stares at the squat, shadowed box and wonders why his God has
deserted him.

∞   ∞   ∞

"You are a pretty one, Marje. Why aren't you married?"

The girl blushes, but at the same time she is secretly irritated. Her masters, the Planckfelts, work her so hard that when does she find even a chance to wash her face, let alone look for a husband? Still, it is nice to be noticed, especially by such a distinguished man as the Artist.

He is famous, this man, and though from Marje's perspective he is very old—close to fifty, surely—he is handsome, long of face and merry-eyed, and still with all his curly hair. He also has extraordinarily large and capable-looking hands. Marje cannot help but stare at his hands, knowing that they have made pictures that hang on the walls of the greatest buildings in Christendom, that they have clasped the hands of other great men—the Artist is an intimate of archbishops and kings, and even the Holy Roman Emperor himself. And yet he is not proud or snobbish: when she serves him his beer, he smiles sweetly as he thanks her and squeezes her own small hand when he takes the tankard.

"Have you no special friend, then? Surely the young men have noticed a blossom as sweet as you?"

How can she explain? Marje is a healthy, strong girl, quick with a smile and as graceful as a busy servant can afford to be. She has straw-golden hair. (She hides it under her cap, but during the heat and bustle of a long day it begins to work its way free and to dangle in moist curls down the back of her neck.) If her small nose turns up at the end a little more than would be appropriate in a Florentine or Venetian beauty, well, this is not Italy after all, and she is a serving-wench, not a prospect for marriage into a noble family. Marje is quite as beautiful as she needs to be, and yes, as she hurries through the market on her mistress's errands, she has many admirers.

But she has little time for them. She is a careful girl, and her standards are unfortunately high. The men who would happily marry her have less poetry in their souls than mud on their clogs, and the wealthy and learned ones to whom her master Jobst Planckfelt plays host are not looking for a bride among the linens and crockery, have no honorable interest in a girl with no money and a drunkard father.

"I am too busy, Sir," she says. "My lady keeps me very occupied caring for our household and guests. It is a difficult task, running a large house. I am sure your wife would agree with me."

The Artist's face darkens a little. Marje is sad to see the smile fade, but not unhappy to have made the point. These flirtatious men! Between the dullards and the rakes, it is hard for an honest girl to make her way. In any case, it never hurts to remind a married man that he is married, especially when his wife is staying in the same house. At the least, it may keep the flirting and pinching to a minimum, and thus save a girl like Marje from unfairly gaining the hatred of a jealous woman.

The Artist's wife, from what Marje has seen, might prove just such a woman. She is somewhat stern-mouthed, and does not dine with her husband, but instead demands to have her meals brought up to the room where she eats with only her maid for company. Each time Marje has served her, the Artist's wife has watched her with a disapproving eye, as if the mere existence of pretty girls affronted Godly womanhood. She has also been unstinting in her criticism of what she sees as Marje's carelessness. The Artist's wife makes remarks about the Planckfelts, suggesting that she is not entirely satisfied with their hospitality, and even complains about Antwerp itself, making unfavorable comparisons between its weather and available diversions and those of Nuremberg, where she and the Artist keep their home.

Marje can guess why a cheerful man like this should prefer not to think of his wife when it is not absolutely necessary.

"Well," the Artist says at last, "I am certain you work very hard, but you must give some thought to the other wonders of our Lord's creation. Virtue is of course its own reward—but only to a point, after which it becomes Pride, and is as likely to be punished as rewarded. Shall I tell you a story?"

His smile has returned, and it is really a rather marvelous thing, Marje thinks. He looks twenty years younger and rather unfairly handsome.

"I have much to do, Lord. My lady wishes me to clear away the supper things and help Cook with the washing."

"Ah. Well, I would not interfere with your duties. When do you finish?"

"Finish?" She looks at his eyes and sees merriment there, and something else, something subtly, indefinably sad, which causes her to swallow her sharp reply. "About an hour after sunset."

"Good. Come to me then, and I will tell you a story about a girl something like you. And I will show you a marvel—something you have never seen before." He leans back in his chair. "Your master has been kind enough to lend me the spare room down here for my work—during the day, it gets the northern light, such as it has been of late. That is where I will be."

Marje hesitates. It is not respectable to meet him, surely. On the other hand, he is a famous and much-admired man. When her day's work is done, why should she (who, wife-like, has served him food and washed his charcoal-smudged shirts) not have a glimpse of the works which have gained him the patronage of great men all over Europe?

"I will . . . I may be too busy, Sir. But I thank you."

He grins, this time with all the innocent friendliness of a young boy. "You need not fear me, Marje. But do as you wish. If you can spare a moment, you know where to find me."

*   *   *

She stands in front of the door for some time, screwing up her
courage. When she knocks, there is no answer for long moments. At last
the door opens, revealing the darkened silhouette of the Artist. "Marje.
You honor me. Come in."

She passes through the door then stops, dumbfounded. The ground-
floor room that she has dusted and cleaned so many times has changed
out of all recognition, and she finds her fingers straying toward the cross
at her throat, as though she were again a child in a dark house listening to
her father's drunken rants about the Devil. The many candles and the single brazier of coals cast long shadows, and from every shadow faces peer.
Some are exalted as though with inner joy, others frown or snarl, frozen
in fear and despair and even hatred. She sees angels and devils and
bearded men in antique costume. Marje feels that she has stepped into
some kind of church, but the congregation has been drawn from every
corner of the world's history.

The Artist gestures at the pictures. "I am afraid I have been rather
caught up. Do not worry—I will not make more work for you. By the
time I leave here, these will all be neatly packed away again."

Marje is not thinking of cleaning. She is amazed by the gallery of
faces. If these are his drawings, the Artist is truly a man gifted by God.
She cannot imagine even thinking of such things, let alone rendering
them with such masterful skill, making each one perfect in every small
detail. She pauses, still full of an almost religious awe, but caught by
something familiar amid the gallery of monsters and saints.

"That is Grip! That is Master Planckfelt's dog!" She laughs in delight.
It is Grip, without a doubt, captured in every bristle; she does not need to
see the familiar collar with its heavy iron ring, but that is there, too.

The Artist nods. "I cannot go long without drawing, I fear, and each
one of God's creatures offers something in the way of challenge. From
the most familiar to the strangest." He is staring at her. Marje looks up
from the picture of the dog to catch him at it, but there is something
unusual in his inspection, something deeper than the admiring glances
she usually encounters from men of the Artist's age, and it is she who
blushes.

"Have I something on my face?" she asks, trying to make a joke of it.

"No, no." He reaches out for a candle. As he examines her he moves
the light around her head in slow circles, so that for a moment she feels
quite dizzy. "Will you sit for me?"

She looks around, but every stool and chair is covered by sheaves of
drawings. "Where?"

The Artist laughs and gently wraps a large hand around her arm. Marje feels her skin turn to gooseflesh. "I mean let me draw you. Your face is lovely, and I have a commission for a Saint Barbara that I should finish before leaving the Low Countries."

She had thought the hand a precursor to other, less genteel intimacies (and she is not quite certain how she feels about that prospect) but instead he is steering her to the door. She passes a line drawing of the Garden of Eden which is like a window into another world, into an innocence Marje cannot afford. "I . . . you will draw me with my clothes on?"

Again that smile. Is it sad? "It is a bust—a head and shoulders. You may wear what you choose, so long as the line of your graceful neck is not obscured."

"I thought you were going to tell me a story."

"I shall, I promise. And show you a great marvel—I have not forgotten. But I will save them until you come back to sit for me. Perhaps we could begin tomorrow morning?"

"Oh, but my lady will . . ."

"I will speak to her. Fear not, pretty Marje. I can be most persuasive."

The door shuts behind her. After a moment, she realizes that the corridor is cold, and she is shivering.

"Here. Now turn this way. I will soon give you something to look at."

Marje sits, her head at a slightly uncomfortable angle. She is astonished to discover herself with the morning off. Her mistress had not seemed happy about it, but clearly the Artist was not exaggerating his powers of persuasion. "Can I blink my eyes, Sir?"

"As often as you need to. Later I will let you move a little from time to time so you do not get too sore. Once I have made my first sketch, it will be easy to set your pose again." Satisfied, he takes his hand away from her chin—Marje is surprised to discover how hard and rough his fingers are; can drawing alone cause it?—and straightens. He goes to one of his folios and pulls out another picture, which he props up on a chair before her. At first, blocked by his body, she cannot see it. After he has arranged it to his satisfaction, the Artist steps away.

"Great God!" she says, then immediately regrets her blasphemy. The image before her looks something like a pig, but covered in intricate armor and with a great spike growing upwards from its muzzle. "What is it? A demon?"

"No demon, but one of God's living creatures. It is called 'Rhinocerus,' which is Latin for 'nosehorn.' He is huge, this fellow—bigger than a bull, I am told."

"You have not seen one? But did you not . . . ?"

"I drew the picture, yes. But it was made from another artist's drawing—and the creature he drew was not even alive, but stuffed with straw and standing in the Pope's garden of wonders. No one in Europe, I think, has ever seen this monster alive, although some have said he is the model for the fabled unicorn. Our Rhinocerus is a very rare creature, you see, and lives only at the farthest ends of the world. This one came from a land called Cambodia, somewhere near Cathay."

"I should be terrified to meet him." Marje finds she is shivering again. The Artist is standing behind her, his fingers delicately touching the nape of her neck as he pulls up her hair and knots it atop her head. "There. Now I can see the line cleanly. Yes, you might indeed be afraid if you met this fellow, young Marje. But you might be glad of it all the same. I promised you a tale, did I not?"

"About a girl, you said. Like me."

"Ah, yes. About a fair maiden. And a monster."

"A monster? Is that . . . that Nosehorn in this tale?"

She is still looking at the picture, intrigued by the complexity of the beast's scales, but even more by the almost mournful expression in its small eyes. By now she knows the Artist's voice well enough to hear him smiling as he speaks.

"The Nosehorn is indeed part of this tale. But you should never decide too soon which is the monster. Some of God's fairest creations bear foul seemings. And vice versa, of course." She hears him rustling his paper, then the near-silent scraping of his pencil. "Yes, there is both Maiden and Monster in this tale . . ."

∞   ∞   ∞

Her name is Red Flower—in full it is Delicate-Red-Flower-the-Color-of-Blood, but since her childhood only the priests who read the lists of blessings have used that name. Her father Jayavarman is a king, but not *the* king: the Universal Monarch, as all know, has been promised for generations but is still awaited. In the interim, her father has been content to eat well, enjoy his hunting and his elephants, and intercede daily with the *nak ta*—the ancestors—on his people's behalf, all in the comfortable belief that the Universal Monarch will probably not arrive during his lifetime.

In fact, it is his own lack of ambition that has made Red Flower's father a powerful man. Jayavarman knows that although he has no thought of declaring himself the *devaraja,* or god-king, others are not so modest. As the power of one of the other kings—for the land has many—

rises, Jayavarman lends his own prestige (and, in a pinch, his war elephants) to one of the upstart's stronger rivals. When the proud one has been brought low, Red Flower's father withdraws his support from the victor, lest that one, too, should begin to harbor dreams of universal kingship. Jayavarman then returns to his round of feasting and hunting, and waits to see which other tall bamboo may next seek to steal the sun from its neighbors. By this practice his kingdom of Angkor, which nestles south of the Kulen hills, has maintained its independence, and even an eminence which outstrips many of its more aggressive rivals.

But Red Flower cares little about her plump, patient father's machinations. She is not yet fourteen, and by tradition isolated from the true workings of power. As a virgin and Jayavarman's youngest daughter, her purpose (as her father and his counsellors see it) is to remain a pure and sealed repository for the royal blood. As her sisters were in their turn, Red Flower will be a gift to some young man Jayavarman favors, or whose own blood—and the family it represents—offers a connection which favors his careful strategies.

Red Flower, though, does not feel like a vessel. She is a young woman (just), and this night she feels herself as wild and unsettled as one of her father's hawks newly unhooded.

In truth, her sire's intricate and continuous strategies are somewhat to blame for her unrest. There are strangers outside the palace tonight, a ragtag army camped around the walls. They are fewer than Jayavarman's own troop, badly armored, carrying no weapons more advanced than scythes and daggers, and they own no elephants at all, but there is something in their eyes which make even the king's most hardened veterans uneasy. The sentries along the wall do not allow their spears to dip, and they watch the strangers' campfires carefully, as though looking into sacred flames for some sign from the gods.

The leader of this tattered band is a young man named Kaundinya who has proclaimed himself king of a small region beyond the hills, and who has come to Red Flower's father hoping for support in a dispute with another chieftain. Red Flower understands little of what is under discussion, since she is not permitted to listen to the men's conversation, but she has seen her father's eyes during the three days of the visitors' stay, and knows that he is troubled. No one thinks he will lend his aid (neither of the two quarreling parties is powerful enough to cause Jayavarman to support the other). But nevertheless, others besides Red Flower can see that something is causing the king unrest.

Red Flower is unsettled for quite different reasons. As excited as any of her slaves by gossip and novelty, she has twice slipped the clutches of her aged nurse to steal a look at the visitors. The first time, she turned up her nose at the peasant garb the strangers wear, as affronted by their raggedness as her maids had been. The second time, she saw Kaundinya himself.

He is barely twenty years old, this bandit chief, but as both Red Flower and her father have recognized (to different effect, however) there is something in his eyes, something cold and hard and knowing, that belies his age. He carries himself like a warrior, but more importantly, he carries himself like a true king, the flash of his eyes telling all who watch that if they have not yet had cause to bow down before him, they soon will. And he is handsome, too. On a man slightly less stern, his fine features and flowing black hair would be almost womanishly beautiful.

And while she peered out at him from behind a curtain, Kaundinya turned and saw Red Flower, and this is what she cannot forget. The heat of his gaze was like Siva's lightning leaping between Mount Mo-Tam and the sky. For a moment, she felt sure that his eyes, like a demon's, had caught at her soul and would draw it from her body. Then her old nurse caught her and yanked her away, swatting at her ineffectually with swollen-jointed hands. All the way back to the women's wing the nurse shrilly criticized her wickedness and immodesty, but Red Flower, thinking of Kaundinya's stern mouth and impatient eyes, did not hear her.

And now the evening has fallen and the palace is quiet. The old woman is curled on a mat beside the bed, wheezing in her sleep and wrinkling her nose at some dream-effrontery. A warm wind rattles the bamboo and carries the smell of cardamom leaves through the palace like music. The monsoon season has ended, the moon and the jungle flowers alike are blooming, all the night is alive, alive. The king's youngest daughter practically trembles with sweet discontent.

She pads quietly past her snoring nurse and out into the corridor. It is only a few steps to the door that leads to the vast palace gardens. Red Flower wishes to feel the moon on her skin and the wind in her hair. As she makes her way down into the darkened garden, she does not see the shadow-form that follows her, and does not hear it either, for it moves as silently as death.

∞   ∞   ∞

"And there I must stop." The Artist stands and stretches his back.

"But . . . but what happened? Was that the horned monster that followed her?"

"I have not finished, I have merely halted for the day. Your mistress is expecting you to go back to work, Marje. I will continue the story when you return to me tomorrow."

She hesitates, unwilling to let go of the morning's novelty, of her happiness at being admired and spoken to as an equal. "May I see what you have drawn?"

"No." His voice is perhaps harsher than he had wished. When he speaks again it is in softer tones. "I will show you when I am finished, not before. Go along, you. Let an old man rest his fingers and his tongue." He does not look old. The gray morning light streams through the window behind him, gleaming at the edges of his curly hair. He seems very tall.

Marje curtseys and leaves him, pulling the door closed behind her as quietly as she can. All day, as she sweeps out the house's dusty corners and hauls water from the well, she will think of the smell of spice trees and of a young man with cold, confident eyes.

∞   ∞   ∞

Even on deck, wrapped in a heavy hooded cloak against the unseasonal squall, Father Joao is painfully aware of the dark silent box in the hold. A present from King John to the newly elected Pope, it would be a valuable cargo simply as a significator of the deep, almost familial relationship between the Portugese throne and the Holy See. But as a reminder of the wealth that Portugal can bring back to Mother Church from the New World and elsewhere (and as such to prompt him toward favoring Portugal's expanding interests) its worth is incalculable. In Anno Domini 1492, all of the world seems in reach of Christendom's ships, and it is a world whose spoils the Pope will divide. The bishop who is the king's ambassador (and Father Joao's superior), who will present the pontiff with this splendid gift, is delighted with the honor bestowed upon him.

Thus, Father Joao is a soldier in a good cause, and with no greater responsibility than to make sure the Wonder arrives in good condition. Why then is he so unhappy?

It was the months spent with his family, he knows, after being so long abroad. Mother Church offers balm against the fear of age and death; seeing his parents so changed since he had last visited them, so feeble, was merely painful and did not remotely trouble his faith. But the spectacle of his brother Ruy as happy father, his laughing, tumbling brood about him, was for some reason more difficult to stomach. Father Joao has disputed with himself about this. His younger brother has children, and someday will have grandchildren to be the warmth of his old age, but Joao has dedicated his own life and chastity to the service of the Lord Jesus Christ, the greatest and most sacred of callings. Surely the brotherhood of his fellow priests is family enough?

But most insidious of all the things which cause him doubt, something which still troubles him after a week at sea, despite all his prayers and sleepless nights searching for God's peace, even despite the lashes of his own self-hatred, is the beauty of his brother's wife, Maria.

The mere witnessing of such a creature troubled chastity, but to live in her company for weeks was an almost impossible trial. Maria was dark-eyed and slender of waist despite the roundness of her limbs. She had thick black curly hair which (mocking all pins and ribbons) constantly worked itself free to hang luxuriously down her back and sway as she walked, hiding and accentuating at the same moment, like the veils of Salome.

Joao is no stranger to temptation. In his travels he has seen nearly every sort of woman God has made, young and old, dark-skinned and light. But all of them, even the greatest beauties, have been merely shadows against the light of his belief. Joao has always reminded himself that he observed only the outer garments of life, that it was the souls within that mattered. Seeing after those souls is his sacred task, and his virginity has been a kind of armor, warding off the demands of the flesh. He has always managed to comfort himself with this thought.

But living in the same house with Ruy and his young wife was different. To see Maria's slim fingers toying with his brother's beard, stroking that face so much like his own, or to watch her clutch one of their children against her sloping hip, forced Joao to wonder what possible value there could be in chastity.

At first her earthiness repelled him, and he welcomed that repulsion. A glimpse of her bare feet or the cleavage of her full breasts, and his own corrupted urge to stare at such things, made him rage inwardly. She was a woman, the repository of sin, the Devil's tool. She and each of her kind were at best happy destroyers of a man's innocence, at worst deadly traps that yawned, waiting to draw God's elect down into darkness.

But Joao lived with Ruy and Maria for too long, and began to lose his comprehension of evil. For his brother's wife was not a wanton, not a temptress or whore. She was a wife and mother, an honorable, pious woman raising her children in the faith, good to her husband, kind to his aging parents. If she found pleasure in the flesh God had given her, if she enjoyed her man's arms around her, or the sun on her ankles as she prepared her family's dinner in the tiny courtyard, how was that a sin?

With this question, Joao's armor had begun to come apart. If enjoyment of the body were not sinful, then how could denial of the body somehow be blessed? Could it be so much worse in God's eyes, his brother Ruy's life? If there were no sin in having a beautiful and loving wife to share your bed, in having children and a hearth, then why had Joao himself renounced these things? And if God made mankind fruitful, then commanded his most faithful servants not to partake of that fruitfulness, and in fact to despise it as a hindrance to holiness, then what kind of wise and loving God was He?

*   *   *

Father Joao has not slept well since leaving Lisbon, the ceaseless movement of the ocean mirroring his own unquiet soul. Everything seems in doubt here, everything seems suspended, the sea a place neither of God or the Devil, but forever between the two. Even the sailors, who with their dangerous lives might seem most in need of God's protection, mistrust priests.

In the night, in his tiny cabin, Joao can hear the ropes that bind the crate stretching and squeaking, as though something inside it stirs restlessly.

His superior, the bishop, has been no help, and Joao's few attempts to seek the man's counsel have yielded only incomprehending homilies. Unlike Father Joao, he is long past the age when the fleshly sins are the most tempting. If his soul is in danger, Joao thinks with some irritation, it is from Pride: the bishop is puffed like a sleeping owl with the honor of his position—liaison between king and pope, bringer of a mighty gift, securer of the Church's blessing on Portugal's conquests across the heathen world.

If the bishop is the ambassador, Father Joao wonders, then what is he? An insomniac priest. A celibate tortured by his own flesh. A man who will accompany a great gift, but only as far as Italy's shores before he turns to go home again. Now the rain is thumping on the deck overhead, and he can no longer hear noises in the hold. His head hurts, he is cold beneath his thin blanket, and he is tired of thinking.

He is a only a porter bearing a box of dead Wonder, Joao decides with a kind of cold satisfaction—a Wonder of which he himself is not even to be vouchsafed a glimpse.

∞   ∞   ∞

Marje has been looking at the Nosehorn so long that even when the Artist commands her to close her eyes, she sees it still, printed against the darkness of her eyelids. She knows she will dream of it for months, the powerful body, the tiny, almost-hidden eyes, the thrust of horn lifting from its snout.

"You said you would tell me more about the girl. The flower girl."

"So I shall. Let me only light another candle. There is less light today. I am like one of those savage peoples who worship the sky, always turning in search of the sun."

"Will it be finished soon?"

"Tale or picture?"

"Both." She needs to know. Yesterday and today have been a magical time, but she remembers magic from other stories, and knows it does not last. She is sad her time at the center of the world is passing, but underneath everything she is a realistic girl. If it is to end today, she can make her peace, but she needs to know.

"I do not think I will finish either this morning, unless I keep you long enough to make your mistress forget I am a guest and lose her temper. So we will have more work tomorrow. Now be quiet, Marje. I am drawing your mouth."

∞   ∞   ∞

As she steps into the circle of moss-covered stones at the garden's center, something moves in the darkness beneath the trees. Red Flower turns her face away from the moon.

"Who is there?" Her voice is a low whisper. She is the king's daughter, but tonight she feels like a trespasser, even within her own gardens.

There is a tiny rumble of thunder in the distance. The monsoon is ended, but the skies are still unsettled. He steps out of the trees, naked to the waist, moonlight gleaming on his muscle-knotted arms. "I am. And who is there? Ah. It's the old dragon's daughter."

She feels her breath catch in her throat. She is alone, in the dark. There is danger here. But there is also something in Kaundinya's gaze that keeps her fixed to the spot as he approaches. "You should not be here," she says at last.

"What is your name? You came to spy on me the other day, didn't you?"

"I am . . ." She still finds it hard to speak. "I am Red Flower. My father will kill you if you do not go away."

"Perhaps. Perhaps not. Your father is afraid of me."

Her strange lethargy is at last dispelled by anger. "That is a lie! He is afraid of no one! He is a great king, not a bandit like you with your ragged men!"

Kaundinya laughs, genuinely amused, and Red Flower is suddenly unsure again. "Your father is a king, little girl, but he will never be Ultimate Monarch, never the *devaraja*. I will be, though, and he knows it. He is no fool. He sees what is inside me."

"You are mad." She takes a few steps back. "My father will destroy you."

"He would have done it when he first met me if he dared. But I have come to him in peace and am a guest in his house and he cannot touch me. Still, he will not give me his support. He thinks to send me away with empty hands while he considers how he might ruin me before my power grows too great."

The stranger abruptly strides forward and catches her arm, pulling her close until she can smell the betel nut on his breath. His eyes, mirroring the moon, seem very bright. "But perhaps I will not go away with empty hands after all. It seems the gods have brought you to me, alone and unguarded. I have learned to trust the gods—it is they who have promised me that I shall be king over all of Kambuja-desa."

Red Flower struggles, but he is very strong and she is only a slender young girl. Before she can call for her father's soldiers, he covers her mouth with his own and pinions her with his strong arms. His deep, sharp smell surrounds her and she feels herself weakening. The moon seems to disappear, as though it has fallen into shadow. It is a little like drowning, this surrender. Kaundinya frees one hand to hold her face, then slides that hand down her neck, sending shivers through her like ripples across a pond. Then his hand moves again, and, as his other hand gathers up her sari, it pushes roughly between her legs. Red Flower gasps and kicks, smashing her heel down on his bare foot.

Laughing and cursing at the same time, he loosens his grip. She pulls free and runs across the garden, but she has gone only a few steps before he leaps into pursuit.

She should scream, but for some reason she cannot. The blind fear of the hunted is upon her, and all she can do is run like a deer, run like a rabbit, hunting for a dark hole and escape. He has done something to her with his touch and his cold eyes. A spell has enwrapped her.

She finds a gate in the encircling garden wall. Beyond is the temple, and on a hill above it the great dark shadow of the Sivalingam, the holy pillar reaching toward heaven. Past that is only jungle on one side, on the other open country and the watchfires of Kaundinya's army. Red Flower races toward the hill sacred to Siva, Lord of Lightnings.

The pillar is a finger pointing toward the moon. Thunder growls quietly in the distance. She stumbles and falls to her knees, then begins crawling uphill, silently weeping. There is a hissing in the grass behind her, then a hand curls in her hair and yanks her back. She tumbles and lies at Kaundinya's feet, staring up. His eyes are wild, his mouth twisted with fury, but his voice, when it comes, is terrifyingly calm.

"You are the first of your father's possessions that I will take and use."

∞   ∞   ∞

"But you cannot stop there! That is terrible! What happened to the girl?"

The Artist is putting away his drawing materials, but without his usual care. He seems almost angry. Marje is afraid she has offended him in some way.

"I will finish the tale tomorrow. There is only a little more work needed on the drawing, but I am tired now."

She gets up, tugging the sleeves of her dress back over her shoulders. He opens the door and stands beside it, as though impatient for her to leave.

"I will not sleep tonight for worrying about the flower girl," she says, trying to make him smile. He closes his eyes for a moment, as though he too is thinking about Red Flower. "I will miss you, Marje," he says when she is outside. Then he shuts the door.

∞   ∞   ∞

The ship is storm-tossed, bobbing on the water like a wooden cup. In his cabin, Joao glares into the darkness. Somewhere below, ropes creak like the damned distantly at play.

The thought of the box and its forbidden contents torments him. Coward, doubter, near-eunuch, false priest—with these names he also tortures himself. In the blackness before his eyes he sees visions of Maria, smiling, clothes undone, warm and rounded and hateful. Would she touch him with the heedless fondness with which she rubs his brother's back, kisses Ruy's neck and ear? Could she understand that at this awful moment Joao would give his immortal soul for just such animal comfort? What would she think of him? What would any of those whose souls are in his care think of him?

He drags himself from the bed and stands on trembling legs, swaying as the ship sways. Far above, thunder fills the sky like the voices of God and Satan contesting. Joao pulls his cassock over his undershirt and fumbles for his flints. When the candle springs alight, the walls and roof of his small sanctuary press closer than he had remembered, threatening to squeeze him breathless.

Father Joao lurches toward the cargo hold; his head is full of voices. As he climbs down a slippery ladder, he loses his footing and nearly falls. He waves his free arm for balance and the candle goes out. For a moment he struggles just to maintain his grip, wavering in empty darkness with unknown depths beneath him. At last he rights himself, but now he is without light. Somewhere above, the storm proclaims its power, mocking human enterprise. A part of him wonders what he is doing up, what he is doing in this of all places. Surely, that quiet voice says, he should at least go back to light his candle again. But that gentle voice is only one of many. Joao reaches down with his foot, finds the next rung, and continues his descent.

Even in utter blackness he knows his way. Every day of the voyage he has passed back and forth through this great empty space, like exiled Jonah. His hands encounter familiar things, his ears are full of the quiet complaining of the fettered crate. He knows his way.

He feels its presence even before his fingers touch it, and stops, blind and half-crazed. For a moment he is tempted to go down on one knee, but God can see even in darkness, and some last vestige of devout fear holds him back. Instead he lays his ear against the rough wood and listens, as a father might listen to the child growing in his wife's belly. Something is inside. It is still and dead, but somehow in Father Joao's mind it is full of terrible life.

He pulls at the box, desperate to open it, knowing even without sight that he is bloodying his fingers, but it is too well-constructed. He falls back at last, sobbing. The crate mocks him with its impenetrability. He lowers himself to the floor of the hold and crawls, searching for something that will serve where flesh has failed. Each time he strikes his head on an unseen impediment the muffled thunder seems to grow louder, as though something huge and secret is laughing at him.

At last he finds an iron rod, then feels his way back to the waiting box. He finds a crack beneath the lid and pushes the bar in, then throws his weight on it, pulling downward. It gives, but only slightly. Mouthing a prayer whose words even he does not know, Joao heaves at the bar again, struggling until more tears come to his eyes. Then, with a screeching of nails ripped from their holes, the lid lifts away and Joao falls to the floor.

The ship's hold suddenly fills with an odor he has never smelled, a strong scent of dry musk and mysterious spices. He staggers upright and leans over the box, drinking in the exhalation of pure Wonder. Slowly, half-reverent and half-terrified, he lowers his hands into the box.

A cloud of dense-packed straw is already rising from its confinement, crackling beneath his fingers, which feel acute as eyes. What waits for him? Punishment for his doubts? Or a shrouded Nothing, a final blow to shatter all faith?

For a moment he does not understand what he is feeling. It is so smooth and cold that for several heartbeats he is not certain he is touching anything at all. Then, as his hands slide down its gradually widening length, he knows it for what it is. A horn.

Swifter and swifter his fingers move, digging through the straw, following the horn's curve down to the wide rough brow, the glass-hard eyes, the ears. The Wonder inside the box has but a single horn. The thing beneath Joao's fingers is dead, but there is no doubt that it once lived. It is real. Real! Father Joao hears a noise in the empty hold, and realizes that he himself is making it. He is laughing.

God does not need to smite doubters, not when He can instead show them their folly with a loving jest. The Lord has proved to faithless Joao that divine love is no mere myth, and that He does not merely honor chastity, He defends it. All through this long nightmare voyage, Joao has been the unwitting guardian of Virtue's greatest protector.

Down on his knees now in the blind darkness, but with his head full of light, the priest gives thanks over and over.

∞   ∞   ∞

Kaundinya stands above her in the moon-thrown shadow of the pillar. He holds the delicate fabric of her sari in his hands. Already it has begun to part between his strong fingers.

Red Flower cannot awaken from this dream. The warm night is shelter no longer. Even the faint rumble of thunder has vanished, as though the gods themselves have turned their backs on her. She closes her eyes as one of Kaundinya's hands cups her face. As his mouth descends on hers, he lowers his knee between her legs, spreading her. For a long moment, nothing happens. She hears the bandit youth take a long and surprisingly unsteady breath.

Red Flower opens her eyes. The pillar, the nearby temple, all seem oddly flat, as though they have been painted on cloth. At the base of the hill, only a few paces from where she sits tumbled on the grass, a huge pale form has appeared. Kaundinya's eyes are opened wide in superstitious dread. He lets go of Red Flower's sari and lifts himself from her.

"Lord Siva," he says, and throws himself prostrate before the vast white beast. The rough skin of its back seems to give off as much light as the moon itself, and it turns its wide head to regard him, horn lowered like a spear, like the threat of lightning. Kaundinya speaks into the dirt. "Lord Siva, I am your slave."

Red Flower stares at the beast, then at her attacker, who is caught up in something like a slow fit, his muscles rippling and trembling, his face contorted. The nosehorn snorts once, then turns and lumbers away toward the distant trees, strangely silent. Red Flower cannot move. She cannot even shiver. The world has grown tracklessly large, and she is but a small thing.

At last Kaundinya stands. His fine features are childish with shock, as though something large has picked him up by the neck and shaken him.

"The Lord of all the Gods has spoken to me," he whispers. He does not look at Red Flower, but at the place where the beast has vanished into the jungle. "I am not to dishonor you, but to marry you. I will be the *devaraja,* and you will be my queen. This place, Angkor, will be the heart of my kingdom. Siva has told me this."

He extends a hand. Red Flower stares at it. He is offering to help her up. She struggles to her feet without assistance, holding the torn part of her gown together. Suddenly she is cold.

"You know your father will give you to me," he calls after her as she stumbles back toward the palace. "He recognizes what I am, what I will be. It is the only solution. He will see that."

She does not want to hear him, does not want to think about what he is saying. But she does, of course. She is not sure what has happened tonight, but she knows that he is speaking the truth.

∞   ∞   ∞

Marje is silent for a long time after the Artist has finished. The grayness of the day outside the north-facing window is suddenly dreary.

"And is that it? She had to marry him?"

The Artist is concentrating deeply, squinting at the drawing board. He does not reply immediately. "At least it was an honorable marriage," he says at last. "That is something better than rape, is it not?"

"But what happened to her afterward?"

"I am not entirely sure. It is only a story, after all. But I imagine she bore the bandit king many sons, so that when he died his line lived on. The man who told me the tale said that there were kings in that place for seven hundred years. The rhinocerus you see in that drawing was the last of a long line of sacred beasts, a symbol to the royal family. But the kings of Cambodia have left Angkor now, so perhaps it no longer means anything to them. In any case, they gave it to the king of Portugal, and Portugal gave its stuffed body to the Pope after it died." The Artist shakes his head. "I am sorry I could not see it when it breathed and walked God's earth."

Marje stares at the picture of the Nosehorn, wondering at its strange journey. What would it think, this jungle titan whose ancestor was a heathen god, to find itself propped on a chair in Antwerp? The Artist stirs. "You may move now, Marje. I am finished."

She thinks she hears something of her own unhappiness in his voice. What does it mean? She gets up slowly, untwisting sore muscles, and walks to his side. She must lean against him to see the drawing properly, and feels his small, swift movement, almost a twitch, as she presses against his arm.

"Oh. It's . . . it's beautiful."

"As you are beautiful," he says softly. The picture is Marje, but also not Marje. The girl before her has her eyes closed and wears a look of battered innocence. The long line of her neck is lovely but fragile.

"Saint Barbara was taken onto a mountain by her father and killed," the Artist says, gently tracing the neck with his finger. "Perhaps he was jealous of the love she had found in Jesus. She is the martyr who protects us from sudden death, and from lightning."

"Your gift is from God, Master Dürer." Marje is more than a little overwhelmed. "So are we finished now?"

She is still leaning against his arm, staring at the picture, her breasts touching his shoulder. When he does not reply, she glances up. The Artist is looking at her closely. From this close she can see the lines that web his face, but also the depth of his eyes, the bright, tragic eyes of a much younger man. "We must be. I have finished the drawing, and told you the tale." His voice is carefully flat, but something moves beneath it, a kind of yearning.

For a moment she hesitates, and feels herself tilting as though out of balance in a high place. Then, uncomfortable with his regard, her eyes stray to the portrait of the Nosehorn, watching from its place on the chair, small eyes solemn beneath the rending horn. She takes a breath.

"Yes," she finally says, "you have and you have. And now there are many things I must do. Mistress will be very anxious at how I have let my work go. She will think I am trying to rise above my station."

The Artist reaches up and briefly squeezes her hand, then lifts himself from his chair and leads her toward the door.

"When I have made my print, I will send you a copy, pretty Marje."

"I would like that very much."

"I have enjoyed our time together. I wish there could be more."

She drops him a curtsey, and for a moment allows herself to smile. "God gives us but one life, Sir. We must preserve what He gives us and make of it what we can." He nods, returning her smile, though his is more reserved, more pained.

"Very true. You are a wise girl."

The Artist shuts the door behind her.

ABOUT THE AUTHOR

Tad Williams is currently thirty-eight years old. He's an expatriate Californian, living in London.

He says: "I am primarily a novelist, but I have also published short stories, newspaper journalism (op ed, concert reviews), magazine articles (both on fiction and on technology), and have written television and film screenplays (all unproduced, so go ahead and sneer). Besides the States, the UK, and the Commonwealth, I have also been published in France, Spain, the Netherlands, Germany, Italy, Japan, Poland, and Brazil, and maybe some other places they haven't told me about. Since I can't read the languages of most of those countries, I am forced to take my publishers' word that those are actually my books between the covers and not old issues of *Popular Mechanics*.

"I am half-owner of a multimedia company, Telemorphix, Inc. We produce an interactive television show called *Twenty-First Century Vaudeville*. It's too weird to explain—it's better if you just see it—but we think it's pretty cool. We put it on the air over a year ago in the U.S. in San Francisco and it's now playing in Boston; we're doing our best to produce it in the UK as well.

"I have held a variety of other jobs, including over a decade's work as a radio talk show host in the Bay Area. My best-known show, *One Step Beyond*—as well as its companion venue, *Radio Free America*—was an investigative political show syndicated in several large media markets (New York, Los Angeles), which focused on controversial political subjects like clandestine intelligence, the drug-and-gun trade, and political crimes and assassination. I did all this with the unlikely (and perhaps unfortunate) radio nom-de-microphone of 'Nip Tuck.' We were perhaps the first radio program in America to investigate the background of the Iran/Contra scandal—many of the major players had already been profiled on our show long before the story broke. We developed a cult following, and although I quit doing the show a few years ago, it is still being rerun in many areas.

"Someday I will write the perfect novel, give up fiction, and really start working on that tryout for *Jeopardy* (the American game show)."

Tad's novels: *Tailchaser's Song* (DAW Books, 1985); *The Dragonbone Chair* (DAW Books, 1988); *Stone of Farewell* (DAW Books, 1990);

Child of an Ancient City (with Nina Kiriki Hoffman; Atheneum, 1992); *To Green Angel Tower* (DAW Books, 1993); *Caliban's Hour* (HarperCollins, Fall, 1994). All the foregoing titles published in the UK by Legend (Random House). Coming up from DAW: OTHERLAND—a tetraology consisting of (probably) *Otherland, River of Blue Fire, Mountain of Black Glass*, and *Sea of Silver Light*.

DAVE WOLVERTON

—◅◁▥▥৶▥▥▷▸—

WE BLAZED

Peter: **Dave Wolverton** is the author of several novels, including a *Stars Wars* bestseller. He has also written much short fiction. He lives in Oregon with his family, and his résumé—properly checkered—includes a job as a pie maker. I don't know why that should delight and fascinate me so much, but it does.

Janet: Dave is one of the few people I know who owns—and has actually read—the Mormon book I ghostwrote in one of my hungrier years. He is also one of the few people who doesn't think I'm crazy for living in Las Vegas. Dave is a fine, often "literary" writer, with a fundamental belief in dotting i's and crossing t's, no matter what his subject matter. Those who know him best as a *Star Wars* author would be well-advised to dig deeper. It was his other novels and his short fiction which first caught my attention.

We Blazed

K AITLYN PROMISED TO LOVE ME FOREVER,
and whether that was ten thousand years ago, or a hundred thousand, or
more, I didn't know.

One morning three years past I had wakened and begun hunting for
her in this strange land, a land where banana plantations were carved precariously from the sodden forest, a land where the chatter of green parrots
and peeping of frogs and whirring of insects filled the jungle. Strangely,
there were no monkeys; it was as if God had discarded them.

I walked the muddy roads, often passing caravans of men of questionable descent—small men with enormous black mustaches, men too
dark to be European, too stocky to be African. They walked barefoot and
wore baggy cotton outfits called *tahns,* dyed in solid reds and yellows,
yet always the men's attire was so stained by the road as to have faded to
an uncertain gray. Their breath smelled of anise and curry, ginger, red
pepper and spices too obscure to be named.

As for the women—well, they ran when they saw my skin, translucent and gleaming like pearl. It was an unnatural whiteness, and, like my
height, it marked me as someone unique. The immortal.

Sometimes I'd walk into a village, a collection of huts made of mud
and sticks, and the women would run, shouting "N'carn! N'carn!" They
would grab their small daughters and flee, afraid that I would rape four-
year-old girls. The men would draw short, curved daggers from their
belts and try to herd me, drive me from the village.

Sometimes they'd cut me and watch disbelieving as the wounds
closed. The first time it happened, when a young father tried to gut me, I'd
been frightened, and the dagger had hurt terribly in my belly, an invasive

cold chunk of metal. I'd thought it would kill me, so I'd pulled the dagger from my attacker's hand and concentrated on giving him as good as I got, slicing him from navel to sternum, then twisting the blade into his heart. The blood had poured over my fists, and the smelly little man coughed and slumped forward, his wrists limp over my shoulders, like a drunkard who'd passed out while dancing in my arms.

I'd thought it would feel good to repay him for his hospitality, and if I'd died then, I'd have felt justified. But immediately after the attack I looked down as my own wounds painfully began to close. The cries of the dead man's children, the wailing of his wife, followed me from the village that day, and haunted me for many months to come.

I never took vengeance on one of them again.

For a long time, I hid from the people. But outside their huts at night, I'd sit in the darkness and listen, until I learned some of their language.

I knew my name, Alexander Dane, though my friends, when I still had friends, used to just call me Dane. But I did not know *what* I was. Sometimes I imagined I could sense vague roots to these people's words. They called me N'carn, and I imagined I was the *incarnate* or the *reincarnated,* some being they had known before, reawakening into this age. But if that were the case, why did they fear me?

I could not be killed. If I did not eat, I felt pangs of hunger but did not starve. Could I be a ghost?

Once I found an ancient city that might have been New York. Dark men there were mining the junkyards, where they'd hit veins of aluminum mingled with other metals. I saw crumpled Coke cans, flattened and fused by age, interspersed with ancient bricks and liquid RAM casings and Barbie dolls. But the miners there were digging at two hundred feet.

How many years had passed? A million? I had no memory of any interval between some vague date near 2023 and the time that I woke to begin searching for Kaitlyn. The earth had warmed, and that could have happened in only a few centuries, but some mornings the sun seemed to rise redder and colder than I remembered. How many millions of years would it take for the sun to grow cold? Had it been that long, or was I imagining things?

Did it matter? Kaitlyn promised to love me forever. If ten thousand years had passed, or a million, it should not have mattered.

Or could it be that these differences in the world were not really exterior to me? Could the difference really only be in the way this new body perceived things? On nights when the myriad stars threatened to set the heavens afire, or on days when the wildflowers in the meadow smelled too alive or that the perfect blue summer sky was not white enough on the horizon, I imagined that perhaps I was only dreaming, or that I was living someone else's dream of Earth.

In the spring I found the river that would lead to Kaitlyn—a muddy, churning flow that carved its serpentine way through broad flatlands. The natives called it the Ki'tack River, but it could have been the Congo or Mississippi, and I would not have been able to tell.

I only knew that such a mighty dark river would have to lead to her.

When Kaitlyn and I were young, we'd sung together in a band called Throat Kulture. Our first big hit had been called "River of Darkness," and as I saw the Ki'tack, the chorus began playing in my head:

> *(Me)* "There's a place, we're all going to . . ."
> *(Kaitlyn)* "River of Darkness,"
> *(Me)* "And I'll be waiting, there for you.
> You can't escape, a love so true"
> *(Kaitlyn)* "River of Darkness"
> *(Me)* "Yes, I'll be waiting, there for you. . . ."

So I followed the straight road that paralleled the river. Along the muddy track, I'd often find crossroads leading to small villages. One never knew how far back into the jungle such villages might be—twenty yards, or twenty miles. And I could not tell who might live in the villages. There were no signs in the sense that we use. The art of writing words had been forgotten by these people.

But there *were* signs, of a sort, to show who would be in each village. At the crossroads, villagers would pile mud, which over the decades would bake in the sun, and in this mud would be many small cubbyholes. A cubbyhole might contain a parrot feather tied to a twig, telling the traveler that in this village lived a man named Parrot Feather married to a woman named Twig. I had no idea what name Kaitlyn would use, so I personally checked almost every village.

One hot afternoon, I stepped off the road to let a small caravan pass. The sun had dried the road to dust over the past several weeks, and the elephants in the caravan were churning the dust as they walked. One reached down with its trunk and threw dust onto its head to ward off the stinging flies—much to the dismay of its mahout, who began cursing the elephant and beating its ears with a stick.

As I stepped from the road, I noticed an unpromising crossroad that led to a small village. The village road was covered with short grass, attesting that it was seldom used. The village would be far away, I suspected. I glanced at the cubbyholes with their pieces of obsidian, dried beetles, and salamanders carved from wood. The village marker was situated under a fig tree, its leaves dusty and denuded from the passing elephants, but on the far side of the tree, away from the road, were a few sweet figs. My stomach was tight from hunger, so I pulled down a fig, brushed the dust from it, and began to take lunch, when I noticed something strange.

On the bottom of the village marker, near the back, was an ancient seashell—a snail shell that might have been the yellow of dawn at one time. I'd been traveling upstream for a year, and I was a thousand miles from the ocean. It was unlikely that anyone would have been named Yellow Seashell so far inland. I knew it was hers. Kaitlyn loved seashells, and her favorite color was yellow.

I stepped under the trees and found that the buzzing of stinging flies was louder there. For a long time I followed the ancient trail through a boggy track, and once I stopped while a pair of wild water buffaloes lowered their black heads and stared at me, as if to charge. Sometimes I heard alligators croaking in distant pools, but other than that, there was little sign of life in the deep woods.

As I hiked throughout the afternoon, storm clouds swept overhead, bringing the first rain in days. After five miles, when I came out of the jungle, I found the road following the broad river, its waters almost black under dark skies. A rooster crowing and the grunts of pigs alerted me when I neared the village—that and the fact that the road was heavily trampled here.

But just before I reached the village, I found something that disturbed me. Beside the road, lying in the mud, was an ancient statue carved of granite.

It wasn't a big statue—perhaps only four feet tall. But it caught my attention because it was a statue of me, my face twisted in a grimace, squatting, naked, holding over my head a huge twisted horn, as if I were in the act of impaling someone with it.

I went to the statue, grunted as I hefted it upright. The left side of the face was covered in black mud and rotted leaves, but I felt sure that it was me. My face had never been twisted so savagely in rage, but everything else—the size, the musculature—all was mine except for one thing: the figure had balls but no penis.

The statue was old. Stone had flaked off the face, as if it had been lying here for millennia. At the feet of the statue were three rotting eels among the leaves, a gift left for some dark god.

I went into the village.

A circle of perhaps twelve huts squatted beside the riverbank. Since it was raining, everyone was inside. A small herd of black-and-white pigs rooted beside the smoking remains of a cooking fire. A pole above the fire held the carcass of a giant blue catfish, four feet long, waiting to be cooked. A family of red chickens nervously stood in the lee of a hut, pecking for grain by the villagers' grinding bowls, waiting for the last drops of rain to fall.

One of the huts was much larger than the rest—perhaps sixty feet in diameter. I knew that this must be the headman's hut; it was enormous. Smoke poured from the smoke hole at its top, and from inside I could hear singing.

There were no electric guitars or keyboards in this world. Some musicians struck up a tune on conga drums, panpipes and hand harps. A woman began singing in the nasal local dialect. It was Kaitlyn.

My heart began beating hard, and my mouth felt dry. I wondered if Kaitlyn would look the same, or if she would be wearing another body. Had she and I somehow been reborn, to meet in this new world? That is how I felt, reborn. But aside from the unnatural luster of my skin, the way I glowed like starlight on water in the darkness, I looked the same.

I recalled when I'd first met Kaitlyn singing in a little club in Soho, a willowy eighteen-year-old woman going on fifty, with long blond tresses.

She'd been a slave to designer drugs like Ecstasy, VooDew, and Scythe, an idealist who couldn't handle a fucked-up world, so she fucked herself up whenever she could. But that girl could wail.

She strutted across stage to the dizzying pyrotechnics of an AI-mastered light show, a hologram of a red phoenix tattooed to her forehead, and you could feel the blaze from her, a thrill like electroshock.

We'd shared the quest for fame. For awhile it seemed we'd made it. But when the road wore us down, Kaitlyn quit blazing and started wearing greens and blues. We moved to the 'burbs, bought a house with a big backyard. Then I woke up here.

I walked into the headman's hut. It had a dark corridor with walls made of tapestries that smelled like hemp, painted in bright batik patterns of ivory and emerald.

At the end of the hall was a large open room, with a couple dozen people sitting round a fire. Firelight flickered yellow on their faces, and I smelled the local bread cooking beside the fire, bread made with several kinds of grain, along with dried garbanzo beans, and flavored with cumin and other spices.

In the shadows at the far side of the room, several men and women were playing pipes and drums. Naked children danced around the fire while Kaitlyn wailed for them.

She stood between me and the fire, with her back to me, swaying gently, crooning in the local gibberish. The children gazed up at her, dark eyes shining with adoration.

Kaitlyn looked much the same, long wheat-blond hair curling down over her thin hips, bones protruding slightly through her forest-green *tahn*. Only her skin was different—shining and opalescent, like mine. As if light had been captured in her pores and were leaking through.

The villagers watched her sing with rapt attention, and none noticed me until I was right behind her, then one woman gasped and pointed at me.

I didn't know quite what to say, so I walked up behind Kaitlyn and whispered in her ear, "Hey, babe, it's me, Dane," then kissed her temple above the eye.

Kaitlyn turned and stared at me half a second in disbelief, then slapped my face.

Around the room, men drew daggers while women grabbed their daughters and hid. The room filled with shouts and whirling bodies. Kaitlyn twisted from my arms and tried to cross the room, calling "Abim! Abim!" It was the masculine form of the word, "Water," and only the feminine form was ever used when speaking about water, so I knew she was calling a man. In her haste, Kaitlyn tripped over a small boy and fell into the lap of a woman who played the harp.

But from the darkened corners, a man bellowed and charged. I saw at once that he was large—skin of dark brown, black hair cascading over his shoulders. Unlike others, he did not wear a *tahn*. Instead he wore short pants of white cotton, a vest of cream-colored silk that exhibited the rippling muscles of his arms and chest. I knew at once that he was rich, for he wore sandals of thick leather in a style that only the richest people affected.

He lunged into the light, and I gasped. He was at once the most handsome and powerful man I've ever seen—a face with strong lines, gray eyes glimmering like dark ice. And as he rushed at me, he pulled a scimitar from a sheath at his side, whirling it over his head.

He stopped between me and Kaitlyn, and I heard women weeping and shouting "N'carn!" The dark men at my back were growling and had pulled their knives, began circling me, yet they all stayed away more than an arm's length, as if afraid I would charge them.

There were nine of them, and one man kept dancing in close, as if wanting to be the first to score. He kept shouting in his local dialect, "Kill it! Kill it!"

But Abim shouted, "No, you cannot kill him! Stay back!"

The little man danced in with his knife, a gleaming blade shaped like a horn. I didn't want to fight him, but I also knew that if he scored on me, it would hurt like hell.

He lunged and struck a shallow gash on my calf. There was a time when I'd thought that as a star, I might need to know some self-defense just to hold "my people" off. I remembered enough from my tae kwon do classes to kick him in the face. Blood spurted from it, and he staggered backward, little worse for the encounter.

"It is me you want!" Abim shouted at me dangerously. "I am the one who desecrated your altar! It was *I* who made the women quit leaving sacrifices! Your fight is with me!"

I'm sure he thought he was being noble as hell, but I frankly didn't give a damn who'd desecrated my altar. Still, his shouting made the other men stop, as if willing to let me and Abim battle it out. They seemed relieved, as if believing that once I'd ripped off Abim's head, I might somehow be appeased enough to let them alone.

The problem was, I didn't really want to fight. I'm just a rocker with a colonial-style house in the Jersey suburbs.

I asked Kaitlyn in English, "What the hell is going on here?"

She stared at me, uncomprehending. "He's come for me!" she shouted in the native dialect. Abim's eyes widened.

"No!" Abim seemed unwilling to admit that I'd want Kaitlyn. "It is a sacrifice he wants—a virgin! One of us must give him a daughter!"

"Samat!" I shouted at him like a trader in the marketplace. *"K'tarma Kaitlyn!"* No, I want Kaitlyn, and I pointed at her.

Abim glanced down at Kaitlyn, still sprawled on the floor behind him. She gazed up at him lovingly, imploringly, and Abim charged me and swung his sword.

His scimitar arced gracefully, and as the fire flickered on the blade, it glinted yellow like the sunrise. It hit my neck, and I felt the smallest jolt as blade cleaved through bone, then I was tumbling backward, my head slamming down then bouncing on the dirt floor with a mind-numbing thud.

My head rolled to a man's dirty bare foot, landed in a platter of bread, and I was looking up. I tried to blink crumbs from my eyes, and the man above me looked down and screamed in horror, kicked at my face.

I could not die then, no matter what they did to me.

For the next several moments, I was kicked across that floor by one man, then another, all of them too terrified to stop.

I shouted for mercy, but since I had no lungs, no words came from my mouth. Once I saw Abim hacking the arms from my headless torso, but mostly I saw only darkness, the spinning room, the callused brown toes kicking at me.

At last my head stopped rolling across the floor, and Abim peered down at me, asking "Are you dead yet, demon?"

I said nothing, was afraid to move my lips or blink.

"No, he's not dead," Kaitlyn said. And she rushed near me. She huddled at Abim's side touching his shoulder hesitantly, reassuringly.

Two little girls with dark hair came to Kaitlyn. They were both old enough that they wore clothes. The youngest was probably six, the older ten. They clutched at the forest-green cotton leggings of Kaitlyn's *tahn*. "Mother, mother?" they cried in terror.

Kaitlyn held them tenderly and whispered, "Hush, my little orchids." And as I saw the girls look up at her with their angelic faces, a sense of regret washed through me. Their hair was a muted brunette—Abim's dark black mingled with Kaitlyn's blond. But the girls' dark eyes shone like obsidian, nothing of Kaitlyn in them.

Kaitlyn had sometimes said she wanted children, but I'd never taken her seriously. At first, when we were new as a group, just out on the road, I'd pointed out that a lot of Throat Kulture's popularity was based on her looks. She looked really blazing, and it wouldn't do to have her belly hanging out over her pants. So we'd waited.

Later, when we moved to the 'burbs, she sometimes talked softly about "doing the family thing," but so far, I hadn't been able to give up my dreams of going back on tour.

But seeing her, there with the girls, Kaitlyn looked so natural as a mother, so at peace, that I felt as if I had done her wrong.

"How can the demon not be dead?" Abim asked Kaitlyn, squatting over me. He held his sword tightly, gripping its black hilt with both hands.

"A new body will sprout from its head, in time. You cannot kill such a creature." Kaitlyn whispered at his back. She spoke with obvious authority, for like me, her skin shone with her immortality.

"And what if I hack the head in two?" Abim asked.

"The demon will grow back—in a week, a month. You cannot kill it."

"N'carn," Abim intoned his name for me reverently, watching me with wide, superstitious eyes.

"Yes, the unicorn," Kaitlyn whispered. Her eyes went unfocused, reflective, as if she were looking deep into her past. "I remember him. . . ."

My heart leapt. Yes, it's me, Dane, I wanted to say. If she remembered me, I thought, then she would remember that she'd loved me, that she'd promised always to love me. But as quickly as the moment of reflection had begun, it ended, and she looked away, as if I were only a stranger she'd heard of long ago.

Abim grunted, satisfied for the moment that I could not harm him. "It is my fault he is here," he apologized to the others. "I threw down the altar. Perhaps if we give him a sacrifice, he will leave. A virgin. He likes virgins?"

Kaitlyn's nostrils flared wide with fear. "Yes, yes, it likes virgins. . . ."

We Blazed   517

A vague memory stirred in me of a time when I'd first been dating
Kaitlyn. She hadn't joined the band yet, had in fact only come to listen to
us play in the basement of a friend's bar. He'd let us practice there mornings, as long as we gigged his place once a week.

Our lead guitarist, Scott Walsh, was jamming just for Kaitlyn, thrashing on stage, as if he had ten million fans in the basement. He could really
crank that ax, almost as good as me, but I couldn't play lead and sing lead
at the same time, so I stuck to the base. Anyway, Walsh always felt that I
was competing with him for the ladies, so he told Kaitlyn that we'd have
to quit practice early because I had a date.

Kaitlyn had smiled at me a little, and said, "Oh, he's gonna thrill one
of his fans?"

And Walsh had laughed, "Only if she's a virgin. Dane likes his fans
nice and tight."

I let the comment slide, and a few months later, while he was out riding his Harley, Walsh was so stoned that he hit a semi and got his head
siphoned through the grill. But six years later, after we'd been married for
four of those years, Kaitlyn and I made love on the sofa one night, and
afterward Kaitlyn surprised me by asking, "What did Walsh mean when
he said you only liked virgins?"

Her voice held accusation, as if she'd secretly believed over the years
that Walsh and I had had some kind of contest, popping virgins. I said,
"Man, I don't ball my people," and it was true. After I met Kaitlyn, I'd
never thought twice about another woman, but she knew that I wasn't
being totally honest. I'd sampled my share of sweet meat.

"Who will we sacrifice?" Abim asked. "Arrota? N'kot?" he named
some girls.

"They're too young," Kaitlyn said. "Besides, what mother would let
that monster have them? How can we decide to give another mother's
daughter to such a creature?" and Abim looked back mournfully at his
own daughters.

"W'karra?" he said. The oldest of Kaitlyn's two little girls trembled—she could not have been more than ten— and she clung to Kaitlyn's
leg.

The little girl looked up at her mother and father dutifully, as if willing to give her life if they asked.

"But how will the monster rape her, without a body?" Abim wondered
aloud. His brows knit together in concentration, and he glanced at me.

"No!" I mouthed the word, trying to tell him that I did not want the child.

Abim's eyes grew wide, frightened. "Look, it talks!" he shouted excitedly, and he urged Kaitlyn and the others closer. "It does not want a virgin!"

"Kaitlyn," I mouthed. "I want Kaitlyn!" But Abim seemed not to understand. In truth, I believe he knew what I was saying, but he did not want to admit it to me, at least not in front of Kaitlyn.

"I do not understand you, demon," he said. And he took my head, turned it over on the dirt floor so that my face was toward the floor.

He sat down with his people to hold a counsel. "What should we do with this demon?" Abim asked.

"Kill it! Kill it!" they all said. "Get rid of it!"

"But how?" Abim asked. "My wife is immortal, like it is. She says it cannot be killed. Given time, a new body will grow from the head!"

"Burn it!" someone said.

"No," Kaitlyn answered. "You cannot kill the demon with fire. Even if you cook it whole, it will grow back, when the fire cools."

"Bury it then!" someone else said. "Dig a deep hole, and bury it under rocks."

"And what then?" Kaitlyn asked. "The body will grow back, and it will dig its way up from the grave."

"Feed it to the alligators," someone suggested, but his voice faltered when Kaitlyn's expression showed that this, too, would not work.

"I know what to do," Abim said at last. "I will keep the head nailed to a post, and each day, when a new body is growing, I will prune it off again."

There was mumbling approval from the others within the hall, and I feared they would indeed take me then, keep me nailed to a post forever.

But someone said, "And what if jackals come into the village at night and drag the head away? What then? The demon will simply come back and take vengeance on us all!"

That news seemed to sober them, until at last Abim said. "Then I will cook him in a fire that never cools."

"And where is that, my love?" Kaitlyn asked.

"Northwest of here—a three-day run—in the pool of fire at Flaming Mountain."

"The volcano?" Kaitlyn asked. "Even that might not kill him, I fear. In time, even volcanoes cool."

"But that will be ten thousand years from now," Abim said. "And even if it does cool, what then? The demon will be buried deep under rocks. How will it claw its way out?"

"Would it work?" Kaitlyn asked, a thrill of hope in her voice. There were grunting murmurs of assent from the wild men who crowded around my head.

It was the best plan they could devise. So Abim fetched a hemp sack that had once held oats, and he shoved my head in, blocking out all light. While his people prepared food for his journey, Abim dropped my head outside the hut.

I heard Kaitlyn whimpering, talking to him tenderly, asking him to return soon. Never had Kaitlyn spoken to me with such desperate yearning. She told him that she loved him, that she would be waiting for him and would not sleep until he slept beside her.

I heard Abim kissing her passionately while his daughters cried in the background, full of concern.

A pig found the sack I was in, came and began grunting, sniffing at its contents. It nudged me over, and Abim shouted to startle the pig. The pig squealed and ran off. Abim swung the sack over his back, and in moments we were bouncing along the road as Abim ran through the jungle.

I began growing again in the sack. I did not grow quickly, as I did when someone merely cut me. Instead I felt it first as a tingling, a little nub at the base of my neck where the tailbone began to poke through my scabby neck wound. In a few hours, the healing began to quicken, a powerful burning sensation in four quadrants as hands and feet began to take form.

By nightfall, I could move my stubby little fingers, and wiggle my toes. Almost I could maneuver around in the sack, but my head vastly outweighed my body.

So it was that Abim must have noticed the new shape of the sack, for just after sunset when he stopped to make camp, he pulled me out of the bag, looked at my new torso.

He laid me on the ground. I tried to twist over and crawl off, but Abim merely turned his head aside in disgust and sliced off the new growth of body. When he finished, he pulled it away—the torso of an infant— and hurled it into the tall reeds outside camp.

Abim set my head on a fallen log, barkless and bleached white with age, and he stared at me as if afraid to look away while he ate a brief dinner of jerky and spiced bread.

"I do not hate you, demon," Abim muttered darkly, and I watched him, a man as handsome and muscular as any I've ever seen, and I thought about him rutting with Kaitlyn, the woman who'd promised to love me forever. At that moment, though he did not hate me, I hated him.

"I would not cut off your body, if it would not grow back," he apologized, as if suggesting that by force of will I could stop regenerating myself. He tore at his jerky with strong, even teeth, and said softly, "I would feed you if I could, but now you have no belly to fill."

He stared at me, and I mouthed words begging him to let me leave, to let me walk away and never return. Whatever Kaitlyn had once felt for me, it was over, promises aside. I wondered again if I were a ghost on some eternal quest for the woman I loved. If I were, would my spirit now rest?

Abim watched my lips move, but became frustrated. "I cannot tell what you are trying to say!" he shouted. He went on the far side of the fire, threw himself on the ground.

I lay watching him. Abim tried to sleep, but he fretted and kept rolling over, eyeing me.

I heard the snarling and chuckling of hyenas in the brush, tearing at an infant's body.

At last Abim fell asleep, and a new body began to emerge and take shape on me. Testing, I reached out with tiny hands, kicked with infant's feet.

I managed to fall off the log without waking Abim, and I began crawling to him. My small lungs would not let me talk, not with my large esophagus and voice box, but I hoped that if I got close enough, I would be able to whisper to him, plead with him to let me go.

I worked at reaching him for a long hour, till a silver fingernail of moon rose, gauzy through the high, sheer clouds. I was only halfway across the camp.

Abim woke, howled in dismay when he saw that I'd been struggling toward him. "What did you think to do, demon?" he accused. "Would you have bitten out my throat!"

He charged me, and, in one vicious swipe, pared away my body, then hurled my head back into his bloody sack, and began loping through the tall grass.

Once, I heard a lion roar in the darkness, and Abim called to it softly, "Hey, my brother, I do not want to be eaten this night. Go away." The lion did not attack. A while later I heard the occasional croak of an alligator, the plop of frogs leaping into deep water. Abim was jogging beside the river, in the darkness.

Abim talked to me incessantly for the next two days. He apologized for what he felt he must do. Five times he pruned away that which grew on me, then hid me in his rucksack.

My presence unnerved him. He could not rest. When he managed to sleep fitfully for a moment, he would waken afterward, complaining that in spirit I had come to him in his dreams. What he believed I said, what troubling commentary I may have given him, I will never know. But I'm sure I will haunt his dreams across the years to come.

I had time to think during those travels. I'd believed that the people of this land referred to me as the *Incarnate* when they called me N'carn. But Kaitlyn had referred to me as the unicorn.

It was a word only she could have known in this land, for it was no longer in these people's vocabulary. Kaitlyn was the only other immortal I'd met. She was far older than the others. She must have given me that title, I realized.

So, some things began to make sense. When I saw Kaitlyn with her daughters, that felt right all the way down to my marrow. Kaitlyn loved children, had wanted them for years.

And her belief that I had specifically tried to seduce virgins—I could see where such memories might come from.

But the statue in the village, the penisless statue of me holding that strange horn, striking someone with that horn, that unicorn's horn? I couldn't understand that.

And I reasoned that Kaitlyn might have sculpted that statue in ages past. She'd admitted that she remembered me. But where would she have gotten such an image as that shown on the statue? What could I have done that would make her dim memories of me into something so monstrous? And why would she call me "the unicorn"?

I wished desperately to talk to Abim, to question the man. On the morning of the final day, while I still had an infant body, I managed to plead that he would let me speak.

But Abim hacked off my torso, and whispered fiercely, "I know what you want, demon! You came for Kaitlyn. You cannot have her, and I will not listen to you beg!" He shoved me in the sack for the last time.

Later that day, he brought me out into the mountain air. The scent of the sky was sweet with jungle, malodorous with the bite of sulfur. Abim stood on the lip of a volcano, and showed me the pools of burning lava below. Plumes of smoke rose from the ground, and chunks of black rock floated at the edge of the lava, like ice in some fuming drink.

"Here, demon"—Abim shouted, laughing maniacally—"this is where you will stay, stay for eternity! Kaitlyn is mine now!" His hands were shaking, and Abim sobbed. He turned me to face him. His own face was dirty from jungle pollens and dust so that his tears made clean rivers down his cheeks.

I mouthed the words, "Mercy. Have mercy on me." Abim watched my mouth move, his face frozen in horror.

"I cannot have mercy!" Abim said. "Kaitlyn will always be mine! You are immortal, like her. But this thing, too, you must know: Kaitlyn has loved me forever. She loved me in the beginning of the world, and I do not die like other men. I stopped counting after ten thousand years of life, and that was many, many thousands of years ago. Her love for me has made me immortal, too. So if you come back again, ever—you must contend with me!"

Abim's lips were trembling as he made his threats. Perhaps he feared that in some distant future, it would be me throwing *his* head into a volcano. But I doubted it. I do not really believe he feared death as much as he feared separation from Kaitlyn, the woman he loved.

In that final moment, I decided that I liked the man. The things he was forced to do in order to get rid of me were wounding his soul, which suggested that he was a compassionate man. And he loved Kaitlyn and her daughters, was willing to do anything for them.

And Kaitlyn loved him, more, I realized, than she'd ever loved me.

I hoped they would be happy once I was gone, and if I'd had a voice, I'd have told Abim so.

At last, he took me by the hair and cocked his muscular arm, then hurled me as far as he could. For a moment I lofted over the flowing lava. I looked out above the bowl of the volcano, at skies so blue they hurt my eyes, and I felt the hot thermal winds rising up off the lava.

I was not afraid. I am immortal. And I mouthed the words to Abim, "I forgive. . . ."

All too soon I dropped into the pool of fire. Every inch of skin became a searing pain. I tried to close my eyes, protect myself. I wished to die with all my soul.

Nothing helped, and I seemed to burn for an eternity.

∞   ∞   ∞

I opened my eyes, cleared them from fog. There was a hot pain at the base of my neck where my neural jacks met the interface to an artificial intelligence owned by a small corporation called Heavenly Host.

I was reclining in a comfortably darkened room in a plush leather chair, the low humming of compressors the only sound. In front of me sat the Heavenly Host AI in a vast glass cryochamber, the brown filaments of its neural net floating like the groping roots of some strange plant in the clear blue gel of liquid memory.

A technician stood at my side, studying my face. "How did it go, Mr. Dane? Did you find out what you wanted?"

I had to let my head clear for a moment. More than three years of memories were jamming in my head. My thoughts had never felt so tangled.

I remembered slowly. I'd come here to Heavenly Host, bringing a memory crystal that Kaitlyn had given me last year on our wedding anniversary. This was one of those places that sold immortality to the dead. By downloading your thoughts and dreams and memories, you could create your own universe in virtual reality, your own heaven, and live there for what seemed like forever.

On our last anniversary, Kaitlyn had given me her download on a gray Mitsubishi memory crystal in a box with black velvet lining, and said, "Now, if I die, you and I can still live together forever. I'll always love you."

I'd thought even then that it was a strange gift. Hell, Kaitlyn is only twenty seven, hardly old enough to be obsessing about death.

"How long was I in there?" I asked, nodding toward the AI, still waiting for my head to clear.

The technician cleared his throat. "Realtime? Less than point-oh-four seconds. Every hundred years is equal to one second, realtime."

I thought about that. It had taken about fifteen minutes from the time that we'd plugged in Kaitlyn's memory crystal to the time that we got my own consciousness downloaded and on-line. I hadn't had a complete download. Instead, I'd asked to go in "cold," not knowing how I'd come to be there. I'd wanted to view Kaitlyn's heaven objectively.

But during that fifteen minutes that it took to do my partial download, Kaitlyn had lived in her VR heaven for ninety thousand years.

The technician shook his head. "I can see by your frown that you didn't get what you wanted. It happens that way sometimes. They're all living at light speed in there"—he nodded vaguely toward the AI, the Heavenly Host—"even more than we're living at light speed out here. They forget things a little slower than we do, but they do forget. It helps give them the illusion, over time, that they really are living forever. Even if they understand at first how they got there, the memory fades. But sometimes things get lost, changed from what we expected, or hoped."

I considered what he said. I don't think that the VR world that Kaitlyn's subconscious created was her idea of heaven. She'd once told me she believed that global warming would turn most of the world into a jungle in the far future, and she expected mankind to breed out racial differences until we were all dark, one uniform color. I think her mind must have played tricks on her, creating the VR world she'd expected rather than one she wanted to inhabit for eternity.

Then again, perhaps her world wasn't far from her ideal.

"No, no, it wasn't a total loss," I tried to reassure the technician. I looked up at the fellow. He was no one to me, just a nerdy, hatchet-faced guy who was charging me a lot of money. But he'd heard of Throat Kulture, said we blazed, and I felt I owed him some explanation.

"Kaitlyn slashed her wrists last night," I said. There was a hollowness in my chest. I didn't want to divulge such private information, but he'd learn about it in the tabloids tomorrow anyway.

"Ah, hell," the tech swore softly. "She okay?"

"Yeah, yeah," I said. "She'll make it fine, but I been thinking, and I couldn't figure it, you know? We've got everything—money, fame, a nice house." I just recalled that we'd been on tour for the last six months, and the band was doing better than ever. That was a memory I hadn't taken into the Heavenly Host with me. "So I just couldn't figure it. But now, I've got some clues."

"Good," he said, a verbal slap on the back, a gesture he was too intimidated to give.

I let him unplug the neural jack at the base of my neck, then got up to go.

"You want me to turn your wife's program off?" the tech asked, gesturing to the AI.

I looked at the mass of neural netting in its blue gel, thought for a moment. It cost a shitload of money to run that program for an hour.

"No," I said, "let it run for the night, give her a couple million years. She's happy in there." And she hadn't been happy in a long time. I'd realized last night, after I first found her bleeding in a tub where the warm water had gone crimson, that she had to have been thinking about this for months. That's why she'd given me the memory crystal for our wedding anniversary.

I took the people tube home, cramped among the unwashed bodies of street punks who stared at me in awe and the clean aloof business class on their commute home from the city. I seldom used public transit, but right now I needed the comfort of warm bodies around me.

And as the tube lurched through its starts and stops, I thought about what I'd learned.

I'd believed that Kaitlyn and I were living our dreams, but after seeing her VR heaven, I realized now that we'd only been living *my* dreams. She wanted something else from life.

I thought about Abim, the man she'd created to be her perfect lover. It stung me that she would make something like him, when she could as easily have re-created me. I thought about the children she wanted, the tours she would throw away.

I wondered at how, in the Heavenly Host, her image of me had become so warped, so distorted over time. Her people had made sacrifices to keep me away, I realized in horror.

And I wondered why she called me the "unicorn." I did not have to look far.

When I got home, I had the house turn the lights on to their brightest, so that all shadows fled from the house. Everything was pristine and glistening white inside.

And I just stood for a moment in the doorway and looked at the far wall in shock. On the wall just inside our doorway is an old picture of me and Kaitlyn and Walsh, back when Throat Kulture had just formed. It's flanked by some platinum records, with "River of Darkness" on the right.

I hadn't really noticed it in years, but in the picture, I saw that strange pose, the one I had in the statue. Only in the picture I'm holding my guitar upside down and making a jabbing motion, as if to impale my fans. My face is twisted in a grimace. Three really blazing women are spotlighted on the floor at my feet, groping for me on stage, and I realize that there is something sexual, almost pornographic, in my gesture, something I hadn't seen before. At the time, I'm sure that I'd made that gesture innocently, just part of the stage show. But as I looked closely, it was as if my guitar were a giant dildo, and I was jabbing the women, balling them all.

I wet my lips, my heart hammering, and looked up closely at the picture. I reached up and touched it with a forefinger that is almost all callous after years of playing, fingers that can touch but seldom feel. And on the soundboard to that old white guitar, an instrument I'd discarded years ago, I found the faded manufacturer's logo: a blue unicorn.

I went to the fridge to get a beer to settle my nerves, and I wondered how I could get Kaitlyn to love me forever, to dream about me forever, to let her know how desperately I loved her.

Then I called my agent on the vidphone to tell her that Kaitlyn and I were canceling our tours, that from now on we might only release recordings—if we didn't retire completely.

I put on a clean shirt for my visit to the hospital. Before I left the house, I stood for a long minute by the front door under the brilliant lights, listened to the silence.

I stilled my breathing and I thought, this is how the house would sound if Kaitlyn were dead. Empty. Hollow.

Then I breathed again and thought of the sweet dark-eyed daughters of Kaitlyn's dreams. I struggled to imagine what this house would sound like in some future year, when the cheering of crowds at our stage shows had faded from memory.

Sometimes when I compose, I can close my eyes and hear a song in my head before it is ever played. Now, as I listened, I could hear the sound of my breathing multiplied so it became the breathing of several people, a whispering that gradually grew loud enough to fill the void of these rooms. Almost as I stood at the door, I could hear a tumult echoing from the future, the clattering of footsteps tumbling, the giggling of girls laughing with delight as they raced toward me through the living room. A sweet longing came over me as I imagined how Kaitlyn and I would give flesh to these dreams, give flesh to children like unwritten songs waiting to be played on our guitars.

About the Author

Dave Wolverton began working as a "prize-writer" in college during the 1980s, and quickly won several literary awards. He first hit the best-seller lists in science fiction with his first novel *On My Way To Paradise,* which won the Philip K. Dick Memorial Special Award as one of the best SF novels of 1989.

His novels *Serpent Catch* and *Path of the Hero* also received high acclaim. *Star Wars: The Courtship of Princess Leia* placed high on the New York Times and London Times best-seller lists, and was soon followed by the highly successful, *The Golden Queen* (Tor Books, August 1994). Dave's next novel, *Beyond the Gate,* was released by Tor in hardcover in the summer of 1995.

Dave has also published short fiction in magazines such as *Asimov's* and *Tomorrow,* and in numerous anthologies.

In 1992, Dave became the Coordinating Judge for the Writers of the Future contest. Among other things, he edits their anthology and teaches at their workshops. He has been a prison guard, missionary, business manager, farmer, a technical writer and editor, and a pie maker. He currently lives in Oregon with his wife and four children.